India's Indigenous Immigrants
Story of Assam, Sylhet Referendum, NRC, and more...

Subir

Ukiyoto Publishing

All global publishing rights are held by

Ukiyoto Publishing

Published in 2024

Content Copyright ©Subir

ISBN 9789360492670

All rights reserved.

No part of this publication may be reproduced, transmitted, or stored in a retrieval system, in any form by any means, electronic, mechanical, photocopying, recording or otherwise, without the prior permission of the publisher.

The moral rights of the author have been asserted.

This book is sold subject to the condition that it shall not by way of trade or otherwise, be lent, resold, hired out or otherwise circulated, without the publisher's prior consent, in any form of binding or cover other than that in which it is published.

Disclaimer

This book is an academic exercise, reflecting the author's perspective on the socio-political milieu of Assam, based on personal experiences and extensive research. It is not intended to offend any individual or group sentiments. The contents are believed to be true to the author's knowledge. Any legal disputes arising from the contents of this book should be filed within the jurisdiction of Kolkata.

www.ukiyoto.com

"UNTIL THE LION LEARNS TO WRITE, EVERY STORY WILL GLORIFY THE HUNTER".

An African Proverb

A Tribute to Martyrs

Kamala,
THE Youngest and only female martyr,
&

Martyrs Tarani Debnath, Chandicharan Sutradhar, Sukamal Purkayastha, Kumud Das,
Kanailal Neogi, Sachin Pal, Sunil Sarkar, Hitesh Biswas, Birendra Sutradhar, Satyen Deb [1]
In
Bengali Language Movement.

They made the supreme sacrifice opposing the Assam Government's iniquitous Official Language Act in 1960, which designated Assamese as the only official state language besides English. On the morning of May 19, 1961 (the very next day after Kamala's matriculation exams had ended), these brave souls fell to the bullets of the security forces while holding a protest demonstration in Silchar, a district town in Assam. Sixteen-year-old Bengali girl, Kamala, thus became the first female language martyr of the world in modern times. [2]

Their sacrifice did not go in vain. As a result of the bloodshed of these brave Bengalis, the insensitive government eventually had to concede and restore Bengali as an official language in the (then) Cachar district of Assam.

My eyes are moist as I pay humble homage to these brave souls.

ॐ शान्ति, शान्ति, शान्तिः Om Shanti, Shanti, Shanti.

Subir

Contents

Prologue	1
Pre-Colonial Era of Assam	9
The Story of OPIUM	39
The Emergence of Assam	51
The Colonial Era of Assam	84
Divide et Impera: Genesis of Assamese-Bengali Discord	116
Apartheid in India	142
The Cabinet Mission Plan	164
The Sylhet Referendum	211
Post-Independence Era's Truncated Assam.	271
Inglorious ill-treatment of students in Assam Valley	312
NELLIE,	322
The Assam Agitation	373
IMTD Act of 1983.	448
The Dreaded 'D'	462
Assam NRC	480
Epilogue	539
About the Author	*590*

Prologue

Why this book?

"Bengalis are the root of all evils in Assam, and the Sylheti Bengalis are the worst of the lot," calmly commented one of my Assamese friends while we were chatting during our routine evening tea at the Gauhati University canteen. He was responding to a sharp remark from another Assamese classmate: "The Bengalis came to Assam in large numbers with the British, occupied our lands, grabbed all the job opportunities and small trades, imposed their language on us, are not prepared to learn the Assamese language, and now oppose our mother tongue, Assamese, becoming the medium of instruction in our schools and colleges in Assam!"

This conversation took place in the early 1970s when I was pursuing my postgraduate studies in Physics at the University as a boarder in one of its hostels. During that period, the state government had declared Assamese as the sole medium of instruction in colleges affiliated with Gauhati University. Our discussion at the canteen centred on protests by Bengalis and other communities against this decision.

I am a Sylheti Bengali. [1] Although I was born and brought up in Assam and often overheard the perfunctory Assamese utterance "বঙালে দেশখন খালে" (Bongale deshkhon khale) [2], meaning 'the Bengalis have spoiled the state,' yet my friend's sweeping remark against my community was a rude shock to me. Besides, the reproval came from one of my closest friends, who was neither ignorant nor illiterate but a fellow postgraduate student who had known me from childhood as we grew up together in Shillong as neighbours. I wondered: What on earth had made my father come from his ancestral home in Sylhet to Gauhati Cotton College in Assam in the early 1920s for graduation? Why had he joined services under the Government of Assam and not in other parts of the country? What sin did I commit in my previous life for which I was born in Shillong (the then capital of greater Assam) and joined a postgraduate course at Gauhati University? As a Bengali, why am I considered a pest in Gauhati and a parasite on the soil of Assam? I cursed myself and my entire Bengali community for being such a nuisance to the people of Northeast India.

Alas! Instead of voicing a strong protest against that absurd and unfounded allegation, I was somewhat apologetic. I hurried back to the hostel to hide my disgraced self within the four walls of my tiny room. I allowed this to happen because I did not know the truth. And sadly, no one had made me aware of the reality of our past. During those days, neither did I have any inclination nor means to know the fact. Hence, I had to leave the canteen quickly with my tail tucked between my legs.

As I gradually became aware of the injustices inflicted upon the Bengalis in North-East India, particularly the betrayal of Sylheti Bengalis by a faction of Assamese leaders during the Referendum of Sylhet District at the time of the country's partition, I couldn't forgive myself. I still harbour guilt for my ignorance at that time, which rendered me defenceless against those egregious verbal assaults. At that moment, I failed my community by failing to provide the necessary defence for the Bengalis.

Today, I aim for our descendants to grasp the truth that eluded me in the past. Henceforth, the Bengali youth of North-East India must hold their heads high when faced with such baseless allegations. Furthermore, they should be equipped to offer a fitting response to any misinformed individual who might question the legitimacy of Bengalis in the North-East, particularly in Assam. That is the primary objective behind my endeavour to publish this book.

Besides, this book would spread awareness in the country about some concealed realities of Assam. It includes the previously unknown and unused oxymoron "Indigenous Immigrants" Subir coined to precisely describe the Bengalis in Assam, who initially emerged with the branding of the entire community residing in Assam as 'immigrants' by a British diktat in the early 1920s. During that time, the province of Assam, as well as the undivided province of Bengal, were part of India, and both were Bengali-majority provinces. There was no international border between them. Yet, the British colonial rulers mischievously designated the Bengalis residing in Assam as 'immigrants', giving the wrong impression that they came from a foreign country. That is why the qualifier 'indigenous' to the misnomer 'immigrant' became necessary to distinguish Bengalis, who are indigenous to India, from real 'immigrants', as seen elsewhere in the world.

It was over two years after the "independence" of India that I was born in Shillong in 1950. At that time, the States of Arunachal Pradesh (the erstwhile North-East Frontier Agency or NEFA), Nagaland, Meghalaya, and Mizoram were also part of Assam. My father was born on 8th April 1907 in Sylhet, then a district of Assam province in India. After graduating from Assam's Cotton College, Gauhati, he worked in the Assam Government and permanently resided in Shillong since the early 1930s. Had my mother tongue been Assamese or Khasi, I would have been recognized as a "son of the soil" in Assam or Meghalaya. But, in reality, I am not a "son of the soil" in either of the two States. The laws of the land do not recognize me as such. The reason is: my mother tongue is Bengali—one of the 22 officially recognized languages under the Indian Constitution, and one of the most widely spoken languages, ranking 6th in the world, spoken by nearly 230 million people worldwide! [3] Is it not an unacceptable reality that perpetuates the wrong perception of 'Assam for the Assamese,' 'Bihar for the Biharis,' 'Gujarat for the Gujaratis,' and so forth? It makes me wonder: India is then for whom—only for people like me?

Still, I am grappling with the question: Am I not a son of an Indian couple born on Indian soil? As a bona fide citizen, to which State's soil in India do I belong? Or am I a stateless Indian? Is it essential to link my mother tongue with any specific soil of my motherland? Why is there so much injustice in store for a Bengali like me from the day I was born in Shillong, which is part and parcel of my motherland India? Whom should I hold accountable for such an anomaly? After all, I am not an "illegitimate son of India" or a nomad deserving of this treatment! As a citizen of "independent" India by birth, born to a legitimate Indian couple, it should have been my birthright as per the preamble of the Indian Constitution to enjoy "equality" before the law in this Christian-majority State of Meghalaya. I expected my right to enjoy all the facilities and privileges legally granted by the Constitution to its citizens to be upheld. I wanted my rights to be duly protected and opportunities made available to me in equal measures. Nevertheless, I am told that the law of the land was so framed and tinkered with from time to time that people like me are placed at a disadvantageous position in many places in India.

Although I belong to a community that is in the minority in the state of Meghalaya, the law of the land does not recognize my Bengali community as a "minority." The Minorities Commission of India cannot address the discrimination against me by the state's majority population as it is not for minority people like me! I am told that the word minority has not been defined by our lawmakers. So, the Bengalis, even though a minority in Meghalaya, cannot claim this status in the state. There is an uneven playing field around me and for my children in almost every sphere of life in this region, because I speak Bengali, practice Hinduism, and do not belong to a caste that comes under the purview of the 6th Schedule of the Constitution of India. Many times, the so-called "son-of-the-soil" has harassed us by asking my fellow Bengalis and me to go back to Bangladesh - because of our mother tongue; I was discriminated against while pursuing my education in the state, and I had to encounter inequity vis-à-vis the 'son-of-the-soil' in my quest for gainful employment with the state Government and also in the matter of taxation on my earnings - to name a few!

Ironically, before the country's independence, my father could purchase land in Shillong in his name. However, after independence, as a citizen of "independent" India, I lost that right! I cannot buy any landed property in Shillong or any part of Meghalaya in my name. Not only did I lose my right to buy land in Shillong in my name, but I also lost my right to sell the house in Shillong that I had inherited from my father to anyone other than a tribal. The law of the land prohibits me from doing so. Since childhood, I have experienced this type of discrimination and silently tolerated the inequities in "independent" India. The so-called "sons-of-the-soil" of Assam, Meghalaya, and other states of North East India may be unaware of these ground realities prevalent in "their" states. It would be kind of them to remember these bitter truths when they raise their voice against the perceived discrimination by what they call 'the mainstream Indians' in 'mainland' India.

This book is also an attempt to bring home this point, not only to the people of North-East India but also to the entire nation, which is more or less unaware of many facts 'unique' to this region. I want the liberals, the experts, and the intelligentsia who often advocate the cause of the North-easterner in debates at TV studios, and rightly so, whenever there are any unfortunate incidents involving the "son-of-the-soil" of the North East, to be aware of these realities. Furthermore, I hope that the narrative of my plight and the discrimination against my community in this book will be an eye-opener to Indian intellectuals and crusaders who fight for the universal right to equality.

Renowned authors and celebrated poets often exquisitely express the pleasure and ecstasy a lover experiences upon receiving a love letter in their choicest words. However, I can't convey the pain and trauma that someone goes through upon receiving a so-called "love letter," as it is colloquially known in some states in North East India. It's nothing but an extortion note from underground extremists demanding cash. I've received it; I know its horrifying effects. I still carry the terrible experience deep within me! But I won't be able to narrate those excruciating feelings like a poet or an author.

Nonetheless, it is a fact that I received one such "love letter" on November 9th, 1995. It was delivered to me by hand inside the branch premises of the bank where I was working. The horrific experience was preceded by the death of a local staff member of the same branch, killed by a stray bullet that often flies in the skies in certain pockets of North-East India even today. It pierced his heart one Sunday morning while he was gossiping with friends standing in front of his home, located somewhat close to my official residence in that state. The unfortunate incident occurred barely a couple of months before I received the "love letter". Add this to my continued stay with my spouse and two minor children at the official residence on the first floor of the branch building. Fear always gripped me, dreading flying bullets hitting my back at any moment. It more or less sums up my ordeal of those days. Nevertheless, the "love letter" is still with me as one of the most freakish mementoes of my days in North-East India.

Although I was given blanket permission by the bank to close the branch if needed, neither did I desert the bank nor oblige the extortionists. I stayed on to provide uninterrupted services to the customers. Later, I learned that my track record saved me from any harm by the extremists, but that's a different story altogether. Meanwhile, during the same period, it was reported that an officer of a central public sector undertaking posted in the same state, upon receiving a similar extortion letter, tried to flee but was shot dead while handing over the charge of his office overnight. The relevance of the narration in this book is to invalidate the notion that Bengalis are cowards and run away from difficult situations. Those aware of the ground realities of the region would know that cases like this, where Bengalis bravely faced similar threats in the North Eastern states, are plenty. Furthermore, it is to prove that the allegations are mostly fabricated and often motivated and aimed at tarnishing the image of a community.

My dream to become a physicist was shattered due to communal disturbances in Assam; my efforts to join Meghalaya state government services proved futile because of my mother tongue. My children could not find a level playing field when they grew up in North-East India. Yet, despite all this, I did not abandon my beloved "Seven Sisters" until I needed to send my children outside this region to meet their growing needs for better educational facilities and avail of more extensive career opportunities. By the way, the Seven Sisters (States) is a popular term for the contiguous states of Arunachal Pradesh, Assam, Meghalaya, Manipur, Mizoram, Nagaland, and Tripura before the inclusion of the State of Sikkim into the North Eastern Region of India.

In North-East India, I have seen the shocking manifestation of violence and the ugly face of communal disturbances, their casualties, and the mindless killings from point-blank proximity and survived. In the early 1970s, one late evening, just after finishing dinner, I had to flee the Gauhati University hostel along with some other Bengali students at a minute's notice. It was after receiving a tip from my Assamese friend about the imminent danger of communal violence likely to be unleashed targeting the Bengali students. We spent that night at the nearby Maligaon Railway Station platform. Then, at the crack of dawn, I left for my home in Shillong. My pursuit of a Master's Degree as well as my student life thus came to an abrupt end!

Prima facie, it might appear that we had overreacted and unreasonably panicked, but the incidents narrated in chapter 10 of this book titled "The Inglorious Harassment of Students In Assam Valley" should be enough to justify our action. Weeks later, I went back to the hostel to collect my belongings from the room. When I saw my prized possession, the alarm clock, a gift from my father after my graduation, lying in pieces on the floor along with my damaged books, torn notes, and all - scattered all over the room - I could not hold back tears running down my cheeks.

Next, I came face to face with a fierce mob near Shillong's Don Bosco Square when some of us were rushing back home from our office at Laitumkhrah. It was one early afternoon. Suddenly, a curfew was declared in the wake of communal riots in the town. Then, unexpectedly, one tribal friend of mine emerged from nowhere, whisked me away from the scene of the unruly gatherings, and almost dragged me to the nearby NCC office inside the premises of St. Edmunds College. It was the same college from where both of us had graduated together. Hours later, in the evening, I was escorted by two Army personnel in a military van to the safety of my home in the Laban locality.

I cannot forget the gruesome scene I witnessed on the ground floor of "Bawri Mansion," a commercial building, at Dhankheti, Shillong, on January 5th, 2001. Around midday, five innocent people - three employees and two Khasi customers, including one lady - were mowed down by bullets from AK rifles. Strangely, or perhaps not, no one has been arrested for the heinous crime to date, as far as my knowledge goes. I could not count the exact number of dead bodies lying on the floor inside the TV merchandise shop 'Aristo' by name. The inside of its showroom was filled with the smoke of automatic gun fires. I even heard numerous shots sprayed by two or three members of an extremist group who reportedly came to kill the Bengali proprietor of the shop. The upper floors of "Bawri Mansion" housed our Zonal office. The incident occurred when we came down to the corridor of the ground floor during our recess period. The weird scene became more dreadful as the smoke gradually cleared to reveal the horrible display of stray dead bodies alongside some injured victims lying on the floor and blood oozing out from them. The pungent smell in the air, painful shrieks and moans from the wounded completed the devastating sight.

Even today, I vividly visualize these and many more shocking incidents, which I had the misfortune of witnessing with my own eyes as I moved from state to state in North-East India in connection with my official commitments. Yet, during more than half a century of my life that I spent in the region, I received so much love, affection, respect, and help from different people, especially from many of "the sons & the daughters of the soil," that even the encounters with unpleasant happenings could not obliterate my happy reminiscences of the Seven Sisters. I still carry nostalgic recollections of North-East India, particularly of the memories of my golden childhood days, which I had spent in Shillong. I shall cherish these unique treasures in my heart as long as I live.

The write-up that follows in the subsequent chapters might be somewhat unpalatable to a few individuals, groups, or communities. It is because of the unconcealed but factual narration of the realities which existed in the past or are prevalent at present as I released my pent-up emotions gathered over the decades - rather frankly. However, my endeavour always was not to hurt anyone's sentiment unnecessarily. At times, I used forceful language that might sound harsh and unkind as I tried to argue the case in favour of the humiliated community. However, if I have messed up in striking a balance between reality and civility somewhere, I assure my readers that it's unintentional or unavoidable.

All possible efforts have been made to present an honest and fair picture of reality as I have seen, heard, and understood. In the introduction to the book "Planter Raj to Swaraj," the eminent historian and author Amalendu Guha wrote: "It is possible that even an honest, dispassionate historian's perception might get unconsciously derailed because of his ethnic or class identity." Thus, it is natural for this representation to be somewhat tilted in a particular direction because, essentially, the entire narration is depicted from the viewpoint of one specific individual. I recognize that there would be a scope of debate on my perception and assessment. Also, there would be room for incorporating additional views and alternative facts. These are welcome, but in no way should they reject or negate my perception per se – because the narrations are honest, sincere, and nothing but the truth - to the best of my knowledge.

It would be my privilege if someone would take the trouble of sensibly pointing out, without vilification or ad hominem, where exactly I went wrong, if at all, in the opinions I have expressed in this book. I am only too eager to correct myself if I have made a mistake in my assessment - even now. Similarly, if my views are found to be well-placed, I expect pragmatic individuals to take the necessary actions according to their own abilities to make a difference in the undesirable state of affairs in the region - keeping in mind the interests of India as a priority.

I confess that I made liberal use of many books, research papers, oral statements of persons with firsthand knowledge, and online reports from various websites to supplement my personal experience and perception to complete this story. I have tried to acknowledge and give credit wherever it's due, but any omissions that might have occurred inadvertently are regretted.

Last but not least, there are many good things in Assam and North-East India, including its people, traditions, and culture. However, any portrayal of these must wait for now. Over 19 lakh people are currently facing the prospect of being declared "stateless" persons. Their names have not appeared in the final list of Assam NRC. This 19 lakh is not merely a number nineteen with five zeros attached to it. They are not just statistical figures, scientific digits, or mathematical integers. They represent over nineteen lakh uniquely woven flesh, blood, bones, and whatnot, wrapped under some special skins of individual living souls - separately called human beings - comprising adult men, women, youngsters, kids, toddlers, and infants. Like you and me, they have hunger in their stomachs, taste in their mouths, and, above all, carry a heart that can feel pain, pleasure, and ecstasy. These days, they are terrified of their uncertain future, for soon they might be declared "illegal immigrants" in India.

Therefore, it is not the time for opening pleasantries, to sing praise, or to write about the right things in Assam. It's time for the people of India to know the realities. They need to be told the other side of the story and the whole story of Assam that has remained untold, unpublished, and unending so far. It might make a huge difference in understanding what is really at stake. So let us begin at the beginning.

****

Chapter 1.

Pre-Colonial Era of Assam

There was nothing called Assam before the advent of the British in this part of the country. Professor Nandana Dutt, Department of English, Gauhati University, Assam, discussing the formation of Assam and the Assamese identity in her book "Questions of Identity in Assam: Location, Migration, Hybridity," among other things, wrote:

"Till a few centuries back, there was nothing like the Assamese. Instead, there were Bodo, Dimasa, Karbi Koch, Ahom, Tiwa, Mising, Sonowal, Moran, Motok, Chutiya, Bamun, Sudhir, Kayastha, Kalita, etc. It was only with the advent of the British that the earlier term 'Aham' (often used to refer to the Ahom kingdom) became Assam. Similarly, with regard to language, along with many tribal languages, there existed the dialects known as Kamrupi, Goalparia, and Darangi. The standardization process, as a result of which the Sibsagar dialect came to be recognized as the Assamese language, was also due to the proselytizing efforts of the American Baptist missionaries. From the time the British arrived, almost all the inhabitants of Assam came to be known as the Assamese. In the list of communities, [1]Deka now includes "Bongali, Rajasthani, Bihari, Sikh, and Mymensinghia" [1]

Note: [1]Kanaksen Deka, litterateur, journalist, and Sahitya Sabha president (2005-07), attempting to answer the question, 'So, who were the Assamese?'

Although there are differences of opinion on whether the name Assam was derived from the term 'Ahom', renowned academic and author in English and Kannada, Journalist M.S. Prabhakara, who served as a correspondent for The Hindu for many decades in Assam and South Africa, wrote, among other things,

> The earliest reference to the name in a European language, provided by Hobson-Jobson, is dated c. 1590,
>
> > "The dominions of the Rajah of Asham join to Kamroop; he is a very powerful prince, lives in great state, and when he dies, his principal attendants, both male and female, are voluntarily buried alive with his corpse".

The "Rajah of Asham" was part of the Ahom dynasty that ruled over the territory of what is now Assam for well nigh six centuries - and gave the land and the language its name. [2]

Similarly, deliberating upon this issue in his book "A History of Assam," Sir Edward Gait also indicated his inclination to support such a possibility as he said, "There is, I think, no doubt (the name Assam) is derived from the present designation of the Ahoms." [3] Besides, since 1996, the date 2nd December has been celebrated in the state as Assam Day, Asom Divas (অসম দিৱস), Axom Divox, or Sukaphaa Divox, commemorating the arrival of the founder and first King of the Ahom kingdom, Chaolung Sukaphaa, in Namrup, Assam, and accordingly, this date is regarded as the founding date of the Ahom Kingdom. [4] It buttresses the assertion that the name Assam has its origin in the term 'Ahom' and the "Ahom kingdom." Therefore, from the above discussions, it can be affirmed, with a reasonable degree of certainty, that the name Assam was derived from the term 'Ahom,' and it came into being with the advent of the British in this part of the country, and then almost all the inhabitants of the Ahom Kingdom came to be known as the Assamese.

Interestingly, the word Assamese in English generally represents both the people of Assam and their language. But in the local parlance, i.e., the Asamiya language, the descendants of the Tai (Mao-Shan sub-tribe) people who accompanied Sukaphaa to the Brahmaputra valley and settled with him in the Ahom kingdom were known as the Ahoms. During those days, the ordinary citizens of the Ahom kingdom became known as the 'Ahomiyas'. Over the years, the term 'Ahomiya' evolved into Asamiya (sometimes spelt differently, like Asomiya, Oxomiya, and so forth).

After the British annexation of the Ahom kingdom in 1826, its geographical boundary started expanding as more and more territories were subjugated by the British and added to it. The process continued relentlessly. Consequently, Assam's population also grew ceaselessly. However, in general, the people of many newly added territories were not considered Asamiya or Ahoms, although, in English, the people of Assam in general became commonly known as the Assamese. For the major communities from Bengal, Bihar, Rajasthan, and so on, their usual names, like Bengali, Bihari, Rajasthani, and so forth, remained in vogue. Similarly, the people of the newly acquired adjoining hills and plain territories were named after their respective tribes, such as Khasis, Jaintias, and Garos for the hillmen; and Bodo, Kachari, Karbi, Miri, Mishimi, Rabha for the plains tribes.

Then, there were a few groups of Assamese Muslims; five sub-groups among them, Goriya, Moriya, Julha, Deshi, and Syed, have recently been recognized officially as the "indigenous" Assamese Muslim communities, setting them apart from Bengali-origin Muslims, who are known as Neo-Assamese or Neo

Asamiya. They declared the Asamiya language as their mother tongue in the census records.

Recently, a new adjective, 'ethnic,' applied to the Assamese, has been gaining popularity. According to the renowned Professor of Political Studies at Bard College in New York, Sanjib Barua, "The 'ethnic Assamese' can be distinguished from Assam's many 'immigrant' communities and the 'tribal' communities - the latter two, in recent years, less likely to be sympathizers with Assamese sub-nationalism." [5]

Significantly, during the Ahom rule, it was different. The following paragraph, quoted from "The North-East Frontier – The Land, The People and Their Early History" by Sudhindra Nath Bhattacharya, Lecturer, Department of History, Dacca University, provides a remarkable perspective:

"Another peculiar feature was the feudal organization of the Ahom society. At the apex was a ruling aristocracy consisting of the king and the descendants of the original noble families, who accompanied the traditional Ahom conqueror from his mountain home across the Patkoi range. These are so-called **"genuine Assamese,"** whose number at the time of Mir Jumla's invasion is computed by his [1]*waqianavis* at not more than 20,000. They furnished the chief officers of the state – Gohains, Baruas, Phukans, and each of them had a band of personal followers at his beck and call whose number varied according to his own status. The middle stratum of society was filled up by men of the plains, who formed the majority of the population. They were the **Assamese proper**, "with many Bengali affinities, defective in physical strength, endurance, and martial spirit." At the base were the vast body of slaves, some being Mongoloid serfs, but most of them **Bengali prisoners of war, Hindus, and Muslims.** They were a discontented set of people, comparable to the [2]Helots of ancient Sparta – politically dangerous and socially degraded. [6]

Note: [1]*waqianavis* - a medieval royal functionary in charge of news writing.

[2]Helots were in a sense state slaves, bound to the soil and assigned to individual Spartans to till their holdings.

Until August 15th, 1947, the present-day states of Arunachal Pradesh, Nagaland, Mizoram, Meghalaya, and the Sylhet region, presently in Bangladesh, were part of the Assam Province of British India. However, in the partition of 1947, India lost the Sylhet region of Assam to (East) Pakistan. In the post-partition period, Arunachal Pradesh, Nagaland, Mizoram, and Meghalaya separated from the Assam state.

Located in North East India, between the latitudes of 24° and 28°N and longitudes of 90° and 96°E, and south of the eastern Himalayas, today's Assam, or Axom as pronounced locally, covers an area of 78,440 sq. km. Squeezed amidst the young mountains in Upper and South Assam and the old mountains in Lower Assam are the two valleys of the state, the Brahmaputra and Barak rivers, separated by the Barail range. Geographically, Assam, connected to the rest of India via a 22-km land strip in West Bengal, popularly known as the "Chicken's Neck" near Siliguri, is the gateway to its neighbouring states: Arunachal Pradesh, Nagaland, Mizoram, Meghalaya, Manipur, and Tripura. Assam also shares an international border with Bhutan and Bangladesh. Assam's political borders are Arunachal Pradesh in the east, West Bengal, Meghalaya, and Bangladesh in the west, Arunachal Pradesh, Bhutan in the north, and Nagaland, Manipur, Mizoram, Meghalaya, and Tripura in the south, accounting for nearly 2.4% of India's total geographical area. It boasts amazing natural views, with numerous valleys, rivers, creeks, waterfalls, and abundant natural resources to meet the ever-growing needs of Generation Z or the post-millennial generations. Today, Assam is the largest state in North-East India. [7]

The prehistoric and proto-historic periods of North-East India are shrouded in mystery as very little is known about the region during that time. However, references in the great epics, the Ramayana and the Mahabharata, as well as in the Vishnu Purana, Kalika Purana, and Yoginitantra, suggest the existence of a country known as Pragjyotisa in this part of India during ancient times. Later, its name was changed from Pragjyotisa to Kamrupa. In classical Sanskrit literature, Pragjyotisa and Kamrupa are mentioned alongside each other. Kamrupa is also cited as a frontier territory in the well-known Allahabad inscription of Samudragupta. It is believed that the province's name was subsequently changed from Pragjyotisa to Kamrupa (also referred to as Pragjyotisha or Pragjyotisha-Kamarupa), which wielded significant influence in the Indian subcontinent during the classical period. Along with Davaka, Kamrupa is recognized as one of the first historical kingdoms of present-day Assam. [8] [9]

"What is Kamrupa? The most simplistic and generally shared definition is the 'earliest kingdom of Assam' or the 'ancient past of Assam'. However, the implication of this definition is far more complicated than historical reality. The importance of Kamrupa was accentuated by a group of nationalist historians/antiquarians of Assam since the early twentieth century when the search for the past, or more precisely, redefining the past emerged as a fundamental constituent of the making of Assamese identity. Their main concern was to find a proper place for Assam in the mainstream of Indian history and civilization. Kamrupa became an entrance through which Assam could connect itself with the rest of the subcontinent. It constituted a historical region where 'there are sacred myths and symbols, held by significant groups within the area, regarding the relationship of people to their past and geographical entity. Although considerable progress has been made in the quantitative compilation of textual, epigraphical, and archaeological information on the early Brahmaputra Valley, the writings on Kamrupa have been mostly limited to a dynastic history, emphasizing **a unilinear political continuity of the region from the past to the present. A number of controversial issues either remained unsolved, or they were conveniently erased from the dominant history writings** on Kamrupa, which underlined the coherence of language, ethnicity, religion, and culture of the region. This coherence, mostly imagined and retrospectively imposed, became an important basis for the exclusive regional identity against neighboring regions and the political aspiration to justify the dominance of the Hindu majority over other minorities." (Emphasis by Subir)

That was Research Fellow Jae-Eun Shin in her paper "REGION FORMED AND IMAGINED: Reconsidering the temporal, spatial, and social context of Kamarupa", which appeared in the book "MODERN PRACTICES IN NORTH EAST INDIA: History, Culture, Representation" edited by Lipokmar Dzuvichu and Manjeet Baruah. From the analysis of the temporal, spatial, and social context of Kamarupa, Jae-Eun Shin concluded that the definite history prior to the Varmans still remains uncertain. The first solid historical evidence of Kamarupa appearing as a peripheral kingdom under Gupta influence belonged to the fourth century. None of the dates assigned to the legendary ancestors in ancient times was historically tenable. [10]

The earliest historic record of Kamarupa is found in the account of the Chinese pilgrim Hiuen Tsang, who visited the region in 640 AD. It appears from his account that the whole of the Brahmaputra valley, Koch-Behar, and Bhutan were included in Kamrupa. At that time, a Hindu king named Bhaskara Varman was the king of Kamarupa, which was pretty strong and prosperous, according to Hiuen Tsang's report.

After Hiuen Tsang's visit, the history of Kamrupa again became obscure, and the veil got lifted a little when Pralambha founded a dynasty around the year 800 AD. From the sketchy information available, it transpired that the dynasty ruled for about 200 years, and then it gave way to the Palas dynasty, which ruled the Kamarupa Kingdom from the 9th to 11th centuries. The first Pala ruler of the Kamarupa Kingdom was elected, which probably explains the name of this dynasty as "Pala". Ratna Pala was the most noted sovereign of this dynasty.

There was another Pala dynasty in Bengal (8th to 12th century). But, unlike the Palas of Kamarupa, who were Hindus, the Palas of Bengal were Buddhists. The Pala dynasty of Kamarupa ended when it was invaded by Gaur (name of medieval Bengal), King Ramapala (1072-1126) - the Pala of Bengal. King Ramapala made Timgyadeva the governor of Kamarupa, who ruled between 1110 and 1126. Subsequently, however, Timgyadeva threw off the Pala King's control and started to rule independently for some years. He was then attacked and replaced by Vaidyadeva under Ramapala's son Kumarapala. Vaidyadeva (or Vaidya Dev) ruled between 1126 and 1140. He, too, declared independence within four years of his rule after the death of Kumarapala. The Ramacharita of Sandhyakara Nandi refers to the fact that Rama Pal, King of Gauda, conquered Kamarupa. It is believed that the Kamarupa King conquered by Rama Pal was Jayapal. [11] [12] [13]

However, with the advent of the Ahoms, detailed accounts of their kingdom were recorded in the [1]**'Buranjis', which** are historical chronicles first written on the instructions of Ahom king Sukaphaa, who established the Ahom kingdom in 1228.

Note: [1]Buranji in the Ahom language literally means "a store that teaches the ignorant"; 'bu' is ignorant person, 'ran' means teach, and 'ji' stands for the store. [14]

Interestingly, there were two kinds of *Buranjis*: one maintained by the state (official) and the other by families. Many such manuscripts were written by scribes under the office of the *Likhakar Barua*, based on state papers, diplomatic correspondences, judicial proceedings, etc. Others were written by nobles or individuals under their supervision, sometimes anonymously. These documents reveal the chronology of events, language, culture, society, and the inner workings of the state machinery of the kingdom. They were written in a "simple, lucid, and unambiguous but expressive language with utmost brevity and least exaggeration." The tradition of writing Buranjis survived more than six hundred years well into the British period, lasting a few decades after the demise of the Ahom kingdom. [15]

In the early 13th century, a group of Shan tribes called themselves Tai, meaning "celestial origin," wandered about the hilly region of the Patkai hills on India's northeastern border with Burma, occasionally raiding Naga villages. These were the progenitors of the Ahoms, and their original home was somewhere in the ancient kingdom of Pong. Their leader, Sukhappa, along with eight nobles and 9,000 men, women, and children, crossed a river called the Khamnamjang on rafts and arrived at Nongdnyang Lake. Some Nagas attempted to resist his advance, but Sukhappa defeated them and perpetrated frightful atrocities on those he captured. He caused them to be killed and roasted, compelling their relatives to eat their flesh. The ghastly barbarity created such widespread terror that the other Nagas of the neighborhood hastened to make their submission. Leaving one of his nobles to rule the conquered country, Sukhappa proceeded onward. After trying different places for several years, he arrived at Charaideo, about 30 km from Sibsagar town in present-day Assam (India), and built a city there. The neighboring country at that time was in possession of the Morans. Sukhappa fought with and defeated these tribes. Afterward, he wisely adopted facilitatory measures by treating them as equals and encouraging intermarriage, thereby welding them all into one nation. Many Morans then adopted Ahom rites and customs, but their language continued to be Bodo. With time, the local chieftaincies of Barahis, Mataks, Chutiyas, Kacharis, and a few other ethnic communities were also subjugated. Thus, the migrant Tai-Ahoms established a small kingdom known as the Ahom Kingdom, with Sukhappa as the first king (1228-1268), and Charaideo, about 30 km from present-day Sivasagar town, as their first capital.

The Tai-Ahom and Hindu versions of a legend attribute a divine origin to Sukhappa's ancestors. The Ahom society consisted of seven privileged or noble clans (staghar/satghoria) from which all important state officials were appointed. Kingship and positions of high officials (Gohain) became hereditary within designated families. Sukhappa appointed his two chief counsellors, Burhagohain and Barogohain, from the next two traditionally important clans, Chao-frongmung and Chao-thaomung, respectively. The third counsellor position, Barbarua and Barphukan, was created to meet the kingdom's growing administrative needs. These posts were not hereditary but could only be filled from the state's twelve specified families (barogharia). While kingship was hereditary, the approval of the nobles was required for a king's accession. The king also had the authority to delegate any duties to a high official.

Sukhappa led the adventure and was a distinguished military leader. He belonged to the Chao-pha clan, from which only the Tai-Ahoms could normally select their chief. Popular belief suggests that Chaolung Sukaphaa was a Tai prince originally from Mong Mao, now part of the Dehong-Dai Singhpho Autonomous Prefecture in Yunnan, China. Presently, Sukaphaa is regarded as the first Assamese. His coronation took place on 2nd December 1228. Since 1996, 2nd December has been celebrated as Sukaphaa Divas or Asom Divas to commemorate the coronation of the first Ahom king. As the founder of the Ahom kingdom, Sukaphaa, also known as Siu-Ka-Pha, is considered the architect of present-day Assam.

Initially, Sukhappa exploited the subjugated tribes like the Morans and the Baharis, who had not yet advanced beyond tribalism. He benefited from their personal services by appointing them as suppliers of firewood, honey, and water, among other tasks. Meanwhile, there was a considerable increase in the number of ruling tribes, both through natural growth and conversion, and to some extent, through new immigration via marriage ties. This necessitated the cultivation of more food crops and the clearing of additional lands. Consequently, the system of obligating one man from each family to provide service to the state was introduced. However, even this was insufficient to meet the growing internal demands and the potential threat of Mughal aggression. Consequently, the existing practice of exacting personal service from subjects was gradually expanded.

As the Ahoms expanded their territorial boundaries and their various requirements increased, the formalization of exacting personal service from subjects occurred in 1609 AD through the establishment of the paik system by Momai Tamuli Barbarua, an Ahom official, under the patronage of King Susenghphaa (1603–1641) or Pratap Singha. Under this system, excluding nobles, priests, high castes, or slaves, every adult male between the ages of 16 to 50 was registered as a paik for state service. The smallest unit of the paiks, called a 'got', consisted of four paiks. When one or two paiks from the 'got' served the state, the remaining three or two were responsible for household affairs. Paiks in a 'got' rotated their service to the state, with each paik serving for three to four months annually. Some paiks were organized into professional khels, each performing specific productive work. For example, boat-building khels were overseen by a Phukan (e.g., Naosaliya Phukan), and smaller khels, like bow-makers, were overseen by a Barua (e.g., Dhenu-Chocha Barua). The system was structured to meet both the economic and military needs of the state.

In times of emergency, a single paik in a 'got' had to carry the workload of his other comrades, making his life miserable. The concealment of a paik was considered a serious offence, which was dealt with very severely. The paiks were not free to pursue independent trade and thereby improve their material conditions. Their pattern of living was fixed by the state, which they had no right to alter. Only by paying commutation money of three rupees per head per annum could a paik sometimes obtain an exemption to enjoy this privilege. In order to enjoy this privilege, some paiks borrowed money from the well-to-do and, unable to pay the debt, became bondsmen and, consequently, slaves. Some even bribed the officers to conceal their names, whereas others took shelter in the satras (Vaishnava monasteries).

The paiks could be mobilized at short notice by the respective heads of the khels working through their subordinate officers, with some preliminary knowledge of their duties, civil and military, being imparted to each paik by his previous service to the state. However, they had to undergo a refresher course at their allotted headquarters and intensive training especially needed for the occasion before proceeding to the battlefield. The Barbarua was usually the commander-in-chief of present-day upper Assam and the Barphukan of present-day lower Assam. In times of emergency, the three Gohains and also the king took to the battlefield.

The paik system enabled the king to maximize the utilization of manpower both in times of war and peace. It proved an effective weapon to fight external enemies and therefore continued to thrive until there was an external threat. However, no sooner was the danger over than the paik system also began facing popular resistance. As the Ahoms fought the Mughals and the rebellious chiefs, the need for more men in the armed forces and in wartime construction, and more money to meet the expenses thereof, compelled the king to resort to a ruthless exploitation policy. Consequently, people's dislike for this system grew silently, and resentment took the form of popular rebellion towards the close of the Ahom rule.

Nevertheless, during the Mughal wars, the Ahoms constructed impregnable forts at strategic points, which evoked admiration from the enemy. The espionage system of the Ahoms was highly developed. Overall, the technical skill, courage, and general excellence of the Ahom army received appreciation from the Persian chroniclers covering the Mughal wars. On the strength of such military strategy and the efficiency of the army, the Ahoms earned the credit of being "one of the few races in India who could stem the tide of Mughal conquest."

Yet, face to face with the rebellious subjects of the Ahom kingdom, their defence system soon cracked even before the British and the Burmese armies were on the rampage. The reason is apparent. The Ahom army was comprised mostly of commoners only. Many among them participated in the revolt against the state dispensation. It made a difference. Although a household troop of 6,000 men commanded by the Bhitarual Phukan and a unit of musketeers called Konwar Hilaidaris, consisting of the king's sons, relatives, and very trustworthy youths of the kingdom were available for the king's protection, the absence of an exclusive regular and disciplined army proved disastrous. Besides, the paik system was effective as long as the king enjoyed the loyalty of his subjects, plus his ministers and bureaucracy were upright. But, the deficiency in both prerequisites proved ruinous to the Ahom kingdom. [17]

The Chronicler Shihabuddin Talish, who travelled with Mir Jumla, the Subahdar of Bengal in Eastern India under the Mughal Emperor Aurangzeb, during his 1662 expedition to the Ahom Kingdom, recorded, among other things, that:

"It is not the custom here (Ahom Kingdom) to take any land tax from the cultivators, but in every house, one man out of three has to render service to the Raja, and if there is any delay in doing what he orders, no other punishment other than death is inflicted. Hence, complete obedience is rendered by the people to the biddings of their Raja." [18]

Reproducing some of the accounts of Shihabuddin Talish in his book "A History of Assam," Sir Edward Gate wrote: "The contemporaneous account by a foreign observer, albeit somewhat critical, is of special interest, as it mentions many matters on which the indigenous records are silent." In the present context of our story, only two selected parts of the account are depicted below, which provide a glimpse of the contemporary state of affairs prevailing in the Ahom kingdom:

"... Narrow are the gates by which outsiders can enter or exit from this country, and slow are the feet on which its natives can travel to other countries. Their **kings neither allowed foreigners to enter their land nor permitted any of their own subjects to leave**. ..."

"....... The wives of the Rajas and peasants alike never veil their faces before anybody, and they move about in the marketplaces with bare heads. Few of the men have two wives only: most have four or five, and they mutually exchange wives or buy and sell them. Adoration among these people takes the form of kneeling down. The peasants who go to the Raja, or the nobles who have an audience with him, after bending both knees, sit down in the kneeling posture, keeping both eyes fixed on the ground. They shave their hair, beard, and moustaches. If any of the natives act contrary to this practice in the least particular, they say that he has adopted **the manners of the Bengalis,** and they cut off his head ....." [19] (Emphasis by Subir)

It needs to be mentioned here that this part of our country remained virtually cut off from the rest of the Indian subcontinent for a long time due to its geographical location, separated by numerous hills and rivers interspersed by deep valleys, and partly due to the deliberate isolation policy of the Ahoms. Most of the inhabitants settled along the fertile banks of the Brahmaputra River or on the banks of its tributaries. These alluvial plains were bordered by the wilderness of tall grass beyond which lay inhospitable and impenetrable jungles. The mode of transport was primitive. The only means of communication was by boat, elephants, or palki (Palankeen). Wheeled traffic was unknown. Even the bullock cart made its appearance only after the advent of the British. Under these circumstances, the Brahmaputra was the only highway connecting this region to India. The extremely long and tedious journey, coupled with adverse climatic conditions, were additional hazards that hindered the movements of men and material both inside and outside of North-East India. [20]

It is believed that the 14th Ahom King Suhungmung (1497–1539) was the first Ahom king to adopt a Hindu name: 'Swarga Narayan'. He and his successors were named 'Swargadeo' (Lord of Heaven). By the middle of the 16th century, the Ahoms were in control of almost all of present-day eastern Assam. After the 1682 Battle of Itakhuli, much of the control of Koch Hajo fell into the hands of the Ahoms. Thus, the Ahom kingdom gradually expanded and dominated most of the Brahmaputra River valley in the 16th to 18th centuries. By bringing the various indigenous ethnic groups and regions under one ruler and one governing polity, the Ahom kingdom eventually became the largest and most powerful among the pre-colonial principalities in North-East India.

By the end of the 17th century, the Ahoms were the unchallenged masters of almost the entire Brahmaputra valley, except the Goalpara region, with many tributary chiefs and princes owing allegiance. During this period, the Ahoms had to fight and subdue many tribes. The Moran and Barahi tribes were easily subdued and assimilated through marriage. Over the following three centuries, the Ahoms brought more powerful Chutiyas and Kacharis under their effective control, and by 1536, they were the foremost power in the region. Nevertheless, the emergence of the Koches to the west of their territory checked their expansion policy to a considerable extent.

The Ahoms and several other tribes were admitted into Hindu society but as peasant castes of low status. The Ahoms retaliated by not admitting high-caste Hindus to the top administrative crust of the state. Their society was not open to immigration unless it was on state initiative. After embracing Hinduism, the **Ahom kings invited high-caste Hindus to strengthen their newly adopted system. Bengal was found to be one of the most suitable sources for such importation.** It was an important centre of religio-cultural activity and conveniently located geographically. Artificers were also invited from Bengal. Numerous schools were established for the Brahmins. The Vaidikbrahmins came to the Ahom kingdom in the early sixteenth century and received the title Kamrupia-brahmins. The Rarhi-brahmins immigrated in the following century. Similarly, *ganaks* or *acharyas* also came from Bengal. The immigration of caste Hindu families into the kingdom increased during the reign of Sibsingha (1714-1744) [21] (Emphasis by Subir)

It is said that Ahom Kings ruled their territory for nearly 600 years from 1228 to 1826 AD and successfully resisted Mughal assaults by defeating their army seventeen times or so. However, some records show that out of all the Mughal incursions on the Ahom kingdom between 1615 and 1682, the Mughals actually won the wars at least six times. For example, in the conflict of 1637, the Mughals captured the whole of Kamrup. In another conflict, initially, Ahom King Jayadhwaj had to abandon his capital, but the battle continued with ups and downs for both the warring sides. Finally, a humiliating treaty had to be signed by King Jayadhwaj Singha at Ghilajharighat on 23rd January 1663, known as the Treaty of Ghilajharighat, to buy peace from the Mughals. Under the treaty, the Ahoms ceded western Assam to the Mughals and promised a war indemnity of Rupees three lakh plus ninety elephants. Besides, the king had to hand over his only daughter Ramani Gabharu as well as his niece to the harem of the Mughal emperor. Additionally, the king had to transfer Kamrup to the Mughals with a promise to pay heavy war compensation. Although these instances indicate that the conflicts were not one-sided, the reality is that the Ahoms could eventually push back the Mughals out of their Kingdom every time. In 1682, the conflicts between the Mughals and the Ahoms ended with the victory of Ahom King Gadadhar Singha when he regained Kamrup up to the Manas River in the battle of Itakhuli. That was the last major conflict between the Ahom and the Mughals. [22] [23] A YouTube video by StudyIQ Education titled "How Ahom defeated Mughals 17 times? Facts about Ahom Military Commander Lachit Borphukan" narrates the story interestingly.

Note: After the treaty of Ghilajharighat, Ramani Gabharu was reportedly taken to Dhaka and then to Delhi. She spent 10 years in Delhi and finally married Aurangzeb's third son, Muhammad Azam Shah. Ramani converted to Islam and took the name of Rahmat Banu. She accompanied her husband, Azam Shah, to Dhaka when he became its Subahdar in 1678. Fifteen months after he assumed charge of the Subahdar, Azam Shah left for Delhi accompanied by his other two wives, leaving Ramani Gabharu in Dhaka. In 2007, Bangladeshi economist and author Dr Abdun Noor wrote about the lost Princess Ramani Gabharu in his Bengali novel Bicholito Samay (Uncertain Times). The USA-based Dr Noor was searching for the Ahom Princess's lost trail and wondered why Ahom and Mughal histories were silent on the latter part of her life!

Source: Khosa, Aasha. "Bangladeshi author Dr Abdun Noor continues his search for the lost Ahom Princess". Awaz the Voice

One of the most prominent kings of the Ahom kingdom was the 17th King of the Ahom Dynasty, Susenghphaa (1603–1641). He was commonly known as Burha Raja (Old King) because he occupied the throne rather late - at the age of 58. His reign saw an expansion of the Ahom kingdom to the west, the beginning of the Ahom-Mughal conflicts, and a reorganization of the kingdom with an expanded Paik system and reoriented village economy. His spread to the West was underlined by the two new offices he created: the Borbarua and the Borphukan. The alliances Susenghphaa formed with the rulers of Koch Hajo resulted in a formation that successfully thwarted Mughal expansion. The administrative structure he created survived until the end of the Ahom rule.

The most well-known personality during the Ahom period, however, was Lachit Borphukan (1622-1672), who fought bravely against the Mughal Empire and successfully prevented them from taking control of the entire Ahom kingdom. An expert in the art of Guerrilla Warfare, Lachit served as the commander-in-chief of the Ahom kingdom. His utmost dedication and incomparable sincerity towards the King and the kingdom made him legendary. Every year, on the 24th of November, the people of Assam celebrate his birthday as Lachit Divas all over the state to honour the bravery and extraordinary efforts put in by Lachit Borphukan in winning the Battle of Saraighat.

In Indian history, the Battle of Saraighat was one of the most significant events, highlighting the importance of naval forces. It took place on the banks of the Brahmaputra River in Guwahati in March 1671 and was one of the greatest naval battles fought on a river. The Ahoms emerged victorious under the able leadership of Lachit Borphukan, who thwarted all attempts by the Mughals to deceive them. Despite his ill health, Lachit Borphukan resisted the Mughals' attempts to occupy the kingdom with his superior expertise in Guerrilla Warfare.

These days, the Lachit Borphukan gold medal is awarded to the best cadet from the National Defence Academy. The medal was instituted in 1999 to inspire defence personnel to emulate Borphukan's heroism and sacrifices.

The Ahoms reached the pinnacle of their glory during the reign of the early Tungkhungiya kings - a sub-branch of the Ahom dynasty that ruled the Ahom kingdom from 1681 till the end. The great king Rudra Singha (1696-1714) even mobilized his army, intending to extend his reach to the Karatoya River, the western boundary of the erstwhile kingdom of Kamrupa, thereby aiming to liberate the whole of eastern India from the yoke of the Mughals.

However, after Rudra Singha's death, his eldest son Sib Singha (1714-1744) ascended to the throne and assumed the Ahom name Sutanpha. He was heavily influenced by Brahman priests and astrologers, leading to the predominance of Hinduism as the primary religion. As a result, the Ahoms, who adhered to their traditional beliefs and tribal customs, were marginalized and viewed as a separate and degraded class.

To exacerbate matters, his chief queen, Phulesvari (one of the names of the Hindu Goddess Durga), was even more devout. In her fervent adherence to Sakta Hinduism, she committed an act of oppression with far-reaching and disastrous consequences. On one occasion, upon learning that Sudra Mahantas of the Vaishnava persuasion refused to worship Durga, she ordered Moamaria and several other Gosains to be brought to the Sakta shrine, where sacrifices were being offered. She caused the distinguishing marks of the Sakta sect to be smeared with the blood of the victims upon their foreheads. The Mahantas never forgave this insult to their spiritual leader, and half a century later, they rose in open rebellion.

As mentioned earlier, the Ahom rulers followed a policy of isolation in their relations with the West, meaning Mughal India. They feared that any relationship with Mughal India might result in the loss of their sovereignty and territorial boundaries. Accordingly, no Assamese trader was allowed to leave the kingdom, and strict vigilance was kept over the movement of Mughal traders. However, after the end of the Ahom-Mughal wars, this restriction was relaxed, and European merchants made the best use of this opportunity. Several outposts were established to monitor the transit of goods, but all duties were to be paid at the frontier outpost, usually called Assam *chauki* by the British. The *chauki* was supervised by one, and occasionally by two officers called Duaria Barua. The territory around the *chauki* was administered by another officer called Kandahar Barua. The Duaria Barua was supposed to pay an amount of Rs.90,000/- to the Ahom government, but only Rs.26,000/- of the amount reached the royal treasury. Barphukan used to conduct all trades with Bengal. The Duaria Barua, who had wide discretionary powers, used to inflate the rates of the customs duties fixed by the government and receive advances from the Bengal merchants for Assam goods. Sometimes, he used to trade with specific individuals and breach the terms of the contract. Hence, the officers associated with the Assam-Bengal trade, the Duaria Barua, and the Barphukan, particularly the merchants concerned, could amass considerable wealth.

Moreover, soon after the threat of external aggression receded and the Ahoms consolidated their strength, a feeling of superiority began to develop among the nobilities. They distinguished themselves as members of the ruling class, causing division even among themselves, between rulers and the ruled. The yearning for wealth, power, and recognition gave rise to corruption within the Ahom administration. The members of the ruling class started exploiting those they governed, leading to entanglements in personal conflicts among the aristocracies. This created an atmosphere of clan against clan, family against family, and man against man.

Furthermore, the rulers became so immersed in religious practices that worship and oblations took precedence over their duties to the state. Power-hungry nobles and officers began to override the authority of the king, initiating the disintegration of the Ahom kingdom. [24] [25]

The primary source of revenue for the Ahom kingdom was the commutation money realized from the *paiks* exempted from periodic corvee (unpaid forced labor) service, rent paid by *paiks* for cultivated lands beyond the tax-free allotment, and other miscellaneous duties. However, with the privileged classes such as Brahmins, astrologers (Ganaks), and priests increasingly acquiring rent-free (*lakheraj*) and semi-rent-free (*nisfkhraj*) lands, many of which later transformed into a kind of feudal lords, the kingdom's revenue resources dwindled. Consequently, various additional duties were levied on the common people, such as water tax for fishing, taxes for crossing rivers, sales tax, wealth tax, marriage tax, and more, to compensate for the shrinking revenue. Additionally, heavy taxation was imposed on people hereditarily engaged in collecting gold, iron, etc.

The growing imposition of such taxes, compulsory corvee labor, extreme socio-economic repression, and exploitation by the ruling class, contrasted with the steady progressions of class differences in society towards the end of the Ahom rule, set the stage for the peasant upsurge known as the Moamoria rebellion (1769–1805). [26]

The terminologies Moamaria, Mayamara, Matak, or Moran are often used indiscriminately and synonymously in various contexts. However, there are controversies regarding whether these terms are interchangeable or if this confusion arises due to crude generalizations. Biswadip Gogoi, a Junior Resource Person (JPR) at the National Translation Mission, Mysore, in his article titled "The Matak, Mayamara Sect, and Moamaria Revolt: A Brief Revisit," published in the Integrated Journal of Social Sciences on December 16, 2015 (Integr. J. Soc Sci., 2015, 2(1), 23-27), intricately discusses this question. [27] Without delving deeply into the subject, for the limited purpose of our story, let us consider the perspective of Sir Edward Gate, as cited by Biswadip Gogoi in the aforementioned article:

> "The terms Moran, Matak, and Moamaria are often used indiscriminately, but they are quite distinct. Moran is the name of a tribe, and Mayamaria (or Moamaria) refers to that sect, while Matak

refers to the country once ruled by the Bar-Senapati. The term 'Matak' is a ¹Shingpho word."

Note: ¹"Singpho," the local pronunciation of "Jingpho," is a dialect spoken by the Singpho people of present-day Arunachal Pradesh and Assam, India.

Today, the Morans are probably best known in Assam's history for the Moamaria revolt, which ended the Ahom dynastic rule, eventually paving the way for the founding of British colonial rule in this part of the country. Led by the Morans of present-day Upper Assam and orchestrated by Mayamara Mahanta, the Moamaria revolt drew support from various disciples of the Mayamara sattra. They were also joined by various other tribal groups oppressed and exploited by the ruling class through the paik system. At that time, the Moamaria revolt was instrumental in creating an autonomous territory, Matak Rajya (Matak State), with Bengmora, present-day Tinsukia, as the capital under the headship of Sarbananda Singha. Despite being from different castes, tribes, and communities such as Moran, Chutiya, Kachari, Ahom, Bihia, Kaivartas, Kalitas, Kayasthas, etc., these people joined hands to take part in the uprising.

Before delving into how commoners expressed their anguish against the ruling class of the Ahom kingdom, it is essential to shed light on Mahapurusha Srimanta Sankaradeva (1449-1568) to provide the episode of the Moamaria rebellion with proper perspective.

It was a watershed moment in the annals of the Ahom kingdom's political history when, in the 16th century, Srimanta Sankaradeva (1449-1568) established Mahapuruxiya Dharma. This proselytizing religion was open to all, including Muslims and tribesmen. Sankaradeva was a multifaceted genius, a forerunner of the Bhakti Movement, and a strong advocate of Vaishnavism. The Neo-Vaishnavite cult propounded by Sankaradeva transformed and modernized contemporary society with its classless ideology. His way of life and teachings were unique and different from other branches of Hindu philosophies, welcoming everyone, irrespective of caste, creed, and sex, into this order. The Mahapuruxiya Dharma, started by Srimanta Sankaradeva, offered an escape route for those working under the Paik system. The Sattras (Neo-Vaishnavite monasteries) became a safe haven to evade compulsory labour for those seeking to escape the "Paik" system, which was the backbone of the Ahom state.

Neo-Vaishnavism, initiated by Sankardeva, opposed idol worship, while idol worship was an integral practice within Brahminical and Sakta ritual forms. Consequently, Brahmins became adversaries to the Vaishnavas concerning religious beliefs and practices. As expected, conflict arose between the Ahom rulers and the Sattaras, as the former viewed the Vaishnavas and their Sattaras (monasteries) as a challenge to their established religious order. The Ahom rulers feared the steady influx of thousands of subjects into the burgeoning Sattaras, away from the grip of the Paik system. They worried that charismatic Sattra Gurus, swaying many high-born individuals, would undermine the Ahom king's authority over the populace.

Hence, mainstream sects and the Shakti order launched vigorous theological assaults and urged compliant kings to suppress or eradicate the nonconformist Sattras. Periodic campaigns ensued, resulting in the destruction of many Sattras and the deaths of prominent priests and followers. For example, in 1650, Moyamoria guru Nityanandadev was killed by order of Ahom king Surampha or Bhogaraja. In 1691, another Moyamoria guru, Vaikunthanathdev, also known as Saptabhujdev, was killed during the reign of King Supaatpha or Gadadhar Singha. While a few Sattaras retaliated, others either could not or chose not to respond effectively. There were instances where the tension between the two schools of thought escalated, prompting Sankaradeva himself to seek refuge in the Koch kingdom during the reign of Suklemung to evade persecution.

The Brahmins effectively employed the state apparatus against the Vaishnavas, particularly the Moamorias. On numerous occasions, Moyamoria Mahantas were publicly insulted by Ahom kings and royal officials. The mistreatment of the Moamorias provoked such outrage that it sparked their rebellion against the oppressive state forces, leading to over 35 years of Moamaria rebellion (1769–1805). This rebellion played a significant role in ending the 600-year dynastic rule of the Ahoms.

The first Moamaria revolt commenced in 1769 AD, sparked by an act of brutality perpetrated by the arrogant Kirtichandra Barbarua over what seemed like a trivial incident. In the month of Aswin (September/October 1769), two Moran disciples of Moyamoria satra, Nahar Khora Saikia and Ragha Neog, went to offer their regular tributes of elephants to the Ahom king. They incurred the displeasure of Barbarua, purportedly for bringing him a lean elephant and for not paying their respects to him before presenting themselves to the king. Enraged, Barbarua ordered Nahar's ears to be severed and Ragha to receive twenty lashes. This incident incited the Morans, led by Ragha Neog and Nahar Khora Saikia, to launch a revolt against the ruling class, known as the 'Moran revolt' in Assam's history.

The revolt swiftly spread throughout upper Assam, with individuals from various castes, tribes, and communities spontaneously joining the uprising. Assisted by ordinary paiks, they liberated the territory north of the Burhidihing River. On 21st November 1769, the rebels seized control of the Ahom capital, Rongpur, and enthroned Ramananda, Nahar Khora Saikia's son. The Ahom king, Lakshmi Singha, Kirtichandra, and several other key officials attempted to flee but were promptly captured. The rebels placed the king under house arrest, executed Kirtichandra and other officials, and assumed control of the kingdom's administration.

All significant positions traditionally held by scions of aristocratic Ahom families were now made accessible to commoners. Three common Mataks ascended to the positions of the three great Gohains: Ragh Neog became the Borbarua, a Kanri paik assumed the role of Borphukan, and two common Ahoms were appointed as Gohains at Sadiya and Marangi. An ordinary paik was dispatched to Guwahati as Borphukan.

However, the inexperienced rebels, lacking in statecraft, failed to institute a new order. Instead, they began emulating the unpopular practices of their former leaders. Ragh Neog seized the wives and daughters of numerous nobles, confining them to his harem. As some rebel officers started mimicking the behaviour of the old nobility, discontent grew among many rebels. Four months after seizing power, they departed the capital under the leadership of Govinda Gaoburha. Seizing this opportunity, some of the old nobility assassinated Ragh on 14th April 1770. With the assistance of Kuranganayani, an Ahom queen from Manipur, they reclaimed the capital. Amid the ensuing chaos, almost all the key leaders, including the head of Moyamaria Sattra and his son, were executed.

Upon the loyalists' recapture of the capital, the remaining Moamaria rebels in Sagunmuri, led by Govinda Gaoburha, attempted to overthrow the king once more. This uprising, too, bore the hallmarks of popular support. The rebels primarily wielded bamboo staves and clubs as weapons. In one engagement, both the Borpatrogohain and the Dhekial Phukan were killed, and the Borgohain narrowly escaped. The rebels advanced toward Rongpur, only to be met at Thowra by forces comprising the Burhagohain, the new Borpatrogohain, the Borgohain, and a cavalry detachment from the Manipur king. In the ensuing battle, the rebels were defeated; Govinda Gaoburha was captured and subsequently executed. Following this, the Burhagohain systematically razed villages and executed remaining leaders, resulting in many rebels and their families perishing from starvation during the siege. The surviving populace was then dispersed and resettled in different areas. This suppression process spanned almost a year, marking the end of the first phase of the Moamoria rebellion.

Meanwhile, during the internal disturbances connected to the Moamaria rebellion, a disastrous famine struck the lower Gangetic Plains of India between 1769 and 1773. An estimated 10 million people died of starvation and famine-triggered epidemics, mainly affecting the Bengal and Bihar regions. However, the Ahom kingdom could not escape the catastrophic consequences, experiencing starvation deaths and famine-triggered epidemics. The famine hit the rural poor the hardest, pushing families to adopt increasingly desperate means of survival. This took a toll on the demography, as food scarcity worsened due to the adverse impact on agricultural production during the uprising. Even individuals of the highest castes were reportedly forced to consume wild fruits, roots, and the flesh of cows, buffaloes, dogs, and jackals.

The second phase of the Moamaria revolt began in 1782 AD. The royal persecution unleashed by the Ahom administration to control rebellious subjects, particularly the heavily tortured Moomarias in the previous revolt, instilled a deep-seated yearning for revenge among the populace. This sentiment gradually spread to areas where the influence of sattras was marginal. Disgruntled people began to organize themselves under the guise of kirtan (community prayer songs) and other religious congregations. By 1782, numerous secret organizations emerged to retaliate against imperial oppression. In April, during the Ahoms' spring festival, Bohag Bihu, an armed group of Moamaria rebels launched a sudden attack on a convoy of the Ahom king. Despite the king managing to escape, the rebels entered the capital and captured several important royal officials. However, they were eventually overpowered within a couple of days by the massive royal onslaught.

The Ahom administration then unleashed an unprecedented, ruthless reign of repression in retaliation. Since most rebels were ordinary peasants belonging to the Moyamaria faith, all Moamarias were subjected to severe retribution. Thousands of farmer paiks lost their lives, and many fled to neighbouring kingdoms. This had a severe adverse impact on agricultural production, pushing the economy of the Ahom kingdom to the verge of collapse. The remnants of the paik system, reorganized after the first upsurge, fell into disarray under the latest chaotic situation.

The third phase of the Moamaria revolt took place between 1786 and 1794. Following two consecutive revolts by the people, the Ahom administration became vulnerable to a great extent. In the border areas of the kingdom, the government substantially lost its authority, retaining control only in the core areas surrounding the capital. Rebel forces began to organize in the border areas, where many had deserted their homes in response to ruthless royal repression.

Gradually, several leaders emerged among the rebels, all from humble backgrounds of downtrodden peasant-artisan communities. In a very short period, the rebels brought a vast area in the northeast frontier of the Ahom kingdom under their control. Meanwhile, a group of rebels freed the Moamaria sattradhikar (head of the sattra), who was held captive in Aoniati sattra, and set it on fire along with the sattras of Garmur and Dakhinpath, as well as all royalist sattras on the river island Majuli. These sattras adhered to Vedic principles and had Brahmin sattradhikars. The rebels then executed the sattradhikars of Bareghar and Budhbari sattras, which belonged to the Kala samhati, for collaborating with the royal side.

These successive triumphs of the rebel forces over the royal forces attracted many paiks to join their ranks. They gradually marched towards Ahom's capital, Rongpur. The Morans, under the leadership of Sarbananda from the eastern part of Assam, also advanced towards Rongpur, and both forces surrounded the capital. In this tense situation, as the Moamarias approached the capital's gates, King Gurunath Singha convened consultations with his ministers to determine the next course of action. The ministers recommended a retreat to Gauhati due to the hostile and dangerous attitude of the people of Rongpur. Consequently, the king and important nobles vacated the palace at midnight on January 19th/20th, 1788, using the pani-duar (river gateway). The king departed in such haste that he left behind his queens, who, accompanied by their maids, proceeded on the same night to Lechang under the Premier Escort and the newly appointed Dihingiya Sarudeka Barbarua. The following morning, the Moamarias captured the capital, Rongpur.

Purnananda Burhagohain, a high-profile minister in the Ahom government, and the Dihingiya Barbarua took immediate steps to retake the capital and prevent the old Ahom capital, Garhgaon, from falling into the hands of the Moamarias. After fierce battles, the rebels entered Garhgaon and set fire to all the houses in the city. Subsequently, the Moamarias began to bring villages into submission, and some common people on the Ahom side also began to surrender themselves to the insurgents. After taking possession of Garhgaon, one division led by a leader named Pabha proceeded to Charaideo, where they set fire to the temple buildings and destroyed the properties.

Again, within a very short period, the popular rebel forces extended their authority to many areas. The rebels ransacked pockets wherever they encountered resistance from any remnant royalist forces. However, the rebel leaders did not attempt to establish a centralized administration over the liberated areas. Harihara Tanti, who hailed from an artisan community in weaving, ruled over a large tract on the north bank of Brahmaputra. His lieutenant, Howha, became the ruler of Majuli. Sarbananda became Raja in the Moran habitat in the northeast part of the Ahom kingdom. Another rebel leader and distant kin of the late Maomora Sattradhikar, Bhart, was chosen as the king of Rongpur. The new regime then tried to bring peace to the state ravaged by civil war.

After fleeing from the capital Rangpur, Gaurinath Singh took shelter in Gauhati, where his position was also not safe. Disturbances broke out in Darrang relating to controversies over the succession to the throne. Gaurinath Singh imprudently interfered in the matter, dismissed the claim of the Koch prince Krishnanarayan as Raja of Darrang, and managed to make Bishnunarayan the Raja. As a result, disgruntled Krishnanarayan raised a revolt against the Ahom king and started finding ways to capture power in Darrang. Both Ahom king Gaurinath Singh and Darrang Prince Krishnanarayan initiated steps to enlist some outside help. That was the backdrop against which the Barkandazes entered the chaotic scene in the Ahom kingdom, adding a critical dimension to the complexities arising out of the Moamaria rebellion.

Barkandazes were typically comprised of disbanded soldiers from Muslim armies or Zamindars. Following the collapse of states like Awadh, Bengal, Bundelkhand, and the decline of Mughal power, native soldiers found themselves unemployed. Consequently, these ex-soldiers turned to plundering, roaming highways and provincial borders, preying on traders, pilgrims, and travellers. Bundelkhandes weren't large organized groups; rather, they operated in small bands of fortune hunters, often transforming into mercenaries or armed ruffians lacking ethics, moral conduct, or loyalty. They were willing to offer their services to anyone who provided money and resources.

The Barkandazes included Sikhs, Rajputs, Muslims, and fighting Sanyasis from various provinces, ranging from Bengal to Lahore. They formed bands of Sanyasis and Fakirs, using religious pilgrimages as a cover to beg, steal, and plunder across Bengal, terrorizing its people. Their depredations "unhinged the rural administration of Bengal" and became commonplace occurrences. Among them, the barbarities of Manju Shah were particularly notorious.

Equipped with horses, camels, rockets, and various arms, Barkandazes Sanyasis and Fakirs typically offered their services with a matchlock and a sword, relieving their employers of the need to supply weapons. Local Zamindars employed them to intimidate villagers, disgruntled rebel princes and nobles enlisted them against the state, and even officers of the East India Company utilized them in times of emergency.

When King Gaurinath Singh sent a letter from Gauhati to the Company's Resident, Hugh Bailey, at Goalpara seeking military assistance to regain his lost power and position in the northeastern region, Bailey managed to dispatch some Barkandazes who had formerly served under him. As these Barkandazes proceeded toward Gauhati, they were intercepted by Krishnanarayan. King Gaurinath Singh then contacted Daniel Raush, the former salt revenue officer at Goalpara. Raush sent seven hundred Barkandazes under Subedar Chait Singh and assured King Gaurinath that he would write to Calcutta for more if the force proved inadequate. Gaurinath Singh, in turn, deployed these Barkandazes to aid Purananda, who had been resisting the Moamarias in the present-day upper Assam area. However, the Moamarias killed most of the Barkandazes in a battle fought near the river Kakila. Thus, despite his vigorous efforts, Puranananda could neither drive out the Moamarias from Rangpur nor protect Garhgaon and Charideo. All his other companions either deserted him or were killed on the battlefield. Consequently, he sailed downwards, intending to join the king.

On the other hand, when the British turned down Krishnanarayana's appeals for support in capturing Darrang and Kamrup, he began recruiting men from the Company's territories on his own initiative. He gathered around 3000 Barkandazes from Bengal and elsewhere through agents like Phatik Barua of Darrang, Dhir Singh Jamadar of Punjab, and others. Many Assamese recruits joined this group. The Barkandaz force was commanded by Munder Khan, formerly a Subedar in the Company's service.

In December 1791, Krishnanarayan entered Assam, captured Darrang, and proclaimed himself the Raja. He also seized north Gauhati and spread rumours that they were acting with the authority of the Bengal government. Krishnanarayan and the Barkandazes ravaged the country, leaving the people virtually defenceless against these unsympathetic foreign elements. Gaurinath Singh and his ministers were unable to stop them.

Gaurinath Singh then began making overtures for a political settlement with Krishnanarayan, who was willing to accept it. However, at that time, he was effectively a prisoner in the hands of the Barkandazes. Despite his desire to proceed with a political settlement, Barkandaz leaders Hari Singh and Durjan Singh prevented Krishnanarayan from accepting such a proposal. They made unreasonable demands and defied directives from the Bengal government. Additionally, they threatened to forcibly conquer the entire Ahom kingdom. More Barkandazes entered the kingdom via Jogigopa.

Meanwhile, plundering and killings in the Ahom kingdom escalated to such an extent that the deteriorating situation became a concern for the Bengal government. The Barkandazes grew increasingly arrogant, disregarding warnings from the British government and asserting that they were within Company territories and not subject to the Bengal government or its officers. With the Moamaria rebellion on one hand and the disturbances caused by the Barkandazes on the other, the situation in the Brahmaputra valley quickly became chaotic and uncontrollable. Calls for military assistance to expel the Barkandazes and suppress the Moamaria rebellion began reaching the British government from various sources. The ongoing lawlessness in the region also severely impacted British business interests.

Considering these factors, Governor-General Lord Cornwallis eventually decided to dispatch "an active and prudent officer" with six companies of soldiers to drive the Barkandazes out of the Ahom kingdom and restore Gaurinath Singh to authority.

Captain Thomas Welsh, renowned for his distinguished military career in India, was chosen for this expedition. He arrived in Goalpara on November 8th, 1792, where he met with Raush and Bishnuarayan, who had been expelled from Darrang. He also encountered Gaurinath Singh near Nagarbera Hill, on the southern bank of the Brahmaputra. Gaurinath had fled from Gauhati due to depredations committed near his residence by a group of Moamarias under the leadership of Borgai Raja. Welsh captured Gauhati, facilitating Gaurinath Singh's re-entry into the city on November 25th, 1792.

Captain Welsh initiated negotiations with Krishnanarayan and the leaders of the Barkandazes, who defied Welsh's directive to come to Gauhati within 10 days and prevented Krishnanarayan from leaving their custody. With more Barkandazes entering the kingdom, Welsh decided to take action. He successfully seized Aswakranta Hill, a stronghold of Krishnarayan and the Barkandazes, forcing them to retreat to Darrang. Hundreds of Barkandazes lost their lives during the retreat to Bhutan, where they burnt and destroyed many villages along the way.

Welsh restored Gaurinath to his position and mediated a compromise between King Gaurinath and Krishnanarayan, who was accepted as the Raja of Darrang by Gaurinath. The 400 Barkandazes who remained with Krishnanarayan surrendered at Gauhati, where they were promptly disarmed and dispersed after receiving their overdue salaries. Many other groups of Barkandazes remaining in the kingdom were also defeated in various encounters. <u>Captain Thomas Welsh concluded his expedition in May 1794.</u> [29]

Meanwhile, the Moamaria rebels kept their resistance alive in several parts of the northeast of the Ahom kingdom. The kingdom had organized a new army based on the British model to combat the rebels by this time. This army was trained, armed with guns, and received regular salaries. Many Hindustani sepoys serving under the British were recruited into this army.

However, the rebellious zeal of the Moamarias had not diminished, yet their defeats against the British greatly weakened them. Furthermore, in the prevailing chaos and confusion, the earlier communication network among the rebels was dismantled. Under such circumstances, it became very difficult for the Moamaria rebels to withstand the royal attacks. Yet, Bharat continued his rebellion against the Ahom army until he was killed in 1799 after a fierce battle. Then the royal force engaged in a protracted conflict with the Moran kingdom founded by Sarbananda until 1805 when both forces became exhausted and entered into an agreement recognizing each other's jurisdiction. The Morans resumed their traditional vassal obligations to pay in raw cotton, ivory, and elephants to the Ahom king. With this, the long and bloody struggles among different classes in the Ahom kingdom and its tributaries came to an end.

Though the Moamoria rebellion ended in failure, it played a significant role in demolishing the exploitative paik and khel system. The revolt eventually compelled the state to transition toward a money economy. The introduction of a salaried army by the reinstated Ahom king in the late 1990s was notable. The chaos caused by the Moamaria revolts hindered the growth of feudalism that had begun spreading in the Ahom kingdom. The pervasive disorder and internal conflicts between the kings and the nobles eventually invited the Burmese to the already devastated and depopulated Ahom kingdom - throwing its people out of the frying pan into the fire!

Dibrugarh University History Professor S. L. Baruah succinctly articulated that position with the following words:

> "Any repressive or atrocious rule is still called in Assam Manar Din or the Burmese reign of terror. Indeed, it was under the Burmese that the people of Assam experienced the extreme horrors of death and destruction. The Burmese played the final scene of the tragic drama of the fall of the Ahom monarchy. But the event was not an accident; it was only the culmination of the political forces long at work in the eastern and western frontiers of the kingdom of Assam. The kings and the nobles of Assam, by their cupidity and short-sightedness, expedited the process of the conflict of the imperial powers. The result was most disastrous for the people of Assam." [30]

On 28th October 1793, John Shore succeeded Lord Cornwallis as the British Governor-General of Bengal. Following this change in the incumbency of the Bengal Governor-General, a radical shift in British policy towards North-East India occurred. John Shore was not prepared to take on any avoidable political commitments, especially in a region that lay outside the sphere of the Company's domain. Therefore, Captain Welsh was recalled despite repeated pleas from Ahom King Gaurinath for the retention of the British troops. Consequently, the Ahom kingdom lapsed into its former state of anarchy and internal strife.

The situation deteriorated further when even the Ahom court became divided following the premature death of Gaurinath Singha in 1795. His successors, first Kamaleswar Singha (1795-1811) and then Chandrakanta Singha (1811-1818), were mere puppets in the hands of Purnananda Buragohain, the prime minister. The latter became the virtual ruler of the upper part of the Ahom kingdom, i.e., present-day upper Assam. Badan Chandra Barphukan, the king's viceroy in the lower part of the Ahom kingdom, i.e., present-day lower Assam, bitterly opposed this personal rule of the Buragohain. Their hostility was so deep-rooted that the Buragohain sent a senior officer with adequate force to arrest the Barphukan and bring him to the capital. Upon learning about this, Badan Chandra fled to Calcutta to seek British aid. Failing to convince the British, he turned to other quarters for help. During his stay in Calcutta, he came into contact with the political agents of the Burmese government and expressed his desire to approach the king in Burma for assistance. Badan Chandra later accompanied the agents to the Burmese capital, Amarpur, and appeared before the Burmese monarch, Badawpaya (1781-1819), appealing for military aid. In his interview with Badawpaya, he stated:

> "I have come from the country Mung-pet-ching (a corrupt form of the term Vaisali, which stands for the whole of India) of the east. There is no king worth the name in Weissali (Assam). It has become a deserted dominion, and its people are passing through a time of great distress. For this reason, I, considering you as the Sun God, have come to you after overcoming so much hardship and danger on the way. Whomever I met on the way in these hills, in the dales and the river, I asked about you and have arrived here at last." [31]

The Burmese, ever anxious to extend their dominion westwards, made their appearance on the scene in 1817. A Burmese army crossed the Patkai and eventually reinstated Chandrakanta to his rightful position. Badan Chandra was appointed Premier with the designation Mantri Phukan. The Burmese were paid one lakh rupees as remuneration, in addition to offering suitable presents to their commanders. Furthermore, an Ahom princess, Hemo Aideo, the daughter of an Ahom prince named Baga Konwar, who represented Chandrakanta's own sister, was handed over to the Burmese General to be presented to their king along with 50 elephants. Hemo Aideo received a rich dowry.

Although Badan Chandra and Chandrakanta now presented themselves as all-powerful, most nobles soon realized that they had brought humiliation to the Ahom kingdom by offering subsidies and a princess to the Burmese monarch. From then onwards, the Burmese began to treat the Ahom kingdom as a vassal state, as according to their custom, **offering a princess was equivalent to the acceptance of allegiance.**

Anyway, shortly after their withdrawal, Chandrakanta was deposed and mutilated in order to disqualify him from claiming the throne. Purandar Singha, another scion of the royal family, was crowned in his place. Chandrakanta again appealed to the Burmese, who returned with a larger force in 1819 under the command of Ala Mingi. After putting up mild resistance, Purandar Singha fled to Gauhati and took refuge in Chilmari, Bengal. Chandrakanta was reinstated to the throne by the Burmese.

However, Chandrakanta soon realized that the Burmese attitude towards the Ahom kingdom had undergone a radical change. In 1817, they had retreated of their own accord, content with a large indemnity, a princess, and a vague acknowledgement of their suzerainty by the Ahom king. But the second time around, in 1819, they appeared to have territorial designs. The new Burmese king, Ba-gyi-daw, was determined to bring the Ahom empire under Burmese domain. In these circumstances, Chandrakanta found himself increasingly sidelined, a mere puppet at the hands of the Burmese. Without hope of receiving help from any quarter, Chandrakanta was left with no option but to flee to British territory. From there, he made several abortive attempts to recover his lost position. However, the Burmese king viewed the developments with serious concern. In 1822, he sent one of his greatest generals, Minigmaha Bandula, with an army of 30,000 men and forced Chandrakanta into submission. The Burmese installed another member of the Ahom royal family, Jogeswar Singha, as the new puppet ruler of the kingdom, but the de facto ruler was Minigimaha. It virtually marked the end of nearly 600 years of Ahom rule in Northeast India.

Soon, a reign of terror unleashed by the Burmese army became the order of the day in the conquered kingdom, in retaliation for Chandrakanta's earlier abortive attempts to regain power. The Burmese plundered and burnt villages, committing indiscriminate atrocities on innocent citizens. The helpless people suffered untold misery.

Major John Butler, who arrived in Assam in 1837, recorded a story of mass killings by the Burmese in 1819-20 on the bank of the Kalang River. After decapitating 50 persons in a single day, the Burmese placed many men, women, and children on a bamboo platform inside a house made of bamboo and thatch. They then set fire to the house, and 200 persons were consumed by flames in a few minutes. People fled to remote jungles and neighbouring countries to escape the horrors and cruelties of mutilation and death. [32]

In the words of an eyewitness, Maniram Dewan, an Assamese nobleman in British India:

> "The Burmese, in attacking a rich man's house, would tie him with ropes and then set fire to his body. Some were flayed alive, others burnt in oil, and still others were driven in crowds to village Namghars or prayer houses, which they then set on fire... It was dangerous for a beautiful woman to encounter a Burmese, even on a public road. Brahmanas were made to carry loads of beef, pork, and wine. The Gossains were robbed of all their possessions. Fathers of damsels whom the Burmese took as wives quickly rose to affluence." [33]

A similar account was given by the renowned Assamese author Dutiram Hazarika, who was privy to the last king of the Ahom dynasty, Purandar Singha:

> "A number of men and women would be shut up in a house, which would be set on fire afterwards. Youthful virgins were forced to become their wives. The people fled to distant parts of the country, where they were plundered and killed by the Dafalas and other wild tribes. Villagers were robbed of their property and subjected to inhuman tortures if they couldn't produce their money. The fathers of beautiful maidens had great favour with the Burmese. They would be readily admitted to their fold, dress as Burmese, and commit excesses upon their countrymen. The people taking shelter in forests did not fare better, and babies in the arms died due to starvation and the death of their mothers. The Burmese dishonoured all women they came across on the roads and thoroughfares. The ugly and unattractive ones were left to the mercy of fate, while their more beautiful sisters enjoyed the continued patronage of the Shan invaders. Daughters were molested in the presence of their parents, and wives before their husbands." [34]

Meanwhile, relations between the Burmese and the British had become strained. The Burmese had plundered villages in Habraghat in Rongpur and encroached upon British possession of Goalpara. It was also rumoured that General Mingimaha was contemplating a full-scale attack on Goalpara. In 1823, the Burmese occupied the island of Shahpuri on the Chittagong frontier. They had forced Gambhir Singh, the Raja of Manipur, to surrender and expelled Govinda Chandra, the Raja of Cachar. The Burmese preparations for an impending three-pronged attack on Bengal made the situation all the more alarming for the government. Apart from being a security threat, Burmese activities on the frontier also hindered British commercial interests in the region. These circumstances compelled the East India Company's government to review its prevailing policy of non-intervention.

In November 1823, David Scott was appointed as Agent to the Governor-General of the North-Eastern Frontier in addition to his current duties as Commissioner of Rangpur. As early as July 1822, David Scott, as Agent to the Governor-General of the North-East Frontier, had informed the government:

> "The Burmese, having obtained complete mastery of Assam and a person of that nation having been appointed to the supreme authority, the country may now be considered as a province of the Burman empire." [35]

Scott's continued reports of the alarming situation on the frontier convinced the Governor-General-in-Council to adopt strong measures to punish and restrain the Burmese. Reviewing the encroachments of the Burmese in Arakan, Assam, and Cachar, the council adopted a resolution concluding that the Burmese activities must be regarded as having placed the two countries in a state of actual war. The British declared war against the Burmese on 5th March 1824. Some British forces were led by Lieutenant Colonel Richards, who advanced up the Brahmaputra and occupied Rongpur. Soon after, the Burmese were expelled from Cachar and Manipur. However, on the Chittagong front, the British troops suffered a crushing defeat at Ramoo. Nonetheless, the Burmese did not advance further as their General Minigmaha Bandula was recalled to Ava. In February 1825, General Campbell marched north at the head of two columns, one proceeding by land and the other by the Irrawaddy River. The Burmese occupied a strongly fortified position at Danabyu, 60 miles northeast of Rangoon, under the command of Bandula. On 1st April 1825, Bandula was killed by a rocket, and with his death, all resistance practically ceased.

Meanwhile, simultaneous campaigns in Arakan, Tenasserim, Pegu, and Upper Burma had taken a heavy toll on the Burmese. The death of General Minigmaha Bandula in April 1825 compounded their problems. In September 1825, the Burmese proposed a truce. However, negotiations failing, the British resumed their advance towards Ava, the capital of Burma (1364-1841). The Burmese then again proposed peace, and the treaty terms were discussed. Later, a treaty was signed by the two parties, and a truce was agreed upon until the 18th of January to enable the envoys to obtain necessary ratification from the King. As the ratified treaty did not arrive, General Campbell occupied Malun and Pagun-Myo and continued his march towards Ava. At Yandao, 45 miles from Ava, a Burmese delegation met General Campbell again, conveying the King's agreement upon the terms and delivered 25 lakhs of rupees, the first instalment of one crore of war indemnity demanded by the British. Accordingly, General Campbell signed the peace treaty from the British side, and Governor of Legaing, Maha Min Hla Kyaw Htin, from the Burmese side at Yandabo on 24th February 1826. [36] [37] [38] [39] [40]

Sir Edward Gate, in his book "A History of Assam," narrated the condition of the people of the Ahom kingdom after the expulsion of the Burmese as follows:

> The condition of the Brahmaputra valley at the time of the expulsion of the Burmese was most deplorable. No less than thirty thousand Assamese had been taken away as slaves, and a well-known native authority was of the opinion that the invaders, by their barbarous and inhuman conduct, had 'destroyed more than one-half of the population which had already been thinned by the intensive commotion and repeated civil wars.' Those who survived had been so harassed by long-continued wars and repeated acts of oppression that they had almost given up cultivation and lived chiefly on jungle roots and plants, and famine and pestilence carried off thousands that had escaped the sword and captivity. The Ahom nobles and the great Gosains, with few exceptions, had retired to Goalpara after losing the whole or bulk of their property; and large numbers of the common people followed them. The former eventually returned to their homes, but the poorer refugees did not, and their descendants still form a large proportion of the eastern part of Goalpara. [41]

Interestingly, Sir Edward Gate, in the same chapter of his book "A History of Assam," mentioned that Goalpara, including Garo Hills but excluding the Eastern Duars, was originally administered from Rangpur and, as such, formed part of the province of Bengal (under the Mughal rule). Later on, it was transferred to the East India Company by the Mughal Emperor's 'Farman' on the 12th of August 1765. Therefore, it is clear that Goalpara was not a part of the Ahom kingdom before the Burmese took over, as many people believe today. The refugees and their descendants, forming a large proportion of the eastern part of Goalpara, were displaced persons from the Ahom kingdom.

It is to be noted that the internal disturbances arising out of the Moamaria uprising, coupled with the effect of the Bengal famine (1769-1773) followed by the Burmese invasion, had a near-annihilating consequence on the demography of the Ahom kingdom. Before the Moamaria rebellion (which started in 1769), its population was estimated at two and a half million (or 25 lakhs). Immediately **after the Moamaria revolt and the Burmese invasion, the estimated population came down to 7 lakhs.** [42] Therefore, during these intervening 57 years, instead of registering a natural growth of population, the Ahom kingdom ended up with an incredible decline of 18 lakhs in its population, which is a drop of 72% of its people! Considering the natural population growth that must have occurred during the period, it won't be an exaggeration to say that **about 3/4th or three out of every four persons of the Ahom kingdom perished between 1769 and 1826.** (Emphasis by Subir)

Thus, *the British appeared in the Ahom kingdom at the worst hour of its peril. Wrecked by repeated ravages of the Burmese onslaught, the people heaved a sigh of relief. They welcomed British rule with 'unbounded joy' and cherished 'sanguine hopes of peace and prosperity under its protection.* It marked the end of nearly 600 years of the Ahom kingdom. The British Colonial rulers annexed the territory in 1826. Nevertheless, before delving into the colonial period of Assam's history proper, the economic importance of opium to the British and its far-reaching ramifications in shaping Assam's future need to be narrated briefly. This will help in understanding how it played a significant role in the large-scale influx of 'outsiders' into the depopulated and desolated territory.

So, it's now over to 'The Story of OPIUM' in the next chapter.

* * * * * * *

Chapter 2.

The Story of OPIUM

"কেপা-কানি বিহৰ শেষ ।
কানীয়াৰ নাই জ্ঞানৰ লেশ ॥
হায় হায়! কি ঘোৰ ক্লেশ ।
কানিয়েই খালে অসম দেশ ॥"

"Dwindled is the opium stash,
Fading its induced stupor from the scholar's head!
Oh! The trauma and the suffering,
My beloved Assam - doomsday is beckoning!" *

(*English adaptation by Subir)

This stanza is from the concluding part (Section IV, Third Scene) of the Assamese satirical drama "Kaniar Kirtan" (The Carol of Opium Eaters), composed in 1861 by the eminent Assamese lexicographer, writer, and social reformer Hemchandra Barua. In the satire, he lamented the cancerous spread of the habit of opium consumption in Assamese society, predicting it to be a sign of the approaching doomsday. [1]

In the article "On the Evils of Opium Eating: Reflections on Nineteenth-Century Assamese Literary Reformist Discourse," Kawal Deep Kour, a PhD candidate in Narcotics at IIT Guwahati (Assam), wrote the following in the 'Abstract':

Acknowledgement of the evils of opium eating also echoed in several literary outpourings of the nineteenth century, which sought to combine entertainment and reform. Facilitating an understanding of the nineteenth-century reformist discourse are two Assamese satirical texts by Hemchandra Barua and Dutiram Hazarika. They enable an evaluation of the perception of the Assamese mind in the nineteenth century towards issues of social reform. Both texts reveal a strong sense of antagonism towards those traditions which nurture the perpetuation of social practices such as opium consumption, which, as widely upheld by Christian missionaries, medical opinion, and social reformers, had resulted in both physical and mental degeneration of the people. The idea that opium addiction was synonymous with backwardness and degeneration made the intelligentsia adopt as its agenda the amelioration of the "opium evil." These texts, resorting to the use of satire, wit, and humour, spearheaded an innovative reform agenda. [2]

"The universal use of opium has converted the Assamese, once hardy, industrious, and enterprising, into an effeminate, weak, indolent, and degraded people," wrote the famous Assamese writer Anandaram Dhekian Phukan in his Memorandum to A.J.M. Moffat Mills (1819–1859). Andrew Moffatt Mills was deputed to investigate the conditions of the province of Assam in 1853. In his Report on the Province of Assam, Mills summarily agreed with what Anandaram Dhekial Phukan thought and thus claimed that

"..... 3/4ths of the population are opium-eaters and men, women, and children alike use the drug." [3]

It was in this context that "Kaniyar Kirtan", along with Dutiram Hazarika's "Rasik Puran" (1877), played a decisive role in determining the trajectory of the reformist discourse. Drawing inspiration from the zeal of Bengal's Raja Rammohun Roy and the revolutionary tenor of Ishwar Chandra Vidyasagar, Hemchandra Barua's Kaniyar Kirtan reveals his detestation for redundant social customs and religious hypocrisy and a genuine concern for social reform. His reformist temper drew sustenance from his interactions with the intelligentsia of Bengal through the medium of Orunodoi as well as from the writings of Anandaram Dhekial Phukan and Gunabhiram Barua. Their writings were relevant to the times and directed against social evils.

The menace of widespread opium consumption in Assam figured prominently in intellectual discourses as an evil practice that needed immediate redressal. Accordingly, Anandaram Dhekial Phukan submitted a Memorandum to Mr Moffat Mills, arguing that opium had universally been the sole cause of undermining the health and physical condition of the entire population. It was used by the young as well as the old. He urged the government to provide speedy and effective remedies to preserve the country from degradation.

Composed in 1861, Kaniyar Kirtan reflected the sensibility of a social crusader. It set for itself the avowed objective of ameliorating the sufferings consequent upon indulgence in opium, the pain of a society witnessing a continuous decay of human values due to its hypocrisy and superstitions. Kaniyar Kirtan was written in the form of dialogues dominated by satirical elements. Each scene is divided into darshan (acts). Barua's satire is ruthless, devoid of sympathy and is often set in contrast with the jovial, with brilliant wit and the inimitable twist of words and expressions. [3]

Anandaram Dhekial Phukan was one of the pioneers of Assamese literature. His most significant contribution to Assamese society was reinstating the Assamese language to its rightful place in Assam. He was instrumental in replacing Bengali with the Assamese language as a medium of instruction in Assam's schools and courts. Given his perception of the condition of the Assamese people highlighted in the memorandum he had submitted to Mills, and coming from such a person of the stature of Anandaram Dhekial Phukan, whose love for Assam was palpable, it can be well imagined what impression the British and others had carried at that time about the local population when they were looking to employ people for various jobs in Assam during the colonial days!

> "Assam was known in the past as the "black spot" of India, owing to the heavy consumption of opium there, both oral and smoked. Opium had, in fact, been the bane of the economic and social life of the Assamese people. It appears from history that opium was a closely guarded preserve of the Ahom royal family during the Ahom rule of Assam. The habit was gradually acquired by the nobility and high court officials, and eventually, it became universal. Poppy cultivation was undoubtedly extensively carried out throughout the land. When Assam was annexed by the British as a result of the Treaty of Yandaboo in 1826, the situation remained much the same. The then administration found a source of income from opium at once and lost no time in making the opium trade a state monopoly. Steps were also taken to suppress the cultivation of poppy by the peasants, solely with a view to advancing the interests of government revenue. Poppy cultivation was so freely and extensively carried out that government measures to suppress it met with stiff opposition everywhere, culminating in the "poppy revolution" at Phulaguri in the district of Nowgong in the late 'nineties. The rebellion was put

down with a firm hand, but not without casualties on both sides. After this, the government continued its monopoly by auctioning off the opium shops. Until the year 1919, there were no effective restrictions on the sale and consumption of opium. Until then, the policy was to lessen consumption by raising the treasury price, reducing the number of opium shops, restricting the limit of private possession, and raising the permitted age of consumers. In spite of this policy, the guiding factor was revenue and not the moral, social, and economic uplift of the people. During 1918/19, the total sale of opium stood at 1,324 ^{1}*maunds* 26 seers, yielding a revenue of Rs. 3,391,522." [4]

Note: [1](1 maund = 37 kg 312 gm, 1 seer = 932.8 gm.)

The above paragraph is quoted from the abstract dated 1st January 1958 of the Opium prohibition campaign in Assam, authored by Assam Excise Commissioner, Shri E. H Pakyntein (IAS).

Opium is the dried or inspissated juice of a capsule of the garden poppy, poppy opium or white poppy plant Papaver somniferum species of flowering plant in the family Papaveraceae. There are various types of poppies, like the white poppy, purple poppy, and red poppy. The white variety of poppy was largely grown in the Bengal region. The purple variety gave the highest yield, nearly three times as much morphine as the white variety. It grew luxuriantly in Rajputana and Central India. The red flower variety with dark seeds was cultivated in the Himalayas. In reality, opium is the juice which oozes out from the unripe capsules of the plant after the artificial removal of the petals or after the petals have fallen naturally. [5]

According to Sir Edward Gait, author of "A History of Assam," the inhabitants of the Brahmaputra valley were addicted to the use of opium to a degree unknown anywhere else in India, but it is not known exactly when this perilous habit was introduced in the valley. However, it was fairly common in 1793 when British Captain Welsh found Raja Gaurinath so completely abandoned to the opium habit that he was often quite incapacitated for the transaction of public business. The widespread and immoderate consumption of the drug was noticed by Robinson and other writers, including Mill, who in 1853 said that **"three-fourths of the population are opium eaters, and men, women, and children alike use the drug."** (Emphasis by Subir)

During those days, the people themselves used to grow poppies in their gardens. When the heads had reached the proper size, diagonal incisions were made, and they used to collect juice on two-inch strips of cloth, which, when fully saturated and dried, were rolled up in little bundles, known as Kani in the local basilect of the Brahmaputra valley in Assam, and kept till these were required for use. [6]

Initially, during the days of the Mughal invasion in the seventeenth century, only a few rich people of the Ahom kingdom knew about opium and its use. The vice of opium addiction was limited to the elites in Ahom society during those days until the middle of the next century. According to Maniram Dewan, an early nineteenth-century chronicler, the poppy was first cultivated by Rajput Barkendazes at Beltola, in the vicinity of Gauhati, during the reign of King Lakshmi Singh (1769-1780). It was through them that the common people were introduced to the Poppy plant and its use, and after that, the habit of opium consumption spread the length and breadth of the Ahom kingdom. Captain Thomas Welsh, who commanded the East India Company's expedition during the period from November 1792 to May 1794, observed that poppy was "growing in luxuriance in most of the lower provinces" of Assam and that the reigning monarch Gaurinath Singh (1780-95), was an opium addict.

The following paragraph quoted from Amalendu Guha's "IMPERIALISM OF OPIUM: ITS UGLY FACE IN ASSAM (1773-1921)" is very significant:

> "The Assamese were not yet acquainted with the manufacture of 'merchantable opium' that could be locally procured in considerable quantity. Welsh recommended that 'a few boat-loads of opium' be sent from Bengal for sale. It was widely believed that **Welsh**'s several hundred sepoys were **primarily responsible for spreading the opium habit in Assam.** A large number of Hindustani ex-sepoys from Bengal, who were recruited by King Kamaleswar Singh (1795-1811), also played a similar role in popularising the opium habit and poppy cultivation." [7] (Emphasis by Subir)

The professed policy of the British colonial government in Assam between 1826 and 1919 was one of progressively restricting the opium trade. It underwent three significant changes during this time period. The first phase, from 1826 to 1860, saw a policy of non-interference regarding the production and consumption of kanee (homemade opium). During this phase, while private individuals were allowed to cultivate poppy, the government authorized the sale of *abkaree* (government-exercised) opium at a cheaper price. Consequently, the availability of *abkaree* opium led to increased drug abuse, rather than controlling the growing problem, as the government prioritized revenue collection.

The second phase began on May 1st, 1860, when home cultivation of poppy was banned throughout Assam, forcing opium addicts to rely solely on government-supplied opium. This phase continued until 1874, when a separate Assam Province was established, separating three Bengali-dominant districts and the Assam division from the Bengal presidency. Administratively, this period was marked by strict monopoly control. Opium was obtained from government treasuries under license at a price that, while not prohibitive, aimed to deter excessive consumption. There were no restrictions on the quantity an individual could purchase at one time. Licenses for retailing the drug to consumers were granted to "respectable persons" without any fee or security requirements. License holders were free to set their own prices for opium, selling in quantities not exceeding five tolas (1 tola = 11.66 grams) to one person at a time. Licenses for *madak* and *chandu*, two different opium preparations, were auctioned off to the highest bidder, with a minimum bid set at four rupees per month for each license. The Board of Revenue, Lower Provinces, closely monitored opium sales to track fluctuations in trading. The policy during this period aimed at maximizing revenue while minimizing consumption.

Due to the low price, which was set at Rs. 14/- per seer in 1860 (1 seer = 0.933105 kg), and increased availability of the drug, opium consumption in Assam proper nearly tripled, from 625 *maunds* in 1860-61 to 1,837 *maunds* in 1874-75. Correspondingly, revenue during the same period soared from Rs. 2,14,857/- in 1860-61 to Rs. 11,94,564/- in 1874-75.

A four-and-a-half times (456%) increase in revenue in less than fifteen years! Thus, the government's opium policy aimed to maximize revenue through monopoly in the trade.

Immediately after the constitution of the Assam province in 1874, further changes were introduced in the excise administration of the newly emerged province. This was known as the 'fixed licence-fee system'. Under this system, any person could open any number of shops for the retail sale of the drug upon payment of a fixed amount for each shop. The imposition of license fees reduced the number of licenses from 5076 in 1873-74 to 3977 in 1874-75, yet no significant decrease in consumption was observed. In 1877, the fixed license-fee system was replaced by the *'mahal* system'. Under this system, each district was divided into several *mahals* (or revenue divisions), and the right to sell opium in a particular *mahal* was put up for auction, granting the purchaser exclusive freedom to sell opium within that specified area. However, the *mahal* system proved unsatisfactory as authorities struggled to control the *mahaldars* (persons holding *mahals*), leading to a rapid increase in smuggling. In 1884, it was decided to revert to the old system of licensing individual shops. [8]

The British Raj faced fierce criticism of its opium policy within the metropolitan country itself. Verbal attacks against the opium monopoly were integral to the free-trade agitation until the mid-nineteenth century. However, by 1888, the Society for the Suppression of the Opium Trade led this agitation, gaining support from democratic sections of British society. Due to pressure on the British Parliament, the Royal Commission on Opium was appointed in 1893.

Many shocking facts about the situation in Assam came to light. Apart from the legal supply, certain quantities of contraband opium were regularly smuggled into Assam from Rajputana and other areas by Marwari and Nepali traders. The lower classes generally spent 10 to 20 per cent of their income on opium. In 1893, it was observed that some veteran consumers in the district of Lakhimpur spent up to about half of their income on the drug. These observations provided only a rough idea of the proportion of household income spent on opium. A small sample study further revealed that, on average, more than a quarter of cash requirements were for purchasing opium, while only 9 per cent related to the land revenue demand.

The Royal Commission's findings and recommendations were disappointing. It did not feel that British India had any moral obligation to stop opium exports to China as long as the latter country was permissive. It held that 'the temperate use of opium in India should be viewed in the same light as the temperate use of alcohol in England'. The Commission found that the objectives and workings of the opium monopoly were legitimate and satisfactory.

The government's excise policy hit the Assamese peasant society hard, not only economically but also morally. During 1874-1905, the habit of taking the drug in its most injurious form, i.e., smoking, increased rapidly, raising the proportion of smokers from an initially estimated 5 to 10 per cent to above 50 per cent of the addicts. By the end of the nineteenth century, opium smoking had infiltrated Hindu religious practices and become a congregational ritual (*kaniya-sava*), eating into the very core of Assamese society. Although there was an enhancement of price from time to time, it still kept the drug within reach of the peasant, apparently to squeeze him more.

The 'achievement' of progressively restricting the opium evil by the British colonial rulers, from the Indian point of view, was frustrating. In Assam proper, an exceptionally high per capita rate of opium consumption persisted.

As much as 1,557 maunds out of the entire province's consumption of 1,686 maunds in 1880-81, and 1,201 maunds out of 1,291 maunds in 1900-01, were consumed in Assam proper alone. There was a continuous increase in opium consumption after 1897-98, while the selling price remained unchanged at Rs. 37 per seer for nineteen years until 1908-09. The total consumption in Assam proper was at its lowest in 1897-98 (1,128 maunds) and 1901-02 (1,126 maunds), but thereafter it recorded an increasing trend that persisted until the Non-Cooperation movement of 1921-22.

Against the internationally accepted norm of 6 seers per 10,000 people, which could be safely allowed to the concerned population, consumption was as high as 267 seers in 1891 for the indigenous Assamese population; and it gradually increased to 287 seers by 1921. This was a net outcome of the colonial taxation policy in operation, and that too in the name of containment of opium. Opium was the most important source of the province's revenue, second only to land. A maund of opium would cost the treasury Rs. 290/-, ex-factory in 1883-84, but it brought forth a gross revenue of Rs. 1,040/- when sold at Rs. 26/- per seer. It was a gold mine for the government, not to be easily surrendered!

Besides the government, some planters and traders also allured the Assamese peasants with opium to gain economic advantage. For instance, S. E. Patel, a planter, told the Royal Commission of Opium that some ten to twelve years from 1863, he used to regularly issue about 40 lbs. of the drug every month to his labourers – and this constituted half of the wage bill – to serve as circulating media over the area of 200 square miles where his Assamese labourers were recruited. Another planter, E. P. Gilman, also informed the Commission that he used to sell opium to Assamese villagers. Haribilas Agarwala, an Assamese planter, ran a lucrative opium shop, although he recommended to the government a policy of gradual eradication of the evil. As long as opium was not a contraband commodity and money invested in it paid dividends, there was no shortage of distribution for the drug. [9]

In the Ahom kingdom, the consumption of opium was considered a luxury reserved for the nobility and upper classes of society. However, by the time Assam was annexed by the British in 1826, a large number of people from all classes had begun indulging in opium. Since 1860, when a governmental decree banned all private cultivation of poppy in Assam, the use of opium among the higher classes fell out of fashion. Nevertheless, its consumption among the working classes and labourers persisted, leading to significant economic and social repercussions for the province. This earned it the dubious distinction of being labelled "a land of abundance inhabited by lazy people." **It soon became a serious concern for the British rulers,**

especially as European tea planters settled in Assam and began demanding a prompt solution to acute labour shortages in tea gardens. (Emphasis by Subir)

By the mid-1860s, the recruitment policy of labourers from other provinces was well underway. By the early twentieth century, Assam had gained notoriety as 'a black spot of India' due to its extraordinarily high level of opium consumption. The average annual consumption rate of opium among the indigenous Assamese population in 1901 was as high as 275 seers, which further increased to 287 seers per ten thousand of the population by 1921, compared to the standard of 6 seers per ten thousand people set by the League of Nations. [10]

Opium has euphoric effects on the brain, causing relaxation and relief from pain. It is so potent that users often feel completely relaxed and sedated, prompting many to continue abusing the drug. Persistent opium abuse significantly increases the risk of addiction. Prolonged use of this powerful sedative can have devastating consequences on both physical and mental health. Opium also inhibits bowel movement and dries out the mucous membranes in the mouth and nose. Consequently, the drug is medically utilized to treat conditions such as moderate to severe pain, diarrhoea, and abdominal cramps, as well as an antitussive (cough suppressant), and for surgical preparation. While constant lethargy and drowsiness are the most evident short-term side effects, the most perilous long-term effects include lifelong liver and kidney damage, weakened immune system leading to increased susceptibility to illness, persistent mental fog (even during abstinence), and notably, impotence.

In 1826, the British intervention in rescuing the Ahom kingdom from the Burmese invasion and annexing it to India undoubtedly left many shattered, shocked, and dazed. However, it is inconceivable that the Assamese, many of whom were devout followers of revered figures like Mahapurush Srimanta Sankardev, and Madhavdev, among others, would be so mentally degraded and demoralized to the extent described: *"three-fourths of the population are opium eaters, and men, women, and children alike use the drug."*

The answer perhaps lies in the following excerpt from the article "Opium: Popularity and Consequences in Colonial Assam, India" by Sanjib Kumar Chetry, as directly restated. The article was published in the International Research Journal of Social Sciences, E-ISSN 2319–3565, Vol. 5(2), pages 41-45, in February 2016:

"The people have, however, brought the opium habit upon themselves. When kala-azar made its appearance, an idea was floated by some cases, it bore fruit, and several young men and women took to the drug in apprehension of malarial fever. Kali Ram Chaudhari, Extra Assistant Commissioner, Nagaon, wrote:

> 'I myself have seen instances of the conversion of total abstainers into opium-eaters. I should not be understood to say that there was no opium-eating before the appearance of the Kala-azar. There were certainly a large number of people who used to take opium in one kind or another.'

But when the British government came to know that the general people of Assam also had a weakness for opium, taking advantage of this situation, the British made it an article of universal consumption for the people of Assam, and by doing so, they augmented their revenues by leaps and bounds. Consequently, the number of opium eaters had grown rapidly. Sir Andrew John Moffatt Mills, in the course of his official tour and inquiry in 1853, found that 75% per cent of the people of Assam were opium eaters. It was presumed rightly that within 28 years of British rule (1826-53), opium consumption became the most universal.

While the Government was convinced of the damaging effects resulting from excessive opium use, it was of the opinion that 'its use has, with many, almost become a necessity of life, and in a damp climate like Assam, it is perhaps beneficial if taken with moderation.' In the same vein, Johnston Long, Civil Surgeon of Sibsagar, also wrote in 1853 that 'the unrestricted use of opium amongst the peasantry of Assam is not of very old data'." [11]

"Use of opium as a household remedy in India was widespread and extensive," wrote Researcher W V Gita in the research paper titled "History of opium and its impact on society under the British," mentioning that it was widely used as a household remedy for its supposed prophylactic or curative effects against malaria. People also believed that opium reduced the danger of delta fever, rheumatism, and many other diseases. [12] These lines bolster Sanjib Kumar Chetry's contention, as quoted above.

Besides, while diseases like malaria, diarrhoea, influenza, and abdominal pains were quite common in the region, the availability of any sort of dependable medical facilities was conspicuous mostly by its absence. In such circumstances, people had no choice but to depend on household remedies or local quacks in the event of any illness in the family or to take any preventive measures. Perhaps this triggered the onset of opium abuse in some pockets of the Brahmaputra valley. Subsequently, the British colonial rulers cleverly exploited the prevailing weak spots in Assam to their maximum advantage.

In 1907, an anti-opium conference was held in Upper Assam's Dibrugarh town at the initiative of local workers. It urged the government to check the rot and recommended the formation of a temperance association. A similar conference was held in the same venue wherein, apart from forming a temperance association, suggestions were made for opening a public register of opium eaters, as had been successfully done in Burma. The Hague Convention of 1912, where voices against excessive opium eating were raised, undoubtedly strengthened the hands of the supporters of opium prohibition. The net result of all this was the appointment of a committee headed by A. W. Botham, with three other Assamese members, to go into the details of the opium question and suggest remedies, if any. The recommendation of the Botham Committee was a big disappointment.

Against this backdrop of events, resentments against the official opium policy began to manifest in Assam. The lead was originally taken by the Assam Association (founded in 1903), which focused its attention on all matters of public importance. It initiated a strong agitation against the Excise Policy of the Assam government and demanded the total prohibition of opium. In a memorable speech delivered during the budget session of the Assam Legislative Council in 1919, Rai Bahadur Phanidhar Chaliha, an active member of the Assam Association, boldly declared that the Excise department of the government had become 'an eyesore to the educated Indian community and to all who have the welfare of the country at heart. He characterized the income derived from opium as 'tainted money' and demanded the complete abolition of this 'immoral trade'. For his remark, Chaliha was chastised by the Chairman of the Council, and in protest, he resigned from the Council.

Similarly, Ghanashyam Baruah, another member of the Association, championed the cause of Assam and suggested certain measures. However, he was not supported by the non-official members of the Council and consequently, his resolution was defeated. No wonder the official policy remained virtually unchanged, and any attempt to introduce prohibition was disfavored. It became clear that no positive steps towards eradicating the opium menace would be forthcoming from the government. That was the moment when Congress came into the picture. With the beginning of the non-cooperation movement, Congress launched a vigorous campaign against opium.

"Make Assam free from opium and have swaraj from me," Gandhiji used to tell the leaders of the Assam Pradesh Congress Committee. The picketing of opium shops and the persuasion of opium-eaters not to indulge in this drug were the chief features of the Congress program during the non-cooperation movement. The sustained campaign against opium abuse eventually started showing results. Opium revenue progressively fell from 38,26,000/- to Rs. 10,07,000/- between 1927-28 and 1938-39. Addressing a gathering at Sibsagar on 24th February 1939, the then Premier of Assam and popular Congress leader, Gopinath Bordoloi, appealed to all sections of people to extend their full cooperation towards ensuring the success of the Kanee Barjan Andolan (The "Give Up Opium" Campaign). When Md. Saadulla was installed as the Premier of Assam for the third time, he declared 26th February 1941 as Opium Prohibition Day. He brought all non-excluded areas of the province under the opium prohibition scheme with effect from 1st March 1941. Thus, by adopting a progressive opium prohibition program, the new Saadulla government accelerated the trend established by the Bordoloi government. The people of all communities of Assam responded enthusiastically and began to work sincerely towards the movement's success. It is remarkable that what the government could not do in nearly a hundred years was, to a great extent and with minimum effort, done by the people themselves. [13] [14]

* * * * * * *

Chapter 3.

The Emergence of Assam

"There are places
- the Indian state of Assam is one -
where the slaughter of children is a form of political expression."

Shillong-born Professor of Political Studies from Assam, Sanjib Barua, quoted the above line from the editorial of an American magazine, The New Republic, on page xix in the Preface of his book "INDIA against itself: ASSAM AND THE POLITICS OF NATIONALITY." In an apparent reference to the Nellie Massacre, the Professor was articulating on the 1983 carnage in Assam that made international headlines. He added, inter alia, "The editorial, though not well informed about the circumstances of violence, made a number of breath-taking assertions about its significance." What such a shocking international headline on a massacre that took place in our country does to the psyche of any patriotic Indian or, for that matter, the ordinary people of India in general, is difficult to assess and articulate, but perhaps such a shameful incident could have been avoided if we were well-informed and kept our people fully aware of the truthful history, especially the factual story behind the emergence of Assam Province in 1874.

During their colonial rule in India, the British distorted the contemporary historical accounts on such a scale that it severely polluted the communal atmosphere of the land, sowing the seeds of mutual hatred and animosity between the major communities inhabiting Assam. Instead of mending the misrepresentation in the post-colonial era, we disregarded the falsification. Meanwhile, the seeds of antipathy and animosity planted by the colonial rulers under their 'divide and rule' policy germinated and grew into a full-grown deadly tree playing havoc in Assam even today as the elephant in the room – a metaphorical idiom in English. The massacre mentioned in the previous paragraph is one of its major ramifications. It is, therefore, essential to go over the emergence of Assam fleetingly and comprehend the realism that might, in the future, go a long way in preventing such mishaps from recurring.

Assam came into being with the arrival of the British in this part of the country. The territory is described as an ethnic and cultural mosaic, comprising Ahoms, Bodos, Koch Rajbonshis, Santhalas, Mishings, Dimasas, Kukis, Hmars, Zemis (Nagas), Karbis, and numerous other smaller tribes, with a major presence of Bengalis followed by the Asamiyas. Many Biharis, Oriyas, and Nepalis, among numerous plains tribal and hill people, all living side by side in unison, have undoubtedly made it a mini India.

The British archival records suggest that officials and merchants of the East India Company (EAC) used the word 'Assam' from the beginning of their relations with the Ahom Kingdom to denote the territory under the rule of the Ahom kings. For instance, as early as September 1785, on the representation of some merchant adventurers, the EAC Court of Directors had resolved to extend the Company's salt trade into the neighbouring 'kingdom of Assam'. Two years later, the Governor-General-in-Council had appointed Hugh Baillie as the 'Superintendent of the Assam-trade' with headquarters at Goalpara. The term 'Assam' also appeared in titles of publications authored by some British officials. Thomas Welsh, who led an expedition in 1792 to help the Ahom monarch suppress the Moamaria uprising, wrote his 'Report on Assam 1794'. John Peter Wade's 'An Account of Assam' was compiled in 1794-1800. Francis Buchanan-Hamilton wrote 'An Account of Assam' in 1808-09.

The 24th February 1826 Treaty of Yandabo, signed at the end of the First Anglo-Burmese war, which became the basis of the British annexation of the Ahom kingdom, provided that the king of Ava renounced all his claims upon 'the principality of Assam and its dependencies'. However, the Ahom kings never used 'Assam' in any of their documents, inscriptions, or coins. The Buranjis, the medieval chronicles of the Ahom kingdom, referred to their land as 'Asom' and its people as 'Asomiya'. These terms are still in colloquial use today. [1]

In the "H K Barpujari Endowment Lectures MAKING OF BRITISH ASSAM," [1]Professor J. B. Bhattacharjee enunciated, among other things, that:

> "Assam was constituted into a province by the British rulers of India to meet the colonial needs of a viable province in the north-eastern part of their Indian empire. It was accomplished in stages by subjugating the erstwhile Ahom kingdom or Assam proper and its neighbouring hitherto independent hill tribal areas in several

instalments and annexing those to the Bengal presidency and thereafter by separating the Assam division from Bengal (in 1874) and transferring to it not only the adjoining hill districts but also three traditionally Bengal districts (namely, Goalpara, Sylhet, and Cachar) from the Cooch Behar and Dacca division.

In the province of Assam, so created by the British, the Assam proper or the traditional Assamese heartland formed only a small part, and the Assamese people a minority. The Assamese, the Bengali, and a large number of tribal groups were indigenous in their respective areas, but each one was a minority in the total population of the province, thereby creating conditions for each group to suffer threats to ethnic and linguistic identity.

The problem was complicated further when the British named it 'Assam' (deriving the name from the Ahom kingdom) despite the multi-ethnic and multi-cultural character of the province. The name carried the impression of the legitimacy of an Assamese (i.e., Asamiya) predominance in the entire province, including the traditionally non-Assamese areas.

Thus, the seeds of discord were planted, and the quest for identity and ethnic and linguistic assertions culminated in movements for administrative reorganization and the creation of a multi-ethnic, multi-cultural province denying the people the right to linguistic states." [2]

Note: [1]Professor J.B. Bhattacharjee retired as one of the most senior professors at North-Eastern Hill University, Shillong, in 2006. He was the founding Vice-Chancellor of Assam University, Silchar, and served as a visiting scholar at various universities in the UK and USA for short periods. He authored 15 books, edited around 30 collections, contributed to more than 300 research papers, and supervised the research work of over 50 scholars for their M.Phil and Ph.D. degrees. He presided over the modern India section of the Indian History Congress in Gorakhpur in 1989 and the History and Culture section of the Indian Social Science Congress in Bangalore in 1991. Professor Bhattacharjee has been an honored Fellow of the Institute of Historical Studies, Calcutta since 1991. In appreciation of his significant contributions to history, the Asiatic Society, Kolkata, conferred upon him the prestigious Sir Jadunath Sarkar Gold Medal, as reported in The Shillong Times dated April 23, 2016.

Earlier in this book, it was observed that from the latter part of the eighteenth century, cracks began to emerge in the nearly six hundred years of the Ahom monarchy's foundation under the strain of power struggles, civil rebellion, and Burmese brutality. In response to appeals from the fugitive Ahom king and others, the British entered the Ahom kingdom and expelled the Burmese after prolonged and intense wars.

Following their pillaging in the Brahmaputra valley, a contingent of the Burmese army invaded the plains of Cachar with little resistance from Cachar king Govindachandra, who fled his capital to save his life. The Burmese military then turned their attention to Manipur, engaging in their customary spree of killings, plunder, and torture of innocent civilians. Meanwhile, the exiled king of ¹Cachar, Govindachandra, made impassioned pleas to the British East India Company for assistance. The geopolitical situation of the region had reached a point where the Company could no longer ignore the presence of the Burmese army in their vicinity without jeopardizing its own interests in the region.

¹Cachar: In the Sylheti-Bengali dialect of the former Sylhet district of Assam, Kachar, or Cachar, signifies a stretch of land situated at the base of a mountain. [3].

That was the backdrop against which the British struck hard at the root of the Burmese campaign towards the end of 1823. The decisive battle was fought on 13th February 1824 at Badarpur on the bank of the Surma River. The Burmese army was forced to retreat after suffering heavy losses. The British reinstated Govindachandra to his throne in March 1824, but the king had lost all capacity to govern. After a couple of months, he entered into a treaty with the Company and placed his territory under British protection. After their Cachar campaign, the British army marched against the Burmese in the Brahmaputra valley, and by 1825, the Burmese army was completely routed. Next, the British army drove out the Burmese occupational force from Manipur.

As briefly narrated earlier, the British then entered Burma, fought against the Burmese army, and eventually signed the Treaty of Yandabo on 24th February 1826. The king of Ava renounced all claims upon 'the principality of Assam and its dependencies'. Since then, the Ahom kingdom came under the British East India Company's domain and became a constituent of political India. Incidentally, from the 15th century, Europeans used the term Ava as a synonym for central and northern Myanmar. [4]

British Officer David Scott played a pivotal role in the war against the Burmese. As the Agent to the Governor-General, it was his responsibility to oversee the civil administration of the areas reclaimed by the British forces from the Burmese occupation. Following the conclusion of the Burmese war through the Treaty of Yandabo, the British reinstated rulers such as Raja Gambhir Sing of Manipur, Raja Gobindra Chandra of Cachar, and Raja Ram Singha of Jaintia to their respective monarchies. However, Assam remained under the jurisdiction of the Agent. In 1826, Assam was formally annexed to British territory and **placed under the Government of Bengal.** On 3rd

December 1828, David Scott was officially appointed as the Commissioner of Assam, while still retaining his positions as the Agent to the Governor-General and the Commissioner of North-East Rangpur (later renamed as 'Goalpara district'). With Scott's appointment as Commissioner, **Assam became a Division or Commissionership within the Bengal Presidency.** Interestingly, as David Scott simultaneously held the positions of Commissioner of Assam and Commissioner of North-East Rangpur, the latter region inadvertently became part of the jurisdiction of the Commissioner of Assam.

Regarding the colonial rulers' relationship with nearby tribal peoples, their primary objective was to maintain peaceful relations through a policy of non-interference. This allowed them to exploit the region's natural resources without obstruction from the hill tribes. Initially, they continued the measures devised by their Ahom predecessors.

The Ahoms were more or less successful in dealing with the tribespeople by adopting a conciliation policy backed by a display of force when conciliation failed. The first choice of the Ahoms was to prevent the tribesmen from harassing the people in the plains by granting them a subsidy, called 'Posa' (maintenance) in the Assamese language, which was expected to provide the tribes with part of their subsistence. But it was no guarantee against tribal raids. The hillmen might at any time descend on the villages in the plains and carry off captives and property. Punitive expeditions to punish the guilty hillmen were usually sent by the Ahom government in such eventualities. The policy adopted by the British initially was no different from the Ahom policy except in its methodology of paying the subsidies. During Ahom rule, the hillmen generally collected their allowances directly from the villagers, while during British rule, they received them from the government.

The first significant shift in British administrative policy was the introduction of the Bengal Eastern Frontier Regulation in 1873, commonly known as the Inner Line Regulation. Under Section 2 of the Regulation, the state authority prescribed an "inner line" to limit the movement of "British Subjects". Section 4 gave the authority power to provide a permit for passing or residing in any of these "inner line" areas. This regulation aimed to protect the culture and identity of the tribes in the region, giving them some autonomy to look after their personal tribal affairs. The regulation prohibited "British Subjects" from entering the protected or restricted areas. (Post-independence, the term "British Subject" was replaced by "Citizens of India". The Bengal Eastern Frontier Regulation continues to apply in present-day Arunachal Pradesh, Nagaland, Mizoram, and Manipur states.) The Inner Line Regulations marked the extent of the revenue administration beyond which the tribal people were left to manage their own affairs - subject to good behavior. No British subject or foreigner was permitted to cross the Inner Line without permission, and rules were laid down for severely circumscribed trade and acquisition of lands beyond the Inner Line under special circumstances. The communities staying beyond the 'Line' were seen as belonging to a different time regime – where slavery, head-hunting, and nomadism could exist. The Inner Line was expected to enact a sharp split between the modern and the primitive.

Another purpose behind introducing the Inner Line was to prevent friction with the tribal people. The government's decision in this matter was based on two principal considerations. The first was the troubles already erupted on the Naga Hills border between the Nagas and the tea planters. The second was a similar danger which, the government feared, was latent in uncontrolled contact between the Hillman and the speculators in the encroached rubber-producing districts. The distressing ramification of applying BEFR in the area was the feeling of alienation among the local people living within the same political boundary of the country. [5] [6] [7] [8]

In April 1833, the restoration of the Ahom monarchy in Upper Assam became imperative due to the extremely deplorable situation prevailing there. The Singphos and the Khamtis, independent hill tribes in the vicinity, frequently raided the plains, leading to reports of mutually destructive and deadly warfare pouring in almost regularly. The involvement of disgruntled officials from the former government in various conspiracies, and their connivance with warring factions, resulted in complete lawlessness. The total revenue collected in 1832-33 fell far short of Upper Assam's establishment expenses. To reverse this trend, the British government restored an Ahom prince on an experimental basis. Consequently, on 24th April 1833, Purandar Singha was installed as the ruler of Upper Assam on the condition that he would pay the British an annual tribute. Thus, the young Ahom king, approximately twenty-five years old, was tasked with addressing a myriad of irretrievable problems that had plagued the country for over half a century. Despite his sincerity and best efforts, Purandar Singha could not improve the situation. To exacerbate matters, he defaulted on the payment of the annual tribute and appealed for a reduction in the amount, but the British government did not favourably consider his appeal. Instead, Major Adam White, the Political Agent, assumed charge of Upper Assam, which was integrated into the Assam Commissionership in October 1938.

The first external territorial unit to be added to Assam proper was North-East Rangpur, which the British had established as a special administrative unit before the occupation of the Ahom kingdom by separating three thanas—Goalpara, Dhubri, and Karaibari—from the old Rangpur district of Bengal to effectively deal with the problem of Garo raids into British villages in Bengal. Later, the British authorities rechristened North-East Rangpur as the Goalpara district. Apart from administrative reasons, there were no historical, ethnic, linguistic, or cultural considerations in incorporating Goalpara from the Bengal Presidency into the Assam division. However, for a brief period of only three years, in 1658, the Ahoms occupied Goalpara. Contrary to popular belief these days, it was not a regular part of the Ahom kingdom. In reality, in the establishment of British Assam, the first step toward the territorial expansion of the Assam division was the integration of Goalpara.

Then, the annexation of Upper Assam was completed by the resumption of Matak, or the territory of the Moamaria Chief, popularly known as Barsenapati, on 26th December 1839, after the British government issued a general proclamation whereby Captain Vetch assumed charge of the entire Matak territory between Budidihing and Dibong. Thus, Matak became a part of the Assam Commissionership.

During the first few years of British rule, when Garo Hills were treated as a part of Goalpara, the Garos were a terror to the people on the plains. Initially, the government took some conciliatory measures for some years and followed the policy of non-interference but without much success. Some villagers of the remote villages in Garo Hills were adamant and did not accept the new administration. In 1866, the Garo Hills were partially brought under British control. Soon they secured the allegiance of more villages. The Garo Hills were organized into a district with headquarters at Tura in 1869. Some remote villages refused to fall in line, and whenever they got the chance, they attacked public servants and protected villages. In 1872-73, a well-organized drive was, therefore, carried out against the rebels that demolished the remaining posts of resistance in Garo Hills.

A significant acquisition of the newly constituted Commissionership of Assam was the territories of the Khasi and Jaintias. The Jaintia hills formed a part of the historic Jayantia Kingdom, while the Khasi hills were divided into several principalities called Hima (meaning 'state'), each ruled by a chief called Syiem. The British authorities in Calcutta maintained political and commercial relations with the Raja of Jayantia and the rulers of the Khasi states ever since their accession to the Diwani of Bengal, which brought them to the frontier of these states bordering the Sylhet district of Bengal. Several Sylhet-based European companies were engaged in trade with the Khasi-Jaintias. The Khasi-Jaintia hills were an important source of supply of limestone, sillimanite, and a few more items for the whole of eastern India.

The successive collectors and other British officers of Sylhet also made great fortunes by indulging in private trade with the Khasi-Jaintias. However, the British followed an unwritten policy of non-interference with these hills.

Anyway, soon after the annexation of Assam, the British could foresee the strategic importance of direct road communication from lower Assam in the Brahmaputra Valley to Cachar and Sylhet in the Surma Valley through Khasi Hills and Jaintia Hills. The proposed road would reduce the length of the march from Lower Assam to Sylhet. Besides, it would also enable the British to keep the Khasi Chiefs under control and facilitate trade and commerce by having easy access to the markets. As the proposed road would pass through the principality in these hills, they induced one of the constitutionally chosen chiefs or 'Syiems' of Nongkhlaw, U Tirot Singh, to consent to an Agreement (Treaty No. LXXXIV – Aitchison). By this treaty, Tirot Singh placed his territory under British protection. He also agreed to supply materials and labourers for constructing the proposed road through his principality. However, there were some disputes, and the Khasis resisted the construction works, resulting in skirmishes between the British and the Khasis. Eventually, after the death of U Tirot Singh in 1835, a settlement could be reached. The British conciliated with the Khasi Chiefs and promised them some customary rights and privileges.

The relationship of the Jayantia Raja was not very friendly with the Collectors of Sylhet and the British merchants, who always wanted to gain some undue concessions from the Raja. The British officials also used to dispute over the traditional privilege hitherto being enjoyed by the Raja of Jayantiapur to levy transit duty on the cargo passing through the river Surma. By framing the Raja for some alleged crime despite the investigation report not establishing his guilt, the Governor-General-in-Council resolved to confiscate the possessions of the Raja in the lowlands as a punishment for his guilt and leave him in charge only of the hills. However, Raja Rajendra Singh declined to continue as the ruler of the hills after the fertile agricultural and revenue-yielding tracts in the Sylhet plains were taken away from him. Accordingly, the kingdom of Jayantia was annexed in 1835. Thus, the Jaintia Hills, the Khasi Hills, and the Garo Hills, all three constituents of present-day Meghalaya, were annexed by the British in the nineteenth century.

The proclamation annexing the Jayantia kingdom was followed by distributing the plains of the erstwhile Jayantia kingdom to the neighbouring districts. The southern part was attached to Sylhet in Bengal on geographical and cultural considerations. Similarly, the northern plains in the Brahmaputra valley, namely, vassal Chieftaincies of Gobha (a Tiwa Kingdom), Dimarua, Neli (or Nellie, close to the erstwhile capital of the Gobha kingdom with a substantial Tiwa population), Khola, etc., were incorporated into the Nowgong district.

The Nowgong district of Assam proper was further expanded by incorporating a portion of the Dimasa kingdom of Cachar that had, in the meantime, been annexed by the British. Another 'protected state' under the Treaty of Badarpur (1824), Cachar or the Heramba kingdom at that point in time, like the Jayantia kingdom, had three distinct divisions, namely (i) South Cachar, or the Cachar plains, which was an extension of the Bengal plains from Sylhet and populated predominantly by Bengalis, (ii) North Cachar or the hills division, which was the Dimasa tribal heartland, and (iii) Central Cachar in the bordering areas of the Brahmaputra valley (Kapili-Dayung-Dhansiri valley, or the modern Daboka-Hojai-Lumding area), peopled mainly by Dimasa, Hojai, Lalung, and other tribes and communities like the Bengalis. Gavindachandra was reinstated as the Raja of Cachar (as mentioned earlier) after the Treaty of Yandabo. However, political and social tensions persisted in the state. In 1830, Gavindachandra was assassinated, and after that, in 1832, the British annexed South Cachar. In 1836, they made it a district, Cachar, within the Dacca Commissionership on geographical and cultural considerations. Then in 1854, when the British resumed North Cachar on the grounds of maladministration, they incorporated it into the Cachar district of the Dacca division. [9] [10] [11]

Integration of the Naga Hills was quite challenging. It's vital to note that "Naga" is a generic term encompassing more than 20 major tribes and numerous sub-tribes, each with specific geographic distributions. Though they share many cultural traits, the tribes maintain high isolation and lack cohesion as a single group. The Konyaks are the largest tribe, followed by the Aos, Tangkhuls, Semas, and Angamis. Other tribes include the Lothas, Sangtams, Phoms, Changs, Khiemnungams, Yimchungres, Zeliangs, Chakhesangs (Chokri), and Rengmas. There are about 60 spoken dialects that vary even from village to village. Presently, Nagamese ("Naga Pidgin"), a typical broken Assamese dialect, serves as their lingua franca, while English is the state's official language. Many Nagas also speak Hindi.

Initially, the British government was not prepared to take over the Naga Hills but aimed only at protecting their subjects in plain areas from Naga raids. However, after trying various methods from 1833 to control the Nagas without success, the British finally decided to annex the Naga Hills. In 1866, the Naga Hills District was created, with Samaguting as the District headquarters. As part of the program to civilize the Nagas, which the government thought was the only way to prevent raids, a school and a dispensary were opened in Samaguting. Trade was encouraged, and some roads were also constructed. Subsequently, efforts were initiated to persuade the Naga Chiefs to come under British protection. Afterwards, for administrative convenience, the British government divided the Naga Hills into three categories:

- The administrative areas,
- The controlled political areas, and
- Areas beyond political control.

In administrative matters, the Nagas paid house tax as a sign of submission to British authority, in return for which they received British protection. In 1878, the district headquarters was shifted from Samaguting to Kohima, the heart of the Naga Hills. Following this move, raiding activities greatly diminished but did not cease entirely.

However, in October 1879, Political Officer Mr Damant and 35 of his sepoys were shot dead while attempting to enter Khonoma village. He was the third British officer killed in the Naga Hills within a short span. Shortly after Mr. Damant's death, the government dispatched a strong military force against Khonoma village. After a fierce battle, the British emerged victorious and imposed severe punishment on the local Nagas. Subsequently, other Angami villages, including Khonoma, fell one after another. Gradually, this process of annexation extended to other Naga areas. By 1885, the Lotha areas were annexed, and a British officer was stationed at Wokha. Then, in 1889, the Ao areas were also annexed, with the headquarters established at Mokokchung. Similarly, more and more Naga villages in present-day Zunheboto and Phek districts were brought under British political control. Nevertheless, the so-called trans-Dikhu tribes, i.e., the Eastern Nagas, among which the Konyaks were the largest tribe, remained un-administered throughout British rule. [12] [13]

Interestingly, the Lushai Hills were geographically linked to Assam only through the Cachar plains. The British came into contact with the Lushais directly from Cachar and the Chittagong frontiers, and indirectly through the princely states of Tripura and Manipur. The occasional raids and head-hunting adventures within British territory provided justification for intervention. Of the two frontiers, Cachar was more exposed to such raids and plunder, particularly after establishing tea gardens in the plains bordering the Lushai Hills.

The Deputy Commissioner of Cachar held the additional charge of handling affairs in the Lushai Hills. He succeeded in persuading some Lushai Chiefs in the bordering areas to accept tributary status in return for annual rewards and British protection. The Deputy Commissioner of Chittagong also did the same in his frontier. However, the situation in the Lushai Hills became threatening due to mutually destructive warfare and a fresh wave of Lushai immigrants from the Burmese side. Between 1855 and 1861, several representatives of the Lushai-Kuki villages urged the Cachar authorities to help their Chiefs against the invading clans. Throughout the 1860s, many raids were reported from Cachar and Chittagong. Economic blockades and minor punitive actions from time to time failed to achieve the desired results.

In 1869, moderately strong punitive expeditions to the Lushai Hills from Cachar and Chittagong also proved more or less ineffective. Accordingly, in 1871, two military expeditions, one from Cachar and the other from Chittagong, were dispatched to the Lushai Hills. It was considered a great success as most parts of the hills were reduced to submission, fines imposed on them were realized, captives held by the tribes were released, guarantees were obtained for free passage for government officials in the future, and survey parties completed the mapping of 6,500 square miles of new and difficult territory, filling the gap which had hitherto separated the survey of Chittagong from that of Cachar. Yet, outrages on the borders and warfare within the hills were reported throughout the eighties. The course of events culminated in 1889-90, in which the governments of Bengal, Assam, and Burma (then a British province) jointly took part.

According to Dr. Pum Khan Pau, Assistant Professor at Visva Bharati University, Santiniketan (India), after the British announced the annexation of Upper Burma on January 1st, 1886, ending the Konbaung dynasty and Burmese independence, the Third Anglo-Burmese War formally ended, although resistance to British rule continued for another four years. The annexation of Upper Burma led to the encirclement of the Chin-Lushai Hills by British territories, resulting in a marked shift in colonial frontier policy from non-intervention to intervention. These hill tracts were a common source of trouble in Arakan, Chittagong, Cachar, Upper Burma, and Manipur, and colonial sources often cited it as a necessary pretext to change their policy. Though there is no doubt that the hill tribes often carried out raids and depredations in the plains under British control, an in-depth study of colonial records also revealed that the underlying objective of the British to annex the Chin-Lushai Hills was largely due to the need, they felt, to cut through the 'un-administered' hill tracts and connect Bengal and Burma. In other words, after the fall of Upper Burma, the British began to change their perspective and began to see the strategic importance of the Chin-Lushai hill tracts. Consequently, the British had to change their colonial frontier policy and started intervening in the affairs of the hill tracts.

In the joint expedition of the governments of Bengal, Assam, and Burma, the British forces from Burma took charge of the Chin Hills territory up to the Burmese frontier. At the same time, the Cachar column brought the North Lushai Hills under its control, and the Chittagong column took charge of the South Lushai Hills. The Cachar column established Fort Aizawl, and the Chittagong column established Fort Lunglei. Thus, the colonial rulers proclaimed the whole of the Lushai Hills as British territory. The Chief Commissioner of Assam appointed a Political Officer at Aizawl, and the Lieutenant-Governor of Bengal posted a Political Officer at Lunglei. In the process, the North Lushai Hills became a district in Assam and the South Lushai Hills a district in Bengal. Thus, the Chin-Lushai Tract was annexed by the British after the combined expedition of 1890-91 and divided the tract into three units.

However, before long, the Government of India felt the need to unite its two districts, the North Lushai Hills and the South Lushai Hills, under a single authority on both political and financial grounds, as it would result in an annual savings of two lakh rupees. On May 13th, 1893, the Government of India asked the Chief Commissioner of Assam to effect the transfer as early as possible. The Assam Chief Commissioner initially opposed the idea because it would entail an additional financial burden and administrative responsibility on the Assam administration but ultimately had to give in to the Government of India's persistence. Accordingly, on April 1st, 1898, the southern district was amalgamated with the north, and the united Lushai Hills District was placed under the Chief Commissioner of Assam. [14] [15]

The story of the emergence of Assam wouldn't be complete without touching upon the unique manner in which the erstwhile NEFA territory came under its jurisdiction during the British colonial rule in India. The North-East Frontier Agency, popularly known as NEFA earlier, is a mountainous territory of some 32,000 square miles that lies in the shape of a scythe to the north and east of the Brahmaputra valley. Approximately 20 major tribes inhabit this area with distinct ethnic, linguistic, and cultural individuality. The major tribes, from east to west, include the Monpas, Akas, Daflas, Apatanis, Adis, and Tagins. In the Northeast and east of the territory, which sweeps around the head of the valley, there live Idus, Taraons, Kamans, Khampts, Singphos, Tangsas, Noctes, and Wanchos. Each tribe is divided into numerous clans, which are generally exogamous, and characterized by the custom of marrying only outside the limits of their clan. The number of clans dividing the tribal groups can be gauged from the fact that the Idus, for instance, number only about 10,000, and there are about 450 clans. A habitation so sharply divided into small groups had never formed a single political unit. From time immemorial, not only the tribes but also the clans and, in certain cases, the villages had led to separate existences. The NEFA area was thus inhabited by an assortment of tribes, independent of each other, varying in language and culture, without any common bond under the shadow of mutual fear and hostility.

Scenically, it is one of the most magnificent but relatively unexplored countries in the world, with the rich natural splendours of the eternal snow on the high Himalayan range, deep gorges, torrential rivers, dense forests teeming with wildlife, and many colourful, warlike tribes. It is more varied and impressive than the far-famed northwest frontier of India. Yet, until very recently, it remained relatively unknown to the outside world. The only reason was that, unlike the northwest frontier, it was never in the past a gateway for invasions into the heartland of India.

Initially, the policy adopted by the British towards the northeastern tribal population at different times was one of non-interference. They wanted to leave the hillmen alone if the latter did not disturb the peace in the plains. The only problems the British had to deal with concerning the tribes, strictly speaking, were local in character until the end of the nineteenth century. However, in the early twentieth century, what was considered as local problems assumed an international dimension at the NEFA frontier. It was a complex situation involving a global heavyweight, where the government had to bear in mind its touchy relationship with various tribes inhabiting hills at the border areas. So, the British were in a dilemma.

In July 1909, the Political Officer in Sikkim, Charles Bell, who had considerable knowledge of Tibet, cautioned the Indian Government against the Chinese designs in that country. Though it was about seven months before the Chinese occupation of Lhasa, the capital of Tibet, the mounting activities of the Chinese in eastern Tibet convinced Bell that the Chinese were next going to turn their attention to the contiguous tribal area north of Assam. He advised the British administrators in India to take immediate steps to prevent the tribal region from falling into Chinese hands. Since the area was likely to be fertile, it could support large numbers of troops. Therefore, the Chinese occupation of this tract would constitute a threat to Assam. Unfortunately, Bell's warning went unheeded by a government that had not yet awakened to the implications of Chinese activities in Tibet.

Earlier, in 1903–04, British forces, under the command of the Indian Political Officer Colonel Francis Younghusband, invaded Tibet. After failed negotiations and a series of battles in which Younghusband's modern weaponry vanquished Tibetan forces, the British entered Lhasa and imposed a treaty on the Tibetans. Commonly known as the Younghusband Mission of 1904, the term "mission" is a misnomer. Except for a handful of imperial officials and journalists, the Tibetan Frontier Commission comprised military forces and would be more correctly termed 'The British Invasion of Tibet'. Since 1792, the Tibetan government had forbidden Europeans from entering their realm, and several thousand Tibetan soldiers died resisting Younghusband's advance from India to Lhasa. But the euphemism 'mission' became the standard term because the British disliked the idea of their forces invading the largely defenceless Himalayan realm, known in popular mythology for its monks, monasteries, and spiritual mysteries. The subsequent withdrawal of the British from Lhasa created a power vacuum, enabling the Chinese to re-establish their authority at Lhasa.

The main purpose of the Younghusband Mission was to keep Russia - and not China - out of Tibet. Britain favored a stronger position of China in Tibet as a counterpoise to any Russian interference there. Consequently, the Anglo-Chinese Convention of 1906 provided that the preservation of Tibet's integrity should rest with China and that China, but no other Power, should have the right to concessions in Tibet. Besides, the Anglo-Russian Convention of 1907 precluded both Russia and Britain from seeking concessions in Tibet, stationing representatives at Lhasa, and entering into negotiations with Tibet except through the intermediary of China. These two conventions not only eliminated the possibility of Russian interference in Tibet; they also tied the hands of Britain in Tibet and left that country entirely at the mercy of China, who had already been alerted by the Younghusband Mission. The only reason why Britain entered into such self-denying treaties and allowed China a free hand was that she was afraid of Russia alone and did not consider the weak Manchu empire a probable source of danger. But China seized this opportunity, pushed troops through eastern Tibet, and finally occupied Lhasa on February 12th, 1910.

Almost immediately after occupying Lhasa, the Chinese began probing the tribal country north of the Assam plains. For instance, in May 1910, a Mishmi Village Chief reported that two Tibetans had brought him an order from the Chinese to cut a track from Tibet to Assam, but he had refused to obey, saying - though without authority - that he was a British subject and, as such, he would take orders only from the Assistant Political Officer, Sadiya. In June 1910, another Mishmi Village Chief reported that the Chinese had planted two large flags near the Yepak River in the Lohit Valley. In March 1911, there were reports that the Chinese were engaged in making a road along the left bank of the Lohit towards Tinai (or Tini), a village opposite Walong. There were other reports, too, suggesting undue Chinese interests in the region. When these reports of Chinese activities in the Mishmi country were combined with a report that the Chinese had sent an official with a military escort into the Hkamti country in Upper Burma, it appeared that they were probably trying to converge on the Brahmaputra valley from both the northeast and southeast. The Chinese did not confine their activities to the Mishmi section alone; they also became active in the other sections of the frontier. For example, in July 1911, a report from Peking indicated that the Chinese had seemingly included the Abor country within the region of Pome and were contemplating the dispatch of an expedition down the Dihang from Kongbu. At about the same time, information was received from certain elephant catchers of the arrival of four men in a Hazarikhowa Aka village north of Tezpur. They appeared to have been a Chinese party. Before long, the Chinese also started probing into other tribal areas north of Assam. Such a brisk Chinese penetration in the tribal country on the border of Assam caught the British unprepared.

Unwittingly, the British administration had been neglecting the northeast frontier as long as they did not foresee any danger from the Chinese on that front. Consequently, when the Chinese suddenly displayed brisk activity on that frontier, the plains of Assam lay dangerously open to a determined thrust from that area. When in August 1910, Charles Bell repeated the warning, Lhasa had already fallen to the Chinese, and the first Chinese probes in the Mishmi Hills had been reported. By the way, the Mishmi Hills are on the northeastern side of present-day Arunachal Pradesh, and on its Chinese side, they form the southern parts of Nyingchi Prefecture in the Tibet Region.

This lack of knowledge of the northeast frontier as late as 1910 contrasted sharply with the relatively detailed understanding of India's northern and north-western frontiers, which the British had come to possess by that time. This contrast was surprising given that the British had come into contact with the northeast frontier about twenty years before, in 1826, with the annexation of Assam, while their direct contact with the northwest and an indirect one with the northern frontier through Kashmir was established only after the annexation of Punjab in 1849. The explanation perhaps lies in the fact that while the northern and north-western frontiers faced the mighty threat of Russia striding across Central Asia in the nineteenth century, in the Northeast, the weak Manchu empire in China apparently posed no such danger at all. Consequently, when the Chinese suddenly displayed brisk activity on that frontier, the severe vulnerability of the plains of Assam was laid bare.

The threat potential of the Chinese raid in the region had an added dimension for the British colonial rulers, given that the stake of the European capital in tea alone was enormous. For example, only in Assam's Lakhimpur district were there over 70,000 acres of tea gardens, turning out over 30 million pounds of tea annually and employing over 200 Europeans and over 100,000 Indians. Besides, these gardens lay at the foot of the hills, inhabited by tribal people. Then there were several other industries as well.

For instance, the coal industry had an output of over a quarter million tons a year. Accordingly, considering the exigency and after protracted deliberation on the pros and cons of the various options available to the British in the new situation, the policy of non-interference, which had been devised to meet the local problem of tribal hostility, was eventually abandoned, and a forward policy was adopted in September 1911.

The Viceroy of India, Lord Charles Hardinge, who initially did not favour any interference in the tribal territory, thus parted with the policy of non-interference once and for all. He admitted the utility of that policy so long as the problems on this frontier had been purely local in character. But circumstances had radically changed with Chinese intervention. "We consider that our future policy should be one of loose political control, having as its object the minimum of interference compatible with the necessity of protecting the tribesmen from unprovoked aggression, the responsibility for which we cannot avoid, and of preventing them from violating either our own or Chinese territory; and, while endeavouring to leave the tribes as much as possible to themselves, to abstain from any line of action or inaction as the case may be, which may tend to inculcate in their minds any undue sense of independence likely to produce results of the nature obtaining under somewhat analogous conditions on the northwest frontier of India." This was the first time that Hardinge advocated the idea of "loose political control" of the tribal area, meaning thereby to create a buffer which was to be protected from outside invasion but not to be interfered with in its internal affairs - an idea which had been first suggested by Bell.

The new approach was described as a policy of 'loose political control'. Its purpose was to leave the tribespeople free in their internal affairs but at the same time to leave them in no doubt that they were under British control. In other words, the tribal country was not brought under direct administration, but no intrusion from the north into the tribal lands was to be tolerated henceforth. The practical difficulty was one of the reasons why the government did not try to bring the area under direct administration, which would have unmistakably proved that it was Indian Territory. Moreover, the government had to take into account their past experience with the warlike tribes, who certainly had the capacity to cause infinite trouble in their inaccessible mountains if administrators directly interfered with their way of life.

Thus, by September 1911, the colonial rulers' official approach toward tribal-related issues finally underwent a fundamental change. Consequently, on 21st September 1911, Hardinge submitted a full statement of his north-east frontier policy. It was pointed out that the first objective of his government was to obtain a strategic frontier line "between China cum Tibet and the tribal territory from Bhutan up to and including the Mishmi country, and this should... now be the main object of our policy .... the question of a boundary well defined and at a safer distance from our administrative border has become one of imperative importance and admits of no delay...." To meet the strategic requirements of such a line, Hardinge recommended, subject to such modifications as might be found necessary as a result of the survey and explorations in the coming days.

But, in the absence of an immediate occasion for introducing the new policy, it would have been difficult for the British to suddenly initiate the new active policy without drawing the unwelcome attention of the Chinese who were taking an interest in the tribal area. So, the crafty colonial rulers used the killings of some British officers and their party by the Abors. Then, on the pretext of avenging the massacre, they sent an expedition to those areas as a first step towards implementing the "loose political control".

The government took advantage of the opportunity to stage two allied operations on the frontier - the Mishmis mission and the Miri mission - with the primary aim, in common with the Abor expedition, of exploring and surveying the tribal country to define an Indo-Tibetan boundary. The proposed expedition had several principal objectives:

a) It was to avenge the massacre of the British party and to arrest the culprits.

b) It was to visit the Abors in their villages and make them clearly understand that, in future, they would be under British control, which, for the time being, would be of a loose political nature.

c) It was to compel or persuade any Chinese officials or troops who might be met in the tribal territory to withdraw to the north of the 'recognized Tibetan-Chinese limits'.

d) The tribal country was to be explored and surveyed as much as possible so that on the information thus acquired, proposals for the alignment of an Indo-Tibetan boundary line could be based.

Anyway, the operations in the hills in 1911-12 resulted in several measures for protecting the frontier, which fall into two broad categories:

- Establishing outposts.
- Constructing roads.

However, while the Mishmi country - the most threatened section of the frontier - received the greatest attention, there was no such proposal for the Miri section, which was the least threatened and the least known of all the parts of the frontier.

After the successful close of the military operations, the expedition set itself to fulfil the second objective. The double purpose was to explore the tribal country and establish friendly relations with the Abor communities. The hostile Abors were given to understand that they would be under British control in the future. The most important of the terms imposed on them was that, in the end, they were to obey all the government's orders and not disturb the trade with the plains. Small parties were dispatched in different directions under Bentinck, Colonel McIntyre, Captain Molesworth, and Captain Dunbar, who visited many Abor villages. These visits to other parts of the Abor country dispelled a long-standing erroneous idea about the Abors. They were discovered, after all, to be not as bad as they had been previously thought to be. Similarly, the other parts of what was to be known as NEFA were covered by several British expeditions.

Extensive surveys and exploration on the frontier during 1911-13 revealed a relatively comprehensive picture of this border area for the first time. There were suggestions at different official levels - individual officers on the frontier, the Local Government, and the Government of India - for the best possible boundary alignment. When a clear idea of the area's geography and the limits of Tibet finally emerged, the Government of India took the opportunity of the Simla Conference to settle with the Tibetan Government a commonly agreed Indo-Tibetan boundary.

It's interesting to note that, earlier, under the Bengal Eastern Frontier Regulation (BEFR) 1873, the British introduced the 'Inner Line' that represented the limits of administration of the territory. In addition, now the colonial government's political control, sans any administrative control, extended up to another limit called the 'Outer Line'. At the same time, the position beyond the Outer Line was not explicit. Though the government had not regularly exercised any control beyond the Outer Line, they had done so occasionally by sending punitive expeditions into the hills. But ordinarily, excepting such occasions, the Outer Line was the limit to government control. However, the crux of the confusion - whether the Outer Line could be considered the external frontier of India - was unclear.

While the British were preparing themselves to face any eventual Chinese attack on the NEFA region, on the other side of the frontier, the Chinese revolution, which broke out in 1911, swept away the Manchu dynasty and considerably weakened their hold on the regime. Besides, frequent skirmishes between Tibetans and the Chinese were happening as the former were lately busy settling down in Tibet. The Tibetans seized the opportunity of the fragile government to roll back the Chinese invasion of Tibet. However, the Chinese did not stop trying to reconquer Tibet. Consequently, disturbances continued in the eastern marches of Tibet.

The British knew that a fresh Chinese invasion of Tibet would seriously threaten India's frontiers, as had happened after the fall of Lhasa to the Chinese in 1910. Hence the British wanted to settle the disputes between Tibet and China and bring peace and stability to Tibet. For this purpose, the Simla Conference was convened under the presidency of the British plenipotentiary, Sir Henry McMahon. Charles Bell assisted McMahon as an adviser on Tibetan affairs and Archibald Rose, the British Legation in Peking, as an adviser on Chinese affairs. The Tibetan plenipotentiary, Lonchen Shatra, and the Chinese plenipotentiary, Chen I-fan (or Ivan Chen), represented their respective countries. The conference continued from October 1913 to July 1914. Although the conference's main objective was stabilizing Tibetan-Chinese relations and, particularly, defining the boundary between Tibet and China, on the sidelines of the meeting, Bell and Lonchen Shatra also negotiated the Indo-Tibetan border of India's northeast frontier and eventually determined the boundary of India's northeast border on a map drawn on two sheets of paper on a scale of eight miles to an inch. That way, out of the process of discussions on the sidelines of the Simla Conference emerged the Indo-Tibetan boundary, now known as the McMahon Line.

Significantly, in the course of negotiation, the Tawang tract and a considerable area north of it, between the main Himalayan range and the Se La range, which had long been considered Tibetan territory, were included on the Indian side, with the condition that Tibetan ownership in private estates on the British side of the frontier would not be disturbed. These private estates included monastic estates as well as those belonging to private individuals, not under the Tibetan Government's ownership. However, the Tibetan Government sought the right to appoint the Head Lama of the Tawang monastery. Since such a practice couldn't be allowed in British territory, it was decided that the Tibetan government would be consulted before the appointment of a new Head Lama. This resolution removed obstacles to drawing the boundary line westward along the main range from Gori Chen through the Menlaka thong La to the Bhutan border.

Apart from strategic reasons, there were several other factors influencing the inclusion of Tawang on the British-Indian side. It was deemed advisable to soon establish a North-Eastern Agency to oversee political matters related to Sikkim, Bhutan, Tibet, and the frontier tribes. Tawang was considered an ideal location for the agency's headquarters due to its strategic position. Additionally, Tawang lay on the shortest route between India and Lhasa, making it operationally advantageous to relocate the Political Officer's office from Gangtok (Sikkim) to Tawang, closer to Lhasa. Moreover, Tawang's climate was suitable for Tibetans, Bhutanese, Sikkimese, frontier tribesmen, and plainsmen alike. Considering these factors, it was deemed preferable to relocate the headquarters of the Political Officer in Sikkim, who served as the Government of India's advisor on Tibetan affairs, from Gangtok to Tawang.

The Indo-Tibetan boundary negotiation was finalized by an exchange of notes between McMahon and Lonchen Shatra on the 24th and 25th of March 1914. However, McMahon was well aware that the new boundary had been determined with insufficient knowledge of the area. Hence, he believed that if further information were acquired in the future pointing to the desirability of modifying the boundary anywhere, given the cooperative attitude of the Tibetans throughout the negotiation, the British should also show a similar attitude regarding Tibetan interests, "although no obligation to do so has been mentioned in the agreement." Accordingly, the Indo-Tibetan boundary had, by and large, become a settled fact in 1914.

Yet, it was only a half-finished job not completed by actual demarcation on the ground. It would have been an extremely difficult task in this high Himalayan terrain, as McMahon later said in an address to the Royal Society of Arts in November 1935: "For great lengths of it lofty mountain ranges and watersheds buried in eternal snow facilitated verbal definition and rendered demarcation on the ground... either impossible or superfluous." Besides, by 1914, the Tibetans had repelled the Chinese invaders. Consequently, the northeast frontier of India was free from all Chinese pressure, and with Tibet being friendly towards the British, there was no likelihood of a Tibetan threat on this frontier. Thus, the McMahon Line became the demarcation line between the Tibet region and Assam's NEFA region. [7] [16] [17] [18]

Anyway, there is confusion in some academic circles as to whether NEFA was a part of Assam. This confusion stems from NEFA being placed within the administrative supervision of India's Ministry of External Affairs. Nevertheless, British-born anthropologist, ethnologist, tribal activist, and author Dr. Verrier Elwin clarified the factual position in his book "A Philosophy of NEFA", published in 1959 by Sachin Roy on behalf of the North-East Frontier Agency, with a foreword by Jawaharlal Nehru, the (then) Prime Minister of India. The relevant paragraph, which clarifies the actual position, is quoted below:

> "**The NEFA administration:**
>
> **The North-East Frontier Agency is constitutionally a part of Assam,** with which it will be united when it reaches a sufficient state of development. It is administered by the Ministry of External Affairs, with the Governor of Assam acting as agent to the President. The administrative head is the Adviser to the Governor, and his Secretariat is situated in Shillong where he is assisted by a Legal Advisor, an Advisor for Tribal Affairs, a Financial Advisor, and the Heads of Departments for Health Services, Engineering, Education, Agriculture, and Forests whose work is coordinated by a Development Commissioner. The Advisor is also responsible for the unified and coordinated control of the Assam Rifles to the Ministry of External Affairs through the Governor." [19] (Emphasis by Subir)

Moreover, as recently as on 3rd February 2022, in an article that appeared in the Indian Express titled "Explained: At the root of Assam-Arunachal Pradesh border dispute, a committee report from 1951", its author Tora Agarwala, who covers the Northeast for the newspaper, shed some more light on the issue. Only some selected portions of the article relevant to this story are quoted below:

> "Bone of contention: 1951
>
> Arunachal Pradesh, **which was earlier a part of Assam,** shares a boundary of roughly 800 km with the state - with frequent flare-ups reported along the border since the 1990s.
>
> ……….. After Independence, the Assam government assumed administrative jurisdiction over the North East Frontier Tracts, which later became the North East Frontier Agency (NEFA) in

1954, and finally, the Union Territory (UT) of Arunachal Pradesh in 1972. It gained statehood in 1987.

However, before it was carved out of Assam, a sub-committee headed by then Assam chief minister Gopinath Bordoloi made some recommendations in relation to the administration of NEFA (under Assam) and submitted a report in 1951. Based on the Bordoloi committee report, around 3,648 sq km of the "plain" area of Balipara and Sadiya foothills was transferred from Arunachal Pradesh (then NEFA) to Assam's then Darrang and Lakhimpur districts.

'This remains the bone of contention between the two states as Arunachal Pradesh refuses to accept this notification as the basis of demarcation,' said a senior government official from Assam, closely involved in inter-state border-related matters.

Arunachal Pradesh has long held that the transfer was done without the consultation of its people. "It was arbitrary, defective, and no tribal leader from Arunachal Pradesh was consulted before the land was transferred. They just decided to draw a line between the hills and plains," said Tabom Dai, General Secretary, of All Arunachal Pradesh Students' Union (AAPSU). According to him, Arunachal had customary rights over these lands, considering the tribes living there would pay taxes to Ahom rulers. Assam, on the other hand, feels that this demarcation as per the 1951 notification is constitutional and legal." [20]

The article mentioned above backs the assertion that NEFA was, in fact, included in Assam province during the British colonial rule in India.

So far, we have seen that the British found it administratively advantageous to group the diverse areas on Bengal's Northeastern frontier into Assam and initially followed a policy of non-interference with most of the hill men. Then, under the Bengal Eastern Frontier Regulation Act, 1873, they framed regulations restricting the entry and regulating the stay of outsiders in designated areas, introducing the Inner Line Area concept. Later, the idea of "loose political control" of the tribal areas was adopted to augment the defence of their commercial interests when Lhasa had fallen to the Chinese, and the first Chinese probes in the Mishmi Hills were reported. However, this exercise was secretly followed by a futile idea to integrate the frontier marches in North East India with the hill regions of upper Burma in what came to be known as the Crown Colony proposal (we shall discuss it later in this chapter). It was not because the vast multitude of tribespeople in this long border stretch had anything in common except their Mongoloid racial features. In reality, the British saw in the growing antipathy to the plains people of India and Burma an opportunity to forge together a political entity that would tolerate the limited presence of British power even after the end of their colonial rule in India. So the British were only too keen to amplify the hills-plane divide that they could so far infuse into them steadily. Thus, the Government of India Act 1919 (Montagu-Chelmsford reform) provided powers to the governor-general to declare any tract a 'Backward Area' and bar the application of normal provincial legislation there. Within a decade, the Garo Hills, the Khasi-Jaintia Hills, the Mikir Hills, the North Cachar Hills, the Naga Hills, the Lushai Hills districts and the three frontier tracts of Balipara, Lakhimpur, and Sadiya were all designated as Backward Areas. The Simon Commission recommended designating these Backward Areas as Excluded Areas. The 1935 Government of India Act recognised the Backward Areas of Assam as Excluded Areas of the North-East Frontier Tract (Now Arunachal Pradesh), Naga Hills District (now Nagaland), Lushai Hills Districts (now Mizoram), and the Garo Hills, the Khasi-Jaintia Hills (later to become Meghalaya), the North Cachar Hills District, and the Mikir Hills were reconstituted as 'Partially Excluded Areas. The princely state of Tripura and the princely state of Manipur remained beyond the scope of this reorganization (and our story, as well). [31] The origin of the Sixth Schedule of the Indian Constitution can also be traced back to the Government of India Act, 1935.

Assam, as it emerged during British colonial rule in India, was formed around the nucleus of the Ahom kingdom, encompassing a collection of territories inhabited by people speaking over 400 languages/dialects, with diverse backgrounds, descent, and distinct ethnic, linguistic, and cultural identities. In essence, the British amalgamated the following major territories and a few other minor principalities or sovereign states in the formation of Assam during their rule in India:

a) The Ahom kingdom, primarily the Brahmaputra valley with the westernmost boundary extending up to the Manas River, inhabited mostly by Assamese-speaking people.

b) The three districts, Goalpara, Cachar, and Sylhet, of Bengal, whose entire population were largely Bengali-speaking.

c) The Garo Hills, the Khasi Hills, and the Jaintia Hills – now part of the state of Meghalaya.

d) The Dimasa kingdom, the Matak kingdom, the Heramba kingdom, etc.

e) The territories of over 20 major Naga tribes and numerous sub-tribes, constituting the present state of Nagaland.

f) The land of the Mizos, now the state of Mizoram.

g) The erstwhile NEFA, or present-day Arunachal Pradesh, is inhabited by some 20 major tribes and numerous sub-tribes and clans.

"This was an impossible province but for the imperial diktat. In the entire history of British imperial expansion and their unfettered prerogative to make or mar provincial boundaries throughout India, one fails to notice a single instance where as many as eight territorial units, inhabited by more than twenty-five times of ethnic groups having a great many dialects and languages unintelligible to the nearest neighbour mutually unconnected in historical memory, were put together to form a new province," as the renowned historian and author from Assam, Rajen Saikia, averred. He was speaking eloquently in his Sectional Presidential address in the Modern India Section of the Indian History Congress in its seventeenth session (2009-2010). In the same speech, among other things, Saikia also said:

> "The diktat of 1874 created such an amalgam of unwilling units that everyone suspected the other and loved to live with a sense of exclusiveness and total disregard for the core province. It was an artificial administrative construct and there was nothing like emotional unity among the constituents. Every unit was committed to the idolatry of its own geography, racial memory and community interests. It seems as though every unit had a silent but strong resolve not to belong. To belong is to get lost." [21]

So far, the transformation of the territorial boundary of British Assam, starting initially with the Ahom Kingdom (considered as the nucleus, or the core, of Assam proper) up to the integration of today's Arunachal Pradesh (the erstwhile North-East Frontier Agency (NEFA)), has been broadly reviewed except for its elevation to a full-fledged province in 1974. What necessitated Assam's blending with three of Bengal's districts and how it was done were left out in between - purposefully. That aspect was undoubtedly the most crucial phase in the making of British Assam and hence, left for the finale!

It is a well-known fact that after the [1]Sepoy Mutiny (1857-59) was over, the British Crown took over the administration of India, ending nearly 100 years of rule of the East India Company. Since then, the process of decentralisation of the British administration in India was initiated. The question of relieving the Government in Bengal of the burden of administering the 'unwieldy, too large and heterogeneous' Bengal Presidency and 'making it convenient for the administration' was started, and the matter was under active consideration of the British Secretary of State for India, who was in charge of the Indian administration in Whitehall.

Note: [1]The Indian Rebellion of 1857, or India's "First War of Independence against British".

At that time, there was a pressing need to elevate the Assam division of the Bengal Presidency from a Commissionership Province to a full-fledged Province under a Chief Commissioner. Discussions began at the official level in Calcutta, the capital of British India. Earlier, a similar attempt had been made when the three commissionerships of Tenasserim, Pegu, and Martaban were merged into the Chief Commissionership of British Burma in 1862. However, this did little to alleviate the burden on Fort William in Kolkata from its extensive and unwieldy responsibilities. Nonetheless, high-level discussions persisted to create a new province under a Chief Commissioner by carving out certain portions of the Bengal Presidency, following the model of the 1862-Burmese experiment, to effectively address emerging needs. The urgency increased after the Orissa famine of 1866. Certain quarters alleged that the Lieutenant-Governor had failed to pay adequate attention to the distant and peripheral divisions of his jurisdiction, resulting in catastrophe in those areas. Consequently, it was agreed that the outlying areas should be separated from the presidency for better administrative efficiency. However, there were differences of opinion regarding which areas should be carved out to constitute the new Chief Commissionership.

Significantly, until the 1850s, British policy was to avoid the hills in their colony, but tea altered this traditional approach. The discovery of the indigenous tea plant in the Assam division of the Bengal Presidency in the early 1830s, and subsequently in Cachar and Sylhet, both in the Dacca Division of the same Presidency in the mid-1850s, changed the course of history and the fate of the natives in the North-East region of India. In the late 1860s and early 1870s, 'Tea mania' became evident in England. Many ambitious European entrepreneurs believed that owning a few tea bushes in India's North-East would lead to immense wealth. It was a 'Great Rush' in the Indian context to become rich overnight. Many influential British politicians also joined the rush. Consequently, within the corridors of power, the Tea Planters became a force to be reckoned with. Soon, they demanded the creation of an exclusive province to safeguard their interests and ensure the efficient utilization of state resources.

It may be recalled that on 29th March 1857, the first shot that initiated the Indian Rebellion of 1857-58 was fired by Sepoy Mangal Pandey of the 34th Regiment of the Bengal Native Infantry (BNI) at his commanding officers of the East India Company at the Barrackpore ground near Kolkata. This event, and Pandey's subsequent punishment, fueled more resentment among the sepoys of the Bengal Army, ultimately contributing to the Revolt of 1857. The world's largest anti-colonial uprising in the nineteenth century began here, with Hindus and Muslims fighting together, shaking the foundation of British rule in India. Consequently, the British Parliament passed the Government of India Act 1858, which transferred the government and territories of the East India Company to the British Crown, ending the company's rule over British territories in India, which came directly under the British government. Therefore, the first census operation in India in 1872 was carried out to devise a long-term strategy for preventing such a concerted revolt against British rule. The census report showed that in Bengal, Muslims outnumbered Hindus. The idea of dividing the unreasonably vast Bengal Presidency along Hindu-Muslim communal lines, which was becoming a potential hub of revolutionary activities, is believed to have matured from that census report.

Besides various colonial interests aimed at facilitating exploitation through the British policy of 'divide and rule,' the eventual decision to amalgamate the whole of Assam Commissionership, Goalpara, and Garo hills of Cooch Behar Commissionership, plus Cachar and Sylhet districts of Dacca Commissionership division, seemed to have emerged from the common fact that these territories, in particular, were exposed to frequent tribal attacks. Both Cachar and Sylhet were vulnerable to Lushai invasions, Goalpara and Assam to Garo incursions, and rampant Naga attacks in Assam villages. Additionally, the growing influence of the Tea planters might have also favoured the merging of three tea districts - Assam, Cachar, and Sylhet - in the establishment of the British Assam Province in 1874.

Thus, Assam was merged with three Bengali-dominant districts of Sylhet, Cachar, and Goalpara and elevated to a full-fledged province under a Chief Commissioner in 1874. "Making of British Assam," authored by J. B. Bhattacharjee, contains the text of the H. K. Barpujari* Endowment Lectures delivered by Bhattacharjee at the Institute of Historical Studies, Kolkata, on 24th and 25th March 2008. The following paragraphs, quoted from his said book, provide a vital facet on the emergence of Assam Province in 1874 **that rarely finds mention** anywhere in dominant historical narratives, non-fiction stories, research papers, newspaper columns, journals, weblogs, or any form of storyline concerning the contemporary account of Assam. It's an enlightening eye-opener:

> "Evidently, Assam became a province in British India for the first time in 1874. It was headed by a Chief Commissioner under the direct control of the Governor-General of India and consisted of (i) the five districts of Assam proper, viz., Kamrup, Darrang, Nowgong, Sibsagar, and Lakhimpur[1] (which together more or less corresponded to the erstwhile territory under the Ahom kings), (ii) three hill districts, viz., the Khasi-Jaintia Hills, Naga Hills, and Garo Hills (which were independent territories before the British occupation), and (iii) three transferred districts from Bengal, viz., Goalpara, Sylhet, and Cachar. The new province comprised a total area of more than 54,000 sq. miles, with a population of nearly 4,250,000 and gross revenue of about 52.5 lakhs. Shillong became the capital of Assam.

Table I				
Area, Population and Revenue of the Chief Commissionership of Assam				
	Districts	Area (Sq. Miles)	Population	Gross Revenue (Rs.)
Assan Valley	Goalpara	4433	444761	245796
	Karmpur	3631	561681	1155466
	Darrang	3112	236009	596293
	Nowgong	3421	256390	640240
	Sibsagar	2811	296589	914098
	Lakhimpur	11906	121267	486538
Hill Areas	Garo Hills	3390	80000	NA

	Khasi-Jaintia Hills	6650	141838	107801
	Naga Hills	4900	68918	6495
Surma Valley	Sylhet	5415	1719539	790544
	**Cachar	5000	205027	292691
Total		**54669**	**4132019**	**5235962**

Note:

i) Area of Lakhimpur then included the Frontier Tracts, inhabited by various native tribes, which were later transferred to NEFA (that became Arunachal Pradesh later on). The actual area under the administration was only 3,145 sq. miles, and the rest was under political semi-control.

The total area of the province was later added to 13,175 sq. miles of the Lushai Hills district, which was transferred to Assam in 1898. This would take the total area of the Commissionership to about 67,000 square miles. Considering that parts of the Naga Hills were added after the formation of the district, the area of the Chief Commissionership would increase." [22]

*Professor H. K. Barpujari, in the words of the author, "is widely acclaimed as the 'Doyen of the Historians of the Northeast', particularly for his first major work, namely, Assam in the Days of the Company (Gauhati 1963), which remains a masterpiece of historical research on Colonial Assam for almost half a century".

**The district of Cachar, lying beyond the Shillong plateau, is an extension of Gangetic Bengal, washed by the Barak River, and is separated from the Brahmaputra valley by the Shillong plateau.

The following are representations of the same data (Table I above) in two other forms. In Table II, the district-wise gross revenue figures are sorted from the highest to the lowest, and in Table III, the percentage of Bengali-speaking people against the Assamese-speaking people and others is sorted.

Table II

Gross Revenue District-wise of the Chief Commissionership of Assam (From Highest to the Lowest)

Valley	Districts	Area (Sq. Miles)	Population	Gross Revenue (Rs.)	Seial No
Assan Valley	Karmpur	3631	561681	1155466	1
Assan Valley	Sibsagar	2811	296589	914098	2
Surma Valley	**Sylhet**	**5415**	**1719539**	**790544**	**3**
Assan Valley	Nowgong	3421	256390	640240	4
Assan Valley	Darrang	3112	236009	596293	5
Assan Valley	Lakhimpur	11906	121267	486538	6
Surma Valley	Cachar	5000	205027	292691	7
Assan Valley	Goalpara	4433	444761	245796	8
Hill Areas	Khasi-Jaintia Hilla	6650	141838	107801	9
Hill Areas	Naga Hills	4900	68918	6495	10
Hill Areas	Garo Hills	3390	80000	0	11

Thus, it can be seen that **the gross revenue of Sylhet was the third highest** among all the districts of the newly created Assam Province.

Percentage-wise Bengali-speaking people against the Assamese-speaking people and others

Districts	Originally From	Linguistic Dominance	Population Absolute Number	Percentage to total Population[1]
Goalpara	Bengal	Bengali	444761	
Sylhet	Bengal	Bengali	1719539	
Cachar	Bengal	Bengali	205027	
Total Bengali-speaking people			**2369327**	**57.34**
Karmpur	Ahom Kingdom	Ashomiya	561681	
Darrang	Ahom Kingdom	Ashomiya	236009	
Nowgong	Ahom Kingdom	Ashomiya	256390	
Sibsagar	Ahom Kingdom	Ashomiya	296589	
Lakhimpur	Ahom Kingdom	Ashomiya	121267	
Total Assamese-speaking people			**1471936**	**35.62**
Garo Hills	Hill Region	Tribal dialect	80000	
Khasi-Jaintia Hilla	Hill Region	Tribal dialect	141838	
Naga Hills	Hill Region	Tribal dialect	68918	
Total population speaking various tribal dialects			**290756**	**7.04**
Total population of Assam Province			**4132019**	**100.00**

[1]Although the population of the three Bengal districts was almost entirely Bengali-speaking people, the population of the five erstwhile districts of Ahom territory was not entirely Assamese. Since the annexation of Assam in 1824, many Bengali-speaking people were shifted by the British to the Assam division for administrative purposes. Besides, several plains tribal communities and hill tribes also inhabited the Assam division before its upgrade to Assam Province in 1874. Still, for simplification, it is assumed that the entire population of the erstwhile Ahom territory was Assamese, like the total population.

It is vital to note from the above tabular data that in the newly created province that came into being in 1874, Bengalis constituted 57.34% of its total population. At the same time, the Assamese people (Asamiyas) comprised less than 36% of the province's population. Additionally, Sylhet district was ranked third in terms of gross revenues among all the districts.

Oddly enough, the province carried the appellation Assam—a term originating from the Ahom Kingdom ruled by the Ahoms. In other words, the Bengali-majority province was given a name derived from the Ahom kingdom, renowned as the land of the Ahoms or the Assamese, without consideration of the fact that in the new province, the Assamese were a minority with less than 36% of the total population, as opposed to the Bengali population of over 57%.

As time went by, the notion gained currency that Assam was primarily the land of Assamese, despite the influx of Bengalis being so significant that they outnumbered the Assamese. Towards the end of the nineteenth century, the British actively encouraged large-scale migration of Bengalis from neighbouring East Bengal into Assam to bolster revenue and address increasing food scarcity. This exacerbated fears among the Assamese of being further outnumbered by Bengalis in their homeland. The British, for their part, exacerbated tensions between the two communities through incendiary rhetoric and unfriendly actions.

In this ongoing narrative, it's often overlooked that many of these Bengalis, whose roots trace back to East Bengal, are also indigenous to the British-created Assam. Consequently, few realize today that Bengalis from the former Goalpara, Cachar, and Sylhet districts, and their descendants now scattered throughout Assam, are indeed indigenous to Assam and not immigrants. While parts of Goalpara and Cachar remain within present-day Assam, a small portion of Sylhet district also falls within its borders. Whether or not these indigenous Bengalis have maintained connections with their counterparts in East Bengal (present-day Bangladesh) is irrelevant to their status as natives, migrants, or immigrants in Assam.

Nevertheless, many in the state mistakenly believe that all Bengalis of East Bengal origin in Assam are migrants or immigrants, which is factually incorrect. This misconception has played a significant role in fueling animosity towards Assam's Bengali population, contributing to numerous controversies in the state.

Besides, the fact that a part of Bengal's territory went into the formation of Assam in 1874, where the Bengalis were the aboriginal population, i.e., the indigenous people of the British-created Assam province all along, was overlooked and gradually became obscured. Significantly, a tiny part of Sylhet district (now in Bangladesh) comprising three and a half Thanas remained in Assam (India) as per the award of the boundary commission at the time of partition. The indigenous population of that part and their descendants are also indigenous to present-day Assam.

Be that as it may, renowned Professor from North-East India, J.B. Bhattacharjee, voicing his opinion on this topic, wrote, among other things, that:

> "..... the naming of the province 'Assam' had far-reaching ramifications which surfaced more vigorously in the post-independence period. The slogan 'Assam for Assamese' directly emanated from the name of the province given by the British rulers and it did not take care of the fact that the larger portion of the British province was made up of historically non-Assamese areas. While the Assamese people were legitimately concerned about their linguistic rights and cultural identity in their homeland or Assam proper, the assertion of Assamese identity for the entire province of Assam threatened the identity of the indigenous people in the historically non-Assamese portion of the province. The indigenous people in their respective traditional homelands within the enlarged British province thus suffered the crisis of identity and violation of human rights for each community to live with their language and culture. The things could be different if the naming of the province was in the pattern of the 'North-West Frontier Province', and as proposed by the Government of India at the time of the partition of Bengal (1905), i.e., the 'North Eastern Province'. The national leadership after independence also failed to honour the decision at the Calcutta Congress (1917), which resolved in favour of linguistic states. The concerned section of the Constitution of India simply listed 'Assam' as one of the states in the Union, ignoring the multi-ethnic and multi-lingual character of the State. The State Reorganization Commission (SRC) too did no right no wrong. The

result was the series of ethnic movements for the unmaking of British Assam" [33]

With this encapsulated portrayal that went into the making of Assam by the British in India, let us now focus on some important aspects of the COLONIAL ERA OF ASSAM in the next chapter.

******

Chapter 4.

The Colonial Era of Assam

The British East India Company's rule in the Indian subcontinent commenced after the defeat of Nawab Siraj-ud-Daulah of Bengal in the Battle of Plassey on 23rd June 1757. Initially, Northeast India did not attract the British much due to its sparse population, with hardly any sign of surplus revenue-yielding potential or indications of existing economic activities. However, as discussed earlier, the frequent barbarous atrocities unleashed by the Burmese on the Ahom Kingdom wiped out more than half of its population. This population was already reduced significantly by repeated civil wars, infighting amongst the nobility, famine, and deadly diseases. As a result, the Ahoms were forced to seek the help of the British in Calcutta, the then capital of British India. At the invitation of the Ahom King, the British entered the territory ruled by the Ahom kings and eventually drove the Burmese forces away from this part of the country.

Initially, the British did not intend to occupy the region. In fact, earlier in 1824, the East India Company's Government had proclaimed to the people stating:

> ".... we are not led into your country by the thirst for conquest; but are forced, in our own defence, to deprive our enemy of the means of annoying us. You may therefore rest assured that we will......re-establish...... a Government adapted to your wants and calculated to promote the happiness of all classes."

However, at the end of the war, a new situation emerged wherein the British considered it expedient to revise their earlier stand. Haunted by fears of a renewed Burmese invasion, it was undoubtedly strategically crucial for the alien Britons to ensure that the region did not relapse into anarchy. But there was another equally important factor that largely influenced their decision not to vacate the region immediately. It was the subsequent realization of the business potential of the land. After all, the East India Company was primarily a commercial concern, and therefore it was motivated to a large extent by financial considerations while making major decisions. Accordingly, the entire Brahmaputra Valley and the adjoining hill areas were finally brought under British dominion (as already discussed). [1]

Here is an interlude that is very significant to the rest of the story. On 26th September 1792, King George III sent a special delegation comprising over 100 members from England led by British Ambassador Earl George Macartney to China to meet Chinese Emperor Qianlong on a vital mission. The mission was to officially wish the Chinese emperor a happy eighty-third birthday on behalf of King George III of England. Alongside that little birthday greeting, Macartney was to negotiate the matter of free (or at least freer) trade between Britain and China. Currently, the British were limited to one port: the city of Canton (now known as Guangzhou). British traders were not allowed to land anywhere else in China, causing frustration due to this forced bottleneck. The Chinese had their reasons, of course. They had observed the actions of Europeans elsewhere in the world and had no intention of becoming another colony. After nearly 11 months of journey, the delegation arrived in Beijing on 21st August 1793, and Emperor Qianlong granted them an audience on 14th September 1793.

The expedition spared no expense in attempting to change the minds of the Chinese. The British East India Company had agreed to sponsor all of it. Therefore, Macartney had brought a fortune in gift items from Britain to impress the emperor. Yet, the delegation failed to influence the Chinese ruler.

This outcome was a disaster for Britain. They needed this trade deal more than one might usually imagine. Britain was heading towards an economic flashpoint, popularly known as a balance of payment crisis. The situation was such that imports were significantly higher than exports, almost depleting the country's physical money to pay for its purchases. At the centre of this economic tornado was the humble, calming cup of tea – the tea for which Assam was to become renowned worldwide subsequently.

When the English people first became acquainted with tea, they fell in love with it. It became a national obsession. The demand for tea in Britain became so huge that at the beginning of the 19th century, the duty on tea accounted for 10 per cent of Britain's total revenue. However, the only way to obtain tea was from China. Unfortunately, the Chinese had no interest in British goods. So, even as tea imports to Britain surged, the British could not sell anything to China. The Chinese would only accept silver – equivalent to hard cash. Soon, the Treasury of the British Empire was running out of silver. The British didn't have enough money to pay for their tea habit.

Simultaneously, the British had another problem: their new colony in India wasn't as profitable as they had hoped. They had shifted from controlling a network of trading posts in India to becoming an imperial power. They governed the land and raised money through taxes. It was the era of Company Raj. But as imperial wars to conquer more and more land (so they could earn more) dragged on, they found that they were spending an increasing share of their newly gotten funds on the wars themselves. So they needed a new way to make money off this hard-won colony.

And then, somewhere in the mechanical mind of the British Empire, a cog clicked and fell into place. Two problems became one solution. They put their colony to work to produce something that the Chinese would buy, even if they didn't want it: OPIUM. You can drink it, eat it, and smoke it. It gets you high – and it is addictive. And after a while, it becomes hard to stop using it. And there is nothing better for a seller than a product you can't stop buying. Over the eighteenth and nineteenth centuries, the British transformed most of the farming economies of the Bengal Presidency into opium-producing machines. **The British were knowingly getting millions of people addicted for profit, not just in China but also in India. Even when they passed laws against opium at home, they produced it in India and sold it in China!** Their agents smuggled the drug illegally into China, exchanging it for tea. Suddenly, the balance of trade leaned the other way. Silver started flowing back out of China into British hands. (Emphasis by Subir)

The above interlude is based on an episode from Thomas Manuel's book, "Opium Inc.: HOW A GLOBAL TRADE FUNDED THE BRITISH EMPIRE". It was first published in India in 2021 by HarperCollins. [2] Earlier, in chapter 2, titled "The Story of OPIUM," we caught a glimpse of the dire effects of opium on the people of Assam that resulted from such a duplicitous role played by the British colonial rulers in India.

Soon after Assam was annexed by the British, making it a part of the Bengal Presidency, a botanical garden in Calcutta, after scientifically examining a few samples of tea-like plants growing wild in some parts of North-Eastern regions of India, confirmed in the early 1830s these as an indigenous variety of the tea plant. They named them Camellia Assamica. It was a fascinating serendipity for the British at that time. The discovery of the indigenous tea plant and the large stretches of land lying waste in the Brahmaputra Valley caught their particular imagination so much that it changed their attitude towards Assam. When the Charter Act of 1833 ended the East India Company's tea trade monopoly with China, the Company officials were desperately trying to establish an alternative source of tea under its exclusive control. Eventually, the British opened the first tea garden in India at Lakhimpur, Assam, in 1835 and started the commercial production of tea in the same year. In 1836, the first batch of tea produced in Assam was sent to Calcutta. In 1838, the first twelve chests of manufactured tea made from indigenous Assam leaf were shipped to London via Calcutta and sold at the

London auctions. It paved the way for forming the 'Bengal Tea Association' in Calcutta and the first joint-stock Tea Company - the 'Assam Company' in London. On witnessing its success, other companies were formed to take up tea cultivation in Assam. [3] [4]

As Assam Tea started gaining popularity with the British by the 1840s, even the demand for tea from China, as well as the flow of silver to China, decreased significantly. To the British colonial rulers, the inclusion of Assam in India thus became the cherry on the cake. To cultivate the special crops in Assam, the Waste Land Settlement Rules were formulated for the first time in 1838. Broadly speaking, Waste Land is the land left fallow or covered with jungle or uncultivated land that was not likely to be taken up for the cultivation of ordinary crops. However, the British Government altered Assam's wasteland rules in different ways to safeguard their commercial interests. At times, they even connived at breaching the rules. The special cultivation initially meant cultivating commercial crops such as tea, coffee, sugarcane, etc. Later on, for all practical purposes, cultivation of all other crops except tea had been relegated to the background. Maximum efforts were directed towards the growth and extension of tea cultivation, and very liberal and flexible rules were framed to grant wasteland to the planters.

Significantly, the government's objective was to attract European Capitalists and not to encourage local businessmen to invest in tea. As a result, the participation of local entrepreneurs in the tea industry was negligible. Moreover, as the most essential requirement of the tea industry, which is labour, was extremely in short supply in the sparsely populated Assam, the government cleverly increased the rate of revenue on land to such an exorbitant extent that by 1872-73 there was a 100% increase in the total land revenue demand of the Brahmaputra Valley. The idea was to make the ordinary cultivations un-remunerative and thereby dissuade the locals from farming on their own land to make a living. However, despite being subjected to such heavy taxation, the local Assamese people did not come forward to work as wage labourers. Under the circumstances, the planters were forced to bring labourers for the tea industries in Assam from other provinces of India - such as present-day Bihar, Jharkhand, Orissa, Uttar Pradesh, Uttarakhand, Madhya Pradesh, Andhra Pradesh, and Tamil Nadu.

There were various reasons why the local people did not want to work in the tea gardens. Some of these, according to Researcher Julee Duwarah, were:

1. At that time, the population density was very sparse in Assam. Large areas of land were uninhabited and unused. Therefore, local people

were not interested in working in the tea gardens, preferring to focus on their own cultivation on those large lands.

2. On the other hand, under the rule of the indigenous kings, the local people became dignity-conscious and free-minded. So, they did not show interest in serving under 'outsiders' at the tea gardens, preferring to maintain their free lifestyle.

3. Due to excessive consumption of opium, the local people were becoming lazy. Therefore, they did not want to work hard in the tea gardens. [5]

Nevertheless, it's fascinating to note that tea had a far-reaching impact both on metropolises like London and peripheries like Sylhet, Cachar, and Assam. While Assam tea had already entered the London auctions in 1838, in the Dacca division of the Bengal Presidency, indigenous tea was found in the Cachar district in 1855 and the Sylhet district in 1856. In Cachar, the first tea garden was opened within one year in the cold weather of 1855-56, and in the Sylhet district, systematic tea cultivation started in the year 1860 - close to the hills, which were extremely malarious and surrounded by dense jungle. [6] Until the 1850s, British policy was to avoid the hills in their colony, but tea altered the traditional policy. In the 1870s, planters differed in their opinions of the kinds of soil most suited for the growth of tea, but at that time, there was no doubt that 'the virgin soil of the dense forests at the foothills, where the climate is hot and moist, and where tea is often found indigenous, is the best'.

Opening up land for tea in the jungle was a 'man's job'; often enough, the pioneers on the estates had extremely 'primitive quarters', where disease and discomfort made life 'arduous'. Nonetheless, by the late 19th century, tea had made great progress, becoming a global commodity, and it soon won the hearts of women in the metropolis. Tea became the 'great white hope' for progress. 'Tea mania' became visible in the late 60s and early 70s of the 19th century and seized people's minds. Ambitious entrepreneurs began to scramble wildly for tea shares and tea lands. It was the 'Great Rush' in an Indian context to get rich overnight. Tea planters in the early 1870s, according to a certain Edward Money, "were a strange medley of retired or cashiered Army and Navy officers, medical men, engineers, veterinary surgeons, steamer captains, chemists, shopkeepers of all kinds, stable keepers, used up policemen, clerks and goodness knows who besides'. Every man thought owning a few tea bushes was to realize wealth. It all contributed to forming a shifting frontier on the Eastern border of the British Raj.

Tea planters required a separate province of their own to fulfil their metropolitan imagination. They had long demanded the creation of an exclusive province to ensure their interests and the efficient use of state tools. Very soon, every branch of the administration was overhauled. Consequent to the growth of tea plantations and migrant labour coupled with increased work, special regulations were drafted to provide for growing local needs. That was the backdrop, according to some experts, under which a new province was created in 1874, carving out three Bengali-dominated districts, Sylhet, Cachar, and Goalpara, along with the Assam division from the Bengal Presidency and amalgamating them together to form the Assam province, in sync with the appellation 'Assam Tea" that started gaining popularity globally.

Besides tea plantations, the expansion of agriculture was another key reason behind the incorporation of the three districts into the new province. For instance, Goalpara was not chosen for tea cultivation, but it was a district supplying the bulk of the food crops and labourers. The district also produced surplus rice for the consumption of tea garden workers. Archival evidence suggests that in the late 19th century, Sylhet was known as the granary of Bengal, and it attracted agrarian labourers, particularly during the harvest seasons from neighbouring Mymensingh and Tripura (Modern Comilla & Noakhali) to Sylhet. Archival and other sources also suggest that access to the nearby Chittagong port for tea export was another driving force that had inked the new map in the Eastern frontier of the British Raj. [7]

Interestingly, unlike other commercial crops such as rubber, sugarcane, etc., tea production commenced within a very short time of its plantation. Therefore, tea cultivation got prime importance from both the government and the planters. However, the large-scale expansion of tea cultivation that took place eventually resulted in the decline of rice cultivation. So, the local people also suffered to a certain extent. It is important to remember that tea supported only a little more than one-seventh of the number dependent on ordinary agriculture. Therefore, the need for colonization of the vast wastelands of the province was acutely felt not only by the European capitalists but also by some of the local educated people, given Assam's acute shortage of population, the reluctance of the local people to work as wage labourers, and the priority attached to the rapid growth and extension of the tea industry. Accordingly, in 1874 almost a hundred Assamese people submitted a petition to Lord Northbrook (Viceroy of India from 1872 to 1876), in which they urged the Government to bring 'outside-people' into the province to augment Assam's population and thereby strengthen its economy.

Because of the hefty profit margins in the tea industry, both planters and the government continued to place strong emphasis on its expansion. Consequently, they made every possible effort to rapidly extend tea cultivation. Accordingly, the government formulated very liberal and flexible rules for granting wasteland to tea planters. However, the large-scale expansion of tea cultivation resulted in the shrinking of general agricultural lands in the province, leading to a decline in food production over time.

By the turn of the 20th century, thousands of acres of land in the north of the Brahmaputra, near or at the foothills, had been claimed by tea plantations. Consequently, restrictions were imposed against trespassing in these plantation areas, which had previously been freely accessible to local tribes. The tribal people also lost their free access to the woods, which were declared Reserved Forests under the Assam Forest Regulation of 1891. Subsequently, it became a punishable offence for tribal people to hunt, shoot, fish, cut any tree, or collect any forest produce in the Reserved Forests.

Previously, hillmen had supplemented their meagre economy by hunting, fishing, rubber-tapping, elephant-catching, and gathering other forest products in the hills and foothills, which extended up to the Brahmaputra valley. However, during British rule, the available land area for tribal people significantly decreased due to the expansion of tea plantations and the establishment of reserved forests. This adversely affected the economic conditions of tribal communities to such an extent that land issues became the catalyst for severe tribal outrages.

Then there was another problem. In the rubber-producing districts of Assam, it was the practice of the government to lease out the rubber mahal (i.e., the right to buy the rubber produced in the district) by annual auction. However, very little of the rubber used to come from within the settled revenue limits; the hillmen would bring much of it from their tribal lands lying beyond the British jurisdiction. However, the farms let out in each district would take it for granted that they not only had the right to buy the India-rubber produced in the districts, but also the foreign caoutchouc, i.e., India-rubber collected in and imported from the territory beyond the British, civil and revenue, jurisdictions. This system had been working well until independent European speculators came in. They disputed the claim of the lessees of the rubber mahals to a monopoly of the rubber brought from outside the British territory.

The government now faced a potentially dangerous situation. It feared that the speculators might cheat the hillmen, leading to tribal disturbances. The government of India also realized that if the speculators were allowed to advance into the hills, to take advantage of the ignorance of the tribe members, and perhaps even to buy up from them the right to collect forest produce, the difficulties which had arisen from the unrestrained extension of tea-planting on the frontier may soon crop up in a new and even more dangerous form. Envisioning the hillmen getting cheated by unscrupulous speculators in the developing situation, the government faced a potentially hazardous situation that, they feared, could lead to tribal disturbance. [8]

That was the backdrop against which the British colonial rulers introduced the Bengal Eastern Frontier Regulation of 1873 – commonly known as the Inner Line Regulation. The regulation empowered the government to draw an Inner Line to prohibit British subjects or any person from going beyond the line without a pass issued by the district authority concerned; to confiscate any rubber, wax, ivory, or other jungle produce found in possession of any person guilty of violating this regulation; and to prohibit any person, except the original inhabitants of the districts concerned, from acquiring any interest in land or the product of land beyond the Inner Line without official sanction. The government could even extend the last prohibition to the original inhabitants of the districts. This regulation also provided for the protection of wild elephants. These restrictions were so stringent that they were supposed to check the expansion of tea plantations, rubber industry activities, etc., into the tribal country and restrict the likely undesirable contacts between the ignorant tribe members and sharp speculators in caoutchouc-related dealings. However, the Inner Line regime also impeded the hitherto free communications and contacts between the ordinary people of the hills and the plains.

As Assam witnessed tremendous growth in the tea industry during the last three decades of the 19th century, it required improved infrastructure, particularly in communications. Hence, the construction of railways started in 1881. The Assam Railways and Trading Company, formed in 1881, undertook the construction work of the Dibru-Sadiya Railway. The first railway line was opened in 1882 from the Dibrugarh steamer 'ghat' (a flight of steps leading down to a river) to Jaipur road. During this period, numerous roads, waterways, and railways were built in the tea districts connecting the plantations. In 1847, a steamer service on the Brahmaputra was established by the government between Calcutta and Gauhati (960 km), but due to a shortage of steamers, it could not be continued regularly. In 1856, the Government Steamer Service was extended from Gauhati to Dibrugarh.

Four years later, the Indian General Steam Navigation Company entered into a contract to run a pair of vessels every six weeks from Calcutta to Dibrugarh. In 1905, a daily steamer service was started between Dhubri and Gauhati in both directions as a natural consequence of the extension of the Eastern Bengal Railway to Dhubri in 1902. The railway served a large number of important tea gardens and provided an outlet for the coal and oil from Makum.

It may be recalled that at the time of British occupation, Assam had a ravaged economy with a sparse population. The essential civic infrastructure like medical facilities, road communication, and educational institutions, in the modern sense of the term, was almost absent. The erstwhile Ahom rulers hardly paid any attention to supporting trade and commercial activities; the monetary economy was non-existent, and barter was the standard mode of transaction. The black fever (kala-azar) epidemic originating in Garo Hills spread to Goalpara in 1883 and throughout Assam, subsequently from 1888. The epidemics, plus other diseases, coupled with the near absence of suitable medical facilities, resulted in a high mortality rate in the region. Throughout the 19th century and in the early decades of the 20th century, the so-called towns of greater Assam, in a real sense, were a small assortment of some semi-permanent tiny accommodations of government servants and traders with narrow roads and minimal civic amenities or just some "glorified villages." Only Sylhet, with 14,407, followed by Gauhati and Barpeta, were the three towns where the population exceeded more than 10,000 each in 1881. There were barely 15 or so "towns" where the population was more than 5,000 each. Throughout the period 1881–1931, the urban population as a percentage of Assam's total population remained below 2%. [9]

Except for land, practically all other requirements for the production, manufacturing, and service sectors, including the all-important labour force, had to be brought from outside the province. From 1826 to 1873, when British capital was infused into Assam's economy and necessary infrastructure started to develop, human resources such as traders, bankers, lawyers, doctors, and clerks had to be imported from its Sylhet District or other Indian provinces as necessary support staff. Marwari traders-cum-money lenders monopolized the internal trade. With the advantage of their early exposure to English education, administrative work, and professional services, Bengali clerks, doctors, lawyers, and teachers monopolized government jobs and private professions. The British administration was not inclined to set up appropriate educational infrastructure because it could recruit from Bengal's surplus of educated and skilled personnel at a lower cost. Thus, the Brahmaputra Valley continued to suffer from a shortage of educated and skilled personnel. In contrast, the share of the population from Surma Valley and outside the province, especially from adjacent Bengal, grew rapidly in Assam proper. Moreover, employers often discriminated against Assamese people due to their alleged opium addiction, as discussed earlier in Chapter 2 of this book.

However, with the expansion of various economic activities revolving around the tea industry, the valley's population also increased. This created immense pressure on the hitherto self-sufficient economy of the state because the Assamese people produced minimal surplus beyond what was needed for their own consumption. The government also did not encourage them in any manner to produce more than their requirements. Under these circumstances, planters had no alternative but to import food items at very high prices. The government began to realize the urgency of extending ordinary cultivation as a necessity and focused its attention on finding ways and means to start food cultivation in Assam on a large scale.

With demand from tea factories and the railways, coal output increased from 50 tons in 1872 to more than 277,000 by 1905-06. The oil fields developed by the British capital in the 1890s increased annual crude oil production from 882,000 gallons in 1900-01 to 2,733,000 by 1905-06. For supplying packing boxes and scantlings to the tea industry, as many as fourteen sawmills were functioning in 1901. Simultaneously, infrastructure for telecommunications and other facilities also began to develop. All these required huge capital and human resources. However, practically all other inputs were brought from outside the province except for land.

The land-abundant Brahmaputra Valley could not cope with the ever-increasing requirements of food grains to feed its growing population with locally grown food. The annual import of food grains into the Valley rose from 0.3 million maunds around 1872 to about 0.7 million maunds during the last five years of the 19th century. As the gap between demand and supply widened, the prices of food grains started to increase. Many starvation deaths were reported in Nowgong during the bad seasons of 1896. On October 16th of that year, troops had to be called out to suppress a riotous outburst against the Banias (an occupational community/caste of businessmen in India) who had cornered the grain market. Conditions were further worsened by the great earthquake of 1897, which caused many deaths and havoc over many hundred acres of farmland. [10]

This was the background against which the British government decided to accede to the earlier demands of Assamese nobles and gentries to import people to this sparsely populated province and colonize Assam on a large scale. However, this government decision was also influenced by certain other considerations. First, it would supply labour to the province of Assam; secondly, it would alleviate population pressure in the congested parts of India and serve as an effective measure against famine. Besides, encouragement to the people thus brought from outside to cultivate in the wastelands of Assam would help improve the state's economy and increase the government's revenue income.

In the meantime, with the dawn of the 20th century, jute cultivation and factory production of jute products increased worldwide. This necessitated the expansion of jute cultivation from Bengal to Assam. Ample land was available in five districts of the Brahmaputra valley: Naogaon, Lakhimpur, the eastern part of Darrang, as well as the east Duars region of Goalpara, and the Barpeta division of Kamrup, which proved ideal for jute cultivation. F.J. Monahan, the Assistant Director of Assam Land Records and Agriculture Department, prepared a detailed report on the prospects of jute cultivation in the Brahmaputra valley and recommended immigration and settlement of peasants from East Bengal. The Calcutta Chamber of Commerce emphasized the immediate commencement of jute cultivation in Assam by importing cultivators from Bengal. Thus, alongside addressing the shortage of food production, jute cultivation became another factor driving the British colonial rulers to encourage cultivators from Bengal to migrate to Assam.

The "Gazette of India" of 1899 published a report stating, "Closely connected with the prevention of famine lies the question of the movement of people and their distribution for employment." The report highlighted the significant advantages of people moving to the province of Assam and the benefits the Government of India could derive from it. Moreover, the increasing demand for jute on the eve of the 20th century allowed colonial officials in Assam to encourage East Bengal cultivators to extend jute cultivation in Assam.

Meanwhile, under the encouragement of Zamindars of Goalpara, some peasant cultivators from Bengal had already entered and settled in the riverine tracts of Goalpara. The Census Report of 1911 revealed an inflow of Bengal cultivators from the bordering districts of Dacca, Bogura, Rangpur, and Mymensingh to Assam in search of vacant land for cultivation. Gradually, this influx shaped the population composition of the Brahmaputra valley.

With the increase in influx, the nearly homogenous nature of the tribal populations of the 19th century soon changed to a heterogeneous population of non-tribal communities, resulting in complex ethnic, linguistic, and religious differences, mainly in the Brahmaputra valley. **Push and pull**

factors also played significant roles in the migration of East Bengal cultivators to Assam. The scarcity of food grains, shortage of human resources for land reclamation, the extension of jute cultivation, and the absence of any restrictive laws (after all, both Assam and Bengal were Bengali-majority provinces within the same country) created a pull factor for the migration of East Bengal peasant cultivators to Assam. Colonial officials viewed land-abundant Assam as a solution to East Bengal's problem of land scarcity. Conversely, overpopulation, land shortage, abnormal price hikes on food grains, and Zamindari oppressions pushed a sizable section of East Bengal's agricultural population towards Assam.

The motive of the colonial officials was also partly political, aiming to balance the Hindu and Muslim populations of Assam. This strategy was undoubtedly one of the striking features of colonial political control through their 'divide and rule' policy. Statements from Lord Curzon, Viceroy, and P.G. Mellitus, Revenue Member, suggest they also considered Assam capable of absorbing the surplus population of other provinces.

In the absence of any suitable settlement scheme or officer to regulate settlement, migrants started settling wherever vacant lands were available. Under the squatting system prevailing in Assam, newcomers were allowed to settle without hindrance on any government wasteland except reserved land. After migrants cleared jungles and prepared land for cultivation, they were provided with an annual patta by the relevant authority. [11]

It is pertinent to mention here that geographically, the Brahmaputra Valley of Assam consists of three classes of land: (A) The chapori or riverine tracts along the Brahmaputra Valley. (B) The central tracts contained the bulk of the population and consisted of land under permanent cultivation. (C) The submontane tracts are situated in the foothills or lower slopes of a mountain range. The tea gardens were located in the (B) tracts or the central tracts.

Regarding the land belonging to 'A' tracts, i.e., chapori areas along the Brahmaputra river, it was seen that the so-called "East Bengal immigrants" (as commonly categorized in the dominant history of Assam) had begun to settle there of their own accord in small numbers ever since Assam became a part of Bengal Presidency and subsequently remained amalgamated to Bengal's Cachar, Goalpara, and Sylhet districts up to 1947. It is noteworthy to recall here that Assam also remained merged with East Bengal once again for 7 (seven) years at a stretch from 1905 to 1912.

Once the government decided to populate the unutilized vacant stretches of land in Assam for growing food crops locally by the expansion of ordinary cultivation on a large scale, it also had to decide where the colonists would be settled. The Brahmaputra Valley, as mentioned above, consists of three categories of land - the submontane region, the central plain tracts, and the char or chapori areas of the Brahmaputra. The central tracts were generally inhabited by the local people. Most of the tea gardens were also located here. The submontane regions were inhabited by some tribes. The land was not generally suitable for ordinary cultivation. Initially, this category of land was considered fit for tea cultivation but was soon found unsuitable for the purpose. Accordingly, considering all these aspects, the government decided to allow the char or chapori areas for the settlement of the colonists. (Char-chaporis are shifting riverine islands of the Brahmaputra River and its tributaries.)

Initially, considering the need for the cultivation of food grains and the sparse population of the province, the Chief Commissioner of Assam (1902–05), Bampfylde Fuller, suggested that the Assam administration should endeavour to colonize the wasteland with the help of the authorities of the Assam Bengal Railway. He felt the labourers who had come into the province in the temporary service of the railway or its contractors should be encouraged to take up cultivation in those lands. Fuller regretted that large numbers of immigrants were permitted to leave the province, which so urgently needed colonists, without making some attempts to induce them to settle down on the other. It was directed that the concession might be extended to the bona fide settlers not employed on the railway, but the preference should be given to railway employees and 'foreigners'. A set of rules and a form of lease embodying the terms of the concession were issued. The attempt of the government, however, failed to obtain a satisfactory response, and according to the Deputy Commissioner of Nowgong district, up to June 30th, 1906, only 25 acres of land had been settled under these rules.

Similarly, the government made another attempt to populate the deforested areas of the Nambor forest in the (then) Golaghat subdivision in the district of Sibsagar. The authorities offered very liberal terms to the prospective cultivators to attract the colonists. The first three years of land occupation were made revenue-free, and then a nominal rate of 3 annas a bigha was imposed. Liberal terms were also granted to the mauzadars (the administrative official responsible for a mauza, i.e., district). Despite these attempts, however, the government was not successful in colonizing the area with the people from the Surma Valley. The remoteness of the tracts and the pestilential climate of the region were considered to be two major obstacles in colonizing the Assam Valley. The government, therefore, considered that under the circumstances, selecting a better group of colonists was essential to making the colonization process fruitful.

Soon, the government realised that a positive result in their efforts depended heavily on selecting the right group of colonists who could survive in the pestilential climate of the Assam Valley. At the same time, it must consist of people with a proven track record of being hardy cultivators. Sir Henry Cotton, Chief Commissioner of Assam (1896-1902), believed that the coolies brought from Bihar and North-Western provinces were useless for jungle clearing and would also succumb to malaria far more rapidly than the more hardy and indigenous tribes from other parts. According to him, "There is every reason to suppose that they would make good cultivators when the land is cleared, and the miasma is blown away, but they ought never to be employed as the pioneers of cultivation." He also believed that although the aboriginal tribes were bad agriculturists, they were good at jungle clearing. Therefore, these tribes must be the prelude to the migration of regular agriculturists.

Noticeably, there was a natural flow of migrants to the Assam Valley from the districts of Eastern Bengal, particularly from Mymensingh (located on the bank of the Brahmaputra River on the East Bengal side) and Pabna (located on the north bank of the Padma River). They arrived in small groups and generally wished to take up the nearest lands available for cultivation they met on their journey. The Mymensingh and Pabna migrants went to the 'A' and 'B' tracts mentioned above but did not go to the 'C' tracts. The Government realized that being more or less from the same climatic zone, they should be in a better position to withstand the hostile climate of Assam. Besides, they were sturdy workers too.

Considering these positive aspects, the Government decided to encourage their settlement in the province. The Government promoted their inflow by providing a better communication system and facilitated their settlement by providing lands on easy terms, etc. The prime reason behind this support to them (85 per cent of whom were Muslims) was their suitability as 'settlers' in Assam. Accordingly, the flow of these settlers into the province began in the last decade of the 19th century, though initially, it was not on a very large scale. [12]

The migration of people from East Bengal, especially Bengali Muslims from Mymensingh and its adjoining areas to Assam's Brahmaputra Valley, received a boost after the amalgamation of Assam with East Bengal, forming the new province of Eastern Bengal and Assam in 1905. The government further encouraged this by establishing railway communication with Eastern Bengal and making train fares affordable for migrant labourers and their families intending to settle in Assam. Consequently, the migration of people from East Bengal into the Brahmaputra Valley of Assam continued to increase.

Moreover, in the labour-starved economy of the Brahmaputra Valley of Assam, slavery as an institution played a significant role until the first half of the nineteenth century. An estimated 5 to 9 per cent of the population were enslaved individuals and bondsmen, with a considerable number working on agricultural farms. The old Ahom aristocracy, Brahmin, and Mahanta landowners heavily relied on slaves and bondsmen to cultivate their vast agricultural lands, including the 'devottar,' 'brahmottar,' and 'dharmottar' lands. When the British colonial rulers abolished the slavery system in 1843, it substantially impacted the Assamese gentry due to the acute labour shortage resulting from the abolition. The so-called 'adverse impact' of the abolition was widespread and severe, with Brahmin slave-holders in the Kamrup District even organizing a protest demonstration and submitting a bunch of 1000 petitions seeking permission to retain their slaves and bondsmen. [Guha, Amalendu. p. 9."Planter Raj to Swaraj"]

Therefore, when the flow of cheap Muslim migrants from neighbouring Bengal began, they were welcomed by the Assamese gentry, Mahantas, landlords, and all with open arms to address the scarcity of labourers. This influx of migrants was the icing on the cake for the new East Bengali settlers in Assam. Consequently, by the end of the second decade of the 20th century, it was observed that migrants extended their settlements to the central tracts in addition to the char areas, which were specially earmarked for them. [13]

It needs to be mentioned here that for the new settlers, it was not easy to come from East Bengal to Assam, occupy wasteland, and start cultivation in an unknown destination where there was no organization, private or official, to assist them in undertaking the settlement. Most of the available lands had to be reclaimed first and made suitable for human habitation. The lands were highly unhealthy and infested with malaria and wild animals. The expenses of the journey, reclamation of land, and building of abodes were substantial. As the migrants were strangers to this land, there was an element of uncertainty in entering into any transactions involving land purchases from the Assamese. Instances were not wanting where a seller wanted back his land after receiving the stipulated amount.

Considering their desperate needs in the new environs full of hazards calling for great labour and sacrifice, a certain amount of roughness and intolerance was perhaps inevitable. Still, admittedly, the migrants became peaceful over time. However, here in Assam, two groups of people with different ancestries, religions, customs, and habits, economic conditions, cultures, and languages came face to face; hence, some unpleasant confrontations of these initial contacts were not wholly unexpected. But, at a later stage, some vested interested groups of people misused the memories of such confrontations for political propaganda.

Greed for land is universal among men, and it was not unnatural in a society permeated by inequality and injustice to take advantage of the fluid situation. Accordingly, some migrants acquired large blocks of land with a 'Speculative Motive.' The Assamese themselves also had done so as there were no restrictive laws against it. However, such transactions were not limited to the newcomers and the local inhabitants. They also became objects of exploitation by the wealthier sections of their own community, government officials, and the non-official public. It is not, however, only the landholders and leading men among the immigrants who allegedly made money out of newcomers, but there were many instances of Assamese speculators also, especially in the earlier days in Nowgong, who made large sums of money by selling lands to the migrants. Besides, the Deputy Commissioner, Nowgong, was reportedly able to provide many instances of corruption among the land records staff in settling lands, altering lines, and giving pattas, etc.

Again, instances were not lacking wherein newcomers to the province were fleeced right and left by indigenous inhabitants and the Matbars and Dewans - the leading men of their community. Thus, many of these migrants became prey to unscrupulous individuals. Eventually, a time came before long when, due to their numbers as well as the politicization of so-called immigration, the whole issue attained a new colour and interpretation. The migrants became unwanted people in the province despite contributing significantly to the growth and development of Assam. After being maltreated and oppressed, the attitude of the migrants as a class hardened against the locals, especially the political and community leaders. The Assamese and the Bengali Muslims sought to resolve the problem politically but failed. Thus, the politicization of an essentially economic issue turned into a sociological and political predicament.

From various primary sources and corresponding letters, it could be gathered that the Assamese people had continued to transfer lands within the lines of restriction under the provision of the then-existing law. There was no bar for selling periodic patta land to a migrant, making the problem more complex. Debendra Kumar Mukherjee, Assistant Director of Land Records, who went for an inspection in the Dihing circle in April 1924, found that lands belonging to the Assamese people were fast passing into the hands of immigrants in those areas where there existed no line of division. He apprehended that if the land transfer continued at such a rate, within a few years, all such villages would be held exclusively by the so-called immigrants.

Therefore, until the Deputy Commissioner took special measures by marking out the blocks of land owned by the Assamese people and preventing further land transfer to the immigrants, he saw no hope in protecting the Assamese people. While giving the reason behind the transfer of lands to the migrants, the Assistant Director of Land Records, in his report, pointed out that the Assamese people could not resist the temptation of high prices offered by the Mymensinghias and thereby sold their possessions. He realized that the Assamese people failed to foresee the result of such action, and if it continued, they would be compelled to leave their ancestral place sooner or later and migrate elsewhere.

Interestingly, one section of the people viewed the migrants as criminals who must be removed bags and baggage, while the other section claimed them as saviours. They said that before the coming of the Mymensinghias, they suffered from floods, but since they settled on the land, there had been no flood at all. Also, there could be no doubt that these migrants had greatly added to the prosperity of their land. [14]

As the new settlers from East Bengal spread beyond the char areas, it led to conflicts with the native people, followed by mutual hatred and distrust. The government and politicians later exploited these sentiments to further their selfish agendas.

While the genesis of the lingering Assamese-Bengali discord can be traced back to the aforementioned sequence of events, the unabated incitement provided by British administrators from time to time to widen the fissure between the two major communities in Assam is the main reason for the never-ending communal disharmony in the province since those days. We shall delve into this as we progress.

Unfortunately, neither the Assamese nor the Bengalis could discern the insidious 'divide and rule' game the British colonial rulers played in the immigration dynamics during their rule. Instead, both communities, sometimes knowingly but mostly unwittingly, played into the hands of the shrewd Britons without questioning their true intentions. Significantly, the term 'divide and rule' has fallen out of use in India since the end of British rule. Instead, 'polarization' has emerged as its new incarnation, continuing to afflict Assam and the North-East, as well as other parts of India, as a 'parting gift' from the British colonial rulers.

In any case, much to the dismay of the Assamese people and amidst public anger and mass protests in Bengal, the British partitioned Bengal in 1905, believing it to be the hub of India's independence movement led by the Congress party. The Viceroy of India, Lord Curzon, announced the partition plan on 19th July 1905, which was implemented on 16th October 1905 primarily to quell revolutionary activities against British rule in the Indian subcontinent and to punish the Bengali middle class for their widespread support and participation in the freedom movement. Accordingly, the eastern part of Bengal was detached from the Bengal Presidency, and the Chief Commissioner's Province of Assam was merged with it to form a new province, thereby ending Assam's separate status as a province.

As the partition plan for Bengal and the reports of the new province being named "North Eastern Province" became known, the first President of Asom Sahitya Sabha, Padmanath Gohain-Barua, raised the alarm. Acting as a mouthpiece of Assamese society, Gohain-Barua, in an editorial comment in Assam Banti on 10th July 1905, expressed fear that the name Assam would be obliterated forever. In another editorial, he urged Assamese people to stand up in protest against the merger itself. Later, however, reluctantly accepting the creation of the new province as a settled fact, pleas were made for retaining at least the word 'Assam' in its designation. [15] With efforts from various quarters, the proposal to change the name to "North Eastern Province" for the new province could somehow be shelved, much to the relief of some Assamese people. Ultimately, the new-born province was named 'Eastern Bengal and Assam', retaining Assam in its title, with the headquarters of the province in Dacca and Shillong as its Summer Capital.

Moreover, in his thesis submitted for the degree of Doctor of Philosophy at the University of London titled "THE NEW PROVINCE OF EASTERN BENGAL AND ASSAM, 1905-1911," researcher Mohammad Kasim Uddin Molla also wrote that the British Secretary of State for India, suggesting a change in the name of the new province, wrote:

> "I have reason to think that the important commercial interests represented by the tea industry would complain if the name of Assam, now so widely known in the markets of the world as the chief source of Indian tea, were to disappear from the list of Indian provinces; and I should be disposed to prefer "Eastern Bengal and Assam" as the name of the new Lieutenant Governorship."

Accordingly, the province was eventually named 'Eastern Bengal and Assam'. [16]

Nevertheless, the archival materials indicate that the partition of Bengal was a well-thought-out plan by the British to unite the Mohammedan population of Eastern India and reduce the 'politically threatening' position of the 'Hindu minority' in undivided Bengal. At that time, the province of Bengal, the hub of India's radical revolutionary activities against British rule, caused utmost concern to the colonial rulers. For instance, in the Bengal Presidency, Bipin Chandra Pal of (Habiganj) Sylhet district was the renowned Pal of the "Lal-Bal-Pal" triumvirate, known to be one of the chief architects of the Swadeshi Movement. Besides, Eastern Bengal was the most densely populated portion of the densely populated Bengal. It needed room for expansion and could only expand towards the East. So, far from hindering national development, the British gave it a vast scope to develop and enable Bengal to absorb sparsely populated Assam. These were the possible political benefits of the plan that the British Colonial rulers envisaged. To the British administrators: "the advantage of severing these eastern districts of Bengal, which are a hotbed of the purely Bengali movement, unfriendly if not seditious in character, and dominating the whole tone of Bengal administration, will immeasurably outweigh any possible drawbacks...". They considered: "... Bengal united is a power; Bengal divided will pull in several different ways". In the final analysis, the British administrators decided: "Bengal is very densely populated; that Eastern Bengal is the most densely populated portion, that it needs room for expansion and that it can only expand towards the East. So far from hindering national development, we are really giving it greater scope and enabling Bengal to absorb Assam." [17] It is another example of the British policy of 'Divide and Rule' to tame the rebellious Bengalis to the extent possible. Thus, the seeds of the Hindu-Muslim communal divide with a cunning twist of Assamese-Bengali racial rivalry were also planted in Assam. The root cause of the present imbroglio in Assam is this mischievous British policy, the ugly manifestation, and the far-reaching ramifications of which are still perceptible in Assam!

Significantly, the first advocate of 'Muslim separatism' concerning Eastern Bengal and Assam was perhaps Lord Curzon. In a statement made at Dacca on February 18th, 1904, he claimed that in partitioning Bengal, he was carving out a Muslim Province. However, the statement's significance did not resonate well among the educated Muslims as was expected at that time. Lord Curzon also asserted that this was investing the Muslims of East Bengal with a unity they had not enjoyed since the olden days of the Muslim rulers and kings. Nevertheless, the seeds of 'Muslim separatism' thus sown by British rulers showed results four decades later. A separate Muslim country, Pakistan, eventually emerged in 1947. [18]

Following the partition of Bengal in 1905, the province of Assam again merged with East Bengal. The flow of agricultural labourers from East Bengal into Assam picked up simultaneously (as mentioned earlier). These Bengali migrants were primarily agricultural labourers, about 85 per cent of whom were Muslims from the adjacent Mymensingh and nearby areas. The

British bureaucracy provided inducement by allotting them land in uninhabited "char areas" where they had to wage a heroic battle day in and day out against poisonous insects, wild beasts, deadly diseases, and all odds to start farming. They soon populated the 'unwelcome' riverine countryside of Assam, contending with floods, rains, epidemics, erosion, and dedicating themselves to developing the land to make it suitable for agriculture. In the process, the new settlers succeeded in transforming the land, which was once nothing but wilderness, into productive fields. With their incredible stamina, earnest efforts, and knowledge of superior techniques in land development and cultivation, the Bengali Muslims toiled, suffered, fought against all odds, and even sacrificed their lives to survive in the unfriendly environment of Assam, introducing newer varieties of seeds and significantly increasing food grain production. Within a short time, these 'Mymensinghis' or the 'Miya ', as they were pejoratively called, hailing from East Bengal, introduced jute, mung-pulse, and several other crops in the Brahmaputra Valley, resulting in a significant growth of agricultural output in Assam.

Note: [1] "Miya" is derived from "mian," an honorific of Persian origin commonly used throughout the subcontinent when addressing a Muslim gentleman. According to Professor Yasmin Saikia, the Hardt-Nickachos Chair in Peace Studies, "etymologically, the word 'miya', of Urdu origin, means a man of social standing, a gentleman. In Assam, however, it pejoratively refers to the outcast Bengali Muslims. Today, some Miya poets and artists use the term self-referentially to highlight the humiliation they suffer."

Earlier, in Kamrup and Goalpara, agricultural workers were extremely scarce. In Central and Upper Assam, they were practically non-existent after the abolition of the slave system discussed earlier. So gradually, the Assamese gentry also started to welcome these cheap laborers for the agricultural development of their large but mostly unused fields. Thus, the new settlers from East Bengal, primarily comprising 'Mymensinghi' Muslims, began to spread to other areas of Assam. Side by side, the Bengali Hindus not only formed the backbone of Assam's administration by then, but they were also at the forefront of providing other essential services in education, healthcare, legal aid, as well as trade and commerce. Thus, with the joint efforts of the so-called 'outsider' Bengalis, the British could achieve leapfrog growth and economic improvement in Assam. The following two paragraphs, in parts, quoted from the Sectional President's Address in Indian History Congress 2009 by Assam's author and history Professor Rajen Saika, provided a glimpse of how the Assamese population viewed the 1905 Partition of Bengal:

> "In the Eastern Bengal and Assam Legislative Council, Manikchandra Barua, the leader of the Assam Association, remarked that 'the partition in its present shape was a mistake' and that 'by partition, Assam has suffered the most.' The political geography of

the fleeting province had devastating results. It declared open sesame to the migration of peasants from eastern Bengal to the lower Assam districts. Large-scale migration to Assam was possible because of railways. The Assam Bengal State Railway, connecting the Chittagong port and Lumding in central Assam, was completed by 1905. That was the highway of migration. In good time, the north bank was connected to Calcutta. Several feeder lines, both in upper and lower Assam, strengthened the railway network. The process of mass migration began in 1905, but it was detected only at the time of the census of 1911. Those who entered Assam and occupied land never cared even to apply for it. A government report of 1907 reveals, 'It is practically impossible to insist on a formal application and an enquiry being made prior to occupation of wasteland in all cases in Assam, where the area of waste available for settlement is so great, and raivats are continually reclaiming small plots. If formal application were made, in all such cases, our revenue establishments would be unable to deal with the mass of business they will entail.' The pity was – there was no government machinery to give effect to their scheme in a planned manner. Another dimension was linguistic. To secure the support of the Muslims of Dhaka and Mymensingh, Curzon publicly told them that in the grouping, it was their Bengali language spoken by fourteen and a half million people that would thrive, not Assamese spoken by one and a half million. 'Assamese ... will be one to disappear,' he said. So, there was not the least apprehension about moving from Bengal to Assam. For the migrating peasants, the opening had come as a godsend. Those peasants from Bengal had a pivotal role in the extension and commercialization of Agriculture. But when their number swelled into alarming proportions, the government and the political leaders woke up to the seriousness of the situation and tried to devise ways and means to control if not totally stop the migrants into Assam from taking up lands for settlement." [19]

In the face of stiff opposition from the Bengalis, the British had to annul the partition of Bengal on December 12, 1911. After keeping it attached for another seven years to East Bengal, the British administration formally reverted Assam to its old status of a Chief Commissioner's Province with effect from April 1, 1912. Thus, the three populous Bengali-speaking districts of Goalpara, Sylhet, and Cachar, the five by and large Assamese-speaking districts of Brahmaputra Valley (Kamrup, Nowgong, Darrang, Sibsagar, and Lakhimpur) - together known as Assam proper, and underdeveloped adjoining hills districts, speaking diverse tongues, once more became amalgamated as the Province of Assam.

> "It is significant that, in the nineteenth century, the enlightened section of the Assamese middle class welcomed large-scale immigration of productive labour and skill from other provinces and did not suffer from the 'xenophobia' of the later periods. It was convinced that no economic progress was feasible unless the then-depopulated condition was restored to normalcy. Guniram Barua, a nineteenth-century Assamese intellectual, estimated that no less than a million people could be immediately settled from outside on the wide acres of Assam. He enumerated three factors that were favourable to such immigration: (i) cheap and fertile land, (ii) attractive earnings for skilled labour and craftsmen in view of the local skilled manpower shortage, and (iii) the prevailing conditions of easy matrimony into local families."

That was Assam's renowned historian, economist, and poet, Amalendu Guha, in his well-researched book "Planter Raj to Swaraj" [20].

We have discussed earlier that after the British annexation of Assam in 1826, as the European capital started flowing into the financial system of Assam, its economic transition began, which saw the gradual end of the barter system, the introduction of a monetized economy, and the building of new infrastructures. Tea cultivation started in the late 1830s; later, coal mining began, and then sawmills were established to exploit the vast forest wealth. In 1890, oil exploration began at Digboi, and in 1893 the first oil refinery started at Margherita, both in upper Assam. The construction of railways was launched in 1881 to transport the products. With all these developments, the inflow of people from 'outside' of the so-called Assam proper started, including a considerable number of Bengali-speaking people from the Surma Valley, Goalpara, and the adjacent Bengal Presidency.

That was the period in which the transition from decades of peaceful coexistence to the era of conflicts between the "Babus" (Bengalis) and the "Dangariyas" (Assamese) kicked off. With the advantage of their early initiation into English education and exposure to British India's administrative system, the Bengalis monopolized government jobs and other professions in Assam. The emerging Assamese middle class, emerging from a previously relatively closed society, suddenly found themselves exposed to a completely alien work system. Naturally, they were in a disadvantageous position in the new competitive scenario.

In 1874, when Assam was separated from the Bengal Presidency to create a separate Chief Commissioner's province, the new province continued with its nomenclature 'Assam'. However, the majority population of the province was Bengali-speaking people. Besides, the newly formed province's territorial boundary also underwent a sea change. It was much larger than the Ahom Kingdom, or Assam, first annexed by the British in 1826 with just about Assam proper. Subsequently, the three Bengali-dominant areas of Sylhet (now in Bangladesh), Cachar, and the greater Goalpara, as well as the tribal-dominated areas of today's Meghalaya, Nagaland, Mizoram, and Arunachal Pradesh, were included, which more or less finally made 'Assam' under British rule.

The metamorphosed province covering all these additional territories continued with the appellation "Assam". However, a British-sponsored misconception began to circulate among some Assamese leadership that 'Assam was for the Assamese' – meaning, for the Asamiyas (Assamese-speaking people) only. The presence of a large number of Bengali-speaking people in Assam was initially frowned upon, which gradually developed into resentments, frictions, and conflicts between the Assamese on the one hand and the Bengali plus other communities and tribal populations on the other hand.

Interestingly, Persian was the state language in Bengal for more than 600 years, from 1203 to 1837 AD. Persian language and literature reached the highest stages of development during the Mughal period. By the middle of the 19th century, however, the importance of Persian faded in Bengal. The use of Persian as an official language was prohibited by Act No. XXIX of 1837 on the 20th of November 1837. Some localities feared that many of their people, who did court-related work, would be jobless if they were to switch to a new script. Extensive protests followed immediately in Bengal. A memorandum, signed by 800 dignitaries from Kolkata and another by 481 dignitaries from Dhaka, both Hindus and Muslims, was submitted to the British government, demanding the withdrawal of this directive. Despite the objections of many dignitaries from Calcutta and Dhaka, the declaration was enacted against the people's wishes making the law effective from the First Day of December 1837. [21]

Accordingly, Bengali became the official language of the Bengal Presidency. Though in most parts of the Brahmaputra valley, the vernacular language of the people of the pre-British period of Assam has a long history of existence, and Ahomiya (or Asamiya) and its forms were the lingua franca, it was not taught as a subject in the absence of schools in the modern sense of the term. The elite studied Sanskrit in the tol - the prevalent schooling system. Besides, the intelligentsia were also, to some extent, influenced by Persian, the court language of India at that time. Nevertheless, the British government introduced the modern schooling system in Assam for the first time in the mid-nineteenth century, with Bengali as the medium of instruction because, by then, Persian had been replaced by Bengali as the official language of Assam, as was done in Bengal. At that time, Assam was headed by a commissioner and was still under the Bengal Province. For almost a decade, the language policy of the British colonial government remained unquestioned, and it did not meet with any protest. On the contrary, the Assamese elites used the language in their writings and quite often even in their conversations.

It is noteworthy that before the arrival of the Christian Missionaries in North-East India, the Bengali scripts were being used by the Khasis in Meghalaya. The Métis in Manipur also used the Bengali scripts. There is virtually no difference between the Assamese and the Bengali scripts except for two alphabets. There is also a strange similarity between these two speeches - although both are distinctly separate languages. Nevertheless, on their arrival in Assam, the Christian Missionaries started to patronize and promote the Assamese language to win over the local population. It was their time-tested method to make a rapid inroad into the psyche of the inhabitants, where they landed for the first time to spread Christianity.

Between 1830 and 1840, an English author named Nathan wrote the Assamese grammar and Dr. Miles Brown prepared the Assamese-English dictionary. These missionaries were the first to set up a printing press in Assam. In 1846, the missionaries published the first Assamese-language monthly newspaper/magazine '*Orunodoi*' from Sibsagar, Assam, mainly for proselytization. They picked up the Ahomiya version spoken in the Sibsagar district that eventually became the *likhito* (written) or the standardized Assamese language. Associate Researcher [1]Jayeeta (Jo) Sharma's research paper "The making of 'Modern' Assam, 1826-1935" also reviewed how the Ahomiya version spoken in the Sibsagar district eventually emerged as the primary language in Assam. The following few lines are quoted from the said research paper:

> In late medieval Assam, ujani Asamiya, the dominant idiom around Sibsagar, the heartland of the Ahom kingdom, had also emerged as the primary written language. This accompanied a state-building process where a 'Sanskritising' Ahom regime, in its transition from clan to region hegemony, added more and more of Indic cultural ingredients to its public image. Concomitantly, its own Tai language productions were displaced into the esoteric realms of astrology and

divination. By the late seventeenth century, most of the courtly patronage for written texts was directed towards the Assamiya vernacular that philology would subsequently discover to be of 'Sanskritic' parentage. At the same time, this written register easily fluctuated according to use - the Assamiya used in the buranji chronicles produced under court patronage was not the same as that in the caritputhis emerging from the satras. But, this vernacularization does not mean that court and monastery had broken decisively with the cosmopolitan languages that had previously circulated across wide swathes of Asia. Thus, we see that the satras continued to contribute to the Sanskrit sacral tradition as well as to the Brajabuli literary culture associated with Vaishnavite devotionalism.'

One example of a precolonial written variant that might have challenged the growing monopoly of ujani Assamiya was Kamrupi, the dominant idiom in Lower Assam, where Ahom authority had been constantly contested by both internal and external forces. Nonetheless, the association of court patronage with ujani Assamiya meant that the latter could develop a culture of civility that Kamrupi never managed. From the seventeenth century, a new cultural ingredient, the Indo-Persian, entered this territory as the Ahom encountered the Mughal. One lasting feature of this was that Kamrupi came to possess a much larger incidence of Hindustani and Persian words than the ujani Assamiya. During the nineteenth century, Kamrupi was sporadically championed by some publicists whose origins in Lower Assam made it their 'mother tongue', and the American Baptist missionaries briefly toyed with the idea of nurturing that 'dhekeri'[2] idiom in their print productions. But the greater part of the colonial intelligentsia continued to emerge from the caste Hindu and Ahom families of Upper Assam. Ultimately, ujani Assamiya's greater access to 'symbolic capital' meant that both the first printing press and a claim to be the official vernacular came from an Upper Assam location. Aided by missionary and colonial interlocutors, this intelligentsia was the prime agent in ordering ujani Assamiya into a modern Assamese print language and in relegating its Lower Assam companions to the status of rustic dialects. [22]

Note: [1] An Associate Professor of History at the University of Toronto.

[2] Haliram Dhekial Phukan noted that the people of Upper Assam dismissively used the term "dhekeri" for the inhabitants of Lower Assam, signifying their slow, plodding manner of speech in their dialect. The word "dhekeri" itself originated from a pargana within the medieval Koch kingdom. By the early twentieth century, there was some effort to redress this stereotype by periodicals such as the Bahi, which declared in an editorial that the two languages, Assamese and Kamrupi, were one and the same.

Interestingly, the main reason for the missionaries to select this particular form of Assamese language, according to an 1852 report of Assam Mission, was that they considered it to be the best-suited vehicle of communication between the numerous communities and tribes, with as many speeches and dialects prevalent in the region. It was more or less during those years that the Assamese-Bengali rivalry began to manifest slowly.

Surprisingly, almost a decade after the new language policy became operational, initial protests against the government's language policy in Assam came from the American Baptist Missionaries and a few educated Assamese elite sections of people. Later, some people went to the ridiculous extent of suggesting that some Bengali Amlas (officers) had misled the British to believe Assamese was an off-shoot of the Bengali language. The planned propaganda told the people that some mischievous Bengali misled the British administration, stating that Assamese wasn't an independent language but a debased form of the Bengali language. According to the misinformation, the Amlas did this with the evil intention of imposing the Bengali language in Assam, which was to the detriment of the Assamese people. Consequently, the Colonial rulers introduced the Bengali language in Assam's schools and courts.

Given the introduction of the Bengali language in Bengal itself had met with protests from the Bengalis, especially both from Calcutta and Dacca, the suggestion that people of the same Bengali community tried to impose their language in Assam is no doubt ludicrous. The reason for spreading such unfounded information is rather apparent. It does not require the IQ of a rocket scientist to guess the source of the grapevine.

Meanwhile, Assamese leader Anandaram Dhekial Phukan carried on a sustained campaign with the British over the language issue for 40 long years. Finally, in 1873, the British changed their policy and introduced Assamese in schools and courts in Assam alongside the Bengali language. According to the 'Assam Portal', a premier web portal from Assam: The period between 1836 and 1873, nearly four decades (37 years), is referred to as the Dark Age for the Assamese language. [23]

As the Bengali language remained the province's official language from 1836 to 1873, many authors described it as a clear sign of 'Bengali chauvinism,' infuriating the Assamese community more than anything else. Besides, in the imperial administration, the supposed supercilious outlook and the alleged ruthless attitude of the Bengali functionaries towards the local people are said to have also supplemented the building up of animosity between the two major communities in Assam. The Bengali *Amlas* of those days are still held liable for the so-called 'imposition' of the Bengali language on the people of

Assam for nearly four decades from 1836 to 1873, and certain ill-informed Assamese people are still resentful for the evil act of what is called the wicked Bengalis.

Nevertheless, the British government's documents and records bear irrefutable testimonies that all these were bogus propaganda. Yet, the false notion of some unscrupulous Bengali hands behind the introduction of the Bengali language in Assam at that time was readily accepted by many innocent people in Assam. The planned propaganda was unleashed to incite Assamese-Bengali discord as part of the British 'Divide and Rule' policy to create animosity between the two major communities in Assam. Dr. Shibnath Barman and Prasenjit Choudhury, in their book "BASTAB NE BIBHRAM' written in the Assamese language (Guwahati, 1986), delved into this topic critically. Besides, prolific writer Dr. Devabrata Sharma in his thoroughly researched book titled "ASOMIA JATIGATHAN PRAKRIYA (DWITIYA KHONDO) - ASOMOT BHASA ANDOLONOR 'TRAGIC TRILOGY' (PROTHOM PORBO) 1960 SONOR BHASA ANDOLON pretty intricately addressed the issue. He illustrated how severely the Bengali community was denounced for their alleged involvement in what a few Assamese intelligentsia thought was a shrewd imposition of the Bengali language on the people of Assam during those days.

Notably, many articles published in the missionary mouthpiece followed the method of compare and contrast, focusing on the worst of the local religions, cultures, and their way of life with those of their own best. By showing everything Indian in a poor light, they attempted to establish the superiority of Christianity and artfully tried to proselytize the local people. Besides, they were also instrumental in creating an intense cleavage between the two major communities, the Assamese and the Bengalis, in Assam through their malevolent writings. [24] [25] [26] For instance, in an anonymous article subtitled in English as "The Assamese and the Bengali Languages," published in the *Orunudoi* in November 1854, the two languages, Bengali and Assamese, are allegorically presented as mothers. One was loved and appreciated, the other disowned. Ironically, the mother who is loved is the stepmother, Bengali, and the biological mother, Assamese, pines away for her children.

The article begins with young boys wandering away from their village and encountering a woman clad in tattered rags. Startled, they flee in fear, shouting and screaming. Their stepmother consoles and calms them then sets out to confront the 'witch' who frightened her sons. Upon meeting the woman, she inquires about her identity and the reason for her unsettling appearance and behaviour. The woman, representing the Assamese language, responds:

> "Oh Mother, why do you inquire about my misfortune? There is little to speak of. My plight is such that death may be preferable. What more can I divulge about my sorrowful tale? You already know it all. Nevertheless, since you've asked, I shall recount. Assam is my homeland; the Assamese language is my name. Those youths who fled from me in terror are my offspring. From their infancy, I taught them to utter 'father,' 'mother,' 'brother,' yet now that they've matured, they've forsaken me for you."

The anguish of the symbolic mother intensifies the prevailing disillusionment over the growing 'Bengalisation' of the native populace. Articles in the Orunudoi detailed the adverse effects of Bengali language influence, suggesting it was only due to British patronage that Bengali attained its elevated status and prestige. In the same vein, the 'Assamese Language' laments:

> "Oh Mother, you now recoil from me in disgust. But consider your former state. Did you possess this refined demeanour before the English rulers ascended to power? Hear me out. Though my ungrateful children have abandoned me, the 'Sahabs' of the mighty nation, America, have offered me sanctuary and nurturance." [27]

During that period, much like the other provinces in India, Assam was not configured into a homogeneous entity based on ethnological, linguistic, or cultural criteria. However, owing to the name Assam, Assamese leaders were misled into disregarding the shifting geography and demographic makeup of the transformed province, markedly different from the Assam annexed by the British in 1826. Since Assam's establishment as a province in 1874, it became evident that the Bengali-speaking population constituted the largest linguistic group within the province. Regrettably, this significant reality was overlooked. Furthermore, due to the association with the name Assam, it was tacitly assumed that the province was predominantly inhabited by Assamese-speaking people, the Asamiyas.

Unfortunately, the discord and animosity arising from the official language dispute hindered the much-needed integration between the Bengali and Assamese-speaking communities. Moreover, within the corridors of power at the time, Bengali was often favoured over Assamese in conversation. From the perspective of the Assamese community, it seemed that the 'immigrant' Bengalis not only secured most of the new opportunities in "Assam" but also brought with them a new culture, language, and a sense of dominance, posing a threat to Assamese society on various fronts. However, this sentiment did not immediately manifest as anguish or jealousy towards the perceived Bengali dominance; it evolved over time. Years later, the attitude of the

Assamese community towards Bengalis underwent a significant shift, eventually turning into resentment and animosity.

Notably, History Lecturer Madhumita Sengupta, following a thematic examination of five selected books, penned an article titled "HISTORIOGRAPHY OF THE FORMATION OF ASSAMESE IDENTITY: A REVIEW." This article was featured in the bi-annual academic journal Peace and Democracy in South Asia (PDSA), Volume 2, Numbers 1 & 2, 2006. The books under review were:

(i) "Planter Raj to Swaraj: Freedom Struggle and Electoral Politics in Assam, 1826-1947" by A. Guha;

(ii) "A Burning Question" by H. Gohain;

(iii) "Roots of Ethnic Conflict: Nationality Questions in North East India" by S. Nag;

(iv) "Social Tensions in Assam: Middle-Class Politics" by A.K. Baruah; and

(v) "India Against Itself: Assam and the Politics of Identity" by S. Baruah.

The concluding comments on the issue of the formation of Assamese identity, quoted below, allude to some interesting questions confronting the controversy surrounding the Assamese-Bengali language in Assam:

"Conclusion: Reflections on the Formation of Assamese Identity

At the outset, I would like to mention that despite my proposed critique of the existing literature, the aforementioned works have made a significant contribution to this area of historical research. Apart from drawing academic attention to this rather neglected region of the Indian subcontinent, the works of Amalendu Guha, Hiren Gohain, and Sanjib Baruah, in particular, have been responsible for shifting the focus away from the so-called supercilious attitude of the immigrant Bengalis, which remains unverified, to the economic content of the grievances of the Assamese middle class. The role of colonial administrative policies in encouraging immigration and hence in the emergence of an Assamese identity has also been highlighted, which is a far cry from the way immigration has been portrayed in official accounts as being entirely spontaneous. Nonetheless, the literature surveyed so far throws up certain obvious questions that merit a closer look.

Firstly, to what extent was the earliest attempt to locate the self the outcome of perceived wrongs of the kind referred to earlier? For a people to be antagonized by an assault on their language, the prior existence of community consciousness (in this case, the sense of belonging to a linguistic community) is essential. However, if we presume that this did exist, then the arguments of these authors do not stand, and we cannot trace the formation of the Assamese community to the event in 1836, i.e., the introduction of Bengali as the official language. We cannot, however, argue in favour of the existence of this kind of community consciousness in Assam prior to 1836 because this would make it difficult for us to explain the lack of protests until 1853. Differences of opinion in Assamese society regarding the markers of identity would also be difficult to explain. Rajen Saikia points out that from 1836 when Bengali was introduced to 1853, there was no perceptible reaction against the decision. The protest came up loud and clear only in 1853 when A.J.M. Mills, Judge of the Sadar Dewani Adalat, visited Assam on an official inspection tour. After all, the language itself was being standardized all this while. In fact, what needs further exploration is the role of the missionaries in emphasizing the distinctness of the Assamese language. However, the question remains as to whether we can regard even language standardization as a sufficient explanation for the formation of community consciousness in Assam. Should we not take into account the impact of Renascent Bengal on the earliest ideologues, considering the fact that most of them had spent some time in Calcutta - the hub of Bengal? It may be noted that Anandaram Dhekial Phukan, one of the earliest exponents of the Assamese language, was himself patronized by Major Jenkins for receiving higher education in Calcutta. He became a regular contributor to Orunodoy, the paper which played a pioneering role in instituting Assamese as the official language, only on his return from Calcutta. Although a sound case can be prepared only on the basis of more evidence, prima facie, it seems that the final verdict on the creation of Assamese identity cannot be pronounced without reference to the impact of Calcutta in particular and Bengal in general on young Assamese minds. The researcher must also consider the impact of the growing anti-colonial consciousness throughout the country on the people. There were bound to be several 'others' in the story of the self-definition of the Assamese. In other words, the introduction of Bengali and the employment of Bengalis in government offices surely contributed to the growth of community consciousness among a section of the Assamese-speaking population, but the latter cannot claim sole credit for the phenomenon, perhaps not even the credit for being the initiator. Such a perspective becomes obvious, especially in the light of the selection of markers of identity in the 19th century. In fact, this very selection itself is suspect for a variety of reasons. How was this selection carried out, and what prompted such a selection? In other words, how did language become so important to the people? What happened to the other markers? Why was language so important even after 1873? It has already been shown that the inclusion of Sylhet cannot explain this adequately. In fact, why did language continue to retain its importance even when the demographic structure was changing in the 20th century owing to immigration? After all, the insistence on language was tampering with the very composition of the community and also alienating the tribal elements that were acknowledged as integral to the Assamese community. Was the projection of language as the only marker of identity not proving to be self-destructive? Why did the intellectuals not realize this? What was blurring their vision?

Finally, did the movement of the Assamese in the 19th and 20th centuries reflect the concerns of the urban middle class alone? Fresh research that offers answers to these questions is needed to provide us with a comprehensive picture of the nature and genesis of the movement for an Assamese identity, filling, in the process, gaps left by existing studies on the subject. For the moment, it can only be said that the selection of markers of identity by Assamese intellectuals in the 19th and 20th centuries led to a complete transformation and, subsequently, the disintegration of the previous identity markers. In other words, what I am proposing is that a new community emerged in Assam in the 19th century with a predominantly, although not yet exclusively, linguistic identity. I do not regard this community as a so-called ethnic group, for if such a thing existed, then this could only have been prior to the 19th century, and with a character quite distinct from the way it is perceived by available literature. It is, however, my conjecture from the foregoing literature survey that the emergence of a linguistic community in the 19th century was something entirely novel and that it synchronized with the politicization and disintegration of specific ethnic boundaries in colonial Assam. [28]

The entire northeastern region is surrounded almost entirely by international borders, except for the 60-kilometer-long and 22-kilometer-wide Siliguri Corridor in the Indian state of West Bengal, also known as the "Chicken's Neck", which connects it with the rest of the country. Thus, the geographical location of Assam and its neighbouring areas is special, as Madhumita Sengupta, Lecturer, Department of History, Rani Birla Girls' College, Kolkata, mentioned in her paper while delving into the roots of Assam's 'ethnic' turmoil in her study. Likewise, the deliberations in the next chapter, "Divide et Impera: Genesis of Assamese-Bengali Discord", also centred around figuring out the source of the 'ethnic' tensions in Assam. So, let's see if answers to the queries raised by Madhumita Sengupta in the conclusion to her review paper lie in some measure in the next chapter.

****

Chapter 5.

Divide et Impera: Genesis of Assamese-Bengali Discord

"History pulls you by your ears far more brutally than a teacher in the classroom or a parent at home".

On the 26th of March 1886, George Francis Hamilton, Secretary of State of India, wrote to Curzon:

> "I think the real danger to our rule in India, not now, but say 50 years hence, is the gradual adoption and extension of Western ideas of agitation organization, and if we could break educated Indians into two sections holding widely different views, we should, by such a division, strengthen our position against the subtle and continuous attack which the spread of education must make upon our system of government. We should plan educational textbooks so that the differences between communities are further strengthened.

Again, in a letter dated 14th January 1887, Secretary of State Viscount Cross wrote to Governor-General Dufferin:

> 'This division of religious feeling is greatly to our advantage, and I look for some good as a result of your Committee of Inquiry on Indian Education and teaching materials'.

Thus, under a definite policy, the Indian history textbooks were so falsified and distorted as to give an impression that the medieval period of Indian history was full of atrocities committed by Muslim rulers on their Hindu subjects, and the Hindus had to suffer terrible indignities under Islamic rule. There were no common factors in social, political, or economic life."

Against this background, Dr B. N. Pande, a freedom fighter, social worker, and parliamentarian, noticed by chance that the following line found a place in a history textbook authored by Mahamahopadhyaya Dr Har Prashad Shastri, Head of the Department of Sanskrit, Calcutta University. It was approved as a history course book for high schools in Bengal, Assam, Bihar, Orissa, U.P., M.P., and Rajasthan.

> "Three thousand Brahmins committed suicide as **Tippu** (Sultan) wanted to forcibly convert them into the fold of Islam."

On inquiry and after many reminders, Dr. Shastri replied to Dr. Pande that he had taken that from the Mysore Gazetteer...

However, Dr Pande's subsequent investigation revealed that the episode of the suicide of 3,000 Brahmins was nowhere to be found in the Mysore Gazetteer, and no such incident had taken place. On the contrary, Pande discovered that the Prime Minister of Tippu Sultan was a Brahmin named Punaiya, and his commander-in-chief was also a Brahmin named Krishna Rao. Additionally, Tippu Sultan used to allocate annual grants to at least 156 temples. Dr Pande then approached Ashutosh Mukherjee, the Vice-Chancellor of Calcutta University at the time, and requested proper action against the offending passages in the textbook. Promptly, Ashutosh Mukherjee replied that the history book by Dr. Shastri was no longer part of the curriculum. However, the same suicide story reportedly resurfaced later in the history textbooks prescribed for some Junior High Schools. [1]

That was just one instance, among many others, demonstrating how the British rulers began implementing the detestable "Divide et Imperia" policy in India. It became a cornerstone of British administrative policy, signifying the strategy of gaining and maintaining power by breaking up larger concentrations of any force into smaller pieces, which individually would possess less authority than the original larger entity. Commonly known as the "divide and rule" policy, the British colonial rulers cunningly applied it, including in India. This strategy allowed a relatively small number of British to govern millions of Indians for nearly 200 years.

While the British most successfully implemented the policy in India by fostering division along Hindu-Muslim communal lines throughout the country, in Assam, they added an additional layer by introducing the Assamese-Bengali linguistic divide alongside the Hindu-Muslim communal tensions, further complicating matters. The Hindu-Muslim communal conflict, combined with the Assamese-Bengali linguistic contest, proved disastrous for Assam.

Like the Hindu-Muslim communal tension in the country, which was mainly based on this distorted history, a similar misperception was created in Assam over the years regarding Bengalis. It was believed that Bengalis in Assam were immigrants, as discussed in the previous chapter. The narrative suggested that they arrived with the British rulers and subsequently seized most economic opportunities, employment avenues, and vast areas of territory. In the process, many factual historical realities were conveniently sidelined to distort the overall picture. Therefore, this chapter attempts to clear the confusion and set the record straight, to the best of its ability.

In the narrative of the making and unmaking of Assam by the British, the reality is as follows: for 48 years initially, Assam remained within the Bengal Presidency as a division from 1826 to 1874 until it was elevated to a province of British India under a Chief Commissioner. In the newly created Assam province, the majority of the population was Bengali-speaking. Then, for six years, Assam remained attached to Eastern Bengal due to the partition of greater Bengal in 1905. Additionally, until the end of British rule in 1947, three Bengali-dominant districts - Sylhet, Goalpara, Cachar - and the Brahmaputra valley's Assam proper remained amalgamated in the British-created Assam Province, alongside present-day states of Meghalaya, Mizoram, Manipur, and Arunachal Pradesh.

It is noteworthy that while in 1947, Sylhet district was lost to Pakistan in a disputed referendum, the Bengali-dominant regions of Cachar and Goalpara remained integrated into the present-day Assam state. Furthermore, a small portion, comprising only three and a half *thanas* (Police Stations) of the erstwhile Sylhet District, remains in Assam even today. Incidentally, these three and a half *'thanas'*, along with their adjacent part of Cachar with a significant concentration of Sylhet-origin people, were supposed to be named EAST SYLHET, akin to West Bengal on the other side. This proposal circulated during the partition days but ultimately did not materialize for reasons unknown.

It is noteworthy that the Assamese and Bengalis shared a long history of living together in peace and amity, with any communal friction between the two communities being unheard of. In the chapter on the Pre-colonial history of Assam, it has already been mentioned that in the 11th century AD, King Rampala, the fifteenth ruler of Bengal's Pala dynasty, conquered Kamarupa, which was the early historical kingdom of Assam. Rampala appointed Timgyadeva as the governor of Kamarupa, who ruled between 1110 and 1126. In addition to the Palas of Bengal, historical sources suggest that the Senas and Baidya Dev kings of Bengal also ruled Progjyotishpur-Kamrupa until 1113. Moreover, in 1142, a Bengali Brahmin minister of Baidya Dev became the king of Progjyotishpur-Kamrup. The rule of that dynasty existed until circa 1191. During these periods, numerous people from Bengal came and settled in Pragjyotishpur-Kamrupa, leaving a lasting impact on the Mongolian-origin, the Mon-Khmer-origin, and other hillmen and plains people inhabiting the territory. There are also numerous historical references that endorse the arrival of Bengalis in various parts of present-day Assam at different times. The following paragraphs cite some of those instances, among many others.

Assam's great Vaishnavite saint and reformer Srimanta Sankardev was born into the Baro-Bhuyans family, believed to have originated from Bengal. Although there are several versions of Sankardev's ancestry, the widely accepted version is presented in the Guru Charitra, which also matches the account in a Bengali book by Bidhan Chandra Purkayastha. Accordingly, both variants are briefly narrated here.

The origin of the Baro Bhuiyan of Nowgong as per the Guru Charitra or the Sankar Charitra:

Kamatapur Raja Durlabh Narayan once went to war with another Raja named Dharma Narayan, who styled himself Gauresvar or Lord of Gaur (the modern district of Sylhet was known as Gaur). When peace was concluded, Raja Dharma Narayan sent seven families of Brahmans and seven families of Kayasthas to Durlabh Narayan. He settled them on the frontier as wardens of the marches, granting them lands and slaves. The most capable among them was a Kayastha named Chandivar, who became their leader. Their headquarters were established at Paimaguri, where they earned the people's gratitude by erecting an embankment. Subsequently, the Bhutiyas raided and abducted several people, including Chandivar's son. However, Chandivar, along with the Bhuiyas, pursued the raiders and rescued the captives. He later settled in Bardowa in Nagaon, where his great-grandson Sankaradeva was born. *(This version is considered authentic by Vaisnava scholars in Assam.)* Incidentally, "*Baro*" means twelve, but in reality, there were more than twelve chiefs or landlords, and the term "baro" signifies 'many.'

The version in the Bengali book by Bidhan Chandra Purkayastha:

Assam's great Vaishnavite saint and reformer Srimanta Sankardev was born into the Baro-Bhuyans family. During the 13th century, at the request of Kamatapur King Durdabh Narayan, the King of Gouda sent seven Brahmin families and seven Kayastha families to reside permanently in Kamtapur. The leading figures of the seven Brahmin families were: i) Krishna Pandit, ii) Raghupati, iii) Rambor, iv) Lohar, v) Baryan, vi) Dharam, and vii) Madhura. The head of the Kayastha families was (a) Srihari, (b) Sripati, (c) Sridhar, (d) Chidananda, (e) Sadananda, (f) Hariboro, and (g) Chandibor, whose fifth-generation offspring was the great Vaishnavite Saint and Social Reformer Srimanta Sankardev. Kusumbar Bhuyan was the father of Sankardev, and his mother's name was Satyasandhya. [3]

In the 12th century, the Chutia King Sonagiri Pal, alias Gouri Narayana, united the Chutias of northeastern hilly tracts of Sonagiri, Ratnagiri, Nilgiri, and Chandragiri regions to fight against the Ahoms. At that time, a Bengali king named Bhadrashan ruled the plain region of the foothills. Some scholars believe that the prevailing worship of Goddess Ma Kali was started by the Chutias under the influence of these Bengalis.

When the great Koch king Naranarayana visited the Kamakhya Temple with his brother Chilarai, the Great General of Koch Kingdom, they found the temple in complete ruins. Narayana renovated the temple in 1565 A.D. He also gave royal patronage to the temple. [4] At the invitation of King Naranarayan, several Vedic Brahmins arrived at the Nilacal hills near present-day Guwahati. After the renovation of the Kamakhya Temple, these Brahmins were entrusted with the duty of performing regular worship and other related works of the temple. During those days, many Bengalis were encouraged by providing tax-free lands to settle in this part of the country. That was the period when many skilled Bengali workers were also provided with tax-free lands to settle permanently here.

In circa 1612, a Dhaka Zamindar named Shatrujeet attacked the Darang kingdom, and by defeating its king, Pariksheet, he became the ruler of Pandu and Gauhati. Later, his rule extended up to Dhubri. The army and other personnel who accompanied Shatrujeet, mostly Bengali-speaking people, gradually spread to the central and western regions and eventually started inhabiting those places, which are present-day Assam.

Similarly, there are many other historical accounts and archival records of the arrival of Bengalis in Assam at different times and instances. In the long run, all the Bengali-speaking people who arrived prior to the annexation of the territory by the British assimilated with the local people and adapted their customs, dispelling their Bengali identities. Presently, they are part and parcel of Assamese society.

After the British annexation of Assam, which was initially made a division of the Bengal Presidency, the scenario changed significantly. This time, instead of Bengalis becoming a part of Assam, the division of Assam literally became a part of Bengal. Later, when the British transformed Assam into a separate province by amalgamating three districts of Bengal (Sylhet, Cachar, and Goalpara), and Assam division, along with some hills, it turned into a Bengali-majority province. Bengali-speaking people accounted for over 57% of Assam's population, although its nomenclature continued as Assam.

In the new scenario, over 57% of Bengali-speaking inhabitants constituted the majority. As a matter of course, they did not assimilate into the minority Assamese-speaking people, who comprised less than 36% of the province's population by then. In prevalent history books, this reality remained sidelined. Apparently, the Britons left the reality purposely shrouded as per their long-term game plan. The fact that Bengalis in Assam province did not assimilate into Assamese culture and society became a topic of discussion. It thus widened the crack that had already developed between the Assamese and Bengali communities resulting from the rivalry for limited job opportunities, etc. With the shaded reality, an opportunistic historical narrative could thus be fabricated that a large number of Bengalis, Muslims and Hindus, arrived in Assam during the British colonial period, overwhelming the Assamese people in their native land and threatening their language, culture, and lifestyle.

There is no doubt that many migrants from other parts of Bengal, too, came to the Bengali-dominant Assam during that period. However, the vital fact that Assam was *ab initio* attached to the Bengal Presidency since its annexation or that it was a Bengali-majority province during British rule in India did not find any mention in the history books. This omission persisted even in post-colonial India.

Consequently, with the making and unmaking of Assam, the demographic status of the metamorphosed Assam registered a profound transformation in the pattern of its population distribution. The British colonial rulers, known for their knack of running with the hare and hunting with the hounds, soon started playing their dirty tricks, resulting in British-sponsored communal disharmony between the Hindus and Muslims on one hand, and the Assamese and Bengalis on the other. This was in keeping with the infamous 'divide and rule' policy of the British colonial rulers. One of the most dreadful manifestations of this policy was the introduction of a unique 'Line System' in Assam, which will be discussed in the next chapter.

Author Abhinav Chandrachur's book, 'REPUBLIC OF RELIGION: *The Rise and Fall of Colonial Secularism in India,*' opened up a new perspective in this context. Among other things, Chandrachur wrote that:

> "Secularism in British India arose from a disdain for 'heathen' Indian religions. During the early period of European colonialism in India, Hindus were referred to as Gentoo, akin to 'gentile' (Latin: gentiles). Christian writers often referred to heathens as gentiles."

The British colonial government deemed Indian religions like Hinduism or Islam as 'heathen', thus refraining from declaring any as the official religion of India. Furthermore, they refrained from imposing Christianity on Indians, fearing widespread public outrage despite it being their preference. Consequently, the British opted to artificially impose secularism in India by separating religion and the state, despite its incomplete presence in England.

Author Chandrachur contends that England was not secular during its colonial rule over the Indian subcontinent and afterwards. Throughout much of the nineteenth century, individuals in England could be imprisoned for merely denying 'the truth of Christianity in general or of the existence of God', under charges of 'blasphemy'. Until the mid-1850s, students at Oxford and Cambridge universities had to pledge allegiance to the thirty-nine articles of the Church of England. As recently as 2015, a member of the royal family could be barred from inheriting the Crown by marrying a Roman Catholic. Presently, the monarch of England must be a Protestant Christian, holding titles such as 'Defender of the Faith' and 'Supreme Governor of the Church of England'. The government still appoints the Archbishop of Canterbury, while senior bishops hold seats in the House of Lords by virtue of their positions.

What then motivated the colonial government to secularize Indian laws and institutions and provide English education to Indians? According to Chandrachur, "the colonial rulers' decision to secularize laws and institutions and offer English education to Indians was, at some level, intended to facilitate the spread of Christianity in India by diminishing Indians' reliance on their own indigenous religious customs and institutions."

British officials pursued three initiatives through the adoption of a policy dubbed 'secularism' (a term relatively new and imprecise) in India. Firstly, they delegated the management of temples, historically overseen by Indian rulers, to trustees, thus segregating religion from the state. Secondly, the colonial administration afforded heightened protection to minorities, often fueling a sense of paranoia that they would be defenceless without imperial intervention. Thirdly, the government strategically encouraged Christian missionaries to propagate Christianity.

In 1835, Thomas Babington Macaulay articulated in his infamous minute that English education should be introduced in India because instructing Indians in languages such as Arabic and Sanskrit would entail imparting 'false history, false astronomy, and false medicine' associated with a 'false religion' and an 'absurd theology'. Macaulay's father, Zachary, an evangelical, had advocated for colonial officials to permit Christian missionaries in British India. Macaulay and his cohorts believed that education dispensed in government institutions would be 'exclusively secular'. Notably, at that time, England lacked secular public education for schoolchildren. The intent behind this secular education was to pave the way for the propagation of Christianity in India.

In the mid-nineteenth century, Austrian-born Aloys Sprenger assumed the principalship of the colonial government's madrasa in Calcutta. During his tenure, Sprenger authored a book denouncing Islam as a false religion and forbade students from participating in religious ceremonies during class hours.

Since 1854, the colonial government's policy dictated that education in government institutions must be secular, although grants-in-aid could be allocated to private educational institutions offering both secular and religious instruction. However, this stance shifted in 1915 with the enactment of a law by the imperial legislative council establishing Banaras Hindu University. This move was unprecedented as it sanctioned the provision of religious instruction and examinations in Hinduism, despite the university's statutory establishment with the Governor-General as its 'Lord Rector' and the Lieutenant-Governor-General as its 'Visitor'. Subsequently, Aligarh Muslim University was established in 1920, where teachings in Muslim theology were incorporated. Therefore, in terms of educational policy, secularism was initially introduced by the colonial government to propagate Christianity in India but later abandoned to mitigate India's disloyalty to Britain and potentially deepen internal divisions.

In essence, the astute British rulers introduced 'secularism' in India to foment discord among its populace as part of their notorious 'divide and rule' strategy. Despite their genuine desire, they refrained from mass conversion to Christianity immediately, fearing widespread backlash and public outcry. Instead, they initially segregated religious activities from the political affairs of the state and labelled it secularism. Subsequently, they exploited religion to sow communal divisions among different communities and advocated for the establishment of religious-based educational institutions. Ultimately, they utilized education as a tool for Christian proselytization to secure their exclusive constituency. Consequently, in the remote hills of North-East India, where formal education was nearly nonexistent among the local population, missionaries, aided by government support, began establishing a significant number of schools in villages and towns as preliminary steps towards converting the local populace to Christianity. [5]

Previously, in 1885, a British member of the Imperial Civil Service and political reformer, Allan Octavian Hume, founded the Indian National Congress (INC), often simply referred to as Congress, to establish a platform for civil and political dialogue among educated Indians. At that time, the Viceroy of India was Lord Dufferin, who gave his approval for the first session of Congress. Very soon, Congress became a central organization for Indian nationalism. The party demanded that educated Indians be given a greater share in the Government. However, Viceroy Dufferin became wary and felt that Congress might become a threat to the British Raj. So, he requested the Congressmen to focus their sessions and meetings on non-political social reforms. Despite this, Congress did not yield. Consequently, Dufferin adopted other techniques to suppress the influence of Congress. He approached the wealthy to ask them to withdraw their patronage from the INC. Additionally, he implemented a rule that prohibited government employees from participating in Congress meetings. Subsequently, the Viceroy began seeking the assistance of loyal, pro-British individuals. Among them were the educationalist Syed Ahmad Khan and linguist Shiv Prasad. Both were instructed to initiate an anti-Congress movement in the country. Consequently, around 1887, Syed Ahmad Khan began delivering speeches against the INC. During this period, Congress was advocating, among other things, for:

1. The ICS examinations to be conducted in India.
2. Indians to have a say in the budget formulated by the British Government.
3. Indians to be able to influence the budget, at least to some extent.

However, Syed Ahmad Khan vehemently opposed all these demands and advised people to distance themselves from Congress. He also began discussing the Two-Nation theory in his speeches. Khan warned that Muslims were in peril, asserting that once the British departed, Hindus would torment Muslims, followed by invasions from French, Portuguese, and German forces who would abuse Indians. Consequently, he argued, it would be in the Muslims' best interest to support British rule. Despite Syed Ahmad Khan's advocacy for modern Muslim education, exemplified by the establishment of a college in 1875, now known as Aligarh Muslim University, his inflammatory speeches and anti-Congress activities had significant repercussions. By the early 1900s, a segment of the elite Muslim population strongly embraced the Two-Nation theory. Against this backdrop, the All-India Muslim League was established in 1906. Evidently, the British sought to exploit the Divide and Rule policy, thus endorsing the All India Muslim League. Subsequently, the League petitioned Viceroy Minto for separate electorates for Muslims. Congress vehemently opposed this stance. Even Congress leader Muhammad Ali Jinnah initially opposed separate electorates, despite later advocating for partition. At this juncture, figures like Sarojini Naidu, a prominent freedom fighter, regarded Jinnah as an emblem of Hindu-Muslim unity.

But the British saw another opportunity to use "Divide and Rule" here and approved separate electorates. Giving separate electorates to Muslims meant that there would be some reserved seats for which only Muslim candidates could contest elections, and only Muslim voters could vote. The British Raj approved this by the Indian Council Act 1909, also known as the Morley-Minto reforms. But the British did not stop there. The Indian Act of 1919 was passed later, wherein similar representation was given to Sikhs, Europeans, and Anglo-Indians. Their "Divide and Rule" policy was prospering, and more cracks started forming among the country's various religions. It led to a small section of Hindus becoming paranoid that nothing was being done for them. Their interests were being overlooked. That's why, similar to the All India Muslim League, a Hindu League was formed. It was named Akhil Bharatiya Hindu Mahasabha, founded by Madan Mohan Malaviya. After this, in 1925, a person named Keshav Baliram established another Hindu organization named Rashtriya Swayamsevak Sangh (RSS). Thus, on the one hand, some Muslims believed the 'Muslims are in danger' narrative; on the other hand, some Hindus started fearing that the 'Hindus are in danger'. The distorted version of Indian history that the British started teaching in schools during those days buttressed such apprehensions. The British showed how Hindus resisted Muslim rulers in history. Then, the separate electorates were further extended to depressed classes, women, and labourers through the enactment of the Government of India Act of 1935.

In 1909, an Indian Service officer, Lieutenant Colonel U. N. Mukherjee, wrote some letters to a Kolkata-based newspaper. He titled the letters "Hindus: A Dying Race!" In those letters, he spoke of his fears about how Hindus were in danger. The Muslim population was increasing rapidly, and after some years, the Hindu population would peter out. The same concerns persist even after 100 years. He feared that Muslims would take over the whole country. On the other hand, some Muslims were afraid that Hindus would take over the country. The fear generated among the two major communities in India soon turned into Hindu-Muslim religious riots, which eventually led to the partition of the Indian subcontinent in 1947. [6]

How blatantly the cunning British rulers persisted with their notorious 'Divide and Rule' policy and continued their 'run with the hare and hunt with the hounds' approach could be noticed from the remarks made by a British Census Superintendent, C.S. Mullan, in the Assam Census Report 1931, which became viral, especially since the immigration issue in Assam afterwards became a political hot potato. The legacy of Mullan's Census Report 1931 activated, to a significant extent, the Assamese-Bengali discord. This civil servant was the chief author of the Assam Census Report of 1931. "He wrote during the year 1921-31,

> *the immigrant army* had almost completed the *conquest* of Nowgong. The Barpeta subdivision of Kamrup has also fallen to their *attack*, and Darrang is being *invaded*. Sibsagar has so far escaped completely, but a few thousand Mamensinghias in North Lakhimpur are an *outpost* which may, during the next decade, prove to be a valuable basis for *major operations*. Whosesoever, the *carcass*, have the *vultures* be gathered together. *Where there is a wasteland thither flock the Mamensinghias.*"

It's revealing that while, on the one hand, the British incentivized the settlement of the stout hardworking East Bengali Mamensinghias in the vast wasteland of Assam to meet its food shortage and augment revenue, as narrated earlier in this chapter, on the other hand, the *British Census Superintendent* recorded a stern message for the Assamese people to be on their guard against the new settlements in Assam, calling it (by using military terminology) as a kind of 'conquest', 'attack', and 'invasion' of their homeland. In this regard, the eminent historian Amalendu Guha wrote in his book "Planter Raj to Swaraj",

> "Mullan tried to peer into the future and mischievously forecast the future course of this 'invasion'. He prophesied that Sibsagar would ultimately remain the only district where an Assamese race would find a home of its own. The motivation behind such irresponsible and unfounded utterings was clear. He wanted the Assamese and the immigrants to be set against each other." [7]

Guha then wrote about how Mullan's prophecy of 1931 provided a rationale for the chauvinism that was to plague Assam for many years to come:

> "An article on the gloomy future of the Assamese nationality was published in 1937 by Jnananath Bora, a leading intellectual of the province, in Dainik Baroti (Jorhat), the mouthpiece of the Samrakshini movement. Bora argued that unless Sylhet was separated, unless Assamese was declared as the **only medium of instruction in schools**, and unless the influx of settlers stopped, it would be difficult for the Assamese to survive as a nationality. He was only echoing a cry raised on the floor of the Council the previous year: 'Now, sir, can this be a reward from God that the Assamese people should confine themselves to Sibsagar alone .... we will not allow this to be'."

Thus, Mullan succeeded in creating a lasting division between the Assamese and Bengali communities, so much so that in almost all scholarly deliberations, discussions, debates, and research papers on the immigration issue of Assam, it is pretty common to find his defamatory comments—**even in the present day**—distorting the knotty question of Assam's 'immigration' issue to a great extent. In this context, the renowned historian of North-East India, Amalendu Guha, penned the following lines supporting this assertion. However, this contention seldom appears in books and academic papers covering this controversial question. Guha wrote:

> "So mischievous and blatantly fallacious were Mullan's observations that even the Governor, in his address to the Council on 6 March 1933, thought it expedient to quote the same 1931 Census Report to point out that:
>
>> In spite of the large increase in the population of Assam at every Census since 1901, the **percentage of speakers of Assamese in the total population has remained very steady**. It is clear from the figures of the increase in speakers in Assamese in this Census that **the language is at present in no danger of supersession**. (Emphasis by Subir)

Time has proved that the Governor was right and Mullan was wrong. Indeed, Assam's population has been growing since 1901 due to the influx of outsiders into the province. Yet, the percentage of Assamese-speaking people in it, instead of decreasing, continued to register an increasing trend in every Census report even before Assam's disintegration started in the 1960s. [8]

Besides, in another article titled "EAST BENGAL IMMIGRANTS AND BHASANI IN ASSAM POLITICS: 1928-47," Guha continued:

> "The Assamese public was noticeably agitated over the outsider issue. So long in all Government schools in the Brahmaputra valley, attended by both Bengali and Assamese pupils, there was an arrangement for teaching through the medium of the respective languages. But, under the changed circumstances, the Government decided to close down Bengali classes in these schools and encourage setting up new aided schools exclusively for Bengali children in 1935. **Thus, another wedge was driven between the Assamese and the Bengalis through segregated school education.** Scared by legislation relating to money-lending and tenancy, the influential urban middle class became increasingly panicky about their future status under the Provincial Autonomy in the local power structure" (Emphasis by Subir). [9]

Another aspect of Mullan's 'mischievous and blatantly fallacious' observations seems to have remained unassessed so far. In his sickening remarks, the British officer likened **Assam's wasteland** to a carcass (a dead animal's body) and equated the East **Bengali settlers in Assam to a vulture** known to scavenge discarded wastes for food. A wasteland, farmland, or woodland – any type of land that is part of our motherland – is revered not only by the Assamese people but by every Indian in general. To liken any portion of our motherland, be it in Assam or anywhere else, to a carcass is indeed **condemnable and unacceptable**, like comparing the so-called Mamensinghias with a vulture – if not more. And that too, **coming from one** of the likes of those who **intruded into India** from the far-off country of **England to loot our wealth, ruin our economy, impoverish our population**, and whatnot for nearly two hundred years. Yet, instead of condemning Mullan for showering such brazen insults, historians, academicians, and intelligentsia quote his timeworn observations to highlight the so-called rampant 'immigration' of Bengalis in Assam from the neighbouring East Bengal during the British colonial period. In the process, Mullan's uncalled-for aspersion on Assam's native lands has remained unquestioned, providing legitimacy to the offending affront and building an image of Mullan as the Malthusian poster boy of Assam!

> "The 1931 census report was not the first time that the British government acknowledged the threat of Muslim immigration into Assam. In 1911 also, the census commissioner pointed to the danger

of immigration by calling it 'a peaceful invasion of Assam by the advancing hordes of Mymensinghia army.' However, the mystery was that even with repeated acknowledgements of the danger of Muslim immigration into Assam, the British administration continued the policy of encouraging Muslim immigration from East Bengal to Assam until independence. A number of political historians believe that Mullan's statement was part of the British government's policy of divide and rule. They argue that the anti-colonial struggle gained momentum at that stage in India, and the British administration tried to sow division between Hindus and Muslims in Assam through such comments. It should be acknowledged that when the British administration itself was responsible for large-scale immigration into Assam, such a comment by a colonial officer must have had some strategic relevance."

That was Dr. Monoj Kumar Nath, Associate Professor, Department of Political Science, Dibrugarh University (Assam), articulating in his book "The Muslim Question in Assam and Northeast India" [10].

In any case, by the Government of India Act (1919) passed by the Parliament of the United Kingdom, the [1]Dyarchy system was introduced for the provinces, marking the first introduction of the democratic principle into the executive branch of the British administration of India. The first was composed of executive councillors appointed, as before, by the Crown. The second was composed of ministers chosen by the governor from the elected members of the provincial legislature. The administrative subjects under the control of Indian ministers included local self-government, education, public health, public works, agriculture, forests, and fisheries.

Note: [1] The Dyarchy principle was a division of the executive branch of each provincial government into authoritarian and popularly responsible sections.

In 1935, the Dyarchy system ended when the Government of India Act 1935 was enacted, ushering in the concept of popular government through collective responsibility and **peripheral** provincial autonomy. With the election to the Legislative Council held in 1937, under the Act of 1935, Assam entered into the parliamentary system. However, 34 out of 108 seats were reserved for Muslims in the Assam Legislative Council under the 1935 Act.

During 1939–45, virtually every part of the world was involved in a conflict called the Second World War. The principal belligerents, Great Britain, France, the United States, the Soviet Union, and, to a lesser extent, China, known as the Allied Forces, were pitted against Germany, Italy, and Japan, called the Axis powers. In 1942, the British suffered a defeat in Singapore, and the Japanese force invaded the world's largest exporter of rice, Burma, hindering India's procurement of rice. At that time, India used to buy more than 15% of its overall rice requirement from Burma. On 16th October 1942, the whole east coast of Bengal and Orissa was hit by an unprecedented cyclone, and the autumn crops in many core rice-producing areas failed. Despite this, the British administration did not stop exporting rice from Bengal, which fed Indian and British troops in the Middle East. It resulted in the Great Famine of Bengal (1943), causing starvation deaths of some three million people in Bengal. Against this backdrop, the British launched the 'Grow More Food' campaign for India to overcome the famine's effects.

Nevertheless, under the banner 'Development Scheme', the Saadulla government in Assam had previously initiated a policy to develop all the cultivable land as quickly as possible and share it among the various communities. Then, when the British launched the 'Grow More Food' campaign, the Saadulla government decided to settle the so-called immigrants on new land primarily for growing food crops - particularly all varieties of paddy. The government even proposed to open village grazing areas for cultivation which were considered too large for the needs of the local people. In 1943, grazing reserves in the districts of Kamrup, Nowgong, and Darrang were regularized, and new areas were offered to immigrants for settlement of land on the Assamese side of the invisible line of the infamous Line System. Saadulla's adversaries in Assam saw it as a pro-immigration policy of his government. Governor-General and Viceroy of India, Lord Wavell, when he visited Assam in 1943 described this proactive role of the Muslim League ministries in increasing the migration of agricultural laborers from Bengal as the immigration of Muslims and said:

> "The native Assamese are lazy and likely to be ousted by more pushing but less attractive Bengali Moslems. The chief political problem is the desire of the Moslem ministers to increase this immigration into the uncultivated Government lands under the slogan "grow more food", but what they are really after is "grow more Moslems". [11]

Governor-General Wavell's phraseology, "grow more Moslems," in contrast to the "grow more food" programme, went viral as soon as the comments became public. Even in contemporary discourse on Assam's socio-political narratives, this phrase, "grow more Moslems," is quite popular, akin to British Census Superintendent C.S. Mullan's terms such as 'Land hungry Mymensinghies,' 'immigrant army,' 'aggression,' and so forth. However, Wavell's comment on Saadulla's efforts to alleviate the crisis of food shortage in the country at that juncture is deemed unbecoming of the Governor-General, especially given that 3 to 4 million people died of starvation under his watch during the British-induced famine in neighbouring Bengal province in the same year, 1943, when Wavell himself served as India's Viceroy and Governor-General.

It's worth recalling that during the Bengal famine of 1943, out of a population of 60.3 million, an estimated 2.1 to 3.8 million Bengalis died of starvation. This occurred because British Prime Minister Churchill deliberately diverted essential supplies from civilians in Bengal to support European stockpiles. He infamously remarked that the starvation of Bengalis mattered much less than that of the sturdy Greeks. When British officials voiced concerns over the deaths resulting from his decision, Churchill callously wrote in the margin of the file, 'Why hasn't Gandhi died yet?" All of this occurred under Wavell's tenure as Governor-General and Viceroy of India. Therefore, Wavell's comment on Saadulla's efforts to "grow more food" being equated to "growing more Muslims" is not surprising coming from Churchill's faithful deputy. On the surface, Wavell may have made these comments with the tactical design of inciting Assamese people against Bengalis, yet **his sweeping remark labelling the Assamese community as lazy was unacceptable, appalling, and reprehensible.** Significantly, while the phraseology "grow more Moslems" (or "grow more Muslims") persists, any form of rebuke or condemnation of Wavell's blanket criticism against native Assamese is conspicuously rare.

Be that as it may, nowhere else in India was World War II so directly felt by the populace as in North-East India. However, the cunning British colonial rulers adeptly concealed the truth about the significant events that followed under the guise of a Japanese invasion of India, leaving few Indians aware of the reality today. It's a factual story of North-East India that warrants telling, hence narrated briefly here for all to understand the level of deception employed by the British rulers in India.

In early 1944, the Indian National Army (INA), popularly called Azad Hind Fauj, led by Netaji Subhas Chandra Bose, successfully penetrated India's Mao frontier of North-East India. As the INA, with support from the Japanese army, tried to proceed from the border regions towards India's mainland to liberate the country from British alien rule, the deceitful Britons began their misinformation campaign. British Prime Minister Winston Churchill knew the truth. He feared that if Azad Hind Fauj entered any populous region inside India, it would lead to a country-wide revolt against the British Raj that would surely demolish the British rule in India. So, his government camouflaged the INA's forward march as a Japanese invasion of India and launched desperate radio broadcasting campaigns and wide newspaper reporting to mislead the world.

Earlier, on 21st October 1943, Netaji had announced in Singapore the formation of India's first independent government in exile. This Azad Hind Government enjoyed the recognition of Japan, Croatia, Indonesia, Germany, Italy, Thailand, Burma, and a few other countries. Soon after that, on 30th December 1943, when the Japanese liberated Andaman, Netaji went there to hoist the flag of independent India, making it the first Indian territory freed from British rule.

However, before entering the Indian Territory, the INA and the Japanese had an agreement that provided, inter alia:

a) The two armies would work in conjunction.
b) Officers and soldiers of the Azad Hind Fauj would be governed by their own military law (The INA Act) and not by Japanese law and police.
c) The Japanese force would transfer control of the liberated territories to the Azad Hind Fauj.
d) The only flag permitted to fly over Indian soil would be India's National Tricolour. [12]

Netaji had taken great care to maintain clear terms with the Japanese on all matters, including the currency notes of the Azad Hind Government, in the liberated areas in India, where the National Bank of the Azad Hind would be the only authorized bank. History bears testimony that the Japanese fully honoured their promises. The INA Memorial Complex at Moirang in Manipur (India) houses a collection of letters, photographs, badges of ranks, and other war memorabilia, with INA currency notes inscribed with Netaji's portrait adorning the tiny museum, buttressing this fact. The INA received massive support from local tribal groups of Naga and Mizo extractions when they entered India through its northeast frontier. Tribal villages like Taungian, Ukhrul, Tiddi, Sanghak, Molan, Morse, Tamu, Kabaw, and Hangdam voluntarily submitted to the INA. The Tricolour Flag of the Azad Hind flew over these villages for several months. The Subash Brigade occupied Kohima after a pitched battle on 8th April 1944. The Bahadur Group of INA led the operations in Manipur. After encounters with the Allied forces, this group occupied the Mairang and Bishenpur areas. The Imphal valley was then besieged. The Azad Hind Fauj remained in possession of about 1500 square miles of territory in Manipur for about six months. Major General A. C. Chatterjee, appointed by the Azad Hind Government as Governor of the occupied territory, took charge of civil administration. The Nikhil Manipuri Mahasabha joined Azad Hind en bloc under the leadership of M. Koireng Singh, H. Nilmani Singh, et al.

At that time, the Indian National Congress had asked party leaders in Assam to resist the Japanese. Yet, some prominent Congress leaders of Assam, like Lakshmi Prasad Goswami and Debakanta Barua, publicly announced their resolve to welcome the advancing liberation forces led by Netaji. Meanwhile, India's political parties like the Forward Block, Revolutionary Communist Party, and the Congress Socialists in Assam started preparations to welcome the INA. The rumour that the INA had already crossed Kohima on its way to the Brahmaputra valley had motivated a section of patriotic youths in Assam. They prepared to receive the INA men at Lumding and formed a local unit of the Forward Bloc. In Naga Hills, Z. A. Phizo, who later headed the underground Naga movement, and his followers joined the INA. Additionally, many people from Cachar, Manipur, and Naga Hills moved to the liberated areas to work for the Azad Hind, despite the strict vigil of the British army on the borders. [13]

On April 8th, 1944, the Subash Brigade of the Azad Hind Fauj occupied Kohima, the present capital of Nagaland, after a pitched battle. Netaji Subhash Chandra Bose stayed at Ruzazho village for nine days and appointed Shri Poswuyi Swuro DB as the 1st Administrator of the Azad Hind Government at Ruzazho village, Nagaland. Netaji Bose also appointed 10 Gaon Burhas (Village Chiefs) during the same time. However, the British-Indian army surrounded 15,000 Japanese troops at Garrison Hill in Kohima and engaged them in warfare from April 5th to 18th, 1944. The battle continued around Kohima until mid-May, after the British Army received reinforcements. Faced with stiff resistance and 53,000 dead and missing on the Japanese side, including INA personnel, Commander Sato's division had to withdraw from the war. The INA also suffered significant losses in men and material during this retreat. About fifteen hundred INA members were captured in the battles of Imphal and Kohima and during the subsequent withdrawal. Additionally, some were captured during the 14th Army's Burma Campaign, bringing the total to 16,000 of the INA's 43,000 recruits. When the INA retreated due to compromised supply lines and the withdrawal of Japanese forces, Z. A. Phizo and M. Koireng organized another attack on the British, but they were all captured and jailed in Rangoon along with the INA prisoners. [14] [15]

"When you go home, tell them of us and say for your tomorrow we gave our today," reads an epitaph written by English classicist John Maxwell Edmonds in the War Cemetery in Kohima, the capital of the Indian state of Nagaland. It is in memory of the 2nd British Division of the Allied Forces soldiers who lost their lives during the Kohima War fighting the army that came to liberate India from British colonial rule. Sadly, the fact that numerous INA soldiers also laid down their lives in this battle in their bid to free India from British colonial rule finds no mention here. Most people are unaware of the supreme sacrifice made by the soldiers of the Indian National Army, also known as the Azad Hind Fauj, led by Netaji Subhas Chandra Bose.

It would, however, be a blunder to trivialize the pitched battle the British forces fought against the combined Azad Hind Fauj and the Japanese Forces around Kohima and Imphal in 1944 as Netaji Subhas Chandra Bose's senseless, futile escapade was to liberate India from the mighty British superpower in the World War II days. On the contrary, the British soldiers' struggle to repel INA's attack on them to liberate our country with the help of Japan was declared the 'greatest ever battle involving British forces' in a contest by the National Army Museum in London. [16].

The story does not end here. The British administration wanted to give exemplary punishments to the 16,000 captured INA soldiers as mentioned earlier, so that no Indians would dare to take up arms against them in the future. They arranged for their trials in the Red Fort, Delhi, to be widely publicized. In the first of these trials, in an attempt to play the communal cards - one Hindu, one Muslim, and one Sikh - Colonel Prem Sahgal, Major General Shah Nawaz Khan, and Colonel Gurbaksh Singh Dhillon, who had previously worked in the British Indian Army, were charged on multiple counts, including severe charges of treason.

During the war, there had been a complete blackout in India of any news about the INA. While young Indians had been listening to Bose's broadcasts, their newspapers contained almost no reports about the INA's actual role as India's liberation army that fought for its independence. So, when the newspapers began to carry detailed information about the INA trials, the vast majority of Indians heard for the first time about the heroic fighting by an ill-equipped and poorly-supplied freedom army of soldiers and civilian recruits, local men and women of northeastern India. The first and most significant of the highly publicized military trials began on 5th November 1945 inside Delhi's Red Fort.

To cut a long story short, protests in sympathy with the accused INA soldiers erupted throughout the country, with several killed in police firing. The Raj also observed with increasing disquiet and unease the spread of pro-INA sympathies within the troops of the British Indian forces. The British colonial rulers realized they could no longer use it to suppress such a movement owing largely to nationalistic and political consciousness in the troops ascribed to the INA. They understood that their time was up in the Indian sub-continent.

The effects of the INA trials brought a decisive shift in British policy in India. Soon after the swearing-in of a newly elected Labour government in Britain headed by Clement Atlee in September 1945, Prime Minister Atlee expressed his Government's intention of creating a Constituent Assembly for India that would frame India's Constitution - as a prelude to granting independence to India without disturbing its unity. Accordingly, Atlee sent a Cabinet Mission that arrived in New Delhi on 24th March 1946. [17] It will be touched upon briefly in the subsequent Cabinet Mission chapter 7. But, the fact of the matter is the "failed" military onslaught of the INA in the North-Eastern battlefront and the Red Fort trials of 1945-1946, not the "peaceful" Quit India movement, primarily impacted the British decision to quit India. The colonial rulers could read the writing on the wall, resulting from their preposterous decision to put the INA men on trial at the Red Fort.

Sadly, these historical realities are hidden in our history books. Consequently, the valiant roles played by many ordinary men and women of northeast India have missed the light of day till now. Nevertheless, this INA episode demonstrated that the emotional unity, the idea of patriotism, and the sense of belonging among the common people of various communities and tribes of this part of our country had remained intact despite sustained efforts made by the British with all the ingenuity they could muster to divide Indians based on their religion, race, and regions they belonged. It was one of the rare occasions when the infamous policy 'Divide and rule' (Latin: divide et impera) failed to work for the British as the Indians forged unity. Its result is there for everybody to see. The mighty British were forced to beat a hurried retreat from India.

Interestingly, as India was inching towards freedom, the idea of a **Crown Colony** for the hills of Assam germinated in the minds of the colonial rulers. It was to be a unique colony, populated by warlike tribes of Northeastern India and Burma who were 'slowly civilizing' and converting to Christianity, ruled by benign tribal-loving British administrators in bush-shirts and hats; a misty, forested and isolated Shangri La, away from the heat, poverty, and opinionated crowds of the vast Indian plains. The idea was initially kept top-secret, but soon it gained popularity and a degree of acceptance – both among some tribal chiefs as well in the British bureaucracy. The way maps were being redrawn across the world, anything was possible. Singapore, Bermuda, Aden, and Gibraltar were already British crown colonies, and so was the 'fragrant harbour' of Hong Kong. Circumstances narrowly prevented the creation of another such entity on the Indian subcontinent.

Imperialism in the 18th and 19th centuries was marked by the British takeover of various parts of the world. By the height of British imperialism,

Britain ruled over territory in every hemisphere of the world; however, to the colonial rulers, no territory was more important than India, the "jewel in the crown." India's convenient location on key trade routes and its abundant natural resources made it the most important colony in the world. The British forced Indians into low-level jobs to establish absolute control, extracting millions of rupees worth of raw materials and then selling the finished goods back to India, effectively "milking" the country heavily.

Consequently, they were able to exploit the Indian people, leaving them ruined, impoverished, and entirely reliant upon British officials. With devastating consequences, Britain established complete control over India because it was the "[1]jewel in the crown."

Note: [1] "Jewel in the crown" means the best or most valuable part of something.

The Crown Colony project was a clandestine plan conceived and discussed at the highest circles in the British Government to establish a British colony comprising the hill areas of North East India and the tribal areas of Burma. Nevill Edward Parry first conceived the proposal. He was earlier the Deputy Commissioner of the Garo Hills (1924-1928) and later the Superintendent of the Lushai Hills. In a memorandum to the Simon Commission in 1930, Parry mentioned that the object of creating the Crown Colony by carving out the hill areas of North East India and adjacent Burma was to safeguard the future existence of these regressive tribes who were not fit to govern themselves. Another proponent of a separate administration was Dr. John Henry Hutton, an anthropologist and the Deputy Commissioner of the Naga Hills. They outlined the idea in a memorandum to the Simon Commission. Hutton argued that the hill people were racially, historically, culturally, and linguistically different from the people of the plains of Assam, while their administration was on wholly different lines. Therefore, Hutton and Perry suggested the formation of a North Eastern Frontier Province to comprise as many of the backward tracks of Assam and Burma as would be conveniently included in it. The plan was to create a unique colony, populated by war-like tribes of India and Burma who were 'slowly civilizing' and converting to Christianity, ruled by 'benign tribal-loving British administrators'.

Throughout the colonial period, the northeastern part of our country was treated by British administrators differently from the rest of India. The core of the colonial policy was to keep this region's numerous indigenous tribal groups separated and isolated. Accordingly, with the Eastern Bengal Frontier Regulation of 1873, an 'Inner Line Permit' (ILP) System was introduced to protect the culture and identity of indigenous tribes in the region, which allowed them some autonomy to look into their personal tribal affairs. The regulation prohibited "British Subjects" from entering Assam's protected or restricted areas. Similarly, in 1935, the hill areas were demarcated and divided into 'Excluded Areas' and 'Partially Excluded Areas'.

All the while, British colonial officers were considering the creation of a small nation under their control, covering India's strategically important borders with Tibet and Burma. In British opinion, the hill tracts of North-East India were an ideal location for such a Crown Colony, given that the region was isolated, lacked significant trade links, the tribes scarcely shared any customs and traditions with mainland India, they were largely animist or Christian, and had minimal political consciousness. Separation from India was inherent in the plan. The proposal envisaged that the level of control would undoubtedly have to be "very considerable for a time, but it is essential that it should come from Whitehall and not from India, to which the hill tracts are entirely alien." This secret plan was discussed at the highest levels of the colonial administration. The Secretary of State for India, Leo Amery, was so impressed with the plan that he gave a copy to Professor Reginald Coupland, who used it in his third and final volume on the constitutional problem in India. Reginald Coupland thus is sometimes, but quite inaccurately, credited with masterminding the Crown Colony Scheme as the 'Coupland Plan'. The plan had considerable support among the British, but due to its secrecy and delayed disclosure, it could only garner intermittent tribal support. The idea of a direct link with Britain appealed to many tribal leaders, particularly from the Khasi-Jaintia Hills and Lushai Hills. Reverend L Gatphoh, a clergyman representing the Jaintia Hills, hoped his hills would come under the Protectorate. In the opinion of several hill leaders, the 'White devil' would be somewhat preferable to rule over them than the 'Brown devil'.

When Jawaharlal Nehru and Assam Premier Gopinath Bordoloi learned about the British plan for a Crown Colony in northeastern India, it alarmed them. They strongly opposed the design of constituting a separate territory by carving out Assam. Apprehending trouble from the leaders of India as well as from the Burmese leaders negotiating the independence of Burma with the British rulers at the time, the proposal for a Crown Colony was shelved. The British realized it was ill-timed and conceived too late to shape their own Protectorate.

Some leaders like Reverend JJM Nichols Roy from the Khasi and Jaintia Hills had been convinced by Pandit Nehru to opt for India. Nichols Roy sent a Memorandum to the British Parliamentary delegation on 29th January 1946, in which he openly expressed his disagreement with the proposed Crown Colony. Among his reasons for disagreement were the many oppressive and unjust rules of the British officers, especially the administrative styles of the

Political Officers in the Khasi and Jaintia Hills. He categorically stated that the Protectorate would not be economically viable, apart from arguing that: "The hill people of Assam should get their own share of independence and they should be connected to the province of Assam".

In Lushai Hills (later Mizoram), the powerful organization Mizo Union opposed the plan. The Union was against the existence of a Chief-ship because a Crown Colony would only mean the perpetuation of the Chiefship. The Mizos favoured autonomous status for the Lushai Hills within the Province of Assam. Similarly, few Garos wrote to the British Parliamentary delegation in February 1946 opposing the plan.

In the Naga Hills, the Naga People's political organization, the Naga National Council (NNC), was convinced to join India with the promise of granting enormous autonomy. The Council passed a resolution in June 1946 at Wokha, demanding autonomy within Assam and opposing the Crown Colony. Assam Premier Gopinath Bordoloi had played a crucial role in convincing many tribal leaders of the advisability of their remaining within India.

Thus, the Crown Colony in North-East India was a near miss! Once it did not materialize, many colonial administrators were disappointed. ARH Macdonald, Superintendent of the Lushai Hills (now Mizoram), wrote in March 1947, apparently with a heavy heart and philosophical tone:

> "My advice to the Lushais, since the very beginning of Lushai politics at the end of the war, has been, until very recently, not to trouble themselves yet about the problem of their future relationship with the rest of India; nobody can possibly foretell what India will be like even two years from now, or even whether there will be an India in the unitary political sense. I would not encourage my small daughter to commit herself to vows of lifelong spinsterhood, but I would regard it as an even worse crime to betroth her in infancy to a boy who was himself still undeveloped."

The 'divide and rule' was deeply ingrained in the British colonization policy. It was evident; that when the Britons were forced to withdraw from India, their parting gift for the people of the sub-continent was the creation of Pakistan! They also dreamt that a Crown Colony in North-East India was a possibility – a small nation sharing borders with India, Bhutan, Bangladesh, Tibet, and Myanmar. Nevertheless, it would have been financially unviable, fractured on tribal lines, and poorly administered once the British administrators left for greener pastures. Just imagine Naga, Mizo, Kuki, Meitei, Garo, Kachin, and Chin insurgencies raging in the small land-locked country. A relapse into India and Burma was eventually plausible, albeit with much turmoil and a setback to the idea of a plural India. Thankfully, the borders remained where they were. India just missed having one British Overseas Territory on its northeastern periphery, the Crown Colony, breathing down its neck all the time. [18]

Although India managed to avoid the breakup of some of its hills in its northeastern perimeter and then foiled the dubious British plan to create a 'crown colony' in this region, the cunning British rulers managed to leave behind numerous 'indigenous immigrants' (an oxymoron coined by Subir) in the region surreptitiously. How they did it is ingenious! In an official directive, they wittingly ruled that Assam's Bengali population, who formed the majority in the province since its inception, should henceforth be designated as "immigrants". The common appellation "immigrant", as we all know, represents a foreigner coming to a different country to live there permanently. The Muslims from Mymensingh (Mymensihghis) and the Hindus from Sylhet (Sylhetis) were the main objects of the British diktat. They used the term "immigrants" as if the Bengalis came from a FOREIGN country.

During those days, Sylhet was within the same Assam province, and Mymensingh was adjacent to Assam in British India, with no international boundary in between. Thus, the term "immigrant" for this group of Bengalis was a complete misnomer replete with the ulterior motive of creating the impression during those days that the Bengalis, both Hindu and Muslim, were 'foreigners' in Assam. Tellingly, the tea garden coolies and ex-coolies who, during those days, came to Assam from present-day Jharkhand, Bihar, U.P, and even from a far-off place like Chennai were NOT labelled as 'immigrants'. The fact that the same British order clarified this point on the tea garden coolies and ex-coolies exposed the hidden agenda of the British colonial rulers of those days.

Unfortunately, from that moment on, the inappropriate appellation 'immigrant' for the Bengalis became a much-used qualifier to describe a Bengali of East Bengal/Pakistan (now Bangladesh) origin. This adjective 'immigrant' attempted to ingrain the false notion among Assam's innocent people that the Bengalis did not belong to India. The indiscriminate use of this loose term soon became vogue among the citizens living in North East India, especially in Assam, giving the impression that all Bengali residents are of foreign origin - illegally staying in Assam.

Additionally, a perception was also created that the 'immigrant' Bengalis only came from Bengal into Assam in large numbers in search of jobs and lands during the Colonial era. Thus, obscuring the truth that Assam Province was entirely formed in 1874 with the amalgamation of (then) Assam division of Bengal Presidency with Bengal's three heavily populated districts. Accordingly, over 57% of the province's population were Bengalis from the beginning. What is more unfortunate is after the end of British rule in India, the indiscriminate use of this misleading term 'immigrant' for the Bengalis in Assam persisted non-stop.

Today, many people remain unaware that the "indigenous immigrants" were neither freeloaders nor free riders in Assam. A significant portion of them are actually Aboriginal residents or their descendants in the state, hailing from regions such as Sylhet, Cachar, or Goalpara. Even other settlers in Assam, who arrived during British rule, did not solely rely on support without reciprocating. Rather, Assam heavily depended on this group of people at a certain point in time, particularly for achieving much-needed self-sufficiency in food and modernizing the region. In this context, the following two paragraphs are quoted from Researcher Hussain Eusub's research paper, "A History of Muslim Politics in Assam," which are quite telling:

> "S. N. Mackenzie, Commissioner of the Assam Valley Division, was perplexed regarding the government's immigration policy. He viewed executive orders aimed at curbing immigration and altering land settlement methods for immigrants in Assam as unwise and unbeneficial. Moreover, he opposed measures intending to change the issuance of periodic pattas. Mackenzie found it illogical to issue immigrants only annual pattas, which he believed would deprive them of rights enjoyed by Assamese locals. He conceded that immigrants had indeed contributed to the development of the country, a feat that Assamese locals could have achieved years ago had they possessed the same initiative and industry as immigrants. Personally, Mackenzie favoured a policy of non-interference unless there was an urgent need for legislation.
>
> Mackenzie was informed by H.C. Barnes that the government's policy was not to restrict immigration from Mymensingh. However, when control over the Assamese and Bengali populations became necessary, the government chose to intervene and implement control measures." [20]

In the early part of the 20th century, as the influx of the Muslim population from the adjacent Mymensingh district of East Bengal into Assam continued, the local population grew wary. They felt threatened by the prospect of being outnumbered and displaced from their ancestral homeland, Assam, which had been a Bengali-majority province since 1874 when the British created the Assam province. This reality was unknown to the local people. Interestingly, alongside the Assamese, there are **many other indigenous groups in Assam whose numerical strength is much smaller than that of the Assamese. Yet, they never expressed fear of being overwhelmed by the Bengalis and displaced from their native lands** because the British never instilled similar paranoia in them.

Nevertheless, to alleviate the concerns of the local Assamese middle class and forestall the mounting rural tension, colonial district officials in Nowgong devised an administrative measure known as the Line System in 1916, which was extensively implemented in 1920.

The Line System purportedly aimed to safeguard the local Assamese against potential disruptions in demographic and social balance, and ultimately against social conflict. It delineated specific areas where new settlers resided and earned their livelihoods. Certain areas were exclusively reserved for the so-called 'indigenous' population. This mechanism effectively segregated the Bengali-speaking Muslim population from the indigenous communities of Assam. When viewed through the lens of apartheid, a political system that divides people based on race, gender, class, or other factors, this Line System in Assam aligns with the infamous Apartheid System of South Africa – the most extreme manifestation of Divide et Impera. Yet, many people in India, including Assam, remain unaware of it.

Thus, we transition to the next chapter, "Apartheid in India: Assam's lesser-known Line System."

* * * * * *

Chapter 6.

Apartheid in India
Assam's Lesser-known Line System

It's unbelievable but true! Apartheid, or "separateness," a system of institutionalized racial segregation and discrimination, was in existence in Assam during British rule in India, much before the expression earned a sense of disgust and loathing from its South African connection, familiarity, and notoriety. As already mentioned, in 1916, the Colonial district officials in Nowgong of India's Assam province devised an administrative measure known as the Line System "to appease the Assamese middle class and prevent rural tension." [1] Its actual implementation started in the 1920s.

Under the Line System, the Bengali Muslims of India's Mymensingh District of East Bengal, which was then in India - adjacent to Assam – barely 150 KM away, were required to settle only in certain earmarked areas of the Brahmaputra Valley in Assam. Initially, the line system was not a clear-cut British government policy. Instead, the British administration encouraged the settlement of Muslims in Assam from its neighboring districts of East Bengal to improve agricultural production, especially food crops. These extremely hardworking Bengalis were employed as agricultural laborers to augment the agronomic revenue of the British rulers. The Assamese gentry also welcomed these Bengalis with open arms and facilitated their resettlement on the soil of Assam.

The Line System was initially devised by J.C. Higgins, Deputy Commissioner, Nagaon (also termed Nowgong), in 1916. It was the result of his personal initiative. A few British district officers then started following it in the early decades of the 20th century in the wake of the large-scale arrival of Muslims from East Bengal. The Colonial Government, and later on, the successive Provincial Governments of Assam in British India, did not interfere in enforcing the Line System but more or less formalized it in the districts of Lower Assam, except for Goalpara district, where the system was reportedly not introduced.

In an Assam University research paper, Researcher Bodhi Sattwa Kar wrote:

> "For the first time in 1913, the problem of agricultural immigrants and the need to prevent interference with the indigenous Assamese had begun to attract the attention of the colonial Government.

Interestingly, both the Assamese middle class and the Colonial Government earlier encouraged immigration to settle in the wasteland considering the economic prospect of the province. In view of the increasing number of immigrants, the colonial bureaucrats like Deputy Commissioners considered steps to meet the situation. A plan was framed in 1916 and was first applied in Nowgong, according to which the new coming immigrants should not be allowed to settle anywhere they liked but would be confined to certain areas in villages demarcated by lines. J.C. Higgins, Deputy Commissioner, Nowgong, in his order in 1923 officially inaugurated the Line system though it had already been implemented and in operation in 1920. The Government could devise no better measure to tackle the immigration problem of settlement and as the number of newcomers increased gradually, the Government gave their approval vide letter No.2132 R, dated August 1925." [2] (Emphasis by Subir)

This discriminatory system was supposedly designed to protect the local Assamese against any possible disturbance of demographic and social balance and eventually against any social conflicts. With the introduction of this mechanism, the provincial government segregated the new Bengali-speaking Muslim settlers from the 'indigenous' Assamese communities of Assam.

Under the Line System, the following four broad demarcations were made:

(i) villages reserved exclusively for the 'indigenous' communities,

(ii) villages meant for the "immigrants" (the new settlers were being described with the misnomer "immigrants" although they too belonged to India),

(iii) villages in which a line was drawn on the map or the ground, on one side of which the "immigrant" could settle, while the other side was earmarked for the 'indigenous' communities, and

(iv) villages where both the immigrant and indigenous people could settle.

There is a striking resemblance between the 'Line System' implemented in Assam in the 1920s and the 'Apartheid System' followed in South Africa from 1948 to the early 1990s. The 'unparalleled brutality' in enforcing evictions under the "Line System" in Assam was vividly documented by Abdul Matin Choudhury, representing the Surma Valley Muslims, and by Syed Abdur

Rauf, representative of Immigrant Muslims from Barpeta, in their joint NOTE OF DISSENTS in the Report of the Line System Committee (1938). **This report is a publication of the Assam Government of British India.** The racial and communal discrimination that formally began in Assam in 1920 and those in South Africa from 1948 were synonymous with the word apartheid. While the dictionary meaning of apartheid is "a political system in which people of different races are separated," Wikipedia describes it as "a system of institutionalized racial segregation and discrimination that existed in South Africa (its origin in Assam being hitherto unknown), which was characterized by an authoritarian political culture based on white supremacy. It encouraged state repression of Black African, Colored, and Asian South Africans to benefit the nation's minority white population."

Remarkably, as early as March 1936, well before the apartheid system started in South Africa, Abdul Mazid Zioshshms, a Council Member, complained in the Assam Legislative Council that: "….. on the one hand, the Indians were protesting against the inhuman and indiscriminate attitude of the South African government towards Indians, then why similar sympathy should not be shown towards Bengali immigrants." He also stated that: "for political reasons, the immigrants were counted upon, but when their purposes were served, they were thrown aside." [3] Abdul Mazid Zioshshms was speaking in support of a resolution by Nuruddin Ahmed demanding the abolition of the Line System, as he felt it had hindered the assimilation of immigrants into Assamese society.

It is pertinent to mention that the legality of the Line System was deemed doubtful by the Advocate General of Assam. Section 298 of the Government of India Act 1935 stated:

> "No subject of His Majesty domiciled in India shall, on the grounds of only religion, place of birth, descent, colour or any of them, be ineligible for office under the Crown in India or be prohibited on any such grounds from acquiring, holding, or disposing of property or carrying on any occupation, trade, business, or profession in British India."

Even the Karachi Resolution of the Indian National Congress passed in 1931 granted every citizen of India the right to 'move freely throughout India and to stay in any part thereof.' Jawaharlal Nehru also condemned the Line System in no uncertain terms. In his book 'Unity of India,' he commented:

> "The present Line System seems to me obviously a transitional affair which cannot continue as such for long …… To keep it as it is seems to be undesirable. The principle is bad, and we cannot encourage it

in India. It is also bad to confine immigrants to a particular area and so prevent them from being assimilated by the people of the Province." [4]

Besides, according to author Anindita Dasgupta:

"The operation of the Line System clearly demonstrated the half-heartedness that went into its making. The Line was an irritant to the migrants, while it also did not satisfy the natives. The new restriction did achieve one thing, however: the line sharply outlined the differences between the two communities: the natives and the migrants. Clashes between the two communities became more frequent and sometimes even turned violent. On the other hand, the British managed to retain their control over local resources by overseeing the allotment and disbursement of landholdings, designing 'enclaves' of communities, changing cropping patterns (because the natives and migrants had different priorities and expertise in agriculture), and dividing Assam's population into two opposing units, by controlling and regulating their access to the province's limited resources." [5]

On 16th March 1936, a resolution was brought by its member Nuruddin Ahmed in the Assam Council demanding the abolition of the Line System. He felt that it had stood in the way of absorbing the immigrants into Assamese society. In support of his resolution, he said that the immigrants had long been suffering from disadvantages and hardships under the Line System, which were:

(1) The immigrants could not be engaged as 'adhiers' or 'bhagidars' by the owners of annual lease lands outside the Line, as persons engaging them might lose their land as per Assam Land rules.

(2) The land prices remained low due to restrictions on both the immigrants and local people from acquiring lands outside their reserved areas.

(3) The Line System effectively obstructed the assimilation of immigrants with the Assamese people despite earnest solicitude expressed by the Assamese people for it. Moreover, the Line System indefinitely delayed the granted rights and privileges of immigrants.

(4) It instilled in the immigrants a feeling of segregation and inferiority, which they would not appreciate.

(5) It fostered a sense of animosity and rivalry between the immigrants and the local people.

(6) Due to the lack of close cooperation between the two sections of the population, the development of the different districts of Assam was generally hampered.

(7) The Line System facilitated, to a great extent, the exploitation of immigrants by non-immigrant Bengalis and even interested Assamese people by encouraging them to remain separate and not integrate themselves into Assamese society.

Mr. L.A. Roffee, a European member, expressed sympathy with the indigenous Assamese people who might be overwhelmed, but ultimately, the weaker must yield to the stronger. The indigenous people must strive for their own advancement. Mr. W.L. Scott, the Revenue member, emphasized that the Line system could not be allowed to persist indefinitely. He argued that the immigrants had severed ties with their places of birth and should be regarded as residents of Assam. He acknowledged that the barriers separating communities of different economic levels were artificial and that the indigenous people must either rise to the level of the immigrants or be overshadowed by them. In supporting the demand for the abolition of the Line System, other members also cited various reasons, such as:

(a) Similar rules do not apply to the ex-tea garden labourers and up-country people, who were mostly Hindus;

(b) By abolishing the Line System, immigrants could easily be assimilated into the Assamese people;

(c) It is undesirable and unfair that settlement rules should be harsh for one group of settlers and lenient for others;

(d) Since the Indians were protesting against the inhuman and indiscriminate attitude of the South African government towards Indians, similar sympathy should be extended to Bengali immigrants;

(e) For political reasons, the immigrants were relied upon, but once their purposes were served, they were cast aside;

(f) The Line System not only hindered the expansion of immigrants but also fostered racial distinctions among different communities.

However, the resolution was defeated by seven votes to twenty. All seven supporters were Muslims, and almost all the Hindu members of the Council voted against the motions. The members representing the government did not vote. [6]

"In the Budget Session of 1940, the immigrant leader Abdur Rouf accused the Congress of being 'hypocritical preachers of Hindu-Muslim Unity as their principles and professions are but poles apart.' In his opinion, "they are very particular about providing land to the tigers, rhinos, buffaloes, and other wild beasts to roam in, but they won't give land to the landless immigrants to live upon …. Some twenty lakh bighas of land have been kept as grazing reserve for half-a-lakh of buffaloes. On the other hand, one lakh human souls are going to perish for want of food, clothing, and shelter". Another League member remarked: "**It is really surprising that the exponent of the Indian National Congress, which is pledged to the one-nation theory should raise on the artificial barrier between Indian and Indian** against the peaceful settlement in vast cultivable wasteland lying fallow for centuries, only on the ground that they happen to be Muslims" [7] (Emphasis by Subir)

The profound significance of the other Muslim League member's perilous remark in this context cannot be lost sight of given that the one-nation theory propagated by Congress eventually failed to influence the Muslim League, leading to the partition of India. While here, the Muslim League member alleged that the Congress in Assam was not practising what they were preaching.

> "If, Sir, your ancestors came to Assam with Mirzumla or Ahom kings, if you came as invaders, despoiled the population, usurped the land and settled here, you will be called an indigenous Assamese, you will be treated as pet child, you will be shown all the favour that benign government can bestow. But, Sir, if your ancestors came as pioneers, if they developed the country, if they cleared the jungle and made prosperous villages and habitable tracts if they contributed to the development of the province, you will be treated as a pariah in your land, and you will be saddled with all the difficulties and all the disadvantages that human ingenuity can invent. Sir, a more unjust, a more illogical, and a more absurd system, it is difficult to conceive ……………. a sort of vested interest is created in favor of the so-called **indigenous population** to the detriment of the interest of the **so-called immigrants**." (Emphasis by Subir)

That fiery speech, quoted in parts above, was delivered by Abdul Matin Chowdhury, a Muslim League leader of national status. It continues to stand out as a charter of the rights of the so-called 'immigrant' Muslims in Assam, showing the sense of injustice felt at the time in the later part of the 1930s when Assam politics was overwhelmed by the question of whether the Line System should go or stay. (Abdul Matin) "Chowdhury repeated the specific charge that while migrants from Madras, Ranchi, and elsewhere were welcome to settle in Assam, the objection was raised towards the predominantly Muslim settlers from Bengal. Just as Jinnah's 'two-nation' theory was about to be asserted, Chowdhury warned against the political fallout of this policy of segregation, stating, 'it closes all avenues of approach and reconciliation between the two major races inhabiting the province. The political ramification of this policy is disastrous' [8]

That was a prophetic oration indeed from Abdul Matin in 1937 - **one decade in advance!** The two major communities in Assam were on the brink of a cataclysmic break-up. As feared by the Muslim League leader, the disaster did befall soon after 10 years, causing catastrophe, calamity, and misery to millions of people. A separate Muslim country, Pakistan, came into being in eastern India too. The million-dollar question today is whether the demand for a separate homeland exclusively for the Muslims in this part of India, against the (then) existing situation, was justifiable or not. It's time now for historians to dispassionately and fairly examine it. Likewise, the role of Syed Muhammad Saadulla in Assam politics in the 1940s should also be judged accordingly, especially whether Saadulla had good reasons to support the cause of Pakistan in the prevailing circumstances in those days.

Subsequently, a nine-member Line System Committee was appointed under the Chairmanship of F. W. Hockenhull, where Abdul Matin Chowdhury was also made a member. The Committee consisted of the following members:

1. F.W.Hockenhull	- Chairman Planning
2. Sarveswar Barua Hindu	- Member Assamese
3. Kameswar Das Hindu	- Member Assamese
4. Rabi Chandra Kachari	- Member Plains Tribal
5. Dr Mahendra Nath Saikia	- Member Depressed Class
6. Abdul Motin Choudhury	- Member Surma valley Muslim
7. Syed Abdur Rauf	-Member Barpeta immigrant Muslim.
8. Khan Bahadur Sayidur Rahman	Member Assamese Muslim
9. A.G.Patton	Member Revenue Secretary

The composition of the committee gave representation to all interests concerned (except the Bengali Hindu community). The committee spent 6 days in Nowgong, 2 days in North Lakhimpur, 2 days in Mangaldai, 4 days in Barpeta, and 2 days in Gauhati. They examined witnesses and paid visits to those villages where the problem was acute. In addition to questioning numerous individuals during their tours, the committee formally recorded an examination of 20 officials and 24 non-official witnesses. The committee considered visiting Goalpara, but upon receipt of a report from the Deputy Commissioner of Goalpara, who informed that the Line system was neither in force nor necessary to introduce, the subject was dropped. [9]

The committee members interviewed and examined a cross-section of society and public leaders. Syed Abdur Rouf, representing the immigrants, strongly pleaded for the abolition of the line system, while the overwhelming majority of the interviewed persons wanted its retention to protect the indigenous people against the influx of people from outside. The general consensus of the committee was that the line system was a temporary mechanism created to check the unrestricted inflow of immigrants into open areas and to protect the demographic composition against disruption and disturbance. It was recommended that 'no land should be settled with immigrants coming to the province henceforward.' There were three dissent notes, which contained sentiments for the abolition of the line system and objections to the contention of the committee, which branded the 'immigrants as undesirable neighbours.' The line system continued, but it could not check the influx and settlement of immigrants in various parts of Assam. [10]

The committee submitted its 34-page, 9-chapter joint report in 1938 with a SUMMARY AND CONCLUSION in the 9th Chapter. While some members preferred to abolish the Line System, some favoured its retention in the present form. The committee then worked out conflicting views and submitted their recommendations as a united committee, with three Notes of Dissent.

The first dissent note was submitted jointly by Rabi Chandra Kachari, Kameswar Das, and Sarveswar Barua; the second was submitted jointly by Abdul Matin Choudhury and Syed Abdur Rauf; and the last one by Dr. Mahendra Nath Saikia. The notes carried widely conflicting views. The lone exception who did not dissent from the report was Khan Bahadur Sayidur Rahman, representing the Assamese Muslims. Interestingly, the three Notes of Dissent were submitted by as many as six members out of seven (excluding two Government nominees), elected members of the committee.

The Line System committee agreed that it is undesirable at present to relax all restrictions on immigrants in the matter of where they should or should not take up land. They admitted that the habits and customs of immigrants, acquired under a different system of land tenure and economic life in Bengal, conflicted materially with the indigenous people of Assam. Therefore, to avoid collisions and protect the interests of simple-minded, peace-loving people, especially the tribal races of Assam, it was desirable to retain a certain amount of control in indicating the areas where immigrants might settle.

The Enquiry Committee recommended abolishing the artificial restrictions imposed on immigrants acquiring land titles, and no barriers should be placed on how immigrants acquire land through purchase. Steps should be taken to protect local people from oppression, and they should be duly warned of any intention to remove the lines. They should also be allowed to migrate elsewhere if they wish.

The committee favoured reserving large areas of the province for the expansion of indigenous cultivation, which would be fostered by the extension of the Development Scheme. It also recommended encouraging the settlement of immigrants in areas that had proven unattractive to Assamese people in the past. Additionally, it recommended extending colonization schemes where they already existed and initiating new ones if necessary.

The Enquiry Committee recognized that the time had come to end the haphazard method of settlement by squatting (taking up land without application). The land was becoming more valuable and scarce, and uneconomic methods of cultivation (such as prevalent jhum cultivation in the hills and fluctuating cultivation in plains) must be discouraged.

However, the committee expressed the view that without firm administrative resolve, avoidance of unnecessary interference, and the presence of adequate and competent staff to enforce executive orders, the recommendations would hold no value. [11]

Out of the three NOTES OF DISSENT, one was submitted jointly by Rabi Chandra Kachari (Member, Plains Tribal), Kameswar Das (Member, Assamese Hindu), and Sarveswar Barua (Member, Assamese Hindu). The first point they made, as quoted below, is quite significant:

> "At the outset, however, we would like to mention certain undamental points of difference between us and the majority. We look upon the Assam Valley as the home of the Assamese people – who have a vested interest in the soil of these districts – which they successfully defended against hordes of invaders in pre-British days. If they had the sovereign power today, they would still resist the occupation of the lands hereby **outsiders** against their will by armed force if necessary. When the Assamese people welcomed the British Government as their rulers, they did not anticipate that the new

rulers **would invite foreigners** to come in such large numbers so as to swamp the indigenous population. The present Government, therefore, has a sacred duty to the Assamese as the guardians of their rights and privileges to protect them from the onrush of Eastern Bengal immigrants. Development of the province from the point of view of land revenue should not be the only consideration – nay not even the main consideration." (Emphasis by Subir) [12]

According to the joint NOTE OF DISSENT by Abdul Matin Chaudhury (Member Surma Valley Muslim) and Syed Abdur Roup (Member Barpeta Immigrant Muslim), there was a relentless accusation against the East Bengal Immigrants as a class and a race. The problem, essentially economic and administrative, was converted into communal, racial, and political. A broad outlook and catholicity of views were conspicuously absent. Bigotry and parochialism predominated. Under the sub-heading DISCRIMINATION, the note mentioned that every rule or regulation framed and issued, any reservation made, should apply equally to all, irrespective of whether they are "indigenous" or "immigrants." According to the Note, discriminatory provisions create bitterness and resentment, perpetuate racial antagonism, impede the growth of friendly relations between the two races, and retard the process of their being welded into a nation.

Regarding allegations of forcible possession of Assamese land, the Deputy Commissioner of Nowgong reported having observed that immigrants got into the Assamese Line by means of sale, subletting, and in a few cases by gift, e.g., an immigrant Muhammadan marrying an Assamese girl. Regarding the Assamese people being compelled to sell their land because of oppression by the immigrants, the note mentioned that the Deputy Commissioner (DC) had considered that these were greatly exaggerated. In fact, the DC reportedly found in many transactions between Assamese and immigrants that the immigrants had lent money to the Assamese even without any bonds sometimes, and the Assamese, having no means to pay back the money, ultimately had given their land to the immigrants. These were absolutely *bona fide* dealings.

According to the evidence of some prominent local personalities and many government officials, including a few Colonisation officers, the immigrants had by then settled down as peaceful citizens, and friction with their Assamese neighbours was practically non-existent. The grievances of letting loose cattle in some Assamese peoples' land, and pilfering of paddy, according to the Note of Dissent, were by no means frequent occurrences, and these could easily be dealt with by the application of the Cattle Trespass Act and by the ordinary law of the land, if necessary. Even diligent research into the history of a decade could hardly unearth more than a handful of cases of kidnapping and murder where immigrants and the Assamese were involved. The whole allegation of the immigrants being undesirable neighbors falls to the ground when seen from the fact that throughout the Valley, inside the Assamese Line, thousands of immigrants were employed by the Assamese people themselves, as sub-tenants and Adhidars, living in close proximity to the Assamese, cultivating their land, and harvesting their paddy. The immigrants were welcome as serfs to middle-class Assamese people but debarred from acquiring independent status, and the Line System served as a convenient instrument for the purpose.

The narrative under the sub-head LANGUAGE AND CULTURE exposes the blatant reality and is hence depicted below in its totality:

> "The spurious character of the opposition to immigrants, on economic grounds, is evident from the persistency with which it is urged that the East Bengal immigrants must 'assimilate' with the Assamese by 'adopting their language and culture.' The word 'assimilation' hardly admits of precise definition. To ask a Bengali to give up his mother tongue and inherited culture, of which he is as proud as an Assamese of his own, in exchange for a patch of land – to which he is as entitled as an Assamese – is to ask him to barter away his birthright for a mere mess of pottage. **This attempt to convert the Bengali immigrants into Assamese, under the duress of economic pressure, is foredoomed to failure. Years of German rule failed to compel the people of Alsace and Lorraine to adopt the German language and German culture; where the mightiest forces, in other parts of the world, have failed, the protagonists of Assam Sanrakhini are not likely to succeed. Minorities in all parts of the world cling tenaciously to their own language and culture. The League of Nations everywhere concedes to minorities this inalienable right. It is one of the fundamental rights that no one would light-heartedly agree to relinquish.** Taking advantage of the numerical superiority of Assamese in Local Boards, in the Assam Valley, and of the economic helplessness of the immigrants to start educational institutions unaided, systematic attempts are being made to impose Assamese as the medium of instruction even in primary schools. Boys of tender age, living in compact immigrant areas, segregated from contact with Assamese boys of similar age, never hearing Assamese spoken either at home or outside are required to have their lessons in Assamese when they attend elementary school. No wonder the progress of

education amongst immigrants is retarded, and one has to tour many a mile before coming across an Immigrant Matriculate. Grants from Local Boards are refused to primary schools that use Bengali as a medium of instruction. So the practice has grown in many schools of boys keeping two sets of books. One in Assamese and the other in Bengali, the former for inspection by Visitors and the latter for actual use. The position would have been ludicrous if it were not so tragic too. No one objects to Bengali Immigrants 'learning' to speak the Assamese language. In many cases, it may be a necessity for daily intercourse in life, but to insist that the 'Immigrant from East Bengal, Sylhet and Cachar should adopt' it, is an entirely different proposition. There ought to be limits to which even blatant aggressive Jingoism can go. This digression into controversy over 'language' and culture has been necessitated by the fact that during the course of our enquiry, this topic loomed large in the statements and oral evidence of the Assamese witnesses and the cultural conquest of the immigrants and their 'assimilation' into the Assamese fold has been a prominent plank in the Assamese program. **The question of the Line System has thus been complicated by the introduction of this irrelevant and extraneous consideration.**" (Emphasis by Subir)

Under the sub-head PROBLEM OF THE LANDLESS PROLETARIATS, the dissent note highlighting its vital urgency wrote that the number of landless people in the immigrant areas of the Brahmaputra Valley was so numerous that new words had been coined to signify the class. "They go by the name of "Wala" in Nowgong and "Utuli" in Kamrup and other districts. They own no homestead land of their own, and live with their families and children, either in the huts built on other people's land, or in houses of relatives and friends; they earn their precarious living by working either as casual labourers or, in some cases, as Adhidhars or by sharing in the cultivation of the scanty area held by their relatives and not infrequently, as absolute dependents on them. These people have migrated permanently to Assam and are bona fide natives of the province. This unfortunate class of people leads the most pitiable existence having no sunshine in their dreary life, no rays of hope for the future. Grinding poverty degrades, debilitates, and degenerates them, reducing them to the scums of society, to which they are a danger and a menace. Driven to desperation by hunger, many of them have trespassed into Government Grazing Reserves and built houses there for themselves and their wives and children, as an alternative to taking shelter under the open canopy of the sky." Its most important cause was the rigidity of enforcement of the Line System. As the system of land settlement failed to keep pace with the enormous increase in the immigrant population since 1921, the position was completely metamorphosed, particularly in Barpeta and Nowgong. Another important cause of creating landless peasants was reportedly the annual changing of course by the mighty river the Brahmaputra and the river Beki which washes away the lands of the immigrants and thereby compels the settlers to search for fresh fields and pastures. The note, underscoring the urgency to solve the problem, mentioned:

"The situation is grave and serious and demands immediate and concentrated attention of the Government and of all those who are interested in the well-being and prosperity of the province."

Significantly, there was a mention in the Note, **"it is a travesty of truth to suggest that train-loads of immigrants are daily pouring in from Eastern Bengal" – an allegation that was commonly levelled against the first Premier (referred to as Prime Minister) of Assam - Syed Muhammad Saadulla.** (Emphasis by Subir)

The description under the sub-head EVICTION, being another controversial reality, is also quoted from the Note of Dissent in its entirety:

> "With regard to evictions, we feel it is our duty to sound a note of warning. We have been told that in Barpeta and Gauhati subdivisions, evictions are being carried out with unparalleled brutality. On arrival at Barpeta, we were informed that on 21st December last, a large number of houses had been burnt in Koragori Grazing Reserve, and many families, with women and children, had been rendered destitute and homeless. On receipt of this information, one of us, Maulavi Abdul Matin Chaudhury, hastened to the spot, stayed there for two days, made a personal investigation, and recorded the statements of several persons affected. Two of the statements are included in this note of dissent, indicating the method employed in evictions.
>
> The story of Koraguri Reserve was repeated at the village Pukuripar, Mauza sub-Chamaria, in the Gauhati subdivision. About 58 families had been residing there for the last 6 or 7 years. On 26th January, only two days after the Line System Enquiry Committee left Gauhati, an Eviction Party raided the village of Pukuripar and burnt the entire village to ashes, rendering about 200 persons, including women and children, homeless. It is alleged that hardly any opportunity was given to the people to remove their belongings and that even articles of daily use, taken out of the house, were thrown

into the fire again. A copy of the Holy Quran was also partially burnt in the all-consuming flames – a most sacrilegious incident that no Muslim can contemplate without pangs of pain, horror, and dismay. The burnt copy of the Holy Quran was shown to us and is in our possession now.

These are incidents that any Government claiming to be civilized and humane ought to be ashamed of. But Koraguri and Pukuripar do not conclude the story. Thousands of families are under notice of eviction in Barpeta and Gauhati subdivisions for the technical offence of occupying land beyond the lines. These they have acquired, either by purchase or reclamation. There are thousands who built their houses in villages two to four years ago, and notices of evictions are now hanging over their heads like swords of Damocles. These people are now living in a state of suspense and trepidation. We are emphatically of the opinion that no eviction should be carried out of persons who are in occupation of lands acquired either through purchase or reclamation, and pattas should immediately be issued to them. The status quo should be maintained. While millions of bighas of Government Khas land are lying waste, the Government must not grudge them a few thousand bighas of land, which they have reclaimed and for which they are prepared to pay revenue. If under exceptional circumstances, it may be found absolutely necessary to evict a few isolated individuals, lands must be provided for them in the vicinity before they are asked to evacuate. Turning people out of their houses into the wilderness must be avoided at all costs, and whatever method it may be necessary to employ, in the rarity of eviction cases, burning of the houses must not be one of them.

(The Report of the Line System Committee 1938 contains both the Vernacular version and its English translations. The English translations as appeared in the report are quoted below, verbatim)

STATEMENT MADE BY LALITA, WIFE OF KANAI NAMASUDRA, ON 20TH JANUARY AT KARAGARI, BARPETA SUBDIVISION

My name is Lalita. (Four daughters from 1 to 10 years of age.) Rice was just cooked; the children had not yet taken their food when the house was set fire to. Belongings were not allowed to be brought out. I stood outside only with a basketful of rice. They did not allow me to take out anything. They said, 'Today it is not your house, it is ours.' Those who came to burn the house and the graziers said this and abused me in obscene language. Two Dharoi (mat), two Jhap (door), and two Koches (fishing instruments) which the children had made for fishing, all these too were burnt. In another were materials for building a house – Rua, Aton, Pita, Kushi – these were also not allowed to be taken out and were burnt. They rebuked us if we attempted to take anything.

STATEMENT MADE BY ALLADHI, WIFE OF JAFAR, ON 19TH JANUARY 1938, AT KORGURI RESERVE, BARPETA

My name is Alladhi [Nasiron (6 months), Tosiron 2 years, Bishu (3 years), Basiron (5 years), 11 children in all]. On the day of the occurrence, many persons came and began abusing me in various ways. My children began crying. Those people set fire to the house. Taking the youngest baby in my lap, I hugged the other kiddies with my arm. In the house, there was paddy, there was rice, and there were four kathas, there were three Patunies; there three ten rupee notes. I did not bring out anything. My husband was not at home, he had gone to the hut. The graziers set fire to the house. I, with children, began shrieking. I have a brother at Nalirpam; I proceeded towards his house. After I had gone a little way, one man came and caught hold of my clothes. I began to cry loudly, and the children also began to cry, and he left my clothes. I went across to the other side, from where my brother accompanied me.

After setting fire to his house, they tried to snatch away the kathas and cloth of my brother for throwing them into the fire. Finding my brother resisting, they assaulted him and gave a cut blow with a Dao (generally used by the Assamese).

Shillong ABDUL MATIN CHAUDHURY
31st January 1938 SYED ABDUR ROUF [13]

Like the conflicting views of the members of the Line System Committee, the Assam Legislative Council members also differed to a large extent in their approach to implementing the committee's recommendations. The views of the two major political parties, the Congress and the Muslim League, were somewhat on communal lines. While Congress had adopted a rigid stand against the settlement of more immigrants and was hell-bent on evicting those who settled in unauthorized areas, the Muslim League was firmly in favour of a lenient approach towards the issues concerning the immigrants not only because the new settlers were Muslims but also for the reason that there was an economic angle beneficial to Assam Province as a whole.

For the Assamese Hindus, in particular, the fear of being swamped by the Bengali Muslim population seemed more dangerous than the threat of poverty and underdevelopment. It was evident in 1939 when a bill was presented in the Assam Legislature to impose a tax on agricultural income aimed at taking care of the revenue deficit of the province. Participating in the debate, its member Abdul Matin Chaudhury criticized the government with another stinging speech:

> "...... He (Hon'ble Finance Minister) says the Bill is solely intended to wipe out the provincial deficits. I have always held, and I never missed an opportunity of expressing it, that there is enormous scope for expansion of the revenues of this province by developing the unsettled areas of land lying idle and fallow; hundreds and thousands of landless people are clamoring for land, but the Government will not provide for these landless people. If they only do so, there will be enough money not only to wipe off the deficit but also to meet the requirements of the Government. The All India Congress passed the Resolution on Fundamental Rights at Karachi, which was proclaimed as the Magna Carta of the people of India. When it is a question of blackmailing the Assam Oil Company, Congress remembers its Karachi Resolution. But when it is a question of dispensing with a "domicile certificate for the Bengali settlers or the question of granting land to the landless immigrants, the Karachi Resolution is put on the shelf. The Hon'able Fakhruddin talks of the masses. His duty is to give land to the landless. It is the racial prejudice of the Congress Government that is at the root of all financial difficulties in Assam. I am not prepared to agree to the imposition of taxes on Agricultural income when better, and less onerous methods are available to the Government....." [14]

After six months of the publication of the Line System Enquiry Committee Report, the Saadullah Coalition Ministry resigned on 13th September 1938 when faced with a no-confidence motion. It was succeeded by a Congress-Coalition Ministry headed by Gopinath Bardaloi. The ministry took no action for fourteen months and resigned in November 1939 as per the decision of the central leadership of the Congress party to protest against Viceroy Lord Linlithgow's action of declaring India to be a belligerent in the Second World War without consulting the Indian people. But on the eve of the resignation, the government issued a resolution, which instead of modifying the Line system, worsened the position of immigrants. The main features of the Bardaloi government's resolution were:

(i) Denial of land settlement to anybody in the village and professional grazing reserves;

(ii) Regulated settlement of landless people, including immigrants, on available wastelands, subject to a holding of 30 bighas per family; and

(iii) Eviction of all immigrant squatters from areas declared protected tribal blocks in the sub-montane region.

The declaration of the Bardaloi government caused widespread resentment among immigrant leaders. They found a platform in the first session of the Assam Provincial Muslim League Conference held at Ghagmari on 18 November 1939. The new Saadulla Ministry, which assumed office after Bardaloi's resignation, rejected the policy laid down by Bardaloi, aligning with the sentiments expressed in the Assam Provincial Muslim League Conference. [15]

Saadulla adopted a policy of extending colonization areas for immigrants and re-examining the necessity of reserving such large areas for professional graziers. Moreover, the Development Scheme under Saadulla was viewed by the Congress party as an attempt to allocate all available land among immigrants. Later, under the 'Grow More Food Campaign', the restrictive 'Lines' were withdrawn in several villages to enable immigrants to obtain a land settlement on the Assamese side. All these steps were strongly criticized by the Congress as well as Assamese Hindus, who saw it as an attempt by the Muslim League Ministry to integrate Assam into the scheme of Pakistan.

In November 1944, after officially abstaining for about three years, when the Congress Assembly party resumed legislative activities, Gopinath Bardaloi expressed alarm and apprehension about how the Saadulla Ministry was handling the land development policy. The opposition suggested that an all-party conference reconsider the land settlement question. The Governor also hinted at a similar course of action in his address to the Assembly. Saadulla accepted the offer without prior consultation with the Muslim League Party. An all-party Conference was duly held under Saadulla's chairmanship on 16-19 December 1944 to recommend a suitable land settlement policy. According to the recommendations of the Conference, it was decided that:

a) No more settlements would be allowed on Grazing Reserves except for encroachers until 1st January 1938.

b) A uniform land settlement plan for all districts for landless people, including outsiders who arrived before 1st January 1938.

c) District-wise reservation of thirty per cent of land for future expansion.

d) After settlement under the new plan, annual pattas would be abolished in the rest of the province except in Tribal areas.

e) Creation of tribal belts forbidding settlement of others in those areas.

However, the resolution was not acceptable to the immigrant Muslims. A meeting of the Assam Provincial Muslim League Council held at Gauhati under Bhasani's chairmanship on January 28, 1945, demanded the total abolition of the Line system. Congress also refused to back the resolutions for various reasons. Because of the stiff opposition from both Congress and the League, Saadulla feared his own position and came forward to make an agreement with Gopinath Bardaloi and Rohini Kumar Choudhury. Bardaloi was ready to support Saadulla under certain conditions. The first and foremost condition was that there should be a reconstitution of the Cabinet and a review of the land settlement policy. The agreement between Saadulla, Bardaloi, and Rohini Choudhury included the revision of the land settlement policy to protect the interests of the local people, especially the tribal people of Assam. Accordingly, a new ministry was reconstituted, and the revenue portfolio was handed over to Rohini Choudhury, somewhat appeasing the sentiments of the Assamese people. However, the formation of the new ministry was opposed by Tayebulla, the President of the Assam Pradesh Congress Committee (APCC), who did not approve of the tripartite agreement. Later on, Bardaloi, too, withdrew his support on the grounds of the non-implementation of the agreement by Saadulla.

In October 1945, the Assam Legislature was dissolved. But Saadulla was allowed to continue as the head of a caretaker government until the general election was held in January 1946. On February 11, 1946, the Congress under Gopinath Bardaloi came to power. The government immediately took up the eviction issue and decided to evict immigrants from the professional grazing grounds. This prompted the provincial Muslim League Committee to form a Committee of Action headed by Bhasani, which directed the Muslim League workers to agitate against the eviction policy of the Congress government all over the province. By then, the All India Muslim League Legislator's Convention was held in Delhi in April 1946. It demanded the inclusion of Assam in Pakistan. Thus, the immigrant issues and the policy of land settlement, which were originally socio-economic issues, became politicized along communal lines, resulting in the demand for Assam's inclusion on the map of Pakistan. [16]

Those were the days during March-June 1946 when the British Cabinet Mission was holding talks with Indian national leaders on transferring powers to Indian hands without partitioning the country. After the Indian leaders failed to arrive at any mutually acceptable scheme, the Cabinet Delegation and the Viceroy declared the Cabinet Mission Plan (discussed in the next chapter) of a three-tier federal government on May 16, 1946, in favour of a grouping system in which both Bengali majority provinces, Assam and Bengal, were placed in the same group. Congress and the Muslim League had also originally agreed to the plan.

In this context, the comments of Maulana Abdul Kalam Azad, former Minister of Education of India and a former Congress President (1939 - April 1946), in his book "India Wins Freedom: The Complete Version," are most significant: *"The only objection raised from the Congress side was by certain leaders from Assam. They were possessed by an inexplicable fear of Bengalis. They said if Bengal and Assam were grouped together, the whole region would be dominated by Muslims."* [17] It was a watershed moment establishing an intense political milieu that eventually sealed the fates of millions of people on the Indian subcontinent.

In that severe political tug-of-war, Muhammad Ali Jinnah declared August 16, 1946, as 'Direct Action Day' and called for Muslims all over the country to suspend all businesses. It was to pressure the British government to relent to the Muslim League's demand of creating a Muslim-dominated Pakistan by dividing India based on religion. It marked the beginning of several acts of violence throughout the country spread over a couple of days, including the dreadful Calcutta Riots with their tremendous negative impact on Hindu-Muslim relations. Luckily, there was no major communal outburst in the Brahmaputra valley, although tensions prevailed in different parts of Assam.

However, the political situation in Assam became further complex when the Bardaloi government decided to resume eviction towards the end of November 1946. Against this backdrop, the Presidents and Secretaries of Assam's Muslim League met and decided it was "high time that drastic action is taken in respect of tyranny, misrule, and atrocities of the government unprecedented in history". Saadulla condemned the proposed execution of the eviction plan as "an act of vendetta and entirely unbecoming of an enlightened government in these times when the shortage of foodstuffs is causing havoc in various lands."

The situation took a serious turn when Bengal Premier Suhrawady sent a telegram to his Assam counterpart, Bardoloi, to hold up the eviction programme until he had an opportunity to discuss the question with him. In a separate statement, All India Muslim League member of the Committee of Action, Abdul Matin Choudhury, declared that eviction "will disturb the peace of Assam". Moreover, the Congress in Assam was confronted with the difficult task of resisting the Cabinet Mission Plan.

Still, the Congress ministry was not averse to any solution. In fact, Bardoloi wrote a letter to Saadulla expressing his eagerness to negotiate provided encroachers, who re-encroached upon the reserves from which they were evicted earlier, evacuated voluntarily and peacefully. This stand was also endorsed by a meeting of the Congress Parliamentary Party. In a conciliatory effort, the Working Committee of the Provincial League met on November 17-18 and considered the statement made by Saadulla that the Congress Premier approached him for a peaceful solution to the question of eviction. "In view of the communal tension throughout the country and the serious repercussions that will result from such a thoughtless policy of the Government of Assam", the Working Committee expressed its preparedness to submit to the arbitration of Liaquat Ali representing the Muslim League and Nehru as the Congress representative. However, Assam Premier ruled out the question of arbitration without any representation from the government and declared: "In dealing with the question of eviction, we are only dealing with lawbreakers and persons who have acted directly against constituted authority and law and order".

The Premier later made it known that the government was not treating the whole question as anything but an economic one. In his view, the government was trying to implement an equitable distribution scheme of land. However, to the Assamese Hindus, the question of the immigration of Muslims into Assam was inseparably linked with the establishment of Pakistan. Obviously, they found no sense in pressing a solution of the League brand down the throat of Assam.

The Bardaloi government's persistence with the decision of large-scale eviction of so-called illegal immigrants from Assam eventually precipitated communal tension followed by the civil disobedience movement by the Provisional Muslim League in Assam. It soon turned into a battle cry for Pakistan. Another dimension of the immigrant problem was the language issue and valley rivalry between the Brahmaputra Valley and Surma Valley of Cachar and Sylhet region. Initially, under the encouragement of Colonial officials, Bengali Muslim immigrants readily identified themselves with the

Assamese people. But later, when communal tension precipitated due to the large-scale eviction drive, they started to assert their Bengali identity.

Earlier, towards the end of January 1947, the League Working Committees of Bengal and Assam held their Joint Session at Bahadurabad "to discuss problems arising out of the Ruthless Eviction Operation by the Government of Assam." The conference thought eviction was not a communal problem and was not an insult against the Muslims, but it constituted **"a challenge and a threat to the Bengalee people and the spirit at work was the anti-Bengali bias of the Assamese-dominant Government of Assam."** [18] (Emphasis by Subir)

Towards the end of April 1947, an attempt was made to solve the problem, but it failed. Governor Akbar Hydari suggested settling immigrants on the north bank of the Brahmaputra. However, Bardoloi believed this would only embolden the Muslim League to incite further disorder and lawlessness in the province.

Sir Benegal Narsing Rau, I.C.S, who had served as Secretary to the Government of Assam during the Saadulla ministries, met with Saadulla to address the immigrant issue. The Committee of Action authorized Saadulla to negotiate based on the Muslim League's demands. Meanwhile, agitation intensified in Sylhet and Cachar, with meetings and processions held in defiance of prohibitory orders.

In response, the Assam government arrested several Muslim League leaders, including Moinul Haque Choudhury of Silchar, A. Latiff, Jalaluddin Ahmed Choudhury of Karimganj, and Baris of Sylhet. A volunteer named Aklas was killed in Sylhet during police firing. Amidst this tension, negotiations between Saadulla and B.N. Rau faltered. The Assam Provincial Muslim League Committee accused the government of unjustified police firing, leading to the deaths of innocent demonstrators in Mankachar and Sylhet. Consequently, they saw no merit in continuing negotiations.

Saadulla, as Chairman of the Action Committee, instructed various District Committees of Action to intensify the Civil Disobedience Movement. However, it was too late, as the Assam government had already adopted a tough stance against the movement.

The announcement of the Mountbatten Plan on June 3, 1947, which proposed the partition of India and the creation of Pakistan for Muslims, along with the referendum in the Sylhet district of Assam, altered the situation significantly. This development relegated the Line System, originally introduced by the colonial government to control immigrant settlers from Bengal to Assam, to a secondary concern. However, it underscored how this system, intended to manage immigration, ultimately contributed to the division of India along communal, religious, racial, and cultural lines. The colonial strategy of "divide and rule" successfully sowed seeds of lasting animosity between Hindus and Muslims, as well as Bengalis and Assamese. [19]

Ironically, when the Labour Party came to power in post-war Great Britain and its new Prime Minister, C. R. Attlee, sent a Cabinet Mission to facilitate the transfer of power to Indian hands without partitioning the country, the three Cabinet Committee members and India's penultimate Viceroy, Lord Wavell, despite their protracted mediation with Indian leaders, failed to bridge the communal and linguistic schism created by British rulers in India. While they successfully narrowed the Hindu-Muslim communal divide to a large extent, the British-sponsored antagonism between Assamese and Bengalis in Assam proved too deep to overcome. Consequently, the Cabinet Mission failed. The vital details of the Cabinet Mission Plan, against the backdrop of Assam's role in its collapse - a seldom discussed poignant tale – are narrated in the next chapter.

* * * * * * *

Chapter 7.

The Cabinet Mission Plan

On 9th March 1966, the Prime Minister of the United Kingdom, Harold Wilson, announced in the House of Commons that the closed period for official records would be reduced from fifty to thirty years. He also stated, among other things, that the practice of publishing selected documents relating to external relations, which had hitherto been confined to the two great wars, should be extended to include some selected periods of peacetime history. For some years, a project to publish documents from the India Office Records was already under discussion. Against this backdrop, the British Prime Minister, in reply to a written question in the House of Commons, announced on 30th June 1967 that the first of the new series of selected documents to be published would relate to the Transfer of Power in India. Soon after that, the British Government decided to entrust the task of publication of the records of the Transfer of Power in India to independent historians with unrestricted access to the records and freedom to select and edit documents.

Accordingly, the Smuts Professor of the History of the British Commonwealth at Cambridge, P. N. S. Mansergh, was appointed Editor-in-Chief, and Mr E. W. R. Lumby was appointed Assistant Editor. Lumby fulfilled his duties until his death on 23rd January 1972. By that time, the first three volumes in the Series had been published, and the fourth was in an advanced stage of preparation. Sir Penderel Moon, O.B.E., sometime Fellow of All Souls College, Oxford, was appointed Assistant Editor in September 1972 when Volume IV was about to go to press and the editing of Volume V had just begun. Penderel Moon assisted Professor Mansergh until the completion of the series, THE TRANSFER OF POWER 1942-7 Volume XII.

Thus, the priceless series of authentic records of British Government documents relating to the crucial period between 1942 and 15th August 1947 was made public in the twelve-volume book titled THE TRANSFER OF POWER 1942-7 with a distinctive subtitle for each Volume starting with "Volume I The Cripps Mission January-April 1942" and ending with "Volume XII The Mountbatten Viceroyalty Princes, Partition, and Independence 8 July-15 August 1947. These documents have been extensively referred to and quoted in this book, including the above two paragraphs and the following statement, which is generally known as the Cabinet Mission's Plan:

Statement by the Cabinet Delegation and His Excellency the Viceroy

(as issued in New Delhi on 16th May 1946)[1]

L/P&J/10/42: ff 53-5

1. On March 15th, just before the dispatch of the Cabinet Delegation to India, Mr. Attlee, the British Prime Minister, stated:

"My colleagues are going to India with the intention of using their utmost endeavours to help her attain her freedom as speedily and fully as possible. What form of Government is to replace the present regime is for India to decide; but our desire is to help her set up forthwith the machinery for making that decision."

* * *

"I hope that India and her people may choose to remain within the British Commonwealth. I am certain that they will find great advantages in doing so."

* * *

'But if she does so elect, it must be by her own free will. The British Commonwealth and Empire is not bound together by chains of external compulsion. It is a free association of free peoples. If, on the other hand, she elects for independence, in our view, she has a right to do so. It will be for us to help make the transition as smooth and easy as possible.'

2. Charged in these historic words, we—the Cabinet Ministers and the Viceroy—have done our utmost to assist the two main political parties to reach an agreement upon the fundamental issue of the unity or division of India. After prolonged discussions in New Delhi, we succeeded in bringing the Congress and the Muslim League together in a Conference at Simla. There was a full exchange of views, and both parties were prepared to make considerable concessions in order to try to reach a settlement, but it ultimately proved impossible to close the remainder of the gap between the parties, so no agreement could be concluded. Since no agreement has been reached, we feel that it is our duty to put forward what we consider the best arrangements possible to ensure a speedy setting up of the new constitution. This statement is made with the full approval of His Majesty's Government in the United Kingdom.

3. We have accordingly decided that immediate arrangements should be made whereby Indians may decide the future constitution of India, and an Interim Government may be set up at once to carry on the administration of British India until such time as a new Constitution can be brought into being. We have endeavoured to be just to the smaller as well as to practicable ways of governing the India of the future and will give a sound basis for defence and a good opportunity for progress in the social, political, and economic fields.

4. It is not intended in this statement to review the voluminous evidence that has been submitted to the Mission; but it is right that we should state that it has shown an almost universal desire, outside the supporters of the Muslim League, for the unity of India.

5. This consideration did not, however, deter us from examining closely and impartially the possibility of a partition of India; since we were greatly impressed by the very genuine and acute anxiety of the Muslims lest they should find themselves subjected to perpetual Hindu-majority rule. This feeling has become so strong and widespread amongst the Muslims that it cannot be allayed by mere paper safeguards. If there is to be internal peace in India, it must be secured by measures that will assure to the Muslims control in all matters vital to their culture, religion, and economic or other interests.

6. We, therefore, examined in the first instance the question of a separate and fully independent sovereign State of Pakistan as claimed by the Muslim League. Such a Pakistan would comprise two areas: one in the northwest consisting of the Provinces of Punjab, Sindh, North-West Frontier, and British Baluchistan; the other in the northeast consisting of the Province of Bengal and Assam. The League was prepared to consider adjustments of boundaries at a later stage but insisted that the principle of Pakistan should first be acknowledged. The arguments for a separate State of Pakistan were based, first, upon the right of the Muslim majority to decide their method of Government according to their wishes, and secondly, upon the necessity to include substantial areas in which Muslims are in the minority, in order to make Pakistan administratively and economically workable. The size of the non-Muslim minorities in Pakistan comprising the whole of the six Provinces enumerated above would be very considerable, as the following figures show:

	Muslim	Non-Muslim
North-Western Area		
Punjab	16217242	12201577
North-Western Province	2788797	249270
Sindh	3208325	1326683
Br Baluchisthan	438930	62701
	22653294	13840231
	62.07%	**37.93%**
North-Eastern Area		
Bengal	33005434	27301091
Assam	3442479	6762254
	36447913	34063345
	51.69%	**48.31%**

The Muslim minorities in the remainder of British India number some 20 million dispersed amongst a total population of 188 million. These figures show that the setting up of a separate sovereign State of Pakistan on the lines claimed by the Muslim League would not solve the communal minority problem; nor can we see any justification for including within a sovereign Pakistan those districts of the Punjab and of Bengal and Assam in which the population is predominantly non-Muslim. Every argument that can be used in favor of Pakistan can equally, in our view, be used in favor of the exclusion of the non-Muslim areas from Pakistan. This point would particularly affect the position of the Sikhs.

7. We, therefore, considered whether a smaller sovereign Pakistan confined to the Muslim majority areas alone might be a possible basis of compromise. Such a Pakistan is regarded by the Muslim League as quite impracticable because it would entail the exclusion from Pakistan of (a) the whole of the Ambala and Jullandur Divisions in the Punjab; (b) the whole of Assam except the districts of Sylhet; and (c) a large part of Western Bengal, including Calcutta, in which city the Muslims form 23.6% of the population. We ourselves are also convinced that any solution which involves a radical partition of the Punjab and Bengal, as this would do, would be contrary to the wishes and interests of a very large proportion of the inhabitants of these Provinces. Bengal and Punjab each have their own common language and long history and tradition. Moreover, any division of the Punjab would of necessity divide the Sikhs, leaving substantial bodies of Sikhs on both sides of the boundary. We have, therefore, been forced to the conclusion that neither a larger nor a smaller sovereign state of Pakistan would provide an acceptable solution for the communal problem.

8. Apart from the great forces of the foregoing arguments, there are weighty administrative, economic, and military considerations. The whole transportation, postal, and telegraph system of India has been established on the basis of a united India. To disintegrate them would gravely injure both parts of India. The case for a united defence is even stronger. The Indian armed forces have been built up as a whole for the defence of India as a whole, and to break them in two would inflict a deadly blow on the long traditions and high degree of efficiency of the Indian Army and would entail the gravest dangers. The Indian Navy and Indian Air Forces would become much less effective. The two sections of the suggested Pakistan contain the two most vulnerable frontiers in India and for a successful defense in depth, the area of Pakistan would be insufficient.

9. A further consideration of importance is the greatest difficulty that the Indian States would find in associating themselves with a divided British India.

10. Finally, there is the geographical fact that the two halves of the proposed Pakistan State are separated by some seven hundred miles, and the communications between them both in war and peace would be dependent on the goodwill of Hindustan.

11. We are, therefore, unable to advise the British Government that the power which at present resides in British hands should be handed over to two entirely separate sovereign States.

12. This decision does not, however, blind us to the very real Muslim apprehensions that their culture, political, and social life might become submerged in a purely unitary India, in which the Hindus, with their greatly superior numbers, must be a dominating element. To address this, the Congress has put forward a scheme under which Provinces would have full autonomy subject only to a minimum of Central subjects, such as Foreign Affairs, Defence, and Communications.

Under this Scheme, Provinces, if they wished to take part in economic and administrative planning on a large scale, could cede to the Centre optional subjects in addition to the compulsory ones mentioned above.

13. Such a scheme would, in our view, present considerable constitutional disadvantages and anomalies. It would be very difficult to work a Central Executive and Legislature in which some Ministers, who dealt with Compulsory subjects, were responsible to the whole of India while other Ministers, who dealt with Optional subjects, would be responsible only to those Provinces which had elected to act together in respect of such subjects. This difficulty would be accentuated in the Central Legislature, where it would be necessary to exclude certain members from speaking and voting when subjects with which their Provinces were not concerned were under discussion.

Apart from the difficulty of working such a scheme, we do not consider that it would be fair to deny other Provinces, which did not desire to take the optional subjects at the Centre, the right to form themselves into a group for a similar purpose. This would indeed be no more than the exercise of their autonomous powers in a particular way.

14. Before putting forward our recommendation, we turn to dealing with the relationship between the Indian States to British India. It is quite clear that with the attainment of independence by British India, whether inside or outside the British Commonwealth, the relationship which has hitherto existed between the Rulers of the States and the British Crown will no longer be possible. Paramountcy can neither be retained by the British Crown nor transferred to the new Government. This fact has been fully recognized by those whom we interviewed from the States. They have at the same time assured us that the States are ready and willing to cooperate in the new development of India. The precise form which their cooperation will take must be a matter for negotiation during the building up of the new constitutional structure, and it by no means follows that it will be identical for all the States. We have not therefore dealt with the States in the same detail as the provinces of British India in the paragraphs which follow.

15. We now indicate the nature of a solution which in our view would be just to the essential claims of all parties, and would at the same time be most likely to bring about a stable and practicable form of constitution for All-India. We recommend that the constitution should take the following basic form:

(1) There should be a Union of India, embracing both British India and the States, which should deal with the following subjects: Foreign Affairs, Defence, and Communications; and should have the powers necessary to raise the finances required for the above subjects.

(2) The Union should have an Executive and a Legislature constituted of British Indian and State representatives. Any question raising a major communal issue in the Legislature should require, for its decision, a majority of the representatives present and voting of each of the two major communities as well as a majority of all the members present and voting.

(3) All subjects other than the Union subjects and all residual powers should vest in the Provinces.

(4) The States will retain all subjects and powers other than those ceded to the Union.

(5) Provinces should be free to form Groups with executives and legislatures, and each Group could determine the Provincial subjects to be taken in common.

(6) The constitutions of the Union and of the Groups should contain a provision whereby any Province could, by a majority vote of its Legislative Assembly, call for a reconsideration of the terms of the constitution after an initial period of 10 years and at 10-year intervals thereafter.

16. It is not our object to lay out the details of a constitution on the above lines but to set in motion the machinery whereby a constitution can be settled by Indians for Indians. It has been necessary, however, for us to make this recommendation as to the broad basis of the future constitution because it became clear to us in the course of our negotiations that not until that had been done was there any hope of getting the two major communities to join in the setting up of the constitution-making machinery.

17. We now indicate the constitution-making machinery which we propose should be brought into being forthwith in order to enable a new constitution to be worked out.

18. In forming any Assembly to decide on a new Constitutional structure, the first problem is to obtain as broad-based and accurate a representation of the whole population as possible. The most satisfactory method obviously would be by election based on adult franchise, but any attempt to introduce such a

step now would lead to wholly unacceptable delays in the formulation of the new Constitution. The only practicable alternative is to utilize the recently elected Provincial Legislative Assemblies as the electing bodies. However, there are two factors in their composition that make this difficult. First, the numerical strengths of the Provincial Legislative Assemblies do not bear the same proportion to the total population in each Province. Thus, Assam, with a population of 10 million, has a legislative Assembly of 108 members, while Bengal, with a population six times as large, has an Assembly of only 250. Secondly, owing to the weightage given to minorities by the Communal Award, the strengths of the several communities in each Provincial Legislative Assembly are not in proportion to their numbers in the Province. For example, the number of seats reserved for Muslims in the Bengal Legislative Assembly is only 48% of the total, although they form 55% of the Provincial population. After careful consideration of the various methods by which these inequalities might be corrected, we have come to the conclusion that the fairest and most practicable plan would be as follows:

(a) to allot to each Province a total number of seats proportional to its population, roughly in the ratio of one to a million, as the nearest substitute for representation by adult suffrage.

(b) to divide this provincial allocation of seats between the main communities in each Province in proportion to their population.

(c) to provide that the representatives allotted to each community in a Province shall be elected by the members of that community in its Legislative Assembly.

We think that for these purposes, it is sufficient to recognize only three main communities in India: General, Muslim, and Sikh, with the "General" community including all persons who are not Muslims or Sikhs. As the smaller minorities would, upon the population basis, have little or no representation since they would lose the weightage which assures them seats in the Provincial Legislatures, we have made the arrangements set out in paragraph 20 below to give them full representation on all matters of special interest to the minorities.

19. (i) Therefore, we propose that there shall be elected by each Provincial Legislative Assembly the following numbers of representatives, each part of the Legislature (General, Muslim, or Sikh) electing its own representatives by the method of proportional representation with the single transferable vote:

Table of Representation	

SECTION A

Province	General	Muslim	Total
Madras	45	4	49
Bombay	19	2	21
United Provinces	47	8	55
Bihar	31	5	36
Central Provinces	16	1	17
Orissa	<u>9</u>	<u>0</u>	<u>9</u>
Total	<u>167</u>	<u>20</u>	<u>187</u>

SECTION B

Province	General	Muslim	Sikh	Total
Punjab	8	16	4	28
North-West Fronter Province	0	3	0	3
Sind	<u>1</u>	<u>3</u>	<u>0</u>	<u>4</u>
Total	<u>9</u>	<u>22</u>	<u>4</u>	<u>35</u>

SECTION C

Province	General	Muslim	Total
Bengal	27	33	60
Assam	<u>7</u>	<u>3</u>	<u>10</u>
Total	<u>34</u>	<u>36</u>	<u>70</u>

Total for British India	292

Maximum for Indian States	93
Total	385

Note - In order to represent the Chief Commissioners Provinces, there will be added to Section A the Member representing Delhi in the Central Legislative Assembly, the Member representing Ajmer-Merwara in the Central Legislative Assembly, and a representative to be elected by the Coorg Legislative Council. To Section B will be added a representative of British Baluchistan.

(ii) It is the intention that the States should be given appropriate representation in the final Constituent Assembly, which would not exceed 93 based on the calculations adopted for British India. However, the method of selection will have to be determined through consultation. In the preliminary stage, the States would be represented by a Negotiating Committee.

(iii) The representatives thus chosen shall meet at New Delhi as soon as possible.

(iv) A preliminary meeting will be held at which the general order of business will be decided, a chairman and other officers elected, and an Advisory Committee (see paragraph 20 below) on the rights of citizens, minorities, and tribal and excluded areas set up. Thereafter, the provincial representatives will be divided into the three sections shown under A, B, and C in the Table of Representation in sub-paragraph (i) of this paragraph.

(v) These sections shall proceed to settle the Provincial Constitutions for the provinces included in each section and shall also decide whether any Group Constitution shall be set up for those provinces and, if so, with what provincial subjects the group should deal. Provinces shall have the power to opt out of the Groups in accordance with the provisions of sub-clause (viii) below.

(vi) The representatives of the Sections and the Indian States shall reassemble for the purpose of settling the Union constitution.

(vii) In the Union Constituent Assembly, resolutions varying the provisions of paragraph 15 above or raising any major communal issue shall require a majority of the representatives present and voting from each of the two major communities. The Chairman of the Assembly shall decide which (if any) of the resolutions raise major communal issues and shall if so requested by a majority of the representatives of either of the major communities, consult the Federal court before giving his decision.

(viii) As soon as the new constitutional arrangements have come into operation, it shall be open to any Province to elect to come out of any Group in which it has been placed. Such a decision shall be taken by the new legislature of the Province after the first general election under the new constitution.

20. The Advisory Committee on the rights of citizens, minorities, and tribal and excluded areas should contain full representation of the affected interests. Its function will be to report to the Union Constituent Assembly on the list of Fundamental Rights, the clause for the protection of minorities, and a scheme for the administration of tribal and excluded areas. It should also advise on whether these rights should be incorporated into the Provincial, Group, or Union Constitution.

21. His Excellency the Viceroy will forthwith request the Provincial Legislatures to proceed with the election of their representatives and for the States to set up a Negotiating Committee. It is hoped that the process of constitution-making can proceed as rapidly as the complexities of the task permit, so that the interim period may be as short as possible.

22. It will be necessary to negotiate a Treaty between the Union Constituent Assembly and the United Kingdom to address certain matters arising out of the transfer of power.

23. While constitution-making proceeds, the administration of India must continue. We attach the greatest importance, therefore, to the immediate establishment of an interim Government with the support of the major political parties. It is essential during this interim period that there be maximum cooperation in addressing the difficult tasks facing the Government of India. In addition to the heavy task of day-to-day administration, there is the grave danger of famine to be addressed; decisions must be made on many matters of post-war development that will have a far-reaching effect on India's future; and there are important international conferences in which India must be represented. For all these purposes, a Government enjoying popular support is necessary. The Viceroy has already initiated discussions towards this end and hopes to soon form an Interim Government in which all portfolios, including that of War Members, will be held by Indian leaders enjoying the full confidence of the people. The British Government, recognizing the significance of the changes in the Government of India, will provide the fullest measures of cooperation to the Government

so formed in accomplishing its administrative tasks and in facilitating as rapid and smooth a transition as possible.

24. To the leaders and people of India, who now have the opportunity for complete independence, we would finally say this: We and our Government and countrymen had hoped it would be possible for the Indian people themselves to agree upon the method of framing the new constitution under which they will live. Despite the efforts we have shared with the Indian Parties, and the exercise of much patience and goodwill by all, this has not been possible. Therefore, we now present to you proposals which, after listening to all sides and much earnest thought, we trust will enable you to attain your independence in the shortest time and with the least danger of internal disturbance and conflict. These proposals may not completely satisfy all parties, but you will recognize with us that at this supreme moment in Indian history, statesmanship demands mutual accommodation.

We ask you to consider the alternative to acceptance of these proposals. Despite all the efforts made by us and the Indian Parties together for agreement, we must state that in our view there is little hope of a peaceful settlement by agreement of the Indian Parties alone. The alternative would therefore be grave danger of violence, chaos, and even civil war. The result and duration of such a disturbance cannot be foreseen; but it is certain that it would be a terrible disaster for many millions of men, women, and children. This is a possibility which must be regarded with equal abhorrence by the Indian people, our own countrymen, and the world as a whole.

We, therefore, present these proposals before you with the profound hope that they will be accepted and operated by you in the spirit of accommodation and goodwill in which they are offered. We appeal to all who have the future good of India at heart to extend their vision beyond their own community or interest to the interests of the whole four hundred million Indian people.

We hope that the newly independent India may choose to be a member of the British Commonwealth. We also hope that in any event, you will remain in close and friendly association with our people. But these are matters of your own free choice. Whatever that choice may be, we look forward with you to your ever-increasing prosperity among the great nations of the world, and to a future even more glorious than your past.

Foot Notes:

[1] In the course of proceedings in the Constituent Assembly on 19th December 1946 and 20th January 1947 discrepancies were noted between the text of the Mission's Statement of 16th May 1946 as issued in India and that issued in a

White Paper in London (Cmd.6821). Constituent Assembly Debates, Vol.1, No.9, PP. I39-4I, Vol. II, No. I, p.252.

As a result, the India office carefully compared the two texts. Thirty-three discrepancies were noted. Almost all were minor; about half were caused by the insertion or omission of the definite article. The more important discrepancies are: (1) The third sentence of para. 18 in Cmd. 6821 begins: '(The only practicable course is to utilize....' (2) The first sentence of para. 20 in Cmd 6821 begins: 'The Advisory Committee on the rights of citizens, minorities and tribal and excluded areas will contain due representation of the interests affected....' (3) In the last sentence of para. 23 in Cmd. 6821, the words 'in the Government of India' were omitted. (4) The third sentence of the second sub-para. Of para. 24 in Cmd 6821 begins: 'The gravity and the duration of such disturbances...'

The main cause of these discrepancies was that the version in Cmd. 6821 was based on the Fourth Revise (No. 268) with later amendments. The Fourth Revise had been telegraphed to London in cipher and small errors crept in at the ciphering, transmission, or deciphering stages. However, in the case of the discrepancy in para. 20 noted above, an amendment to the Fourth Revise sent to London by the Mission was not made to the text. (See No. 268, note I.)

On 23rd January 1947, Mr. Turnbull indicated in noting on this subject that the text of the Statement issued in India should be taken as definitive. L/P&J/10/42: ff 3-15.

[Note in original:] All population figures in this statement are from the most recent census taken in 1941. [1]

The above statement by the Cabinet Delegation and His Excellency the Viceroy, Lord Wavell, on 16th May 1946, is reproduced from the book "THE TRANSFER OF POWER (1942-7) Volume VII. It is commonly called the Cabinet Mission's Plan, which offered **'the last opportunity for preserving the country's unity'** - in the words of the eminent Supreme Court lawyer and political commentator, A. G. Noorani.

The Plan contained the Cabinet Mission's proposals in the wake of the failure of Indian political parties to agree mutually on the constitutional future of independent India. The members of the Cabinet Mission were Lord Pethick-Lawrence, Secretary of State for India, Sir Stafford Cripps, President of the Board of Trade, and A.V Alexander, First Lord of Admiralty.

Gandhi's immediate response to the Cabinet Mission Plan was very promising. According to him: *It* (the proposal) *contained the seed to convert this land of sorrow into one without sorrow and suffering.* In an article in Mahatma Gandhi's famous English-language weekly Harijan ('Children of God'), he wrote:

"Speaking after the evening prayers, Gandhiji referred to the sweet Bhajan sung by Shri Suchetadevi. 'The poet says we are inhabitants of the country where there is neither sorrow nor suffering.' Where was such a country to be found in this world? He had traveled fairly widely but he had not come across such a country so far. The poet had later described the conditions for the attainment of such a State. It was easy to observe them individually. For one who really and truly was pure at heart, there was no sorrow or suffering. But it was a difficult state to attain for the millions. Nevertheless, he wanted India to be such a country.

He had told them yesterday to examine independently other people's opinions of the statement of the Cabinet Delegation when they saw it. They had to examine it not from a parochial standpoint but that of the whole country. They should examine it from the point of view of a country which would be without sorrow or suffering. He would give them his own reaction. He did not want to contradict himself by asking them to follow his ideas if they did not appeal to them. Everyone should think for himself and herself. They were to weigh opinions and adopt only those they had assimilated.

He had glanced at the document last night. He read it carefully in the morning. It was not an award. The Mission and the Viceroy had tried to bring the parties together but they could not bring about an agreement. So they had recommended to the country what in their opinion was worthy of acceptance by the Constituent Assembly. It was open to that body to vary them, reject them, or improve upon them.

There was no 'take it or leave it' business about their recommendation. If there were restrictions, the Constituent Assembly would not be a sovereign body free to frame a constitution of independence for India. Thus the Mission had suggested for the Centre certain subjects. It was open to the Assembly, the majority vote of Muslims and non-Muslims separately, to add to them or even reduce them. It was good that they were not described as Hindus, Muslims, Sikhs, and other religious communities. That was an advance. What they aimed at was the absence of religious divisions for the whole of India as a political entity. And it was open to the Assembly to abolish the distinction which the Mission had felt forced to recognize. Similarly about grouping. The Provinces were free to reject the very idea of grouping. No province could be forced against its will to belong to a group even if the idea of grouping was accepted. He instanced only two things to illustrate his point. He had not exhausted the list of things which seemed to him to be open to objection or improvement.

Subject to the above interpretation which he held was right, he would tell them the Mission had brought forth something of which they have every reason to be proud.

There were some who said the English were incapable of doing the right thing. He did not agree with them. The Mission and the Viceroy were as God-fearing as they themselves claimed to be. It was beneath their dignity as men to doubt a person before he was proved to be untrue to his word. The late Charlie Andrews was every inch of him an Englishman who had died slaving for India. It would be grievously wrong to doubt in advance every one of his countrymen. Whatever the wrong done to India by British rule, if the statement of the Mission was genuine, as he believed it was, it was in discharge of an obligation they had declared the British owed to India, namely to get off India's back. It contained the seed of to convert this land of sorrow into one without sorrow and suffering."[A]

[A]"Mr. Gandhi's (The document on the file is in the form of transcript and carries the date 'Delhi. 17.5 46.')" [2]

Within four days, Gandhiji drafted another article on the same subject, which was published without significant alteration in Harijan on 26th May 1946.

"AN ANALYSIS

After four days of searching examination of the State Paper issued by the Cabinet Mission and the Viceroy on behalf of the British Government, my conviction abides that it is the best document the British Government could produce under the circumstances. It reflects our weakness, if we would be good enough to see it. The Congress and the Muslim League did not, could not agree. We would grievously err if at this time we foolishly satisfy ourselves that the differences are a British creation. The Mission has not come all the way from England to exploit them. They have come to devise the easiest and quickest method of ending British rule. We must be brave enough to believe their declaration until the contrary is proven. Bravery thrives upon the deceit of the deceiver.

My compliment, however, does not mean that what is best from the British standpoint is also best or even good for India. Their best may possibly be harmful. My meaning will, I hope, be clear from what follows.

The authors of the document have endeavoured to say fully what they mean. They have gathered from their talks the minimum they thought would bring the parties together for framing India's charter of freedom. Their one purpose is to end British rule as early as may be. They would do so, if they could, by their effort, leave a united India not torn asunder by internecine quarrel bordering on civil war. They would leave in any case. Since in Simla two parties, though the Mission succeeded in bringing them together at the Conference table (with what patience and skill they could do so, they alone can tell), could not come to an agreement. [2]Nothing daunted, they descended to the plains of India and devised a worthy document for the purpose of setting up the Constituent Assembly which should frame India's charter of independence, free of any British control or influence. It is an appeal and advice. It has no compulsion in it. Thus, the Provincial Assemblies may or may not elect the delegates. The delegates, having been elected, may or may not join the Constituent Assembly. The Assembly having met, may lay down a procedure different from the one laid down in the Statement. Whatever is binding on any person or party arises out of the necessities of the situation. The separate voting is binding on both the major parties, only because it is necessary for the existence of the Assembly and in no otherwise. At the time of writing, I took up the Statement, re-read it clause by clause, and came to the conclusion that there was nothing in it binding in law. Honour and necessity alone are the two binding forces.

What is binding is that part of it which commits the British Government. Hence, I suppose, the four members of the British Mission took the precaution of receiving the full approval of the British Government and the two Houses of Parliament. The Mission is entitled to warm congratulations for the first step in the act of renunciation which the Statement is. Since other steps are necessary for full renunciation, I have called this one a promissory note.

Though the response to be made by India is to be voluntary, the authors have naturally assumed that the Indian parties are well-organized and responsible bodies capable of undertaking voluntary acts as fully as, if not more fully than, compulsory acts. Therefore, when Lord Pathick-Lawrence said to a press correspondent: "If they do not come together on that basis, it will mean that they will have accepted that basis, but they can still change it by a majority of each party they desire to do so," he was right in the sense that those who became delegates, well aware of the contents of the Statement, were expected by the authors to abide by the basis unless it was duly altered by the major parties. When two or more rival parties meet together, they do so under some understanding. A self-chosen umpire (in the absence of one chosen by the parties, the authors constitute themselves one) fancies that the parties will come together only if he presents them with a proposal containing a certain minimum, and he makes his proposal, leaving them free to add to, subtract from or altogether change it by joint agreement.

This is perfect so far. But what about units? Are the Sikhs, for whom the Punjab is the only home in India, to consider themselves against their will, as part of the section which takes in Sindh, Baluchistan, and Frontier Province? Or does the Frontier Province also against its will belong to the Punjab, referred to as "B" in the Statement, or Assam to "C" although it is a predominantly Non-Muslim Province? In my opinion, the voluntary character of the Statement demands that the liberty of the individual unit should be unimpaired. Any member of the sections is free to join or not join it. The freedom to opt out is an additional safeguard. It can never be a substitute for the freedom retained in paragraph 15(5) which reads:

"Provinces should be free to form Groups with executives and legislatures, and each Group could determine the Provincial subjects to be taken in common."

It is clear that this freedom was not taken away by the authors by section 19 which "proposes" (does not order) what should be done. It presupposes that the Chairman of the Constituent Assembly at its first meeting will ask the delegates of the Provinces whether they would accept the group principle and if they do, whether they will accept the assignment given to their Province. This freedom inherent in every Province and that given by 15(5) will remain intact. There appears to me to be no other way of avoiding the apparent conflict between the two paragraphs as also the charge of compulsion which would immediately alter the noble character of the document. I would, therefore, ask all those who are perturbed by the group proposal and the arbitrary assignment, that if my interpretation is valid, there is not the slightest cause of perturbation.

There are other things in the document that would puzzle any hasty reader who forgets that it is simply an appeal and advice to the nation showing how to achieve independence in the shortest possible time. The reason is clear. In the new world that is to emerge out of the present chaos, India in bondage will cease to be "the brightest jewel" in the British Crown; it will become the blackest spot in that crown, so black that it will fit only for the dustbin. Let me ask the reader to hope and pray with me that the British Crown has better use for Britain and the world. The "brightest jewel" is an arrogation. When the promissory note is fully honoured, the British Crown will have a unique jewel as of right flowing from the due performance of duty.

There are other matters outside the Statement that are required to back the promissory note. But I must defer that examination to the next issue of *Harijan*.

M. K. GANDHI

[1]The document on the file is in the form of a draft and is dated 'New Delhi. 20.5.46'. Evidently it is the draft sent by Mr Gandhi to Sir S. Cripps which is referred to in No. 347. The draft was published without significant alteration in *Harijan* on 26th May.

[2]In the published version, this sentence reads: 'Since in Simla the two parties could not come to an agreement, the Mission succeeded in bringing them together at the Conference table (with that patience and skill they could do so they alone could tell)' [3]

Thus, to Gandhi, the plan was 'the best document the British Government could produce in the circumstances' that 'contained the seed to convert this land of sorrow into one without sorrow and suffering'. Also, Congress and the Muslim League accepted the Cabinet Mission Plan at one stage, and a solution to the communal question without partitioning the country was in sight for a while. [4] Then, how come, as we all know, the partition of India happened on 15th August 1947? What exactly took place in the intervening period of about fourteen months, between May 1946 and July 1947?

Quite a few disagreements between the concerned stakeholders cropped up in the early months after the issuance of the Cabinet Mission's statement. All the controversies, except one, were eventually more or less sorted out through discussions and interventions of the Mission delegates and the Viceroy of India. On the flip side, Assam's determined opposition to its grouping with Bengal in Group C, as envisaged in the Cabinet Mission Plan, finally turned out to be too great to overcome.

Interestingly, the majority of the populations in the two adjacent provinces of Bengal and Assam were Bengalis, as discussed earlier in Chapter 3 of this book. When the British created the Assam province in 1874, Bengalis constituted over 57% of its population, compared to less than 36% of the Assamese people. Since then, especially from the early 20th century, the number of Bengalis in Assam has been increasing due to the large-scale influx of people from Bengal into Assam. In fact, the renowned historian of Assam, Amalendu Guha, wrote forthrightly in his book "Planter Raj to Swaraj" (page 23), "Under the circumstances, the Bengali linguistic group rapidly increased in number from census to census through immigration. It continued to outnumber the Assamese even in the new province (created by the British in 1874) well until the partition of Assam in 1947."

Expectedly, therefore, the Cabinet Mission grouped the two adjacent Bengali-dominant provinces of Assam and Bengal in the same group in its Plan. Although the Bengalis of Assam and Bengal, both Hindus and Muslims, did not oppose the grouping as envisaged in the Cabinet Mission's Plan, the Assam Congress Committee led by Gopinath Bordoloi refused to accept being in the same group as Bengal. Its determined opposition for that reason resulted in the collapse of the Cabinet Mission Plan to grant independence to a united India, which eventually led to our country's partition.

In his journal article titled "Collapse of the Cabinet Mission's Plan", renowned Indian lawyer and political commentator A. G. Noorani wrote, "Documents on the Transfer of Power 1942-7, Volume VIII: The Interim Government (3 July - 1 November 1946)" by Nicholas Mansergh and Penderel Moon should make every Indian sad; **"for it documents the collapse of the last opportunity for preserving the country's unity".**

A selected portion of Noorani's article is quoted below:

> "The Cabinet Mission's statement of May 16, 1946, proposed a loose federation confined strictly to defense, foreign affairs, and communications and endowed with the 'powers necessary to raise finance required' for these subjects. There were to be three sub-federations in the forms of groups of provinces, two of them comprising the 'Pakistan Provinces' in the east and the west. The plan explicitly allowed the legislature of a province to secede from a group immediately after the first general elections. In striking contrast, no province could opt out of the Indian Union. All it could do was to demand 'reconsideration of the terms of the constitution after an initial period of ten years and at ten-yearly intervals thereafter.'
>
> Doubtless, after a preliminary meeting of the Constituent Assembly, the members had to 'divide up into the three sections' which were to 'proceed to settle the provincial constitutions for the provinces included in each section, and .... also decide whether any Group Constitution shall be set up for those provinces and, if so, with what provincial subjects the Group should deal. Provinces shall have the power to opt out of the Group in accordance with the provisions' mentioned earlier namely after the general elections – not before it.
>
> Grouping Controversy
>
> Would it have at all been possible for a united Bengal to draft such a Constitution for Assam as to prevent it from opting out of Group C or for a united Punjab and Sind, likewise to prevent NWFP from

leaving Group B? (Group A comprised the rest of the Provinces) By what conceivable gerrymandering could such an outrage have been perpetrated? If it were, that would have ground enough to regard as a breach of the agreed proposals. On the other hand, consider the gains. As Maulana Azad explained then, 'all schemes of partition of India have been rejected, once and for all.' P. R. Lele, a veteran Congressman, and able publicist rightly asked 'could a triumph like this come without price, without some sacrifice?' The Congress refused to pay the price – grouping of the provinces.

The Muslim League's movement for Pakistan could not have retained its momentum once the Constituent Assembly had begun drafting a Constitution for a united India with the Congress in an overwhelming majority in the Assembly. The opportunity was a challenge to the statesmanship of the majority party. But the Congress was in no mood for compromise. [5]

Earlier, when the Labour Party came to power in post-war Great Britain, its new Prime Minister, C. R. Attlee, on 19th September 1945, expressed his government's intention in the House of Commons that a Cabinet Mission would be sent to India to facilitate the process of the transfer of power. The Mission's aim would also be to help the Indian leaders decide the form of government that would suit them after the transfer of power. Accordingly, the Cabinet Mission arrived in New Delhi on 24th March 1946. By that time, Gopinath Bardaloi came to power in Assam on 11th February 1946, which was soon followed by the eviction of the so-called immigrants. The INA trials, which began at the Red Fort in November 1945, propelled the Indians to defy British rule, and reports of Hindu-Muslim communal riots poured in from various parts of India. Both the rulers and the ruled had the growing feeling that India could no longer be directly governed as a colony and that its independence would come in a form determined primarily by the nature of the confrontation. Thus, the Mission had to deal with a major obstacle: the two main political parties, the Indian National Congress and the Muslim League, did not see eye to eye with each other. They had fundamental differences over India's future. While the Muslim League wanted the Muslim majority provinces of India to constitute a separate sovereign state of Pakistan, the Congress wanted a united India. At the Shimla Conference, the Mission attempted to facilitate an agreement between the Muslim League and the Congress. When this failed, the Mission came out with its proposal - the Cabinet Mission Plan. [6] It remains relevant even today in comprehending and making sense of the historical developments in Assam and North-East India - both before and after its collapse in 1947.

Significantly, the period of the Second World War, particularly following the 1942 movement suppressed by the British rulers by 1944, slackened Gandhiji's grip on a politically awakened India. Large sections of Indian nationalists became increasingly aware that, for the final bid for power, the Gandhian method would not suffice. The new mood, drawing inspiration from Bose's exploits abroad, found expression in the post-war national upsurge. All previous movements seemed insignificant compared to the unique atmosphere that prevailed. Assam, too, modestly shared this new spirit, although most of the Congress leaders were still under Gandhiji's influence. The public trials of the INA personnel as war prisoners between November 1945 and May 1946 at Delhi's Red Fort galvanized the whole country and pushed India towards complete freedom. Everywhere – including Assam – demonstrations were held to demand the unconditional release of the war prisoners and their rehabilitation as national heroes. Even after the British Cabinet's decision on January 22, 1946, to send its mission soon to negotiate the transfer of power, troops had to be called out. Scores of people were shot to suppress an anti-British upheaval and barricade resistance in curfew-bound Calcutta. Hartals and demonstrations to protest against the massacre were held in Assam, Bengal, and other provinces. A distinguishing feature of this anti-British imperialist upsurge was the growth of popular initiative. Students, office employees, workers, and slum-dwellers – Hindus and Muslims – unitedly moved into action with Congress, League, and Communist flags in their hands.

Peaceful hunger strikes and work stoppages by defense personnel made headlines and had a cumulative effect, given the wide sympathy for the INA prisoners. The Royal Indian Navy (RIN) revolted at Bombay and Karachi in February 1946, taking a distinctly political turn. Large-scale fraternization developed between the sailors and citizens. The historic uprising 'laid bare in a flash all the maturing forces of the Indian revolution – their points of strength as well as weakness. Even after their eventual surrender, open outbursts of discontent persisted. There were fresh acts of defiance in the air force and the army – in Calcutta and Jabalpur. In Assam, preparation for the all-India railway strike, which was to start on June 27, 1946, became a rallying point for all anti-imperialist political forces. The Railway Board had to concede almost all the demands to avoid the strike.

If the national scene had its credit side during post-World War II, it had its debit side, too. The British Cabinet Mission's negotiations with national leaders in March-June 1946 and the Congress and League leaders' squabble over its offer of transferring power to Indian hands vitiated the atmosphere. Failing to arrive at a scheme approved by all parties, the Mission declared itself in favor of a three-tier federal government with only three subjects – defense, foreign affairs, and communications – vested in the center, as per the statement of the Cabinet Delegation and the Viceroy issued in New Delhi on May 16, 1946, depicted at the beginning of this chapter. A novel feature in the Plan was that the groups might have, if they so wished, legislature and executives forming an intermediate layer of government between those in the provinces and the Union.

Under the Plan, the representatives of the provinces were to divide themselves into three sections – A, B, and C, after a preliminary session of the proposed Constitution Assembly was over. Section C was to consist of Bengal and Assam. Each section was to decide its own provincial and group matters. The Constituent Assembly members supposed to sit in Section C were going to be almost evenly balanced, as shown below:

Composition of Sections under Cabinet Mission Plan			
	General	Muslim	Total
Bengal	27	33	60
Assam	7	3	10
Total	**34**	**36**	**70**

[7]

Interestingly, although there were 34 General seats and 36 Muslim seats on the basis of proportional representation in the Bengal-Assam group as a whole, it is believed that the 36 Muslim seats included one Congress Muslim who, in all probability, would vote against the Muslim League. Thus, the League and the General were effectively equal with 35 seats each. [8]

It may be mentioned here that soon after the arrival of the members of the Cabinet Mission in India, they, along with the Viceroy of India, Lord Wavell, started discussions with several Indian leaders to critically evaluate the prevailing situation in the country and feel the pulse of various leaders. One such meeting took place between them and Assam Premier Gopinath Bardoloi on April 1, 1946, barely one and a half months before the formal announcement of the Cabinet Mission Plan. The minutes of the said meeting are reproduced below:

"Minutes of the meeting between Cabinet Delegation,
Field Marshal Viscount Wavell and Mr Gopinath Bardoloi
on Monday, 1 April 1946 at 4.50 pm
L/P&J/337/: pp 39-42

SECRET

Mr. Bardoloi said, in response to a question from the Viceroy, that he was prepared to make a statement regarding what he regarded as the best method of achieving a political settlement. However, he desired to clarify from the outset that the Congress President alone was competent to speak on the general question, and he could only offer his personal opinion. He believed that under a Constitution akin to that of the United States, a genuine reconciliation between the Muslim League and Congress could be achieved. The Center would need to retain responsibility for communications, defence, foreign relations, and special powers for emergency measures, along with the right to levy taxes for these purposes. However, he argued that complete separation as desired by Mr Jinnah was unnecessary. Instead, empowering the units further would suffice. He urged Mr Jinnah to consider this perspective, dismissing the notion of two nations as fallacious. He warned that if Mr Jinnah insisted unreasonably on this point, it might be necessary to proceed without accommodating him. The process of granting Muslims a share in the administration, he emphasized, must be democratic.

In his view, if Mr Jinnah's stance were accepted, it could lead to civil war. However, if he refused to reach an agreement, independence must still be granted, even if it meant proceeding without him. He insisted that no one should be allowed to halt the progress.

If provinces were to be based on linguistic divisions, as desired by Congress for many years, Bardoloi suggested that they should enjoy greater autonomy than under the 1935 Act. He proposed limiting the Center's powers, with residual powers resting with the provinces. He envisioned a United States of India, with the main executive functions remaining with the provinces.

Regarding immediate possibilities, he pointed out that if Mr. Jinnah were to reach an agreement with Congress, achieving a settlement would be easier. He stressed that near-failure of agreement due to unreasonableness should not obstruct the transfer of power. He proposed establishing a government at the Center immediately, by inviting provinces to nominate individuals to a panel from which the Viceroy could select his interim government. Even if Sindh and Bengal stood apart, 27 out of India's 32 crores would be represented. He believed that Punjab would also join. The provisional government, formed in this manner, would be tasked with convening a Constituent Assembly, negotiating with Mr. Jinnah if necessary, drafting a constitution for the new India, and conducting negotiations with the princely states. He emphasized the need for the British government to clearly indicate that power had genuinely been transferred to the provisional government, warning that any delay in the transfer would be highly dangerous.

Conditions in Assam

He then described the situation in Assam. The province (including Sylhet) had functioned as a unit for 3,000 years. The Ahom kingdom had persisted until the British arrival. At that time, Sylhet was part of Bengal, and although there were several attempts by Muslims to conquer the province, in 1901, excluding Sylhet, Muslims comprised only 7% of the population. The juncture of Assam with Bengal in 1905 led to a significant influx of Muslims, resulting in the Muslim population growing from 3 lakhs to 13 lakhs in the Assam valley proper. Only Muslim immigrants had entered, and now, with Sylhet district included, Muslims constituted 33.7% of the population. Bardoloi deemed Mr Jinnah's proposition that the entirety of Assam should be included in Pakistan preposterous.

In response to SIR STAFFORD CRIPPS, **Mr. Bardoloi stated that the Congress would not object to the transfer of Sylhet to Bengal**, as its people and culture were predominantly Bengali. Before 1874, the district was administered by a Commissioner. In 1874, it was decided to include the district as part of Assam. In 1924 and again in 1926, the Assam Legislative Council passed a resolution that the district should be transferred to Bengal, and a similar resolution was passed by the Bengal Legislative Council in 1826. However, the Muslims of Sylhet now opposed the separation of the district from Assam, as they gained advantages in terms of representation in government services, etc. Additionally, **Sylhet being a permanently settled deficit district, maintained by the people of the Assam valley,** strained relations between the two regions were likely. This was the primary argument for cutting off Sylhet from the Province.

Assam was a province with considerable resources, but the Government of India, by absorbing royalties on oil, had taken a significant amount of money out of it. Approximately 260 million lbs. of tea were produced every year, 90% of which was exported. However, the export duty was realized by the Government of India in Calcutta, resulting in lost revenue for the Province. In return, despite being one of the poorest, the Province received only 30 lakhs in subvention from the Central Government. To enable Assam to utilize its resources in its own interest, Bardoloi felt that the fullest possible autonomy should be granted to it.

Responding to a question from the Viceroy, **Mr Bardoloi disagreed that there was a large area of uncultivated land in Assam,** dismissing it as Muslim League propaganda. He mentioned that the Muslim League had been sending Muslims to occupy grazing areas, and these settlers from Bengal were harming cattle and oppressing the inhabitants. Sir Mohammed Sa'adulla had agreed that they should be evicted, but so far, nothing had been done. The present Government intends to carry out its policy in accordance with the agreement. Bardoloi emphasized that **it was incorrect to claim that there was vacant land available,** as much of the land was submerged under water for a large part of the year. While there were underdeveloped areas in the hills, denudation needed to be avoided, and most of the land would be required to create economic holdings. Even in the valley, once land had been allocated for those with uneconomic holdings (e.g., less than one acre), there would not be enough land to go around. Finally, he refuted the claim that the Congress was preventing the export of grain from the Province.

The Hill Tribes

Regarding the position of the hill tribes, Mr. Bardoloi expressed his desire to present a memorandum[1] by the Rev. J.J.M. Nichols-Roy, a Khasi Christian and Minister in the current Assam Government. The hill people were also keen for some degree of autonomy. While the tribes in the north of Assam were generally still somewhat primitive, relations between the hill people in the south and those in the Assam valley were friendly. The Khasis had an advanced form of democratic self-government, and the Jaintias were also in an advanced state of civilization. Mr. Bardoloi believed that these tribes would be willing to be associated with the Assam Government, though they would desire a high degree of autonomy. He expressed a similar hope for Manipur State.

The tribes in the country north of Brahmaputra would continue to be administered by the Provincial Government as at present. Part of the cost was now being met from provincial revenues, and the expenses of the Assam Rifles were shared between the Central and Provincial Governments. While some provision for external defence would be necessary, Mr Bardoloi felt confident that Provincial resources were adequate to cover the administration of this area. Sir Stafford Cripps pointed out that the matter would require arrangement between the Centre and the Provinces, a sentiment with which Mr Bardoloi concurred.

THE SECRETARY OF STATE indicated that **the delegation wished to explore the situation at this stage. If there were to be a Pakistan region, including Eastern Bengal, Sylhet might be included with Eastern Bengal. Did Mr Bardoloi agree that on this hypothesis, the remainder of Assam could unite with the main part of India? Mr. Bardoloi responded that the loss of Sylhet would not significantly affect communications between Assam and the rest of India.**

Furthermore, Mr. Bardoloi stated that he was firmly against Pakistan. However, he noted that the land tenure, etc., in Sylhet, was similar to those in Bengal, and if there were a hypothetical United States of India, the district should form part of the Bengal area rather than the Assam area. He expressed confidence that Congress would be willing to meet the expenses of the tribal areas, though external defence would have to be funded by the Centre.

The Constitution-Making Body.

THE SECRETARY OF STATE informed Mr. Bardoloi that one purpose of their visit was to accelerate the setting up of a Constitution-making body. What were Mr. Bardoloi's views on the best method of selecting such a body? Mr. Bardoloi replied that he thought it unnecessary to delay for adult franchise, and representatives should be sent to sit with people from other Provinces. The selection need not, however, be limited to people with seats in the Legislature. The best people would be wanted, and there should be power to send names from any part of India, and for the Constitution-making Body to co-opt in case of need. All communities should, as far as possible, be represented. Even if Mr Jinnah did not agree to the Interim Government, the Provinces should have the right to send in a panel of names, not necessarily from the Province itself. Panels of names could be submitted by each Government as responsible to the Legislature; i.e., they would be selected rather than elected.

In conclusion, Mr. Bardoloi asked whether he could take any message from the Delegation. Sir Stafford Cripps said that he felt it was for the Indians to help at this stage, and the Secretary of State added that their cards had been placed on the table. They intend to make the independence of India an accomplished fact and were whole-hearted and sincere in this attempt." [9] (Emphasis by Subir)

Nevertheless, as soon as the Cabinet Delegation and the Viceroy issued the New Delhi statement on 16th May 1946, the Assam Provincial Congress Committee (APCC) President consulted his Working Committee and telegraphically appraised the Congress high command of Assam's resentment against the grouping clause. Assam Premier Bardoloi, who was then in New

Delhi, placed before the APCC (All-India Congress Committee) Working Committee a memorandum to the same effect on 19th May. In June, a nine-member Congress delegation from Assam met the Working Committee, then in session in New Delhi, and presented yet another memorandum. [10] However, former Assam Premier Md. Saadulla supported the grouping and advanced the following arguments in its favour:

a) If Assam stood out of Group 'C', her geographical position as a northeastern frontier with Bengal interposed between her and the rest of the country would make it unsuitable and impracticable to join any other section. Therefore, she must submit to the Group Constitution or remain alone as a single unit.

b) The financial interests of Assam would suffer as her main income came from the European Planters who paid either in Calcutta or London.

c) For law and order, she would have to maintain a huge force of her own.

d) Assam's refusal to join the Section with Bengal would adversely affect their mutual relationship. Considering Assam's high dependency on Bengal in many areas, such a step would be unwise.

Saadulla felt that Grouping and the subjects which the Group Constitution would take over would be a matter of mutual understanding and adjustment between the two provinces. [11]

Besides, according to Researcher Monolina Nandy Roy, the Bengali-speaking people of the Surma-Barak valley were inclined to welcome the grouping proposal of the Cabinet Mission at least as a partial approach to the greater Bengal of their desire, though recognizing the inadequacy of this method. As a result, a wider split occurred between the Congresses of the two valleys. **The Surma Valley Congress leaders (under the West Bengal Congress Committee) lost no opportunity to welcome the grouping plan.** [12] (Emphasis by Subir)

Nevertheless, the Congress leaders at the national level thought they found a face-saving clause in paragraph 15 of the Cabinet Mission's statement. According to them, this clause could be construed as suggesting inherent freedom on the part of a province to join or not join a section. Therefore, they advised that, even if Congress accepted the Plan, the Assam legislature could, by mandatory resolution, direct its representatives to the Constituent Assembly to shun the section it was supposed to join. Hundreds of meetings were held around the Brahmaputra Valley of Assam province throughout May, June, and July to record vehement protests against the grouping clause.

Resolutions to that effect were forwarded to national and government leaders, as well as to the press.

At the instance of the Congress Party, the Assam Legislative Assembly passed the historic, mandatory resolution on 16th July 1946, by which it was resolved that the provincial constitution could be framed only by Assam's own representatives to the Constitution Assembly and that it would be detrimental to the province's interests if they joined others in a section for that purpose. The original suggestion to do so had come from Nehru and Patel when an APCC delegation met them in Delhi on the 8th and 9th of June 1946.

In its operative part, the resolution directed all the ten representatives of the province to sit in the Constituent Assembly only to frame the Union Constitution and to sit in an exclusive meeting or meetings attended by them alone to frame the provincial constitution. When the resolution was moved, the League members refused, after recording their protest, to take part in further deliberations and voting. They nevertheless participated in the election to the Constituent Assembly. Under the system of proportional representation with single transferable votes for the purpose, seven Congressmen and three Leaguers were elected.

On 10th August, the Working Committee of the AICC accepted the Cabinet Mission Plan and proposed to proceed with the Constituent Assembly. The League was also committed to the Plan. But meanwhile, because of the Assam legislature's mandate, the situation changed. 'This clearly repudiated one of the fundamental terms of the statement of 16th May,' said Jinnah in the course of an angry statement on 12th August, 'and this is an instance of how the majority acted, although it is highly doubtful whether the Assam Assembly was competent to give such a mandate to the representatives of the Constituent Assembly. [13]

The Muslim League proclaimed 16th August 1946 to be observed countrywide as 'Direct Action Day' to press for their demand for a separate Muslim homeland after the British left the Indian subcontinent. On that day, large-scale Hindu-Muslim communal riots flared up in Calcutta that started in the morning with altercations between the supporters and opponents of the Muslim League-backed 'bandh' (a general strike). Between dawn on the morning of 16th August 1946 and dusk three days later, the people of Calcutta hacked, battered, burned, stabbed, or shot 6000 of each other to death, and raped and maimed another 20000. The dreadful slaughter, which turned Calcutta into a charnel house for seventy-two hours, is important because it did more than murder innocent people. It murdered hopes too. The infamous riot known as the "Great Calcutta Killing" changed the shape of India and the course of history. The clashes continued for four days resulting in 5,000 to 10,000 dead and some 15,000 wounded.

The "Great Calcutta Killing" report and its catastrophe prompted Viceroy Wavell to make an unannounced air dash to Calcutta on August 25-26 (1946). He spent two-and-a-half hours on a tour of some riot-affected areas of the metropolitan city. [14] While in Calcutta, Wavell also spent some time in consultation with Khwaja Nazimuddin, who was a member of the All India Muslim League Working Committee and had the ear of Mr Jinnah. Nazimuddin had come forward with a proposition. The Cabinet Mission's Plan for Indian independence had been based on the idea of a Federal India with three groups. The most important element in the federal structure, of course, would be Group A, controlled by an overwhelming majority of Hindus. It would always be more powerful than Groups B (Muslim-dominated) and C (with a slight domination of the Muslims). That was an arrangement the Muslim League had accepted until Nehru's maladroit repudiation of the grouping scheme. Nazimuddin now proposed to Wavell that Congress should make a declaration that they had accepted the Cabinet Mission Plan not as they interpreted it, but as the Cabinet Mission had intended it. The scheme, in other words, should be given a chance to work. In these circumstances, Nazimuddin told Wavell, the Muslim League might reconsider its rejection of the scheme and decide to come into the interim Government.

Soon after his return to New Delhi, Wavell called Gandhi and Nehru to meet him on the evening of 27th August 1946. At the meeting, visibly upset, Wavell described to the two Congress leaders the enormity of the crime against humanity and civilization committed by Muslims and Hindus alike in Calcutta during recent days and stressed the guiltiness of both communities for it. He admitted that, as an Englishman, he had no right to judge the actions of the Indian political parties, but as long as he was Viceroy of India, he felt it necessary to do all in his power to prevent any more massacres of this kind. The dialogues which then followed between Wavell on one side and the Gandhi-Nehru duo on the other were noteworthy.

> Wavell put the question frankly to Gandhi and Nehru: "Will you give me the guarantee the Muslim League is asking for? 'Give me a simple guarantee that you accept the Cabinet Mission Plan,' asked Wavell.
>
> 'We have already said that we accept it,' replied Gandhi, 'but we are not prepared to guarantee that we accept it in the way that the Cabinet Mission set it out. We have our own interpretations of what they propose.'

'Even if those interpretations differ from what the Cabinet Mission intended?' Wavell asked.

'But of course. In any case, what the Cabinet Mission Plan really means is not what the Cabinet Mission thinks but what the interim Government thinks it means," replied Gandhi.

Wavell pointed out that the interim Government's opinion, as things were at the moment, would almost inevitably be pro-Congress and anti-Muslim League since the League was boycotting the Government. How could it be unbiased?

Gandhi replied that he was not concerned with bias. He was simply concerned with the legal basis of the discussion. Legally, this was a matter for the interim Government to decide. Once the interim Government was in power, such matters as the Muslim League's ambitions and artificial anxieties could be voted upon, but not before.

'But don't you see,' exploded Wavell, in an unusual burst of temper, 'it will be a Congress Government! They are bound to be lacking in impartiality.'

Pandit Nehru interrupted at this point. 'You misunderstand the composition of the Congress Party, your Excellency, not, I may say, for the first time. The Congress is not pro-Hindu or anti-Muslim. It is for all the people of India. It will never legislate against the interests of the Muslims.'

Wavell replied, 'But whose Muslims, Pandit Nehru? Yours, the Congress Muslims, the so-called stooges? Or those of the Muslim League? Can't you see that the necessity of this moment is to satisfy the Muslim League that you are not trying to do them down? It is a moment - possibly the last we have - to bring the League and the Congress together. And all I ask is a guarantee. Will the Congress commit itself to a declaration, a declaration which will satisfy the Muslim League and assure the continuation of a stable and unitary government?' Wavell reached into his drawer and pulled out a paper. 'This is what I have in mind.'

The declaration ran thus: 'The Congress is prepared, in the interests of communal harmony, to accept the intention of the statement of 16th May (the Cabinet Mission statement reproduced at the beginning of this chapter) that provinces cannot exercise any option affecting their membership of the sections or the groups if formed, until the decision contemplated in paragraph 19 (vii) of the Statement of 16 May is taken by the new legislature after the new constitutional arrangements have come into operation and the first general elections have been held.'

Gandhi handed it over to Nehru, who read it and said: 'To accept this is tantamount to asking Congress to put itself in fetters.'

Wavell replied: 'So far as the Cabinet Mission Plan is concerned, that is what I feel you should do. When Congress accepted the Cabinet Mission Plan in the first place, I cannot believe that you did so, not knowing its implications. If so, why did you accept it at all? The plan for dividing the country into groups was implicit. You cannot now turn round and say that you did not realize that is what was intended.'

Gandhi: 'What the Cabinet Mission intended and the way we interpret what they intended may not necessarily be the same.'

'This is lawyer's talk,' said Wavell. 'Talk to me in plain English. I am a simple soldier, and you confuse me with these legalistic arguments.

Nehru: 'We cannot help it if we are lawyers.'

Wavell: 'No, but you can talk to me like honest men interested in India's future and welfare.' Dammit, the Cabinet Mission made its intentions as clear as daylight. Surely we don't need to go to law about that or split legal hairs, either. As a plain man, the situation seems to be simple. If Congress will give me the guarantee for which I ask, I think I can persuade Mr Jinnah and the Muslim League to reconsider their refusal to join the interim Government. We need them in the Government; India needs them, and if you are seriously concerned over the dangers of civil war - and you must know as well as I that the danger is great - then you need them too. In the circumstances, I feel that it would be unwise, even perilous if I allowed Congress to form an interim Government on its own.'

Gandhi: 'But you have already announced that the Government will come into being. You cannot go back on your word now.'

Wavell: 'The situation has changed. As a result of the killings in Calcutta, India is on the verge of civil war. It is my duty to prevent it. I will not prevent it if I allow Congress to form a Government which excludes the Muslims: they will then decide that Direct Action is the only way, and we shall have the massacre of Bengal all over again.'

Nehru: 'In other words, you are willing to surrender to the Muslim League's blackmail.'

Wavell (with great heat): 'For God's sake, man, who are you to talk of blackmail?'

So far as Nehru and Gandhi were concerned, it was the end of Wavell as a Viceroy with whom they could deal. That night both of them sat down to write letters. Gandhi first penned a cable to Mr Attlee, the Labour Prime Minister, in which he expressed concern over the Viceroy's state of mind. He was, he said, 'unnerved owing to the Bengal tragedy'. He needed to be bolstered by 'an abler and legal mind'.

The above-mentioned proceedings of the consultation Viceroy Wavell had with Khwaja Nazimuddin in Calcutta and what transpired at the meeting he had with Gandhi and Nehru on 27th August 1946 have been reproduced from the book "The Last Days Of The British Raj" by Leonard Mosley, British journalist, historian, biographer, and novelist. [15] Later, in the same chapter under the caption 'THEY'VE SACKED ME, GEORGE', Mosley added:

> "On the morning of 19 February 1947, the Viceroy was having breakfast with George Abell when the dispatches were brought in. One of the cables marked 'private and confidential' was handed to the Viceroy, who opened it, read it through, and then went on eating his egg. Abell was on sufficiently close terms with his Chief to realize, from the set of Wavell's face, that something had happened, and he waited to be told. There was five minutes' silence. At last, Abell said:
>
> 'Anything important, sir?'
>
> Wavell: 'They've sacked me, George.' A long pause, and then: 'They were quite right, I suppose.'

On 20th February 1947, Mr Attlee announced in the House of Commons that power would be transferred into the hands of a responsible Indian Government by a date not later than June 1948. He also announced the resignation of Lord Wavell as Viceroy and his replacement by Admiral Viscount Mountbatten. His tribute to Wavell's unrelaxing efforts was polite but cool. As he said afterwards, 'I came to the conclusion that Wavell had shot his bolt.' [16]

On his return from Calcutta, and before meeting Gandhi and Nehru, Viceroy Wavell also sent a telegram dated 27th August 1946 to Lord Pethick-Lawrence (Secretary of State for India and leader of the Cabinet mission to India in 1946), in which he wrote, among other things:

> "I see no hope at all of avoiding further and more serious rioting in Calcutta and elsewhere in India unless some settlement at the Centre.

Some members of the Muslim League are obviously desirous of coming to terms if possible, but Jinnah appears to still be quite intransigent. Nazimuddin told me that an unequivocal statement by Congress that Provinces could not opt out of Groups except as laid down in the Statement of May 16th might cause the League to reconsider the Bombay resolution, or if I or HMG stated plainly our intention not to permit Congress to put any other interpretation on grouping except that meant by the Mission." [17]

Maulana Abul Kalam Azad, the Congress President from 1940 to 1946, played a crucial role in formulating the Cabinet Mission Plan. He was also closely associated with the sequence of events emerging from this vital issue all along. In his book "India Wins Freedom," Azad graphically narrated the activities of some of our prominent political leaders and the happenings during those days that eventually led to the collapse of the Cabinet Mission Plan. India lost the last chance to remain united and free of British colonial rule. The under-noted paragraphs are quoted from that book:

"Both Congress and the Muslim League had originally accepted the Cabinet Mission Plan, which meant that both had accepted the Constituent Assembly. So far as Congress was concerned, it was still in favour of the Cabinet Mission Plan. The only objection raised from Congress was by certain leaders from Assam. They were possessed by an inexplicable fear of Bengal. They said that if Bengal and Assam were grouped together, the whole region would be dominated by Muslims. The objection was raised by leaders from Assam immediately after the Cabinet Mission announced the Plan. Gandhiji had initially accepted the Cabinet Mission Plan and declared that 'the Cabinet Mission proposal contains the seed to convert this land of sorrow into one without sorrow and suffering.' He went on to say in Harijan, 'After four days of searching examination of the State paper issued by the Cabinet Mission and the Viceroy on behalf of the British Government, my conviction abides that it is the best document that the British Government could have produced in the circumstances.' Gopinath Bardoloi, the Chief Minister of Assam, however, persisted in his opposition and submitted a Memorandum to the Congress Working Committee opposing the grouping of Assam and Bengal as proposed in the Cabinet Mission statement.

In the Working Committee, we felt that we should not reopen the question of grouping. In order partly to meet the objection of our colleagues from Assam, but mainly on grounds of principle, we did, however, raise the question of European participation in the election of the Constituent Assembly. I wrote to the Viceroy that Congress might reject the whole of the Cabinet Mission's proposal if the European Members of the Bengal and Assam Legislature participated in the election to the Constituent Assembly either by voting or by standing as candidates. The objection was met, as the Europeans in the Bengal Assembly made a declaration that they would not seek representation in the proposed Constituent Assembly. In the meantime, however, Gandhiji's views changed, and he gave his support to Bardoloi. Jawaharlal agreed with me that the fears of the Assam leaders were unjustified and tried hard to impress them. Unfortunately, they did not listen to either Jawaharlal or me, especially since Gandhiji was now on their side and issued statements supporting their stand. Jawaharlal was, however, steadfast and gave me full support.

I have already said that the League's rejection of the Cabinet Mission Plan had caused us a great deal of anxiety. I have also mentioned the steps which the Working Committee took to meet the League's objection. This we did by passing a resolution on 10 August in which it was clearly stated that despite our dissatisfaction with some of the proposals contained in the Cabinet Mission Plan, we accepted the scheme in its entirety. This did not, however, convince Mr Jinnah, as he held that the Working Committee did not still state in categorical terms that the provinces would join the groups envisaged in the Cabinet Mission Plan. The British Government and Lord Wavell generally agreed with the League on this particular point.

Looking back after ten years, I concede that there was a force in what Jinnah said. The Congress and the League were both parties to the agreement, and it was based on distribution among the Centre, the Provinces, and the Groups that the League had accepted the Plan. Congress was neither wise nor right in raising doubts. It should have accepted the Plan unequivocally if it stood for the unity of India. Vacation would give Jinnah the opportunity to divide India.

I was all the time trying to iron out the differences through discussions, and Lord Wavell fully supported my efforts in this direction. This was one reason why he was anxious to bring the Muslim League into the Government and welcomed the statement I made on this behalf. He genuinely believed that there could be no better solution to the Indian problem than outlined in the Cabinet Mission Plan. He repeatedly told me that even from the point of view of the Muslim League, no better solution was possible. Since the Cabinet Mission Plan was largely based on the scheme I had formulated in my statement of 15 April, I naturally agreed with him.

Mr. Attlee (Prime Minister of the United Kingdom from 1945 to 1951) was also taking a personal interest in the Indian developments. On 26 November 1946, he invited Lord Wavell and representatives of the Congress and the League to meet in London in another attempt to resolve the deadlock. At first, the Congress was not willing to accept the invitation. Jawaharlal, in fact, told Lord Wavell that there would be no point in going to London for further discussions. All relevant issues had been thrashed out again and again, and it would do more harm than good to reopen them.

Lord Wavell did not agree with Jawaharlal and discussed the matter in further detail with me. He said that if the present attitude of the Muslim League continued, not only would the administration suffer but a peaceful solution to the India problem would become more and more difficult. He further argued that discussions in London would have the advantage that the leaders could take a more objective and dispassionate view. They would also be free from local pressure and the continual interference of their followers. Lord Wavell also stressed the point that Mr. Attlee had been a friend of India and his participation in the discussions might prove helpful.

I recognized the force of Lord Wavell's argument and persuaded my colleagues to change their point of view. It was then decided that Jawaharlal should go on behalf of Congress. The League was represented by Mr Jinnah and Liaqat Ali, while Baldev Singh went on behalf of the Sikhs. The discussions were held from 3 to 6 December but did not yield any results.

The major difference was about the interpretation of the clauses relating to grouping in the Cabinet Mission Plan. Mr. Jinnah held that the Constituent Assembly had no right to change the structure of the Plan. Grouping was an essential part of the plan and any change regarding grouping would alter the basis of the agreement. The Plan had itself provided that after the groups had framed the Constitution, a province could opt out. This, Mr Jinnah said, was sufficient protection for any Province which did not wish to belong to the group to which it was allotted. Congress leaders of Assam, on the other hand, held that a province could stay out from the beginning. It did not join the group at all and could frame its constitution independently. In other words, according to Mr Jinnah, the provinces must first join the group and could thereafter, if they wished, separate. According to Congress leaders of Assam, it could start as separate units and could thereafter join the group if they so wished. The Cabinet Mission had held that the interpretation of the League on this point was correct. Mr Jinnah argued that it was on this basis of the distribution that he had persuaded the League to accept the Plan. Assam Congress leaders did not agree, and after some hesitation, Gandhiji, as I have already said, gave his support to the interpretation suggested by the leaders of Assam. In fairness, I have to admit on this point Mr. Jinnah was, on the whole, right. Both justice and expediency demanded that Congress should have accepted the Plan unequivocally.

On 6 December, the British Cabinet issued a statement in which it upheld the point of view of the Muslim League. [18]

It was in line with the opinion of Lord Jowitt, a Labour Party politician and lawyer who served as Lord Chancellor under Clement Attlee from 1945 to 1951. Pethick-Lawrence, Secretary of State for India, obtained the legal opinion on 2nd December 1946, just one day before the commencement of the said meeting. Among other points, the opinion given by Lord Jowitt on this particular issue of grouping is quoted below:

> "The proposal contained in paragraph 19 (iv), which is part of the proposals for the constitution-making machine, is clear; after the preliminary meeting, the provincial representatives are to form themselves into certain designated sections, and it is for these sections – not for the individual provinces – to settle provincial constitutions. The sections may also decide whether – and if so to what extent – a group constitution shall be set up for any provinces.
>
> I do not agree that it is any part of the recommendations for the constitution-making machinery that the provinces shall in the first place make their choice as to whether or not to belong to the section in which they are placed. No such conclusion can possibly be arrived at without disregarding the perfectly clear words of 19(iv) of the Statement.
>
> The resolution of the Congress Working Committee of 24th May 1946 attempts to justify this construction by the necessity of making paragraph 15 consistent with paragraph 19. But there is no such necessity for the two paragraphs to deal with different concepts; the former contains recommendations as to the basic form of the constitution to be evolved as a result of the functioning of the

constitution-making machine, and the latter contains recommendations as to the construction of that machine itself. In any event, even if there were such a necessity it would be wholly illegitimate to construct an implication therefrom to negate an express term.

I, therefore, conclude that the recommendation involves that it is for the majority of the representatives in each section taken as a whole to decide how provincial constitutions shall be framed and to what extent, if any, they shall be grouped.

I should add that I come to the above conclusion solely on the terms of the Statement itself; if it were legitimate to aid the doctrine of 'contemporanea expositio' it is obvious that my conclusion is reinforced.

JOWITT [19]

Accordingly, the British Government issued the statement dated 6th December 1946, upholding the view of the Muslim League, as mentioned above by Azad. The said statement is also reproduced below:

STATEMENT BY HIS MAJESTY'S GOVERNMENT

The conversation held by His Majesty's Government with Pandit Nehru, Mr Jinnah, Mr Liaquat Ali Khan, and Sardar Baldev Singh came to an end this evening, as Pandit Nehru and Sardar Baldev Singh are returning to India tomorrow.

The object of the conversations has been to obtain the participation and cooperation of all parties in the Constituent Assembly. It was not expected that any final settlement could be arrived at since the Indian representatives must consult their colleagues before any final decision is reached.

The main difficulty that has arisen has been over the interpretation of paragraphs 19(v) and (vii) of the Cabinet Mission's Statement of May 16th relating to the Meetings in Sections, which run as follows:

Paragraph 19(v) "These sections shall proceed to settle the Provincial Constitutions for the provinces included in each section, and shall also decide whether any Group Constitution shall be set up for those provinces and, if so, with what provincial subjects the group should deal. Provinces shall have the power to opt out of the Groups in accordance with the provisions of sub-clause (viii) below."

Paragraph 19(viii) "As soon as the new constitutional arrangements have come into operation, it shall be open to any Province to elect to come out of any Group in which it has been placed. Such a decision shall be taken by the new legislature of the Province after the first general election under the new constitution."

The Cabinet Mission has throughout maintained the view that the decisions of the Sections should, in the absence of an agreement to the contrary, be taken by a simple majority vote of the representatives in the Sections. This view has been accepted by the Muslim League; the Congress has put forward a different view. They have asserted that the true meaning of the Statement, read as a whole, is that the Provinces have a right to decide both as to grouping and as to their constitutions.

His Majesty's Government have had legal advice which confirms that the Statement of May 16 means what the Cabinet Mission has always stated was their intention. This part of the Statement, as so interpreted, must therefore be considered an essential part of the scheme of May 16th for enabling the Indian people to formulate a constitution which His Majesty's Government would be prepared to submit to Parliament. It should, therefore, be accepted by all parties in the Constituent Assembly.

It is, however, clear that other questions of interpretation of the Statement of May 16th may arise, and His Majesty's Government hope that if the Council of the Muslim League is able to agree to participate in the Constituent Assembly, they will also agree, as the Congress has, that the Federal Court should be asked to decide matters of interpretation that may be referred to them by either side and will accept such a decision so that the procedure, both in the Union Constituent Assembly and in the Sections, may accord with the Cabinet Mission's Plan.

On the matter immediately in dispute, His Majesty's Government urge the Congress to accept the view of the Cabinet Mission in order that the way may be open for the Muslim League to reconsider their attitude. If, in spite of this reaffirmation of the intention of the Cabinet Mission, the Constituent Assembly desires that this fundamental point should be referred for the decision of the Federal Court, such reference should be made at a very early date. It will then be reasonable that the meetings of the Sections of the Constituent Assembly should be postponed until the decision of the Federal Court is known.

There has never been any prospect of success for the Constituent Assembly except upon the basis of an agreed procedure. Should a Constitution come to be framed by a Constituent Assembly in which a large section of the Indian population had not been represented, His Majesty's Government could not, of course, contemplate forcing such a Constitution upon any unwilling parts of the country. [20]

Meanwhile, Assam was rocked by another spell of protests. In no circumstances was the APCC agreeable to accepting the grouping as a given fact or the Federal Court as a mediator in the matter. It rushed a delegation to New Delhi to pressure its high command into rejecting the British Government's statement of 6th December 1946. Nehru and Azad tried hard to soften the attitude of the Assam delegation, but they listened to neither since Gandhiji had already thrown his weight on their side. When Bardoloi's emissaries consulted Gandhiji at Srirampur on 15th December, he reiterated: "I told Bardoloi that if there is no clear guidance from the Congress Working Committee, Assam should not go into the Sections. It should lodge its protest and retire from the Constituent Assembly. It will be a kind of Satyagraha against the Congress for the good of the Congress." Accordingly, Bardoloi took a bold stand and informed Nehru, the Congress President, that Assam would stand by Gandhiji's advice of 'framing our own constitution, and grouping accordingly'. A Congress delegation from Assam again met the Working Committee and Gandhiji in Delhi on 4th January 1947.

The AICC met in a plenary session in the first week of January 1947 to review the situation. It was eager to proceed with the Constituent Assembly and was in no mood to retrace its steps. Yet, due to the developing situation during the period, the AICC could not take a clear-cut stand. Its acceptance of the British statement of 6th December 1946 was qualified with many reservations. The unresolved issue over the question of grouping resulted in a problematic political stalemate. Apparently, neither the Muslim League nor the Congress was ready for a compromise. The Labour Government in Britain was faced with a dilemma. Prime Minister Attlee felt that his Government should fix a definite date for the withdrawal of British power from India. He held that once a date line was fixed, the responsibility would shift to the Indian leaders to take a final call. He feared that if the status quo were allowed to continue for long, the Indians would lose faith in the British Government, aggravating the already precarious law and order situation. On the contrary, Viceroy Wavell wished to persist with the Cabinet Mission's Plan to solve their Indian problem. Eventually, Wavell had to resign after he failed to convince Attlee. [22]

On 24th March 1947, Lord Mountbatten was sworn in as Viceroy and Governor-General of India. He replaced Wavell. The Labour Government fully briefed Mountbatten with instruction from Attlee that power must be transferred by 30th June 1948. According to Leonard Mosley,

"Mr Attlee had chosen Mountbatten as the new Viceroy because 'he was an extremely lively, exciting personality. He had an extraordinary faculty for getting on well with all kinds of people, as he had shown when he was Supremo in South East Asia. He was also blessed with a very unusual wife.' He had another quality, too. When he was given a job, he did not like to dawdle on it. Other men might hesitate or cautiously ponder the problem. Mountbatten believed in driving things through, shortcuts if there were any. He approached the problem of India's independence by June 1948, rather than in the manner of a time-and-study expert, who has been called into a factory to knock off the wasteful minutes and get out the product before the target date." [23]

Writing about how the new and the last Viceroy of India, Lord Mountbatten, felt about the Cabinet Mission Plan, Maulana Abul Kalam Azad, in his book "India Wins Freedom," averred that:

Lord Mountbatten did not feel so strongly about the Cabinet Mission Plan as this was not the child of his brain. He wanted to be remembered in history as the man who had solved the Indian Problem. If the solution were in terms of a plan formulated by him, this would bring still greater credit to him. It is therefore not surprising that as soon as he met opposition with the Cabinet Mission Plan, he was willing to substitute it with a plan of partition formulated according to his own ideas. [24]

Interestingly, the record of Maulana Abul Kalam Azad's interview with India's Viceroy Lord Mountbatten at a later date, on 27th March 1947, revealed a fascinating confession of the former. It's reproduced hereunder:

"27

Record of Interview between Rear-Admiral Viscount Mountbatten of Burma and Maulana Azad.

Mountbatten Papers. Viceroy's Interview No. 14.

TOP SECRET   27th March 1947

Maulana Azad is a charming old gentleman who, though he understands English, spoke through an interpreter. He told me first that if he had not been due at that particular moment to leave the presidency of Congress, that party would have accepted the Cabinet Mission's Plan. He said that blame in the first place must be laid on Congress, although it was the Muslim League which was now intransigent. He considered that there was a good chance that I would succeed in 'deflating' Mr. Jinnah; partly by flattering him and partly because he really has nothing to stand on. One of his great objectives was to have ministers in the Central Government, and he had no intention of allowing them to leave it. [25]

Anyway, in the series of discussions, Lord Mountbatten held with several Indian political leaders before the finalization of his plan to hand over powers to the Indian leaders, he also talked to Assam Premier Gopinath Bardoloi on 1st May 1947. The record of this conversation is quoted below:

"271

Record of Interview between Rear-Admiral Viscount Mount of Burma and Mr. Gopinath Bordoloi

Mountbatten Papers, Viceroy's Interview.

Top Secret   1st May 1947

I sat next to Mr. Bardoloi at the luncheon on 1st May. He told me that Assam would make no difficulties about the partition of Sylhet since the general view was that they belonged to Bengal and would be no loss to the rest of the Province. The only people who might kick up a fuss would be the 40 per cent non-Muslim minority in the Sylhet district. I asked him what solution he would prefer for Bengal, from the point of view of Assam. He replied that he would like Bengal to remain unified and join Hindustan since this would give Assam the very best access to the rest of Hindustan. If Bengal remained unified and joined Pakistan, it would virtually strangle Assam. If Bengal remained unified and independent, they would have to negotiate access through Bengal, but it would not be as difficult as if Bengal had joined Pakistan. If they had partitioned, he expected to get access to Hindustan through Cooch Behar and Jalpaiguri. He shared with me the regret that Sir B. N. Rau had failed in his attempt to reach a settlement in Assam recently and attributed this to the shooting that had taken place during his mediation.[1]

Note: [1]In April 1947, Sir B. N. Rau, then on a visit to Assam, negotiated an agreement between Sir Muhammad Saadullah and Mr. Bardoloi on the position of certain immigrants who were being evicted from their lands. However, the agreement was not endorsed by the Assam Committee of Action of the Muslim League. [26]

Before Lord Mountbatten met the Assam Premier Gopinath Bardoloi, he obtained feedback on Assam concerning the issues coming in the way of the Cabinet Mission's grouping formula from Sir Andrew Gourlay Clow, the last British-born Governor of Assam from 1942 to 1947. The Governor's evaluation on the subject is illuminating, as may be seen from the enclosure (reproduced hereunder) to the following letter dated 20th April 1947 from Sir Clow:

183

Sir A Clow (Assam) to Rear-Admiral Viscount Mountbatten of Burma

R3/1/130: ff 213-15

No. 254 GOVERNMENT HOUSE
20 April 1947

Dear Lord Mountbatten,

When I was in Delhi Your Excellency asked me for a note on the relation between the Assamese Hindus' objection to grouping with Bengal and the arrangement of constituencies. The enclosed note will, I hope, explain the position.[1]

Yours sincerely

A. G. CLOW

Enclosure to No. 183.

ASSAM AND GROUPING

The population of Assam at the 1941 census, consisted of (in lakhs)

Caste Hindus	35
Scheduled Castes	7
Muslims	34
Tribals & Christians	26

Muslims, owing to the Bengal famine and other causes, have gained ground since then, and some tribals were recorded as Hindus. But ignoring this, the position broadly is that the caste Hindus, the Muslims, and others form three almost equal groups. In the legislature, however, out of 99 Indian members, the unreserved general seats are 40, and thanks to the Poona Pact, no Scheduled Caste candidate opposed to them has much chance in the 7 reserved seats. The General constituencies contain such a large majority of Caste Hindus that, at the cost of putting some 'stooges', they can command 47 seats plus 3 Indian planting and commercial seats, making 50. Muslims have 34 seats. There are only 15 other seats, of which only 9 are exclusively tribal or Christian. Thus, ignoring the European seats, the Caste Hindus can expect to start with a full half of a house of 99 and in present circumstances have the resources to capture a proportion of the remainder.

2. But on an outright system of separate electorates, the Caste Hindus would start with no more than Muslims, and the intermediate groups, consisting mainly of tribals and Christians, would hold the balance. With the Pakistan issue out of the way, most of these would be as likely to side with the Muslims as with the Hindus. This would be no unnatural alliance, for all these groups are underprivileged, and so are the Muslims. Between the introductions of the reforms in 1937, when about a third of the seats went to candidates associated neither with Congress nor with the Muslims, and 1945, we had Hindu-dominated ministries for about 18 months, a 93 Administration for 18 months, and Muslim-dominated ministries for nearly 6 years. So that, even if there was strictly proportionate representation, the Caste Hindus could no longer rely on dominating the situation. It is, however, conceivable that in Group C, which would have a Muslim majority, the distribution would not be on the strictly proportionate basis indicated by the 1941 census. Muslims might be increased to allow for substantial fresh immigration, backward people might be given weightage, the excluded areas might come in, and further castes might be cut out of the Caste Hindu total and treated separately.

3. Thus the Caste Hindus are apprehensive, and not without cause, that a constitution framed for Assam in Section C would put them in a far weaker position than they hold at present, and perhaps an even weaker position than they deserve. And they would have a poor chance of getting secession approved at the next election, for enfranchised groups might well feel content with a situation that gave them so much power. This is not the only objection the Assamese Hindus have to group: **they dislike the Bengalis even when they are not Muslims. But it is, and has always been the main objection.** At the fight in the All-India Congress Committee in January, one

of our ministers openly avowed it, saying, "There were so many groups in Assam – hill tribes, people from the plains, Ahoms, and so on – and if they all got separate electorates, there would be no hope for the people of Assam to achieve unity in future and opting out of the group would be out of the question."

This was almost an admission of Saadulla's claim that a plebiscite in Assam would vote for grouping. I do not feel as sure as many Hindu ministers seem to be that, under a wide franchise and without separate electorates, Caste Hindu rule will last a very long time. But it will have a far bigger chance of lasting under a constitution framed by the present Assam legislature or the present Constitution Assembly than under one framed by Section C.

If it had been arranged that the Section would frame only the constitution for the Bengal cum Assam group and would accept the wishes of the Assam representatives regarding their own provincial constitution, the opposition to grouping here would have been small. It is not easy to be sure about the position now, but a convention to this effect might diminish opposition sufficiently to permit Assam to enter and cooperate in the Section if it becomes a reality. There is substance in the plea that it is unfair to Assam that its **constitution should be framed by a body in which 5 out of 6 members are Bengalis.** Bardoloi's claim that Assam should not have its constitution framed by Bengal has consequently had some appeal. But I believe that what he fears is that Assam would get a constitution framed by Muslims of Bengal and Assam, with the aid of Scheduled Caste men in Bengal. [27] (Emphasis by Subir)

Note: [1]Lord Mountbatten thanked Sir A. Clow for his letter and note in a letter of 25 April1947. R/3/1/130: f 216.

Nonetheless, soon after Lord Mountbatten began consultations with the country's key political leaders, rumours started circulating that Mountbatten was leaning toward partitioning the country. This stood in stark contrast with the Cabinet Mission Plan, which aimed to avoid the partition of India. Political leaders of all shades had been busy thrashing out the few remaining unresolved issues for the last few months. Maulana Azad feared that partition would be inevitable if a decision were taken hastily. He believed that a better solution, something in line with the scheme envisaged by the members of the Cabinet Mission, might emerge after a year or so. However, by this time, Lord Mountbatten had framed his own proposals and decided to go to London on May 18, 1947, for discussion with the British Government and to secure the approval of his suggestions.

Before Mountbatten proceeded to London, Azad implored the Viceroy not to abandon the Cabinet Mission Plan. In a subsequent discussion lasting over an hour, Azad put forward several arguments against the proposal of dividing India along Hindu-Muslim communal lines, which he believed would invite disaster for the nation. He reiterated his appeal to the Viceroy, urging him to allow some cooling-off period and resume talks with the Indian leaders before reaching the point of no return on the road to granting independence to India.

Lord Mountbatten promised Azad that he would present a complete and accurate picture before the British Cabinet. He assured Azad that he would faithfully report all he had heard and seen during the last two months and bring Azad's views on the matter to the notice of the British Cabinet. His Majesty's Government would have all these materials before making a final decision on the issue.

Mountbatten gave Azad the impression that he was not going to London with a clear-cut picture of partition, nor had he completely abandoned the Cabinet Mission Plan. However, later events proved otherwise. The way Mountbatten acted afterwards convinced Azad that Mountbatten had already made up his mind and was going to London to persuade the British Cabinet to accept his partition plan. His words were only meant to allay Azad's doubts. Mountbatten had not himself believed what he was saying.

Finally, Abul Kalam Azad confronted the Viceroy with a vital question about the large-scale Hindu-Muslim communal riots that were bound to follow if the British Government decided to partition the country based on the Viceroy's recommendation. The actual conversations, in Azad's own words, were:

> "I also asked Lord Mountbatten to consider the likely consequences of partition. Even without partition, there were riots in Calcutta, Noakhali, Bihar, Bombay, and Punjab. Hindus had attacked Muslims and Muslims had attacked Hindus. If the country was divided in such an atmosphere, there would be rivers of blood flowing in different parts of the country, and the British would be responsible for such carnage.

> Without a moment's hesitation, Lord Mountbatten replied, 'At least on this one question, I shall give you complete assurance. I shall see to it that there is no bloodshed and riot. I am a soldier, not a civilian. Once the partition is accepted in principle, I shall issue orders to ensure that there are no communal disturbances anywhere in the country. If there should be the slightest agitation, I shall not hesitate to deploy the Army and Air Force to suppress anybody who wants to create trouble.'

The whole world knows what the outcome of Lord Mountbatten's brave declaration was. When partition actually took place, rivers of blood flowed in large parts of the country. Innocent men, women, and children were massacred. The Indian Army was divided, and nothing could be done to stop the murder of innocent Hindus and Muslims." [28]

Very soon, news from London arrived that the British Cabinet had accepted Mountbatten's proposals. The Viceroy returned to Delhi on May 30th and, on June 2nd, held discussions with representatives of the Congress and the Muslim League. On June 3rd, 1947, Mountbatten announced his Partition Plan. Thus, India ultimately lost a golden opportunity to remain united and free from British colonial rule. The declaration of the country's partition on Hindu-Muslim communal lines on August 15th, 1947, resulted in the greatest man-made human catastrophe on the earth's surface. It triggered riots causing mass casualties and a colossal wave of migration. Millions of people were forced to abandon their homes, seeking refuge in what they hoped would be safer territories. In this way, after nearly a year of uncertainty, the Cabinet Mission's Plan for a solution to the communal question without partitioning India eventually collapsed.

The Muslims headed towards Pakistan, the "land of the pure," while Hindus and Sikhs moved towards what would soon become truncated India, making way for Muslims in the "land of the pure." The days of Raj came to an end amidst upheavals in which not only Hindus and Muslims but also Sikhs and Muslims slaughtered one another. At least fourteen to sixteen million men, women, and children are estimated to have eventually been displaced - travelling on foot, in bullock carts, by trains, and by steamers. According to various estimates, the death toll in post-partition tragedies ranged between 200,000 and two million. Many were killed by members of other communities in riots, while others perished on their way to safety or died from contagious diseases in hastily built makeshift refugee camps. Women were often targeted as symbols of community honour. Nearly 100,000 females, including minors, were raped or abducted in acts of vengeance. The rivers of blood that flowed in large parts of the country due to partition could have been averted had our leaders anticipated the fallout and accepted the Cabinet Mission's Plan to solve the communal question that plagued India.

In the words of Delhi-based Scottish historian William Dalrymple, who is also one of the co-founders and co-directors of the world's largest writers' festival, the annual Jaipur Literature Festival:

> "Across the Indian subcontinent, communities that had coexisted for almost a millennium attacked each other in a terrifying outbreak

of sectarian violence, with Hindus and Sikhs on one side and Muslims on the other—a mutual genocide as unexpected as it was unprecedented. In Punjab and Bengal—provinces abutting India's borders with West and East Pakistan, respectively—the carnage was especially intense, with massacres, arson, forced conversions, mass abductions, and savage sexual violence. Some seventy-five thousand women were raped, and many of them were then disfigured or dismembered." [29]

The Army with tanks and the Air Force with planes never made their appearance as promised by the soldier in Lord Mountbatten to Maulana Abul Kalam Azad. Instead, the statement of the Mountbatten Plan on June 3rd, 1947, to partition India on Hindu-Muslim communal lines only sounded the death knell for the Cabinet Mission Plan - finally shattering all hopes for the budding dream of an Independent United India that the Cabinet Mission Plan had been envisioning for the last year!

* * * * * *

Chapter 8.

The Sylhet Referendum

India missed a golden opportunity to achieve independence without partition by not accepting the Cabinet Mission's Plan. Assam's determined opposition to being grouped with Bengal as proposed in the Cabinet Mission Plan allowed the Muslim League to backtrack on its previous acceptance of the Plan. Consequently, the Cabinet Mission Plan collapsed, and India failed to free itself from British rule without partition. This astonishing turn of events was enabled by the omissions and commissions of our political leaders, as discussed in the preceding chapter.

Nevertheless, the common people of Assam believe that the concerted opposition by the Assam Valley Congress to being grouped with Bengal "saved" Assam from seceding from India and "prevented" the province from being included in Pakistan. However, the truth is that by agreeing to be grouped with Bengal, as the Cabinet Mission Plan had intended, the formation of Pakistan itself could have been prevented. This was essentially the aim of the plan, contrary to what the innocent people in Assam and its neighboring states believed.

To provide clarity and dispel any confusion or misinformation on the matter, **the original text** of the "Statement by the Cabinet Delegation and His Excellency the Viceroy" was reproduced at the beginning of the previous chapter. Additionally, the relevant events between the announcement of the Plan in May 1946 and its failure by May 1947 were briefly narrated there. The Cabinet Mission Plan met its demise when Viceroy Mountbatten announced his Partition Plan on 3rd June 1947.

It was the first time that the Cabinet Mission Plan was discarded, and the partition of British India was officially accepted. The Congress Socialist Party deprecated the acceptance of the Mountbatten Plan as an act of surrender. Readers might find it interesting if a casual reference is made to Lady Mountbatten's significant role in persuading Congress leaders to agree to her husband's plan. In the words of renowned historian Dr. Ishwari Prasad, "By remarkable adaptability of character and pleasing manners, she won the hearts of all the greatest adversaries of the land..." British Prime Minister Clement Attlee also praised the last Vicereine of India, Edwina's role in his

D.O. letter to Mountbatten dated 17th July 1947, *"I know too well that it is well recognized that Edwina has played a great part in creating the new atmosphere. It was a great help having Pug here during this critical fortnight."* [1]

In the prelude to the announcement of the partition plan, there was a reference that His Majesty's Government had hoped for the cooperation of the two major political parties in working out the Cabinet Mission Plan of 16th May 1946, but these hopes remained unfulfilled. It was further stated that the Legislative Assemblies of Bengal and Punjab (excluding the European members) were to meet in two parts, one representing the Muslim-majority districts and the other representing the rest of the provinces. The Muslim-majority districts were specified in the statement. Each part was to decide by a simple majority whether the province was to be partitioned or not. If either party favoured partition, it was to be effected accordingly. In such an event, each part of the Assembly needed to determine whether it would like to join the Constituent Assembly already established or a new Constituent Assembly separately established and composed of representatives of those areas that decided not to participate in the existing Assembly.

The fate of the Muslim-majority district of Sylhet in Assam, a Hindu-majority province of India, was to be decided by a referendum on whether the district would like to remain a part of Assam (in India) or join East Bengal, which would become part of Pakistan **if it was decided that Bengal should be partitioned.** [2] (Emphasis by Subir) On that understanding, the 'partition' of India and the proposal for a 'referendum' on the Sylhet District, if necessary, were 'agreed' by our leaders.

The relevant portion regarding the Sylhet referendum enumerated in the British Government Statement (Mountbatten Plan) of 3rd June 1947 is quoted below:

"45

Statement of 3 June 1947 (as published)[1]

Cmd 7136

INDIAN POLICY

INTRODUCTION

....

....
....

ASSAM

13. "Though Assam is predominantly a non-Muslim province, the district of Sylhet, which is contiguous to Bengal, is predominantly Muslim. There has been **a demand** that, in the event of the partition of Bengal, Sylhet should be amalgamated with the Muslim part of Bengal. Accordingly, **if it is decided that Bengal should be partitioned, a referendum will be held in Sylhet**, under the aegis of the Governor-General and **in consultation with the Assam Provincial Government, to decide whether the district of Sylhet should continue to form part of Assam Province or should be amalgamated with the New Province of East Bengal** if that province agrees. If the Referendum results in favour of amalgamation with East Bengal, a Boundary Commission with terms similar to those for the Punjab and Bengal will be set up to demarcate areas of Sylhet district and contiguous Muslim-majority areas of adjoining districts, which will then be transferred to Eastern Bengal. The rest of the Assam province will, in any case, continue to participate in the proceedings of the existing Constituent Assembly."
.... [3] (Emphasis by Subir)

Note: [1]This statement was made by Mr Atlee in the House of Commons and by Earl of Listowel in the House of Lords at 3.30 pm (Double British Summer Time) and was published in India at the same time.

Furthermore, a personal message from the British Prime Minister Clement Richard Attlee to the people of India, broadcasted on 3rd June 1947, is also reproduced below. This message outlines the backdrop against which the British Government initiated the plan to divide the "great sub-continent," contrasting it with the Cabinet Mission's Plan, which they still believed offered the best basis for solving the Indian problem:

"57

Text of Broadcast by Mr Attlee on 3 June 1947 at 9 pm D.B.S T.[1]

R/30/1/11 : ff 8-9

ANNOUNCER: This afternoon, the Viceroy broadcast a personal message to the people of India. Before broadcasting a recording of the Viceroy's message[2], here is an introduction to it, recorded today by the Prime Minister:

PRIME MINISTER: India, after many centuries of internal disunion, was united under British rule. It has been a prime objective of British policy to maintain the unity that has long preserved peace in that great sub-continent. It has been our hope that this unity might continue when India attained full self-government, which has been, for many years, the goal of British policy in India.

The Cabinet Mission's Plan[3], which we still believe offers the best basis for solving the Indian problem, was designed to this end. But, as Indian leaders have finally failed to agree on a plan for a united India, partition becomes the inevitable alternative, and we will, for our part, give the Indians all help and advice in carrying out this most difficult operation. The two-fold purpose of the plan now put forward is to make possible the maximum degree of harmony and cooperation between the Indian political parties, in order that the partition of India, if decided upon, may involve as little loss and suffering as possible, and, secondly, to enable the British Government to hand over its responsibilities in an orderly and constitutional manner at the earliest opportunity.

It will, I am sure, be obvious to you all – Indian and British alike – that the decision having been made to hand over power, the sooner the new governments can be set up to take over the great responsibilities they are assuming, the better. In order to accomplish this, the plan provides for the handing over of power this year to one or two governments of British India, each having dominion status.

I would make an earnest appeal to everyone to give calm and dispassionate consideration to these proposals. It is, of course, easy to criticize them, but weeks of devoted work by the Viceroy failed to find any alternative that is practicable. They have emerged from the hard facts of the situation in India; they are the result of long discussions by the Viceroy with the Indian political leaders, who will later be broadcasting the plan. And in putting them forward, the Viceroy has the full support of the British Government. The Indians will, I believe, recognize that they are put forward solely in the interests of the Indian people. They may be assured that whatever course may be chosen by India, Great Britain and the British people will strive to maintain the closest and friendliest relations with the Indian people, with whom there has been so long and fruitful an association.

Note: [1]The broadcast went out at 9 pm (Double British Summer Time) on the B,B.C.'s Home Service and at 10 pm (D.B.S T.) on the light programme.
[2]No. 44 (the recording began with the second para)
[3]Vol. VII, No. 303.
[4]No. 45." [4]

According to Viceroy's Personal Reports (Report No. 10) dated 28th June 1947:

"On June 20, the members of the Bengal Legislative Assembly met and decided on the partition of Bengal. At the preliminary joint meeting, it was decided by 126 votes to 90 that the Province, if it remained united, should join a new Constituent Assembly (i.e., Pakistan). At a separate meeting of the members of the West Bengal Legislative Assembly on the same day, it was decided by 58 votes to 21 that the Province should be partitioned and by the same majority that West Bengal should join the existing Constituent Assembly should partition eventuate. It was also decided, by 105 votes to 34 that in the events for partition, East Bengal would agree to amalgamation with Sylhet." [5]

Thus, 20th June 1947 was a sad day for the nationalist Bengalis because the prevailing circumstances compelled them to bury their dream of a United Bengal. Under the Mountbatten Plan, the house proceedings on 20th June resulted in the decision to partition Bengal. It set the stage for (a) the creation of West Bengal as a province of India, (b) East Bengal as a province of Pakistan, and (c) a referendum in the Sylhet district of Assam province to decide whether the district should continue to form part of Assam or be amalgamated with the new province of East Bengal in prospective Pakistan.

In the preface of his book "Bengal: The Unmaking of a Nation 1905-1971," Nitish Kumar Sengupta, academician, administrator, politician, and author, wrote:

"There is no parallel in history to the paradox that while in 1905 a majority of the people of Bengal rejected the British-directed partition of their land and fought against it, only four decades later, in 1947, the same majority asked for a partition of Bengal between the Muslim majority and Hindu majority areas. The explanation lies in the nearly six decades of interaction between the Hindus and the Muslims of Bengal, in the course of which the two communities, after coming close to each other on several occasions, eventually drifted apart and asked for partition." [6]

However, strictly speaking, the Bengalis were not given a clear-cut choice then. They were presented with a **'Devil's Choice'** - either remain in India or opt for Pakistan! The partition of Bengal became inevitable when the Bengali Muslims opted for Pakistan and the Bengali Hindus for India.

Earlier, on 27th April 1947, Bengal Premier H. S. Suhrawardy addressed a press conference in New Delhi in which he put forward a plan for an independent, sovereign, undivided Bengal. Suhrawardy said, "I promise that the future will be unlike the present. Bengal's wealth, peace, and happiness will benefit a great nation. If the Hindus can forget the past and accept the proposal, I promise to fulfil their hopes and aspirations to the full." He also stated that an independent Bengal would have its own constitution and a Legislative Assembly that would make decisions for the country. "We Bengalis have a common mother tongue and common economic interests," he said.

Suhrawardy knew that the partition of Bengal would mean economic disaster for both East and West Bengal since all jute mills, industrial plants, etc., were established in the western part. In contrast, the raw materials and other inputs came mainly from the eastern part of the state, making Bengal indivisible given its economic integrity and mutual dependence. So, to avoid the partition of Bengal that started doing the rounds, he conceived a plan to keep Bengalis united and independent both from India and Pakistan. Suhrawardy had contemplated that the proposed, undivided, independent Bengal would include the districts of Manbhum, Birbhum, and Purnea from Bihar and the Surma Valley of Assam, with the result that there would not be a substantial difference in the numerical strength of the Hindus and the Muslims.

People like Sarat Chandra Bose (elder brother of Subhas Chandra Bose), Kiran Shankar Roy (a disciple of C. R. Das and veteran Congress leader), et al., who were opposed to the Partition of Bengal, supported Suhrawardy's plan. They argued for a united Bengal, independent from India and Pakistan. Netaji Subhas Chandra Bose also was known to have favoured Hindu-Muslim unity and was against the concept of the two-nation theory. It resonated well with many Bengali Muslims. Abul Hashim, the secretary of the Bengal Provincial Muslim League, along with Suhrawardy, pointed out the perils for Bengali Muslims joining Pakistan: "In an Akhand (undivided) Pakistan, they would be under the domination of West Pakistanis, and Urdu would be the state language. They could not expect a better position than becoming peons under the Urdu-speaking judges and magistrate".

Jinnah also agreed with Suhrawardy that the survival of East Bengal by itself was not economically viable since almost all coal mines, minerals, factories, and jute processing mills were in West Bengal.

Sarat Chandra Bose, along with Suhrawardy and Hashim, also approached Gandhi on several occasions with a proposal for an undivided Bengal. Gandhi did lend half-hearted support but advised them to gain the trust of the Hindus first.

On 24th May 1947, the proposal was made public. According to the plan, independent Bengal would decide its relations with the rest of India; there would be joint electorates and adult franchises with reservation of seats for Hindus and Muslims based on their population; an intra-communal ministry in which Hindus and Muslims would have an equal share; Hindus and Muslims would have equal representation in all services including military and police. There would be a 30-member constituent assembly to draft the future constitution of Bengal. The plan also received the support of the British. It carried a better prospect of protecting their commercial interests in Calcutta. On 8th May 1947, when Mountbatten tabled the Partition plan, he made an exception for Bengal, which he argued would be allowed to remain independent if it chose. The British Prime Minister Clement Atlee, too, hoped that Bengal would decide to remain united.

The most vehement opposition to a United Bengal came from Hindu Mahasabha, particularly its leader, Syama Prasad Mukherjee, who was fiercest in his opposition to the United Bengal scheme. The Congress leadership was also against the United Bengal plan. At a meeting on 23rd May, when Mountbatten raised Suhrawardy's plan, Nehru stated in no uncertain terms that Congress would accept a United Bengal only if it decided to stay inside the Indian Union. [7] According to Mountbatten, on Nehru's request, the choice of independence in the case of Bengal and other provinces was removed to avoid 'Balkanisation'. [8] Pakistani-American historian Ayesha Jalal wrote in her book that *although Mountbatten had persuaded London to make an exception for Bengal and allow it to remain an independent dominion, he quickly dropped the plan once Nehru had rejected the proposition out of hand.* [9]

In an article titled "Partition Truths," the renowned scholar A. G. Noorani averred, "The partition of India was a consequence of calculations gone wrong, on the part of both the Congress and the Muslim League." Talking about the H.S. Suhrawardy-Sarat Bose Pact for a United Bengal, independent of both India and Pakistan, Noorani wrote:

> "(Sarat) Bose forwarded to Gandhi as 'a tentative agreement' under a covering letter dated May 23.

Gandhi replied on May 25: 'There is nothing in the draft stipulating that nothing will be done by a mere majority. Every act of Government must carry with it *the cooperation of at least two-thirds of the Hindu members in the executive and the Legislature.*'

Let alone legislation, every executive action, such as a grant of a license, would have been subject to a communal veto. Gandhi would have rejected out of hand any suggestion of such a veto to Muslims in a united India. Rightly so. It is palpably wrong and destructive.

Jinnah accepted the United Bengal idea in a talk with Mountbatten on April 26 ("I should be delighted"). Nehru and Vallabhbhai Patel joined Gandhi in rejecting it. They agreed with the Hindu Mahasabha leader Shyama Prasad Mookerjee in demanding the partition of Bengal *even if India remained united.*

Noorani's article appeared in Frontline magazine, published by The Hindu Group of publications, on April 16, 2014.

Interestingly, "Freedom at Midnight"-famed author duo Dominique Lapierre and Larry Collins interviewed Lord Louis Mountbatten in the years 1971, 1972, and 1973 in England in the course of some twenty work sessions for the book. Among others, the Q&A related to the issue of the proposed United Bengal also figured in their subsequent book "Mountbatten and the Partition of India: March 22 August 15, 1947." This Q & A sequence is reproduced below:

"Q: You were strongly in favour of a united Bengal. Did you believe that partition, if it had to come, would be best not in two but three parts?

A: Yes, this would have been a solution and would indeed be the Bangladesh solution we now have."

You see, what went wrong was that I realized India was not going to let Calcutta go. Now, funnily enough, the Governor of Bengal, dear old Fred Burrows, would have backed me to the hilt. I'd told him it was a good idea because they would then come closer together. I think India disagreed over the fact that it would weaken the centre. You'd have Pakistan, and they felt— mind you, they were idiotic because Pakistan then would only be East Pakistan. I liked the idea very much. If you ask me why it went wrong, you'll have to check the records. I'm sure the Congress Party wanted it thrown out. I still think, in many ways, it was a better idea. I can see why they wouldn't accept it, but it was worth trying. **All the Bengalis were mad keen on it.** I was pursuing every feasible alternative I could think of. I was terribly keen not to have fragmentation. Bengal was 60 million — as big as the British Isles. All the other places were a few odd million. They were not a potentially viable nation as Bengal was. It would have stayed in the British Commonwealth. It had a lot to recommend. But I saw the dangers, and I wasn't surprised when Congress said, "No". But I couldn't turn them down. In retrospect, in view of Bangladesh, it's interesting how right I was to try and keep them together.

Q: Would it be reasonable to say Congress exercised a veto over the creation of an independent Bengal?

A: Yes, I think it would be fair. [10] (Emphasis by Subir)

Note: [1] Q&A - Questions by the authors (Dominique Lapierre and Larry Collins) and Mountbatten's Answers.

When the plan for a United Independent Bengal ran into the sand, joining the upcoming homeland for Muslims, Pakistan appealed more to Bengali Muslims than the idea of continuing in India, dominated by the Hindu-dominated Congress. Accordingly, the Bengal Legislative Assembly voted against joining the existing Constituent Assembly (i.e., India), paving the way for the partition of Bengal. So, as per the above statement of 3rd June 1947, a referendum on Assam's Sylhet district became inevitable to decide whether it should continue to form part of Assam Province or be amalgamated with the New Province of East Bengal (in Pakistan).

It's vital to note that Mountbatten's Partition Plan of India was announced on 3rd June 1947 - only 71 days before India was partitioned on 15th August 1947. More importantly, the Bengal Legislative Assembly had voted on 20th June 1947, which finally determined that a referendum would decide Sylhet district's fate. The referendum took place on 6th and 7th July 1947. In other words, the people did not even get 16 days of official notice of the actual dates of the Sylhet referendum.

"Mistake after mistake," wrote British journalist, historian, biographer, and novelist Leonard Mosley in the concluding chapter of his book, "The Last Days of the British Raj." Then Mosley continued - Wavell, whose plan would at least have kept India intact and united, was dismissed out of hand. In any event, the Cabinet Mission Plan would hold India together, but it was discarded without giving much thought to its wider ramifications. Gandhi changed his mind within a few days on the Plan, which earlier he thought 'contained the seed to convert this land of sorrow into one without sorrow and suffering.' Jinnah's demand for a separate homeland for Muslims was accepted, but no attempt was made to prepare for the fallout! The Labour Government in England was prepared to give independence to the 'United India' by June 1948; then, how was it decided to promise independence to 'divided India' ten months earlier? The partition entailed an international boundary for the newly created Pakistan to be drawn; the Defence Forces, the Police, the Bureaucracy, and hundreds of other important things to be sorted out; and, most importantly, the rehabilitation of millions of people who would be displaced as a result of the partition to be chalked out. All these extra tasks required additional time, yet Mountbatten inexplicably postponed the partition date! Such blunders were avoidable but happened, and not even one person was held accountable, and not even one admitted having made a mistake. And, not one person would answer!

Mosley then added:

> "There are many who believe that they were the victims of a salesman's trick which won them freedom but cost them the unity of the country. With a little patience and a little pragmatism, all the tragedies could have been avoided. Pakistan was the one-man achievement of Mohammed Ali Jinnah, and he died within a year of its foundation. A little patience and a refusal to be rushed would have saved the sub-continent from the devastation the people had to witness. It was Gandhi's counsel and, of course, from the Indian point of view, it was right. [11]

Immediately after his arrival on 24th March, Lord Mountbatten started discussions with political leaders. Having distinguished himself as the longest-serving professional head of the British Armed Forces in his time and with years of armed forces training behind him, Mountbatten stuck to his briefs with military precision and urgency. The first thing he did was to advance the date from June 1948 to August 1947 for Britain to extricate itself from the mess it had created in India. Obviously, this rush was to avoid a possible 'civil war' in India, feared by Mountbatten, and to salvage British reputation as communal conflicts worsened daily across India. He also sought to take credit for completing the job entrusted to him well in time, as was the culture among top bureaucrats in the Colonial period. Accordingly, Mountbatten did not display any humane considerations. When it became clear that India's partition was unavoidable, he did not care for the likely inconvenience of the people or show any concern for their inevitable suffering. Nor did Mountbatten exhibit pragmatism in selecting the dates 6th and 7th of July for Sylhet's referendum when monsoon's fury was expected to be at its peak, and ease of peoples' movement from place to place was likely to be at its lowest in Sylhet district - known for its devastating floods every year. To the ex-Naval Officer, adhering to the target date and executing the assigned task were the only items on the agenda. He did not even consider whether an up-to-date and reasonably error-free list of eligible voters was available, or whether, in the monsoon season, voters would be able to reach the polling stations, primarily located in the flood-prone low-lying areas of Sylhet district. He also disregarded whether the proper infrastructure to conduct voting at such short notice was in place, whether the required number of impartial security personnel could be arranged within such short notice, and so on. These aspects were inconsequential and did not matter to the last Viceroy of India, Mountbatten.

According to author and Vice-Chancellor Bidyut Chakrabarty, the following three important reasons appeared to have governed Mountbatten's insistence on an earlier date:

i) to take credit for himself and thus expose the failure of the Cabinet Mission plan in understanding reality in a proper perspective;

ii) to earn the goodwill of the Congress leaders, particularly Nehru and Patel; and,

iii) an early transfer of power would ensure India's participation in the Commonwealth, as Congress had already committed. [12]

For the Bengalis in Sylhet District, it was indeed a bolt from the blue! The announcement that a referendum would decide Sylhet's fate was a nasty surprise. The 3rd of June 1947 was the inauspicious date when Lord Mountbatten first hinted at the referendum in Sylhet! On the 20th of June 1947, it became inevitable that the people of Sylhet must decide on the 6th and 7th of July 1947 whether to remain in India or become a part of Pakistan. Most of the electorate were ignorant and illiterate. They had never heard the word 'referendum' before, let alone knew its meaning. Yet, the alien British rulers in India expected the people of Sylhet to exercise their irrevocable choice on very short notice and to decide on something that carried a vital bearing not only on their entire life but also on their progenies. The people did not even get a fortnight to take such a momentous decision. Their leaders did not get enough time to reach the people and explain the referendum's meaning, importance, and implications. During those days, very few people had access to the radio news bulletin; television did not even reach India. Newspapers were the only reliable source of information that used to take time to reach the readers and were relatively short in supply. It used to take more than a week on average for the news to reach the nook and corner of the Sylhet district. But who cared? The opposite views of the key political leaders in Assam on the announcement of the referendum were noteworthy. Most of them welcomed the British Government's announcement of the 3rd of June 1947 and were quite satisfied. They seemed elated at the prospect of expelling Sylhet from Assam through the referendum on communal considerations. The referendum proposal was considered more justifiable and democratic than the grouping plan of the 16th of May 1947. Apparently, the thought that India might lose a vital portion of its territory in Assam did not trouble their minds! In this context, the report dated the 5th of June 1947, of Assam Governor Sir A. Hydari to Mountbatten reproduced below from page 154 of THE TRANSFER OF POWER 1942 – 7, Volume XI, by Nicholas Mansergh (Editor-in-Chief) and Penderel Moon (Editor), is self-explanatory:

"86

Sir A. Hydari (Assam) to Rear-Admiral Viscount Mountbatten of Burma (Extract)

Mouintbatten Papers. Letters to and from the Governor of Assam.

GOVERNMENT HOUSE, SHILLONG, 5 June 1947

2. I am very sorry that what in recent months seemed inevitable, namely the rejection of the Cabinet Mission Plan, has in fact happened, and the unity of India has at least for some time been broken; but my Ministers while regretting in principle the partition of India, were relieved at the rejection of the Cabinet Mission Plan with the possibility of Assam having to join a Group with Bengal. They, both Hindu and Muslim (these belonging to the Jamait-ul-Ulema), were pleased with the Announcement and Assam's share in it. Mookherjee, B. K. Das, Abdul Rashid, and Abdul Matlib Majumdar, who all belong to the Surma Valley, are confident that Sylhet will elect to remain with the rest of Assam. Medhi and others do not mind if Sylhet goes to Eastern Bengal; in fact, I suspect that Medhi would be quite pleased if it did. I put the chance at fifty-fifty."

Nevertheless, after the Bengal Legislative Assembly voted on the 20th of June 1947, which finally determined that a referendum would decide Sylhet district's fate on the 6th and 7th of July 1947, Assam Governor Sir Muhammad Saleh Akbar Hydari in his fortnightly report dated the 23rd of June 1947 to the Viceroy Lord Mountbatten, among other things, wrote:

"It is unfortunate that circumstances have compelled the holding of the referendum at a time when a large part of the district of Sylhet is flooded, and a substantial percentage of polling stations will be in the flooded areas. Voters will have to find their way to them as best they can; the only help we can give them is not to indent upon local transport for our own needs."

The list of eligible voters in the referendum could be handed over to the political parties as late as the 26th of June 1947, only 11 days before the date of actual polling. Assam Governor's telegram dated the 5th of July 1947 to the Viceroy bears its testimony. However, the Viceroy soon realized the dire impact of the unholy rush. The belated realization of the undue haste had prompted him to propose the postponement of voting by a possible week or ten days. It was too late then. Mountbatten's telegram dated the 28th of June 1947 to the Governor of Assam bore its proof. In response to Mountbatten's suggestion of the postponement, the Assam Governor had to reply to the Viceroy on the 30th of June telegraphically:

"In deference to your call for utmost speed, arrangements both civil & military have been pushed through to near completion and are now too far advanced to permit postponement." [13]

Thus, the referendum was allowed to take place on the scheduled dates of 6th and 7th July 1947. As expected, what had happened in reality in the name of the referendum could be best termed an ALL-TIME HISTORICAL FARCE - had it not resulted in shocking pain, awful misery, and immense distress to millions of Bengalis. It resulted in a colossal loss to the Sylhetis in the form of their ancestral lands, personal assets, and human lives! To put things in perspective and recognize the real-life plights of the Sylhetis, a quick overview of the history of Sylhet and a recapitulation of its 'in and out' movements between Bengal and Assam in British India would be appropriate.

Ancient Tantric text Shaktisangam Tantra Joginitantra refers to Sylhet as Silhatta. Brihannali Tantra, Devipurana refers to Srihatta as one of the Tantric shakthipeeths. Silhatta or Srihatta evolved from 'Shreehasth' - 'Sree' means 'beauty', and 'hasta' or 'hatta' came from 'hand'. It is also believed that this land was called 'Silhatta' due to the abundance of stone, especially limestone. Over the years, 'Silhatta' evolved into Sylhet. Its people became known as the Sylhetis. Their language, Sylheti, forms the diglossic vernacular spoken by most of the natives of Sylhet, with standard Bengali forming the formal and written language. The patron deity of Srihatta was termed Hattavasini – the goddess who resides in the prosperous marketplace. The advantageous location of the Sylhet region on the banks of the well-navigable Surma-Barak rivers facilitated Sylhet to become an expanded commercial centre from the ancient period.

The history of the Sylhet region begins with the existence of expanded commercial centres that are now the present-day Sylhet City area. Sylhet has a history of conquests and heritage from different types of cultures. In the ancient period, Sylhet was ruled by the Buddhist and Hindu kingdoms of Harikela and Kamarupa before passing to the control of the Sena and Deva dynasties in the early medieval period. After these two Hindu principalities fell, the region became home to many more independent petty kingdoms such as Jaintia, Gour, Laur, and later Taraf, Pratapgarh, Jagannathpur, Chandrapur, and Ita. The Gour Kingdom, established in the 7th century, took part in many battles with its neighbouring states. Eventually, it split into Gour (Sylhet) and Brahmachal (South Sylhet/modern-day Moulvibazar). In 640, the Raja of Tripura Dharma Fa planned a ceremony and invited five Brahmans from Etawah, Mithila, and Kannauj. To compensate for their long journey, the Raja granted them land in a place which came to be known as Panchakhanda (meaning five parts) in Western Sylhet.

The last chieftain to reign in Sylhet was Govinda of Gaur. He was defeated in 1303 by Hazrat Shah Jala Yamani and his 360 Sufi disciples. It marked the beginning of Islamic influence in Sylhet. Shortly after that, Sylhet became a centre of Islam in Bengal. Sylhet was often referred to as Jalalabad during the era of Muslim rule. It was then successively ruled by the Muslim sultanates of Delhi and the Bengal Sultanates before collapsing into Muslim petty kingdoms, mostly ruled by Afghan chieftains, after the fall of the Karrani dynasty in 1576. Described as Bengal's Wild East, the Mughals struggled to defeat the chieftains of Sylhet. After the defeat of Khwaja Usman, their most formidable opponent, the area finally came under Mughal rule in 1612. Sylhet emerged as the Mughals' most significant imperial outpost in the east, and its importance remained throughout the seventeenth century. Among other things like brisk business activities in the area, natural resources, amply skilled labourers, and lascars, the Mughals were primarily attracted to Sylhet for its abundant limestone. Sylhet, especially its Laur regions, was the only known source of limestone at that time. In 1765, Sylhet came under British administration and became a part of the Bengal Presidency that later controlled the Assam division of British India.

When Assam, Sylhet, Cachar, and Goalpara of the Bengal Presidency were carved out, merged together, and transformed into a Chief Commissioner's Province in 1874, Sylhet became a district of the metamorphosed Assam province. Floods perennially ravaged the district, but the land being fertile, there was enough rice production. Until the end of the eighteenth century, the Brahmaputra Valley and Sylhet had one common factor: both tracts were heavily forested where various wild animals, including one-horned rhinos, roamed. Sylhet exported large quantities of paddy, rice, oilseed, limestone, bamboo, dried fish, mattresses, oranges, potatoes, etc., and imported cotton, salt, tobacco, sugar, and mustard oil. In the greater part of the nineteenth century, exports exceeded imports until the world wars. Additionally, when tea became the major export produce of the Assam province in the mid-nineteenth century, its Sylhet and Cachar districts, together known as Surma Valley, also became recognized as tea-growing areas.

Sylhet today is regarded as Bangladesh's spiritual and cultural centre and is often termed the agricultural capital of Bangladesh. The natural resource base of the Sylhet region is considered very strong for the country. The oil/gas reserves and prospecting and production from the Sylhet region are overwhelming. Production data indicate that more than 65% of gas is produced in this region. Most of the gas fields in this region produce a huge quantity of liquid hydrocarbons, including condensate, motor spirit, diesel, and kerosene. Natural oil/gas has been contributing a significant amount of revenue to the national exchequer and meeting the energy crisis of Bangladesh. [14] [15] [16] [17]

On the other hand, Assam was ruled by the British as an extension of Bengal following the annexation of the Ahom kingdom to India in 1826. Thus, Assam and Sylhet were part and parcel of the Bengal Presidency for forty-eight long years. "According to the official correspondence of the East India Company, the move was for administrative convenience and economic benefit, **as Assam alone did not produce enough to sustain itself <u>unless supported by its thickly populated Sylheti-speaking neighbourhood.</u>**" [18] For thirty long years, Sylhet remained with the Assam province - cut off from the more meaningful life of Bengal. Then in 1905, Sylhet, along with greater Assam, was amalgamated into Eastern Bengal to form "Eastern Bengal and Assam" under a Lt. Governor. Again in 1912, Sylhet, along with greater Assam, was reverted to a Chief Commissioner's province when the 'Partition of Bengal' was annulled under public pressure. Sylhet and Assam remained together in the same province for another thirty-five years. Until now, Sylhet and the Sylhetis remained united in India. However, in 1947, India lost the bulk of Sylhet territory to Pakistan and became a part of East Bengal, but a tiny part remained in Assam (India). (Emphasis by Subir)

After that, in 1971, East Pakistan, including Sylhet, gained independence from the Pakistani rulers, forming a new country named Bangladesh. Consequently, following Sylhet's detachment by the British from its parent region Bengal in 1874, the Sylhetis remained Indian citizens, and their homeland Sylhet remained undivided. In 1947, the majority of Sylhetis became Pakistani citizens, while a few fortunate ones remained Indian citizens but were disconnected from their native soil. With Bangladesh breaking away from Pakistan in 1971, Pakistani Sylhetis became Bangladeshis. Thus, the fate of the Sylheti Bengalis, akin to their native land, Sylhet, continued to fluctuate like a political football, subjected to periodic upheavals.

From the outset, after Sylhet's separation from Bengal and its amalgamation with Assam, neither Bengalis nor Assamese preferred cohabitation. Nevertheless, both communities were compelled to coexist as 'unwilling partners,' often advocating for separation. Bengalis aspired to return to Bengal, their original homeland, while many Assamese leaders sought to expel the Bengali population from 'their territory.' As previously discussed, the British administration incorporated Bengali-dominated areas of the Cachar and Goalpara districts into 'Assam proper' (predominantly the Ahom Kingdom) alongside numerous tribal territories. Consequently, a divide emerged between Assamese and Bengali communities, fostered by colonial rulers adhering to their age-old policy of "divide et impera." This discord disrupted the historical tradition of peaceful coexistence between Assamese and Bengali communities. However, geographical proximity, mutual convenience, and peripheral concerns led many Bengalis in Goalpara District to align with the Assamese.

This period marked the onset of the so-called "valley rivalry." The growing friction between the two valleys stemmed largely from limited day-to-day interactions between their inhabitants. Topographical barriers and geographical distance hindered the development of necessary social bonds, impeding assimilation between the two communities. Exploiting this natural division, the British administration pitted Assamese-speaking inhabitants of the Brahmaputra valley against Bengali-speaking residents of the Surma valley, exacerbating tensions to facilitate administrative control. This rivalry significantly influenced Assam's political landscape, particularly in Sylhet's referendum, resulting in the cession of a portion of Indian territory, the Sylhet District, from the Assam province. The resultant wound remains unhealed, with the Bengalis of Sylheti origin continuing to suffer.

Note: ¹The "valley rivalry" stood for the jealousy between the Assamese-speaking population of Assam proper, i.e. the Brahmaputra valley and the Surma valley Bengalis, i.e., Cachar district and Sylhet district collectively.

In their narrative "Assam in the Days of Bhasani and League Politics," co-author Dr. Bimal J. Dev and Dr. Dilip K. Lahiri shed light on a critical perspective concerning the views held by some Assamese leaders regarding Sylhet's inclusion within the Assam province. They write:

"Significantly, the presence of 18 lahks (or 1.8 million) tea-garden labourers in Assam was not objected to, as they did not pose any challenge to the indigenous population from a cultural standpoint. It is noteworthy that the Assam Congress leadership did not oppose the immediate transfer of Sylhet – culturally and linguistically distinct from the Brahmaputra Valley – to Bengal. Indeed, the issue of Sylhet's separation was a major focus of the Congress leadership. Assamese Hindus demanded the transfer primarily on the following grounds:

- A. Provincial autonomy and responsible government, along with administrative efficiency, can only be achieved with a homogeneous unit of government. With Sylhet included in Assam, genuine self-government would not be feasible.
- B. The interests of Sylhet – politically, socially, and financially – diverged significantly from those of the rest of the province.
- C. Financially, Sylhet was consistently in deficit. A reconstituted Assam, following the separation of Sylhet, would be on a more stable financial footing and enjoy improved administrative capabilities.
- D. The system of land tenure and civil court administration differed between Sylhet and the rest of Assam.
- E. The transfer of Sylhet would eliminate the disruptive influence of terrorist violence, which was foreign to the traditions of the people of Assam. Consequently, the Assam Criminal Law Amendment Act would become unnecessary. [19]

With such a ludicrous proposition in 'A' above, the concerned leaders of the Assam Congress wanted people to believe that simply by separating the Sylhet district, they could achieve "real self-government" in Assam. However, this notion seemed far-fetched, considering that the province was home to over two hundred ethnic groups, comprising both plains and hills people with diverse cultures and ways of life, and speaking an equal number of dialects.

The contention in point 'C' above, that "financially, Sylhet was a permanent deficit district," was evidently untrue. If accepted at face value, it implied severe discrimination and exploitation of Sylhet by the Assam administration since the amalgamation of Bengal's Sylhet district and the Assam Province in 1874. The reason behind this assertion is that, at that time:

a) Sylhet district's **gross revenue was the third highest among all the districts in Assam**, as depicted in a tabular format in Chapter 3, "Emergence of Assam."
b) According to the official correspondence of the East India Company, the incorporation of Sylhet into colonial Assam was for administrative convenience and economic benefit. Anindita Dasgupta, Associate Professor of History and Deputy Dean at the School of Liberal Arts and Sciences, Taylor's University, Malaysia, noted that **Assam alone "did not produce revenue enough to sustain itself" unless supported by its densely populated Sylheti-speaking neighbourhood.** [20]
c) Initially, Sylhet was not included in the Assam province. However, within six months, the colonial administration realized the necessity to redraw the map of Assam. **To ensure its financial viability** and in response to demands from professional groups, they decided in September 1874 **to annex the Bengali-speaking and populous district of Sylhet.** Dhaka University Professor Ashfaque Hossain, PhD, one of the leading historians of South Asia, documented this in a journal article published by Cambridge University Press. [21]

The phrase "the contaminating influence of terrorist violence" in point 'E' above obviously refers to the Freedom Fighters of Bengal, who took up arms against British occupation during India's freedom movement. The terms "terrorist" and "contaminating influence" used by the concerned Assam Congress leadership thus expose their standpoint on India's freedom fighters!

Interestingly, Assamese Hindus, Bengali Hindus, and Bengali Muslims—the three dominant groups in Assam—have reversed their positions from time to time on the question of Sylhet's continuance in Assam versus its return to Bengal. This might seem perplexing at first glance, especially to those unaware of the changing ground realities of Assam during those days. However, these apparent flip-flops had their logic.

Many Congress leaders of the Brahmaputra Valley were initially against letting Sylhet remain in Assam. However, there was a time when they feared that Assam minus Sylhet might diminish the province's then-current status with a Governor heading it. Additionally, Sylhet's separation might provoke a similar demand in Bengali-majority Cachar and Goalpara for a merger with Bengal. In fact, Raja Prabhatchandra Barua, one of the founders of the Assam Association, and other Zamindars of Goalpara had already raised such demands in the latter part of the 1910s. [22] So, there was a period when Assamese leaders preferred the Sylhet District to remain in Assam.

However, both Bengali Muslims and Bengali Hindus initially favoured Sylhet returning to Bengal. They even fought together to achieve that goal. Yet, from the early twentieth century, the preference of Bengali Muslims began to reverse. Their new stance was against the separation of the Sylhet District from Assam. Md. Saadulla, the Assamese Muslim leader who by then had become quite popular among Assam's Bengali Muslims, explained the logic in 1926: "As long as Sylhet remained in Assam, Muslims, who constituted one-third of the provincial population, would remain a respectable minority and hold the balance of Assam's electoral politics. But with the Muslim-majority district of Sylhet gone to Bengal, they would lose that position in Assam forever. On the other hand, the change would enhance the proportion of Muslims in Bengal's population, not even 1 per cent." He thus made a case for an undivided Assam in the larger political interests of Muslims in India. [23]

Conversely, the Bengali Hindus of Sylhet District always desired to return to their origin in Bengal. They continued their relentless efforts in that direction until the announcement of the Sylhet referendum in June 1947. The referendum declaration forced the Bengali Hindus of Sylhet to make a complete turnaround. Its logic was also straightforward but misunderstood by many prominent authors. The "Bengal" that the 'Sylheti' Hindus dreamed of returning to all along was in Hindu-majority India, their own country. However, the referendum presented them with an unappealing option of returning to East Bengal in Pakistan, dominated by the Muslim League. This was not what the Hindu Bengalis were anticipating. Thus, the prospect of going back to truncated East Bengal in Muslim League-dominated Pakistan was unacceptable to the Hindu Bengalis. This background led the Hindu Bengalis in Sylhet to make a U-turn just before the referendum and choose to remain in Hindu-majority Assam—in India.

It is noteworthy that Assam was predominantly a non-Muslim province, with Muslims accounting for only 30% of Assam's population. Yet, Sylhet was subjected to the referendum. As quoted earlier in this chapter, the statement announcing the referendum on 3rd June 1947 declared, among other things: "Though Assam is predominantly a non-Muslim province, the district of Sylhet which is contiguous to Bengal is predominantly Muslim. There has been **a demand** that, in the event of the partition of Bengal, Sylhet should be amalgamated with the Muslim part of Bengal. Accordingly, if it is decided that Bengal should be partitioned, a referendum will be held in Sylhet...". (Emphasis by Subir)

In this context, Dr Binayak Dutta, Assistant Professor in the History Department at North-Eastern Hill University, Shillong, wrote an article titled "Event, Memory and Lore: Anecdotal History of Partition in Assam" in the NEHU Journal, Vol XII, No. 2, July - December 2014, pp. 61-76. The following excerpt relevant to our story is quoted from the article:

> "When negotiations began to partition the Indian subcontinent between the colonial state on the one hand and the Indian National Congress and the Muslim League on the other, to create India and Pakistan, the colonial government in its wisdom decided to partition Punjab and Bengal and hold a referendum in the Muslim-majority district of Sylhet in Assam to decide whether it would join the predominantly Muslim state of Pakistan or continue to be a part of Assam and India. Thus, **despite being part of the larger 'non-Muslim' majority province Assam, the district of Sylhet was drawn into the vortex of Partition politics and campaigns.**" [24] (Emphasis by Subir)

On 4th July 1947, a couple of days before the referendum, Secretary of the Sylhet Partition Committee, R. N. Choudhury, wrote to Mountbatten. Among other points, Choudhury notably argued about the illogicality of subjecting Assam's Sylhet district to a referendum.

21. Sylhet's Right to Self-Determination

Letter from R.N. Choudhury to Louis Mountbatten, 4 July 1947 Governor-General (Reforms), File No. 41/20/47-R, NAI

P.55, C.I.T, Shovabazar, P.O. Box No. 12211, Calcutta

Your Excellency,

I confirm having sent you a long telegram, a copy of which is enclosed herewith. This telegram deals with various points of omission and commission relating to the ensuing referendum in the district of Sylhet, which falls due on the 6th and 7th of July 1947. I earnestly hope that the various points raised in my telegram under reference, a copy of which has been enclosed herewith, will receive Your Excellency's kind consideration. Your Excellency's unsparing efforts for the solution of the Indian problem have been so much appreciated everywhere in India and England (and justly so) that I shall probably be regarded as a detractor of a great public man if I happen to disapprove of your decisions in connection with the Sylhet Referendum and if I have to be critical of the methods by which the Sylhet Referendum is being conducted, apart from the big decision in the field of

Indian politics which is having the whole of India in its grip and over which Your Excellency could not be happy yourself.

Now turning to the Sylhet Referendum, unfortunately, the Referendum is very ill-timed, since the feelings of a section of the Muslims of Sylhet have been worked up to a white heat of communal frenzy on the issue of eviction of Muslim encroachers from certain Upper Assam districts. Due to these initial handicaps, the result of the Referendum will be prejudiced to a great extent. Under the circumstances, this moment is hardly a suitable time for fairly ascertaining public opinion on such a vital issue.

I am of the opinion that the case of Sylhet has not been properly represented before Your Excellency. It could have been easily argued that in the present constitutional setup, the existing provinces have been taken as units. It was never contemplated to redraw the boundaries of the provinces throughout India at this stage. Therefore, provincial boundaries have been treated as sacrosanct everywhere. Why should a different principle be applied to the province of Assam alone?

I am of the opinion that there should have been no contemplation to partition the province of Assam, and no Referendum should have been taken at all, according to the British Government Plan as unfolded before the leaders on the 3rd of June 1947, as the special communal situation prevailing in the provinces of Bengal and Punjab was conspicuous by its absence in the province of Assam. The province of Assam has been needlessly dragged into the controversy, and a part of it has been subjected to a Referendum with a view to a most unjust partition of the province to suit the whims of the Muslim League, and Your Excellency's decision (which unfortunately has been supported by Congress leaders) has been to rob Peter to pay Paul. Assam stands absolutely in the same footing so far as the minority is concerned, with other Indian provinces (except Bengal and the Punjab), and as such, different principles should not have been applied to Assam, as distinct from such other provinces.

The contiguity of areas may have great meaning elsewhere, but it should not have any such charm while transgressing the boundary of an existing province. The whole question of the Referendum with a view to partition the province of Assam has been decided in a slipshod fashion, and there ought to have been a vehement protest against holding of the Referendum with a view to partition Assam.

I am of the opinion that the people of Sylhet, especially Hindus, with a view not to embarrass Your Excellency and Congress leaders, shall have to face the Referendum under protest and try their level best to avoid the partition of the province of Assam and transfer of a part of the district of Sylhet to the proposed province of Eastern Bengal, by winning the Referendum in favour of non-transfer.

But since the time is most ill-suited for a Referendum, as the public mind is frantically agitated over the extra-legal activities of the Muslim League on the eviction issue and since the whole affair has taken a communal turn, it is feared that a Referendum at this stage is most likely not to reflect the true opinion of the citizens of Sylhet. Under the circumstances, the citizens of Sylhet, especially the Hindus, reserve their rights to make their self-determination and to keep themselves away from the proposed province of Eastern Bengal, in case the Referendum favours the amalgamation of the district of Sylhet with the proposed province of Eastern Bengal.

At least it should have been possible to effect a partition of the district of Sylhet allowing all the Hindus, resident therein, to remain in the province of Assam by resorting to the transfer of population if necessary (a probability of which has been foreshadowed in Your Excellency's Press Statement dated the 4th of June, 1947), in addition to the provisions of paragraph 13 of the British Government plan. It is unjust to tag Sylhet as any other Muslim Province. The western part of Punjab has not been tagged to Sind and vice versa. Since an outrage has been committed on the citizens of the district of Sylhet and especially on the Hindus and incidentally on the province of Assam, most elaborate safeguards ought to have been provided for such of the citizens as are deadly against a transfer to the proposed Eastern Pakistan. I am afraid this aspect of the matter did not receive full consideration from the authorities concerned.

I have drawn Your Excellency's urgent attention to several matters relating to the referendum at Sylhet in my telegram which require to be set right by Your Excellency immediately. I need not recount them here again to avoid repetition. Their extreme urgency is patent on their faces. What is most imperative is to check the violence of the followers of the Muslim League, in all shapes and forms, and to give protection to all voters right from their village homes to the Polling Booth if the Referendum is held though, as I have suggested, it ought to be postponed sine die. I have no doubt that Your Excellency will have issued appropriate orders in the meantime. The points I have raised are self-explanatory, and I need not dilate upon them anymore here.

Probably, I might add a little information about the votes in the Labour Constituency, which have been shut out very mistakenly from the ensuing Referendum. I am directly connected with a group of Tea Estates both in Surma and Assam Valleys belonging to perhaps the biggest individual tea estate owner in India. I can tell you from my direct knowledge **that tea estate labourers in the district of Sylhet are in no sense a floating population. They are permanently settled in the tea estate areas, living for generations in the same locality. They have lands settled on them in most cases. Therefore, there is no reason whatsoever to discriminate against the labour population in this particular instance. Since Hindus, Muslims, and Christians all are being allowed to take part in the Referendum, why should the labourers be precluded from doing so is a mystery** to every thinking man, especially in view of the importance of labour these days. Since the Labour Constituency Votes were cast in the last Assam Legislative Assembly Election, the eligibility of labour votes being cast in the ensuing Referendum cannot be disputed. These labour voters are as much vitally interested in this Referendum as anybody else. Your Excellency must have been wrongly advised in this matter. I appeal to Your Excellency to issue appropriate orders removing the disability on the labour voters numbering about twelve thousand.

The idea of one undivided India has been and is the only correct solution to the Indian Problem. A departure from this ideal has been a profound mistake and tragedy of the first magnitude. The future will unfold what untold sufferings are yet in store for the inhabitants of this country in the wake of the projected division of India. The proposed Referendum of Sylhet with a view to partition the district is even more regrettable as this contingency could have been avoided easily since **in a similar case it was not found necessary to transfer the Hindu majority areas of the districts in the province of Sind to contiguous Hindu majority districts of the Bombay province.**

It is a thousand pities that Your Excellency went against your own conscience and also against the conscience of the British Government in sanctioning the partition of India only to placate one Mr Jinnah and his irreconcilable followers. The verdict of history will be, I am sure, against this partition, and it will be ranked **as one of the greatest blunders ever made in all history.**

I remain,

Your Excellency's most obedient servant,

(R.N. Choudhury) (Rabindra Nath Choudhury) [25]

Like Assam, Sindh was a province of British India from 1936. It was bordered by Rajasthan and Gujarat in its east and south. The province had a Muslim majority, but several of its eastern sub-districts had a Hindu majority. These sub-districts were contiguous with India. In the 1947 partition of British India, most Hindus fled to India due to communal tensions. As of the 1931

Census, Sindh had about 4.1 million people. About 73 per cent were Muslims, 26 per cent were Hindus, and 1 per cent belonged to other religions, mainly Christianity and Sikhism. The Hindu minority was concentrated in urban areas, while Muslims dominated the countryside. Hindus were an absolute majority in four of Sindh's five largest cities. Larkana and Shikarpur, with populations of 25,000 and 62,000 inhabitants, respectively, were the two largest cities in northwest Sindh. Larkana was 62.7 per cent Hindu, and Shikarpur was 63.5 per cent Hindu. Sukkur, in north-central Sindh, had about 65,000 people, 58.8 per cent of whom were Hindu. Hyderabad, Sindh's second-largest city, had 96,000 people and was 70.5 per cent Hindu. [26] At the time of partition, there was also a demand to include Hindu-majority districts in Sindh in India. The following telegram is a case in point:

"12. Demand for Separation of Hindu Majority Districts in Sindh

Telegram from V.D. Savarkar to President, Sindh Provincial Sabha, and the Chairman of Hindu and Minority Conference, 1 June 1947

S.S. Savarkar and G.M Joshi (Eds), Historic Statements: V.D. Savarkar, p. 198.

PRESS ON WITH ALL POSSIBLE SPEED AND EFFICIENCY THE DEMAND FOR SEPARATION OF HINDU MAJORITY DISTRICTS IN SINDH WITH A VIEW TO JOINING THE HINDUSTAN UNION. PAKISTAN OR NO PAKISTAN, HINDU MAJORITY DISTRICTS MUST BE SEPARATED EVEN IN THE INTEREST OF AKHAND HINDUSTAN ITSELF.

But, unlike the Assam province in northeast India, the province of Sindh in the western part of British India was spared not only a partition but also a referendum!

Naturally, the unusual referendum announcement for Assam's Sylhet district on 3rd June 1947 surprised its Bengali population. There is a perception, especially among the Bengali Hindus, that Gopinath Bordoloi had played a critical role that finally influenced Mountbatten to announce a referendum (that eventually sealed the fate of Sylhet district) in 1947 instead of letting Sylhet continue to remain in Assam as a logical corollary because, after all, Sylhet district was a part of the Hindu majority Assam province. Coming on the heels of his rejection to be in the same group as Bengal as proposed by the Cabinet Mission that eventually resulted in the partition of India in 1947, Bordoloi's alleged role in the final analysis in 'getting rid' of Assam's Sylhet district to Pakistan sent a signal that he was unfriendly to the Bengalis and acted against their interests, given that Sylhet had a heavy concentration of Bengali-speaking people, both Hindus and Muslims[1].

Note: [1]According to the Census of Assam, 1941, the district of Sylhet had a population of 31,16,602 persons. Of this population, 18,92,117 (60.71%) were Muslims and 11,49,514 (36.88%) were Hindus. 69,907 persons were Tribals (2.24%).

The operative word "demand" used in the 3rd June 1947 statement announcing the Sylhet referendum is still shrouded in mystery. The statement also did not elaborate on who had made that demand. Neither the Bengali Hindus nor the Bengali Muslims of Sylhet district had demanded the referendum at that time! So, there is a need to delve into this unsettled question.

The following paragraph quoted from the research paper of Research Scholar Mousumi Choudhury titled "Partition in the East Resettlement and Rehabilitation of Refugees in Cachar a Case Study of Karimganj" is informative:

> "Significantly, the **demand for a referendum was not voiced either by the Hindus or by the Muslims of Sylhet** who enjoyed an enriched inter-community life in their native land. Amalendu Guha argued that "the separation of Sylhet from Assam was chiefly the result of the efforts of the Assamese little nationalists and that after Sylhet was shaken off its back, the Assamese middle class emerged stronger and more ambitious than ever." The demand for Pakistan on a religious basis turned the people of Sylhet ambivalent who had not experienced communal violence earlier. They considered their homeland a unique ambience of unity and fraternity enriched with the contributions of Hajrat Shahjalal and Mahaprabhu Sri Chaitanya. Interestingly, they experienced the quick transformation of their identity from Sylhetis to Hindus and Muslims just on the eve of the referendum." [28] (Emphasis by Subir)

The only time there was a known 'demand for a referendum' was in 1928. Congress member from Surma Valley Basanta Kumar Das had made it. Amalendu Guha narrated its history in "Planter Raj to Swaraj." According to Guha, after the appointment of the Simon Commission, divisive communal politics registered a new dimension in Assam as the question of redrawing the provincial boundaries on a linguistic basis arose. In July 1924, a resolution was moved on the floor of the Third Reform Council for the transfer of Sylhet to Bengal. The Bengali-speaking majority of Cachar felt that if Sylhet was transferred to Bengal, there was no point in Cachar remaining in Bengal. So, demand was also raised to transfer Cachar to Bengal. Accordingly, the resolution was amended to include Cachar in the original proposal. It was passed by twenty-two to eighteen votes. The Government of Assam was committed not to stand in the way provided that Assam's status as a Governor's province remained unimpaired. In its letter of October 1925, the Government of India, however, made it sufficiently clear that Assam's future status as an independent and separate question, not to be linked with that of Sylhet." The issue, therefore, continued to remain controversial.

"In September 1928, the Sylhet question was reopened again in the Council with official backing in an attempt to revise volte-face earlier stand. Hazi Muhammad Bakht Mazumdar, a scion of an ancient Sylhet zamindar family and a Khan Bahadur, moved a resolution on 17 September, asserting that the people of both Sylhet and Cachar were opposed to their transfer to Bengal. It was a direct affront to Congress's stand on linguistic provinces, an 'inspired resolution' in the words of B. K. Das. In an aggrieved and sarcastic tone, N. C. Bordoloi (a popular Assamese leader and a vocal member of the council) told the string-pullers behind it:

> .... you want to have the resolution carried because you want to place it before the Simon Commission. Place this thing before any reasonable man, say to him that the Assam Council has decided the desire of the people by means of the votes of the European planters who forsooth know the desire of the people of Sylhet and Cachar, and by the votes of the European members of the Government, what will he say? Can there be anything more ridiculous than this?"

Analyzing the structure of the Council, Bordoloi pointed out that in a 52-member house (excluding the president), seven officials, eight British planters, and five nominated members, together with two ministers, constituted a solid block of twenty-two who were always moving in one direction. 'So I think it would be better to go to Bengal,' he said, 'if we could go as a whole. It is useless to continue in a province with such a council.' On the other hand, Saadulla would also prefer Assam's merger with Bengal with adequate safeguards rather than parting with Sylhet. In a frantic attempt to stop the resolution, B. K. Das moved an amendment that a referendum be arranged to ascertain the views of all 'chaukidari' and municipal rate-payers of Sylhet and Cachar regarding the transfer question. Nothing short of a referendum based on universal adult suffrage would, however, have proportionately reflected the voice of the Muslims. But neither side was keen on this, although such a measure was suggested in his speech by Dowerah. Das's amendment was rejected by twenty-nine to twelve votes. All thirteen Muslim votes were solidly against the amendment. The original resolution was thereafter passed without division. The debate rang the death knell of the heretofore cleverly contrived Swarajist hegemony in the Council. Never again was the demand for the transfer of Sylhet to Bengal raised in the legislature in the form of a resolution. Muslim members from both the Valleys were henceforth solidly opposed to this idea." [29]

THAT was in September 1928. But what prompted Mountbatten, after nineteen long years, in 1947 to announce the "referendum" for Sylhet district in a Hindu-majority province of Assam is still an unsolved puzzle. Some authors, however, held Basanta Kumar Das, the then Assam's Home Minister of Bordoloi Cabinet, responsible for the referendum. But, it defies logic. It seems that the proposal of Basanta Kumar Das at the Council in September 1928, when there was no question of a division of India into Hindu-Muslim communal lines, was deliberately twisted and linked to Mountbatten's decision of 1947 with a questionable intent of making him, and by default the Bengali Hindus, the scapegoat.

In 1928, Hindu Bengalis favoured joining Bengal IN INDIA, but in 1947 their preference got reversed, as narrated earlier. So, there was no reason for Basanta Kumar Das to support or to "agree" with the referendum. It leads to a notion that maybe the referendum's actual sponsor(s) tried to find an escape route by putting the blame elsewhere. Critical analysis of the following paragraphs of the book "Remembering Sylhet: Hindu and Muslim Voices from a Nearly Forgotten Story of India's Partition" by Anindita Dasgupta would be an eye-opener.

"Both popular and historical writings repeatedly point to a 'disinterest' on the part of Assam Pradesh Congress Committee to exert itself in keeping Sylhet, either before or during the Referendum. The Premier of Assam, and the leader of the Assam Congress, Gopinath Bordoloi himself, however, provides a clue into his role during the Referendum in his own words. Bordoloi had visited Mahatma Gandhi soon after the Boundary Commission (for Bengal and later Sylhet) was set up as he was worried over rumours that there was a conspiracy to include Goalpara, Cachar, and some other parts of Assam into East Pakistan.

The meeting Bordoloi had with Mahatma Gandhi over this issue is vividly described by Bordoloi himself. As he narrated his own fears and worries, the **Mahatma asked him why then, in the first place, Bordoloi had agreed to the Referendum**. When Bordoloi answered that he had played no role in it, Gandhi retorted that nothing could happen in a province without the Premier's knowledge. 'I then told him all I knew', wrote Bordoloi.

"... how Lord Mountbatten, **at a lunch** to which I was invited, said that he presumed that I was indifferent about Sylhet going to Pakistan. I told him, however, that while it was true that a large number of the people of Assam Valley wanted Sylhet to be separated, and at one time, even the Hindus of Sylhet wanted the same, the Congressmen of both the places wanted to live together as they fought a common fight together for ten long years under my leadership for weal or woe. I told him also how Lord Mountbatten met the leader of Sylhet, the then Home Minister of our Cabinet (Sri Basanta Kumar Das), **the same evening** at a garden party how the latter agreed to the Referendum and how the Working Committee of Congress endorsed it. I then put it to him. How can I fight the Working Committee? "(Emphasis by Subir) [30]

It was indeed a skilful and diplomatic answer from Bordoloi! However, his above reply to Gandhi has some significant corollaries:

a) According to Bordoloi, the then Home Minister, Sri Basanta Kumar Das, had 'agreed' to the referendum on the same evening. It means (i) Das did not PROPOSE the referendum to Lord Mountbatten, who obviously was already contemplating the idea of a referendum BEFORE he met Das, and (ii) Mountbatten had merely ASKED for the opinion of the Home Minister on this crucial issue.

b) Bordoloi had met Mountbatten earlier on the same day - at lunch. The question of Sylhet's referendum being so important, it is logical that Mountbatten must have asked for the opinion of Bordoloi as well and not left it at that by merely PRESUMING that Bordoloi was indifferent about Sylhet going to Pakistan. And so, Bordoloi must have (i) also agreed or (ii) evaded a direct answer to the question. By default, it meant that Bordoloi was ALSO agreeable to the referendum, and (c) the only other probability could be that Bordoloi had disagreed or opposed it. But, it is not tenable because, in that case, Bordoloi definitely would have told Gandhi accordingly.

c) If Mountbatten did not ask for Bordoloi's opinion, this would mean either (i) Mountbatten was sure of Bordoloi's support for the referendum or (ii) Bordoloi himself put the idea to Mountbatten.

Thus, Bordoloi's statement to Gandhi that the then Home Minister, Sri Basanta Kumar Das, had 'agreed' to the referendum on the same evening needs to be taken with a pinch of salt. Nevertheless, the above analysis provides a definite clue to the unsolved puzzle of the referendum.

The minutes of the meeting Mr. Gopinath Bardoloi had with the Cabinet delegation and Field Marshal Viscount Wavell on 1st April 1946 have been reproduced in the previous chapter. It may be observed from the same that, in reply to Sir Stafford Cripps, a member of the Cabinet delegation, "Mr Bardoloi said the Congress would not object to the transfer of Sylhet to Bengal...." Besides, according to researcher Monolina Nandy Roy, Bordoloi also stated before the press that he had put the question of the separation of Sylhet from Assam before the Mission without any consultation with the members of the Surma-Barak Valley. There was strong resentment against Bordoloi in the Hindu press for putting up the question of the separation of Sylhet from Assam. As a result, both Bordoloi and the Brahmaputra Valley members of the Cabinet were highly unpopular with the Surma Valley members and the Surma Valley Congress as a whole. [31]

Therefore, the impression Bordoloi tried to convey to Gandhiji that all the Congressmen under his leadership were united in their stand on Sylhet and about his helplessness to fight the Congress Working Committee (CWC) is rather difficult to reconcile. Did Bordoloi really have any intention to "fight the CWC," as he put it, on the issue of the referendum? It seems to be most unlikely. One thing, however, is crystal clear - in his discussion with Mahatma Gandhi over the issue of the Sylhet referendum, Lokapriya Gopinath Bordoloi was rather economical with the truth!

As a patriotic Indian, true nationalist, devout Hindu, and elected Prime Minister of Assam, it was expected that the Premier should register his strong objection to the referendum that might cause, and eventually did, the loss of almost an entire district of his province/country to Pakistan. It was hoped that Premier Bordoloi would look after the interests of the Nation and more so of its people in the Sylhet District of his own province, Assam, irrespective of the religious affinity and linguistic origin of these people. It was desirable at the crisis hour in India that Bordoloi, like any other loyal Indian, would set aside all past likings or dislikings, love or hatred, friendship or hostility, and racial/communal rivalry and focus on the interests of India. All Indians by heart and soul, especially those at the helm of the Assam administration, were expected to take all possible steps to prevent losing its Sylhet district to Pakistan through a referendum. Yet, Gopinath Bordoloi's admission to Gandhi indicated that he did not utter even a mild word of dissent to the Viceroy against holding a referendum on Sylhet. If Bordoloi had done so, he definitely would have mentioned this to Gandhi.

On the contrary, the record of the interview between Rear-Admiral Viscount Mount of Burma and Mr Gopinath Bordoloi (Mountbatten Papers, Viceroy's Interview) dated 1st May 1947 quoted in the previous chapter affirmed that Bordoloi, sitting next to Mountbatten at a luncheon, had told the Viceroy that **"Assam would make no difficulties about the partition of Sylhet since the general view was that they belonged to Bengal, and _would be_** *no loss to the rest of the Province*. **The only people who might kick up a fuss would be the 40 per cent non-Muslim minority in the Sylhet district."** (Emphasis by Subir).

Also, in her book "Remembering Sylhet," recipient of visiting fellowships at the National University of Malaysia and the Institute of International and Strategic Studies, Malaysia, Anindita Dasgupta, who pioneered studies on the oral history of Sylhet's partition, argued that:

> "It is generally believed that the Congress was in favour of retaining Sylhet in India and that the Muslim League was in favour of its partition on the basis of religion. The Sylhet experience, however, suggests that the Congress party was equally swayed by the local politics of language in Assam as by communalism and did not pose major objections to the proposed separation of Sylhet despite allegations of mismanagement of the referendum and demands for a second Referendum. Another reason for Congress's acceptance of the verdict of the July Referendum, despite many accusations of organizational malpractices, was the time factor. In order for India to gain its independence on 15th August 1947, there was no time to organize a second Referendum, though such a request was forwarded by the Sylheti Hindu leaders to the government. Third, communal politics might not have been the only factor behind Partition. As the case of Sylhet shows, the local politics of language played a crucial role in constructing and perpetuating the problem of Sylhet in the Assamese narrative since the late 1870s, which was later merged with the national politics of communalism. The 'valley jealousy' had been around much longer than communal politics, yet during the 1940s, both strands came together in the shape of the July Referendum." [32]

Thus, a definite picture started emerging by connecting all the dots surfaced little by little!

In this context, historian Sujit Chaudhuri, in his seminar paper titled 'a god-sent opportunity,' wrote, among other things, that the Congress high command, in 1946, allowed the Assam Congress to air the proposal for the transfer of Sylhet to Bengal only as a part of a futuristic plan for a reorganization of the provinces within undivided India. Then, Chaudhuri continued:

> "But in June 1947, the situation was totally different. The transfer of Sylhet to Bengal now meant its transfer to East Pakistan, and the Congress high command could in no way sponsor such a proposal.

But to the Assam Congress, it did not matter whether Sylhet went to Pakistan or remained in India. The Bengali-speaking district was regarded as an **ulcer** hindering the emergence of a unilingual Assam. Hence, when the decision for the referendum was announced, Gopinath Bordoloi conveyed to all concerned that **the Cabinet was not interested in retaining Sylhet**." [33] (Emphasis by Subir)

The eminent historian Amalendu Guha, in his book "Planter Raj to Swaraj," wrote:

> "On the Sylhet question, Assamese public opinion, too, remained understandably cold but consistent with its earlier stand. The APCC (Assam Pradesh Congress Committee) election manifesto had pledged to the electorate in 1945-46 that the Congress Party would work to separate Sylhet from Assam. 'Maulana Sahib (Azad) seemed to come to the conclusion that the only alternative to this state of things,' wrote Bordoloi to Patel on 1st February 1946, 'is to separate the Bengali district of Sylhet and a portion of Cachar from Assam and join these with Bengal – a consummation to which the Assamese people are looking forward for the last 70 years.' Bordoloi had let the Cabinet Mission understand in April that Assam would be quite prepared to hand over Sylhet to Eastern Bengal.
>
> A year later, under the changed circumstances (the transfer of Sylhet to Bengal now meant its transfer to East Pakistan), it was no longer possible for the APCC to say this openly. However, Congress control of the Assam administration was so 'correctly' exercised that it hardly provided any advantage to the local Congress (of the Surma Valley) during its campaign in Sylhet to win the referendum." [34]

In other words, in 1945-46, the Congress Party manifesto had pledged to the electorate that it would work to separate Sylhet from Assam, but a year later, in 1947, the circumstances changed. The transfer of Sylhet to Bengal then meant transfer to East Pakistan because Mountbatten had already declared that a referendum would be held in Sylhet under the aegis of the Governor-General and **in consultation with the Assam Provincial Government** to decide whether Sylhet district remained in India or joined Pakistan. Therefore, it was no longer possible for the APCC to say this openly. "(However, as Amalendu Guha insinuates) Congress control of the Assam administration was so 'correctly' exercised that it hardly provided any advantage to the local Congress during its campaign in Sylhet to win the referendum." That was the final nail in the coffin, as far as the question of Sylhet's sacrifice to Pakistan is concerned! (Emphasis by Subir)

In the meantime, encouraged by the widespread Hindu-Muslim communalism that plagued the country on the eve of its partition and influenced by the growing politics of Assamese-Bengali racial rivalry in the province, a few political actors targeted Home Minister Basanta Kumar Das, a Congress leader from the Sylhet District. They tried to shift the blame for the reversal of the Sylhet referendum on Das and, by default, on the Bengalis. Against this scenario, the following few lines quoted from Anindita Dasgupta's book "Remembering Sylhet" are noteworthy:

> "... some others partly hold Basanta Kumar Das responsible for not doing enough in this regard, though Makhan Lal Kar, a volunteer during the Referendum, stated that **Das was informally divested of his portfolio** on the eve of the vote and that, therefore, he could do very little to influence the organization or outcome of the Referendum. Das, he wrote, stuck to the office without power. In fact, Kar also mentioned that Das had made two revealing statements on the eve of the Referendum. He said:
>
> ... there was a promise that the Referendum would be conducted under military supervision with the help of the provincial police. The provincial government have already exhausted all their police and other resources, and it was the inadequacy of the military deployed for the purpose that had made it impossible to conduct the Referendum in a peaceful atmosphere."

Second, Das also pointed out that there was 'organized hooliganism in different parts of the [Sylhet] district and that the police and the army men deployed were not enough to deal with the situation. But the Assam governor, Sir Akbar Hydari, did not take his comments seriously and even informed the national-level Congress leaders that Das' views were not borne out by facts on the ground. [35] In his book in Bengali, *Swadhinata Andoln-e Srihatta* (Sylhet during the Freedom Movement), B. B. Purakayastha wrote that since the national leadership of the Indian National Congress had accepted the verdict of a Referendum, the local-level Congress leaders also demonstrated an enthusiastic approach. Therefore, in spite of being the home minister, Basanta Kumar Das remained only a 'helpless witness of circumstances'.

In reality, at the time of the referendum, while Basanta Kumar Das had actively worked to retain Sylhet in Assam, **no Congress politician from the Brahmaputra valley even visited Sylhet during the referendum period, not to speak of campaigning,** with the lone exception of the popular Assamese politician Rohini Kumar Chowdhury[1]. [36] Interestingly, the newspaper Dawn, dated 17th June 1947, under the caption 'Immediate Dissolution of Assam Ministry Demanded', reported, among other things:

> 'The question of immediate release of political prisoners, now that the Civil Disobedience Movement is no more,' Mr Siddikie[2] said, 'has greatly agitated Muslims of Assam. Taking advantage of the forced absence of our leaders, **arch-Muslim baiters like Mr Basanta Das have set out on a whirlwind tour of Sylhet at the expense of public money for the propagation of the Caste Hindu view** and this is being done under the very nose of Governor Hydari who has not kept it a secret that his sympathies are with the Hindu Congress'. [37] (Emphasis by Subir)

Note: [1]Rohini Kumar Chowdhury was a Member of Lok Sabha, representing Gauhati (Assam) as a member of the Indian National Congress. He was also a member of the Constituent Assembly of India.

[2]Mr. M.H. Siddikie, Secretary, Muslim Chamber of Commerce and Industries, Assam.

So, the role played by Das at the time of the referendum invalidates the perception propagated by certain vested interest groups that he did not do enough or acted against Sylhet remaining in Assam in 1947. It is a fact that later on, Das became a minister in Pakistan, but that per se does not imply any *quid pro quo* or give any credence to the detractors who cast a slur upon him. On the contrary, his becoming a minister in Pakistan was a testimony to his popularity, efficiency, and grit, even in the newly formed Pakistan.

At the same time, the revelation that Basanta Kumar Das was informally divested of his portfolio on the eve of the vote also raises some critical questions. At a time when the law and order situation of the country was highly fluid; when close monitoring and supervision of deployment of security personnel should have been the top priority of the Assam administration; at that critical juncture, when Home Minister Basanta Kumar Das had a vital role to play, particularly in the maintenance of the overall law and order of the province; cutting the wings of Basanta Kumar Das, who happened to be a Bengali Hindu from Sylhet District, with no known reason definitely was something very significant and noteworthy signal that historiographers must look into with magnifying glasses. In fact, the above analytical narration should provide a fresh insight into what prompted Mountbatten to go for Sylhet's referendum since the statement dated 3rd June 1947, is vague. A clear-cut answer to this would set at rest the controversy surrounding the question of why the Sylhet district of a Hindu-majority province of Assam was singled out for the unfair, unjustified, and undue decision for a referendum that caused immense loss to the nation and its people.

Anyway, as soon as the dates of the referendum were declared, a committee was appointed by Jinnah to gear up the electoral activities. He wanted to win the referendum of Sylhet at all costs. At that time, the Muslim League was the ruling party in Bengal. So, Jinnah directed its Premier Suhrawardy to arrange for the necessary support to Assam's local unit of the League, including financial help to meet poll-related expenses. Also, Bengal minister Moazzamuddin Hussain was deputed as a League observer. Moreover, Jinnah's earlier promise in 1944 that the League would protect the rights of the 'Dalits' ensured the support of a section of this community in favour of Sylhet's inclusion in Pakistan. Accordingly, the head of the Scheduled Caste Federation of Bengal, Jogendra Nath Mandal, also a Cabinet Minister in Suhrawardy's Muslim League Ministry in Bengal, arrived in Sylhet as per Jinnah's suggestions. He campaigned for the Muslim League and influenced the opinion of the lower-caste Sylheti Hindus to a great extent.

It was also a watershed moment for many Sylheti Muslims across the globe. Some Muslims working as seamen or earning their livings in England and other foreign countries even came back to Sylhet to participate actively in the referendum. Once a Minister of Assam for several terms, Abdul Matin Chaudhury, in his capacity as the President of the Referendum Committee in Sylhet, invited many famous personalities like the (then) Prime Minister Suhrawardy of Bengal; the former Prime Minister of Bengal Fazlul; the renowned Islamic scholar and the founder of Dhaka's first Bengali newspaper Maulana Akram Khan; the influential industrialist and one of Jinnah's closest political and personal lieutenants Abdul Hasan Ispahani et al. to campaign for the Muslim League. Thousands of Muslim students of schools and colleges in Bengal and Assam were mobilized to work for the cause of Pakistan in the referendum. Numerous local activists worked relentlessly at the grassroots level. A widely circulated and popular Delhi newspaper 'Dawn', whose editor was a famous Sylheti journalist Altaf Hussain was engaged in countering Hindu 'propaganda' against Muslims. According to newspaper reports, rowdy processions, shouting slogans, and drilling of young men were the order of the day. The Muslim National Guards brought from outside (mostly UP and Bihar) flooded the district. Their arrogant presence extended even in the remotest villages and allegedly created panic in the minds of non-Muslim villagers with their appearance in large numbers in the campaign. Their threatening poses and postures scared the non-Muslim populations in the district. It added a new dimension to the already charged atmosphere that radically changed the complexion of the campaign by blatantly articulating the demand for Pakistan in the much-used catchword *"In the name of Islam."* That had an immediate impact on the general population of the Muslim community, especially among the blind followers of Islam and illiterate Muslims.

In contrast, the Assam Provincial Congress (APCC) was virtually an organization primarily comprising Brahmaputra Valley's Assamese nobility, gentry, and upper-caste Hindu community. They had shown hardly any interest in retaining its Sylhet District in Assam (India). It was in keeping with their Election Manifesto of 1945-46. Accordingly, as mentioned earlier, "the Congress control was 'so correctly exercised' that it hardly provided any advantage to the local Congress in the campaign to win the referendum". Unfortunately, while the Bengali Hindus of Sylhet supported the Congress, the Hindu-dominated Congress as a whole failed to support the Bengali Hindus of Sylhet - when required most! Sadly, while the pan-India partition story brought the 'Hindu-Muslim' divide to the fore, a section of the leaders in Assam had added a twist to this story by trying their utmost to settle their old score in the 'Assamese-Bengali' rivalry. It was indeed "a God-sent opportunity" for them to "get rid of Sylhet" and carve out a linguistically homogenous province of Assam. Seemingly, these Congress leaders of Brahmaputra Valley did not hesitate to compromise India's national interests to promote their ethnocentric agenda. Against this backdrop, paragraph 5 of Assam Governor's telegram dated 1st July to the Viceroy reproduced by Dilip Lahiri in his book "Nirbasita Sreebhumi O Referendum Fallout (2nd Part) provides decisive feedback. It reads as follows:

> No one outside Sylhet is particularly anxious to retain the district in Assam. **All my ministers except four Surma Valley ones are lukewarm, and Prime Minister** (Gopinath Bordoloi) has even been publicly criticized for his lack of enthusiasm in retaining Sylhet. The impression of a Ministry strongly determined to keep it, which is one of the objects of League propaganda, is **just not true."** [38] (Emphasis by Subir)

It seems that deliberate attempts were made to conceal some vital information about Assam's Sylhet referendum. One irrefutable testimony of such subterfuge came to Dr. Dilip Lahiri's notice during his research for a book. He mentioned it in his bilingual (Bengali-English) book "Nirbasita Shreebumi (Exiled Sylhet) O Referendum Fallout (Second Part)". Its pertinent portion is quoted below:

> "The report (on the referendum) was prepared in only two copies: one remained with the Governor-General of Assam, and the second copy was sent to Her Highness the Queen of England for records. The Assam Government and its top brass carefully destroyed (the Assam part of the file with referendum contents of 136 pages) the

report for future hegemony with Hindu immigrants of Sylhet and kept the actual history out of bounds till today, i.e., 2016, which was unearthed recently from the British Government's Queens archive in London in 2015." [39]

Note: [1]Dr Lahiri recovered the file through sheer zeal and more than 36 long years of dogged determination in his quest for the truth. He reproduced the facsimile copies of the recovered file's correspondences in his book on pages 86 to 194, "Nirbasita Sreebhumi O Referendum Fallout (Second Part)" published by Kaberi Mandal, Rupkatha Prakashan (Contact: +91 7797460966; email - kaberi0084@gmail.com

During his discussion with Subir, Dr Lahiri asserted verbally that he saw the 'Note Sheet' in Government File No. 1446/20GG/43 with the remark "destroy this file." It had an illegible initial on the Note Sheet. Some correspondence from the retrieved file has been extensively quoted in this book.

While Mountbatten was eager to show to the world that the Sylhet referendum was conducted freely and fairly under his aegis, he had left the entire election process to the Provincial Government, whose neutrality was questionable. It took some critical reports in the Delhi-based newspaper DAWN for the Viceroy to write to the Commander-in-Chief, Field Marshal Sir Claude Auchinleck, on 2nd July 1947 (referendum held on 6th and 7th July 1947) to rush "four British military officers of Indian Army of the rank of Major or thereabouts." The idea behind Mountbatten's sudden move was not "to give Muslim League any handle to allege that the referendum if it should go against them, has not been fairly done." Those were the exact words Mountbatten had used. Accordingly, as the Government records show, one Lt. Colonel and three Majors reached Sylhet on the evening of 5th July 1947, only the day before the referendum. That was how Mountbatten arranged to establish that the referendum was indeed held 'UNDER HIS AEGIS' [40]. That was a royal deception, no doubt!

Similarly, the appointment of H. C. Stork as the Referendum Commissioner was also marred with controversy. Stork was formally relieved from his post of Legal Remembrancer 'to avoid any suspicion of Ministerial direction' only from 1st July 1947, barely a week before the start of the referendum, as the telegram dated 30th July from the Governor to the Viceroy proved. The same newspaper, DAWN, forced the Government to act belatedly with an article commenting, "... we must frankly tell him (Mountbatten) that over the Sylhet Referendum; he is not living either up to his reputation or his standard of fairness" [41].

According to author Dr Dilip Lahiri, the Government exchanged some secret official communications regarding the referendum. As already mentioned, the file containing these papers that remained in Assam was reportedly destroyed. Its second, and only other copy, was sent to Her Highness the Queen of England in London for records. Lahiri managed to recover the file from the British Government's Queens Archive in London in 2015 through more than 36 years of unceasing and determined efforts. He reproduced the facsimile copies of the correspondence in his bilingual (Bengali-English) book titled 'Nirbasita Shreeboomi' or 'Exiled Sylhet'. Some of the above discussions and most of the following deliberations are primarily based on those Government communications [42].

The following two revealing letters from Durga Das-edited book, "SARDAR PATEL'S CORRESPONDENCE 1945-50": Volume V (Control Over Congress Ministries - Indian States' Accession) are also reproduced hereunder,

a) Letter dated 15th June 1947 from Purnendu Kishore Sen Gupta, Member, Executive Committee, Indian National Trade Union Congress, and Organizer, INTUC, Surma Valley, addressed to Congress leader Sardar Vallabhbhai Patel.

b) Sardar Vallabhbhai Patel's response in terms of his letter dated 20th June 1947 addressed to Purnendu Kishore Sen Gupta.

:

P.O. Kulaura,
District Sylhet
15 June 1947

My dear Sardarji,

I crave your indulgence for intruding upon your valuable time, and my excuse for doing so is the very great danger with which our district Sylhet is faced today.

At the very outset, I may tell you that though in Sylhet district Muslims are a majority, during the last general election out of the total Muslim votes recorded, about 26 per cent of the votes went in favour of our nationalist Muslim candidates. The total Hindu votes along with this **26 per cent of the Muslim votes represented an overwhelming opinion against any idea** of Pakistan as far as Sylhet district is concerned and yet, as ill luck would have it, we have to face a referendum to decide the question of whether Sylhet should remain in the Indian Union or be joined with East Bengal. I beg to approach you today for all the help that lies in your power to give us at this critical juncture. Our first difficulty is with the tea garden labour population. There are 221 tea gardens in Sylhet district with a labor population of 197,272. The labourers have only one seat in the Assam Assembly, and they elect their representatives from different zones **by rotation**. As such, the existing electoral roll for the tea garden labourers is confined to one thana only, which has a labour population of 30,522 in 30 different gardens, of which not more than 11,449 are entitled to vote. **The existing electoral roll does not provide any scope for voting to 166,750 labourers** living in 191 tea gardens scattered over the district. The number of actual voters thus deprived of the franchise will not be anything below 50,000. Whatever device is arranged for the representation of labourers in the Legislative Assembly, there is no reason why all of them should not be given full facilities for expressing their opinion on the question of the referendum. Sjt. Jibon Santal, Labor MLA representing these tea garden laborers, has addressed a Memorial to His Excellency the Viceroy praying that a supplementary voters' list may be prepared immediately to give full facilities to all labourers living in the district for recording their opinion on the matter. The entire tea labour force in Assam, including Sylhet, is recruited from Bihar, UP, GP, Madras, Orissa, and West Bengal—all falling within the Indian Union and none from East Bengal, Sindh, or Punjab. It is of utmost importance, therefore, that they should be given the opportunity to exert their full weight in deciding this vital issue. I most earnestly request you to kindly exert all your influence with the Viceroy so that the labourers may get their franchise. Our next difficulty is with our nationalist Muslim friends. They have expressed their desire to remain within the Indian Union, but the Muslim League is determined to resort to any means, as they did during the last election, to win the referendum. It will be extremely difficult for our nationalist Muslim friends to go and record their votes in the face of Muslim League hooliganism unless elaborate measures for maintaining law and order rights in the interior villages are adopted by the Government. The provincial Government should be given all necessary help in this connection by the Central Government. And we absolutely rely on you for this help, without which the whole referendum may be meaningless for us. Our next and greatest difficulty is about finances. Of course, the district will try to help itself as much as possible, but our resources are very limited and the time at our disposal is very short, making it impossible for us to approach all the people in the district. We don't know how we can find the huge amount of money that will be required for the purpose unless all of India comes to our rescue. And for the financial help, we do approach you to take up our cause with the people of the Indian Union. We do wish to remain within the Indian Union, and it will not be possible to do so **unless the people of the Indian Union also kindly extend their helping hand to us**. Some of us may soon meet you for this purpose, and we are confident that you will very kindly give us all the guidance and help necessary in the matter. (Emphasis by Subir)

It would inspire our people greatly if you could kindly visit the district once at your earliest convenience. We require your guidance in organizing our people for the referendum, and the district will remain ever grateful to you if you could kindly spare a few days for our sake.

With best regards,

Yours in the service
of motherland,
Purnendu Kishore Sen Gupta, MLA
Member, Executive Committee
Indian National Trade Union Congress
and Organiser, INTUG,
Surma Valley.

New Delhi
20 June 1947

Dear Friend,

Thank you for your letter of 15 June 1947 regarding the Sylhet referendum. I am afraid we shall have to proceed on the existing basis, and no further changes can be made regarding the electoral rolls. You can rest assured, however, that every effort will be made from here, as well as by the provincial Government, to maintain peace during the referendum.

I am sure that if you organize local opinion in the manner it should be, the verdict of Sylhet will be in the right direction. **It is futile to ask for assistance from outside. The work has to be done, and can only be done, by the local leaders.** (Emphasis by Subir)

Yours sincerely,

Vallabhbhai Patel.

Shri Purnendu Kishore Sen Gupta, MLA. [43]

As previously mentioned, the districts of Cachar and Sylhet, known as the Surma Valley, were under the jurisdiction of the West Bengal Provincial Congress Committee (WBPCC). During that period, an unexpected development occurred in Bengal that hindered the WBPCC from playing a significant role in the efforts to retain Sylhet in Assam, India. The Bengal Legislative Assembly had voted in favour of Pakistan. Subsequently, in a separate session, the MLAs from districts with a Hindu majority voted to partition the province and remain part of India. During this time, inspired by the events in Punjab, a proposal emerged for the religious partition of Bengal. This concept was first suggested at the Tarakeshwar Conference of the Bengal Provincial Hindu Mahasabha (April 4-6, 1947). The conference authorized Shyama Prasad Mukherjee, the principal advocate of the idea, to take all necessary steps to establish a separate homeland for Hindus in Bengal, in collaboration with nationalist elements. The WBPCC promptly embraced this idea and focused on salvaging at least a portion of Bengal from being included in Pakistan. [44] Due to their involvement in the partition of Bengal, the WBPCC couldn't provide significant support to the people of Sylhet in their efforts to retain Sylhet within Assam, India.

Conversely, the Assam Provincial Congress (APCC), largely composed of the nobility, gentry, and upper-caste Hindu community of the Brahmaputra Valley, showed minimal interest (as discussed earlier) in retaining Sylhet District within India. This stance was in line with their Election Manifesto of 1945-46.

In contrast, **nationalist Muslims openly campaigned for India.** Prominent nationalist Muslim leaders and members of the local Jamiat-ul-Ulema, led by Hussain Ahmad Madani, Mahmud Ali, Murmat Ali Barlaskar, Ibrahim Ali Choudhury, Abdul Rashid, Abdul Jalil, and others, organized public meetings and massive rallies to sway Muslim voters. North and South Sylhet were Jamiat strongholds. In 1946, Jamiat candidates were elected to the Assam Assembly from these constituencies with the overwhelming majority over Muslim League candidates. **Hussain Ahmad Madani of**

Jamiat-ul-Ulema consistently opposed the idea of Pakistan and advised all Muslims of Sylhet to vote for an undivided Assam. In response to his call, several nationalist Muslims campaigned fervently to retain Sylhet in India, thereby splitting the Muslim votes. "Frontier Gandhi" Gaffar Khan, a staunch opponent of Pakistan, dispatched many "Red Shirts" to Sylhet to collaborate with local Congress workers. Their joint efforts tipped the balance against Sylhet's inclusion in Pakistan (East Bengal). [45]

Moreover, the Communist Party of India (CPI) also invested significant efforts to influence the referendum in favour of India, working alongside local Congress members after reaching a mutual understanding. Alongside local Congress workers, the CPI formed a 'Joint Volunteers Core' led by member Chanchal Sharma, designated as its 'commander in chief.' Thus, several articulate communists mobilized people, including Muslim nankars, against Sylhet's inclusion in East Bengal. Despite being preoccupied with the Partition of Bengal, Shyama Prasad Mukherjee dispatched workers from the Hindu Mahasabha to mobilize Hindus in support of Sylhet remaining in Assam.

The battle lines were clearly drawn. Bengali Hindus (excluding some 'Dalits') and Muslims of the Organization of Islamic Scholars fought for the country to retain Sylhet district in India, pitted against Jinnah's Muslim League supporters backed by a well-organized 'paramilitary' force of the Muslim National Guard, intent on taking Sylhet from India. Some 'Dalits', led by Jogendra Nath Mondol, worked for Jinnah's Muslim League. The role of Assam Congress during those days and the administrative machinery under its control was controversial. The resulting "push" and "pull" proved too much for Sylhet to remain in India. Yet, patriotic Indians bravely fought against all odds to retain the Sylhet District in Assam until the end!

Meanwhile, the Government announced that the 1946 voters' list would be used in the referendum. A controversial figure, H. C. Stork, was appointed as the Referendum Commissioner to conduct the poll by secret ballots. The Muslim leadership argued that Muslims would be under-represented since the voter list was prepared based on the number of electorates in the previous election. They emphasized that while Muslims constituted 60.70% of the total population of the Sylhet District, they accounted for only 54.27% of the total electoral roll. They demanded the correction of this anomaly and the cancellation of voting rights for tea garden labourers, considered outsiders.

In response to a letter dated June 11, 1947, addressed by Muslim leader Liaquat Ali Khan to Mountbatten raising these issues, Mountbatten's reply in terms of paragraphs 2 and 3 of his letter dated June 25, 1947, reads as follows:

Paragraph 2: "I am afraid I cannot accept your suggestion, which would, I consider, be strictly against the general scheme envisaged in the statement made by His Majesty's Government on June 3. The referenda in Sylhet and Frontier Provinces are, as the statement shows, being held based on electoral rolls for the Provincial Legislative Assemblies. The composition of those Assemblies, their several constituencies, and the electoral rolls for them are **being used as they stand without importing any extraneous consideration.** I am sure that it would be wrong to depart from this principle in the case of the Sylhet District alone."

Paragraph 3: "The presumption in paragraph 2 of your letter that the electors for the Special Constituencies in the Sylhet District will not participate in the referendum is correct." (Emphasis by Subir) [46]

Surprisingly, on the first issue, the Government took the position that electoral rolls must be used as they stood without importing any extraneous consideration. However, **the same logic was not applied concerning the voting rights of tea garden labourers.** The extraneous consideration that the labourers "represent the floating population with little or no stake in the District" (the exact words in the Government noting) was applied, departing from the principle mentioned in the second paragraph above!

Furthermore, as previously highlighted, Secretary of the Sylhet Partition Committee, R. N. Choudhury's communication dated July 4, 1947, pointed out the illogicality of not allowing permanently settled tea garden labourers, who had been residing in the tea estate areas for generations, to vote in the referendum. These labourers inhabited the same locality, owned settled lands, and had participated in the previous Assam Legislative Assembly Election in December 1946. Concurrently, Member of INTUG, Purnendu Kishore Sen Gupta's letter dated June 15, 1947, addressed to Sardar Vallabhbhai Patel, stated that in Sylhet district, there were 221 tea gardens with a labour population of 197,272 who elected their representatives from **different zones by rotation** for the sole seat allocated to them in the Assam Assembly. Accordingly, the existing electoral roll for tea garden labourers only encompassed the inhabitants of one Police Station (thana), consisting of 30 different gardens with a labour population of 30,522. Consequently, out of these 30,522 individuals, only 11,449 (37.51%) were listed on the roll. Overall, the existing electoral roll excluded 166,750 (197,272 minus 30,522) tea garden labourers residing in 191 scattered locations across the district.

In essence, the entire labour population of 197,272 was deemed a 'floating population' or 'outsiders,' thus irrationally and unjustifiably barring them from voting in the Sylhet referendum. Notably, the tea garden labourers were predominantly Non-Muslims, primarily Hindus with a few Animists.

The final result depicted in the following table indicates that if this group of tea garden labourers could have voted, the referendum outcome would likely have favoured India. Consequently, Sylhet would have been part of India today. Moreover, the outcome of the Sylhet referendum is even more regrettable as subjecting the people of Sylhet district in Assam to the ordeal of the referendum and its aftermath could have been easily avoided initially. After all, in a similar scenario, Mountbatten disregarded demands to transfer the Hindu-majority areas of Sind Province to India. Clearly, the treatment was unequal for the people of Assam's Sylhet district.

The final result of Sylhet Referendum:

Srno	Sub-Division	Total Electorate	Vote for Eastern Bengal	Vote for remaining in Assam	Total vote cast	%age of vote cast	**India lost Sylhet to Eastern Bengal by**
1	Sadar	141131	68381	38871	107252	75.99	29510
2	Karimganj	100243	41262	40536	81798	81.60	726
3	Habiganj	135526	54543	36952	91495	67.51	17591
4	S. Sylhet	79724	31718	33471	65189	81.77	-1753
5	Sunamganj	90891	43715	34211	77926	**85.74**	9504
6	Total	547515	239619	184041	423660	77.38	55578

India eventually lost Sylhet to Eastern Bengal (East Pakistan) by a narrow margin of only 55,578 votes! It was a [1]sacrifice of 28,25,282 people; almost all were Bengali-speaking, plus 4,769 sq. miles of Indian land. Sadly, to some 'Indians', it was a good bargain – with a loss of merely 1/18th of its existing area; Assam could 'get rid' of nearly 1/3rd of its unwanted people who had posed a challenge to Assamese dominance in 'their own' state of Assam. [47]

Note: [1]Entire Sylhet district area of 5,478 square miles and population of 3,116,602 according to the 1941 Census report. As per the Radcliffe Award, thanas of Badarpur (47 sq. miles), Ratabari (240 sq. miles), Pathar-Kandi (277 sq. miles), and a portion of the Karimganj Thana (145 sq. miles) remained in India. Thus, a total area of 709 sq. miles and a population of 291,320 persons remained in Assam.

Here is a digression: The Bengalis of East Bengal, who were blinded by the vicious propaganda of the Muslim League in the name of religion, realized their blunder very soon. In the very first sitting of Pakistan's GANAPARISHAD on 23rd February 1948, the bill for making Urdu the national language of Pakistan was placed and subsequently passed - against the will of the Bengalis. The Bengalis didn't object to making Urdu the national language. However, they wanted recognition of their mother tongue, Bengali, as a second national language. At that time, out of the total population of about 6.90 lakh, numerically, Bengalis were the majority in Pakistan, with more than 4.40 lakh strong in number. So, when Urdu was imposed without taking them on board, the Bengalis knew what would be in store for them in the future in the promised Islamic "land of the pure" - Pakistan. That arbitrary decision was enough for the Bengalis to realize that they had just turned from colonial slaves of the British into Bengali slaves of the Pakistanis. The rest is history today — it took barely 24 years for East Bengal to sever its relationship with Pakistan to become an independent country called Bangladesh. The indomitable Bengalis didn't tolerate the assault on their mother tongue. Even the religious bond could not prevent the break-up of Pakistan. In the Post-Mujibur era, there was an attempt to rewire the country as an Islamic State by moving away from what Bangabandhu had envisaged for the people of Bangladesh. But that also failed. In 1989, Bangladesh's top court applied the 'basic structure' doctrine to hold the constitutional amendments converting that country into an 'Islamic State' to be violative of the basic structure of their Constitution. The love for the mother tongue, Bengali, prevailed! It taught a valuable lesson: *In a conflict between religion and language, one's mother tongue triumphs over the religion he/she practices.* [48]

And what happened to Jogendra Nath Mandal? After all, he had made common cause with the Muslim League in their demand for Pakistan, hoping that the Scheduled Castes would benefit from it. Mandal had joined the first cabinet in Pakistan as the Minister of Law and Labour. However, a few years later, he migrated to India after submitting his resignation to Liaquat Ali Khan, the then Prime Minister of Pakistan, citing the anti-Hindu bias of the Pakistani administration. A Sindhi proverb can best explain his situation, "Jini laey moasi, sey kandi nah thia" (You have died for them, but they won't bother to attend your funeral), wrote the newspaper DAWN on 4th November 2015. [49]

Now it's back to the Sylhet Referendum: The most intriguing part of the result was its summary preparation at the final stage of the counting.

According to the secret report dated 26.7.1947 of the Referendum Commissioner, counting was done under strict security cover with elaborate arrangements to maintain the utmost secrecy. Once the counting was over, the Referendum Commissioner HIMSELF prepared the results. The relevant portion of the secret report (that constituted part of the file unearthed from the British Government's Queens archive in London, as already mentioned) of the Referendum Commissioner dated 26.7.47 reads as follows:

> "As the result had to be kept a secret till announced by His Excellency the Governor-General, no representatives of the Parties were allowed to witness the counting, and this produced the inevitable expostulation. The method of counting …….. The pairs of Assistants counted the ballot papers into packets of twenty-five, each packet being tied with string, a further packet being made of the surplus papers over a multiple of twenty-five. The Supervisors checked as many of the packets as possible (a large percentage), and I personally counted all the packets (also checking the numbers in packets taken at random), and the surplus tickets, and **recorded the result in a book that never left my possession. The calculation of totals and percentages was done by me.**" [50] (Emphasis by Subir)

It is evident from the above account that in his anxiety to maintain secrecy (or maybe for some dubious reasons), the Referendum Commissioner did not allow anyone else to cross-check the "calculation of totals and percentage". He did this single-handedly - before the formal announcement of the result. After the official announcement, it is most likely that no one dared, or was allowed, to cross-check the final summary lest any discrepancy or error surfaced. That would have put the Government on the spot. Therefore, the final result that the Referendum Commissioner arrived at and the British Government eventually announced (which devastated the lives of millions of people) lacked verity, transparency, and credibility even from the standard accounting point of view. Alas, after adopting an elaborate method of maintaining the secrecy of the result, the Referendum Commissioner himself violated the single most crucial norm of 'checks and balances' of basic accountancy! It gives rise to a serious question mark on the correctness and reliability of the final result of the Sylhet Referendum! The million-dollar question is: did the Referendum Commissioner do it unwittingly? Or, did he do it wittingly?

The founder General Secretary of the North-East India History Association (NEIHA), Professor J. B. Bhattacharjee, in the JOURNAL ARTICLE Vol. 51 (1990) titled "The Sylhet Referendum (1947): Myth of a Communal Voting," among other things, wrote the following lines:

> "The votes were polled on behalf of four thousand Muslim voters who had died in epidemic malaria two years earlier. The number of ballot papers found in the ballot boxes at the time of counting was in excess of the number issued at the polling station. On inquiry, it was found that the superintendent of Assam Government Press managed to print a few thousand extra papers and put them in the ballot boxes through 'pro-Pakistani' polling staff. The superintendent was later put under suspension.
>
> Basant Kumar Das issued a press statement on the day of the referendum regarding the irregularities.
>
> Sir Akbar Hydari, the Governor of Assam, and Gopinath Bardoloi, the Premier of Assam, however, maintained that the referendum was free and fair and they insisted on the immediate declaration of the result.
>
> **Gandhi later told Bardoloi, "I have heard all about your attitude regarding the separation of Sylhet. Why did you agree to the referendum?"** [51] (Emphasis by Subir)

An extract from a report in the newspaper DAWN dated 9th July 1947 buttresses the allegation of illegitimate manipulation of ballots in the Sylhet referendum. The instance quoted below is merely indicative and not comprehensive:

"27. 'Ballot Boxes in Sylhet Tampered With'

Extract from a report in Dawn, 9 July 1947

Sylhet, Tuesday.

Owing to Mr. Stork's refusal to allow volunteers of each party to guard the ballot boxes, two cases of interference with the ballot boxes were reported on July 6-7 night. At Silam, the Presiding Officer admitted that the locks of the boxes had been found open in the morning.

Local League circles are indignant over the mean and foul tactics of their opponents. They are reported to have thrown a challenge for another referendum under the aegis of the Governor-General even at very short notice.

The most annoying part of the whole thing is that the ballot box was deposited, during the night, at the house of a local zamindar, P. Chakravarty, who has professedly Congress inclinations and it was not guarded by any military troops but only by three unarmed police constables with another unarmed head constable.

At Silam, a place about six miles from Sylhet, the lock of a ballot box was found forced open while at Juri it is reported the side of the box was found to have been broken.

Col. Pearson, specially deputed by Lord Mountbatten, is investigating these cases...." [52]

There were innumerable irregularities in the conduct of the referendum and plenty of allegations of malpractices from the rival parties that had compelled many political leaders to write to Mountbatten to express their concerns. They questioned the neutrality and trustworthiness of the referendum process conducted in Sylhet. Many demanded that the British Government postpone the result declaration pending inquiries into the complaints. The most prominent among the complainants were both Nehru and Jinnah.

The gravity of various complaints raised from different quarters could be gauged from Nehru's letter dated 13th July 1947 to Viceroy Mountbatten. Only the most critical part of his complaint (paragraphs 2 and 3) is quoted below to cite some instances:

> Paragraph 2: "During the last few days, I have received a number of telegrams from Sylhet complaining against a number of malpractices during the referendum. Possibly some of these were received by you also. Today I had a visit from a deputation from Sylhet consisting of Hindus and Muslims. They placed before me a number of allegations supported by various statements and data which together were

formidable. I do not propose to send you now a detailed list of these complaints and the facts which are meant to support them. In brief, they referred **to a state of lawlessness during the referendum in the interior of Sylhet district.** Most of the polling booths had no proper security arrangements and intimidation was exercised by large numbers of armed Muslim National Guards and others who had come from Bengal. Many thousand people who came to vote were forcibly prevented from doing so. There were some incidents of killing voters and others. The district is partly underwater and people travel by boats. Voters coming by boat were not allowed to land.

Paragraph 3: "**A large number of persons voted who according to definite evidence died in the recent epidemics.** Altogether the statements shown to me gave a very extraordinary picture of what took place during the voting in the referendum." [53] (Emphasis by Subir)

Mountbatten right away replied to Pandit Jawaharlal Nehru on the same day, the 13th of July 1947. Its contents are reproduced below:

"Thank you for your letter about the Sylhet referendum, which was opened by Abel at about 7.30 this evening and brought straight to me before I went to the French party.

Mr Jinnah made detailed complaints to me yesterday about interference by the Assam Ministry in the referendum and asked for an enquiry, which I refused. I do not know how good a case he could make out, but I have no doubt that if an enquiry was held there would be a **long and embarrassing contest** which at this stage would, in my opinion, do no good.

In any case, I have already telegraphed the results to London and authorized their release tomorrow, which means that they are probably already in the offices of the newspapers, and to withdraw them would cause a sensation.

I imagine there are always complaints about the conduct of any election or referendum and in this case, the Governor, who is directly responsible under me, has asked for an immediate announcement, which clearly means that he is satisfied.

I am sure, therefore, that we must not stop the announcement of the results tomorrow." [54] (Emphasis by Subir)

Among other issues, Jawaharlal Nehru wrote again to the Viceroy Mountbatten on July 15, 1947, regarding the irregular conduct of the Sylhet referendum, stating:

> "I have received a telegraphic reply from the Governor of Assam regarding the Sylhet referendum. He has provided full particulars. There was undoubtedly intimidation, false impersonation, and incursion of the Muslim National Guard from Bengal. **However, it appears evident that any irregularities that occurred could not materially affect the result of the referendum.**" (Emphasis by Subir) [55]

The truth is, none of these key players wanted a fresh referendum. It doesn't require the IQ of a rocket scientist to realize that the referendum was heavily manipulated. The Viceroy's telegram to the Assam Governor reiterated the complaints he received: **"Experience of Assembly elections has shown that not more than 50 per cent of voters can be recorded at this time** of the year." [56] In contrast, the result showed that **77.38%** of the vote was cast, which on average, indicated 27.38% more people or, in aggregate, nearly **150,000** additional ballots were recorded. Yet, the final conclusion was that it **"could not materially affect the result of the referendum,"** which decided the fate of Sylhet by 55,578 votes more in favour of Pakistan!

The Assam Governor's report on the conduct of the referendum was even more outrageous and ridiculous. There were complaints of rampant impersonation and false voting. However, the high percentage of votes in each constituency was considered 'evidence' to show that it was a free and fair poll. According to the Governor, it also proved that the voters were not intimidated nor prevented from voting and demonstrated that the law and order situation was perfectly normal. Quite the contrary, this high percentage of the average of 77.38% (with the lowest of 67.51% in Habiganj Sub-Division to the highest of 85.74% votes in Sunamganj Sub-Division) in the prevailing situation itself was the most suspicious aspect of the referendum's conduct. The Government's own report mentioned: *"Due to recent floods and heavy rains, the major part of Sylhet district was inundated, and water stood high everywhere, making villages look like small islands."* Additionally, there were reports of incessant heavy rains on polling days, floodwaters inundating several low-lying villages, serious disruption of road communications to the polling booths, artificial scarcity of boats created to foil attempts by villagers to vote, and voters reportedly prevented by the threat of violence and physical harm. [57] [58] Against this backdrop, the high percentage of votes per se should have aroused instant doubt about the fairness of the entire poll process because the adverse ground reports to the Government ruled out *ab initio* the chances of heavy polling.

Furthermore, the report of Lt. Col. C. W. Pearson dated July 11, 1947, to the Referendum Commissioner mentioned, "One Sub-Division was not covered by our 'team,' **SUNAMGANJ**, which was considered to be **too far and so underwater** that observing one or more polling booths would have been **extremely difficult**." [58] Yet, this Sub-Division **recorded the highest (85.74%)** percentage of votes among all the five Sub-Divisions of Sylhet. The British rulers, national-level political leaders, and the Assam administration should have paid due attention to this wake-up call. Yet, they chose not to heed this loud note of warning.

The fact that the key players in the referendum proceedings of Assam's Sylhet district took the heavy polling as a testimony of a free and fair referendum rather than proof of large-scale malpractices like impersonation and false voting as alleged by various stakeholders, in the prevailing ground realities, ignoring the clear warning, speaks volumes of their real intention. The Viceroy rejected the demand for an inquiry, supporting the absurd logic!

The Governor, however, 'arranged' inquiries by the same personnel directly responsible for ensuring a free and fair poll and maintaining law and order but seemingly messed up all these. The authorities never ordered an independent investigation by a responsible, unbiased officer to find the truth.

The Referendum Commissioner's secret report dated 26.7.47 mentioned that when he had visited a Polling-Station (for a few minutes in all likelihood), the Presiding Officer was found to be "not compelling voters to put their ballot papers into particular boxes" as alleged. As if, had the allegations been correct, the Presiding Officer would stick out his neck in the presence of the Referendum Commissioner and openly direct the voters to put the ballot papers into the ballot boxes of his own choice! This single instance of a brief observation was cited by the Referendum Commissioner that complaints were "baseless" – not only in that specific Polling Station but also "equally baseless" elsewhere too! [59]

As protecting voters from intimidation and maintaining law and order were the responsibilities of the Military and the Police, the Referendum Commissioner attached three annexures to that secret report dated 26.7.47. The first one, annexure A, was from Lt. Colonel C. W. Pearson on behalf of all four Military Officers. He denied the allegations and maintained that these were made by "both responsible and irresponsible" persons. Shockingly, what Pearson added in his report, as quoted below, looked nothing less than a political statement - not expected of any disciplined, apolitical defence personnel:

> "It is our considered opinion that the party leaders of both sides, fostered, and in some cases started, these alarmist rumours and that the conduct of these gentlemen in spreading alarm and despondency during the Referendum was as deplorable as the behaviour of the actual populace was admirable and restrained, under the constant bombardment of inflammatory and irresponsible statements made by their leaders. That the Home Minister Mr Das should have given such irresponsible statements to the Press (A.P. I report in the Amrita Bazar Patrika of 8th June) and declared that the Referendum was a "farce" was, we considered, even more deplorable." [60]

Such a manner of expression supposedly authored by an army officer of the rank of a Lieutenant Colonel can only allude to the bureaucratic outburst in an attempt to refute the allegations. Annexure B of the report dated 19.7.47 from the Superintendent of Police (S.P.), Sylhet, was somewhat restrained and business-like and concluded with the following lines:

> "There was a certain amount of intimidation of the minority by the majority community in the interior, but it was not very much. There were very few cases of actual violence". [61]

For a change, the S.P. was not in full denial mode, like all other characters from top to bottom in the hierarchy!

The elaborate report of Mohinder Singh Chopra, Commanding Sylforce in annexure C, also, as expected, denied the accusations and its political overtone marred that too, but it provided some vital clues of the ground reality- as seen in the following excerpts:

"Due to recent floods and heavy rains, the major part of Sylhet district was inundated, and water stood high everywhere, making villages look like small islands."

"Reconnaissance also brought out that the atmosphere of the District as it then prevailed was very tense. The relationship between the various groups representing various shades of public opinion was far from satisfactory."

"Rowdy processions, the shouting of slogans, drilling of young men were the order of the day."

"Non-Muslim population showed apprehension when Muslim National Guards flooded Sylhet from outside. **The National Guards penetrated into the remotest villages and created panic in the mind of the Non-Muslim.**"

6th July 1947: Polling commenced at 0930 hrs, and large crowds assembled at the booths. Due to inclement weather, there was a rush and stampede at the polling stations. It appeared that the staff in the polling station were unable to cope with the voters at a sufficient speed, and the police on duty failed to organize the entry of voters to the booths. **There was a lack of control.**

7th July 1947: Polling was carried out more smoothly on the second day, largely due to the experience gained on the first day. Fracas was reported from two places in the Habiganj Sub-Division. It was alleged that **Muslim National Guards obstructed Hindu voters from entering the booths.** Upon the arrival of the Military, however, crowds dispersed, and order was restored.

Congress and pro-Assam organizations continuously complained that **precautions were inadequate** and desired that the Military and police should have escorted voters from their homes to the polling booths and back. It was **pointed out that this was not the function of the Army and was, in any case, impossible.** The Army could not be expected to be everywhere.

> **In one case, military escort for voters at Kurshi in Habiganj Sub-Division was offered but was refused on the ground that nobody would protect them when the Army went away.**
>
> 9th July 1947: H.E. the Governor arrived and held a conference at Sylforce HQ attended by H.M. (Home) and H.M. (Supplies), D.C. Sylhet, S.P. Sylhet, and C.C Sylforce. The purpose of the conference was to investigate allegations by the Hon. Minister mentioned above that lawlessness prevailed in Sylhet. He was reassured by D.C., S.P., and C.C. Force and by his own personal observation.
>
> It is noteworthy that both Hon. Ministers are residents of Sylhet and hence probably had a less balanced view than a disinterested observer.
>
> GENERAL IMPRESSIONS.
>
> The **number of troops actually available was small**, but this fact was less known to the people of the villages than the fact of their comparatively great mobility and their determination to strike when necessary." (Emphasis by Subir) [62]

A perusal of the full report (including some not quoted here) would indicate that the so-called 'investigation' reports were nothing but self-certification of how efficiently the security forces fulfilled their responsibilities and tried to create an impression that everything was hunky-dory. The reports denied all allegations and rejected the complaints; on the other hand, these were incredibly liberal in showering mutual praise and appreciation on one another - apparently to give some illusory effects.

In any case, it is reasonable to believe that the 'personal' investigations by security personnel themselves were bound to be a futile exercise. Even in normal circumstances, the sight of uniformed armed personnel generates fear among ordinary citizens. The villagers and common people would never open up and dare to speak anything against the security personnel, even if they had genuine grievances against them. The reports also mentioned that during the short period of the referendum, a kind of camaraderie had developed between the different wings of the security forces and the civilian staff. In that circumstance, even if some shortcomings in the discharge of their duty were noticed or found out, it would, in all likelihood, have gone untold because of the solidarity that was reportedly developed.

On top of it, none other than the Home Minister of the province had asserted that there was a breakdown of law and order and that the referendum was a "FARCE". Yet, the administration ignored it completely. In contrast, while the security officers were supposed to be neutral, apolitical, and display some professional ethics and decency, they did not hesitate to vilify by putting some disparaging comments in their reports against Home Minister Basanta Kumar Das. It betrayed their contemptuous attitude towards the political process and the political personalities. Given the tone and tenor of the reports, it's difficult to rule out their chances of being biased due to political or bureaucratic interference. The tone and tenor of the reports reveal that there was **more to how the Sylhet referendum was conducted than met the eye.**

Even the assertion made by the Governor of Assam in his SECRET report dated 14th July 1947 to the Viceroy about Minister (Supply) Mukherji's REPORTED volte-face with hardly any valid justification was not as simple as it looks. After all, these were secret Government communications with very little chance of it coming to Mukherji's knowledge, let alone any possibility of repudiation.

One thing, however, can be said with conviction: all the key players in the Sylhet referendum were in a mad rush. The British Government wanted a quick exit from the mess it had created in India. **Mountbatten feared a country-wide break-out of civil war**[1]. Besides, like any other veteran officer, he also wanted to get the job done hurriedly and earn some credit for the upward trajectory in his professional status. Nehru was yearning for the fruits of power. Bordoloi's aim was **'to get rid'**[2] of Sylhet with its Bengali inhabitants as quickly as possible. Assam Governor Hydari wanted to swiftly steer clear of the most contentious issue of the referendum on his hand and remain in the good books of the British administration. Thus, many disparate strands of the unholy plot came together. All of them wanted to avoid any delay. Agreeing to the demand for a fresh referendum meant procrastinating. So, the appeals had to be rejected on flimsy grounds. None of them gave a damn about what happened to Sylhet or the Sylhetis, who wished to remain in Assam within Hindu-dominated India. It is the bitter truth about the referendum of Sylhet – rather the long and the short of it.

Note: [1]Viceroy's Personal Reports (Report No. 1 April 2, 1947) to Whitehall said: "The only conclusion that I have been able to come to is that unless I act quickly I may well find the real beginnings of a **civil war** on my hands." [63]

Note: ²That was the exact phrase (to get rid of) Sardar Patel used in his letter dated 30th August 1947 to Assam Governor Hydari, though in an unrelated issue but worth noting from the following two letters. Only the relevant paragraphs of these two letters are quoted below:

Government House
Shillong
25 August 1947

My dear Sardarji,

Thank you for your letter dated 21st August regarding Tripura State. It is really a question ....

2.

3.

7.   Now for a passing remark on another subject. With Jalpaiguri cut off from West Bengal by a block of Pakistan, the common-sense course would be to attach it to Assam with which its boundary march. That and Cooch Behar would improve and render safe the Indian Union's communication with her eastern frontier. But I suppose with Sarat Bose* on the warpath and the Bengalis already howling for more territory in place of what they have lost to East Bengal, common-sense must stand down to emotion and so we had better not raise this subject just now!

Yours sincerely
A. K. Hydari

Sardar Vallabhbhai Patel
New Delhi

*Sarat Chandra Bose: Leading Congressman of Bengal, elder brother of Subhas Chandra Bose; member, Interim Government headed by Nehru.

New Delhi
30 August 1947.

My dear Hydari,

Thank you for your letter of 25th August 1947, which I received through your ADC.

2.

3.

4.

5.   As regards Jalpaiguri, the position is very delicate. <u>I am doubtful whether the Assamese themselves would like Bengalis to come in</u>. **They have just managed to get rid of them**. I, therefore, agree with you that we had better not raise it.

Yours sincerely
Vallabhbhai Patel.

H.E. Sir Akbar Hydari

Shillong. [64] (Emphasis by Subir)

The following account, narrated lucidly by Leonard Mosley in his book, "The Last Days of THE BRITISH RAJ," gives an idea about the unholy hurry these people were in during the relevant period. The reckless rush, epitomized by Mosley in the narrative below, ruled out any chance of a fresh referendum, no matter what:

> "On the evening of his arrival, Sir Cyril John Radcliffe, tasked with drawing boundary lines to divide British India into Pakistan and India as two separate countries, was summoned by the Viceroy to meet the Indian leaders. Nehru and Patel were there for Congress, and Jinnah and Liaquat Ali Khan were there for the Muslim League. Sir Cyril modestly pointed out that it was quite a considerable task assigned to him and his two boards of judges. He spoke of the vastness of India, the multitudinous population, and the difficulty of cutting through the great acres of territory on each side of the Subcontinent, dividing it so that communities of people would be cherished, districts saved from division, and towns and villages left

connected with their hinterland. Normally, he pointed out, this was a job that would take even the most careful arbitrators years to decide, but he realized that urgency prevailed. He and his two commissions would do their utmost to help. How long had he got?

'Five weeks,' said Mountbatten.

Before Sir Cyril Radcliffe could express his astonishment and dismay, Nehru interrupted:

'If a decision could be reached in advance of five weeks, it would be better for the situation,' he said.

The others, including Jinnah, nodded in agreement.

It was obviously impossible to explain to any of them that you could not possibly divide a country in such a short time, those injustices would be bound to occur, and that a little time, patience, and research might save endless bickering in the future. It had to be a quick amputation—and that would mean blood." [65]

"The entire operation was both botched and rushed, with the inept handling of the Chairman, Radcliffe, immortalized in the poem 'Partition' by W.H. Auden. Delaying the announcement of the Boundary Commission awards (by Mountbatten) to a period after the date of independence compounded the chaos and mayhem as many a village and town did not know which side of the border it was on. People found themselves on the wrong side of the border on 15 August 1947—flags of both India and Pakistan were flown in regions contested by both communities, Muslim and Hindu." [66]

^'^Unbiased at least he was when he arrived on his mission,
Having never set eyes on this land he was called to partition
Between two peoples fanatically at odds,
With their different diets and incompatible gods.
'Time,' they had briefed him in London, 'is short. It's too late
For mutual reconciliation or rational debate:
The only solution now lies in separation.
The Viceroy thinks, as you will see from his letter,
That the less you are seen in his company the better,
So we've arranged to provide you with other accommodation.

We can give you four judges, two Moslem and two Hindu,
To consult with, but the final decision must rest with you.'

Shut up in a lonely mansion, with police night and day
Patrolling the gardens to keep assassins away,
He got down to work, to the task of settling the fate
Of millions. The maps at his disposal were out of date
And the Census Returns almost certainly incorrect,
But there was no time to check them, no time to inspect
Contested areas. The weather was frightfully hot,
And a bout of dysentery kept him constantly on the trot,c
But in seven weeks it was done, the frontiers decided,
A continent for better or worse divided.

The next day he sailed for England, where he quickly forgot
The case, as a good lawyer must. Return he would not,
Afraid, as he told his Club, that he might get shot.

Partition, 1966 by WH Auden. [67]

Sir Cyril Radcliffe was tasked with dividing India in five weeks. For such a monumental task, requiring years rather than weeks, it truly didn't matter whether he produced his Award in four, five, or six weeks. Given the circumstances, he was bound to sever towns from rivers, villages from fields, factories from storage yards, and railways from goods yards. But urged to move swiftly, he proceeded with desperate urgency. He had his Award ready and written well before the deadline he had been given.

The amputation was executed at lightning speed, just as Mosley had predicted—' it meant blood'. And indeed, it caused profuse bleeding. However, no one could have foreseen the extent of the postoperative haemorrhage. The injury inflicted by the dismemberment was so severe that the bleeding had not ceased altogether. The wound is yet to heal properly, and blood still oozes from its ill-treated parts in the east. Much of the bloodshed could have been prevented by avoiding reckless haste.

Returning to the poignant story of the Sylhet referendum, if we momentarily set aside the dirty politics of linguistic racism, religious communalism, and selfish personal agendas that overshadowed the referendum in 1947, and examine the matter clinically based purely on arithmetic, its result raises a sensitive question: How accurately did the referendum reflect the wishes of the majority of Sylhet's people? Unfortunately, a very insignificant number of the district's total population was able to participate in the **so-called referendum, where 65% of Sylhet's adult population wasn't even eligible to vote!**

According to the latest census reports of 1941, the total population of Sylhet District was 3,116,602. This number would have increased significantly by the time of the referendum in 1947, but for simplicity, let's ignore that. The final result of the referendum, presented in tabular format, showed that the number of eligible voters was only 547,515. In other words, barely 18 out of every 100 persons were entitled to vote. However, presuming that as many as half (50%) of the total population were underage and thus deducted from the total population, Sylhet district's total number of adults would be 1,558,301. This indicates that the names of 1,010,786 adults were not on the voter list. Ineligible voters outnumbered eligible voters at a ratio of almost one to two. In other words, **out of every 100 adults, as many as 65 or so were ineligible to vote.** Consequently, despite all its sound and fury, the Sylhet referendum turned out to be a major deception. What occurred in the name of a REFERENDUM was nothing but a tragic tale of the greatest betrayal to the nation—engineered during the final hours of India's independence!

* * * * * * *

Chapter 9.

Post-Independence Era's Truncated Assam

ˈসিলেট গল, সিলেটি ন গল

Sylhet Gone – Sylhetis Not Gone!

The Cobra Effect occurs when an attempted solution to a problem worsens the situation. The term "Cobra Effect" originated during the British rule of colonial India. The British government wanted to tackle the worrying number of venomous cobra snakes in Delhi. Their strategy was to offer a bounty for every dead cobra. Creating this incentive was initially a successful strategy—many rewards were claimed, and the number of cobra snakes spotted in Delhi started to decrease. However, the greed for the cash reward prompted many enterprising people to start cobra breeding. Soon, the government became aware of the scheme and stopped offering the reward for dead cobra snakes. As a result, the cobra breeders set the now worthless animals free, increasing the cobra population in Delhi. This anecdote shows that the apparent solution to a problem can make a situation even worse. Many such anecdotes throughout history exemplify how linear thinking in the three-dimensional world, involving the human species with the most complex spatial awareness, resulted in the opposite of the intended result.

Note: [1]A word-by-word translation of the Assamese buzzword of the 1950s and 1960s - "সিলেট গল, সিলেটি ন গল" (Sylhet gol, Sylheti no gol): "Sylhet Gone – Sylhetis Not Gone!"

This phenomenon occurred in Assam when it ceded an INDIAN DISTRICT to Pakistan (now Bangladesh) in the referendum of 1947. It is alleged that the thickly Bengali-populated Sylhet district, then in Assam, was obstructing the long-cherished aspiration of a few individuals to make the state unilingual. So, the district, which should have routinely remained in the Hindu-majority PROVINCE of Assam, was subjected to a referendum through sharp political manoeuvring. The intricacies of the plot have been discussed elaborately in the previous chapter of this book. The referendum on Assam's Sylhet district resulted in the permanent displacement of numerous people from their homes, causing countless humanitarian problems. Yet, it did not fulfil a handful of individuals' ill-conceived designs of having a unilingual Assam state in India. Instead, the opposite happened - it opened the floodgate of refugees. The state that allowed its prosperous district to secede from India to 'get rid of' its large Bengali population was flooded with the same Bengali-speaking people. At the same time, Assam lost the Sylhet district's fertile land and copious resources in the process. It was a typical Cobra Effect that took place in the state!

It may be recalled that at the time of the partition of British India, out of seventeen provinces, only eleven of them joined India outright, and three joined Pakistan, whereas the remaining three provinces of Punjab, Bengal, and Assam were apportioned between the newly created Dominion of India and Dominion of Pakistan. Yet, to most of our fellow citizens, the partition of India in 1947 alludes to the break-up of Punjab in the West and Bengal in the East. But there was a third dimension, which seldom finds mention in the numerous stories written on the topic. Thus, the referendum on the Sylhet district through which the Assam Province was drawn into the whirlpool of partition manoeuvrings became a forgotten chapter. Pakistan got the bulk of the Sylhet territory in this power play politics, barring its tiny part that remains attached to Assam in India. Significantly, hardly anyone talks about or mentions this third dimension of India's partition in their deliberations, discussions, or debates! It seems that the controversial referendum on the Sylhet District, passionately fought by a section of the Bengalis of the Sylhet region to retain their land in India during the partition of our country in 1947, is being deliberately played down and eclipsed slowly but surely from our partition history. There are conscious efforts to put a veil of silence over what happened in the Sylhet referendum in British India in 1947. However, the story does not end here. On the one hand, the national 'leaders' agreed to divide the country based on religion, as claimed by the Muslim League. On the other hand, they refused to go for an exchange of the population based on the peoples' religious affiliations.

The final result of the Sylhet referendum that went against India showed that out of the total 4,23,660 votes cast, as many as 184,041 (43.44%) people voted in favour of retaining their native district in Assam. In other words, of the total population of 28,25,282 people in the Sylhet District, at least 43.44% of them, which is 12,27,300 persons, exercised their choice to remain in Assam. Even when their efforts failed to retain Sylhet in Assam, their intention to keep it in Assam state in independent India must be appreciated and honoured. Unfortunately, this expectation remained unacknowledged and unfulfilled.

After the partition of India on 15th August 1947, Sylhet became a part of (East) Pakistan based on the referendum result. At that time, numerous Sylhetis, who favoured Sylhet to remain in Assam, wanted to return to Indian soil. But, they were left behind to fend for themselves in the newly created Muslim country, Pakistan, although they longed to be in their homeland, India. When they thought of crossing over to the Indian side of the newly drawn international boundary in the eastern sector, the Indian administration dissuaded them from entering their own country. At no point in time did the leaders of Pakistan and India think of population exchange, though a few leaders in India favoured this alternative. Unfortunately, on this vital issue, the contrary opinion prevailed.

Yet, numerous Sylhetis were desperate to return to India. In fact, the Noakhali Riots of October 1946 and the immediate aftermath of the partition violence forced many of them to abandon their native land and rush to India with their family. Initially, mostly the middle class or the upper-middle-class people who already had some near and dear ones gainfully engaged in Assam migrated to India. The display of passion generated in the Noakhali massacre and the violence in the aftermath of the partition were wake-up calls to them. They brought their family to safety in Assam and elsewhere at the first warning signal sounded in East Bengal. The communal riots of 1950 proved to be the last nail in the coffin for those migrants who had stayed back and tried their best to cling to their native land as long as possible. They were cautious and reluctant to move out of their comfort zone to an unknown territory. They knew it would be difficult to re-establish themselves in a new land. Yet, the safety of their lives and family members eventually forced them to seek refuge in India - their own country. Later, with the announcement of the introduction of passports, the minority community in East Pakistan realized that the borders were getting sealed and that was their last chance to make it to the other side legally. Therefore, 1952 once again saw an increased influx of migrants coming from East Pakistan in the months preceding the introduction of passports. Consequently, the buzzword *'Sylhet gol, Sylheti no gol'* of the 1950s and 1960s started doing rounds in Assam.

In-between and after that too, trickles of Bengali Hindu refugees into Assam, Tripura, and West Bengal persisted all along as a result of their continued persecution in the newly created (East) Pakistan. Simultaneously, under economic compulsions, the Bengali Muslims continued to relocate themselves to Assam and West Bengal. The Assamese landlords welcomed Muslim migrants in Assam as cheap agricultural labourers. Thus, the unabated influx of Bengali Muslims persisted with patronage from the politicians who treated them as a "vote bank." The Assamese gentry also welcomed them for engaging them in menial works.

During the partition days and until he breathed his last on 5th August 1950, Gopinath Bordoloi headed the Congress ministry in Assam. Bordoloi's alleged involvement in getting 'rid of' the Sylhetis from Assam signalled that he was unfriendly to the Bengalis and acted against their interests. Accordingly, in this book, Bordoloi's role as the Prime Minister of Assam in British India has been fiercely criticized for, so to speak, giving away Assam's Sylhet district to Pakistan on a platter - as historical facts and figures suggest. Nevertheless, before reviewing his role as the first Chief Minister of Assam state in post-partition India, the following anecdotal account of Gopinath Bordoloi is presented to put the records in perspective.

Subir knew a Bengali gentleman who was privy to intimate details about the Bordoloi family. On being asked explicitly about Gopinath Bordoloi, the gentleman confided in Subir that Gopinath was beyond reproach - as a person. As if to reinforce the statement, he added that Bordoloi was fond of Bengali people and their culture and loved to read Bengali books, recite Bengali poems, sing Bengali songs, and so on. Did Gopinath Bordoloi despise the Bengalis? Surprisingly, the answer to this pointed question was an emphatic – "NO"! What were the compelling reasons then that made Gopinath Bordoloi act in a manner which looked as if Bordoloi was inimical to the interests of the Bengalis - especially in Assam? "It was his political compulsion," was the answer. "In those days of utter chaos and endless confusion, which prevailed during India's pre-independence period, Bordoloi had to resort to these manoeuvres for his political survival," the gentleman added. The following paragraphs on Bordoloi are based on Subir's conversations with the Bengali gentleman and some research works.

During those crucial days when the British colonial rulers were being shown the door, Gopinath Bordoloi had to face many challenges in safeguarding the interests of his homeland. One such serious complication was the 'Crown Colony' plan the colonial rulers were secretly drawing for the hills of Northeast India. Hardly any discussion appeared on the subject since our country's independence. The Crown Colony plan has been briefly touched upon in chapter 5 of this book. Bordoloi's vital contribution as the Chairman of the subcommittee of the Indian Constituent Assembly on Assam Tribal and Excluded Areas eventually thwarted the covert plan of 'Crown Colony', thereby preventing the loss of many hills of Northeast India.

During Gopinath Bordoloi's reign as Assam Chief (Prime) Minister, a serious rift surfaced between the Government and the party organization. This confrontation became apparent at the time of Debeswar Sarmah's election to the post of party president in 1949. Sarmah was initially a supporter of Gopinath Bordoloi's policies about controlling the flow of immigrants into the state and the protection of tribal lands. However, this support turned into resentment against Bordoloi when he was not offered a place in the Gopinath Bordoloi ministry. Post-independence, some confrontations also developed within the Bordoloi Cabinet due to disagreement in conceptualizing government policies regarding the refugees from East Bengal. Such a clash reportedly took place between him and his Minister in charge of Finance, Revenue, and Legislative Departments, Bishnuram Medhi, on the entry of refugees and providing them employment. Medhi strictly expressed his dislike for the continuous flow of refugees from East Pakistan. For him, refugees should not be given jobs, putting the local people's interests at stake. On the other hand, Bordoloi had taken a softer stand on the issue of refugees and employment.

The renowned historian from Assam, Amalendu Guha, perhaps evaluated Gopinath Bordoloi most explicitly on pages 188 and 278 of his book "Planter Raj to Swaraj" with the following few lines:

> "However, a careful reader of Tayyebulla's memories and Bordoloi's correspondence with Gandhiji and other leaders cannot but conclude that **Bordoloi knew the game of politics rather too well.** Despite many shortcomings and contrary to Governor Reid's impression, he had enough gift of leadership to have his way at every critical stage, and with popular support. This was because he could always strike a balance between national and narrowly Assamese interests, as subsequent events indicated."

> "Bordoloi cared neither for prizes nor for the dictates of his party's high command when Assam's interests were concerned. With Gandhi's blessings, he led a successful resistance to the proposed inclusion of Assam in Group C of the Cabinet Mission Plan acceded to by the All India Congress Committee (AICC). People widely believed that Assam was saved from being a part of Pakistan. It was he, again, who flagged off the Sylhet referendum to comply with the public opinion of his constituencies, the Brahmaputra Valley, thus inviting a rebuke from his mentor, Gandhiji. His mission in life was to serve Assam to the best of his abilities and with vision."

As a human being, Lokpriya Gopinath Bordoloi, as he is lovingly called, was undoubtedly a 'Lokpriya' (meaning 'loved by all') gentleman. He had an upright character. Among others, a large section of the Bengali population, who came in personal contact with this gentleman, also held a high opinion of Bordoloi. He belonged to the Brahmin Diavajna (astrologer) caste. His family history traces an enlightened family originally from Uttar Pradesh. His mother passed away when he was just twelve years old, after which he was raised by his eldest sister Shashikala Devi. In 1910, Gopinath Bordoloi married Surabala Devi, who belonged to an enlightened family in North Gauhati. As an ardent follower of Mahatma Gandhi, Gopinath led a simple life and dressed in Khadi. He was a real gentleman endowed with softness and humility. His love of Tagore's songs was so passionate that he hired an expert to learn them at a certain point, suggested one report.

On 5th August 1950, Gopinath Bordoloi died of a heart attack while in office at 60, putting his family in a harsh financial condition with no family pension and provident fund. His residential building, which was under construction, was incomplete. He had made no savings and absolutely no provision for his family members. He had 4 sons and 5 daughters. Two eldest daughters were married, and three unmarried daughters were school-going. While his 3 sons were at school and college, the youngest son still had one year to start schooling. Gopinath Bordoloi's two brothers were of meagre income, and one had a family of 8 children. The brothers lived together in a family of four, with one widowed sister of Bordoloi staying with them.

Though Gopinath Bordoloi's pay was Rs.2,000/-, he drew only Rs.1,500/- and surrendered the remaining Rs.500/- to the Government. It was considered unwise for the Government at the Centre or the State to grant a biggish one-time ex gratia payment and a monthly family pension as a special case to Bordoloi's family that would create a precedent. Accordingly, it was decided to give scholarships to his children and the total amount of his surrendered pay aggregating to Rs.10,000/- or so to Mrs. Bordoloi. [1] Former Prime Minister Atal Bihari Vajpayee conferred upon him India's highest civilian Award, Bharat Ratna, posthumously in 1999 – nearly 50 years after his bereavement in August 1950.

Be that as it may, Superintendent of Census Operations 1951 for Assam, Manipur and Tripura, R. B. Vaghaiwalla, ICS, in the 1951 Assam Census Report, among other things, wrote the following;

> "Though Assam's loss in area as a result of this partition is negligible (it has lost only 1/18th of its existing area) it has lost very nearly 1/3rd of its entire present population and along with it the vast paddy lands and the tea, lime and cement industries of Sylhet; the far-reaching effects of this loss will continue to be felt by Assam as well as India for many years to come." [2]

In other words, the separation of Sylhet from Assam was a loss of under 6% of the state's land area but more than 33% of its population; almost all were

Bengali-speaking people. According to the initial scheme of British India's division on the Hindu-Muslim communal line, this split should not have happened in the first place. Nevertheless, the Census Superintendent Vaghaiwalla did read the writing on the wall quite correctly when he recorded in the census report that *'the far-reaching effects of this loss will continue to be felt by Assam as well as India for many years to come'*. The breakup of Sylhet from Assam happened concurrently with the severance of East Bengal from India. As a result, the partition left barely a 27 KM wide stretch of land at Siliguri in West Bengal, known as 'Chicken's Neck', wedged between East Pakistan (presently Bangladesh) to the west and China to the north to keep all the Northeastern states, including Assam delicately bound to the rest of India. The entire region became almost surrounded by foreign countries on all sides barring the slender 'lifeline' of the Siliguri corridor to keep the Northeastern states united to the mainstream of India by land.

According to the Ministry of Development of the North Eastern Region, responsible for the matters relating to the planning, execution and monitoring of development schemes and projects in the North Eastern Region:

> "During the period of British rule, the Brahmaputra and Barak-Surma rivers were used extensively for transport and trade between northeast India and the port of Calcutta (now Kolkata). With the growth of the tea industry, these rivers became important carriers of trade. The East India Company started the water route along the Brahmaputra from Kolkata to Dibrugarh in 1844 and steamships were introduced by the Joint Steamer Company in 1847. At about the same time Silchar was linked with Kolkata along the Barak-Surma-Meghna navigation channel. However, with the partition of India in 1947, water transport received a serious blow as a foreign country was born between northeast India and the port of Kolkata." [3]

Besides, both rail links and road communication, which existed through East Bengal, making it rather easy for to and fro movement between the Northeast and the rest of India, got cut off. The flourishing trade between the neighbouring districts like the Khasi & Jaintia Hills of present-day Meghalaya in India and the Sylhet district of East Pakistan, today's Bangladesh, virtually came to a standstill. The impact of partition on North-East India as a whole was severe. Many of the present-day problems that engulf the region were mostly the byproduct of the partition of Bengal and trimming off Sylhet from Assam. The Sukla Commission Report submitted to the Prime Minister of India on 7th March 1997 stated that "the North-East was uniquely disadvantaged by a partition which left its external parameter with no more than 2% contiguity with the rest of India... No other part of the country, barring Jammu and Kashmir, has had to bear a comparable burden with severe market disruption, total isolation, and loss of traditional communication infrastructure, pushing regional costs and prices well above national norms, transport subsidies notwithstanding".

Significantly, 'tea,' the most important means of subsistence for the economy of Assam, was dependent on the foreign market through the seaports of Calcutta and Chittagong. But partition robbed Assam of its easy accessibility to the port towns. With the emergence of East Pakistan, Chittagong became a foreign land, and direct routes to Calcutta through East Pakistan were totally snapped away. The region turned into South Asia's third landlocked state, along with Bhutan and Nepal.

The ceding of lands from Bengal and Assam to (East) Pakistan disrupted the traditional economic activities between these territories and East Bengal and deprived the Hill areas of the established market for their agricultural products and handicrafts, which implied an abnormal increase in the prices of fish, and a fall in the price of jute and a few more items of day-to-day requirements. It especially affected the people of the Khasi-Jaintia Hills, Mizoram, and Garo hill districts, which had long been economically more integrated with Eastern Bengal than with the plains of Assam. Earlier, these border people used to sell items like oranges, pineapples, betel nuts, betel leaves, and bay leaves (tej patta), among other things, in Sylhet and used to earn handsome profits for their products. With the separation of irrigated areas in East Bengal, the problem turned more severe because a large tract of provincial and even district boundaries all at once transformed into international borders. [4]

Additionally, though agriculture was the mainstay of Assam before independence, its undivided district of Lakhimpur was the highest revenue-earning district in India mainly because of its tea, coal, timber, and petroleum products. In fact, Assam was the first to produce tea and petroleum oil in the country. Assam's Digboi Oil Refinery (Commissioned in 1901, now in the Tinsukia district) was the only oil refinery in India and the second in Asia. But, today, the state of Assam, in the land-locked North-East region, remains far from being industrialized in the real sense because of the artificial remoteness that resulted from the partition of the country. The inevitable result of the man-made remoteness and near absence of big industries (consequently the less demand for electricity) was that Assam missed the bus when big projects like Bhakra Nangal, Damodar Valley projects, and other similar projects were changing the face of India's economy. Thus, the benefits of the Industrial Revolution remained a far cry from the people of this 'remote' corner of the country while, significantly, no one today talks or writes about the real cause of the self-inflicted remoteness.

Apart from all these adverse impacts exemplified above, the journey between North-East India and other parts of the country also became an arduous and lengthy affair, adding to the few protracted problems the partition had thrown up for the people. Yet, these inconveniences are almost nothing compared to the tremendous miseries that afflicted the Bengalis after the partition. Millions of people were forced to leave East Bengal. Some were pushed out of their ancestral homes under the threat of their lives and properties. The others were compelled by hunger and poverty to leave their families/homes to make a living in West Bengal, Tripura, and truncated Assam. It was mostly Hindus in the former category and Muslims in the latter category. Thus, among other places in India, numerous Bengalis from East Bengal had to relocate to North-East India under compulsion.

Sadly, the partition of the sub-continent was not only a historical event that ended in 1947. It's an unfinished agenda having wide-ranging and deeper ramifications for the lives of individuals and the nation in post-colonial India, especially in the northeastern part of India. Although the 1947 partition of Bengal and the forfeiture of the Sylhet district are no longer a current controversy, the Hindu-Muslim disharmony and the Assamese-Bengali discord set in by the British colonial rulers through their *divide et impera* maxim are still full of vim and vigour. [5] Yet, the common people of the country, particularly Assam, are still not fully aware of the invisible hands at play today in fermenting the communal and racial discords ingrained by the British alien rulers in our system. Suffice it to say that the term 'polarisation'[1] is the reincarnated Indian appellation of the dictum 'divide et impera' of the Romans or the maxim 'divide and rule' of the Britons. Thus, with the exit of the British from India, the practice of 'Divide and Rule' virtually ended in Indian political discourse. It is artfully substituted by the expression 'polarisation', literally a different name for almost the same dictum and maxim.

Note: [1]According to the Cambridge Dictionary, polarisation means "the act of dividing something, especially something that contains different people or opinions, into two completely opposing groups."

Polarizing, or dividing citizens based on community, caste, creed, race, mother tongue, and other factors, is advantageous to the authorities in power to divert people's attention from their basic necessities like the availability of quality education, healthcare services, employment opportunities, plus a dignified life with liberty, equality, and fraternity as enshrined in the preamble of the Indian constitution. Accordingly, the political parties in power keep most citizens of the so-called largest democracy in the world busy and active in practising bigotry between one community against the other, to the extent that the lack of essential amenities rarely becomes the priority demand of the people as a whole. Thus, fraternity becomes the first victim of the democratic principle - recurrent communal riots bear witness to this - closely followed by equality and liberty - in that order — making our democracy per se their casualty since its infancy. As a general rule, the polarization of citizens is done by spreading disinformation, distorting historical truth, and obscuring certain parts of history to facilitate the first two. For instance,

a) Even today, many Indians believe that the partition of British India took place on the Hindu-Muslim communal line as demanded by the Indian Muslims. The truth is only a section of Muslims in India desired it. Many Muslims and Muslim organizations fought AGAINST the demand for India's partition. The All India Azad Muslim Conference (AMC) is a case in point. It was the largest amalgamation of Muslim lower castes and working-class organizations that were against the two-nation theory and Jinnah's scheme of Pakistan. Except for the Muslim League[1], all the important Muslim groups and formations in the country were identified with the objects of the AMC. Its Delhi session in 1940 represented the "majority of India's Muslims". Despite a promising and historic AMC of April 1940, the tempo wavered in the next couple of years. The AMC was the brainchild of Allah Baksh Soomro, British India's 2nd & 4th Premier of Sindh province. He was murdered on 14th May 1943 by hired assigns who sounded the death knell for the AMC. [6]

b) In the emergence of Assam province in 1874, as discussed in chapter 3 of this book, three Bengali dominant districts of Bengal, Goalpara, Cachar, and Sylhet, and the Assam division from the Bengal Presidency were carved out and amalgamated together where over 57% of the population were Bengali-speaking people and the remaining population consisted mainly of the Assamese-speaking population plus other groups of people speaking more than 200 different languages and dialects were below 43%. But, this historical truth that the Bengali-speaking people were predominant and in the majority in the province ***ab initio*** has been blurred in the history book. Thus, the people in Assam are led to believe that only the influx of the so-called 'illegal immigrants' from the adjacent province of Bengal was responsible for making the Assamese people a minority population in their 'own homeland'. It is creating resentment against the Bengali residents of Assam.

Note: [1] In the 1946 election of the Legislative Councils, the Muslim League won by an overwhelming majority. Still, it did not mean that the League represented most Muslims of India, given that the elections were held within narrow and very restricted electorates, which depended on taxation, property, education, government service, and so forth, which also varied from province to province under the sixth schedule to 1935 Act. In other words, the Muslim League wanting partition did not mean that most Muslims favoured Pakistan, given that the majority of Muslims in British India were not eligible to vote because of their poverty, illiteracy, and so on.

As an outcome of the massive polarization that progressively took place among citizens, the post-partition stories of Assam are replete with events based on Little Nationalism. However, before narrating some of these unnecessary, unpleasant, and unacceptable incidents, let us have a look at what Amalendu Guha, the prominent historian from Assam, wrote about Little Nationalism in his journal article in Economic and Political Weekly, vol. 15, titled "Little Nationalism Turned Chauvinist: Assam's Anti-Foreigner Upsurge, 1979-80". The following paragraphs are quoted from Guha's article:

> "Ever since its beginnings in the early 19th century, our nationalism has been developing at two levels – one all-India, on the basis of pan-Indian cultural homogeneities and anti-imperialism shared in common; and another regional (Bengali, Marathi, Asamiya, etc.), on the basis of regional cultural homogeneities. From the very outset, the two nationalisms are found intertwined and dovetailed. Traditionally, an average Indian identifies himself with both nationalisms except in some peripheral areas (e.g., Nagaland and Mizoram), left untouched by the railways and the Indian national movement. Assam is, however, fairly integrated with the rest of India, both economically, culturally, and politically. Like an average Indian, an average Asamiya too is simultaneously aware of both his regional and national identities. Madhav Dev, a 16th-century Vaishnava saint of Assam, wrote in a verse that he was proud of his birth in 'Bharata,' and this fact is often invoked as a symbol of the latter identity. Yet another aspect of the development is that, after the British had quit, no particular nationality could be identified as an oppressor nation in relation to other nationalities within the Union, as the Russians could be in the Czarist State.
>
> The duality of our national consciousness found expression in the articulated attitudes of Dhekiyal Phukan, Bankim Chandra Chottopadhyay, M. G. Ranade, and also later heirs to their tradition. In his presidential address at the annual conference of the Asam

Sahitya Sabha at Dhubri in 1926, Benudhar Rajkhova (1872-1955), for instance, said:

> 'Let all nationalities (jati) of India follow their own paths. The Brahmaputra, the Ganga, the Yamuna, the Kaveri, the Sindh – let all of them go and flow along their respective courses. Let there be no attempts to merge one with the other. Finally, all will converge in the Indian Ocean, that is the Indian nation (mahajati). Troubles will increase if any other method is resorted to for creating the Indian nation.' (Translation by author Guha)

Rajkhova was happy to note in the course of the same address that a large number of Bengali Muslims from the neighbouring district of Mymensingh had settled in Assam, and he predicted that they would all be proud to call themselves Asamiyas in due course. His prediction came out to be true.

Asamiya's little nationalism began to take shape in the 1850s through political mobilization by the Asmiya middle class on the language issue and, later, on job and land issues as well. It generally developed as a comprehensive ideology that underwent organized consolidation during the 1920s. Though basically protectionist and defensive till about 1947, Asamiya's little nationalism had, by then, assumed an aggressive tone as well. For example, while presiding over the annual conference of Asam Sahitya Sabha in 1927, Tarunram Phukan (1877-1939) said:

> We Asmiyas are a distinct nationality (jati) among Indians. Though our language is Sanskrit-based, it is a distinct language. *A rising nationality shows signs of life by way of extending domination over others.* Alas, it is otherwise (with us); we are incapable of self-defence today! We are not only dependent, but even a dependent neighbour is trying to swallow us, taking advantage of our helplessness. Brother Asmiya! recollect your past glory to have an understanding of the present situation. (trans and emphasis by author Guha)

Seeds of chauvinism sown by such speeches were sure to germinate in due course.

However, until about 1947, Asamiya's little nationalism was not a cudgel, and there were no racial or language riots. **As the Asamiya middle class emerged stronger and more ambitious than ever after Sylhet was shaken off its back, its little nationalism started**

degenerating into chauvinism and minority bashing." [7]
(Emphasis by Subir)

It's noteworthy that outside Assam, an Assamese is one who lives in Assam, whatever may be their mother tongue. In Assam, however, Asamiyas or Assamese are those who speak Asamiya and generally live in the six districts of the Brahmaputra Valley. The non-Assamese are those natives of Assam who ordinarily live there and whose mother tongues are not Asamiya or Assamese. They include the Bengalis of Cachar and Goalpara, the Hindi-speaking tea plantation labourers, and the hill people like the Khasis of Shillong. Besides these natives of Assam who are not transient, many Bengalis, mostly from East Bengal, have settled in all the important towns of the Brahmaputra Valley primarily. Some are displaced persons from East Bengal. Many of them have cleared jungles, opened up communications, started cultivation, and rehabilitated themselves in the interior of the Brahmaputra Valley. In the towns of Gauhati, Tezpur, Nowgong, Jorhat, Dibrugarh, Tinsukia, and others, almost half the population consists of Bengalis. They have their own clubs where Bengali plays are staged. Many of them own cinema houses where Bengali pictures are shown. Bengali dailies from Calcutta enjoy a large circulation in these towns. In some of them, Bengali schools are flourishing well. Many Bengalis are thriving as doctors, lawyers, teachers, clerks, and traders. [8]

Former History teacher, Rabindra Sadan Girl's College, Karimganj, Assam, Sujit Chaudhuri, called the disintegration of Sylhet from Assam 'a god-sent opportunity' for the Assamese elite. The following few lines from his paper titled "A 'god-sent' opportunity?" in a February 2002 symposium on 'Partitions in the East: POROUS BORDERS, DIVIDED SELVES' are quoted below to catch a glimpse of how little nationalism in Assam degenerated and initiated minority bashing:

> "The Shillong Times, dated 27 August 1947, published a statement signed by four Jatiya Mahasabha leaders which proclaimed: 'With Sylhet joining Pakistan, Assam has grown smaller in area but attained greater homogeneity which has prompted Assam to be *free and sovereign*. From the days of antiquity, Assam was not only free but indomitable in power... When the (Assam) Congress and the public agitated against the grouping of Assam with Bengal, it was Mahatma Gandhi himself who said that Assam should resist this against the whole world. But now she is grouped with the rest of India, a mightier force than the others. Assam's *sovereignty* was a fact of ages

ago and it should be of the future.' The propagation of the same ideal continued, and *The Assam Tribune*, dated 4th January 1948, reported:

> A meeting of the Asom Jatiya Mahasabha, Kamrup branch, was held on the 1st of January in the church field to discuss the development of the country in all aspects. The President expressed the view that Assam should come out of the Indian Union and become an independent country like Burma or any other country.
>
> Further, 'Sri Ambika Giri Roy Choudhury, General Secretary, Asom Jatiya Mahasabha has this morning sent a telegram from Jorhat to Aliba Imti, President, Naga National Council, Kohima. Sri Roy Choudhury, in the wire, informed the National Council President that the Asom Jatiya Mahasabha workers assembled at Jorhat have expressed their fullest sympathy with their Naga brothers' stand for self-determination.'
>
> It needs to be stressed that in 1947-48, the political environment of India was fluid, and there was nothing 'wrong' if some quarters demanded the secession of Assam from India at a point when the redrawing of the country's frontier lines was already on the agenda.

The transfer of Sylhet to Pakistan was hailed by the Assamese public opinion. The only daily newspaper of Assam, The Assam Tribune, hailed the transfer of Sylhet: 'The Assamese public seems to feel relieved of a burden' (21 July 1947)." But this jubilation was short-lived. The problem of the refugee influx, built within the Partition proposal itself, threatened to neutralize the gains achieved by the ouster of Sylhet. Why? Because most of the refugees crossed over from Sylhet, the district which had been a part of Assam since 1874, to the newly formed Assam again! **Gopinath Bordoloi and his Congress ministry opposed tooth and nail the central government's bid to settle these refugees in Assam.** [9]

After the partition, Assam's linguistic demography changed considerably as the greater part of Sylhet was assigned to Pakistan. It had been estimated that the Assamese constituted one-third of the population in Assam (including Cachar), the Bengalis constituted one-third, and the rest belonged to Tribal and other linguistic groups. In a meeting at Nalbari, Assam, the then Finance Minister Shri Moti Ram Bora stated on the 28th April 1953, that 'out of 96 lakhs population, only 30 lakhs were pure Assamese', according to The Assam Tribune dated 5th May 1953.

Assam was not only for the Assamese demand but also started immediately after the partition. To a delegation of government employees of Sylhet who had been discharged as surplus for having opted to serve in India on the solemn guarantees of the government to retain them on existing terms, Shri Bordoloi said: "The newly accepted policy of his Government was – Assam for the Assamese," according to the Shillong Times dated 29th August 1947. Grieved at this and the policy of exclusiveness followed by the Government of Assam, Mahatma Gandhi remarked in one of his post-prayer speeches: "I have noticed the view expressed that Assam belongs exclusively to the Assamese. In India, if that spirit was to enter every Province, to whom then would India belong? People of all provinces belong to India, and India belongs to all." But nothing daunted, Shri Bordoloi repeated at the Students' Congress held at Golaghat: "Undoubtedly, Assam is for the Assamese," according to the Shillong Times dated 19th October 1947. This policy was finally reiterated through the Governor's Address in the Assam Assembly. **Speaking on behalf of the provincial Congress cabinet,** when the Assam Assembly met on 5th November 1947 for the first time after Independence, in his [1]formal speech, the Governor of Assam, Akbar Hydari, said:

> 'The natives of Assam are now masters of their own house. They have a government that is both responsible and responsive to them. They can take what steps are necessary for the encouragement and propagation of the Assamese language and culture and of the languages and customs of the tribal people who are their fellow citizens and who also must have a share in the formation of such policies. **The Bengali no longer has the power, even if he had the will, to impose anything on the people** of these Hills and Valleys which constitute Assam. The basis of such feelings against him as exist is fear – but now there is no cause for fear. I would, therefore, appeal to you to exert all the influence you possess to give the stranger in our midst a fair

deal, provided, of course, he, in his turn, deals loyally with us'. [10]

Note: ¹The Governor's address to the Legislative Assembly is essentially a statement of policy prepared by the Council of Ministers.

The attitude of the Assam ministry can be gauged from the following government circular issued on 4th May 1948:

'In view of the emergency created by the influx of refugees into the province from East Pakistan territories and in order to preserve peace, tranquility, and social equilibrium in the towns and villages, the government *reiterates* its policy that settlement of land should be in no circumstances made with persons who are not indigenous to the province. The non-indigenous inhabitants of the province should include, for the purpose of land settlement during the present emergency, *persons who are non-Assamese settlers in Assam though they already have lands and houses of their own and have made Assam their home to all intents and purposes*' (Revenue Dept. no. 195/47/188 dt. 4.5.48).

Thus the **Bordoloi ministry pursued a policy that put a ban on the settlement of land not only for the refugees but also for all non-Assamese settlers who might have been living in Assam for generations.** The central government assessed the availability of fallow cultivable land in Assam through a committee headed by Dorab Gandhi, who reported that **18 million acres of cultivable land could be used for the new settlement.**

This figure is also tallied with the Assam government's own assessment as given in its publication, The Problem of Agricultural Development (Assam Government Press, 1946, Table VI, p. 8) and Industrial Planning and Development of Assam (Government of Assam, 1948). The Census of India, 1951, Vol. 1 also reported that in Assam and adjoining areas, 'the percentage of unused land is highest among all the sub-regions of India' (p. 22). The central government insisted that the vast tracts of wasteland in Assam should be utilized for production, as **the available surplus was more than sufficient to accommodate both refugees and indigenous landless people.** [11] (Emphasis by Subir)

On 18th May 1949, Prime Minister Jawaharlal Nehru wrote the following letter to Assam Chief Minister Gopinath Bordoloi:

New Delhi,
May 18, 1949

My dear Bordoloi,

I thank you for your letter of the 7th May. I see you are here in Delhi and I was hoping to talk with you. Meanwhile, I am replying to some matters referred to in your letter.

You mention that Pakistan is carrying espionage in Assam. To some extent, I suppose, this is being done by Pakistan all over India and it is inevitable. But of course, so far as we are concerned, we must try to stop it or find it what they are doing. We do not object normally to particular persons visiting India from Pakistan. But if high officials make a point of coming to India and staying here for a long time, the matter might well be enquired into.

I am surprised to learn that you feel yourself helpless in dealing with the influx of Muslims into Assam. As you know, we have a permit system as between Western Pakistan and India. I do not think there is a permit system in regard to Eastern Bengal and Western Bengal and possibly no such system exists in regard to Assam either. I think you should discuss this matter with Mr Gopalswami Ayyangar. This really has nothing to do with the type of permit system that we have in west. In a sense you have to face a somewhat different problem and surely we ought to be able to devise ways and means to deal with it.

About the influx of Hindus from East Bengal, this is a different matter entirely. **I am told that your government or some of your Ministers have openly stated that they prefer Muslims of East Bengal to Hindus from East Bengal.** While I, for one, always like any indication of a lack of communal feeling in dealing with public matters, I must confess that this strong objection to Hindu refugees coming from East Bengal is a little difficult for me to understand. I am afraid Assam is getting bad a name for its narrow-minded policy.

You say that there is no further land available in Assam. This is a question of fact which can easily be determined. It is patent, however, that **if land is not available in Assam; it is less available in the rest of India which is very heavily populated, barring the desert and the mountains.** What then are we to do with the millions of refugee we have to deal with? Many of them, of course, will be accommodated in East Punjab or roundabout from where Muslims have gone, but we have refugees from Sind, from the North West

Frontier Province, from Baluchistan, from East Bengal etc. Where are these people to go if each province adopts the attitude Assam apparently has done? **Are we to push them out of India or to allow them to starve and die out?** Obviously not. Therefore we have to absorb them and make provision for them so that they might be good citizens. In doing so, all provinces have to help and cooperate and it will do no good to a province to refuse cooperation in this national work.

The refugee problem is one of the two or three problems to which we give first priority in India at present. This applies to the utilisation of our financial resources also. Our development schemes are thought of in terms of, to some extent, of refugees. If Assam adopts an attitude of incapacity to help in solving the refugee problem, then the claims of Assam for financial help obviously suffer. You say that you have already received two and half a lakh Hindu refugees from East Bengal. That may be so, although there are no precise records. But **evidently Assam Government has done nothing for them**, and they have shifted for themselves.

I think it is important that your Government should look at this question from the larger viewpoint. This is not only essential for India but, if I may say so, for Assam also. **Of all the provinces of India, Assam is the least heavily populated** and there is going to be continuous pressure from all sides including China. No laws will be able to prevent this pressure and occasional influxes. We can deal with this methodically by selecting our people or be swept away by it willy-nilly.

You talk of the communist menace etc. That is no doubt a separate problem. But it is also related to the problem I have touched upon above.

I understand that it has now been decided to have a census of displaced persons taken. There should also be a welfare committee in each district and that deputy commissioner should give rehabilitation facilities to artisans and destitute persons. I am glad this is going to be done and sooner it is done the better. But the main thing is that **this problem has to be looked upon from a different aspect than it has been thus far in Assam**. I understand that Medhi, your Finance Minister, is a strong opponent of any further refugees coming to Assam. I am sending a copy of this letter to him also so that he may know my views on the subject. (Emphasis by Subir)

Yours sincerely

Jawaharlal Nehru. [12]

"On Nehru's advice, Bordoloi met N. Gopalaswami Ayyengar, the Union Minister for Transport, several times. The latter visited Assam in November 1949 to study the situation. Since the problem also existed in West Bengal, he subsequently discussed the idea of a permit system with the Chief Minister of West Bengal, Dr. B. C. Roy. Roy opposed the idea, fearing it would lead to a greater influx of Hindus from East Pakistan. Therefore, Ayyengar suggested an alternative measure: a permit system that would grant the Government of Assam authority to expel such persons from within their borders if it was satisfied that the particular situation justified such expulsion. Bordoloi agreed that the system would benefit Assam, but it fell short of what he was demanding. The result of this initiative was the enactment of the Immigrants (Expulsion from Assam) Act, of 1950. It provided for the removal of all immigrants, except for displaced persons, whose stay was deemed detrimental to the interests of the general public in India or any Scheduled Tribe in Assam. The ordinance was issued in January 1950, and a Bill to replace it received Presidential assent only in March 1950. However, in the wake of widespread communal riots in March 1950, during which Muslim immigrants were targeted, the legislation was kept in abeyance from enforcement due to fears that its provisions would be misused. Nehru therefore advised Bordoloi not to use the law for the time being." [13] Thus, there was the Immigrants (Expulsion from Assam) Act in 1950 **even before the legislation of the Indian Citizenship Act 1955!**

Note: [1]Quoted from NMML occasional paper titled "Nehru and the North East" presented by Prof Sajal Nag[2] at a Conference, 'Rethinking the Nehru Legacy: The Long twentieth century', held at the Nehru Memorial Museum and Liabrary (NMML), New Delhi, on 17-18 November 2014

[2]Prof Sajal Nag is Netaji Subhash Chandra Bose Distinguished Chair Professor in Social Sciences at Presidency University, Kolkata. He specialises in the history of modern North-East India.

Nevertheless, the Bordoloi Government in Assam continued to pursue the policy of Assamisation through executive orders and confidential circulars which were quite unfavorable to the interests of the non-Asamiya inhabitants of the state. Some instances of how this Assamisation policy persisted are narrated in the following paragraphs.

In 1948, Bordoloi announced on the floor of the Assam Legislative Assembly that it was not the intention of the Government to make Assam a bilingual State. For the sake of the homogeneity of the Province, he advised all non-Asamiya people to adopt the Assamese language (Assam Assembly Proceedings, 1948, page 511). On September 26, 1947, Bordoloi, who was also the Minister of Education, passed the following order on a Resolution forwarded to him by Assam Jatiya Mahasava:

> *"Please send this to the Inspectors of Schools to set in terms of the present policy of the Government viz., the Assamese is accepted as a compulsory second language in all schools where it cannot be Assamese completely."*

This was followed by a policy of introducing Assamese as the medium of instruction, even at the primary level. As a result, in the district of Goalpara alone, which was predominantly a Bengali-speaking district, the number of schools with Bengali as the medium was reduced to 3 in 1950-51 from 250 in 1947-48, while the number of Assamese medium schools during the said period rose from 348 to 833.

Starred Question No. 21 (a) (i) (ii) by Shri Santosh Kumar Barua in the Assam Assembly, dated 11th September 1953 (Vide Assam Gazette, dated 10th May 1954, page 2367),

Statement showing the year-wise increase or decrease of the total number of Lower Primary Schools in Dhubri Sub-Division with the medium of Assamese language and Bengali language as the medium, along with their annual expenditure during the succeeding three years immediately after the partition of India and the Sylhet referendum:—

YEAR	ASAMIYA MEDIUM		BENGALI MEDIUM	
	No. of Schools	Expenditure	No. of Schools	Expenditure
		Rs		Rs
1947-48	348	96135	250	66000
1948-49	582	211470	130	48360
1949-50	773	384063	45	4674

Commenting on this, Shri Phani Bora of the Assam Communist Party said at a Press Conference on 27th May 1954 at Gauhati as follows:—

> *"The Assam Government, through their official and non-official agents,* **forcibly sealed off all Bengali Schools in Goalpara district***, denying safeguards of the Bengalees, cultural and linguistic rights. Such imperialist and reactionary actions of the Assam Congress Government were*

responsible for encouraging disintegrating elements in Assam, including Naga Hills." (Emphasis by Subir)

— (A. B. Patrika, 29.5.45).

The infiltration, which initially started in the Assam Valley, extended to other areas as well, including the district of Cachar.

The President of the United Mizo Freedom Organisation, Mr. Lalmawia, in his Memorandum submitted to the States Reorganisation Committee, stated, inter alia, as follows:-

> *"In the heterogeneous State of Assam, where the population of Assamese is not more than 40 per cent, the Assamese people insist that Assamese should be adopted as the State language of Assam. Even before the adoption of Assamese as a State language, the Government of Assam spent a large sum of money spreading the language, even in the far distant district of Lusai Hills."*

Numerous Circulars were issued by the Government of Assam restricting settlement of land, employment in Government services, contracts, licenses for trade and business, and even the matter of admission to schools and colleges to all persons other than those who are indigenous natives or domiciled in the State of Assam. The requisite provisions relating to qualifications for obtaining a domicile certificate in Assam, as disclosed by the Chief Minister of Assam on the floor of the Assembly on the 20th March 1948, are quoted below:

"A non-Assamese must have the following qualifications in order to acquire domicile:—

1. Homestead in the district where he should live continuously at least for 10 years.
2. Desire to live their till his death.
3. Non-possession of any landed property in his native district.
4. Absence of frequent visits to his native place or dist.
5. Absence of Interest or connection whatsoever with the native people."

In this context, a portion of the observation of the States Re-organisation Commission quoted below is revealing:

> "The desire of the local people for the State services being manned mainly by 'the sons of the soil' is understandable but only up to a point. When such devices as domicile rules operate to make the public services the exclusive preserve of the majority language group

of the State, this is bound to cause discontent among the other groups, apart from impeding the free flow of talent and impairing administrative efficiency." (para 849 of S.R.C. Report)

An 'Indigenous' person was defined in the Assam Gazette dated 6th September 1950, on page 1464, as follows:

"Indigenous persons of Assam mean persons belonging to the State of Assam and speaking Assamese language or any tribal dialect of Assam or, in the case of Cachar, the language of the region."

Significantly, the fact that Bengali was the language of the district of Cachar was not mentioned in it. The above definition was formulated in connection with the Assam Census in 1951 when the Assam Government decided to enumerate the size of land-holding of indigenous persons.

Faced with this policy of strangulation, politically, economically, and culturally, the linguistic minorities in the State raised their voice from time to time. On some occasions, these were responded to with mass violence. The first noticeable symptom of violence took place in 1948 at Gauhati and other adjoining areas, directed primarily against Bengali Muslims, all of whom were agriculturists. After the 1950 Riots, the Nehru-Liaquat Pact brought back the Muslim evacuees to Assam shortly before the Census enumerated in 1951. In reply to question No. 13, relating to the size of land-holding, the **Bengali Muslims were made to declare their mother tongue as Assamese;** otherwise, they ran the risk of losing their lands, which were settled annually. The third such disturbance is the well-known holocaust of 1960, which brought widespread havoc and disaster to thousands of Bengali-speaking people in the districts of Kamrup (including Goreswar), Nowgong, Darrang, Sibsagar, and Lakhimpur, i.e., practically throughout the Brahmaputra Valley. [14]. (Emphasis by Subir)

Significantly, the CENSUS OF INDIA, 1951 Volume XII ASSAM, MANIPUR AND TRIPURA PART I-A REPORT, mentioned on page 428:

"Indigenous person of Assam" means a person belonging to the State of Assam and speaking the Assamese language or any tribal dialect of Assam or, in the case of Cachar, the language of the region."

The fact that Bengali was the language of the district of Cachar was not mentioned here in defining the 'indigenous persons of Assam'. The **presence of Bengali-speaking people in Assam was astutely ignored and stifled** by merely specifying: 'in the case of Cachar, the language of the region'! This aspect assumes added significance given that this census report of 1951 eventually became **the foundation on which the first National Register of Citizens (NRC) in Assam was prepared. Subsequently, this 1951 Assam NRC was updated in 2019** to ascertain genuine citizens and foreigners staying in Assam.

In the same census report, Census Superintendent Vaghaiwalla reported:

> "Assam is still one of the few parts of India where language controversies vitiate census information. In the 1941 Census, the language entries were badly vitiated by propaganda, especially in Kamrup and Nowgong districts "and partly among ex-garden labourers. My predecessor was of the opinion that unless corrected, the returns would be useless. In the present Census, the language propaganda and vitiation of census information regarding language were confined mainly to the Dhubri Sub-division of the district of Goalpara. There was brisk propaganda in some parts of Dhubri Sub-division to record "Goalparia" as the mother tongue though there was no such language name. The move derived support from the comments made in the 1931 Census Report by Mr Mullan and from the normal legal rule of the Census viz., to record answers exactly as given by the persons enumerated. I ordered separate sorting for "Goalparia" to find out the exact number before a decision could be arrived at whether they were to be thrown into Assamese or Bengali. These instructions were somehow overlooked by the Tabulation staff: in spite of clear instructions to this effect. As a result, I had to order a re-sorting of the entire Dhubri Subdivision for "Goalparia." On re-sorting, the number of persons who returned their mother tongue as Goalparia were reported to be 2,562 Males and 1,526 Females and finally classified as Assamese **according to the decision of the State Government."** [15] (Emphasis by Subir)

Nevertheless, one of the most dreadful manifestations of the British 'Divide and Rule' policy in India was undoubtedly the introduction of the unique 'Line System' in Assam, discussed elaborately in Chapter 6. Suffice it to say now that in the wake of the massive British-sponsored migration of Muslim agriculturists from East Bengal since the beginning of the 20th century, the local population of Assam became wary when it found mention of this in the 1911 census report. The British administration then segregated the migrant Bengali Muslims from the native Assamese by the Line System. Thus, the cracks created by the British between the Hindus and the Muslims deepened so much that it ultimately resulted in the partition of the country, involving, among other things, the loss of Assam's Sylhet district in 1947. Assam and North-East India thus turned into a landlocked region, surrounded by foreign countries on all sides except the Siliguri corridor.

The partition of India brought about a palpable shift in the prevalent communal conflicts in Assam. From Hindu-Muslim controversies, it turned, to a certain extent, into Assamese-Bengali frictions. For instance, referring to the Confidential Report of Enquiry into Goalpara Disturbances of April 1955, research scholar Wazid Reja Osmani, in his research paper titled "The historical background of the immigration problems in Assam 1946 to 1983," wrote in part:

> "The change in the power structure in Assam in the wake of independence had given the Assamese people political leverage for manipulating the ethnic division of labour which in turn stimulated competition and conflict. Consequently, <u>governmental authority was directed towards</u> **restructuring the ethnic division** of labour which in turn intensified the conflict between the Assamese and Bengali Hindus. For example, in the riots of 1948 and 1950, the starting point was the demand by Assamese youth on the Bengalis to shed the sign of separatism, viz, to replace Bengali shop signboards with Assamese, to **desist from running separate schools for Bengalis and finally to accept Assamese as their language.**" [16] (Emphasis by Subir)

Against this backdrop, the following four paragraphs, among others, selectively quoted from the Report of the States Reorganisation Commission 1955 (SRC), speak for themselves:

> "The genesis of the Purbachal demand is that since the major part of Sylhet (to which Assam remained attached for more than 120 years after its initial annexation in 1826 to the Bengal Presidency) was cut off from India at the time of Partition, the Bengalis in Assam, who used to feel that culturally and even geographically they belonged to Bengal, have found themselves somewhat isolated in what they may now be disposed to regard as an uncongenial environment. It has been represented to us that the activities of the Assam Jatiya Mahasabha and the policies of the local government have not only not reconciled the Bengalis in this part of Assam, but have had quite the opposite result. The Bengali-speaking people have cited, for instance, the fact that the **number of government primary schools in Goalpara district with Bengali as the medium of instruction has fallen from 252 in 1947-48 to 1** at the present time."

"The linguistic complexion of the existing State (Assam) establishes very clearly its composite character, in spite of the very interesting post-1931 spread of Assamese according to the census figures. It is not surprising that the rapid increase in the past two decades in the number of persons speaking Assamese has been disputed, and **the veracity of the 1951 Census figures has been questioned in certain quarters.** We have not deemed it necessary to enter into this controversy, but we would like to draw attention to the fact that in spite of this rapid increase, the **Assamese-speaking population still constitutes only about 55 per cent of the population of the State.**

"We do not desire to make any recommendation about the details of the policy to be followed in prescribing the use of minority languages for official purposes. However, we are inclined to the view that **a State should be treated as unilingual only where one language group constitutes about seventy per cent or more of its entire population. Where there is a substantial minority constituting thirty per cent or so of the population, the State should be recognised as 'bilingual' for administrative purposes.**

"The same principle might hold good at the district level; that is to say, if seventy per cent or more of the total population of a district is constituted by a group which is a minority in the State, **the language of the minority group, and not the State language, should be the official language in that district.** It will also be of advantage if, in bilingual districts, municipal areas, or other smaller units such as taluks, where there are minorities constituting fifteen to twenty per cent of the population, documents which are used by the people at large, such as government notices, electoral rolls, ration cards, etc., are printed in both languages. It should also be permissible to file documents in the courts etc. in the minority language. Likewise, where the candidates seeking election to any local bodies are required to have a working knowledge of a language, the knowledge of a language of such minor language groups should be given recognition." [17] (Emphasis by Subir)

Yet, barely five years after the State Reorganisation Commission 1955 Report, the Assam State Legislative Assembly passed a bill to make Assamese the sole official language of the state amidst one of Assam's worst communal violence episodes against the Bengalis, known as "Bongal Kheda" (meaning "Drive Out Bengalis") in the Brahmaputra valley. "Bongal Kheda" is nothing but an organized campaign for ethnic cleansing in which some unruly gangs of Assamese miscreants attacked the Bengalis *en masse* in both urban and rural areas, looted and set fire to their houses, killed hundreds of innocents, and drove away thousands of them from Assam. The covert tactical support of the local administrations reportedly made it impossible for the Bengalis to retaliate or even to put up a modicum of defence for their lives and properties. While the communal violence flared up in July 1960, the official language bill was passed on 24th October 1960, and the Governor of Assam gave his assent to the bill on 17th December 1960, making it a law that was notified in the Assam Gazette on 19th December 1960 - despite persistent protests by the Bengalis and other communities living in the state.

To gain insight into the origins of the Official Language Movement in post-independent Assam, the following two paragraphs are quoted verbatim from a paper titled "The Assamese Language Issue: An Analysis from Historical Perspective" by Habib Fazlul Basid, a Gauhati University Research Scholar, which appeared in the International Journal of Humanities and Social Sciences, ISSN 2250-3226, Volume 6, Number 2 (2016):

> "Initially started as an elite movement by the Assam Sahitya Sabha (Assam Literary Society organized in 1917), the Official Language Movement of 1960 was spearheaded by the student community comprising the All Assam Students' Federation (under the banner of the Students' Association of Gauhati). The Official Language Movement of 1960, however, was a direct sequel to the appointment of the States Reorganization Commission in 1955 and dates back to the agitation of Assamese as the official state language beginning in 1950. Through two resolutions in 1950 and again in 1959, the Sahitya Sabha stressed the need for making Assamese the official state language. The controversy, however, gained momentum after April 1959, when the Sabha proposed that the Assamese language be declared as the state language in 1960. During Prime Minister Jawaharlal Nehru's visit to Gauhati University on April 17, the students in a body demanded an immediate declaration of Assamese as the State Language. This was reinforced by the Assam Pradesh Congress Committee's (A.P.C.C.) resolution of April 22. However, on May 21, 1960, a huge procession of non-Assamese students was led out from the Khasi National Darbar, shouting slogans to oppose Assamese as the State Language. The disturbances in Assam created by the Assamese students in the form of processions, meetings, and 'hartals' soon began to dominate the situation, leading to violence and widespread destruction of a large number of residences in Assam. This was a matter of concern and sorrow for the

Government of Assam. It was necessary for the Government to enunciate its policy regarding its action to deal with the situation that had arisen. **Despite the S.R.C. Report stating that the Assamese language did not fulfil the formula laid down for an official language and contrary to the non-Assamese opposition, Chief Minister Chaliha introduced the Assamese Official Language Bill** in the Assembly on October 10, 1960. The Bill provided for two official languages - Assamese and, for an interim period, English. The bill passed on October 24, 1960, included safeguards for linguistic minorities as well." [18] (Emphasis by Subir)

As the Assamese Official Language Bill initially sought to impose the Assamese language over a large number of non-Assamese populations in Assam, widespread agitation erupted spontaneously against it in the Bengali-majority Barak Valley and other places in the state. When the Assam Government's attempt to suppress the protest by force failed, it finally gave in to the popular demand but sadly, after eleven Bengali activists, including a young girl of barely sixteen years of age, Kamala Bhattacharjee, sacrificed their lives in police firing at Silchar on May 19, 1961. Ironically, Bimala Prasad Chaliha was Assam's Chief Minister at that time. He represented the people of the Badarpur Assembly constituency of Barak Valley, where more than 90% of the electorates were Bengalis!

Does this mean that Chief Minister Bimala Prasad Chaliha was a prejudiced person? Subir's personal experience, however, tells a different tale. Chaliha, on the contrary, was a very kind, decent, and soft-spoken gentleman, as the following anecdote suggests.

Subir had the special privilege of having a personal acquaintance with Chaliha when he was Chief Minister of Assam, with its capital in Shillong, where Subir grew up. On several occasions, as a teenage boy, he engaged in face-to-face conversations with this renowned Assamese personality. Chaliha used to speak flawless Bengali with an immaculate Bengali accent and always charmed the teenager with his pleasing temperament. Once, there was a happenstance meeting between them at the Borjhar Aerodrome, also known as Gauhati Airport at the time. Subir was there to see off one of his close relatives, and Chaliha had just arrived at the airport from Shillong to catch a flight. After the usual exchange of pleasantries, when Subir mentioned that he was about to go back home, Chaliha offered him the private car that had come to drop him off and assured him that he would return to Shillong soon. If Subir remembers correctly, it was a Plymouth car, and Chaliha graciously allowed him to use the entire chauffeur-driven car for the journey. That unforgettable ride, more than fifty years ago, along the serpentine Shillong-

Gauhati road through the picturesque hilly landscape of present-day Meghalaya, remains cherished in Subir's memory. Thus, the name of Bimala Prasad Chaliha always brings back to him the wonderful remembrance of that day, especially the extraordinary kind gesture Chaliha showed to an ordinary teenage boy. Subir often noticed other kind gestures in him as well.

But what compelled this decent gentleman to act as he did towards the Bengalis in Assam in the 1960s? According to author Rajen Saikia, the hill leaders of Assam were angered by the Assam Official Language Act passed by the State Legislature. The issue had been brewing for quite some time, causing unrest in the state. So, despite being a passionate Gandhian and a liberal democrat, Chief Minister B. P. Chaliha 'dared not to be less of an Assamese if he were to survive in Assam valley politics' [19]. Evidently, Chaliha had to make this choice for his political survival, succumbing to the pressures exerted on him by his adversaries.

'ONE STATE, ONE LANGUAGE' demands in Assam are as absurd as 'One India, One Language', argued poet and commentator Sutputra Radheye. The author put forward multiple reasons in support of this assertion in his article, from which the following paragraphs are quoted:

> "The first reason is the political and social structure of the state. Assam, by its very nature, is pluralistic, including a chromatic variation of communities, languages, and religions, as it wasn't formed on a linguistic basis. Every community has its own ethnic identity, much like India. Thus, a 'state language', which is deeply associated with ethnic nationalism, is not implementable in a diversified civic nationalist state like Assam.
>
> A civic nation or state is nothing but an amalgamation of diverse ethnic identities based on liberal democracy, making it impossible to fuse the miscellany, under the roof of congruity, of one linguistic or cultural identity. The very essence of a liberal state is based on the principles of liberty to endorse the scattering of cultures and languages on the values of liberalism and democracy of identity and self-dignity. Enforcing a language as the 'State language' will put the identity and self-dignity of marginalized ethnicities in jeopardy.
>
> The 'State language' model also contradicts the idea of liberal culturalism, which believes in preserving the ethnic and linguistic groups historically native to the place. Why? Assam was never an Assamese linguistic state. It was always plural with different communities having different mother tongues. Thus, making one language the 'State language' categorizes every other ethnolinguistic

identity in the marginalized section, considering the Assamese-speaking ethno-nationalists as mainstream.

The second reason for my scepticism is the historical context of linguistic hegemony in Assam. In 1960, when the 'The Assam Official Language Act' was passed, it resulted in an outburst of protest in the Barak Valley as the act sought to dilute their self-identity. The same happened in Meghalaya, which was then a part of Assam. As the act declared *"Without prejudice to the provisions of Articles 346 and 347 of the Constitution of India and subject as hereinafter provided, Assamese and English, and when the latter is replaced under Article 343 of the Constitution of India, Hindi in place of English shall be used for all or any of the official purposes of the State of Assam."(The Assam Gazette, October 10, 1960, pp. 623-25)*, the communities in Meghalaya felt marginalized and deprived of self-dignity, resulting in Khasi leaders joining hands with Garo and Jaintia Hill leaders to voice their demand for a separate state. In 1972, Meghalaya attained statehood through their struggle for self-identity."

Barak Valley and Meghalaya were not the only ones threatened by the Act. The Misings also demanded self-rule, as Bora explains in 'The Missing Movement in Assam…': *"Among them were the Misings, who started a movement for self-rule as a means to ensure their cultural and political representation, and, above all, to have the power to control resources in their locality. Mising Agom Kebang, a literary organization of the community, launched a cultural revivalism process to fight against the implementation of the Assam Official Language Act 1960, alleging it as a means of majoritarian dominance."* Linguistic hegemony has also resulted in the demands raised by the Bodo population in the last few decades.

So, what is the connection between all these events? Simply put, it is the power-hungry nature of a linguistic identity to rule over other identities. The third reason for my contradictory stance is purely constitutional. Article 345 of the Indian Constitution mentions the official language, but there is no provision for selecting a state language when it states: *"Official language or languages of a State, Subject to the provisions of Articles 346 and 347, the Legislature of a State may by law adopt any one or more of the languages in use in the State or Hindi as the language or languages to be used for all or any of the official purposes of that State: Provided that, until the Legislature of the State otherwise provides by law, the English language shall continue to be used for those official purposes within the State for which it was being used immediately before the commencement of this*

Constitution." And if Assamese indeed becomes the state language somehow, will it not further affect the structure of Articles 29 and 30? Historically, after the official language act movement, there was the Assamese medium movement. Will history not repeat itself? Post the demand for a state language, will it be for the conversion of all institutions to one linguistic medium?

The majoritarian approach always fuels separatist movements in a civic democracy. It marginalizes communities, dropping bombs of fear into their ethnic identity. Imagine the central government doing the same to Assam through the enforcement of Hindi as the 'National Language', challenging the existence and liberty of self-determination. The same will happen to the minorities in Assam. The Assamese ethno-nationalists have always failed to understand the complexities of civic society, as they tend to live in a utopian world of ethno-nationalism where only their language matters. The hegemony of any ethnicity over the other has been devastating for the world. The struggle for ethnic nationality resulted in the massacre of Jews in Germany, as ethno-nationalists tend to always seek an enemy inside their own house, and live poles away from accepting and acknowledging differences.

And, it is surprising to see how well the ethno-nationalists have adopted the policy of dividing a democracy on the basis of language. In India, ethically, there shouldn't be any state or national language, for the very idea of India is of inclusion and acceptance. Every citizen of India has the right to converse and celebrate their identity. But, this tendency is doing the opposite. More often than not, people of other ethnicities face comments like: *"Assam't thakile axomiya xiki ahibi"* (If you want to live in Assam, you must learn Assamese), which violates their right to self-dignity. A civic nation enables ethno-nationalists to celebrate their identity, and it does the same for other communities; that is, if you speak in Assamese, the other has the equal right to reply to you in Bhojpuri or in Miya dialect. Just as his language can't be forced on you, your language can't be forced on him as well. That's how it works.

But, people must assimilate. Why? Because that's how a civilization grows. People learn the language when there is a necessity. It can't be enforced in a state where people have their own self-ethnic identities. What it will do at maximum is to slow down the process of assimilation, thus dividing society into factions, and a divided society hardly develops. Also, there is a high probability of communities demanding segregation from the state of Assam. Therefore, whatever the future holds, in my opinion, it will not be good for the health of the liberal democracy Assam has. [20]

"HALF A CENTURY onto the Assam State Language Bill – The Poison Chalice".

Under the above caption, S. Kumar Deka, a reporter at the Times of Assam, wrote a highly critical article on the subject, adding, among other things, his take that *"It won't be far from the truth that the language issue became the wedge to break up the cohesion that existed, making it easy for Delhi to apply the long strategy of breaking up Assam."*

The following few lines are quoted from the same article, which was published in the Times of Assam on July 4th, 2012:

> "Subsequent to the language bill, has the Assamese language flourished in leaps and bounds? Yes, **to fool the public**, a governmental department to implement Assamese as the state language was created, which communicated in English and at one stage was headed by a Secretarial level Assamese who studied at Santiniketan and was more at home with Bengali than in Assamese!" [21] (Emphasis by Subir)

Next, in 1972, some Assamese groups demanded that the Assamese language be made the sole language for writing examinations under Gauhati University. Soon, the Bengalis and other communities in Assam again protested. It led to large-scale ethnic riots targeting the Bengalis and others. Widespread rioting was reported throughout the Brahmaputra valley once more. Yet again, the Bengali Hindus were the main target because they were at the forefront of the agitation to prevent the imposition of Assamese. Over 14,000 Bengalis were displaced during the 1972-73 turmoil and fled to West Bengal and elsewhere in northeast India. But the actual extent of Bengali displacement from Assam is far more than these figures suggest. While only those who fled during the disturbances and took refuge in camps in West Bengal were accounted for in government records, thousands took shelter with relatives or relocated by buying up property in West Bengal and elsewhere after selling off their possessions in Assam, escaping government or media notice. And those who continued to leave Assam after the riots had ended, for fear of future attacks, were not taken into account. But if the Bengali Muslims largely escaped attacks by the Assamese during the language riots because they had mostly accepted the Assamese language, they also faced substantial displacement under a draconian scheme called 'Prevention of Infiltration from Pakistan (PIP)', discussed later in this chapter and also during the war with Pakistan in 1965. [22]

The following paragraphs are from the article "In Language Movements of West Bengal and Assam, a Parallel in Governments' Responses" dated July 8th, 2017, by [1]Sangeeta Barooah Pisharoty, Deputy Editor at the New Delhi-based news and opinion website, The Wire. The feedback about Assam's language controversy in the article is significant and relevant to our story.

> At a seminar organized by the Delhi-based socio-cultural organization Jookto in the Nehru Memorial Museum and Library in New Delhi, Ajoy Kumar Roy, General Secretary of a Silchar-based civil society organization, Sammilita Sanskritik Mancha, said:

> The saga of oppression continued. It should be remembered that all higher educational institutions of Cachar were under Gauhati University as there was no university in Cachar at that time (it now has the centrally run Silchar University). On June 12th, 1972, the university's academic council decided that the medium of instruction in all colleges under it would be Assamese, and English would continue simultaneously for the next ten years. Again, the situation in Cachar got heated. Agitation started... The Assam government tried to suppress it by all means... two people died, and ultimately the central government intervened again, and a temporary solution was imposed. According to this, English would continue as the alternative medium of instruction in the colleges of the Cachar district.

> Again, in 1986, through a circular dated 28th February 1986, the Board of Secondary Education (SEBA), Assam, made it mandatory for non-Assamese students from class V onwards to learn Assamese. This circular is known as **the notorious SEBA circular**. It stated that non-Assamese students from class V onwards would have to learn Assamese as the third language instead of Hindi until class VIII, and Assamese would become a mandatory subject from class VIII onwards. Although it might seem less controversial, it's important to note that the circular mentioned Assamese students would learn Hindi as their third language, effectively limiting the number of learnable languages for Assamese students to two, whereas for Bengali students, it remained three.

> Roy recalled that "agitation started, students jumped into it...violence erupted," leading to the unfortunate death of a

student and ultimately prompting SEBA to withdraw the circular. [23] (Emphasis by Subir)

Note [1] Sangeeta Barooah Pisharoty is the Deputy Editor at The Wire, where she writes on culture, politics, and North-East India. She previously worked at The Hindu. Born in Golaghat (Assam), she embarked on her journalism journey in 1996 with UNI, breaking the ceiling to become the first woman from North-East India employed as a journalist in its New Delhi Office.

For the common people in Assam, the issues of the official language and medium of instruction were closely linked to securing jobs, earning a decent living, and maintaining cultural identity. Therefore, to the Assamese community, the dual language policy was perceived as a continuation of Bengali domination in both employment and cultural spheres. Conversely, to the Bengali community in Assam, adopting a unilingual Assamese language system meant the abolition of their mother tongue from school and college education, depriving them of a level playing field. The language controversy, with both economic and emotional dimensions, was exploited by opportunistic politicians for their political gains by pitting one community against the other, thus exacerbating the relationship between the two communities. Moreover, since independence, some Assamese leaders sought to assert their supremacy and attempt "Assamisation" of the state, akin to the "Ahomisation" in the early days of Ahom kings, to realize their long-cherished dream of Assamese dominance. The Bengali Muslims in Assam Valley attempted to avoid being drawn into the language controversy by declaring Assamese as their mother tongue in the census enumerations. Consequently, the language controversy primarily remained a conflict between the Hindus of Assamese and Bengali communities.

However, as mentioned earlier, the Bengali Muslims could not remain wholly insulated from the communal conflicts in Assam. An author and human rights researcher based in Assam, Abdul Kalam Azad, writing about Assam NRC, recalled that: "The legacy of anti-immigrant sentiment in Assamese public sphere for more than a century has created an environment of deadly silence and trauma that has taken control over the lives of several million people across the state." Among other things, the write-up continues:

> "Post Independence, the Muslim community in Assam faced large-scale violence and was forcibly displaced in 1950. Infamously known as 'rioter bosor' (the year of riot) among the community, thousands of Muslims fled the country to take shelter in the then East Pakistan through the open border. Famous Assamese parliamentarian and author Hem Barua wrote that as many as 53,000 such families, who left the country in 1950, came back to Assam under the Nehru-Liaquat Pact.

In 1951, the first National Register of Citizens was prepared to weed out the illegal immigrants from East Pakistan. Since then, the anti-immigrant politics has been feeding the Assamese community with the fear of losing their land, identity and culture. On the other hand, Muslims have been regularly experiencing state-sponsored persecution and mass violence.

'Quit India Notice'

In the late 1960s, several thousand Muslims were forcefully deported to East Pakistan under a draconian scheme called 'Prevention of Infiltration from Pakistan (PIP)', without following any legal mechanism of detection and deportation. The border unit of Assam police used to deport hundreds of Muslims without any hue and cry. Hiranya Bhattacharjee, the former DIG of border police in 1979, stated in an interview with The Wire, "At that time, the process of deportation was on, in spite of the fact that there was no formal agreement with East Pakistan or Bangladesh on deportation. Those days, when we deported thousands, there was no hue and cry. What was happening was considered natural."

Former home minister and chief minister of Assam, Hiteswar Saikia, admitted that 192,079 persons (unofficial figures suggest a much higher number) were deported under the PIP scheme between 1961-69. Professor Monirul Hussain wrote, "Police committed excesses on the Muslims due to certain extra-legal commitments." A border police officer, who was in charge of deporting Muslims under PIP, narrated the horrific stories of forceful deportation to this author. He stated that he resigned from his job due to mental distress caused by the experience of witnessing injustice and inhuman atrocities committed against those Muslims, who were apparently his fellow countrymen. (The individual contacted this author after reading stories of deported Muslims living in a refugee colony in present-day Bangladesh).

After deporting huge numbers of Muslims to East Pakistan, Bimala Prasad Chaliha, the then chief minister of Assam, announced on the floor of the Legislative Assembly in 1969 that 'no more infiltrators were to be found in Assam' and hence, the PIP scheme was to be abandoned." [24]

The PIP scheme and later the PIF scheme reportedly proved ineffective because the process caused excessive delays in identifying and deporting illegal migrants. Subsequently, the Indira Gandhi government enacted the

Illegal Migrants (Determination by Tribunals) Act, of 1983, popularly known as the IMTD Act, which will be discussed elaborately in Chapter 13.

In the context of our earlier discussion about Assam's medium of instruction and the perspective of Bengali Muslims in Assam, the following paragraphs quoted from the research paper of Fakhar Uddin Ali Ahmed titled "Arabic studies in educational institutions of Assam since 1947" are relevant and informative:

> "The Assamese community is a composite community of different castes, and its culture is also a composite culture. In the true sense, none of the communities in Assam could claim its absolute majority; however, a dominant class claimed itself as the language majority by including tribal, tea garden labourers, and particularly Muslims to have Assamese as their language. Tea garden workers are neither entirely Bengali nor entirely Assamese in origin. They came from many parts of India and formed a group of their own. Their language is a mixture of Bengali and Assamese. If the tea garden workers and tribal are excluded, Bengali Hindus and Bengali Muslims will attain a majority based on the Bengali language in Assam. In fact, it was true that the Bengali Muslims were directly influenced by Assamese Hindu intellectuals, for which they willingly accepted to be registered as Assamese in the census of 1951. Thus Assamese could claim their absolute majority. It would be worthwhile to mention the statement of Dr. Birendra Kumar Bhattacharya, Ex-President of Assam Sahitya Sabha. According to him, "The same truth applies to the Muslim immigrants who have occupied citizenship based on a linguistic state. It must be said to the credit of the immigrant Muslims that they have always been at the forefront of the struggle of the state to make 'Assamese' the state language and medium of higher education".
>
> In order to reconstitute Assam as an Assamese state based on the majority language, the Bengali Muslims accepted the Assamese language as their mother tongue and the medium of instruction. They argued that Bengali Muslims, as permanent settlers of Assam, should cooperate and integrate with the local Assamese, just as earlier Muslims, such as the Goria and Maria, had already integrated with the local Assamese. They were nick-named 'Na-Asomia' or New Assamese." [25]

Inherently, in a state where as many as 120 languages were recorded as mother tongues in 1951, and the number rose to 200 in 1971 [26], the 'official' imposition of the Assamese language drew severe backlash from various tribal groups and tea garden labourers, who remained among the most oppressed classes in Assam. These groups faced economic exploitation, as well as social, cultural, and political oppression. The sudden imposition of the Assamese language brought about an identity crisis that had been simmering since independence. Simply put, just as Assamese people in Assam were experiencing an identity crisis due to the large presence of Bengalis in Assam, several tribal groups in Assam also began to feel a similar crisis over the dominance of the high caste ruling class of Assam.

That was the backdrop against which the further disintegration of the British-created Assam followed after the Sylhet referendum in 1947. First, Assam's Naga Hills district and Mon and Tuensang subdivisions of the North Eastern Frontier Agency (NEFA) were merged to meet the demands of various tribal groups, and then a separate Nagaland State was formed in 1963. Next, by bringing together Assam's Khasi Hills, Jaintia Hills, and Garo Hills, the state of Meghalaya came into being in 1972. Assam's Lushai Hills, later known as Mizoram, became a union territory in 1972 and a full-fledged Mizoram state in 1987. Similarly, the remaining part of Assam's North Eastern Frontier Agency (NEFA) became a Union Territory in January 1972; later, it became a full-fledged state of Arunachal Pradesh in 1987.

Additionally, the 'official' imposition of the Assamese language led to more demands for separate states, autonomy, and recognition of mother tongues by various tribes in the areas they dominated. One example is the demand for a separate 'Udayachal' state and 'Bodoland" by the Bodos. When the Bodos launched a massive movement for recognition of the Bodo language in 1974, it was forcefully suppressed by the Assam government. Nevertheless, with sustained agitation by the Bodo people, their language, Bodo, was subsequently made the medium of instruction up to secondary schools. Yet, several constraints and discriminations from the Assam administration reportedly hindered the running of Bodo medium schools satisfactorily. Currently, there is an ongoing fight for a separate state, 'Bodoland", in Assam.

"Assam explodes in an orgy of violence between Bodos and non-Bodos, leaving 30 people dead," under this title, Farzand Ahmed reported the communal violence on 15th September 1989, in INDIA TODAY news magazine, a part of which is quoted below:

> "Even as the fury of the Brahmaputra began to ebb last fortnight, the Assamese anger against the agitating Bodo tribal raged, leaving death and destruction in its wake. For about a week, parts of North Lakhimpur, the Gohpur subdivision in Sonitpur, and the Mangaldoi subdivision of Darrang districts burnt and echoed with the cries of

both helpless Bodos and non-Bodos, who forgot old social bonds, attacking each other as enemies. With 30 people dead, 40 villages gutted, and uprooted people cowering in relief camps, the Bodoland agitation's name stood indelibly etched in Assam's lexicon of violence. …..What was certainly clear was that the growing communal and social divide had been concretized. Said Bijen Kalita, an Assamese youth from Bezpur, now sheltering in a relief camp in Mangaldoi, the district headquarters of Darrang: "We could see the Bodo criminals setting fire to our houses." About 40 km away in Khairabari, Bodos taking shelter in a relief camp also expressed hatred. Said Deb Nath Basumatary, "The preplanned Independence Day arson and killings by Assamese chauvinists with the help of the police prove again that we (Bodos) have no security. The simmering rancour spilt into the open on 10th August when hundreds of Assamese and non-Bodos from north Lakhimpur areas crossed the river Sesha and invaded the Gohpur reserve forest area, which has both Bodo and non-Bodo settlements. This led to a free-for-all for three days inside the 35-sq km reserve forest areas." [27]

Meanwhile, in March 1971, under the code name 'Operation Searchlight', the Pakistani Army carried out a planned military operation to suppress the Bengali nationalist movement in erstwhile East Pakistan. The operation also precipitated the 1971 genocide by the Pakistani Army and caused roughly 10 million refugees to flee to India, while civilian death estimates ranged from 300,000 to 3,000,000. As neighbouring states like West Bengal, Assam, Tripura, and others in India were flooded with Bengali refugees from across the border, it necessitated Indian military intervention. This eventually led to the Pakistani Army's unconditional surrender to the joint command of the Indian Army and Bengal's Mukti Bahini on December 16, 1971, and the declaration of independence of East Pakistan as a new Bengali country named Bangladesh. In due course, most Bengali refugees returned from India to Bangladesh. The formation of a new Bengali country in the neighbourhood of Assam and the alleged leftover refugees from across the border added fuel to the fire.

According to Researcher Wazid Reja Osmani, in the wake of the liberation of Bangladesh, several lakhs of refugees came to North-East India, and most of these, of course, returned under the 'Indira-Mujib' agreement (March 19, 1972), but a few thousand Bengali Hindu war victims stayed" [28] (emphasis by Subir). Nevertheless, there was a perception among a large section of the people that millions of those Bangladeshis, both Hindu and Muslim, illegally stayed back in India and then not only managed to obtain documents surreptitiously to support their claim of being Indian citizens but also enrolled their names in the electoral rolls of Assam.

Interestingly, in a meeting of electoral officers at Ooty, on October 24, 1978, S. L. Shakdhar, the Chief Election Commissioner (CEC) of India, observed:

> "I would like to refer to the alarming situation in some States, especially in the North-Eastern region, from which reports are coming regarding the large-scale inclusion of foreign nationals in the electoral rolls. In one case, the population in the 1971 census recorded an increase as high as 34.98% over the 1961 census figures, and this figure was attributed to the influx of a large number of persons from foreign countries. The influx has become a regular feature. I think it may not be a wrong assessment to make that based on the increase of 34.98% between the two censuses, the increase likely to be recorded in the 1991 census would be more than 100% over the 1961 census. In other words, a stage would be reached when that state may have to reckon with the foreign nationals who may, in all probability, constitute a sizeable percentage, if not the majority, of the population in the State" [29].

Evidently, the CEC was referring to Assam. However, it is not clear from which source the report came to him and how that 'report' was able to determine and distinguish, with a degree of reasonable certainty, between the native and foreign nationals in the electoral roll - a task both the State and the Central Government were finding extremely difficult to assess, even with the Government machinery working overtime on this issue.

Against this backdrop, the following few lines quoted from "Anxiety, Violence and the Postcolonial State: Understanding the "Anti-Bangladeshi" Rage in Assam, India" by Assistant Professor at the Department of Geography in Sikkim University, Rafiul Ahmed, are thought-provoking:

> "The State appears to be under the grip of a Malthusian fever where terminologies like "demographic invasion", "demographic aggression", "demographic time-bomb", "influx", and "infiltration" regularly occupy titles of news reports as well as academic publications in journals and books. The rationalization and naturalization of statistics or rather State-tricks to authenticate the varieties of claims as an improvisation to unsullied personal accounts signifies the establishment of the sacrosanctity of numeral facts. At the heart of this hysteria with numbers is the Malthusian poster boy of Assam, C.S. Mullan, the superintendent of census operations in 1931, who was posted to the region during the British Raj. Mullan

was the chief author of the Census of India in 1931, which for the first time used the term "invasion" in the Assamese context. He instigated what has since the 1930s evolved into a "hate campaign" in the State. To provoke the Assamese against the Bengali, Mullan wrote, "wheresoever the carcases, there will the vultures be gathered together- where there is wasteland thither flock the Mymensinghias". He had further added that "it is sad but by no means improbable that in another thirty years Sibsagar district will be the only part of Assam in which an Assamese will find himself at home." Noted historian Amalendu Guha described Mullan as an irresponsible European civil servant who, in an effort to predict the future, "mischievously" used the word "invasion" to describe the migration of people from East Bengal's Mymensingh district at a time when no national boundary existed. Mullan's verdict on the Bengali invasion makes it possible for those inclined to historicize and authenticate the threat of a Muslim invasion back to the days of the British Raj.

To a large extent, the legacy of Mullan's Census Report 1931 initiated the Assamese-Bengali conflict. The growing resentment towards the Bengalis stemmed primarily from the Assamese middle class's envy, as the Bengalis occupied a majority of the lower-tier administrative jobs in colonial times, especially in the plantation and railways, which were often denied to the Assamese as a matter of policy. The colonial administrative system played a significant role in racializing occupational and employment hierarchies, embittering relations between the Bengali and Assamese middle class. However, this history has largely been obscured. In post-independence India, mutual mistrust manifested in conflicts surrounding language and ethnicity hegemonies. Assam witnessed extensive violence under the Bongal Khedao movement in the 1950s and 1960s, seeking to expel Bengali settlers. The AASU during the 1980s further exacerbated these issues and led to indiscriminate violence and death." [30]

Beneath the smooth surface of normal day-to-day life and the 'business-as-usual' mode prevailing in Assam, there exist unhealthy undercurrents of racism and communalism, 'under the grip of a Malthusian fever', as paraphrased by Professor Rafiul Ahmed. Its general atmosphere sometimes becomes charged through special campaigns designed for unsuspecting innocent youths, resulting in mindless violence, killings, and victimization of 'other' communities, especially Bengalis in Assam. Apart from several organized mass hostilities, there are examples of terrible violence against individual Bengalis in Assam Valley. The following three instances, among many other precedents, are mentioned here to demonstrate how simple it became for innocent individuals to fall prey to senseless killings due to such ruthless hate campaigns.

On January 18, 1980, Dr. Rabi Mitra, a well-known Bengali geologist, was killed by a violent crowd at Duliajan, the Oil India Limited (OIL) headquarters in upper Assam. Earlier, the district administration, backed by police, ordered the dispersal of picketers who, as part of the protest program in the Assam Movement, were blocking the flow of crude oil outside Assam. However, when the picketers refused to disperse, the police resorted to tear gas shelling and then firing, resulting in four deaths and many injuries. Dr. Rabi Mitra had gone to the hospital as a humanitarian gesture to inquire about the victims. Suddenly, a violent crowd dragged him out of his car and killed him in front of the Duliajan hospital for no apparent reason. The leadership of the movement mourned the death of these four individuals, declaring them martyrs of the movement, but they did not include Rabi Mitra in their list as he was neither Assamese nor did he die for the 'cause' of the movement!

Then there was the killing of a middle-aged Nagpur-born Bengali social worker, Sanjoy Ghose, who in 1980 had chosen to join the then-unknown Institute of Rural Management, Anand (IRMA), over confirmed admissions to all three existing IIMs (Indian Institute of Management) – Ahmedabad, Bangalore, and Calcutta! He did it in keeping with his commitment to work for the poorest of the poor. Sanjoy and seven of his colleagues had set up a base on the world's biggest river island, Majuli, on the Brahmaputra River, in April 1996. They started pioneering work to save the island and a large number of Assamese people residing there as it was shrinking due to annual flooding and land erosion. Sanjoy was reportedly abducted on July 4, 1997, by the United Liberation Front (ULFA) of Assam, a separatist outfit operating in Assam and North East India, for the 'cause' of the so-called indigenous Assamese people. A newspaper article in the Deccan Herald on February 9, 2009, claimed that he (Sanjoy) was killed a day after ULFA cadres abducted him on July 4, 1997, and his body, which was never found, was thrown into the swirling waters of the Brahmaputra.

The murderous attack on a postgraduate medical student, Dr Anjan Chakaravarty, in the Gauhati Medical College hostel at midnight of December 11/12, 1979, is another disgraceful instance. During that period, several systematic attacks targeted Bengali students at various hostels of educational institutes in the Brahmaputra Valley. Again, among many such instances at different educational institutions in Assam, only three real-life stories, including that of Dr. Anjan Chakaravarty's murder, collected by Subir literally 'straight from the horse's mouth,' are included in the next chapter - "The Inglorious Harassment of Students In Assam Valley: A Tiny Trilogy." It reflects how dangerously some unscrupulous 'leaders' in our midst, apparently taking cues from the British Colonial Ruler, are trying to contaminate the psyche of our blooming youths to fulfil their personal/party agendas.

****

Chapter 10.

Inglorious ill-treatment of students in Assam Valley
A Tiny-Trilogy
'Worst Possible Manifestation of a Hate Campaign?

It would be extremely difficult, if not impossible, to find a parallel to such real-life stories of hate crimes anywhere else on this planet between students of the same educational institution living together in hostels on the same campus as it took place in Assam! Like elsewhere in the world, here in the Brahmaputra Valley of Assam in India, the students of different communities had been staying together at the same hostels for months - eating, sleeping, and sharing joys, sorrows, and some of the best moments of their lives in perfect harmony. But, like nowhere else in the world, a section of the students suddenly turned to a murdering spree against their hostel mates, targeting the students of a specific community on an inauspicious night! These were obviously done at the instance of their mentors. It happened, not once or twice but repeatedly, during the latter part of the last century, coinciding with or in the run-up to the so-called 'largely peaceful' Assam Agitation. It might not have any bearing on the Assam Movement per se, but these were not isolated incidences or one-off cases. The reports of such incidents had poured in from different locations of the Brahmaputra Valley during that period. Many times, such far-fetched happenings occurred with the same script played by different characters at different venues on different dates where, in all likelihood, its 'producers & directors' were the same. A 'tiny-trilogy', out of many such real-life tragedies, conflating three separate incidents, one each at an Agricultural College, an Engineering College, and a Medical College in Assam, is presented in this chapter to exemplify the realities of those stormy days in the state.

When a section of Assam's leadership found 'ready-made' fall guys, they started blaming everything on them. That was a risk they took, which blurred their vision to such an extent that they stopped seeing things from the proper perspective. They failed to notice the historical distortions described in the earlier chapters. The pestering of the Bengalis in Assam thus continued even decades after the independence of India, and still, any solution to the so-called 'Assam Problem' is nowhere in sight. Very few people outside North-East India are aware of the shocking ground realities. Many newspapers did report the disturbances which took place in Assam from time to time. Yet, stories of this type of exceptional violence targeting the STUDENTS of a particular community inside the hostels of educational institutions in Assam never saw the light of day. Many books, newspaper reports/articles, research papers, and TV talk shows on the Assam Problem 'covered' (a homonym) its perennial tales; yet, never before the manifestation of such unimaginable racial hatred and linguistic chauvinism was depicted as vividly as the following three stories 'uncovered'. And here are the illustrative instances:

Agricultural College

It all started on the evening of May 11, 1970. As the boarders assembled for dinner at the dining hall of Hostel No. 6, Jorhat Agricultural University, suddenly, a fellow Assamese student whispered to Motubabu (as we used to call him in our childhood): "*Please be careful, there might be trouble for you tonight,*" and then vanished. Motubabu was pursuing his graduate degree in Agriculture during those days. He did not take the warning seriously and, as usual, returned to the hostel room after dinner.

All of a sudden - sometimes at midnight perhaps - he woke up to the sound of screaming voices outside his room. He could hardly see anything; the hostel campus was in darkness. "Somebody must have switched off the mainline," Motubabu thought. Then, as he was about to step out of his room and turn left, he suddenly got hit by something on his right shoulder quite unexpectedly. It could have been a stick or an iron rod that Motubabu could not make out. The only thing he could somehow see was that a group of people with their faces seemed to be covered by dark clothes had assembled at the verandah. Instinctively, Motubabu ran for his life!

After running for what seemed like ages, he reached a local cluster of government quarters known as 'NEFA Bari', about 2 Kilometers from the hostel. He was gasping for air. A few Bengali students of the Agricultural University hostel had already assembled there, and some more students joined them soon. Almost all of them were shivering, not because of cold but out of sheer panic. They had spent the night wide awake, apprehending more attacks on them to follow anytime soon, even in that 'NEFA Bari'.

However, the local District Collector (DC), accompanied by some police personnel, arrived at the scene during daybreak. The victims did not have any inkling of how the officials came there, but thankfully all of them were escorted by the police personnel to the 'safety' of Jorhat Circuit House and accommodated there - somewhat segregated. Only when the "all-clear signal" from the local administration came were the students allowed to leave their temporary shelters after about a week.

All the Bengali students were not so lucky on that fateful night. At least 15 of them were reportedly hospitalized in Jorhat Civil Hospital with multiple fractures and cut injuries from the merciless beatings they had received inside the hostels that night. They had to spend about a month in the hospital before being discharged and sent back to their homes.

A couple of months after the incident, the students were called back to the University to resume their studies. Soon after returning, the victims were summoned to the Police Station and subjected to a marathon questioning session. Some victims could recognize the attackers, identify them as their fellow students of the Jorhat Agricultural University, and give their statements to the Police accordingly. By then, it was clear to them that those violent students went from one hostel to another, other than to their own hostels, obviously in a pre-planned manner to create trouble incognito to target the Bengali students.

On return from the Police station, Motubabu, and other victims found a group of student leaders of the Agricultural University Students' Union waiting for them in a hostel room. Some political leaders of Jorhat town and a local MLA were also present in the room. The political leaders assured them of all possible protections from such troubles in the future. But there was a price tag! The victims must not name any of their attackers. In no uncertain terms, they were told to give statements to the Police that they couldn't identify the attackers in the darkness of night because their faces were covered.

As the priority of the victimized students was to complete their studies and build their careers rather than bringing the perpetrators of the heinous crime to book, there was hardly any choice left to them but to oblige their visitors. Later, the victims gave their scripted statements at the Jorhat local court under oath, based on which the Police cases were withdrawn against the perpetrators.

Motubabu is now over 70 and shifted to Kolkata after retiring as a director ranking officer from the Assam Government. In hindsight, he now realized that the local administration must have kept the victimized students isolated in the Jorhat Circuit House not only because of their safety concern, as seemed so at that time, but also because of some ulterior motives. Perhaps they were kept away from the glare of media focus to cover up the news of their fellow students' cold-blooded attacks on them inside the University campus. It was, in all likelihood, done to avoid adverse publicity at the national level that undoubtedly would have tarnished the image of the University and the reputation of the state of Assam. Nevertheless, the memory of this terrible incident from about half a century back still haunts Motubabu at night!

The above realization of Motubabu, to put the records straight, seems to be a conjecture merely on his understanding of the prevailing circumstances at that time or maybe a hunch based on intuition. He did not provide any hard facts to support the conclusion he drew on the alleged ulterior motives of the local administration.

During those days, many other students studying at the Agricultural University also had to flee the hostels – some could escape unhurt, and some of them after getting beaten up. One of them, another childhood friend of Subir, had reportedly spent that night hiding under a road culvert slightly away from the hostel before catching a vehicle to reach his home in Shillong the following day. They all have almost similar frightful stories to tell.

Engineering College

"You must drive away all the Bengalis from Assam if you truly want a solution to your problems. My firm belief is that unless you uproot this community from the soil of Assam, you will continue to have problems securing jobs and seats in the much sought-after Medical, Agricultural, and Engineering Colleges like yours. Very soon, you will find it tough even to run a small 'Pan Dukan' at the corner of your locality because of the competitions they generate. Of course, you may continue with the strikes, demonstrations, bandhs, 'satyagrahas', and similar other legitimate programs from time to time to voice your various demands publicly and to keep up the tempo of the movement, but please always remember that it is the Bengalis who are the root of all your problems. The solution lies in their eviction from Assam."

That was sometime in the latter part of the 1970s, and it was a very influential politician from Assam who was addressing a small gathering of student leaders in a closed-door meeting. I attended the same as one of the Office Bearers of the College Students' Union. Obviously, the speaker did not know that a Bengali student was in the group. My fellow Assamese students were visibly uncomfortable with such a racist sermon from their leader in my presence, but it was "one of those things" that I got used to in my days in Assam. The closed-door meeting was held in the backdrop of a continued students' demonstration in front of a renowned Public Sector Undertaking (PSU) office in support of the demands for job reservation for the students from Assam in its recruitment policy. There were reports that a good number of people from outside the state of Assam were being recruited in that PSU lately.

Later, the politician addressing us became one of the most powerful leaders in Assam and was at the helm of Assam politics for quite a long period. Years later, I happened to watch the same 'leader' in a TV interview on a private TV channel with all-India coverage. He was speaking on various ticklish problems of Assam. But, when he talked at length about the importance of tolerance and amity among the different communities in Assam for its progress and developments, I could not believe my ears and eyes! Was it the same person who, in his address to us at the closed-door meeting, had spewed venom against the Bengalis in Assam and now preaching the values of patience, peace, and harmony in front of a TV camera - keeping a straight face? I was stunned!

Meanwhile, a few days later, in a meeting of the executive committee of the College Students' Union, there was a proposal to submit a memorandum to the Chief Executive Officer of that PSU demanding job reservation to the local aspirants. The initial draft contained, among other things, the notion that there must be a preference for the 'Assamese candidates.' However, at my insistence, backed by irrefutable logic, the language of the memorandum had to be modified to read that there must be a preference for the 'candidates from Assam.' Subsequently, I learned from one of my Assamese classmates that even after accepting my suggestion 'gracefully' to amend the draft, it antagonized certain student leaders so much that they had vowed to 'settle the score' with me at the earliest opportunity. Accordingly, my Assamese friend cautioned me to be on guard from those characters.

Although the atmosphere inside the college campus seemed okay on the surface, soon after that incident, I could feel the stewing tension underneath. There were other minor grievances that the Students' Union also took up for settlement with the College authorities in those days. It was for the common benefit of the students at large. But surprisingly, it appeared that all the issues started to take the colour of the 'Assamese-Bengali' communal overtone at the end of the day. I had a premonition that the undercurrent of the seething tension inside the college campus would explode before long. A couple of months later, a rumour made the rounds that some untoward incidents would occur shortly. Reportedly, the State-level student leaders were not satisfied with the 'performance' of our College Union and sent a message that 'more needs to be done' to promote the larger interests of the community. My local friend gave me enough hints to be ready to leave the hostel at a few minutes' notice and to have adequate cash on me all the time for any emergency requirement. I shared this disturbing news with other Bengali students in the hostels. We were more or less ready to leave our hostels at short notice. All our original mark sheets, certificates, and valuable papers were sent back to our homes by registered posts as a matter of abundant precaution.

On D-Day, when I was about to enter the hostel dining room for dinner, suddenly, a red light appeared on the rooftop of one of our adjacent hostels, and it started revolving. It gave the impression that someone was sending some signal somewhere. Within minutes, the entire College campus plunged into darkness. By that time, I was already inside the large dining hall. It was unusually empty that evening. As I was trying to take a seat for dinner, one middle-aged cook who was quite friendly to me shouted from inside the kitchen in colloquial Assamese, "Forget the dinner, jump from the window to the backyard, escape through the boundary fencing and run for your life."

Instinctively, I did as I was told. Finally, I reached the outer limit of a village, maybe an hour or so later and stopped running to regain my breath. Then I thought that if the villagers found some unknown man approaching their village at this odd hour of the night, they would take me for a thief or someone with evil intentions. So, I decided against entering the village. Somehow, I managed to spend the longest night of my life in a paddy field under the open sky - completely alone.

At the break of dawn, filled with the chorus of birdsong, I heard the ringing bell of an approaching cycle rickshaw. Immediately, I emerged from the paddy field, reached the main road, hailed the rickshaw, and asked how much he would charge to drop me at the Bengali colony a few kilometres away. One look at my dishevelled appearance was enough for the rickshaw puller to snap at me, "Don't bother about the fare. Let me drop you off quickly at your destination. You save your life first."

During the journey to the town, I could understand from him that the screaming I heard emanating from behind the college campus as I was running for my life had alerted them. They lived close to the college campus. They could guess something terrible was happening but did not dare to go inside. Looking at my unkempt appearance, he knew that I was running for my life, and that was enough for him to help me. It explained the strange behaviour of the rickshaw puller. I could only remain grateful to that poor and unknown rickshaw puller for the rest of my life, but I could do nothing else at that moment.

To cut a long story short, I took shelter at the residence of one of my distant relatives in the Bengali colony. Our college was adjourned sine die the next day, and the news reached me immediately. In a couple of days, I headed for my hometown, Shillong. There was a long wait for more than two months, but no news came from the College authorities. I got worried because it was my final year of Engineering College. So, we decided to return to our college after contacting other Bengali classmates scattered in different towns and villages. Before entering our college hostel, we met the Deputy Commissioner and explained our situation to him and our dilemma. He was helpful and accepted our assessment that the situation was not conducive to returning to the hostels. Realizing our tight spot, the local Bengalis in the town came to our rescue. They made available one or two rooms each at their residences and somehow accommodated all of us at different houses in the colony. They also provided our daily food - free of cost. We returned to our hostels with security escorts to collect our belongings a few days later. These were scattered throughout our hostel rooms - partially damaged, burnt, or torn. We salvaged whatever few pieces of books, notes, and clothing found to be worth it. Then we continued our studies from those makeshift accommodations and subsequently appeared at the examination - under strict security cover provided by the local administration.

After reviewing the happenings of D-Day at the hostels, we concluded unanimously that the attackers on that night were none other than our fellow students. What surprised me most was the report that one of my closest friends led the gang, which had proceeded menacingly towards the hostel room that night to target me. His mother had lovingly invited me, as one of his son's close friends, to their residence only a few days before. She had offered me some of the most exquisite homemade Assamese delicacies I had ever tasted. I learned she had personally cooked all those items to give me a special treat. Like any other loving mother and a perfect host, she sat beside me throughout the meal. She took care of the minutest details, making it a memorable dinner for me.

Since then, I have developed a firm conviction that, individually, every Assamese is friendly, decent, and helpful. However, when the group sentiment comes into play, particularly among their young ones, a few get carried away when their mentors and senior leaders arouse their emotions, sentiments, and passion. These so-called leaders never miss an opportunity to raise their hundred-plus years of the racial bogey that the very existence of the Assamese community is in danger, and soon the Assamese race would become extinct under the imminent threat from the overflowing Bengalis in Assam. The constant instigations sometimes become too much for the youths to distinguish between the good and the bad; sometimes, their mental vision becomes blurred, and their friends become foes. Momentarily they lose all their good senses, which makes them do something they soon regret. Perhaps that has been happening in Assam for the last few decades and still happening unabated.

This story was narrated to Subir by one engineer who, in his service life, turned out to be a renowned Gazetted Officer of the Assam state administration. He had earned several appreciations and laurels from the government for his dedicated service. He honourably retired from the post of Director in the Assam Government. He is now settled in Kolkata - leading a peaceful retired life. His name and other personal details are withheld at his request.

Medical College

Those were the most turbulent days during the period of students' agitation in Assam. Normal life almost came to a standstill from the previous day because the agitating students had declared dawn-to-dusk "Bandh" in Assam. The violence that erupted was at its worst in the Kamrup district, where two people had died in police firing, necessitating the deployment of the army. Later on, an indefinite curfew was imposed in several areas.

"Dada, Dada! Open the door; it's very urgent; hurry up!" They were banging at my doors. It was nearing midnight, and I was about to go to bed. This desperate call of familiar voices made me rush to the front door. On unleashing the bolt, I was startled to see two doctors as they just about forced the door open and entered my room. They were nearly out of breath but, with difficulty, uttered together, *"They have killed him!"*

Immediately, I felt that the world was spinning around me. Intuitively, I knew that it was my younger brother Shankar they were talking about. Both the doctors were his classmates, and they were doing their postgraduate courses at Gauhati Medical College in Assam. Shankar had chosen the field of medicine for his specialization, while the other two Bengali doctors had chosen different fields for their doctorate degrees. Today, both are well-known specialist doctors and have excelled in their respective areas of specialization. One is the most renowned doctor in Assam and has made a profound mark at the all-India level. The other specialist doctor is also equally well-known, presently practising in another state of North-East India.

The next thing I could vaguely recollect was that I was moving around like a zombie. I had no energy, feelings, or capability to think, act, or understand what was happening around me at the "Emergency" department of the Assam Medical College Hospital. At that time, the Medical College was in the Panbazar locality of Gauhati, but the hostels were located at Narakashur Hill in the Bhangagarh area. I didn't remember who brought me there and how! The two doctor-cum-classmates of Shankar were mumbling something among themselves, surrounded by some police personnel.

It was sometime in the midnight between the 11th and 12th December 1979 when Shankar was attacked in his Gauhati Medical College Hostel, as I was told later on, and seemingly he had lost consciousness then and there. He succumbed to his injuries the next day, on 12th December 1979.

The only other thing I could still recollect was the last rites of Shankar. His mortal remains were consigned to the flames under massive security arrangements surrounded by a large number of Assam Police personnel. Only a very few close friends and selected relatives were allowed to attend the last rites. My gaze was fixed on the burning pyre, devoid of human feelings.

The entire happenings of those couple of days are saved in my memory merely in a fragmented form like a slide show - as if most of the motion picture film got erased somehow. Alternatively, to be more precise, my recollection of the event is restricted only to three or four slides of a PowerPoint presentation. The remaining slides get lost, thereby taking away its continuity for good.

You know, we were from a family with a very modest income. We used to live almost hand to mouth. My father was an employee of the Assam Government posted at Shillong. We used to stay at a rented house in the Laban locality with my mother, younger brother Shankar, and three sisters. Shankar was the brightest in our family. He always stood first in his class at Laban Bengali Boys' High School during his school days. After completing his Pre-University course from St Edmunds' College, Shillong, and his MBBS degree from Silchar Medical College, Assam, he joined Gauhati Medical College for his postgraduate degree. We had pinned our hopes on Shankar's prosperous professional career. However, his untimely departure was a rude shock that devastated our entire family - shattering our lifelong dream. After that heartbreaking incident, we did not stay in Assam any longer. Many people still remember our beloved brother by his formal name Dr Anjan Chakravarty. He was snatched away from us nearly forty years ago, but I can't forget his innocent face and the sweet tone that used to call me Dada - till today!"

Sitting at his residence on the outskirts of Kolkata on 23rd March 2018, the elder brother Shibu narrated the brutal killing of his beloved brother Dr Anjan Chakravarty, MBBS, at the Gauhati Medical College hostel. Yet, surprisingly, Shibu's face was rather calm, detached, and emotionless - as he recounted one of the many untold, unheard, and unbelievably tragic stories of the Bengali students in Assam, which no one outside their friends and relatives perhaps knows today!

The Fact-Finding Committee appointed by the People's Union for Civil Liberties (PUCL) on Assam Unrest reported, among other things: **"The suspects in this murder case were out on bail within twenty-four hours. We would be pleasantly surprised if the murderers of Anjan Chakravarty were actually apprehended and punished."** The slightly abridged version of the draft (report) released to the press on 28th February 1980 is available online [1].

Recently, a former female student of Gauhati University hinted to Subir about similar harassment she and her fellow students had faced in the University Girls' Hostel during the latter part of the 1980s when they were pursuing their postgraduate degrees. However, she was reluctant to share the details. Anyway, a glimpse of Subir's student life, rather the way it ended at Gauhati University, narrated in the Prologue of this book, should suffice to get a sense of what had been happening during those days.

A special mention needs to be made here about an uncanny similarity in three of four incidents, including Subir's own experience, narrated so far. Prior warnings from fellow Assamese students **saved** the targeted Bengali students from the worst things that could have happened to them. It is not known if the remaining one, Dr. Anjan Chakravarty, who was killed in the Medical College violence, was forewarned about the impending danger. His side of the story will remain untold forever since he is unreachable!

* * * * * * *

Chapter 11.

NELLIE –
Where Bengalis were Butchered In Broad Daylight!

'SOME MAY VIEW THIS TITLE AS ALARMIST - ***GOOD****!*
We must be awake to the assault on democratic values that has gathered strength and devastated numerous homes. The temptation is powerful to close our eyes and wait for the worst to pass, but history tells us that for freedom to survive, we must defend it, and if lies are to stop, they must be exposed

Note: [1]Inspired by one famous quote of Madeleine Albright, US Secretary of State (1997 – 2001).

The smell of human blood still lingers on the soil of Nellie; its air is filled with the blood-curdling screams of wounded men, women, and children crying in pain, agony, and anguish. The people of Nellie remain grief-stricken, even today, haunted by harrowing memories of their close relatives, friends, and neighbours being openly slaughtered in broad daylight. The spine-chilling experience of the mass butchery of their loved ones witnessed before their eyes continues to torment them. After forty years, the survivors still struggle to return to their normal lives, grappling to resume their daily routines like any other ordinary human being. Despite the annual floods that ritualistically drench the Brahmaputra valley, the memories of the heinous crime committed by the brutes in this cluster of villages—commonly known as Nellie—remain undiminished.

In these villages, during the brutal assaults of February 18, 1983, aimed at wiping out the Bengali inhabitants from the soil of Nellie, the pitiless attackers spared not even the newborns, infants, and toddlers.

> *"According to an eyewitness account, a man spots children huddling in a corner trying to hide after their parents have been killed. He takes a swig from his bottle and slices up the kids in one stroke. Another person, after killing quite a few people in an intoxicated state, commits suicide by leaping into the river. Many of*

> *these killers cannot sleep at night because, in front of their eyes, there is only blood and severed heads. Many cry incessantly and cannot eat. My language appears too weak to describe the situation."*

The brutal genocide perpetrated by these merciless people against their fellow humans, especially the young, was sheer insanity—unheard of and unimaginable to any sensible person. Describing the Nellie massacre as one of the most horrific and severe pogroms with few parallels in post-World War II history, Professor Monirul Hussain recorded the aforementioned lines in his thesis "The Assam Movement: A Sociological Study," quoting them from a perspective scholar. [1]

> "Hazara Khatun, with scars from a dagger attack on her face that she survived in 1983, sat on the ground before us and pointed to her empty lap. *'I was cradling my child here,'* she said in a low voice. *'They chopped him into two, down the middle!'*"

"A lifetime is much too short to forget." Under this subtitle, author, columnist, researcher, teacher, and social activist Harsh Mander, who works with survivors of mass violence, recounted some of the gruesome events of the Nellie massacres on the independent platform SOUTH ASIA CITIZENS WEB, the print version of which appeared in the Magazine Section of The Hindu on December 14, 2008. [2] The heart-rending plight of Hazara Khatun, quoted above, was documented by Harsh Mander in that article, where the social activist explained at the outset **"the wisdom of reopening wounds of painful events of such a distant past"** to state government officials and many non-official friends who worked in state development organizations, who had "gently" tried to dissuade him from visiting Nellie. The reason for the **"Journey into the past,"** in his own words, is quoted below:

> "We gathered in the soft sunshine of early winter in an open courtyard. A crowd quickly gathered: the older men with checked lungis and beards could easily be distinguished as people of East Bengali Muslim origin. The women and younger men dressed like anyone from an Assamese village. There were the initial courtesies of traditional welcome, as they offered us customary white Assamese scarves with exquisite red embroidery.
>
> Senior officials of the state government who accompanied me had gently dissuaded me from the visit, questioning the wisdom of reopening wounds of painful events of such a distant past. 'People have moved on long ago,' they assured me. 'What purpose then would our visit serve? It would only revive memories that have long

been buried.' The same advice came from many non-official friends who worked in development organizations in the state. They added that the visit would stir issues that were too bitterly contested in the region. **But the survivors persisted in their resolve that they wanted to be heard.** It was impossible for me to refuse them." (Emphasis by Subir)

The story of the Nellie massacre is not a one-off case but one of many heart-breaking occurrences in Assam. Yet, what made the Nellie genocide truly sickening was the manifestation of its unprecedented cruelty. Snatching a baby from a mother's lap by force and chopping the child into pieces in front of the screaming mother's eyes is not only unimaginable but also the greatest inhuman act any commoner can perhaps imagine. Yet, there is more than one such nauseating incident in the Nellie mass murder that stands out among all other genocides across the globe.

"A woman, with no more than a rag around her waist, screamed uncontrollably. Her breasts bore ghastly lacerations. Abdul Hannan, one of the very few survivors who was now helping collect the wounded, said she was in the sixth month of her pregnancy—aborted when a spear handle was thrust deep into her vagina—and left to die after the marauders spent a few minutes disfiguring her body. She now screamed not with pain but with grief and pointed to the pieces of *a two-year-old, her first, who was torn in two. 'They grabbed his limbs, two from each direction, and pulled him into pieces,' said Hannan, and mumbled as an afterthought, 'Why doesn't she die now?'*"

"Blood, Bodies, and Scars: What I Saw After the 1983 Nellie Massacre in Assam"—under this caption, Shekhar Gupta, Editor-in-Chief and Chairman, narrated the above harrowing incident on February 18, 2019. It started with the lines: "On the 36th anniversary of the Nellie massacre in Assam, which claimed thousands of lives in a few hours, I recall the horrid sights." [3]

All these atrocities occurred purportedly to preserve the so-called separate racial identity of certain human lineages. The brutal violence in the central part of Assam during the early hours of February 18, 1983, has remained the worst case of organized crime recorded in the history of independent India, particularly in Assam. The black mark left behind by the perpetrators on our nation's image will endure endlessly, as the name Nellie has since become synonymous with mass execution during one of the tumultuous days of the Assam Agitation. The six-year-long agitation in Assam, also known as the Assam Movement, is detailed in the next chapter. Nevertheless, in their acts of butchering Bengalis in the Nellie cluster of villages, the perpetrators exhibited such sadistic viciousness in broad daylight that its extraordinarily shocking memories have left a permanent scar of ethnic cleansing in the memory bank of the people at the short end of the stick in Assam.

The fierceness of the assault and the ruthlessness of the aggressors were so horrific that the brutes did not distinguish people by age, infirmity, or sex. From infants less than a year old to harmless adolescents barely ten years and older, from impoverished pregnant middle-aged women with unborn children to grey-bearded elders over seventy years old, irrespective of their biological gender and chronological age, all fell victim to the mindless killings fostered allegedly by supporters of the Assam Agitation, which troubled the Brahmaputra valley of Assam for six long years between 1979 and 1985.

Recounting the horror of Nellie's mass murder, author Taha Amin Mazumder in NewsClick on February 24, 2019, under the caption "Nellie 1983 Revisited: Victims Say They Had Been Barricaded for 6 Months Before the Massacre," wrote the following heart-rending tale of a victim of the mass execution.

> "Romisa Khatun was running aimlessly with her one-and-a-half-year-old son hanging on to her waist. Suddenly, she felt a sharp, stabbing pain in her chest. It was a spear that had pierced through her chest, making a hole through the body, penetrating the bones, the muscles—coming out on the back of the body. Blood gushed out, and she lost her senses. Days later, she woke up in a hospital and asked for her child, but it was too late. She had lost her child; her one-and-a-half-year-old son had been killed. Romisa was 18 years old back then on the 'Black Friday' of February 18, 1983, when the 8-hour-long Nellie Massacre took place in central Assam's Nagaon district (now Morigaon). The carnage is estimated to have left over 5,000 people dead, including the elderly and children. Official reports, however, put the death toll at only 1,819. Now Romisa is 54, but the wound with loose skin hanging around the dent on her chest—that left a hole not just through her body but her mind too, still remains a grim reminder of the massacre that left thousands of people scarred." [4]

This is only one of the many upsetting stories that made the attempted ethnic cleansing in Nellie unparalleled. "Haji Sirajuddin, a survivor of the violence, recounted the horrors of that day to an Indian magazine, The Caravan: *'I remember seeing dead bodies strewn across the paddy fields. The stagnant water in the fields had turned red because of the amount of blood flowing in it. Only human beings are capable of inflicting this kind of violence on each other,"* wrote Communications Specialist and Feminist Research Scholar Maduli Thaosen on February 18, 2020. [5]

Nonetheless, the Bengali-bashing witnessed in Nellie on the morning of 18th February 1983 was neither a first-time incident of its kind nor a singular exemplification of a violent attack on the Bengalis in the history of Assam. Moreover, it would be wrong to presume that only the Muslims among the Bengali-speaking population were at the receiving end of the brutal onslaughts in Assam. For instance, during the same month of February 1983, when the Bengali-speaking Muslims were facing the fury of certain fanatic nationalists of Assam at places like Chaulkhowa, Mukalmua, and Bodhakora in tandem with the brutal blitz in the Nellie cluster of villages, identical bloodbaths also took place shoulder to shoulder in places like Bishnupur, Shantipur Shilapathar in Dhemaji District, Teok, and Hathishal in Jorhat District, and many other places where some jingoistic hoodlums were targeting the Bengali-speaking Hindus. There were many more incidents of similar attacks on innocent men, women, and children in the region for their pronounced fault that their mother tongue was Bengali. However, the severity of the violence and the brutality of the barbarism in Nellie were so enormous, striking, and swift (barely six hours it took to kill the thousands) that it just about eclipsed the news of other vicious onslaughts on the Bengalis carried out in chorus by some racist elements in Assam. Nonetheless, the stories of those violent incidents also trickled out slowly, although belatedly, after the nationwide outcry about the Nellie massacre started to die down gradually.

In the beginning, the leading newspapers of the region played down the Nellie massacre in their reports, but the violence of this magnitude could not be kept under wraps for long; - as the saying goes - 'ill news runs apace' - it caught the imagination of the national media although somewhat tardily. As the messages of Nellie-happenings started to spread, many national and international news reporters made a beeline for Assam. They rushed to the spot to file their stories on their news channels. The wide coverage of the incidents eventually aroused the intellectual curiosity of many experts who tried to get to the bottom of such a large-scale human tragedy. Thus, the topic of Nellie's mass murder found a place in several investigative reports, articles, books, and research papers. The findings of their detailed survey, analysis, and research on the causes behind the broad-daylight butchering of the Bengalis have since been recorded in various news magazines, academic journals, books, and research papers, which are both significant and thought-provoking.

One of the most fearless journalists from Assam, Diganta Sharma, came up with several real-life stories on the Nellie holocaust in his book "Nellie, 1983" written in the Assamese language. It was subsequently translated into Bengali by Dr. Sushanta Kar, a professor at Tinsukia College in upper Assam. In the book, Diganta Sharma furnished what he called 'the first list' of the people killed. It contains the names and ages of 1,447 slain victims - 770 males and 677 females. [6]

Unbelievably, out of the 1,447 slaughtered victims, as per the list, as many as 617 (42.64%) were children less than 10 years old. In other words, out of every 100 people killed in the massacre, nearly 43 little kids were slaughtered, of which 203 babies were 4 years old or less! The most touching is that a total of 53 infants of 1 year or less found a place in the list of 1,447 slain victims. The deplorable story does not end here. The butchers did not spare even nine octogenarian persons in their 80s and five nonagenarians in their 90s!

The Assam police were allegedly sympathetic to the movement and did not take adequate measures to prevent attacks in and around Nellie. The reality will be revealed towards the end of this chapter. Suffice it to say now that many Assam police personnel were not satisfied with the Central Government's decision to hold the election and became very hostile towards the state machinery. Even when some village residents had met the Officer in Charge of the Nagaon police station and requested him to take some action, the concerned officers failed to rise to the occasion - wrote research scholar Alankar Kaushik in his research paper "Violence and Assamese Print Media: A Study of Nellie Violence in 1983".[7]

"Six hundred and eighty-eight criminal cases were filed in connection with Nellie's organized massacre, and of these 310 cases were charge-sheeted. The remaining 378 cases were closed due to what the police claim, of "lack of evidence". But all the 310 charge-sheeted cases were dropped by the AGP government as a part of the Assam Accord; therefore, not a single person even had to face trial for the gruesome massacre. The government gave the survivors of the Nellie massacre a compensation of as little as 5,000 rupees for each death, contrasted for instance with Rs. 7 lakhs that were paid to survivors of the Sikh carnage of a year later in 1984. **Some lives are clearly deemed by the state of being of little worth compared to others.**" (Emphasis by Subir) [7]

According to a report compiled and collected by Main Uddin, Founder and CEO, of Indilens News Team, [9] "the rehabilitation package announced by the government of Assam consisted of the following:

1. Rs. 5000 cash grant to each of the bereaved families for every person killed.

2. Rs. 5000 grant towards the reconstruction of houses destroyed in the recent disturbances.
3. Maintenance of relief assistance on the same scale as in the relief camps up to a period of three months after the return to respective villages till the harvesting of the next crop.
4. Distribution of free seeds at the rate of 10 kgs per bigha subject to a maximum of 20 kgs for two bighas for every agriculturist family for sowing summer paddy.
5. Assistance to replace lost bullocks at the rate of two bullocks per family subject to a maximum of Rs. 1,500.
6. Subsidy of Rs. 500 per family for lost milch cattle.
7. For small traders and businessmen, it was decided to give a business loan of Rs. 2500 per family together with a loan subject to a maximum of Rs. 1000 in an urban area and Rs. 200 in rural areas for the repair and reconstruction of shops damaged in the disturbances and for maintenance relief for a period of one month.

It is noteworthy that the Sikh victims of the massacre that occurred soon after the murder of Indira Gandhi in 1984, a year after the Nellie massacre, were initially given Rs. 35 thousand as compensation for every death (it was raised substantially later on [10]), while the victims of the Nellie massacre were given only Rs. 5 thousand. A Nellie victim lamented this unequal treatment and expressed his anguish, saying that "our life is equal to the cost of 1 kg of fish in the market." Later on, those killed during the Assam agitation were declared as "shaheed" (martyrs) by the government of Assam. The next kin of each dead was given Rs. 35 thousand as an honour to the departed soul. The names of the Nellie massacre were not included in that list."

No matter how elaborately, cunningly, and surreptitiously the so-called 'leaders' and their supporters tried to cover up the guilt of the real perpetrators of the massacre, the truth about the carnage could not be buried deep enough to remain hidden permanently from the inquisitive gaze of the curious onlookers who were ever vigilant on the issues of crime against humanity. The sentinels of human rights were heedless of the risks involved in unearthing the truth. These activists never cared who did it, why or where it happened. The 'leaders' had tried their best to shift the entire blame of the horrendous criminality onto the tribal inhabitants of the surrounding villages, where the indigenous Tiwa (old, pejorative name Lalung) community lived. Yet, all their efforts turned out to be futile. The craftily woven pack of lies fell flat on their faces as more and more right-thinking people came up with new stories, fresh pieces of evidence, and additional perspectives on the barbaric genocide carried out on the unarmed innocent Bengalis during a six-hour-long orgy of violence in at least ten villages of the fourteen Nellie cluster of villages.

The credulous people in the neighbourhood of Nellie were instigated to the extreme and taken for a ride, no doubt, by their so-called 'leaders' by spreading spiteful rumours. From then on, the unsuspecting Tiwas and other natives of the villages surrounding Nellie started believing that their communities would soon be outnumbered and gobbled up by the large-scale arrival of the Bengalis - by now tagged as 'foreigners' - whose presence in their close proximity was painted as a severe threat to the very existence of the aboriginal people of Assam. That was how the Tiwas and other local populations were provoked to uproot the menace from the neighbourhood or bury the 'threats' into the soil of Assam – the sooner, the better. Thus, the groundwork for the worst genocide in post-independent India was skillfully laid.

"The blueprint of the attack was prepared by the All Assam Students Union (AASU)." In the chapter with this belligerent caption, in Assamese language, journalist and author Diganta Sharma quoted India Today news magazine as "...The All Assam Students Union (AASU) is believed to have played a very active part in the massacre..." and then added that the villagers of Nellie had asserted that there was no doubt about the fact that it was the agitators who had engineered the broad daylight carnage, especially at Nellie. The master plan for the genocide was developed by holding a meeting in the neighbourhood. This account is taken from veteran journalist Diganta Sarma's Assamese Book *'Nellie, 1983: Ahom Andolonor Barbarotomo Gonohotyar 'Hotyo Hondyan"* (or, "Nellie, 1983: In search of the truth about the most barbarous genocide of Assam Movement" - in English).

> ***"Assamese people are not responsible for the Nellie incidents; the Lalungs did it"*** *- one Professor sitting in the front row jumped to his feet – as if I had touched a raw nerve - and yelled at me! I was utterly taken aback by the sudden flare-up from an honourable member of the Assamese Hindu community!*
>
> *I was speaking at a seminar on secularism held somewhere in the Dibrugarh district of Assam in the early years of the 21st century. Several intellectuals and highly educated personalities from both Hindu and Muslim communities were present at the session, and the renowned scholar Masidul Hoque was also invited to address the gathering.*

Just as I began to draw attention to certain aspects of the Nellie incidents during my speech, the Professor's unexpected retort forced me to abruptly halt my presentation midway. I was stunned by the shocking outburst from such a well-regarded academician within my Assamese community.

At that very moment, I realized how sensitive these people were on the subject, even after more than a couple of decades since the Nellie massacre! I recognized that individuals like this outwardly aristocratic person in our society, engaged in honourable professions such as lecturing at Dibrugarh University or similar vocations, were actually so stubbornly attached to a narrow, bigoted concept of Assamese little nationalism that they were oblivious to the enormous stigma the Nellie massacre had brought upon the state of Assam. Instead of acknowledging the misdeeds or honestly attempting to bring the real culprits to justice, this so-called intelligentsia in Assamese society was exacerbating the matter for Assam, causing it to become a source of perpetual disgrace for our people.

I hang my head in shame when I see how a handful of individuals in the upper echelon of the Assam Movement are now enjoying all the fruits of the six-year-long nationalist campaign they had initiated. Yet, they failed to honour the sacrifice of the Assamese idealists, which included over 700 martyrs of the Assam Movement. Even worse is the fact that after deflecting all blame for the most condemnable acts during the Assam Agitation onto other communities, they managed to form the government twice in the state, yet they feign ignorance of the 1983 Nellie events as if the massacre of innocent people never occurred!

It's perplexing to see these individuals, who claim to have led the world's largest student agitation, now being the most vocal and assertive in all important political and social affairs in Assam. However, when it comes to the question of the 1983 Nellie Massacre, they become speechless. It is this deadly combination of leadership's deafening silence and the clamorous, oversensitive utterances of a section of the Assamese aristocracy to cover up the genocide that is the most upsetting feature prevalent in the state these days. (English adaptation by Subir)

In this hypercritical tone, the Principal of Jorhat College, Dr. Debabrata Sharma, expressed his unconcealed condemnation of the mass-scale manslaughter at Nellie in the foreword of the well-documented Assamese book "Nellie, 1983," written by Diganta Sharma. Born to a family whose forbears were martyrs in India's freedom struggle as well as the anti-monarchy and caste movement from 1789 to 1806, Dr. Debabrata Sharma suffered grievous injury when some ULFA militants shot him for opposing their theory of de-nationalisation of Assamese people. Yet his undaunted struggle against injustices in society is relentless.

Historically, Nellie was a part of the independent Jayantia kingdom, which became a protected state by an alliance of amity and friendship signed by the Jayantia king with the British on 10th March 1824. The relationship was confirmed after the signing of the 1826 Treaty of Yandabo, by which the Burmese renounced their claims on states and territories in the region. At that time, the Jayantia kingdom included the Jaintia hills and extended to the Surma River on the south and Gobha-Sonarpur on the north. The capital of the kingdom was Jayantiapur in the Barak-Surma valley. The Jaintia hills were predominantly peopled by Jaintias, the Jayantia plains in Barak-Surma valley by the Bengalis, and northern plains or Gobha-Sonarpur (Kamrup-Nagaon) by Lalungs, Dimasa-Kacharis, Jaintias, and others.

The death of Ram Singh, Raja of the Jayantia kingdom, on 25th September 1832, provided the British authority with an opportunity to bargain on the treaty of 1824. Raja Ram Singh was succeeded by his nephew Rajendra Singh. The latter opposed the inclusion of an additional clause requiring the Raja of the Jayantia kingdom to pay an annual tribute of Rupees ten thousand. It infuriated the British authorities. So, on the pretext of the Jayantia Raja's refusal to hand over some alleged culprits to the British authorities, on 23rd February 1835, they resolved to confiscate the possession of the Raja in the lowlands as a punishment for his guilt and leave him only the hills. The British proclamation annexing the Jayantia plains was followed by distributing the territories of the erstwhile Jayantia kingdom to the neighbouring districts. The southern part was attached to Sylhet in Bengal on geographical and cultural considerations. Similarly, the northern plains in the Brahmaputra valley, vassal Chieftaincies of Gobha (a Tiwa Kingdom), Dimarua, Neli (or Nellie), close to the erstwhile capital of Gobha kingdom with a substantial Tiwa population) Khola, etc., were incorporated into the Nowgong district. [11] [12] Thus, Nellie became a part of Assam in 1935. Currently, the Nellie cluster of villages consists of 14 villages – Alisingha, Khulapathar, Basundhari, Bagduba Beel, Bagduba Habi, Borjola, Butuni, Indurmari, Mati Parbat No. 8, Muladhari, Silbeta, Borbori, and Nellie. [13]

From Guwahati, the capital of Assam, Nellie is 70 km east - situated on the highway that leads to Nagaon, the district headquarters of one of the oldest districts in Assam. Erstwhile Nowgong district, which included Nellie village until 1989, was generally agrarian, and villages around Nellie also produced paddy and jute. The villages were inhabited by Bengalis, primarily followers of Islam, Assamese Hindus, and local tribes such as the Tiwas. There were few caste-Hindus in this locality, and most belonged to Scheduled Castes such as the Hiras and the Koibortas, or Other Backward Classes (OBC) such as the Kochs. (The Kochs are said to have indigenous origins.) The villages attacked in the Nellie incident were part of a PGR (Professional Grazing Reserve) called Alichinga Grazing Reserve, which was opened to so-called immigrants in 1943 – wrote Makiko Kimura in her book "The Nellie Massacre of 1983: Agency of Rioters." [14]

By the way, Makiko Kimura, Associate Professor of Tsuda College (Tokyo), was a postdoctoral research fellow of the Japan Society for Promotion of Science and a research associate at the International Peace Research Institute, Meiji Gakuin University (Tokyo). She studied at the Jawaharlal Nehru University (New Delhi) for her PhD degree and visited Nellie for the first time in 2001 to do fieldwork for her PhD research on the anti-foreigner movement in Assam, then again in 2007 to gain a deeper understanding of the violence. She later wrote a book titled "The Nellie Massacre of 1983: Agency of Rioters." It was first published in 2013 by SAGE Publications India Pvt Ltd, New Delhi. Makiko Kimura wrote most of the book while working as a Research Associate at the International Peace Research Institute of Meiji Gakuin University. Like a part of the previous paragraph, a lot more information in this narrative has been sourced from the book of Makiko Kimura on Nellie, including the following paragraph:

> "Before the attack in Nellie, the entire Nagaon District was in turmoil due to the AASU's attempt to block access to polling stations in order to boycott the election. Group clashes took place between different ethnic, religious, and linguistic communities, such as the Assamese Hindus, the tribes, and the Muslims and Hindus of Bengal origin. In Nagaon, the Muslims were supporters of the Congress party, and before the incident, Congress leaders such as Indira Gandhi and Ghani Khan Choudhury visited minority pockets and made provocative speeches. Due to their immigrant origins, the Muslims had decided to vote for the Congress, also hoping that the new government would be able to put an end to the movement. The AASU, however, had its support base in indigenous tribal groups and other Hindus (mainly backwards) in the area, and thus, the tension between the Muslims and the Tiwas increased.....In the southern part, however, the Muslims, who were outnumbered by the Hindus, felt threatened and had reported the possibility of an attack to the police several times before the incident. Some police officers visited the Muslim village and assured them of their safety but did not leave a patrol due to the lack of personnel." [14]

Founder CEO of Indilens Web Solutions, Main Uddin, collected and compiled a report on the Nellie massacre and the Assam agitation. It's available in the public domain on its website. In that report, under the sub-head "Diary: February 1983," a date-wise gist of some important events relating to Assam, starting from 1st February to 22nd February 1983, was listed. It's reproduced below to provide an idea of the prevailing turmoil in the state against the backdrop of which the Nellie massacre took place on 18th February 1983:

Diary: February 1983.

February 1

• All Assam freedom fighters convention under the leadership of ASSU and AGSP.

• Supreme Court rejected Raj Narayan"'s plea for the postponement of the election in Assam.

• Central Government announced Group Insurance benefits for the officials and workers from Assam and outside taking part in the election.

• Bomb blasts in various places in Assam in protest of the election.

• Several footbridges and bridges torched.

• Market burnt down in Dhekiajuli, Sonitpur district

• Group clash in Kamalpur.

February 2

• Police firing at Bordoulguri and Jonaram of Mangoldoi sub-division. 5 killed.

• ASSU alleged that CRPF threw three boys while a bridge was torched.

February 3

• Leaders of the movement declared general non-cooperation of the official programs scheduled from February 5- 22.

• Police firing on civilians protesting the election at Bura, Darrang district. Few killed.

February 4

• Police firing at North Lakhimpur. Several wounded.

• Teachers gathering in protest of the election.

- Wooden bridges burnt down in several places in North Lakhimpur, Darrang and Nagaon
- Body of the supporter of CPI (ML) recovered from Ranjali Reserve, Sivsagar

February 5

- Plying of both private vehicles and state vehicles were stopped.
- Police firing on election protester at Tongla. 4 killed
- 36-hour bandh at Karbi Anglong by two student organisations.
- Bomb blast at a few places
- Bandh in Dibrugarh district
- Centre decided to send 30 battalions of CRPF to Assam.

February 7

- Public meeting at Guwahati JudgesField by the left parties
- Police SI Bipin Mahanta killed in cross-firing by opposition people in Tezpur
- Jorhat judge Nurul Haq kidnapped by miscreants
- Dead body of a Congress worker recovered at Tingkha of Dibrugarh district
- Police –CRPF firing at Titkuri. Several wounded.
- Central government decided to send additional BSF and CRPF teams to Assam.

February 8

- 7 killed in Belsar, Nalbari, following police firing in a rally.
- Bomb blast at Lanka- 3 killed and another 23 injured.
- 7000 employees proceeded towards Assam from different parts of India to hold the election in Assam.

February 9

- Bomb thrown at Cahnd Mohammed, ex-speaker of Assam state Assembly at Athuaguri.

- Police firing at the rallies against election at Kamarkuchi, Samata of Nalbari district – 5 and 2 killed respectively.

- M Rehman was suspended from PWD following a disagreement to build a helipad in Moirabari to be used by the then PM Indira Gandhi for election purpose.

- People killed here and there following protests in various parts of Assam.

- Curfew imposed in many places.

- ASSU announced its programme boycotting the election and arrival of PM in Assam.

February 11

- Police firing at Nalbari, Barpeta etc. 3 killed.

February 12

- Communal violence erupted in several places in Assam. Several houses belonging to minority communities burnt down in and around Boko of Kamrup district and gave birth to communal clash. 9 killed.

- Indira Gandhi spoke to an election rally at Maligaon under strict security arrangements.

February 13

- Communal clash continued in places like Bokulguri, Jagiroad, Lahorighat, North Lakhimpur etc. several killed in police firing and bomb blasts.

February 14

- Election held. Police firing to control protesting mass in different places. Total 19 killed.

- 30 villages burnt down in Darang district.

- Communal clash in Jamunamukh, Nagaon district and and Kamrup district.

February 15 •

Congress- I candidate Satya Narayan of Bishwanath chariali killed by people protesting election.

• Communal clash at Goalpara, Nogaon, Darrang etc. Houses torched and several killed in police firing.

February 16

• Dayanath Sharma, brother of Joynath Sharma, head of All Assam Volunteers Force killed at Chawolkhowa Chapori and another 85 killed in that night.

• Communal clash in DoomDooma. 7 killed.

• Police and CRPF clash at Goalpara. 6 killed in the clash.

• Houses burnt down in Dhubri and Nalbari.

February 17

• Election held for the second phase in 36 state assembly seats and 11 Lok Sabha constituencies.

• Communal clash continued and several killed. Houses torched.

February 18

• Organised massacre at Nellie of Nagaon district. About 2 thousand killed. 16 villages belonging to minority community burnt down.

• Communal clash at Darrang district. 26 killed and four killed in police firing.

• Several clashes in different parts of Assam. Many killed and injured.

February 19

• Attack on linguistic minority at Gareshwar of Kamrup district. Several injured.

• Communal clash at Abhayapuri.

• Lok Sabha election completed at 24 constituencies.

February 21

• Indira Gandhi visited Nellie and Gohpur.

• About 2 thousand people belonging to linguistic minority fled to West Bengal for safety from Goreshwar, Kamrup.

• 48 dead bodies recovered from different parts of Kamrup.

February 22

• Peres de Queler, UN secretary general expressed shock over the Nellie massacre. [16]

In his research paper titled "Violence and Assamese Print Media: A Study of Nellie Violence in 1983," researcher Kaushik Alankar attempted to explore the complexities involved in reporting violence in our societies by diverse media in general and the Nellie violence of 1983 in Assam in particular. The following paragraph is quoted from it:

> "Interestingly, during this period of turmoil, the middle class skillfully used the press and other communication media to create an impression amongst the politically backward sections of the people that the Bengali migrants from Bangladesh, as a community, are opposed to the aspirations of the Assamese, that they are all leftists and that all leftists in Assam are in general agents of Bengali expansionism in eastern India. This stand helped the Assamese middle class to overcome the caste politics of the Ujani Asam Rajya Parishad and the OBC faction and emerge united against the chaos that the divided Congress house. By tracing from the files of the local press, it is interesting to note the initial phase of the agitation. This had initially developed by and large peacefully with blessings from the press through organized intimidations and jingoist wall writings, ceaseless protest meetings fed with myths and false statistics. In 1978, it finally culminated into mass hysteria and led to large-scale anti-Bengali pogroms in January and May-June of 1980. From June 1979 onwards, the press directed its hate campaign exclusively against the so-called Bangladeshis" – all post-1951 East Pakistan migrants and their progeny, most of whom did not possess readily acceptable documents to prove their Indian citizenship in a permissive set-up. Over the months, the movement demonstrated that it could mobilize hundreds and thousands of people without disturbing the peace or creating violence. This was feasible because dissident political and linguistic minorities preferred not to come in

their way by holding parallel meetings and processions to disapprove of some of their slogans and methods. The minorities were submissive in general. Yet incidents of intimidation, arson, and violence continued to mount from August 1979, resulting in an exodus of Bengali and Nepali settlers. Soon, the Government of West Bengal was forced to open two camps in Jalpaiguri district to accommodate them." [17]

Significantly, in the present-day narratives on the so-called "Muslims of East Bengal" of Assam, most authors stop short of naming them as Bengalis who have now settled in the Brahmaputra valley of Assam for decades. They had hailed from Bengal's Mymensingh district and its adjacent areas - presently in Bangladesh. Since the first census enumeration in independent India in 1951, most of them had been declaring Assamese as their mother tongue to secure their foothold in Assam. They speak among them in a typical Bengali ethnic dialect known as Mymensinghee patois. It is now common to call them 'Na-Asamiya', which means 'Neo-Assamese'. Nevertheless, in Assam, they have officially declared Assamese as their mother tongue.

As if in a prelude to the Nellie Massacre, just two days ahead, on 16th February 1983, 109 helpless people were brutally killed in a relief camp at Nagabanda High School (in the Morigaon district of Assam). The villagers of the adjoining villages were instructed by the peace committee of civil administration and police administration to take shelter in the relief camp on 16th February 1983 to escape from the violent attacks of the agitators of the Assam Movement. A large number of people from neighbouring villages took shelter in the school, including women and children. At around 10 o'clock morning, a huge mob led by police personnel attacked the people taking shelter in the school. The police indiscriminately fired on the relief camp. The frightened people closed the doors and windows of the school. Then the agitators set the school on fire. Some people tried to escape through the windows of the backside of the school; some climbed the trees near the school. But they couldn't escape. The agitators killed them on the branches of trees with sharp and long weapons. One hundred and nine dead bodies were recovered, and another few hundred were injured, according to a report by author Abdul Kamal, a researcher and development practitioner based in Assam. The report appeared in Raiot (a webzine from Meghalaya) on 18th February 2018 under the caption "In 1983 NAGABANDA MASSACRE AND THE OTHER SIDE OF ASSAMESE INTELLIGENTSIA" [18]

The next day, on February 17th, 1983, two truckloads of police contingents arrived at Borbori and assured the inhabitants of nearby patrols and full security. Reassured by the security personnel, Nellie residents went to work outside as usual on February 18th, 1983, the day of the massacre. Around 8:30 AM, the village was suddenly attacked by mobs from three sides, pushing the villagers towards the Kopili River. Armed individuals wielding dao, spears, and a few guns advanced towards Nellie in an organized manner. The attackers encircled the whole village, leaving open the side that ended towards the river Kopili. Some attackers were also in boats. [19]

As they advanced, voices blared from loudspeakers, prompting and encouraging the assailants: "Friends, go ahead; we are with you. Please keep on doing your job – there is no need to fear." Those who could run fast managed to escape. The indiscriminate killing commenced around 9 AM and persisted till 3 PM. Most of the victims, over 75%, were children, women, and elderly men aged 60 and above. [20]

Various reports suggest that the attack first targeted a village called Borbori, situated northeast of Nellie. After attacking Borbori, the assailants crossed the national highway and proceeded to attack the Muslim villages south of Kopili. They encircled from the east, south, and north, initiating the burning of houses, mostly thatched. Hemendra Narayan, a journalist with the Indian Express at the time, witnessed and reported the incident.

> In a systematic manner, the houses of Muslim settlements at Demalgaon were set ablaze. As I hurried behind them, hundreds more outpaced me. Soon, one by one, the houses in Demalgaon were engulfed in flames. First, a whitish smoke appeared, and then thick black smoke billowed up. Within half a minute, it was a red glare, and within five minutes, only the bare skeleton of the house remained.
>
> After burning down houses and leaving no place to hide, the attackers commenced killing the Muslim villagers. People began to flee towards the west, where the CRPF was stationed. The immigrants fled to cross Demal Bil (rivulet) to reach Muladhari village. As the houses burned, all the tribals assembled on the high bank. The immigrants could be seen assembled across the rivulet in Muladhari. Others from Alisingha, Silcherri, and Baihati were already there. Arrows and stones were exchanged across the Bil. The shouts and screams reached a crescendo. The situation took a turn when another group of tribals appeared from the eastern side of Muladhari. Vastly outnumbered, Muslims had no choice but to run. However, they were trapped. On one side was the Demal River, and further north, another river, the Kopili. They ran to the west to Bhutnimara village on the foothills, in a desperate bid for survival.

Women and children could not keep pace with the men. One by one, they were hacked to death by hundreds of rampaging tribes.

Those who managed to reach the CRPF camp were able to save their lives, but many women, children, and elderly people were slaughtered. Only when the CRPF troops reached the attack site between three and half-past three in the afternoon did the attackers cease the killings and disperse. According to reports, the massacre left 1819 people dead and several thousand others injured, probably the highest number of people killed with crude weapons. Most of the victims were women and children. The CRPF arrived around 3 PM, and the survivors were taken to the Nagaon police station. Most survivors were housed in the Nellie camp at Nagaon. They returned to their village after 14 days.

The Tewary Commission Report mentioned that the news of the attack reached the police station around half-past twelve. If the police had taken necessary action in time, many killings could have been avoided. It has been alleged that some local police even joined in the raid. [21]

> "In my family, including all my relatives, more than 70 people died. My mother-in-law, grandmother, aunt, nephews, and nieces... They started lighting the houses on fire and came towards us from different directions. After burning down the homes, they started killing the people. We assembled in the field and started running towards the Kiling River. About 10 CRPF personnel were stationed in the western direction. While we were running, many were killed from behind. Those able to reach the CRPF camp were able to survive."

A schoolteacher in Muladhari village recounted this personal experience to author Makiko Kimura during her second visit to Nellie in August 2007, when the researcher found the villagers to be more vocal and outspoken about the loss of life in their own families. The first research trip was in 2001–2002. [22]

Journalists Sumanta Sen and Jagannath Dubashi reported on the Nellie massacre in India Today, ISSUE DATE: March 15, 1983, UPDATED: May 26, 2014. The following account is based on that report:

Ever since the government announced the polls in Assam, the approximately 15,000 Bengali Muslims residing in a cluster of a dozen villages between Jagi Road and Moregaon in Nowgong district knew they would be living on a knife-edge for the next month. The East Bengali origin (mainly from Mymensingh, now in Bangladesh) of these Muslims made them prime targets for the Assamese. Moreover, they had made it clear that they would not heed the poll boycott call given by some Assamese agitators and would participate in the elections. Additionally, raider gangs from the villages had been making forays across the river into the Mangaldoi areas of Darrang district to clash with Assamese rivals.

Thus, the stage was set for one of the most gruesome massacres in Indian history. The polls opened in Nellie on February 14th, 1983, and immediately afterwards, Assamese in the villages surrounding the Muslim pocket held meetings and announced that pro-election Muslims must be socially ostracized, and anybody trading with them would be fined Rs 500.

Meanwhile, news of the slaughter at Gohpur, 133 km from Tezpur, the headquarters of Darrang district, spread, where the Boro tribes, supporters of the pro-poll Plains Tribals Council of Assam (PTCA), were enraged due to intimidation from the Assamese. Together with the volatile tea garden labourers in the Tezpur sub-division, they resented having had vital bridges destroyed. Nobody in Gohpur or even Gauhati knew how the Gohpur killing started on February 14th. The rumor quickly spread that tribal hordes had burned down more than 17 Assamese villages and more than 1,000 people were killed.

Three days later, when police parties finally began scouring the area, it came to light that the Assamese had also hit out: 27 Boro villages were attacked, and torch-wielding Assamese killed at least 30 Boros. The death toll on both sides did not add up to more than 100.

Gohpur, as it turned out, was only the prelude to a grisly theme. On February 16th, five Lalung children were found dead in the Lahorigate area near Nellie. The villagers of Nellie and the surrounding villages were tense with fear and hate. The Lalung tribes were resentful because they felt that the Muslim immigrants - most of whom came to Assam in the '50s and '60s - had occupied prime land once tilled by the Lalungs.

The situation worsened when three Muslim children's dead bodies were recovered at the place where the tribal children's bodies were found. On the same day – February 17th - the Bengali Muslims of Dharamtuli village, one of the Nellie clusters, were forcibly prevented from voting in the second phase of the poll. At the same time, there were reports of Muslim attacks on the Assamese-Hindu villages of Dakchuki, Menapara, and Dhula in the Mangaldoi area across the river.

On February 18th, Friday, at around eight in the morning, a huge mob surrounded Nellie, armed with guns, spears, swords, 'daos' (cleavers), glinting in the morning sun. Cries of "Jai ai ahom!", the rallying slogan of the anti-foreigner agitation that means "Long Live Mother Assam", filled the air.

Nuruddin, a Nellie resident, recalled what happened next: 'We were all standing in front of our house, watching the mob gathering in the distance and wondering what we should do. Suddenly we found the mob running towards us, and as we started fleeing, I fell and felt the running feet around me. Then there was fire and smoke, and I did not know how long I lay there.' Nuruddin was fortunate; he escaped the murderous frenzy of the mob, which was composed mainly of Lalung tribes, though there were some Mikir and Boro tribes as well. Intelligence sources later said that the mob included some Assamese Hindus and Nepalis. It seemed like all the decades of hate and frustration were concentrated in those few bloody hours when the killings continued.

The slaughter and arson occurred mainly in a tiny delta between the small rivers Kopili, Killing, and Demal. The land was very marshy, and the fleeing villagers had no chance to escape. Later, it was estimated that 80 per cent of the dead were women and children because the men ran faster.

As the 'daos' rose and fell with monotonous precision, the women and children tumbled in heaps in the rice paddies. Mothers were still clutching their babies - both slashed and chopped about like hunks of meat on a butcher's slab.

The Muslim villages in the area huddled together as if in a ghetto. Soon, the other villages - Demal, Matiparbat, Borburi, and Dharamtuli among them - were engulfed in bloodlust. The villagers started retreating towards the Demal Bil, a vast stretch of water, and many succeeded in crossing over to the other side and tried to burn the bamboo bridge behind them to keep their attackers at bay. However, the macabre cunning of the attackers became immediately evident - 'dao'-wielding Lalungs from the rear pounced upon the fugitives, and the killings commenced with redoubled fury.

Later, the survivors said they could not organize themselves as the attack had been too swift and sudden. However, it appeared that most of the men were away, and there seemed to be some truth in the report that they had crossed the river to Mangaldoi to attack Assamese settlements there.

In fact, the army cordoned off the Muslims returning across the river on 18th February because they feared reprisals - but this may have prevented many Muslims from reaching their villages when the slaughter was happening.

However, villagers from Nellie and the other settlements saw a sinister design in that women and children bore the brunt of the attack. Says Tahermuddin Thakur: "It looks as if the attackers wanted to make sure of getting rid of the entire new generation and also to ensure that no new births took place."

The stories of the survivors were similar in evoking the stark brutality of 18th February 1983. Nurul, 16 years old, fled with his parents to Demal Bil; the killers caught up with the running family, and Nurul saw first his mother falling and then his father, who was decapitated by one of the hundreds of 'daos' flashing efficiently on that morning, afternoon, and evening. Nurul fell unconscious, for which he could escape the attackers' wrath.

Saifuddin, who had married barely a year ago, said: "We were running with the others when we got separated in the melee. I jumped into a pond along with others, and that is how we got away." Nuruddin lay low while the killings went on, and then when the attackers lost their momentum a bit, "I got up and ran towards some bushes and hid there all night."

Anwar Huq was away when the attackers stormed his village. After he returned, the village was reduced to ashes. Anwar went about like a madman searching for his relatives and suddenly saw his sister lying dead under a tree with her neck slashed. Later, he found that all 20 of his relatives were killed, and he was the only member of his family left alive.

Two days after the massacre, the authorities managed to set up an open-air camp for the survivors in which 2,000 people huddled. Quite a few of them had managed to salvage, of all things, squawking chickens, which were one source of food in the refugee camps. Manik Mia said: "These birds were the only things we had, and we just picked them up and ran for shelter."

It appeared to be a planned attack, as gathered by talking to the refugees. They said that "people from other places" frequently came to Assamese villages - Mukuria, Palaguri, Silbheta - and held closed-door meetings with the leaders of All Assam Students' Union (AASU) that spearheaded the 5-year-long Assam Movement or the Assam Agitation.

According to Abdul Hai of Demai village, many of the attackers were unknown faces but were guided by known AASU boys who led them on shouting "Jai ai ahom" and "Death to the mias".

Even as three army columns moved into the Nowgong district, the authorities began to count the dead. Conservative estimates were 600, but intelligence sources said it would be at least 1,000. In addition, 10,000 were injured or left homeless.

Camp inmates felt that many more had died besides those lying in the fields. Robi said: "I have seen bodies being thrown into the Kopili river the night after the raid." However, he could not identify the people tossing the corpses into the water. When Mrs Gandhi visited the site on 21st February, there was not a single body to be seen in the areas she visited.

The refugees displayed a despairing resolve not to leave the region. Rajab Ali, who lost his mother and brother, said: "Where can we go?" Others are numbed by the inferno into which they were plunged last fortnight. Akram Chowdhury, one of those who emigrated to India from Mymensingh a long time ago, said: "We had been living in peace all these years. Now we are attacked by our neighbours who were friends only the other day." Today,

- Nellie is a graveyard with all the attendant sights, smells, and sounds of death.
- The ghastly hulks of gutted houses.
- The stench of rotting flesh.
- The sound of relatives mourning their mutilated dead

For the survivors huddling over their meagre meals in the camps, protected by armed guards from the madness that prowled the valley, the past was a blood-stained nightmare, the present a daze, the future only uncertainty. Perhaps the vultures were the only ones to be sure of what the future would bring. It knows how to wait; it's a patient bird! [23]

In the report on the "Genesis of Nellie massacre and Assam agitation" compiled and collected by Main Uddin, the founder and CEO of 'Indilens Web Solutions', it is mentioned, among other things, that:

> "The issue of immigration is totally political. If you personally visit these localities which the Assamese claim as Bangladeshi areas, you will discover how many of them are illegal immigrants. Actually, most of these people have been living in these localities for a long time, but because of successive administrative discrimination, their names don't get enlisted in the voter's list. Hence, they remain illegal. Otherwise, there is no reason for successive generations to remain illegal.
>
> As far as infiltration is concerned, the bordering areas are highly porous and the passage of people between India and Bangladesh is mutual. People from both regions cross the border according to their choice. In normal circumstances, it is not an issue. But whenever the Assamese feel like playing with Bengalis' fate and life, they start by calling them Bangladeshi.
>
> However, in southern Assam, about 30% of the entire population is Bengali Hindus (they were either refused from Bangladesh or took shelter voluntarily in India). Since the administration was friendly with them, they got themselves enlisted in the voter list (of 1965,

1966, 1971, and 1975, respectively), consequently becoming legally Indians. Nobody worries or questions about them.

The helpless Bengali-speaking Muslims face double discrimination from two angles. First, being Bengali speakers, they face discrimination from the Assamese authority and people. Secondly, being Muslims, they experience a stepmotherly attitude from the biased Hindu (not all but the majority) officials and the state administration as a whole. So, this is the issue.

If you actually know the issue, you will never even raise the question. And time and again, the Bengali-speaking Muslims in the region have suffered and been questioned for their legitimacy as Indians, but hardly ever have their actual concerns been addressed." [24]

While the official figure for the number of people killed in the Nellie massacre is 1,819 and that of people injured is innumerable, the unofficial figure for the death toll ranges from anything between five thousand and ten thousand. There is, however, no mention of the number of unattended corpses left lying in the open after the violence was over on that day – as usually happens in this type of carnage. Anyway, after nearly four decades of the senseless killings of Bengalis, the specifics of those horrendous events won't make much difference except to take note of the fact that the survivors of the Nellie massacre are yet to get justice. The perpetrators of the terrible crimes, including the foot soldiers, are still roaming free with impunity. Most importantly, the masterminds behind the worst genocide in the post-independent era of India are yet to be unmasked.

Others also cannot escape the guilt of the mass murder. In this tragic occurrence, multiple characters played vital roles behind the scenes, directly or indirectly causing countless violent deaths, grievous injuries, and untold miseries to numerous people. Contrary to popular perception, it's not a single individual or group to be blamed. There are various coteries liable for impropriety and criminality. Some did it knowingly, and others participated unknowingly, culminating in what is believed to be one of the worst-ever ethnic cleansings in our country. Besides, there are several factors that triggered the violence.

While it is not within the bounds of the possibility of the book to deliberate upon the role of each and every camp and clique at length to pinpoint their liability, an attempt has been made in this chapter to provide a broad outline of the actions and activities of some selected groups, organizations, and institutions considered to be the leading players in the state during the turbulent period, especially immediately before and during the mayhem.

People of Nellie believed that the organized massacre on them was planned by the agitators of the Assam movement - according to one India Today report in 1983. The agitators fulfilled their ambition by inciting the neighbouring Tiwa community to carry out the carnage. On April 10th, the then Assam Chief Minister Hiteshwar Saikia reportedly held a press conference and released some papers of AASU activists. Among these were papers prepared by AASU leaders on the religious minority inhabited areas. The report on the press conference was published in a newspaper called 'Janakranti' on April 17th, 1983, which is said to have proved how the organized killing was carried out on people belonging to minority communities, branding them as foreigners. The report also quoted Hiteswar Saikia saying, "Activists of AASU, AGSP are involved in violent activities in the state". [25]

While addressing the question of whether "Land Alienation" was the reason behind the Nellie Massacre or not, Makiko Kimura wrote that the villages attacked in the Nellie incident were part of a Professional Grazing Reserve (PGR) called Alichinga Grazing Reserve, and it was opened to "immigrants" in 1943. From the analysis of documents on grazing reserves and tribal blocks, it could be pointed out that Nellie and its contiguous villages were one of the areas where the "immigrants" started to settle in the 1940s. When the antiforeigner movement began, the movement's leaders raised the issue of land alienation among the indigenous communities to back their claims that the influx of foreigners created socioeconomic problems in Assam.

Makiko Kimura then wrote that the existing literature attributed land alienation as the primary cause of the incident. Before interviewing the villagers, the author thought there could be some problems concerning land between the Muslims and the Tiwas, the Kochs, and the other Assamese Hindus. However, during the group interviews with the villagers, they never mentioned any trouble with their land. In one group interview, the persons interviewed asserted that they did not have any confrontation with Muslims; instead, they had good relations with them and mutually exchanged agricultural products between them. Given the socioeconomic structure of the area, Makiko Kimura summarized that rather than land alienation, some local people in the area saw the antiforeigner movement and the disturbance caused by the election as an opportunity to drive out the Muslims to appropriate their lands.

It was the elections, its boycott called by the AASU, and the subsequent tension which the villagers mentioned as the primary factors to begin rioting and not even the so-called small-scale alleged skirmishes between the Muslims and their tribal neighbours, as being publicized. The image of the "land-hungry Mussalman," caricatured in Mullan's census report, was often exaggerated. Usually, the Tiwas, the Kochs, the Hiras, and other peasants had mortgaged their lands to borrow money from their Muslim neighbours and then lost the mortgaged lands when they failed to repay their loans. [26] Makiko Kimura then added,

> "In the writings of academics and journalists in Assam and the rest of India, the problem of land alienation by the Muslims of Bengali origin has up to now been regarded as the cause of the Nellie massacre. The indigenous peoples in Assam resented losing their land because of the continued Muslim influx. When scholars and journalists try to analyze the cause of the Nellie massacre, they often suggest that the Tiwas were deeply resentful of land alienation. We have already seen that the pan-Indian media, the Indian Express, in particular, reported the cause of the incident as tribal land alienation immediately after the incident took place. It seems that this interpretation is largely accepted by scholars and journalists from Assam. For example, Sanjib Baruah wrote,
>
>> Some of the worst violence occurred in villages around Nellie, an area where the Tiwa people once had their kingdom; much of the area is now settled by Bengali immigrants and their descendants. Tiwas (also called Lalungs) are a "plains tribe" who had lost much of their land to immigrants from East Bengal.
>
> Similarly, the Assamese journalist Sanjoy Hazarika wrote,
>
>> In the case of Nellie and its surrounding villages, those who sold their lands were the Tiwas. Their bitterness grew as they saw the immigrants nourish the soil and grow more crops, making profits on fields which were, until recently, their own.... Perhaps it [the day of the massacre] would be better described as pay-back day.

Clearly, the cause of the massacre given in these two writings was consistent with that of the local movement leaders. It should be noted that most of the local movement leaders in Morigaon were college lecturers or schoolteachers and so-called caste-Hindu Assamese. Being intellectuals, they had better access to the top movement leaders' claims and newspaper reports. It can be said that the local movement leaders' narrative represented the dominant narrative of the Assamese intellectuals.

Nevertheless, land alienation may be one of the reasons for the violence but not the only reason. The slogan of the Assam movement was that Assamese were minorities in their 'own' land and the aliens had stolen their land. The heightened atmosphere of hatred that the Assam movement generated underlined the sinister motif, 'if you attack the Muslims and drive them out, you can obtain their land'. Other cited reasons, such as the kidnapping of girls, supposed threat of attack by Muslims, and operation Brahmaputra spearheaded by the CIA, are part of the rumours that spread before the incident. The threat perception from the Muslims felt by the villagers was crucial when they decided to attack. From their perspective, it was not ideology or land alienation but the more acute and directly felt threat, which made them attack their Muslim neighbour. [27]

The Nellie Massacre on February 18, 1983, believed to be the direct fallout of the elections held on February 14 and 17, 1983, was written about by the renowned journalist from Assam, Diganta Sarma, in his tell-tales book *Nellie*, 1983, written in the Assamese language. According to Diganta Sarma, the plan to attack the villages in Nellie had been made after a few Muslims voted in the election going against AASU's call for the statewide boycott of the vote demanding revision of the voter lists against the backdrop of then Prime Minister Indira Gandhi's decision to give millions of so-called 'immigrants' from Bangladesh the right to vote. "That there will be a massacre in the Nellie area had already been known to the police and the home department bureaucrats. The police also knew about the plan at least 3 days before the ghastly incident. The proof of that finds ground in the fact that Jahiruddin Ahmed, then Nagaon Police Station's officer-in-charge, sent an urgent message to Morigaon's 5th Battalion's commandant, the sub-divisional police officer and Naba Chetia, the officer-in-charge of the Jagiroad police station. However, none of the officials took the message seriously. The Nagaon Police's message sent to the officer-in-charge of Jagiroad Police Station and commandant of the 5th Battalion of Morigaon read:

To:
CO, 5th AP,

INFO, O/C J/Road, PS, SDPO(M)

From, O/C NWG PS, Dt. 15.02.83.

INFORMATION RECEIVED THAT L/NIGHT ABOUT ONE THOUSAND ASSAMESE OF SURROUNDING VILLAGES OF NELLIE WITH DEADLY WEAPONS ASEMBLED AT NELLIE BY BEATING DRUMS (.) MINORITY PEOPLES ARE IN PANIC AND APPREHENDING ATTACK AT ANY MOMENT 9 (.) SUBMISSION FOR IMMEDIATE ACTION TO MAINTAIN PEACE (.)".

There was enough evidence to indicate that the carnage took place with the patronage of the local police and the villagers of the surrounding villages. Many pieces of literature on the Nellie Massacre show that the police had utterly failed to stop the massacre from happening. Can anyone today say that the residents of the neighbouring villages had no prior knowledge of the most loathsome massacre that took place in their next-door neighbourhood, Nellie, on February 18, 1983? [28]

From 1979 onwards, Assam witnessed the consecutive fall of several governments. The Janata Party Government crumbled in 1979 and headed for a split. In December 1980, a Congress (I) government was formed but could not last for more than six months, after which the President's rule was imposed. In 1982, a new Congress government was formed under the leadership of Keshab Gogoi, but it was in power only for two months.

Side by side, many ethnic clashes were reported during the period, especially with the formation of the All Assam Minorities Students Union (AAMSU), which demanded that all those who came to Assam before 1971 be granted citizenship — in direct opposition to the stand taken by AASU. There was also a massive deployment of paramilitary forces in the state. Despite the endless conflicts and the massive resistance from groups like AASU and the general public, the Indira Gandhi–led government in New Delhi decided to call for elections in Assam in February 1983. The leaders of the Assam Movement urged the general public to boycott the Assembly elections.

Yet, the Bengali Muslims across the state chose to ignore the boycott and voted in the assembly elections in defiance of the anti-election protests. In Nellie and surrounding villages, polls opened on February 14, 1983. For Bengali Muslims, voting was the means through which they could effectively prove their claim to Indian citizenship, which was constantly under the shadow of doubt by the ongoing agitations. Many people believed their rebelliousness was the immediate reason for violence against the Bengali Muslims.

In the aftermath of the February 1983 mass killings, the state government set up a Commission of Inquiry in July 1983. It was headed by T. P. Tewary, an officer in the Indian Administrative Service, "to look into the circumstances" leading to the violence that spanned from January to April 1983, "to examine the measures taken by the concerned authorities to anticipate, prevent and deal with these disturbances," and "to suggest measures to prevent the recurrence of such incidents" in the future. In May 1984, after interviewing hundreds of witnesses as well as state officials, the commission submitted its 547-page report. But the report was never tabled in the state Assembly. Its contents remained a closely guarded secret for decades, with a few photocopies circulating among activist groups. It was only after an application was filed by the Centre for Equity Studies under the Right to Information Act that the report's contents entered the public domain.

According to an Indian digital news publication, Scroll.in, dated February 18, 2017, the violence that engulfed the state in those three months grew out of the Assam Movement launched by the All Assam Students Union in 1979. The agitation was aimed at "illegal Bangladeshi immigrants" who had migrated to the state in waves. Matters came to a head when the government scheduled Assembly elections in 1983. It prompted the AASU to step up its agitation and call for a boycott. It divided the population into two camps. One group supported the elections, and the other opposed it. Consequently, violent clashes erupted.

Interestingly, among other things, the report also disclosed another story that emerged from the testimonies recorded in the Tewary Commission – 'that of an administration trying to account for itself and failing' but, according to the report, the commission tried to direct attention to cases of individual guilt. For that fateful morning in Nellie, the report narrowed down the responsibility to three specific officers. The pertinent portions of the news report are quoted below:

> "In Nagaon district, where Nellie is located, the elections had been scheduled for February 14. About 40% of the district's inhabitants were Muslim, many of them immigrants. The Assam agitation had shaded into extremist violence here, and the AASU had come into conflict with the All Assam Minority Students Union. The district had seen blasts and clashes in the three years leading up to the elections. So when the government decided to go ahead with polls, the deputy commissioner expected violence.
>
> The administration was prepared, he said, with polling stations divided into three categories – "safe", "moderately safe" and "unsafe". There were preventive arrests of more than 1,000 people and 22 persons were detained under the draconian National Security Act. On February 16, the army was asked to help with law and order in certain areas of the district.
>
> What, then, went wrong? The Tewary Commission traces it to the wireless message sent on February 15. The officer in charge at Nagaon who sent it had omitted to inform the deputy commissioner and the superintendent of police. Consequently, the district control room, located in Nagaon, remained in the dark. However, the Tewary Commission pins the blame on the three recipients of that

message. They included the commandant of the 5th Assam Police Battalion, who was also in charge of law and order in Morigaon, the subdivisional police officer of Morigaon, and the officer in charge of the Jagiroad police station. All three denied receiving the message, which was delivered to the officer's wife in one case, languished on a table in the other, and in a "put up basket" in the third.

But there was another intimation of impending violence. On the same day, Hindu inhabitants of the village had complained to the deputy superintendent that they feared an attack. KPS Gill, then Inspector General of Police in Assam, had asked the Jagiroad officer in charge to patrol the area and form a peace committee.

On February 17, the officer visited Borbori, one of the 14 villages that would be hit by violence. Residents there had asked him to post armed police at the spot, but he declined, later saying he did not have enough men. The report refutes this claim, pointing out that reinforcements had arrived in time.

The next day, he received word of trouble in Nellie at 10:54 am but chose to send two platoons of the Central Reserve Police Force. He followed hours later, claiming he did not know a path to the village. He also said he was forced to stop and rescue drowning persons in a river on the way. A barely veiled note of amusement enters the report at this point: "On that day, within a period of three hours he is supposed to have rescued two hundred drowning persons, indeed a miraculous task."

The subdivisional police officer of Morigaon was also notified about the violence at 12:30 pm on February 18 but merely passed the message on to his colleague in Jagiroad. It is not clear what lapses the commandant was guilty of, apart from neglecting to check his mail.

The officer in charge at Jagiroad was suspended, and the government ordered disciplinary action against him. The subdivisional police officer from Morigaon was suspended for 10 days but then reinstated. There is no record of action taken against the commandant.

For the deputy commissioner and the superintendent of police, the report has praise: their performance was "in keeping with the high traditions of public services".

Could the tragic events at Nellie have been avoided if the three men had "been more careful with their dak (letters)"? For the most part, the Tewary Commission exonerates the law-and-order machinery: "There were lapses of individuals but the system worked well."

Yet its own findings contradict this statement. In almost every district, it is the same story – trouble starts with the AASU declaring a boycott and extremist offshoots of the agitation implementing it with violence. Roads were blocked, bridges were blown up, and phone lines were cut. Isolated police officers, short of vehicles and unable to communicate, found themselves unable to contain large-scale violence. What system, exactly, was working well?

Disciplinary action, if it was taken at all, was largely restricted to mid- or lower-level officials. The report admits that "Lower formations of the police had a soft corner for the agitation." Many of them were Assamese, and in some places, they had suffered directly from the violence. Besides, four years of policing the agitation had frayed nerves and "demoralised" the police force. When elections were declared, many were reluctant to turn up for poll duty.

In Goalpara district, one senior official admitted that "certain administrative actions", such as mass suspensions and physically forcing government servants to election duty, could have contributed to the violence. Indeed, it was in Goalpara that members of the Assam Police Battalion shot two sentries guarding a polling station on February 16. A crossfire had then ensued between the battalion and the CRPF, killing personnel on both sides. The incident had played a large part in undermining law and order.

Who is to bear responsibility for sending out disaffected, ill-equipped men to deal with raging mobs, for pressing forward with elections even though there were large-scale strikes among government employees? The Tewary report gives a clean chit to the state administration, even defending its decision to hold elections at that volatile moment. It also makes scant mention of the Centre, which was largely absent.

Yet in the years that followed, 688 first information reports were filed for the Nellie massacre, resulting in just 299 chargesheets and no prosecution – the state administration had not thought it necessary to press for justice. And then Prime Minister Indira Gandhi was later asked why she had not responded promptly to the Nellie massacre. "One has to let such events take their course before stepping in," she replied." [29]

As mentioned earlier, although 688 cases were filed for the Nellie massacre, the police filed charge sheets in only 310 cases, which were eventually closed, and not a single perpetrator was punished. In October 1997, the then Assam Chief Minister, Prafulla Kumar Mahanta, told India Today, "The matter was over once the Congress government of the time disbursed compensation."

Then-Prime Minister Indira Gandhi, who visited Nellie after the massacre, stated, "The students and agitators were to blame; they had created a climate of violence by spurning talks with the government." In contrast, the AASU claimed that violence had broken out due to forced elections. That year, Congress won the Assam elections with a thumping majority by securing 91 out of 109 seats.

Two years after the Nellie massacre, the Assam Accord was signed in 1985, fixing the cut-off date to identify foreigners as March 24, 1971, the day before the Bangladesh Liberation War began. In 1985, AGP won the state Assembly elections and formed a government headed by Prafulla Kumar Mahanta. During its regime, about a dozen cases, including that of the Nellie massacre, were withdrawn from various state courts. The murderers of the innocent villagers are still at large. The next of kin of Nellie's victims were given a paltry Rs. 5,000/- each as 'compensation', but they are yet to get justice. It underpins the famous quote of Professor Thomas W. Simon in his book titled "The Laws of Genocide: Prescriptions for a Just World":

> *"When someone kills a man, he is put in prison. When someone kills twenty people, he is declared mentally insane. But when someone kills 200,000 people, he is invited to Geneva for peace negotiations."* [30]

Indeed, this shameful incident is one of the biggest collective acts of violence in postcolonial India that was initially reported widely all over the country and abroad as a "tribal massacre". The distinctive characteristics of the massacre were that barbarism took the form of the rural poor attacking another underprivileged countryside community at the height of the protest movement spearheaded by a student organization in Assam. Unlike collective violence witnessed in urban India, where professional thugs generally start the attacks, troublemakers and criminal elements in Nellie were ordinary villagers from the neighbourhood who were, up till now, quite friendly with the victims. The local police did not promptly take action because of any subjective government order. Here, the government apparently had a will to protect the victims but failed miserably. It appears that because the passion triggered by the student organization's boycott was so widespread, the local police became sympathetic to the professed "cause" of the movement. They avoided taking any effective action. The law enforcement machinery got more or less paralyzed by the friction between the government and the student organization in the process, creating a vacuum in the law implementation approach in the state. Simply put, the government had lost control over the law enforcement machinery. Strangely enough, the animosity between the attackers and the attacked did not sustain for long; the survivors soon returned to their respective villages and started living side-by-side with the assailants like in earlier days! According to Makiko Kimura:

> "The incident was not directly controlled by the top student leaders, but it was an important outcome of the movement... There was a certain decision-making process among the village elders of the Tiwas before the attack... Leaders of the anti-foreigner movement, mainly students and the urban middle class, provided the ideology and legitimacy for ostracizing "foreigners" in Assam. As for the local residents near Nellie—the Tiwas and the Assamese peasants—they suffered from land grabbing by the Muslims. In rural Assam, many people mortgage their land but, unable to pay, have it taken away, and they are subsequently forced to migrate or work as daily wage labourers or adhiyars (sharecroppers). Such a situation is prevalent in Nagaon district, where the colonization scheme was introduced and large-scale immigration took place. In the northern part of the district, the Muslims were already a majority and the indigenous peoples had slowly lost their land. In the Nellie area, the pressure on land was becoming more acute. Under such circumstances, the Tiwas and the Other Backward Classes (OBCs) supported the movement, and the movement leaders and local residents fought a joint struggle." [31]

Independent researcher Rafiul Ahmed's essay, "Anxiety, Violence, and the Postcolonial State: Understanding the 'Anti-Bangladeshi' Rage in Assam, India," offers fascinating insights into this context. The essay was published in PERCEPTIONS: Journal of International Affairs in its Spring 2014 issue, Volume XIX, Number 1. The following paragraphs are quoted from the said essay:

"The State appears to be under the grip of a Malthusian fever where terminologies like 'demographic invasion,' 'demographic aggression,' 'demographic time-bomb,' 'influx,' and 'infiltration' regularly occupy titles of news reports as well as academic publications in journals and books. The rationalization and naturalization of statistics, or rather state tricks to authenticate the varieties of claims as an improvisation to unsullied personal accounts, signifies the establishment of the sacrosanctity of numeral facts. At the heart of this hysteria with numbers is the Malthusian poster boy of Assam, C.S. Mullan, the superintendent of census operations in 1931, who was posted to the region during the British Raj. Mullan was the chief author of the Census of India 1931, which for the first time used the term 'invasion' in the Assamese context. He instigated what has since the 1930s evolved into a 'hate campaign' in the state. To provoke the Assamese against the Bengali, Mullan wrote, 'wheresoever the carcasses, there will the vultures be gathered together—where there is wasteland thither flock the Mymensinghias.' He had further added that 'it is sad but by no means improbable that in another thirty years, Sibsagar district will be the only part of Assam in which an Assamese will find himself at home.' Noted historian Amalendu Guha described Mullan as an irresponsible European civil servant who, in an effort to predict the future, 'mischievously' used the word 'invasion' to describe the migration of people from East Bengal's Mymensingh district at a time when no national boundary existed. Mullan's verdict on the Bengali invasion makes it possible for those inclined to historicize and authenticate the threat of a Muslim invasion back to the days of the British Raj.

To a large extent, the legacy of Mullan's Census Report 1931 initiated the Assamese-Bengali conflict. The growing hatred towards the Bengalis was primarily guided by the Assamese middle class's envy, given that the Bengalis occupied a majority of the lower-tier administrative jobs in colonial times, especially in the plantation and railways, which were often denied to the Assamese as a matter of policy. The colonial administrative system played no small role in racializing occupational and employment hierarchies, which embittered relations between the Bengali and the Assamese middle class. This history, however, has largely been obscured. In post-independence India, mutual mistrust got channelled into many conflicts surrounding the hegemonies of language and ethnicity. Assam witnessed extensive violence under the rubric of the Bongal Khedao movement, which sought to evict Bengali settlers in the

1950s and 1960s. The AASU during the 1980s further fueled these issues and caused indiscriminate violence and death." [32]

The origin of the Nellie massacre and other Bengali-bashing incidents in Assam is generally attributed to land alienation, rampant immigration, students' movement, and so forth. Still, without going into the historical rationality and the contemporary considerations behind the reported mass murders and victimizations of the Bengalis living in Assam, it will not be possible to figure out the underlying rhyme or reason behind such allegations of atrocious inhuman acts. Therefore, to get to the bottom of the fundamental factors responsible for the conundrum, let us quickly go over the story we have studied so far in the earlier chapters of this book. Then, let's try to relate the historical aspects with the up-to-date political and social developments in Assam that should, in the final analysis, explain the concrete cause of the 1983 mass murders of Bengalis in Assam.

What is land alienation? The term alienation is the psychological condition that arises when individuals, or classes of individuals, are detached from their 'species-being.' Thus, the term land alienation, simply put, would mean the dispossession of land of an individual or community following the transfer or change of ownership title or possession. Therefore, in the context of our story, can we not use the term 'land alienation' to describe the dispossession of land and displacement of millions of people in India and Pakistan consequent upon the partition of British India in 1947?

The reality is these millions of partition victims were displaced and detached from their 'species-being,' and there is no reason why their displacement from their native lands should not fall within the ambit of the often-used term land alienation. Thus, the arrival of a large number of Bengalis, both Hindu and Muslim, over a period from East Pakistan (present-day Bangladesh) to Assam, including Nellie, is an issue that has a direct relation to the question land alienation, which can also be considered as the root of the Nellie massacre.

Earlier in the story, we saw how Assam emerged after the advent of the British in this part of our country. Before the arrival of the British, there was nothing called Assam territory, and consequently, there were none known as the Assamese people. Revamped Assam in British India emerged in several instalments with the erstwhile Ahom kingdom, which was annexed by the British in 1826, as its nucleus. The British accomplished it in stages by subjugating the Ahom kingdom and its neighbouring hitherto independent hill areas and annexing those to the Bengal Presidency in a separate Assam division. Then, in 1874, three traditional districts of Bengal - Goalpara, Sylhet, and Cachar - and the Assam division were detached from the Bengal

Presidency and amalgamated to create a new province. It continued with the name Assam. In the Assam province thus emerged, most people (57.34%) were from Bengal. Only 34.60% were from Assam, primarily the Axomiyas (people living in the erstwhile Ahom kingdom) **plus** numerous hills and plains tribes. "The condition for a threat to the Assamese identity was thus created as soon as the Chief Commissionership was constituted (in 1874)." [33]

Notably, the Bengali linguistic group constituted 57.34% of the population of Assam province *ab initio*. According to Assam's eminent historian, Amalendu Guha: "It (Bengali linguistic group) continued to outnumber the Assamese even in the new province well until the partition of Assam in 1947." [34] This reality rarely finds mention in the dominant history of Assam/India. Accordingly, it has seldom been conceptualized and expressed in the discussions on the widespread influx of 'outsiders' in Assam!

From the later part of the 19th century, the British colonial rulers, in their efforts to increase the vast revenue potential of Assam and to meet the food shortage, started incentivizing the agricultural labourers from the neighbouring Mymensingh and its adjoining areas to migrate into Assam after the labourers from elsewhere, both inside and outside Assam, failed to meet the challenges posed by the unfriendly climate and the hostile topography of the province. The members of the landed gentry in Assam also welcomed them. Since then, a heavy rush of Bengalis into Assam caused a deeper apprehension among the Assamese population that they would be overwhelmed by the Bengali migrants in their own land shortly. **At that time, most people were kept in the dark, that in Assam, the Bengalis already outnumbered all other natives, including the Asamiyas.**

Against this backdrop, the 1946 Cabinet Mission Plan to grant independence to India without partitioning the country had failed because some Congress leaders from Assam were opposed to being included in the same group C along with Bengal - as the plan had envisaged - although the majority populations of these two neighbouring provinces, Assam and Bengal, were the Bengalis. It eventually led to the partition of India and Bengal in 1947. At the same time, we saw how India lost to Pakistan in its Bengali-dominated Sylhet district, with a population of more than 31 lakhs that was a part of Assam since 1874 through a controversial referendum due to some omissions and commissions of Assam's Congress leaders. (As per the census report of 1941, the total population of Sylhet District was 31,16,602) Thus, almost the entire East Bengal that shared over 1,000 KM2 border with Assam became a part of Pakistan. By 'getting rid' of this huge number of the Bengali population, the age-old fear of the Assamese community being swamped by the Bengalis fizzled out to a great extent.

After the partition, Assam shared only a tiny part of its border (slightly over 100 KM[1]) with the Bengalis living in West Bengal in India. The West Pakistani rulers dominated the huge Bengali population of East Bengal, which became East Pakistan. Perceptually, a reduction of 90% of [2]Bengali-dominated land on its border was a great relief to a section of Assamese leaders. Consequently: "The dream of building up 'Assam for Assamese' was categorically stated by the Assam Chief Minister Gopinath Bordoloi. But it proved futile, with the [3]Sylheti government employees opting to serve in India after the partition. Rohini Kumar Choudhury, the lone member of the Bordoloi team who opposed the referendum, proved to be correct when he cautioned that 'the problem would persist but not the land. So don't go for the referendum'."

Note: [1]West Bengal border with Assam: Dhubri - 72.90 Km, Kokrajhar – 54.10 Km, **Total 127 km**)

[2]Bangladesh border with Assam: 262 KM, Mizoram 318 KM, Meghalaya: 443 KM, **Total: 1013**;.

[3]Bengalis of Sylhet district origin.

In 1947, the Assamese, particularly the Assamese Hindu middle class, gained control over the government of the newly formed state of independent India. For the first time in a hundred and fifty years, the Assamese were back in power. They used that control to assert the paramountcy of Assamese cultural identity and seek economic and social equality with the Bengali Hindu middle classes – their rivals for jobs in administrative services, professions, and the private sector. In this campaign to assert their culture and improve the employment opportunities of the Assamese middle classes, the Assamese leaders won the support of two migrant communities - the tea plantation labourers and the Bengali Muslims. Both declared Assamese as their native tongue to census enumerators and voted for the Assamese-dominated Congress party. As a result, the Congress party easily won every state assembly and parliamentary election from 1952 through 1977. Even in the 1977 parliamentary elections, when Congress was defeated nationally with only 34.5 per cent of the vote, the party won 50.6 per cent of the votes in Assam.

Additionally, the Bengali Muslims were also afraid of expulsion to East Pakistan, especially after the passage of the Immigrant Expulsion (from Assam) Act by the parliament in 1950. This act, combined with an act passed by the Assam legislature declaring squatter settlements illegal, led many Bengali Muslims to fear that they might be unjustly expelled from the country. Accordingly, the Bengali Muslims sided with the Assamese that mattered the most to the Assamese community to avoid forced expulsion. They supported the state government against the Bengali Hindus on the controversial issue of the official language of the state and the university. Besides, the Bengali Muslims also cast their votes in favour of Congress. Thus, the Assamese-dominated government made Assamese the official language of the state; established a policy of giving preference to the 'sons of the soil' (i.e., Ashomiyas) in employment in state administrative services; appointed Ashomiya teachers in the schools; and pressed for the use of Ashomiya as the medium of instruction in schools, colleges, and universities. [35]

Nevertheless, in 1971, the Bengalis of East Pakistan severed their relationship with West Pakistan to form a new country, Bangladesh. The emergence of independent Bangladesh in Assam's neighbourhood meant that those Bengalis were no longer under the dominance of the Pakistani rulers as before. To the Assamese leaders, it meant a possible comeback of the 'threat' of the predominance of the Bengalis. They perceived that if given the opportunity, a total of 145 million strong so-called "cultural imperialists" Bengali neighbours would attempt to assimilate the relatively small population of 19.9 million (in 1981) people in Assam. To drive the point home, Weiner Myron, American political scientist, and renowned scholar, in his journal article titled "The Political Demography of Assam's Anti-Immigrant Movement," wrote:

> "One should not underestimate the extent to which the peoples of the North-East, and especially the Assamese, have a sense that they are a small people living next to a vast Bengali population eager to burst out of a densely populated region. Bangladesh (in 1980) had a population of 88.5 million, West Bengal (in 1981) had 54.4 million, and Tripura 2 million, for a total of 145 million Bengalis, making them numerically second only to Hindi speakers in South Asia, and the third-largest linguistic group in Asia. Assamese also tend to view Bengalis as "cultural imperialists" who, if given the opportunity, would attempt to assimilate the Assamese, especially since the Bengali language is seen as more "advanced," its literary traditions stronger, and its cultural institutions dominating. [36]

To add fuel to the fire, at least three mutually unrelated back-to-back developments took place after the emergence of Bangladesh that carried much the same frightening connotation of the rising dominance of undesirable elements, Bengalis, in India's northeastern region. It made matters worse for a particular section of the Assamese community. Three back-to-back developments were:

1. The State Assembly Election in Assam took place in 1978, in an unforeseen liberal atmosphere after the 21-month national emergency in India was lifted on 21st March 1977, ending Congress rule at the centre. For the first time, Congress lost, and the Janata Party came to power in Assam. Golap Borbora first headed the Janata Party government from 12th March 1978 to 4th September 1979, then Jogendra Nath Hazarika from 9th September 1978 to 11th December 1979. When this government fell due to internal squabbles, Assam went under the President's rule for 359 days from 12th December 1979 to 5th December 1980. But more significantly, in the Assam Assembly election in 1978, the number of leftist MLAs (communists of different varieties) rose to 23 from 2 in the previous Assembly. The number of Muslim MLAs also increased to 27 from 17. While in popular parlance, communists were regarded as stooges of Bengali nationalism in the Brahmaputra valley, Muslim politicians of all shades were considered by some 'leaders' as protagonists of Muslim Bengal.

2. On 24th October 1978, in a meeting of electoral officers at Ooty, S. L. Shakdhar, the Chief Election Commissioner (CEC) of India observed: "I would like to refer to the alarming situation in some states, especially in the Northeastern region, wherefrom reports are coming regarding large-scale inclusion of foreign nationals in the electoral rolls. In one case, the population in the 1971 census recorded an increase as high as 34.98% over the 1961 census figures, and this figure was attributed to the influx of a large number of persons from foreign countries. The influx has become a regular feature. It may not be a wrong assessment to make that based on the increase of 34.98% between the two censuses, the increase likely recorded in the 1991 census would be more than 100% over the 1961 census. In other words, a stage would be reached when that state may have to reckon with the foreign nationals who may be in all probability constitute a sizeable percentage if not the majority of the population in the state". [36] Although Shakdhar did not specify the state of Assam, it was obvious that the CEC was talking about Assam. It was, however, not clear the source of his report and how that 'report' was able to determine and distinguish, with a degree of

reasonable certainty, between the native and foreign nationals in the electoral roll - a task both the state and the Central Government was finding extremely difficult to assess even with the Government machinery working overtime on this issue. Shakdhar's remark was a reminiscence of the infamous quote of British Civil Servant C.S. Mullan in the 1931 Assam Census. In that, he had inter alia mentioned that if the migration continued unabated, Sibasagar would remain the only district where the Assamese race would find its own home.

3. Myron Weiner's book *Sons of the Soil*, published in 1978, focused on intercultural and interstate migration in some selected regions in India, including Assam, where migrants dominated the modern sector of the economy and examined both the social and the political consequences of India's interethnic migrations. He described the forces that lead individual Indian citizens to move from one linguistic-cultural region to another in search of better opportunities. He attempted to explain their emergence at the top of the occupational hierarchy. In addition, the author provided an account of how the indigenous ethnic groups attempted to use political power to overcome their fears of economic defeat and cultural subordination by the more enterprising, more highly skilled, better-educated migrants. Weiner's book is full of both oblique and direct references to the peculiar relationship that was prevalent between the Assamese and the Bengali Muslims in Assam, such as (i) 'Fortunately for the Assamese, the Bengali Muslims and Bengali Hindus were unable to come together politically,' or (ii) 'There is thus an unspoken coalition between the Assamese and the Bengali Muslims against the Bengali Hindus. It is not a wholly stable coalition, however, since it could be shattered if there were to be a new major influx of Bengali Muslims or if Bengali Hindus and Bengali Muslims coalesce.' Weiner also worked out his own calculation to show that the ethnic Assamese formed only 30.5% of the total population of Assam, whereas Bengali Hindus and Muslims of Bengali origin (now enumerated as Assamese speakers) formed more than 41% of the population. [37]

On the whole, reflecting on Mullan's startling forecast in the 1931 census report of Assam, the emergence of Bangladesh in 1971, followed swiftly by the three consecutive developments mentioned above, posed significant challenges. There were reports that a faction of Asamiya leadership widely distributed excerpts of Myron Weiner's book Sons of the Soil to the native masses to incite them. Motivated media coverage of these issues further inflamed local sentiments. **Together, these events culminated in the launching of the six-year-long (1979–1985) Assam Agitation or Assam Movement.** However, the proverbial 'straw that broke the camel's back was the grapevine in early 1979 that Mrs Indira Gandhi, who was out of Parliament at that time, might contest for the Mangoldoi parliamentary constituency. We shall elaborate on the Assam Movement in the next chapter. Nevertheless, the Nellie massacre of 1983, occurring during the Assam agitation period stretching from 1979 to 1985, has been given precedence in this narrative for its brutality, significance, and relevance, to better understand the Assam Movement.

Before the state election of 1978, regional parties and their supporters raised the issue of Bohiragatos, outsiders in Assam, and their threat to Asamiya's identity. The Asamiya bourgeois press also initiated propaganda against the danger posed by outsiders in Assam. However, the vague campaign against the 'outsiders' failed to garner a significant popular response from the Asamiya masses.

When the Mangoldoi parliamentary constituency fell vacant in early 1979 due to the death of the sitting Janata Party MP necessitating a by-election, there was speculation that Mrs Indira Gandhi might contest for this seat. Many tribal and Muslim populations were expected to vote for the Congress party leader, Mrs. Gandhi. To prevent her return to power post-emergency, opposition parties clamoured for a revision of the electoral rolls, alleging the inclusion of many illegal Bangladeshis' names. Consequently, many Bengali Muslims and Hindus living in Assam for generations were disenfranchised in the Mangoldoi parliamentary constituency. Since then, demands for a revision of the electoral rolls for the entire Assam have gained momentum.

Then, on 6th December 1980, Syeda Anwara Taimur of the Congress party became Chief Minister of Assam, the first Muslim woman Chief Minister of any state in India. The AASU strongly opposed the formation of the Taimur-led government and successfully observed total bandhs in the state to protest on the day she assumed office. A section of the vernacular press began spreading news that the new government would further encourage Muslim immigration and that they would benefit from government jobs and services under the Muslim Chief Minister. [38] This exacerbated the situation. Subsequent political developments forced her resignation after six months on 30th June 1981, putting Assam under President's rule. Mrs Gandhi's second attempt to install a Congress government in the state headed by Keshab Gogoi failed within two months (13th January 1982 – 19th March 1982), leading to the realization that a new Assembly was necessary. What unfolded thereafter and how the election was conducted against the will of a large section of Assamese people is hard to believe!

Magsaysay Award-winning journalist and author Arun Shourie's report in this context is startling and eye-opening. It was published in the India Today issue dated 19th July 2013 under the caption "Arun Shourie turns up the most devastating evidence on violence in Assam". [39] The pertinent parts of Arun Shourie's stunning revelation are covered in the following paragraphs to a great extent. Among other things, it articulated:

The electoral strategy of the party (Congress-I) in Assam during the period was the familiar one:

- Isolate the largest group.
- Gather together the other groups.
- Foment insecurity in them.
- Present 'yourself' as the only available protector.

A single device was available for isolating the largest group, for dividing the people sharply, and for fomenting insecurity in the target groups:

"The electoral rolls should not be purged of the names of non-Indians."

Purging these names had become a matter of principle in the entire Brahmaputra valley. Therefore, if one could only ensure the holding of the elections without rectifying the rolls, everyone would effectively oppose and boycott the elections; half the task would thus be done - without any other effort.

Second, intelligence report after intelligence report assured that if the election is forced on the people without rectifying the rolls, violence would be an inevitable consequence; the violence, in turn, would only heighten insecurity and fear among the target groups.

Third, it was also evident from the reports that a "firm stand" on this issue would be a sufficient signal about who was the only available protector, and who was the only buffer between the target groups and deportation. So, once a "firm stand" was taken on this issue, it would not be difficult to convince large enough electorates that the only way to avoid eviction would be to vote for Congress (I).

And so, the decision was:

*"Elections, yes; but elections at all costs **without revising the rolls**".*

For ramming this sort of election through, the Government needed a pliant election commissioner (whom it soon appointed) and a few men on the spot who would just shut their eyes and ears and go through the motions. To lead the latter coterie, the Government had R.V. Subrahmanian, an officer who had proven his usefulness to the rulers by helping with the clearances for Maruti. Soon after the imposition of the President's Rule in March 1982 and his appointment as the principal advisor to the Governor - in effect, as the ruler of the state - Subrahmanian set about the task of ramming elections – without revisions through.

Meetings were held from May onwards to this end. Officers who showed the slightest reluctance to go through with whatever may be required were put out of harm's way. A commissioner who put his misgivings down in writing was forced to proceed on leave.

A deputy commissioner who, in response to a query about what he would do if a situation developed in which people's lives were unsafe, had said that he might then resort to the part of the Act under which he could cancel the poll, was swiftly shunted to the Secretariat. A small coterie of the select soon emerged: R.V. Subrahmanian, S.L. Khosla, the Chief Electoral Officer, a Commissioner, two Inspectors General of Police, and an all-powerful, unheeding Deputy Commissioner. Several others helped, of course, but they were the cogs.

Members of this coterie, particularly Subrahmanian and Khosla, frequently visited districts to let everyone know that going through with the elections one way or another was all that mattered. Whenever their attention was drawn to the likely violence and disruption, they were told, and explicitly so, that law and order were secondary.

Once the elections were announced on 7th January 1983, this process of acculturating everyone was institutionalized through a Security Coordination Meeting. The meeting began at 4 p.m. every day. About 30 officers attended it. It was a monologue every single day. Subrahmanian would invariably begin with the chant: "Elections must be held come what may, the flag must fly." He would then recite what had been done the previous day and what the priorities were for the day. All discussion was blocked off.

After 4th February, his narration of the polling personnel would take up almost the entire time, arrangements for looking after them, where they would be sent and how, etc. Even as the state burnt, Subrahmanian & Co. dedicated themselves to trivia, to ritual. The stage for a total breakdown, for a war of all against all, began to be set when it became clear that Mrs Gandhi had set her mind on elections.

The earliest exercises of what was liable to develop once the elections were announced indicated that the people would be so enraged that violence would be the inevitable consequence. As per the report, many officers believed, based on their field experience, that holding the election after negotiating the settlement of the foreigners' issue would not be very difficult. But without such a settlement, the organizers of the agitation would strongly resist holding any election, creating large-scale lawlessness.

Initially, an assessment of 120 battalions was made for the actual requirement of security personnel. However, given that the Central Reserve Police Force (CRPF) had only 76 battalions in all, the estimated demand for holding the election was scaled down to 65 battalions so that the concerned authorities could avoid being stigmatized. Nevertheless, the constant insistence of the election authorities in Assam and the bosses in Delhi sealed the channels to convey any inconvenient opinions so that top brass could receive the reports they wanted.

By November 20th, 1982, booth-wise assessments revealed that in approximately 78 (out of a total of 126) constituencies, elections could be held where the voter turnout might range between 30 per cent and 65 per cent. In other constituencies, where large-scale troubles were anticipated, a turnout of anything between 1 per cent and 30 per cent was expected. Overall, the reports suggested that elections would be possible in most constituencies with proper planning and preparation, despite violence and resistance from anti-election forces. This could be achieved by adopting a "counter-strategy" such as (a) holding the poll in three clusters, (b) deploying maximum available force including Home Guards, etc., (c) maintaining a "total alert" to the army as a reserve force, and (d) imposing a total ban on the All Assam Karamchari Parishad and the All Assam Central and Semi-Government Employees Parishad.

Nevertheless, throughout this period, concerned officials in New Delhi received ground reports of actual events from the Special Branch and the Bureau, including updates on the situation in Assam indicating the complete breakdown of the state machinery. They also received reports of killings, arson, group clashes, and government servants refusing to assist in 'illegal' election duties. As tension escalated, a standard format was devised for providing daily and weekly summaries of ground activities. This one-page summary documented events in each district under specific headings: Murder, Railways (sabotage, bomb explosions, obstruction pelting), Bombs (explosions, recoveries), Arson (road bridges, party offices, residences of candidates), and so forth.

From the announcement of elections on January 7th, 1983, until their conclusion on February 21st, the Intelligence Bureau headquarters in Delhi received information about 19,172 "violent incidents," ranging from murder to explosions to assaults. Given the specificity, detail, and accuracy of reports from individual police stations, district police headquarters, and the Special Branch, as well as the thrice-daily Election Situation Reports submitted by the Special Branch, no one responsible for central administration handling election-related work could claim ignorance of the facts.

According to Arun Shourie, the decision to proceed with "elections without revision" contributed to events between February 14th and 18th in four significant ways. In his own words:

> "First, it alienated, indeed enraged, the people throughout the Brahmaputra valley. They felt humiliated and despaired of ever obtaining justice. Consequently, a state like Assam, difficult to police even under the best circumstances, faced heightened challenges.
>
> Second, the decision ruptured the state apparatus itself. The average policeman, resentful, resolved not to suppress his own people on behalf of what he saw as alien occupiers from Delhi.
>
> Third, the priorities of these officers had been perverted. They focused solely on holding elections, neglecting the need for a free and fair poll. Instead, their concern was to ensure the safety of polling officers, prioritizing their well-being over the integrity of the election process.
>
> Finally, the breakdown was so complete that by early February, top police leadership was scrambling from one violent clash to another, attempting to prevent the collapse of forces rather than effectively managing operations from headquarters."

The flight schedules of helicopters indicate that, for instance, K.P.S. Gill, IGP (Law and Order), visited seven to eight district headquarters daily, not to prevent violence but to maintain order and prevent the complete collapse of forces.

Outside forces were of course inducted in large numbers, but the 65 battalions that are said to have been deployed were not as useful as their numbers would suggest. This was due to the fact that when units from outside assist the local police, they are supposed to function under the officer commanding the local unit. However, the senior officers of the CRPF, who would have had to serve under their juniors according to this rule, had not accompanied the units.

Consequently, the units were leaderless. They were also unfamiliar with the terrain, the people, and the language, having to rely on the local Assam policemen for guidance. Moreover, the latter were not merely resentful but hostile; they viewed the presence of the outside forces as an occupation.

      This hostility sometimes erupted into open conflict. At least one instance saw a pitched battle between the Assam Police and the CRPF, resulting in the death of six jawans according to the government's own admission. Sensing both hostility and indispensability, the CRPF units became a law unto themselves: trigger-happy at one moment, sullen and fearful at others. For instance, the men insisted that they would not undertake patrols or any action except in section strength, i.e., in groups of seven or so. Additionally, like everyone else, the CRPF was tied to "election duty".

The fourth factor setting the stage was perhaps the silliest of all. **No situation warranted the induction of the army as much as this one did.** Every intelligence report had urged that the army be kept ready. **However, the chief election commissioner had firmly opposed this idea: <u>the army shall not be called out</u>** for election duty or to maintain law and order. If absolutely necessary, the army may be requested to help protect vital installations only.

The commissioner believed this would be the litmus test: if the state administration called out the army to save lives or maintain law and order, it would indicate that conditions had deteriorated to the extent that a free and fair poll could not be held. However, as exemplified by a single incident, **Subrahmanian & Co would rather sacrifice lives than fail any litmus tests.**

On February 2, a young IAS officer, Harshmohan Cairae, the additional deputy commissioner at Tezpur, sensing that the situation in his district had reached a flashpoint, requisitioned the army and informed everyone via wireless communication. Despite appearances that had to be maintained, the Special Branch also signalled to their headquarters in Gauhati that the officer had indeed requisitioned the army.

No sooner did the information reach Subrahmanian, Khosla and Co than the hit the ceiling. Tremendous pressure was exerted on Cairae to withdraw his order requisitioning the army. He did not budge: the next day his superiors did what he had refused to do, the cancelled the requisition order..........

.... **Elections must be held come what may,"** as Subrahmanian used to say, and given admonition of the Election Commission, elections could not be held if the army was called out. As keeping appearances was more important than saving lives, and the army was kept out. The one officer, Cairae who did what the situation warranted, was swiftly disowned. (He is now on indefinite leave in Moradabad.

The stage was now set: the people were split into warring camps, the average policeman had turned hostile, officers were besieged, an outside force hated, unaccountable, fearful; the one force that could have helped kept out; everyone nailed down to protecting and taking of the two sets without whom the the ritual of elections could not be gone through: the candidates (along with their families) and the polling officers.

When one reads the wireless messages from the field - urgent calls for help, reinforcements, and penultimate warnings - or those sent out from the headquarters - the warnings summarizing the information coming from the field, the urgent reminders that such and thus be done - one is transported into Kafka's world. **Messages of life and death streak over the wireless but no one pays any heed; everyone is busy with "election duty"**. (emphasis by Subir).

Arun Shourie's report in India Today reproduced five wireless messages dispatched by the Inspector General of Police (Special Branch) to all district police headquarters on January 5th, 25th, and 29th, and February 12th and 14th. These messages clearly indicated mounting concerns and the growing urgency of maintaining the state's rapidly deteriorating law and order situation. Yet, since everybody was so occupied with "election duty," no one could heed these messages of life and death.

According to Arun Shourie, Inspector General of Police, Special Branch, Government of Assam, Samar Das, submitted his report to the Assam Chief Minister and others on March 5th, 1983. The report mentioned that 1,383 men, women, and children were butchered in and around Nellie on the forenoon of the 18th of the previous month. The following vital points emerged from the report:

1. The killings did not occur in one isolated village but in ten out of fourteen in the Nellie cluster of villages.

2. Both the district police and the Special Branch in Gauhati had earlier identified these specific areas as likely trouble spots.
3. These villages were not located in remote areas; rather, Nellie was situated right on the national highway, and all the villages were situated across a completely flat plain.
4. The police patrol post of Amsoi was merely a kilometre from Borbori, the village where the most brutal massacre occurred.
5. The Jagiroad police station, under whose jurisdiction the raided villages fell, was nearby, and the 5th Battalion of the Assam Police at Marigaon was also barely 10 km away.
6. Out of the 10 villages under attack, as many as six were among the identified "minority pockets" likely to be attacked. Among these six, two - Nellie and Alisinga - had not only been designated as "minority pockets" in a general sense but were also explicitly pinpointed among the seven "sensitive areas" in the Nowgong district.
7. The lists of "minority pockets" and "sensitive areas" should have routinely reached each district and divisional headquarters, similar to the lists of "anti-socials". As per standard operating procedure, the listed "anti-socials" should have been behind bars as tension mounted.
8. According to police estimates, the mob that descended on Nellie and the surrounding villages numbered 12,000 strong.
9. The individuals comprising the mob did not originate from one village but from a score of villages, some 18 to 20 km away from the impact area.
10. This vast and ever-swelling mob set out around 5 a.m., marching to the beating of drums in broad daylight.
11. The killings commenced in the morning and continued unabated and unrestrained for at least six hours.

All of this bears testimony to the extent to which the law-and-order machinery had been undermined. Moreover, the chronology and timeline of events, just preceding and on the fateful day, are highly significant. On February 16, 1983, merely two days before the massacres in the Nellie cluster of villages, the Jagiroad Police station received specific pleas for help. According to their records, they received information about the killings on February 18 at 10:35 a.m. (cf: entry number 467 dated 18.2.83 in the General Diary of the Jagiroad police station). It's noteworthy that Nellie is located on the national highway, and the other nine villages under attack were connected by rough but drivable roads branching off the highway. The killings began around 8 a.m. However, the police party, accompanied by CRPF personnel, did not reach the area until 3 p.m.

In the concluding part of the India Today article by Arun Shourie, copies of as many as five wireless messages were depicted, recording the terrible fact that 'the police had not just general but specific warnings well before the Nellie massacre date of February 18 about what was liable to happen'. It can be summarized as follows:

a) In a message dated February 10, 1983 – 'a full eight days before the massacre' – instructions were issued by the Nowgong District Police Headquarters to all OCs to ensure adequate Police pickets/mobile patrolling "IN VIEW OF INCREASING INCIDENTS OF VIOLENCE AND ATTACK ON MINORITIES".

b) Three days later and five days before the massacre, on February 13, the DIG of Nowgong instructed the Police to intensify patrolling in minority pockets to prevent any communal troubles, adding that, "INCIDENTS OF COMMUNAL NATURE SHOULD BE DEALT WITH VERY FIRMLY."

c) On the same date, February 13, a second message from the Nowgong SP to all OCs and others was more specific. It read, in part: "INCIDENTS OF COMMUNAL VIOLENCE HAVE BEEN REPORTED FROM SOME PARTS OF THE DISTRICT. IMMEDIATE POLICE ACTION ON THE SPOT OF VIOLENCE IS REQUIRED. ALL PRECAUTIONS TO BE TAKEN TO PREVENT ANY FURTHER FLARE PARTICULARLY IN THOSE AREAS WHERE POLLING IS TAKING PLACE ON 14/2/83."

d) Four days before the Nellie massacre, on February 14, the Nowgong DC sent a message specifically to the Jagiroad Sub-Deputy Collector directing him to keep watch over the communal situation, especially after "today's" poll and to keep in touch with the CRPF commandant, with information also sent to Nowgong Control (room).

e) Three days before the massacre, on February 15 afternoon, the officer-in-charge of Nowgong Police Station sent the most specific of warnings to (i) the Commandant of the 5th Battalion of Assam Police, and (ii) SDO police officer, both stationed at Marigaon, 10 km from the Nellie area, and to (iii) the officer in charge of the police station at Jagiroad itself (Nellie fell under it). It read,

"INFORMATION RECEIVED THAT LAST NIGHT ABOUT ONE THOUSAND ASSAMESE OF SURROUNDING VILLAGES OF NELLIE WITH DEADLY WEAPONS ASSEMBLED AT NELLIE BY BEATING OF DRUMS. MINORITY PEOPLE ARE IN PANIC AND APPREHENDING ATTACK AT ANY MOMENT. SUBMISSION FOR IMMEDIATE ACTION TO MAINTAIN PEACE."

It is evident that under the President's rule, government authorities gave precedence to holding elections in Assam at any cost, turning a blind eye to numerous warnings that violence was imminent if the election was forced upon the people. Yet, the state prioritized the electoral task over the safety and security of its innocent citizens. Thus, the Nellie Massacre occurred.

The extraordinary situation during that election in Assam, which ultimately led to the butchering of numerous Bengalis at Nellie in broad daylight, was poignantly expressed by Arun Shourie in epideictic oratory:

"Messages of life and death streak over the wireless, but no one pays any heed, everyone is busy with 'election duty'!" [39]

As the Nellie Massacre turned 40, an article appeared on the Indian news and opinion website, The Wire, on February 23, 2023, titled "Nellie Massacre: 40 Years Later, a Cautionary Tale for Today's India." Its Assam-born author, Angshuman Choudhury, at the very outset, wrote:

"A killer can kill again. But, can the dead die again? In Nellie, they can. In fact, they have died many times over since that fateful late winter day 40 years ago."

Angshuman Choudhury is an Associate Fellow at the Centre for Policy Research, New Delhi. The following paragraphs are quoted from his insightful soul-searching report on the **"Nellie Massacre: 40 Years Later …":**

> "If one has to go by the total number of people killed in any anti-minority pogrom in post-independence India, the Nellie carnage sits somewhere at the top. The Gujarat pogrom of 2002 and the Bombay riots that followed the Babri Masjid demolition by Kar Sevaks in 1992 come close. And if unofficial accounts are to be believed, more than 7,000 were butchered in Nellie, marking it as the deadliest anti-minority pogrom in modern India.
>
> What makes Nellie particularly unique is that unlike in other similar cases, not a single individual faced justice for the exceptional act of mass murder. The official inquiry report of the Tiwari Commission

remains classified to this day. There is not one memorial in India that commemorates the massacre. In that sense, the violence of Nellie never stopped. It continued in the form of systematic erasure, imposed silences, intellectual obfuscations, and complete denial of justice to the victims. From the Indian state to civil society, everyone participated in this organized memoricide.

I was born in Assam and grew up there. Yet, no one in my family or friends told me about Nellie. I read about it much later in my life. It was not part of collective memory or dinner table discourse in caste Hindu families in the state. But I'm sure everyone who lived through the 1980s – our parents, grandparents, uncles, aunts, or elder siblings – knew about it. They must have also known who the killers were or who incited them. But, most of them had either crafted a subconscious mental story to rationalize their ignorance or simply dismissed it as a stray local clash. Everyone was responsible for Nellie, so no one was responsible for Nellie.

But Nellie didn't happen in a vacuum. It unfolded in the middle of the anti-foreigner **Assam movement (1979-85).** The physical violence flowed directly from the emotive violence generated by the agitation, which sought the expulsion of "illegal Bengalis/Bangladeshis" from Assam. Besides their homemade weapons, the killers were also armed with the ethno-majoritarian vocabularies that the movement leaders propagated day in and day out. [40]

So, it's now over to the anti-foreigner **Assam movement (1979-85)** in the next chapter.

* * * * * * *

Chapter 12.

The Assam Agitation
(1979-1985)

According to the White Paper on Foreigners Issue released on 20th October 2012 by the Government of Assam, Home, and Political Department:

> "The Assam Agitation (1979-1985) was a mass movement against illegal immigrants in Assam led by the All Assam Students' Union (AASU) and All Assam Gana Sangram Parishad (AAGSP) to compel the Government to identify and expel illegal immigrants. While the agitation program was **largely non-violent**, communal incidents were witnessed in some parts of the State, particularly in 1983." [1] (Emphasis by Subir)

The agitation is also called "The Anti-Foreigners Agitation," but its appellation "The Assam Movement" is presently in vogue. The Government of Assam Implementation of Assam Accord wrote under the caption "Martyrs of Assam Agitation":

> "The historic Assam movement was one of the famous movements in post-colonial India mainly led by students of Assam. This movement was started in 1979 under the leadership of the All Assam Students Union (AASU) and the All Assam Gana Sangram Parishad (AAGSP) and officially ended on 15 August 1985 after coming to an understanding with the Government of India which found an official expression in the memorandum of understanding popularly known as the Assam Accord 1985.

> During this period of six long years of the historic movement as reported 855 (later on 860 as submitted by AASU) nos of people sacrificed their lives in the hope of an "Infiltration-Free Assam" in the 1979-1985 Assam agitation." [2]

The Assam Accord, a 5-page document, a Memorandum of Settlement of "Problem of Foreigners in Assam" in English.pdf file is available in the public domain on the Assam Government website. [3] It is also reproduced towards the end of this chapter.

Many renowned Indian intellectuals, including Assamese scholars, and some foreign academics, wrote about the Assam agitation, or the Assam movement, from different perspectives and arrived at diverse conclusions, especially on what provoked the Assamese students to resort to the six-long-years agitation, sacrificing some precious period of their educational lifetime. For instance, American-born Indian sociologist and human rights activist, Gail Omvedt, considered the Assam agitation started not because of the basic Assamese fear of losing jobs to Bengalis but their lands. Myron Weiner, an American political scientist, and renowned scholar of India, saw the Assam movement from the viewpoint of demographic changes. He observed it as the result of the severe breakdown of a precarious political system where populations were in the midst of political, cultural, and economic insecurity. A social scientist from Bangladesh, Abdur Rab Khan, stated that the movement resulted from the rising expectation of the Assamese vis-a-vis the years of neglect towards the legitimate needs of the Assamese people. Assam's renowned historian Amalendu Guha, after critically discussing the movement, said that it was national in form and not free from strong chauvinistic and undemocratic tendencies. Tilottoma Misra, a writer, critic, and translator based in Assam, highlighted economic issues as the driving force behind the movement. According to her, the Assam movement reflected the common people's awareness of the extra-regional big-business stronghold in the state's economy. She likened the status of Assam to a colonial hinterland of India. Similarly, writer Ghanashyam Pardesi perceived Assam as an internal colony within an exploitative national system. At the same time, to renowned scholar, writer, literary critic, and social scientist from Assam, Hiren Gohain, the agitation was a revolt of the impoverished peasants and hard-pressed petit-bourgeoisie youth against intolerable circumstances. In his book "Assam: A Burning Question," he commented, among other annotations, that the movement had roots in the remote past. Its culmination in the form of the Assam movement was a continuation of the movement for a university in Assam during the independence struggle and the movement for an oil refinery and official language in the post-independent period. The former professor and head of the department of English at Assam's Dibrugarh University, Udayon Misra, thought that the movement achieved unity of the community of different segments of Assamese society out of fear of the Assamese people losing their identity. He viewed it as a mass upsurge and the outburst of nationality with a long history of neglect, suppression, and exploitation. Likewise, writer A.K. Baruah viewed the Assam Movement as the result of the genuine fear of the Assamese people losing their national identity. Tarun Gogoi[1] felt that the Assam movement was the consequence of the long feeling of insecurity of the Assamese people about the demographic structure in the state due to the silent invasion by foreigners who were mostly from erstwhile East Pakistan, presently known as Bangladesh. Whereas, according to Prof. Monirul Hussain (Retd) of [2]Jamia Millia Islamia, the Assam Movement refers to the demand made by the AASU and the AAGSP to:

- Put a halt to the illegal immigration of foreign nationals into Assam from neighbouring countries - Bangladesh and Nepal.
- Stop the participation of illegal immigrants in the electoral process in Assam/India.
- Deport all foreigners living illegally in Assam, their traditional homeland of the Asamiyas, to enable the natives to protect their distinct identity threatened by the presence of numerous illegal aliens. [4] [5]

Note: [1]Tarun Gogoi, a Ph D Student (from North East India) at the Jawaharlal Nehru University, Centre For Political Studies.

[2] Jamia Millia Islamia - An Indian Central University.

Some scholars have written that even after independence, the exploitation of Assam as an internal colony of the Union of India continued, which was the primary cause that eventually sparked the Assam movement. Before delving into other vital aspects of the agitation, let us first try to understand why and how such feelings of unfair treatment by the Government in New Delhi toward Assam grew.

In the run-up to the partition of India, both Prime Minister Nehru and Home Minister Patel had expressed their unhappiness at Assam's refusal to accept the Grouping Plan of the Cabinet Mission's Plan, which placed Assam with Bengal. The feeling that the Asamiya leadership got was that, for the good of India, Assam could be sacrificed. Ultimately, Assam's opposition led to the breakdown of the Cabinet Mission plan and consequently, the partition of India in 1947. After the partition, Chief Minister Gopinath Bordoloi's reluctance to accept more refugees from East Pakistan led Nehru to express his unhappiness and even threaten to reduce financial aid to Assam. The seeds of distrust between Assam and the Centre sown during this period were to grow further afterwards.

In 1957, the Centre decided to construct an oil refinery at Barauni in Bihar but not in Assam to process crude oil extracted in Upper Assam, which was to be transported via a 700-kilometre-long pipeline. This decision infuriated the Assamese people, resulting in an agitation that was the first of its kind after independence. All political parties took part in the agitation, coordinated by a Sangram Parishad (Struggle Council). The Centre's rationale that the establishment of the 3.3 million-ton refinery at Baruani was necessary considering its safety from a defence standpoint was seen as a flimsy excuse, adding insult to injury for Assam. People raised the question: how could the Centre ensure the safety of the oil fields in Upper Assam and the 700-kilometre pipeline running through the state if it considered the refinery unsafe in Assam? The eventual concession of a 0.65 million-ton refinery at Noonmati near Gauhati only confirmed that Assam was receiving step-brotherly treatment from the cow belt of India.

Then came the Chinese invasion! The debacle caused by the Chinese invasion, with the rout of the Indian Army at Tawang and the virtual decimation of an entire division of the Indian Army, prompted New Delhi to order the evacuation of the old British district of Tezpur. Nehru made a so-called 'farewell' speech to the Assamese people on All India Radio, broadcast live on November 20th, 1962, in which, among other things, he said, 'My heart goes out to the people of Assam.' It was interpreted in Assam that Nehru had 'abandoned' Assam to the mercy of the Chinese. Such a gesture from the Prime Minister deeply hurt Assamese sentiment and became a poignant topic of discussion among innumerable cultured Assamese families throughout the valley for many years.

Following the Sino-Indian war, the 1960s were difficult years for Assam, with rice shortages and agitations throughout the valley. Despite Assam not being a deficit state for rice, shortages occurred due to hoarding and rice smuggling by the Marwaris to East Pakistan. They had exclusive control of all trade in essential commodities and extensive rice smuggling to East Pakistan. The complete domination of all economic activities by the community in Assam eventually led to a violent agitation on Republic Day in 1968. The rioters were all students at Gauhati, organized as a loose organization called the Lachit Sena. 'The police conveniently looked the other way during the rioting.' Yet, the Centre was not listening. There were rumours that another refinery would be constructed outside Assam. The Assamese people, led by the students, mounted a massive agitation for a second refinery for Assam in 1969. When the state administration was paralyzed for a fortnight as thousands of students from all over Assam courted arrest before the state and central controlled government offices, the Centre agreed to construct a second refinery in Assam at Bongaigaon.

In the 1970s, it dawned on the Assamese people that the three main industries of the state - Tea, Oil, and Coal - were not positively impacting the economy of Assam. The 756 tea gardens in Assam produced 55 per cent of the country's tea and earned foreign exchange of Rs 500 crores. Assam, however, received only Rs 22 crores in sales tax, while West Bengal got Rs 42 crores for 1980 because many tea companies had their Headquarters in Calcutta. In the case of plywood, the state received just Rs 35 lakhs, while the Centre got Rs 80 crores for the same year. The production of crude oil from the oil fields of Upper Assam had risen from 0.1 million in 1962 to 3.5 million tonnes per year in the 1970s due to the discovery of new oil fields. The royalty paid to Assam in 1979 was a mere Rs 42 per tonne. Despite pleas from the state, the Centre refused to raise the state's share of royalty.

Lamentably, for several decades, a vast quantity of natural gas, a source of energy and raw material for a variety of modern industries, was being flared off daily at different oil fields of Assam. Instead of allowing the natural gas to be burnt as waste, it could be gainfully utilized in power generation and for the production of various lucrative items like different types of rubber, plastics, nylon, polyester fibres, paints, dyes, and so on. This could make Assam one of the wealthiest states in India. Yet, because of the almost non-utilization of the natural gas and the by-products of the crude refined in Assam, hardly any ancillary industries came up in the state. On the other hand, many industries that depend on such raw materials from the Assam oil fields kept multiplying rapidly in other states in India. The fact that several polythene industries in the state of Maharashtra were on the verge of being closed down because of the oil blockade in Assam during the agitation period provided a textbook example of how others were benefiting from the resources of Assam.

Besides, during those days, the absorption of Assam's native people in the Central Government offices and Public Sector Undertakings never exceeded 30 per cent. By comparison, local employees had more than 90 per cent representation in other states. The Assamese people were upset with such an anomaly. Thus, the feeling that the Centre was only exploiting Assam's natural resources gained currency among the Assamese people as the 1970s progressed. Similarly, after the transfer of ownership of most big tea gardens from British to Indian capitalists, the new owners started to bring people from other parts of the country to fill up all categories of posts. These people, in most cases, possessed almost no acquaintance with the planting and processing of tea – their only claim to the tea jobs was their 'connections'. In the late 1970s, one could barely see an Assamese Manager or Assistant Manager in tea gardens owned by Indian Capitalists. The Fifth Report of the Employment Review Committee (1976) set up by the Assam Assembly supported the assertion. [6] [7] [8]

Nevertheless, many academics often assert that the root cause of the Assam agitation was the initial import of Bengalis by the British in the colonial days of Assam and the migration that had continued ever since. This generalized assessment could be an oversimplification of the historical fact. Rather, the truth might lie in the answers to the questions: (a) What was the reason that drove the British rulers to import a workforce from outside? (b) Why did the colonial rulers not go for the local human resources to meet their requirements of wage earners, unskilled and skilled labourers, office workers, and all that? Without delving into THOSE aspects, blaming the Bengalis would be simplistic and unfair.

The primary reason behind the initial import of Bengalis to Assam for recruitment was:

> a) The British preferred the Bengali community for their experience through early exposure to the administrative works and procedures adopted by the British in Bengal.
>
> b) In contrast, the Asamiya people were reluctant to take up employment under the British administration. They were more or less self-sufficient in meeting their day-to-day requirements and were mostly satisfied with whatever they used to earn on their land.
>
> c) Besides, initially, the British sought to use high-ranking officials from the Ahom government in their administration. However, these high-ranking Ahom officials could not fit into the Anglo-Mughal administrative structure created by the British in Assam. For example, they had never kept written records; even the judicial proceedings were conducted without recording the statements of witnesses, complainants, or defendants. Moreover, the new administrative offices and titles followed by the British, adapted from the prevalent Bengal governance, such as tahsildar or district revenue collector, were not based on indigenous Ahom administrative structures. No wonder, therefore, that the British increasingly imported trained Bengali officers to work in Assam. [9]

Incidentally, Professor Nandana Dutta of Gauhati University, in her book "Questions of Identity in Assam: Location, Migration, Hybridity," among other things, alluded that British accounts regularly used such features to describe the Assamese as *"a race with no drive, no initiative, as apathetic, object more than subject, always letting things happen to them."* [10] Without entering into the debate whether it was a correct assessment by the British, one can say that the British Colonial rulers' opinion about recruiting the natives of Assam, to a certain extent, might have been influenced by that kind of negative evaluation. Besides, two more factors also could have worked against the local employment seekers: (a) the report of the extensive use of opium in the area and (b) the prevalent dependence on the slave system by the gentry for menial jobs.

As discussed in Chapter 3, since its emergence in 1874, the British-created Assam province was a Bengali-majority province comprising over 57 per cent of Bengali people and less than 36 per cent of its population was the Asamiyas **PLUS** others. Yet, the province carried the appellation Assam - a term originating from the Ahom Kingdom ruled by the Ahoms, known to be the land of the Asamiyas. The reason was, as some academicians believe, Assam Tea had already made its mark as an established brand name in the European market. So the European tea planters preferred the continuance of the name Assam for the land where this particular variety of tea was grown to bolster the brand name. Thus, the British conferred the name Assam, derived from the term Ahom, to the Bengali-majority province they created by amalgamating the three districts (Goalpara, Cachar, and Sylhet) of the Bengal Presidency and its Assam division.

Thus, the British used the name Assam for the Bengali-majority Province, despite the Asamiya people being in the minority in the province. Consequently, as time passed, the impression gained currency that the whole of Assam was the land of Asamiyas, where the Bengalis came in so large in number that they outnumbered the Asamiyas! The fact that a part of Bengal's territory went into the formation of Assam in 1874, where the Bengalis were the aboriginal population, i.e., the indigenous people of the British-created Assam province all along, was overlooked and gradually became obscured.

Next, towards the end of the nineteenth century, the British promoted large-scale migration of the Bengalis from the neighbouring East Bengal into Assam to augment their revenue and meet the increasing food scarcity in Assam. This inflow of the Bengalis from Bengal to its adjacent Bengali-majority province, Assam, termed by the British as immigration, increased the fear among the Asamiyas of getting further overpowered by alien Bengalis in their 'own' homeland. The British did their best to create more friction between the two major communities in Assam over this issue through their scathing utterances, unfriendly actions, and using equivocating words.

In this ongoing misleading narrative, the fact that many of these Bengalis with their roots in East Bengal are also the aboriginal people of the British-created Assam remained obscured. Therefore, very few people can imagine today that these Bengalis of erstwhile Goalpara, Cachar, and Sylhet districts and their progenies of East Bengal origin, since scattered all over Assam, are also aboriginal people of Assam, and **they are not immigrants in the true sense.** While erstwhile Goalpara and Cachar are still in today's Assam, a tiny part of the Sylhet district is also in Assam. This category of the aboriginal

Bengalis of Assam and their descendants may or may not have severed connections with their kith and kin living in East Bengal (presently Bangladesh). One has to bear in mind that, logically, this factor has nothing to do with determining whether they are natives, migrants, or immigrants in Assam.

Yet**, many people in the state still believe that all the Bengalis of East Bengal origin in Assam are either migrants or immigrants, although this is factually incorrect.** This abstraction played a pivotal role in misleading Assam's innocent men, women, and children against its Bengali population, which, in turn, is at the root of many major controversies in Assam, including the Assam agitation. One must keep sight of this critical factor while attempting to find the historical reasons behind the Assam movement. However, the immediate backdrop at which the Assam Movement started was discussed in the previous chapter on Nellie, which is recapitulated in the following paragraphs.

After the emergence of independent Bangladesh in 1971, a possible comeback of the predominance of the Bengalis loomed large in the minds of the Asamiya people. Assam, with a population of 19.9 million, became almost surrounded by 145 million strong Bengalis from Bangladesh, West Bengal, and Tripura. Weiner Myron's journal article titled "The Political Demography of Assam's Anti-Immigrant Movement" rekindled the apprehension among the Asamiyas when Myron alluded, among other things, that if given the opportunity, Bengalis would attempt to assimilate the Assamese, especially since the Bengali language is seen as more "advanced," its literary traditions stronger, and its cultural institutions dominating. At least three mutually unrelated back-to-back developments took place soon thereafter to add fuel to the fire. These were:

- In the Assam Assembly election in 1978, the number of leftist MLAs (communists of different shades) rose to 23 from 2 in the previous Assembly. The number of Muslim MLAs also increased to 27 from 17. While in popular parlance, communists were regarded as stooges of Bengali nationalism in the Brahmaputra valley, Muslim politicians of all categories were considered by some 'leaders' as protagonists of Muslim Bengal.
- On 24th October 1978, in a meeting of electoral officers at Ooty, S. L. Shakdhar, the Chief Election Commissioner (CEC) of India, hinted that a stage may soon be reached when the state may have to reckon with the foreign nationals who may, in all probability, constitute a sizeable percentage if not the majority of the population

in the state. The CEC's apprehension was based on the jump of 34.98% in population between the two censuses.

- Myron Weiner's book "Sons of the Soil," published in 1978, is full of both oblique and direct references to the peculiar relationship that was prevalent between the Assamese and the Bengali Muslims in Assam, such as (i) 'Fortunately for the Assamese, the Bengali Muslims and Bengali Hindus were unable to come together politically,' or (ii) 'There is thus an unspoken coalition between the Assamese and the Bengali Muslims against the Bengali Hindus. It is not a wholly stable coalition, however, since it could be shattered if there were to be a new major influx of Bengali Muslims or if Bengali Hindus and Bengali Muslims coalesce.' Weiner also worked out his own calculation to show that the ethnic Assamese formed only 30.5% of the total population of Assam. In contrast, Bengali Hindus and Muslims of Bengali origin (now enumerated as Assamese speakers) formed more than 41% of the population.

On the whole, reflecting on Mullan's alarming forecast in the 1931 census report of Assam, the emergence of Bangladesh in 1971, soon followed by the three back-to-back developments mentioned above, was highly problematic. Additionally, the motivated media coverage of these issues also aroused local sentiments. All these occurrences, taken together, prepared the fertile ground for the launch of the Assam Agitation.

The straw that broke the camel's back was the by-poll for Assam's Mangoldoi parliamentary constituency. In March 1979, the death of the sitting Janata Party Member of Parliament (M.P.), Hiralal Patgiri, necessitated a by-election for that electoral area. There was talk that Mrs. Indira Gandhi, out of Parliament then, might contest for that seat. In that parliamentary constituency, there were many tribal and Muslim populations. They were expected to vote en bloc for the Congress party, particularly for its leader, Mrs. Gandhi, for her liberal and secular image. Therefore, most of her advisors reportedly made all-out efforts to stop her from returning to power by hook or crook. The opposition parties demanded a revision of electoral rolls, alleging that a substantial number of ineligible voters' names were surreptitiously included. Very soon, written objections were lodged against *47,658 Muslim and Hindu voters accusing them of being illegal Bangladeshis. Such allegations resulted in deleting the names of *36,780 Bengali Muslims and Hindus from the electoral rolls, although they have been living in Assam for generations.

* Source: Bhattacharyya, Hiranya Kumar. p.109 "Betrayal of North East: The Arrested Voice".

The local press widely publicized the controversy over the voters' list raised by the opposition parties. It reignited simmering concerns within the Asamiya community that they were being economically marginalized by the Bengalis, as well as in all other social aspects, threatening their dignity and survival in 'their home', Assam. This instigated the Assamese to act decisively to 'protect' Assam from 'outsiders.' The apolitical image of the All Assam Students Union (AASU), which previously led the movement for making the Assamese language the sole medium of instruction in Assam in 1972, helped AASU to lead the Assam Movement again. It received unparalleled support from some local press, particularly in mobilizing students and the general populace and organizing agitation activities. The national political parties were completely sidelined.

According to research scholar Monirul Hussain, when a section of the local press started raising a hue and cry, reporting an exaggerated number of foreign nationals in Mangoldoi, the non-Asamiya and Na-Asamiya (neo-Assamese) populations became wary of the motives of the press and the state government. Many Hindu Bengalis and Na-Asamiya Muslims living in Assam for generations, including government servants, soon found their names missing from the electoral rolls of the Mangoldoi constituency, including the areas that received the earliest Muslim migrants in Assam in the early 13th century.

An Asamiya Deputy Inspector General (DGP) of Assam Police, who was later dismissed from the service by Presidential order, was allegedly involved in lodging a large number of fabricated complaints using the state police apparatus with tacit support from the government. This action resulted in the removal of the names of numerous Muslims and Hindu Bengalis from their rightful place on the electoral rolls of the Mangoldoi constituency.

Congress leader Dinesh Goswami, who later left Congress and became the leader of the Asam Gana Parishad (AGP) in the Parliament, along with other Congress leaders, submitted a memorandum to the Chief Election Commissioner alleging that the police were used to

> .... deprive a large section of this population of their democratic rights. ...... So far as our information goes, the police officials, on instructions from the government, procured objection forms in large numbers. From the election office at Dispur, they could collect only 10,000 forms, and as these were not sufficient in their view, another 40,000 were printed. The police officer took these forms to rural areas and got the blank objection forms signed by the village headmen and secretaries of village defence parties under intimidation and threat. The police officials themselves then filled up

the blank spaces... The citizens of our country are being deprived of their valuable democratic rights by this dubious method of the government......

Author Hiranya Kumar Bhattacharyya, IPS (Retd), in his book "Betrayal of North East: The Arrested Voice," wrote, among other things, on this subject that 'though quite a few volumes have been written on the Assam Movement, there have been lapses in respect of quoting the correct number of objections filed during this operation, except that Sri Premkanta Mahanta, who, having directly dealt with the matter, had subsequently written a postscript to the Assam Movement and was careful in quoting correct data' in his book written in Assamese that gives a vivid account of how the movement originated but also the correct statistics. Bhattacharyya wrote: 'But before the operation was postponed, already 47,658 objections were filed and the quasi-judicial process for disposing of them as per provisions of ROP Act had commenced. Of these 47,658 objections, 36,780 were sustained. That is to say, 77.17% of objections were found to be correct. As such, the complaint of large-scale harassment to Indian citizens falls flat on the ground.' [11]

Notwithstanding the IPS officer Bhattacharyya's assertion, a glimpse of how the quasi-judicial process functioned in detecting 'foreigners' in Assam has been exhibited in the subsequent Chapter 14 on the 'D' voters in this book that, in turn, would bring to light the hollowness of Bhattacharyya's attempted argument to justify such harassment of Indian citizens.

Very soon, the issue of 'outsiders' divided the people in the Mangoldoi constituency and then the entire state of Assam. Some local Asamiya presses did not even allow any open or democratic discussion in their papers; instead, they aimed only at deepening the fear of the Asamiyas to prepare them for a war against the alleged 'outsiders'. This demonstrated the ideological orientation of those local presses and their tremendous capacity to mobilize public opinion among the Asamiyas.

When the entire political parties of all India levels failed, and the regional right-wing parties and their leadership remained largely unacceptable to the Asamiyas, the obvious choice fell on the All Assam Students' Union (AASU). Until then, the AASU had not become a part of any political party like other student bodies. Organizational, it started as a voluntary federation of the students' unions in 1967, consisting of elected secretaries of student unions. The post-independence expansion of schools and colleges led to the emergence of a space where young people from different parts of Assam could meet. By that time, there were schools in the most remote small towns and villages in Assam; colleges, too, were numerous. Only predominantly Asamiya-speaking schools and colleges seemed to have formed part of this federation, excluding Assam's numerous Bengali or Hindi schools. In due course, it emerged as the most important segment of the new social space for the growth of sub-nationalist politics, providing AASU with an extraordinary organizational base.

Besides, the AASU had an 'apolitical' image before a large section of the Asamiya masses, which was reinforced by the press. Moreover, in 1972, AASU successfully led the movement to make Asamiya the only medium of instruction together with English for college education in Assam. Though the movement ostensibly centred on the issue of the medium of instruction, the ruling classes in Assam exploited it to revive the Asamiya-Bengali conflict after 1960. The AASU had proven records of leading and mobilizing the Asamiya masses successfully on sensitive issues in which existing traditional political parties would hesitate to participate actively. Thus, AASU was the most obvious choice for leading the movement against the 'outsiders' in Assam, especially since in 1974, AASU had demanded the stoppage of the flow of 'outsiders' (bohiragatos) into the state until Assam attained the same position as other developed states of India. They explicitly called their demand a short-term requirement, focusing on building a movement to address the economic backwardness of Assam rather than demanding the expulsion of foreign nationals.

It's pertinent to mention that AASU's success in 1972 attracted many meritorious students with progressive outlooks. They sought to link AASU with the legitimate aspirations of the people of Assam and expressed their determination to fight against the exploitative system. Thus, the students' union attempted to build a mass movement on much-needed economic demands, such as the implementation of progressive land reform in the interest of the peasantry, increased industrialization of Assam under public sector, nationalization of industries owned by big business houses, halt of eviction of poor peasants from Doyeng, Kaki, and Mingmon reserved forests, appropriate measures to control perennial flooding in Assam, government takeover of procurement and distribution of all essential food grains, and similar demands to improve Assam's economy. All these demands were apolitically democratic and progressive.

However, unlike the 1972 movement on the medium of instruction, genuine economic issues and critical requirements of Assam failed to attract mass support. Interestingly, in 1974, contrary to the expectation of the AASU leadership, the Asamiya press did not support the student movement. The Asamiya media was an inseparable part of the Asamiya ruling class, which opposed such progressive demands as land reforms in the interest of peasants or nationalization of various sectors of the economy, nor could they support a movement capable of uniting all sections of the people regardless of race, religion, caste, or language. Hence, there was tactical resistance to campaigns on economic and other vital issues. Accordingly, the ruling class in Assam did not allow AASU to succeed. Additionally, the students' union lacked roots among peasants and the working class, and it was reluctant to link the movement with broader left and democratic forces in the state. In the absence of support from the masses, other democratic forces, and the ruling classes, the state government could suppress the movement without much difficulty, although most of the issues raised through their 21-point charter of demands were legitimate, progressive, and crucial (even now) for eradicating Assam's perpetual backwardness.

Nonetheless, by mid-1979, AASU took up the leadership position for a war against the 'outsiders' (bohiragatos) and prepared the students and others for a mass movement. The student leadership gave the movement general acceptability and respectability, overshadowing the divided regional political parties. However, a coordination body known as All Assam Gana Sangram Parishad (AAGSP) was formed, consisting of AASU, several regional parties, the Assam Jatiyatabadi Yoba Chatra Parishad, the Lawyers Association, and the [1]Asam Sahitya Sabha, which provided strength and social acceptability to the AAGSP.

[1]The Asam Sahitya Sabha, a statewide literary body with an organisational network throughout the Brahmaputra valley with an apolitical image, was also an ally of AASU in their 1972 movement on Assam's medium of instruction issue.

Undoubtedly, there were many conflicts and contests between AASU and AAGSP, but AASU played the most dominant role in leading the movement. The Marwari business community in Assam liberally extended finance for the movement, and the Asamiya bourgeoisie, their press and journalists, the rural gentry, a large section of the middle class including some powerful bureaucrats and high police officials, employees of the state government, contractors, transport operators, owners of Assam's popular mobile theatre groups, and a few socialist and communist renegades stood firmly behind the AASU. So, strictly speaking, the Assam Movement cannot be termed a student movement per se.

On the question of the 'Marwari business community in Assam liberally extending finance for the movement' stated in the above paragraph, the remark is based on the 1989 dissertation on page 179 of "The Assam Movement: a sociological study" Research Scholar Moniful Hussain submitted to the Jawaharlal Nehru University in fulfilment of the requirement for the award of the Degree of DOCTOR OF PHILOSOPHY.

However, the following details in the book "Questions of Identity in Assam: Location, Migration, Hybridity" by Professor Nandana Dutta brought to light, particularly on pages 112 to 113, published in 2012, reveal to some extent how and why the so-called 'Marwari business community in Assam liberally extended finance for the movement'. The relevant portion is quoted below verbatim:

> "Asha's family lived in the third distinctive neighbourhood mentioned earlier, Fancy Bazaar. They were among the earliest migrants from Rajasthan to Assam, with branches of the family also located in [1]Murshidabad to Assam. They were not technically Marwaris, though the distinction would be meaningless in a place where all traders and businessmen were identified by the ubiquitous term 'Marwari'."

Note: [1]Murshidabad is a historical city in the Indian state of West Bengal adjacent to Assam.

> Initially, our family was positive about the movement and its aim of sending back illegal migrants, possibly because of their experience and bitter memories of the partition of Bengal. This residual memory of partition has continued to affect their attitude toward the Bangladeshi migrant and has ensured that the migrant has not been able to make inroads into that particular area of the city – most of the labour employed there is still Bihari. But a gradual irritation set in, especially because of the "donations," which began as polite requests but very soon became intimidating demands with reference made to their outsider status in Assam.
>
> My father's "novelty shop", the only one of its kind at that time and doing good business, became a victim of this regular "donation," sporadically shut down to avoid the unpleasantness that came with a refusal, and in the long run losing customers. This happened to many shops in Fancy Bazaar. On the other hand, the stigma associated with donations remained, and when ten years later, as student members of a local Shakespeare Society, we went to collect donations to put up a play, we were refused by most people and rudely shown the door.
>
> What do you remember of the protests?
>
> The torchlight processions, sometimes silent, sometimes shouting slogans... Joi Ai Asom! As kids, we thought it was fun, and we wondered then at the tension displayed by the adults.

My father and uncles as well as my grandfather's brother had many Assamese friends. They did not change their attitude in any noticeable way. But their visits became less frequent.

My grandfather came home one day with blood on his clothes and face, having roughed up on the street.

The experience in this neighbourhood was different from the other two. The sense of having become a different kind of target – a regular source of larger and larger donations, and the butt of newer hostilities – resulted in the ghettoization that continues into the present. [14]

It is likely that what was true for the Marwaris could also be true, in respect, perhaps of all/many or at least few, of those who reportedly 'stood firmly behind the AASU' as mentioned in the dissertation of Moniful Hussain, discussed earlier.

Anyway, the AASU's aim was initially to evict the 'outsiders' (bohiragatos) from Assam. By outsiders, they meant Indians who came from outside of Assam. These Indians were perceived to control the state's economy. In a few months, though, they changed track and started railing against foreigners, specifically illegal immigrants from Bangladesh. This course correction of the agitation had long been ascribed to the union leaders' eventual realization that the Assamese people were bothered more about Bangladeshi migrants than Indians from other states. However, a former professor of statistics at Gauhati University, Abdul Mannan, turns this thesis on its head. In his book "Infiltration: Genesis of Assam Movement," published in 2019, he showed the change came about in no small measure because of the efforts of two senior police officers, Hiranya Kumar Bhattacharyya and Premkanta Mahanta, as well as the Rashtriya Swayamsevak Sangh. Mannan cites the forgotten memoir of one of the officers to show how they courted the student leaders and persuaded them to redirect popular anger towards Bangladeshi immigrants. The memoir Mannan draws on is "Rajbhaganar Para Kal Thokalaike" – the Assamese title roughly translates as "from dethronement to the plantain grove" – which Premkanta Mahanta wrote and self-published in 1994 with the intention "to help historians with some truths" that might be forgotten.

On 1st October 1978, the new Golap Borbora government of the Janata Party appointed Deputy Inspector General of Police (DIG) Hiranya Kumar Bhattacharyya to head the Border Police Division. Premkanta Mahanta wrote in his memoir that it was a "historic event for Assam", as was his own appointment in the same division the following February. By then, DIG Bhattacharyya had already started identifying and expelling Bangladeshi migrants, Muslim and Hindu, from Nalapara, Mangaldoi, and Tamulpur in Rangia, kicking off a political storm. Mahanta then added: "I affirm that...the six-year-long Assam movement would not have taken place if we hadn't come together at this point". In March 1979, about a month after Mahanta joined the Border Police Division, AASU held a conference in Sibsagar, where Prafulla Kumar Mahanta was elected its president and Bhrigu Kumar Phukan the general secretary. The conference adopted 21 resolutions, one of which spoke of the "menace posed to the existence of the Assamese by the **outsiders** who controlled Assam's economy". The **idea of Bangladeshi** immigrants threatening the state's cultural identity had **not yet been formulated**.

That same month, on the 28th of March 1979 to be precise, the death of Mangaldoi MP, Hiralal Patowari, necessitated a by-election. On the 27th of April 1979, when the customary notice to revise the electoral rolls came out in Mangaldoi, the two police officers feared that Bangladeshi immigrants would try to get their names registered on the rolls – and use it to claim Indian citizenship. Mahanta thought of sending a Border Police Division officer with every Registrar of Voters to thwart their attempt. But, DIG Bhattacharyya pointed out the lack of sufficient time to train the personnel for such a task. Accordingly, Bhattacharyya persuaded Chief Secretary R.S. Paramasivam to ask Chief Election Commissioner (CEC) S. L. Shakdhar for more time to revise the electoral rolls. The CEC gave them an extra week. But instead of trying to prevent Bangladeshi migrants from enrolling as voters, Mahanta wrote that Bhattacharyya "came up with the idea that since more time was granted, the names of foreign nationals on the rolls of 1978 might also be struck off." It was a cumbersome process. The rules demanded that a name be removed from a particular electoral register, a voter from that polling booth must submit a complaint in a form costing ten paise, and another voter from the same booth must second the complaint. The Police officers duo, Bhattacharyya and Mahanta, figured that mobilizing public opinion was the only way to achieve their goal, and accordingly, they launched a publicity blitz. The media began tracking the identification process.

In this context, the following paragraph quoted from an Assam Cadre 1965 batch IPS Officer E. N. Rammohan's book "Insurgent Frontiers Essays from the Troubled Northeast" is noteworthy:

> By the late 1970s, the Assamese people began to feel that the Bengali Muslim immigrant constituting the largest vote bank in the state was fast emerging as a viable political entity. At this time, the sitting member of the Mangaldoi Lok Sabha constituency died, and a by-

election was to be held. When the electoral list was being revised, the Chief Election Commissioner of India expressed concern that a large section of the electorate of this constituency were (sic) foreigners. While the electoral rolls were being revised, a tribunal set up by the State Government declared 45,000 voters of this constituency of 6 lakhs as foreigners. At the initiative of the All Assam Students Union that had been recently constituted, the All Assam Gana Sangram Parishad was formed. It consisted of several regional parties, the Assam Sahitya Sabha, the Assam Jatiyatabadi Yuba Chatra Parishad (AJYCP), and the AASU. It was at this point that political events took a hand. Morarji Desai's Janata Government (at the centre) collapsed as Charan Singh defected, and a coalition Government was formed with the Congress driving from behind. Openly a vote bank of the Congress party, the Immigrant Bengali Muslim lobby began to exert pressure on the Central Government to go easy on revising the electoral rolls of the Mangaldoli constituency. The Chief Election Commissioner, who had originally raised the issue of foreigners in the electoral rolls of this constituency, lost his guts and humbly recanted and stated that the 1977 electoral rolls would serve for this by-election. The government issued orders that no names would be deleted from the electoral rolls. However, by this time, on the basis of the earlier orders issued by the Election Commission, 3,20,000 complaints and objections had already been filed. The Chief Election Commissioner is a Constitutional Authority and could have stood his ground. His humble recantation changed the course of history. The Gana Sangram Parishad started the Assam Movement. On November 6, 1979, a mass rally of students was organized by AASU at Gauhati. Four days later, the first phase of the agitation began, with students and others offering Satyagraha in the manner of the freedom struggle and courting arrest. The response was massive. Thousands of people came up for arrest every day. Naturally, the jails could not accommodate so many people. The government arrived at an understanding with the volunteers. They were formally arrested and released. As the movement gained momentum, the Ganasangram Parishad and the AASU asked all political parties to boycott the elections. [15]

Almost about the same time in March, the AASU conference adopted the resolutions mentioned earlier, which spoke of the menace posed by the 'outsiders'. At the suggestion of the two Police Officers Bhattacharyya and Mahanta, the two AASU leaders (President) Prafulla Kumar Mahanta and (General Secretary) Bhrigu Kumar Phukan were brought from their

University hostels in order to drive home to them the problem caused by foreign nationals. They provided the two student leaders with adequate data and information to bring them around. The student leaders then agreed to prioritize the issue of foreign nationals and the deletion of their names from the voters' list. As a result, on the 23rd of May 1979, the AASU executive committee meeting adopted a resolution calling for a 12-hour statewide 'bandh' the next month to press for the expulsion of "Bangladeshi infiltrators". Thus, the 'outsiders' mentioned in the 21 resolutions adopted in March 1979, cited in an earlier paragraph, turned into "Bangladeshi infiltrators" at AASU's executive committee meeting dated 23rd May 1979, giving the agitation a pan-India acceptance.

As names began to be struck off voter lists in Mangaldoi, Congress leaders complained to the Election Commission that "police had been hatching a conspiracy by indicting genuine Indian citizens as foreigners." The commission ordered a halt to the deportation of alleged illegal migrants and the deletion of their names from the electoral rolls. However, by that time, complaints against 47,658 voters had been received, out of which 36,780 were already identified as foreigners. The controversy over Mangaldoi's electoral rolls became a lightning rod for the Assam agitation. Successive governments fell, and now the student union's war cry was "three Ds" – **detection** of Bangladeshi immigrants, **deletion** of their names from voter lists, and their **deportation**. Assam went into shutdown for nearly a year.

Mahanta's memoir Rajbhaganar Para Kal Thokalaike, despite its openness, did not mention what became of these thousands of people identified as foreigners, prompting the author Abdul Mannan to ask in his book Infiltration: Genesis of Assam Movement: "Were they driven out of Assam, or were they still in Assam? What was the status of their citizenship?" [16] However, ultimately, the Mangoldoi by-election did not take place as the Janata government at the centre collapsed, and all preparations for by-elections to the Lok Sabha were cancelled on August 22nd, 1979.

On September 9th, 1979, a new government was formed in Assam amidst internal disputes in the ruling Janata Party, which collapsed within a couple of months on December 12th, 1979. Thus, the political situation became quite fluid, necessitating the imposition of President's rule in Assam for the first time in its history.

On March 31st, 1980, the All Assam Minority Students' Union (AAMSU) came into existence as an antithesis to AASU under the patronage of Congress. Earlier, on March 3rd, 1980, in discussion with Prime Minister Indira Gandhi, who visited Guwahati to meet the leaders of the Assam movement, the leaders of AAMSU (then at the nascent stage) declared their readiness to accept 1971 as the cut-off year for the determination of illegal foreigners in Assam. Within less than a year of the beginning of the Assam movement, AAMSU emerged as a counterforce to AASU. A countermovement was launched against the Assam movement on May 26th, 1980, by observing 'Demand Day' throughout the state. On-Demand Day, in Howly town of Assam's Barpeta district, AAMSU organized a big rally where four persons were killed in police firing. [17]

Very soon, AMSU became the mouthpiece of the minority community in the region. Its role was quite valuable in some vital issues and selected areas. The Union mainly carried the religious minority with it. The Bengali Hindus were a different force altogether. In the declared non-violent means of movement, sporadic violence drifted the Muslims away from AASU. AMSU's insistence on 1971 as the base year for detecting foreigners divided the Assamese community along communal lines. The hitherto harmonious balance was disturbed. It embedded a feeling of insecurity among the minorities. AASU had to time and again assert that not all minorities are foreigners, but that internally displaced its members as well as the Assamese community. Even without political parties' involvement, there was a communal division. Occasional clashes between the supporters of the two groups, AASU and AAMU, created a lot of frustration among the people. It culminated with the bloody violence in the 1983 Assembly polls in Assam.

Various tribal groups were another factor in AASU's dynamics. The Plain Tribals Council of Assam (PTCA), which came into being in 1966 with the demand for a separate state ('Udayachal') for the plains tribal communities in Assam, was against AASU for historical reasons and, for that matter, the Assamese community as a whole. During the Assam movement, a section of PTCA revived their demand for 'Udayachal' and confronted AASU. Thus, there was a lot of violence between tribal and non-tribal groups. Such developments were very costly for AASU. Consequently, certain relaxations in AASU's stand came about in the post-1983 phase, and the intensity of the Assam movement's program was considerably reduced. [18]

In the Assam movement, people from all walks of life were seen taking part in agitation activities. Children as young as 10 years old to old men and women of 70 or 80 years old participated. Schools and colleges stopped functioning. In fact, all the students in Assam lost a year during the agitation. Though AASU projected it as a national movement, there was a clear separatist undercurrent to the movement. Two constituents of the agitation had secessionist feelings. The different government departments were captive to the movement. The State Police Wireless Organization and the Central Government's Department of Telephones were totally with the movement. AASU's intelligence network was extremely efficient. [19] As the movement progressed, it took various forms, such as calls for all lights to be switched off throughout Assam for an hour in the evening and for all houses to sound gongs in their houses at a designated time. An illustrative (not exhaustive) list of some other modes of protest is as follows:

- Mass picketing of all government and semi-government offices and other establishments, including Banks, Life Insurance Corporation, P&T establishments, Railways, Telegraphs, and PSUs.
- Mass rallies and public processions.
- Mass squatting in front of government and semi-government offices.
- Bandhs or general strikes.
- Offering 'satyagraha' and courting arrest in front of government offices.
- Hunger strikes.
- Gheraos (protests in which agitators prevent the authority from leaving a place of work for a certain period of time or until demands are met).
- Dharna (a mode of peaceful protests to compel the authority to meet certain demands by sitting at their doors).
- Janata Curfew.
- Janata Blackout.
- Torchlight Procession in the evening.
- Satyagraha - a policy of passive political resistance.

The first bandh of the movement, a twelve-hour all-Assam affair, took place on 8th June 1979 to protest the inclusion of the names of illegal foreigners in the voters' list. The spark came with the so-called discovery of inflated rolls in the Mangaldoi parliamentary constituency, as discussed earlier. The first episode of mass picketing called Gana Abasthan Dharmaghat (people's sacrilege), took place on the 6th and 7th of September 1979 in front of the offices of district commissioners, sub-divisional officers, and block development officers. The protestors demanded the detection and deportation of illegal foreigners. From 12th to 14th September, picketing took place before the offices of corporations, banks, and post offices to prevent the employees and the public from entering these office premises, which resulted in clashes between protestors and non-Assamese employees of Nazira Oil and Natural Gas Commission (ONGC) office. Reports of many instances of intimidation to force people to join the agitation were reported on 6th October 1979 for a mass rally in Guwahati when 100,000 participated; on 9th October for the 'drive-out-foreigners campaign'; and from October 12 to 18, 1979, for a week-long protest action of the mass rally that included Satyagraha and courting arrest. The last program saw massive participation, and many still carry memories of the protest agitations, including huge crowds comprising students (both boys and girls), women, and some men. They gathered in and around the market, DC's court, the High Court, and on the roads around Dighali-pukhuri, an area where several educational institutions and their hostels are located, and then walked in disciplined files, shouting slogans in blazing sunlight; many young people fainted in the heat. All female protestors would be dressed in the traditional Assamese attire, 'mekhela sadors', or else it would attract severe reprimands from others, especially elderly participants or the local 'leaders'. The week-long program demonstrated the consolidation of an extremely efficient organizational network giving the appearance of 'spontaneous' mass participation, though the episodes of intimidation and coercion were quite common. Many people received phone calls, were called out by friends, or were summoned by young emissaries, while others were 'collected' as neighbourhood groups and made their way to buses arranged by the leaders.

The next few months saw frequent protest campaigns in the form of longer-duration bandhs. A 36-hour bandh was held between the 3rd and 4th of December. From 5th December to 8th December, round-the-clock picketing took place. On 8th December 1979, all educational institutions were closed indefinitely, and examinations were postponed.

A new course of agitation, the round-the-clock gherao of the residences of candidates for the forthcoming elections, was conducted till 10th December, which was the last date for filing nomination papers for India's parliamentary election. This round-the-clock gherao campaign saw, for the first time, many boys and girls staying out whole nights with parental permission – they were permitted this transgression for the defence of the land. [20]

The oil blockade, another significant form of protest campaign, began on 27th December 1979, stopping the flow of crude oil to the Barauni Refinery in Bihar. It was a part of the Assam agitation. In 1980, AASU's program of the blockade of crude oil supply from Upper Assam to a refinery at Barauni (Bihar) became a regular feature of the protest. After the successful resistance against holding elections in 12 Lok Sabha seats in Assam, the blockade of crude oil in Assam was the most momentous protest action of the movement. Thousands of supporters of the movement on 27th December 1979 moved into various oil installations and refineries in Assam. They stopped the flow of crude oil outside Assam, which led to the stoppage of the functioning of the Barauni refinery in Bihar. The popular response to the oil blockade was overwhelming and total. The supporters picketed the oil installation day and night.

On 18th January 1980, the district administration, backed up by police, ordered the dispersal of picketers at Duliajan, the headquarters of Oil India Limited. When the picketers refused to leave, the police resorted to tear gas shelling and then firing, in which four persons were killed and many injured. Rabi Mitra, a Bengali technocrat and second man (the first being an Assamese) in the OIL's administrative hierarchy at Duliajan when he came to inquire about injured/dead at the hospital, was brutally killed by the mob. The Assamese press and the leadership likened the Duliajan killings to the Jallianwala Bagh of Assam. However, the killings of Rabi Mitra of OIL and the earlier murder of Dr. Anjan Chakravorty on 11th December 1979 at the Guwahati Medical College Hostel gave the Assam movement an anti-Bengali image. [21]

In a related incident, more than a year later, Commissioner of Assam's Plains Division, E. S. Parthasarathy, was killed on 6th April 1981 while he was posted at Jorhat. On the fateful day, around 10:15 in the morning, Parthasarathy got out of his car and briskly walked towards his office to start another week of gruelling work. Moments later, as he sat on his chair, a pressure bomb placed underneath exploded. His body was flung upwards, his lower limbs mangled. Though his aides immediately rushed him to the hospital, death was instantaneous. With that killing, extremist elements in the Assam imbroglio signalled the start of a new violent phase in the Assam movement, a phase anticipated by government agencies but kept at bay by the slow and tedious moves for a negotiated settlement. Parthasarathy, who was 44 when he died, had come to Assam in 1979. An efficient and hard-working officer, he had been in command when the police in the previous year opened fire at Duliajan, killing four picketers, following which rebellious mobs lynched Dr. Robi Mitra of Oil India. At that time, speculation was rife that Parthasarathy was a marked man and that he would pay for the firings. [22]

AASU's main aim behind the massive blockade of oil for nearly one year was to press the government to send back the 'foreigners' who had come to Assam after 1951. In economic terms, this action entailed a huge daily loss to the exchequer. Yet, the movement leaders did not link the oil blockade with the meagre royalty the central government was paying Assam. Besides, AASU also did not relate issues like Assam's industrialization, economic development, and better utilization of the state's precious resources with the blockade for Assam's overall development. Instead, the leaders of the movement convinced the Assamese by emphasizing the continuous immigration from across the border as the root cause of all of Assam's problems, which was, at most, only a part of the entire problem. It was not the primary problem of Assam's backwardness. Anyway, round-the-clock picketing was lifted on 19th April, but the workers continued the non-cooperation. On 7th April, the harsh ¹ESMA (Essential Services Maintenance Act) was promulgated in the state. Police, army, and CRPF started managing the oil installations.

¹ESMA gives the police the right to arrest, without a warrant, anybody violating the Act's provisions. When, from 12th to 17th November 1979, AASU and AAGSP launched a six-day Gana (Peoples') Satyagraha, thousands of people courted arrest in front of D.C. Kamrup. The government declared the educational institutions closed till 22nd November. The West Bengal Chief Minister Mr. Jyoti Basu's reaction to the drive against the foreign nationals was sharp. He asked the union government to immediately take up the matter of harassment of non-Assamese speaking people, hinting that the move to get foreigners out was getting mixed up with the presence of "BAHIRIGATA', Indians from outside Assam – presumably the large number of Bengali-speaking people staying in Assam. His statement altered the influx issue into the Assamese-Bengali clashes, which the state witnessed earlier. The happenings in Assam also disturbed many people outside Assam, especially the people of neighbouring West Bengal. The State Youth Congress and its Chhatra Parishad started road-blockades at some places in West Bengal from 22nd March 1980 to prevent the to and fro movements of the people and the goods between Assam and the rest of India. Thankfully, the ruling CPI (M) government in West Bengal was against any such blockades. Because the government took some strong actions against the activists, the blockade could not last long. By the way, Prime Minister Indira Gandhi also disapproved of the oil blockade in Assam and the road blockade in West Bengal. [23]

Anyway, the oil blockade seemed to have the effect that none of the other programs had had. As a result, the perception gained ground that because the stopping of crude oil affected all of India directly, the central government had begun to notice that something serious was happening in this much-neglected, almost invisible corner of the country. As the mass rallies and satyagrahas continued, other products of the region, including jute, bamboo, and plywood, were also prevented from being taken out of the state. Significantly, the leadership of the Assam movement conspicuously exempted the most valuable items, other than oil, i.e., tea, from the blockade.

Hence, the blockade did not affect the foreign capitalists, the Indian capitalists, and the Assamese tea planters. This suggested the class nexus between the leadership on one hand and foreign, Indian, and regional capitalists on the other.

As already mentioned, the Gana Abasthan Dharmaghat (Mass Squatting Activism in public places) began on the 6th and 7th of September 1979. Classes were boycotted, and students proceeded in a procession to the nearest offices of the Deputy Commissioner (DC), the Sub-Divisional Officer (SDO), the Sub-Deputy Collector (SDC), and the Block Development Officer (BDO). They staged a sit-in strike, raising slogans in support of the AASU charter of demands. This charter included immediate detection and deportation of all foreign nationals from Assam, measures to prevent influx from mainland India, curbing price rise, implementing a long-term policy to address floods, erosion, and drought, ensuring proper utilization of Assam's vast water resources, and addressing all other outstanding grievances of the state's people.

While advocating for the movement democratically and peacefully, on August 30th, 1979, students of Jorhat Engineering College initiated a hunger strike to postpone examinations. Dibrugarh students abstained from classes and hunger strikes to secure the release of arrested movement leaders. At B. Barooah College, Gauhati, students picketed for the non-fulfilment of various demands. Simultaneously, Cotton College students began picketing to press for assurances of fulfilment. However, AASU's call for mass picketing from September 12th to 14th, 1979, garnered little response except in the Golaghat sub-division, where several students were injured due to a police lathi-charge outside the SDO office. The agitation gained momentum with AASU's twelve-hour bandh call in Golaghat, leading to significant disruptions in administrative works across Kamrup, Sibsagar, Jorhat, Golaghat, Nowgong, and Barpeta. Student picketing severely affected essential services such as Posts and Telegraphs, banking operations, private establishments, Assam State Transport Corporation, and the Maligaon Railway Headquarters.

In contrast, AASU's press release alleged police lathi-charges, unnecessary tear-gassing, and large-scale atrocities against peaceful demonstrators. The Assam Tribune reported the arrest of approximately five hundred fifty individuals for violating prohibitory orders, with release occurring after 4 p.m. However, amid peaceful and democratic activities, instances of violence emerged, with agitators disrupting the state's law and order. Reports of violence emerged from various places in the Brahmaputra Valley, including clashes and looting in Kamrup and clashes in the Barak Valley's Karimganj,

Hailakandi, and Silchar areas on January 8th, 1980. Clashes also occurred in Assam's Tulsibari village in the Rangia subdivision of Kamrup district.

Moreover, for two months, the Barpeta, Nalbari sub-division, and parts of the Gauhati sub-division were declared disturbed areas under the Assam Disturbed Areas Act of 1955 and the Armed Forces Special Powers Act of 1958. Police fired tear gas shells, and hundreds of picketers were arrested for violating law and order. Despite the democratic nature of the movement, activism occasionally turned violent, undermining the state's rule of law during the Assam agitation.

Sustained agitation programs such as bandhs, picketing, hunger strikes, and mass satyagraha disrupted administrative processes. Frequent disruptions of national highways and railways due to the agitation impacted the economies of Assam and other northeastern territories, as Assam served as their gateway. The situation deteriorated into a full-fledged confrontation between agitators and the Government of India.

Upon instruction from the Chief Election Commissioner, when the electoral rolls revision process began in Assam for the 1980 Lok Sabha polls, AASU vehemently opposed holding Lok Sabha elections in Assam simultaneously with the rest of the country, demanding the removal of foreign nationals' names from the electoral rolls. They attempted to physically block the parliamentary election process and filed almost 320,000 complaints against alleged immigrants in a single week. Strikes, picketing, and dharnas were held against candidates' submission of nomination papers for parliamentary polls. The agitation's leadership created a stalemate in the electoral rolls revision process. AASU-AAGSP combined efforts called for mass squatting, picketing in front of government offices, and other agitation activities such as mass rallies across Assam, severely impacting government functioning and vital establishments like the Life Insurance Corporation, banks, railways, and post offices. Employees of these establishments openly defied government instructions and participated in the movement en masse. Enumerators refused to work, and the North Eastern Federation of Master Printers declined to print the draft rolls in response to protest calls.

The press and media were reportedly disregarding order during the movement. From June 1979 onwards, the press directed its hatred campaign exclusively against post-1951 East Pakistani immigrants, nearly all of whom were Bengalis. Similarly, immigrants from Nepal were targeted. Amid a widespread upsurge involving mass sit-ins, picketing, satyagraha, strikes, and a mass signature campaign during the 1979-80 parliamentary election period, printing press owners, as an organized body, refused to print electoral rolls for the parliamentary election. On December 10th, 1979, the movement claimed its first martyr. On December 18th, lakhs of people took oaths to continue a lifelong struggle against foreigners. Towards the end of 1979, a state-wide Non-Cooperation Week was observed, followed by a 58-hour Assam bandh at the beginning of 1980. Large-scale killings in Kamrup and repetitive murders worsened the state's law and order. The parliamentary election was boycotted throughout the state except in the Cachar district of Barak Valley. Gazetted officers on election duty refused to cooperate with the government, taking orders from AASU and AAGSP.

From the dissolution of the last Lok Sabha on August 23rd, 1979, to the installation of the Indira Gandhi-led Government in New Delhi on January 14th, 1980, there was hardly any semblance of administration in the state. The election boycott call by the AASU-AAGSP combination exacerbated the state's precarious law and order situation, resulting in the election being held only in two predominantly Bengali-speaking Lok Sabha constituencies in the Cachar district. Elections were cancelled in twelve of Assam's fourteen parliamentary constituencies.

Besides ethnic violence, numerous terrorist attacks on state officials and property occurred during the Assam agitation. As mob violence disrupted law and order in northern Kamrup, the Army was called in to restore control. Additionally, the involvement of the Asom Sahitya Sabha and regional political parties like Purbanchaliya Loko Parishad (PLP) and the Asom Jatiyatabadi Dal (AJD) ushered in a more active and militant phase of satyagraha and picketing. Meanwhile, overt support from the police and state administration for the movement made the state's rule of law highly unpredictable.

Attacks on Bengali minority individuals occurred in Tinsukia and Dibrugarh districts of upper Assam, with the first reported killing being that of a bank officer. The armed forces were given considerable leeway to restore normalcy in areas experiencing large-scale lawlessness, marking the most severe fallout from such incidents. The Government of Assam declared the entire northern part of the Kamrup district, including Barpeta and Nalbari sub-divisions, and North Guwahati and Kamalpur police station areas, as disturbed areas, necessitating Army intervention to maintain law and order. [24]

Professor Monirul Hussain, in his thesis "The Assam Movement: A Sociological Study," noted that to counter protest activities, the State Government announced the closure of all educational institutions on December 8th, 1979. Supporters of the movement began picketing on December 27th, 1979, at various oil installations and refineries in Assam, disrupting crude oil flow outside Assam, leading to the Barauni refinery in Bihar, India, ceasing operations. Concurrently, activities such as Bandh,

Satyagraha, mass rallies, and various forms of protests continued. Despite stiff resistance from agitating students, no eligible candidate was found in all eleven Lok Sabha constituencies in the Brahmaputra valley, resulting in the postponement of elections in the entire Brahmaputra valley. However, in the predominantly Bengali-dominated Barak Valley, where the Assamese population comprised less than 1%, the decades-old Assamese-Bengali divide resurfaced. Despite protests by ASSU and AAGSP, elections for the two Barak Valley seats proceeded. [25]

There is a popular belief that during the early period of the Assam agitation, an armed separatist organization called the United Liberation Front of Asom (ULFA) emerged, reportedly formed by radical AASU members. According to the story, it was established on April 7th, 1979, at the deserted Rong Ghor premises in Sibasagar, where a handful of youth pledged to establish a 'sovereign socialist Assam' for indigenous Asamiya people through armed struggle. However, Retired IPS Officer Ramhohan, narrating the 1983 election scenario in Assam, debunked this myth on page 31 of his book "Insurgent Frontier." In reality, ULFA was formed AFTER the brutal 1983 election, as discussed later in this chapter.

ULFA's main agenda was to gain independence from what they termed 'occupational India' and to expel all 'foreigners' from Assam, which primarily referred to non-Assamese (mostly Bengali) inhabitants. At the organizational level, ULFA had subdivided into political and military wings. Paresh Barua headed the 'military wing' as the outfit's 'commander-in-chief', while Arabinda Rajkhowa led the 'political wing' as the Chairman. Other prominent members included Pradip Gogoi as 'Vice Chairman', and Anup Chetia as the 'General Secretary' of the group. Its organizational structure comprised four zones: East Districts, West Districts, Central Districts, and South Districts. The undivided ULFA had a cadre strength of around 5,000 trained insurgents.

Over the years, ULFA evolved into a feared terrorist group in Assam. Collaborating with other terrorist groups in India's North East such as NDFB, KLO, and NSCN (Khaplang), along with organizations like the Kachin Independence Army (KIA) of Myanmar, ULFA emerged as one of the most potent and violent insurgent outfits in Southeast Asia. Initially, ULFA garnered attention for its Robinhood-type activities. However, it later became entangled in organized crimes such as extortion, drug trafficking, and arms smuggling, causing widespread law and order problems in the region. Ultimately, ULFA's emergence added a new dimension to the fluid political situation in North-East India, particularly in Assam.

Notably, ULFA gained prominence following the rise of the Asom Gana Parishad (AGP) government in the state Assembly Election following the signing of the Assam Accord in 1985. Pakistan's premier intelligence agency, the Inter-Services Intelligence (ISI), reportedly provided training to ULFA militants, especially in terrorist tactics, counterintelligence, disinformation, and the use of weapons. As ULFA grew in power, it established a parallel administration in some areas for a brief period in the early 90s. However, ULFA experienced a sharp decline in acceptability over the years as it became synonymous with terrorist activities. Any sympathy ULFA had until 1998 vanished following its declaration during the 1999 Kargil war that Pakistani infiltrators were 'freedom fighters'. [26]

According to the Union Home Ministry's source in Parliament, from 1979 until December 1982, **just before the assembly election,** there were 272 murders, 1404 assaults, 425 cases of arson, 346 cases of intimidation, 228 cases of mischief, 147 cases of kidnapping, 330 cases of explosions, and 146 cases of recovery of explosives like bombs recorded **attributable to the agitation.** The movement's leadership was accused of targeting minorities - religious and linguistic. The carnage of minorities, both Hindus and Muslims, in North Kamrup in January 1980 resulted in hundreds, including women and children, being killed, thousands wounded, and 20,000 people rendered homeless. [27] (Emphasis by Subir)

Nevertheless, between January 1980 and January 1983, the government and Assam movement leaders engaged in no less than 50 rounds of talks at various levels. In some talks, the government invited opposition parties to participate. All opposition parties advocated for 1971 as the cut-off year, which the movement's leadership did not agree with. This stance politically isolated the AASU leaders from all-India political parties. At the movement's peak, student leaders declared that all-India parties had become irrelevant in Assam due to the Assam movement. The political isolation of the movement leaders at the all-India level also explains why they developed a friendship with RSS and BJP elements despite their differing ideological positions. [28]

Nevertheless, the movement persisted and hopes for an early settlement waned. Consequently, there was a shift in protest actions. By the latter part of 1980, bandhs increased in frequency and duration. Non-cooperation programs with the government, often involving preventing government officials from attending office, became common. Frequent blackouts, curfews imposed by the people, and social boycotts were observed. These actions signalled growing aggression, fostering conditions for greater hostility in neighbourhoods, reducing tolerance levels, and generating individual and collective anger at minor program violations. Most of these operations were neighbourhood-centric, as managing at the unit level was easier. Adolescent boys and girls, feeling empowered against authority, whether parental, adult, or state, often played the most enthusiastic policing roles. This burgeoning violence manifested in the slackening of parental control and the breakdown of traditional social hierarchies. A hierarchy of force replaced these, evident in young boys shoving elderly individuals, often from different communities, on deserted streets or menacingly stalking others. The involvement of many young boys and girls, some in their mid-teens (considering all schools and colleges were closed), was one of the movement's most disturbing aspects. [29]

Anyway, the Assam movement depicted unprecedented gatherings and participation of a large group of people. It showed the power of the masses in stopping the elections and blocking the flow of crude oil from Assam to outside the state. But, the overall law and order situation deteriorated with the beginning of the movement. When the rest of the country went to the polls, the thickly populated northern part of Kamrup district was rocked by civil violence for days, during which the normal law and order machinery collapsed. Highly contradictory and conflicting reports came in about happenings in North Kamrup. The People's Union of Civil Liberties (PUCL) Delhi had sent a fact-finding team to Assam to study violations of civil and democratic rights in the wake of the Assam movement. The team consisted of Prof. G. P. Despande and two other academics, Dhirendra Sharma and Chaman Lal, of Jawaharlal Nehru University, New Delhi. From a week-long investigation of Assam's happenings from 1st August 1979 to 15th February 1980, they found that 23 persons were killed in the Dibrugarh district alone, out of which 17 persons died in mob violence and 6 in police firing, including four declared martyrs. Of the 17 persons who died in mob violence, 1 was an Asamiya and the remaining 16 were non-Asamiyas. In North Kamrup, it was estimated "that 200 to 300 persons died due to mob violence. The administration could establish the identity of only 80 dead bodies, 78 of them belonged to linguistic and religious minorities, and one out of the remaining 2 was a CRPF Jawan. Nearly 25,000 people were rendered homeless as a result of violence and destruction. It is difficult to accept that violence of such scale took place without any organized pre-planning. [30]

Between the 9th and 16th of February 1980, the three PUCL members toured several areas of the state together and separately. They met the leaders of the major political, social, and student organizations and talked to journalists and representatives of linguistic and religious minorities and ethnic communities of Assam. They also met the members of the coordination committee of the Gauhati University Teachers' Association (GUTA) and a few university teachers who were against the agitation. A slightly abridged version of its draft assessments was released to the press on 28th February 1980, which is available in the public domain. It provides the flavour of the early phase of the professed 'non-violent' Assam agitation. Some portions of PUCL's findings are selectively quoted below:

> "This is not the first time that Assam has been rocked with violence since independence. There were communal riots in 1950, 1960, 1968, and 1972. These riots were provoked sometimes by the issue of language. Sometimes these have been directed against outsiders in general, in which people's participation has been phenomenal and 'satyagraha' has been used as a weapon. This agitation is, however, different in that it has been sustained for a long time. There is no doubt that some illegal migration into Assam from Bangladesh has taken place, although the estimates of this migration vary. It is also true, as Jyoti Basu, the chief minister of West Bengal, pointed out in his letter to the Prime Minister, "that the Assamese people (and the Khasis in Meghalaya) do have a genuine fear of being swamped in their own States by people coming across 'the border from Bangladesh and there may be many 'foreigners' residing in Assam". We quote Jyoti Basu because the "Gana Sangram Parishad", the main force behind the current agitation in Assam seems to have identified him as the most hated leader in Assam today. Contrary to what the GSP and the leaders of AASU (All Assam Students Union) and the PLP (Purbanchaliya Lok Parishad) seem to think, the leaders in other parts of India, particularly the Bengali leaders are not unaware of the problem in Assam.
>
> But who are these 'foreigners'? And, indeed, how many of them are there in Assam? The late Hem Barua (ex-MP) had put the figure of 'foreigners' in Assam at seven lakhs in November 1971. The census figures do not make the task of determining the number of legal or illegal immigrants any easier. Nor do they establish the case of the agitators in any conclusive manner. In 1931, for example, the number of Assamese-speaking people in what constitutes Assam today was only 36% of the population. By 1961, it had, in fact, increased to 62%. This raises many important questions, but it is at least arguable that the Assamese-speaking people did not form a majority of the population of what constitutes Assam today well before independence. Since independence, if anything, their number

has gone up, a fact the leaders of the agitation are unable to explain. In any event, we were given widely differing estimates of the "foreigners" or whom the Assamese people describe as "Bahiragata" – a Sanskrit word which means people coming from outside. These estimates varied from 13 lakhs to 77 lakhs. It is probably true, as the leaders of the agitation have claimed, that the rise in Assam's population between 1961 and 1971 is nearly 34 to 35%. This rise, if true, is phenomenal and well above the average for the rest of the country.

Perhaps Assamese are justified in feeling neglected in terms of development. But to relate the neglect to the problem of 'Bahiragata' is patently unrealistic and even mischievous...... "

"........The agitation has been quite successful in terms of the number of people participating in it. During the first phase of the Satyagraha, from November 12 to November 17, as many as 7 lakhs of people are said to have been courted arrest in the city of Gauhati alone. The people at the AASU office claimed a figure of 2 million for the whole of Assam. Of course, as they themselves pointed out, this figure includes any number of people who have participated in the Satyagraha many times over. The Satyagraha is quite simple. People walk to the High Court in Gauhati or in some such office in other towns, court arrested and are released a few hours later.

There have been stray cases of violence on the Satyagrahis. One Khargeshwar Talukdar was alleged to have been killed by the police when a *Morcha* of student Satyagrahis tried to prevent Begum Abida Ahmed, the wife of the late President from filing her nomination papers from Barpeta. Another case of the victim of violence which occurred during the mob clash is that of Dilip Huzuri.

Otherwise, the Satyagraha itself has been rather peaceful. But it could hardly be otherwise. The entire Government machinery is a party to the Satyagraha. On the 13th of February, for example, the staff of the Assam Government itself participated in the Satyagraha. No action against such gross indiscipline has been reported. Nor has Governor L. P. Singh reacted to it in any manner. As one witness told us, "The Government of Assam is running the Movement and the AASU is running the Government."

"The Satyagraha thus has been peaceful for obvious reasons. However, the movement has not been. We collected ample evidence – witnesses, documents, tape-recorded interviews, visits to the sites of burnt and destroyed villages, and to the

wounded and hurt persons — to conclude that whatever be the justification of this movement, tactics, methods, and policies adopted by the leaders and supporters of the movement have willfully violated civil rights and liberties of thousands of citizens of India and have posed a threat to their lives."

This movement gained momentum from the agitation to remove the names of "foreigners" from the electoral rolls. To allow a "mass movement" of this kind to intervene on the question of citizenship of several thousands of people is in itself questionable and clearly dubious. But all the same, it must be recorded that it has resulted in questioning and at times depriving many citizens of their citizenship rights. There are **cases that raise genuine doubts as to whether the movement is against "foreigners" or against the citizens of India.** A memorandum was presented by the Indian Citizens Rights Preservation Committee, Assam, to the President of India (Appendix I). It gives a small but by no means complete list of Indian citizens who sought to be disenfranchised. Copies of this memorandum were sent to the Home Minister, all Members of Parliament, and to the chief ministers of all States. This memorandum was submitted on July 23, 1979, but it has not received any response yet from the Government which was in power then nor from the government which is in power now. The President has not taken any note of the problem in Assam yet. If allowed to work in peace and without intimidation, the above-mentioned committee can prepare a fuller and comprehensive list of genuine Indian citizens whose citizenship rights are questioned.

In addition to these, there have been a number of cases of gross violation of accepted practices of determining the citizenship of people concerned. A more meticulous collection of data when the Assam situation is back to normal or is relatively tension-free would reveal the actual extent of such malpractices........."

".........the worst incidents of violence took place in Mukalmua and Nalbari areas of Barpeta subdivision of Kamrup district. According to the Deputy Commissioner himself, four thousand houses have been burnt, and forty-two persons have been killed. All of them were Bengalis. Two hundred and thirty-five people were arrested. (Most of them were released on bail later). The Deputy Commissioner specifically mentioned that the AASU movement was very peaceful and that what happened in the Nalbari-Mukalmua areas was not their work. We visited the Mukalmua camp where 510 inmates, all Bengali Muslims, are living. In the Chualkhowa area, according to the account given to us by the villagers there, some three to four thousand Assamese people came shouting slogans, armed with spears and other lethal weapons. They set the houses of the Bengali people living in the area on fire, killed many people, and wounded many others.

The most pathetic scenes were witnessed in the Rangafali camp, as well as in the Nalbari area. The camp accommodates more than four thousand inmates, predominantly Bengali Hindus. Among them, we encountered hundreds of badly wounded individuals, victims of truly barbarous attacks. Even infants of a few months old and elderly women aged eighty and above were not spared. Many had their arms and/or legs broken, and basic medical aid and attention had not reached a significant portion of the population. A similar situation prevailed in the Neharbari camp. Reports suggest that the death toll in the Nalbari area may be as high as 400.

The report notably highlights the forced leave of Assam's Chief Election Commissioner K. S. Rao, a South Indian, and the subsequent appointment of an Assamese-speaking official to oversee the citizenship and disenfranchisement operations. This transition added to the arbitrary and indiscriminate nature of decisions regarding the electoral roll. For nearly four months, the Gana Sangram Parishad and the AASU had assumed absolute control of the official machinery, effectively running a parallel government. They either inspired or, at the very least, did not object to wall paintings and posters inciting violence against so-called "Bahiragatas" (outsiders). Examples provided in the report include:

> **"If you see a snake and a Bengali, kill the Bengali first."**
>
> **"Wanted: a Bengali Head - Reward Rs.2,500/-."**

Chauvinistic literature and slogans with strong secessionist overtones also played a role in the turmoil, a fact that movement leaders naturally disclaimed. However, the report includes a few exemplary slogans:

> **"Indian Dogs get out of Assam."**
>
> **"Condemn the Indian Army for raping our mothers and sisters in Assam."**
>
> **"Forget Mother India. Love Mother Assam."**
>
> **"Victory to Mother Assam."**

The report further notes that this climate of hostility stemmed from prevalent chauvinism in Assam, exacerbated by support from the local press. Both The

Assam Tribune and its Assamese counterpart, Dainik Assam, significantly contributed to the hate campaign. These publications blamed outsiders, particularly those from a specific linguistic minority, for various issues within Assam. Allegations were also made against the Gauhati station of All India Radio for propagating chauvinistic views.

To counter the Assamese press's "hate campaign," liberal democratic and progressive individuals formed the 'Gana Sanskriti Bikash Samity.' Under the editorship of Mrs Nirupama Burgohain, a well-known novelist and journalist, they began publishing a new Assamese weekly tabloid called 'Saptahik Janajivan.' However, Burgohain was forced to leave the publication in early 1980 due to her criticism of the treatment of non-Assamese victims of the North Kamrup carnage. Other papers such as Saptahik Kolakhar, Janakranti, and Saptahik Janajivan also played a democratic and secular role but struggled financially and faced attacks on their presses and threats to their staff. Despite these challenges, they persisted in their mission to strengthen democracy and secularism in Assam, prompting the Press Council of India to caution irresponsible presses. [32]

As many of the so-called "foreigners" in Assam were of Bangladeshi (or East Pakistani) [1]origin, the issue was often framed as a confrontation between "the Assamese" and "the Bengalis." Research scholar Makiko Kimura compared news reports, editorials, and articles from newspapers in Gauhati and Calcutta to analyze their role in shaping public perceptions of this controversial issue. The newspapers offered differing views on the cause of the problem, who were victims and offenders, and how to conceptualize the issue, reflecting the deeply divergent perspectives between Assam and West Bengal. Kimura's analysis of articles from The Assam Tribune (Gauhati) and Amrita Bazar Patrika (Calcutta) underscores the divergence in their opinions on the foreign nationals' issue.

Note: [1]The fact that this group of people were Indians before the independence of India on 15.8.1947 and that all of them are of Indian origins never finds mention anywhere.

Overall, newspapers published in Gauhati tended to support the movement, whereas those from Calcutta took a critical stance. Their reporting diverged significantly based on their respective ethnic affiliations, including Assamese, Bengalis, and Bangladeshis. These ethnic labels were fluid and were used to categorize and stereotype articles in their newspapers, thereby shaping people's perceptions of the ongoing situation—a phenomenon often referred to as the agenda-setting function of mass media.

The articles analyzed in both papers spanned from November 1979 to May 1980, covering the first seven months of the movement. Kimura chose this period because it marked the formative stage of the movement, during which the newspapers' opinions were primarily shaped. She compared the narratives of three violent incidents and their portrayals of perpetrators and victims to illustrate the contrasting viewpoints presented by the Gauhati and Calcutta newspapers.

a) The Incidents in North Kamrup: The First Incident of Large-Scale Violence.
b) The Incident in Duliajan: Death of One Bengali and Several Assamese.
c) Counter-Agitation by the All Assam Minority Students' Union: Bangladeshis (Foreigners) or Indian Minorities?

Out of these three incidents, only the narratives of the incident at Duliajan (as already touched upon earlier) in Gauhati newspaper, The Assam Tribune (AT, hereafter) and Calcutta newspaper Amrita Bazar Patrika (ABP, henceforth) are quoted hereunder, as an instance:

> The incident in Duliajan: Death of one Bengali and several Assamese:
>
> On 18th January 1980, police fired at students picketing in front of Oil India Limited in Duliajan in the northern part of Assam. Several Assamese students and a Bengali technical manager of the company were killed.

In a front-page article on this incident, AT reports,

> "At least seven youths were reported to have been killed and more than 100 men and women of different ages seriously injured as a result of firing by the BSF (Border Security Forces) at about 8 a.m. while they were picketing along with thousands of persons in front of the industrial area of Oil India Limited at Duliajan." [The Assam Tribune, January 19]

It also states that AASU had condemned the police firing on peaceful picketers at Duliajan. On the last page, AT writes, "Dr. Robi Mitra, Technical Manager of Oil India Limited, was dragged out of his car by a violent crowd near the hospital at Duliajan and was killed, police said." Moreover, in an editorial on 20th January, an AT editor writes,

> "That ladies were among the victims heightens the ghastliness of the tragedy and wantonness and indiscriminate nature of the police action .... The unfortunate failure to save the life of the OIL official from mob fury, apparently sparked off by the killings, the police and the civil authorities must be held squarely responsible." [The Assam Tribune, January 20]

Thus, AT focuses on the death of the picketers and condemns the police for using gunfire.

Moreover, on 21st January, AT reported,

> "At least 70 Picketers Killed At Duliajan." It states, "The police firing at the Oil Town of Duliajan last Thursday is feared to have turned into an ugly massacre of non-violent and peaceful picketers, according to the assessment of different organizations."

Again on the 25th, AT reports:

> "Over 1000 Dead Bodies were Hidden At Duliajan, Says PLP."

It is clear that AT focuses on the death of the 'peaceful' picketers and doubts that there are more killings. Furthermore, AT condemns the firing by the police and the security forces and claims that the police and civil authorities are responsible for the death of the technical manager.

On the contrary, ABP emphasizes the death of Dr. Robi Mitra. On 19th January, it reports,

> "At least six persons were killed, five of them in police firing and another in mob violence in front of Oil India Limited at Duliajan in Upper Assam this morning. Dr. Robi Mitra, Technical Manager of OIL was dragged out of his car by a violent crowd near the hospital at Duliajan and was killed, police said." [Amrita Bazar Patrika, January 19]

On 21st January, ABP reports the statement by the West Bengal Chief Minister Mr Jyoti Basu. It writes,

> "Mr Jyoti Basu . . . said that apparently regional fanatics were now on a rampage and on a murder spread in Assam and the alarming situation there had not only affected the normal life and procession of Bengalees alone but had equally endangered the personal safety and security of all non-Assamese people alike including those speaking Hindi and Nepalese languages." [Amrita Bazar Patrika, January 21]

From this article, it can be said that Basu interprets the death of a Bengali as a threat to all non-Assamese residing in Assam.

Moreover, on 22nd January, an ABP editorial explains,

> "A young Bengali scientist, Dr. Ra bi Mitra, who was serving as a Technical Manager . . . was stoned to death. . . . This was a case of premeditated murder, not a case of a sudden attack on an individual

by an angry mob .... Dr Mitra was not a Bangladeshi, nor was he a Bengalee living permanently in Assam. . . . If the 'anti-social elements' in Assam succeed in driving away all non-Assamese residents from that state, India will cease to be one country." [Amrita Bazar Patrika, January 22]

ABP stresses the death of one Bengali and claims that this is a premeditated crime by the organizers of the movement, thus concluding all non-Assamese lives are threatened. And it pays little attention to the death of student picketers. As for this incident, there is no difference in the reporting of the facts. But AT clearly emphasizes the police firing and death of the picketers, and ABP condemns the death of one Bengali as caused by the organizers of the movement.

As analyzed by Kimura, all three articles and news reports of AT and ABP differ in the way they describe the victims and the offenders. The distinction between AT and ABP reports became apparent when the typical victims and offenders in the two newspapers were compared by Kimura, side by side, as quoted below:

Newspapers	Victims	Offenders
The Assam Tribune	Indigenous People, Students, Picketers, Local Indian Citizens	Miscreants, Police, Army, Foreigners, Bangladeshis, Immigrants, Linguistics and Religious Minorities.
Amrita Bazar Patrika	Bengali Hindus, non-Assamese, Linguistic Minorities.	Assamese, Regional Fanatics, Anti-social Elements AASU and AAGSP

[33]

Be that as it may, on the 6th of December 1980, Assam got its first woman Muslim Chief Minister when Syeda Anwara Taimur of the Indian National Congress party was sworn in. Anwara Taimur is also the first Muslim woman Chief Minister of any state in Indian history. As mentioned in the previous chapter on Nellie, AASU strongly opposed the formation of the Taimur-led government in Assam and successfully observed total bandhs in the state to register its protest on the day of her assuming office. A section of the vernacular press began to report that the new government under the Taimur Ministry would encourage further Muslim immigration and also benefit Muslims in obtaining government jobs and other services. Soon, the state government imposed press censorship on local publications because such speculative news was allegedly inciting the people. [34] The Taimur government tried to discipline ethnic Assamese government employees, especially senior officials who were known sympathizers of the movement. One of the top police officials was reportedly arrested. There were reports that Taimur's personal secretariat had only 'Muslim' professionals. To some ethnic Asamiyas, these measures appeared as the 'de-Assamesisation' of the state bureaucracy that reinforced the fear of Assamese 'minoritization' by the 'immigrant' powers. Although Taimur was an ethnic Assamese Muslim, she was elected from Assam's Dalgaon[1] Assembly constituency, where there was a heavy concentration of Muslims of Bengali descent. These steps eventually made the already difficult situation even worse. The political developments that soon followed forced her to resign.

Note: [1]Dalgaon is within Mangaldoi Lok Sabha constituency which received the earliest Muslim migrants in Assam in the first part of 13th century.

On June 30th, 1981, President's rule was imposed in Assam for the second time, barely six months after the first, and lasted another 6 ½ months until January 13th, 1982. At that time, Prime Minister Indira Gandhi decided to establish a Congress government in the state. Accordingly, Keshab Chandra Gogoi was appointed Chief Minister of Assam. However, his tenure ended after only 66 days as Gogoi was forced to resign on March 19th, 1982, amid a motion of no-confidence vote against the government. President's rule followed for the third time, lasting 345 days. With the Central rule nearing one year without interruption, the need for an elected government in Assam became urgent.

Like in Assam, the political situation at the Centre was also volatile in the latter part of the 1970s. On July 28th, 1979, Chaudhary Charan Singh was sworn in as the Prime Minister of India with outside support from the Indira Congress and Yashwantrao Chavan of the Congress (Socialist) faction as his Deputy PM. Just before Charan Singh could prove his majority in Lok Sabha, Indira Gandhi withdrew support from his government, forcing his resignation on August 20th, 1979, after just 23 days. He advised President Neelam Sanjiva Reddy to dissolve Lok Sabha. Janata Party leader Jagjivan Ram challenged the advice and sought time to gather support. However, the President decided to dissolve the Lok Sabha and asked Charan Singh to continue as a caretaker Prime Minister. In January 1980, the General elections for the 7th Lok Sabha were held on January 3rd and 6th, 1980. Mrs. Indira Gandhi returned to power, winning over two-thirds majority with 353 out of 531 seats.

Within three days of assuming office, Prime Minister Mrs Gandhi initiated negotiations with the AASU leaders to reach an amicable settlement. In their first meeting with Mrs Gandhi, the AASU submitted a charter of demands, including the 3Ds for illegal immigrants (Detection, Deletion, and Deportation); sealing of international borders to check infiltration; constitutional safeguards for the people of North-East India for the next 15/20 years to protect the identity of the 'indigenous' people; and updating the National Register of Citizens (NRC) of 1951.

The negotiations that followed primarily focused on a mutually acceptable definition of foreign nationals in the Indian subcontinental context and the cut-off date for the detection and deportation of foreign nationals from Assam. However, the two parties could not reach a consensus on a mutually acceptable cut-off date. The government of India also did not agree to accept the AASU's demand for constitutional safeguards for the indigenous population. Between January 1980 and January 1983, the government and the leadership had at least 50 rounds of talks at various levels, but a formal agreement eluded them.

While AASU demanded 1951 as the cut-off year for identifying illegal foreign nationals in Assam against the 1971 cut-off year desired by the Central government, AAMSU demanded that March 25th, 1971, should be the 'base date' for the declaration of foreigners in Assam according to the Indo-Bangladesh treaty of 1972. The Indira Gandhi-led central government promptly accepted AAMSU as a party at the negotiating table on the Assam movement. However, AASU was angered by such a move. The AASU leaders labelled AAMSU as agents of illegal Bangladeshis living in Assam. Consequently, AAMSU mobilized and united the so-called immigrant Muslim community against the Assam movement, leading to frequent clashes between the supporters of the two student unions in Assam during the movement.

During the Assam agitation, the people of the state encountered various forms of violence, broadly classified as (a) brutality perpetrated by the movement leaders and their supporters, (b) counter-violence by the victims, and (c) response by the government, both state and union. The government's response, in the name of maintaining law and order, included, among other things, lathi charge (caning), use of tear gas, arrest, custodial torture, and indiscriminate shooting, resulting in the killing or severe injury of people. The victims' counter-violence was generally in retaliation for the aggression they faced. However, the violence committed by the agitation leaders was both overt and covert, such as the Nellie massacre and stray killings. Particularly in the late seventies, the violence of alienation was marked by beating up individuals who 'looked like immigrants' or similar incidents.

Above all, there was the suppressed violence in organizing thousands of people to participate in the protest agitations. Sometimes many people were made to participate apparently of their own accord but often reluctantly or coerced. While incidents like the Nellie massacre were visible for the world to see, many cases of invisible violence remained unacknowledged, rarely mentioned in narratives of the Assam Movement. Such episodes surfaced later in recollections of the sufferers within the privacy of their homes and occasionally in the writings of a handful of authors when reconstructing memories of violence in their literary works. "Questions of Identity in Assam: Location, Migration, Hybridity," authored by Professor of English at Assam's Gauhati University, Nandita Dutta (first published in 2012 by SAGE Publication India Pvt Ltd), is one such book where the Professor remarkably delves into this aspect.

In this context, Professor Dutta pertinently referred to [1]Homen Borgohain's article, "Asom Andolonor Rajnitiye Bihukou Sporsho Korile" (The Politics of the Assam Movement Has Also Affected the Festival of Bihu), to demonstrate how even Bihu, the most important festival of the Asamiya people, 'was transformed from a predominantly harvest festival strongly grounded in the community into a political weapon.' Professor Dutta quoted the following example given by Homen Borgohain of the huge Bihu procession organized by the movement leaders during the 1982 festival:

> "It (the Bihu procession) was led by the Assamese icon Bhupen Hazarika and Hiranya Kumar Bhattacharyya, the police officer who had resigned from his job and become an important participant in the movement. The procession wended through the city streets, swelling as it passed different residential localities, and culminated in the Judges' field on the banks of the river Brahmaputra, beside the Mahatma Gandhi Road. There a huge political meeting was held, and speeches were delivered on the themes of identity, cultural nationalism and, of course, on the source of danger, the illegal migrant."

Thus, a narrow cultural identity was propagated to bring about divisions within the community through this popular festival, which is otherwise well-known for its all-embracing aspects. [35]

Note: [1]Homen Borgohain (1932 – 2021), an Assamese author, journalist, and President of Assam Sahitya Sabha (2001-2002), was awarded the 1978 Sahitya Akademi Award in the Assamese language for his novel "Pita Putra".

With the failure of talks held in December 1982 and early January 1983, the Government of India expressed its determination to hold elections to the

State Legislative Assembly in February 1983 as, under the terms of the constitution, there was a need to constitute the State Assembly before 28th March 1983 since the last elections were held in the state in March 1977. However, the announcement of the election led to a complete breakdown of law and order amid almost a total boycott of the election process by the agitation leaders. The worst 'Nellie massacre', which occurred on the morning of 18th February 1983, narrated in the previous chapter, bears one among many such testimonies. One more massacre at Chaulkhowachapori in the Darrang district closely followed the Nellie massacre. Again, the victims belonged to the same social group. Another massacre occurred at Silapathar in the Lakhimpur district, where the victims were Hindu Bengalis. Several died at Gohpur in the Darrang district in attacks and counter-attacks. The victims were the Assamese people and the Bodo tribal community. At Chamoria, several Assamese died in rioting. These riots not only killed hundreds of people but also led to the destruction of properties worth crores of Rupees. Those who became destitute in the riots were the ordinary oppressed masses. Rioting became very endemic just before, during, and immediately after the 1983 elections to the state legislature. [36]

Interestingly, in her book "Questions of Identity in Assam: Location, Migration, Hybridity," Professor Nandana Dutta provided insight into the movement and how it took shape to continue for 6 long years. First, it built up an efficient organizational network and a coordination system from its Gauhati University headquarters down the line deep into the rural areas of the Brahmaputra valley. Then, it mobilized people from different communities for various protest actions that gave the impression of a mass support base. However, from the beginning, the so-called 'largely non-violent' bandhs involved the forcible closure of shops, other business establishments, Banks, Government offices, and all. Ensuring its success entailed surveillance to pin down the odd objector or aberrant, pelting stones at the offending shop, or, in the case of office employees, intimidation, physical violence, pelting stones at the individual's house, and shouting slogans usually on the theme of 'betrayal of the motherland.' Neighbourhood surveillance came into play to 'discipline' those who might dare to show disrespect or disloyalty to 'the cause of the motherland.' Participation in rallies, picketing, torchlight processions in the evening, and all similar activities was made 'obligatory.' Otherwise, coercive actions would follow to compel the reluctant people to join the movement. Thus huge crowds, generally comprised of students, both boys and girls, men and women of different communities from almost all walks of life, could be seen in the protest activities. It gave the impression of a mass movement. The most enthusiastic policing was often done by adolescent boys and girls who suddenly felt empowered against authority - whether parental, adult or state authority. This nascent violence began to manifest in the slackening of parental control and the breakdown of traditional social hierarchies. As mentioned earlier, the hierarchy of force replaced these, often evident in the young boy shoving an elderly person, frequently of a different community, on a deserted street or sometimes stalking someone quietly but menacingly. Many would remember that during the movement, the loudest and angriest voices raised were those who had been sent out of the state so that they would not lose an academic year. These were the same students who protested safely on the lawns of India Gate in New Delhi but were among the sharpest detractors of non-participation in protests in the state. [37]

There are many instances of intimidation and bullying in the 'largely non-violent' Assam Movement. These are still alive in the memories of those at their receiving ends. Here is a case in point: An officer of the State Bank of India (SBI) who was posted at the Guwahati Panbazar Branch in Assam had confided to Subir during the agitation period that ensuring participation of the Bengalis - in particular - in the protest activities against the alleged "Illegal Bangladeshis" and compelling them in the loudest sloganeering seemed to be a priority of some leaders and supporters of the movement. The SBI officer felt it reassured the staunch supporters and gave a kind of perverted pleasure to them. Even genuine excuses like personal illness or severe discomfort to the aged employees would not let anyone take 'leave' for a single day from participating in the processions in the streets or sloganeering in front of government offices - even in blazing sunlight. Many people reportedly fainted on the roads as they were not allowed to withdraw from protest activities. The 'indigenous' Assamese were also not spared. Any visible reluctance or lack of enthusiasm in joining the protests would invite appropriate retribution. The Assamese women were expected to wear their traditional 'mekhela sador.' Wearing the 'sari' – generally known as the traditional Bengali attire but quite common and popular ladies' costume in Assam was frowned upon while fighting for the 'cause.' Such casual behaviour would invite severe reprimand from the fanatic supporters of the movement.

The inhuman torture against families who opposed the anti-foreigner movement was a common occurrence during those days. Bijanlal Chaudhury, a college teacher of Assamese literature and distinguished essayist, who opposed the movement, reportedly faced severe threats from the agitators. According to reports, organized gangs followed him and hindered his free movement. The agitation leaders prohibited college students from talking to him or attending his classes under threats of dire consequences. The extent of aversion and hatred against those who opposed the movement was also evident in the treatment of Nirupama Borgohain, an Assamese woman journalist. After she visited some refugee camps and publicized their plight, including accounts of mass killings and arson, she was physically prevented from leaving her house and had to discontinue her work thereafter. [38]

Udayon Misra, former Professor and Head of the Department of English at Dibrugarh University, Assam, in a journal article titled "Immigration and Identity Transformation in Assam," among other things, wrote:

> "The Assamese middle class's insistence on a dominant Assamese identity for the state, and the support given by the ruling Congress party, went a long way in alienating first the hill tribes and then the plain tribes. It was evident that the Assamese middle-class leadership, preoccupied as it was with the struggle to establish Assamese hegemony, had failed to respond to the growing sense of insecurity in the tribal mind. As a result, this sense of alienation came to be expressed in the growth of different organizations, which started demanding political power and social justice." [39]

As Professor Misra mentioned, the growth of different organizations eventually included several villages, districts, and regional associations, which sprang up to represent ethnic aspirations. Some well-known groups among them were:

a) Pragatishil Vhoiyam Janajatiya Parishad (Progressive Plain Tribal Conference),
b) Vhoiyam Janajatiya Parishad (Plain Tribal Conference),
c) All Bodo Students' Union (ABSU),
d) Rabha Student's Union,
e) All Assam Tribal Sangha,
f) Progressive Tribal People Development Council,
g) Mishing Students' Union,
h) Sonowal—Cachari Student's Union,
i) Janajatiya Yuva League (National Youth League),
j) Assam Tribal Women's League,
k) Assam Janajatiya Yuva Kalyan Parisahad (Assam Tribal Youth Welfare League),
l) Assam Janajatiya Yuva Chatra Parishad (Assam Tribal Youth Students' League), and
m) Janajatiya Chatra Sangram Committee (Tribal Student Struggle Committee).

In the 1970s and 1980s, communal clashes in Assam were centred on land, as evidenced by the clash in Gohpur on the eve of the 1983 Nellie violence. It brought to the fore the significance of land-related issues attached to the agitating tribal minds. In Gohpur, the fight was not between local people and foreigners but between tribal and non-tribal Assamese people. Since 1972, the Bodo people have been living in the forest reserves of Gohpur due to border conflicts with the neighbouring state of Nagaland. Bodos were followed by Mishings, Assamese-speaking people, other Indian migrants, and suspected foreigners who squatted in forest areas. The government tried to free the forest land from squatting by these groups of people. Amidst such a situation of landlessness, in 1981, the Assam Plain Tribal People's Council demanded a separate state, Udayachal, and drew the desired boundary for their state. The demand for Udayachal comprised parts of Goalpara district (present-day Kokrajhar District), Kamrup district, and Darrang district in north Assam. This geographical division is very close to today's Bodoland Territorial Council.

These groups and associations of ethnic tribal communities initially supported the Assam agitation spearheaded by AASU. However, due to their small numbers, low literacy levels, and habitation in Assam's interior places, they were less visible in the public arena. Interestingly, despite endorsing the cause of the Assam agitation, they did not hesitate to point out flaws in the movement. Earlier, all these ethnic groups had braved perceived or real threats to the nation (here Assam) together, whether it was the grouping system of 1945-46 or issues of illegal immigration. However, after independence, the rather sluggish growth rate of the communities disappointed almost all tribal people. Besides, during the Assam agitation, the question of Assamese identity became paramount to the leaders of the movement. Despite the whole-hearted support lent by ethnic tribal communities to the AASU-led agitation, there were quite a few anti-tribal incidents, and in 1983, tribal people were the worst sufferers of violence. These developments alerted ethnic tribal people that the Assam agitation might not bring them common prosperity. Accordingly, they became utterly disillusioned and restrained. [40]

Significantly, the Assam agitation initially emerged as a popular movement in the Brahmaputra valley in 1979 and soon gained the characteristics of a people's crusade. However, the campaign did not penetrate the Barak Valley and the two hill districts of Assam. The geographical expanse of the movement was primarily confined to the Brahmaputra valley - the traditional homeland of the Assamiyas plus the erstwhile Goalpara district of the Bengal Presidency to a large extent.

The Asamiya Muslims initially supported the movement. Even during the anti-election period in February 1983, Nurul Hussain, the AASU Vice President and an Asamiya Muslim, presided over the AASU and led the agitational programmes in the absence of its regular President, Prafulla Kumar Mahanta, who was behind bars at that time. However, eventually, the Asamiya Muslims became apprehensive of the close friendship the movement leadership built up with India's right-wing elements. The Nellie Massacre, killings at Chaulkhowa Chapori, and a bomb blast at Balatu Bazar near Hajo forced the Asamiya Muslims to rethink their continuous support for the movement. When Muslim leaders started to raise pertinent questions about the involvement of right-wing elements in some anti-Muslim activities during the Assam movement, they were dismissed. Due to these unpleasant developments, the support base among the Asamiya Muslims eroded substantially, severely affecting the secular credentials of AASU both inside and outside Assam. According to author Sanjib Baruah:

> By May 1983, there was an indication of a split in the AASU. At a secret conclave, several Muslim members of the AASU leadership demanded a correction of a 'pro-Hindu communal tilt'. Their memorandum demanded a 'firm definition' of a foreigner. The press gave some credit to the growing rift between Assamese Hindus and Muslims to the machinations of the Saikia government.
>
> Rifts began to show in other weak links of the Assamese sub-national formation as well. The election violence discussed earlier included some instances of conflict between ethnic Assamese opponents of the election and plains tribal supporters, mainly Bodos. In the following months, important conferences of plains tribal communities made demands that emphasized their distinctiveness from the ethnic Assamese – indeed, demands that smacked of a rebellion from the Assamese sub-national formation. The Saikia government did seem to play a significant role in promoting these rifts. For instance, the government actively patronized the Bodo Sahitya Sabha and promoted it as a rival of the Axom Xahitya Xobha (Ashom Sahitya Sabha) in plains tribal areas. The annual session of the organization was attended by most members of the Saikia cabinet. By contrast, the declining share of government resources and patronage forced the Axom Xahitya Xobha (Ashom Sahitya Sabha) to reconsider its active involvement in the Assam movement. [41]

Even at the beginning of the Assam agitation, the response of the tribal communities to the movement was faint in the tribal areas of the

Brahmaputra valley. This position was further weakened when the AASU demanded the withdrawal of certain constitutional facilities given to the scheduled tribes. In the mid-1980s, AASU declared its intention to prepare a national register of citizens and issue citizenship certificates to the people of Assam. Although AASU later abandoned this decision, tribal communities did not appreciate such moves. They felt they were the original inhabitants of the territory and therefore did not need certificates from those who arrived later. Additionally, they were apprehensive of the Asamiya people's perceived superiority.

Furthermore, the black-tribal people of the tea plantations remained lukewarm to the movement. Initial abrasions alarmed them regarding the movement's supporters, after which both sides kept a safe distance. The campaign also lacked support from Hindu Bengalis in both the Barak and Brahmaputra valleys. Similarly, the movement failed to gain traction among Na-Asamiya Muslim-dominated pockets in old Goalpara, Kamrup, and Nagaon districts. Nepalis throughout Assam were also apprehensive about the movement. Finally, the response of large non-caste groups of Asamiya, such as the Ahoms in Upper Assam and the Koch-Rajbongshis of Lower Assam, was primarily lukewarm.

Significantly, Assam's Hindu Bengalis, Na-Asamiya (Bengali) Muslims and Nepalis together accounted for nearly 40% of the state's population. The Assam movement's leadership did not seek their support but instead indiscriminately labelled them foreigners, making them constituencies for the counter-movement.

In summary, apart from the three communities labelled as foreigners by the movement leaders, and consequently disfavored, the agitation campaign did not penetrate the people of Assam's Barak Valley and two of its hill districts. Additionally, support from several groups in the Brahmaputra valley was either faint or diminished over time. Notable among them were ethnic tribal communities, including Bodo tribes, Asamiya Muslims, black-tribal people of the tea plantation, and large non-caste groups of Asamiya, like the Ahoms in Upper Assam and the Koch-Rajbongshis of Lower Assam.

So, who formed the solid base for the Assam movement? In general, high-caste Asamiya Hindus, including Brahmins, Gonaks, Kayasthas, Kolitas, and Gossain-Mohantas, provided the social support base. Combined, these castes comprised roughly 8% of the state's population and were dominant socially and culturally. Additionally, most Asamiya middle class, traders, contractors, and small capitalists from these caste groups supported the movement. They held influence in state administration, police, professions, educational institutes, and regional press and media. Despite their numerical insignificance, they were influential and formed the primary support base for the movement spearheaded by AASU. Due to their social and cultural prominence in a backward economy, they shaped and upheld the Asamiya nationality. Thus, despite weaknesses in a multi-racial, multi-religious, multi-ethnic society, this numerically small group strongly supported, strengthened and defended the Assam agitation. [42] [43]

Although the Assam Agitation was said to be spearheaded by the AASU, it is evident that behind the student leaders were many senior figures, writers, and college and university teachers who acted as their mentors. However, due to AASU's youthful and innocent public face and the romanticized image of young students leading an ideological battle, the divisive and potentially violent nature of many aspects of the agitation was largely ignored. The failure to recognize this potential for violence in a timely manner had tragic consequences in the long run. The acknowledgement of the national independence movement as a model and the ubiquitous presence of Gandhi's photograph in students' union offices created the impression that this was a powerful Gandhian movement. These factors served to conceal the potential for violence, both from the students themselves and perhaps from their mentors. The portrayal of the movement as 'largely peaceful' in intellectual discussions, reinforced by participants and sympathetic observers, overlooked many of the gross violations as minor and isolated incidents. [44] Thus, scholars sympathetic to the Assam agitation consistently attempted to portray it as peaceful, akin to Gandhian methods of struggle.

As narrated in the previous chapter and this one, linguistic and religious minorities in the state became targets of organized terrorization, with many of them directly suffering from large-scale violence during the six years of the Assam agitation. However, it would be wrong to presume that all these acts were one-sided affairs. In addition to the silent masses of ethnic Asamiyas who did not participate in the agitation programs, the movement leaders and their supporters also endured significant suffering during these six years from state repression unleashed by the government to quell protest movements. Their pains, miseries, and hardships were no less than those experienced by their targets. In certain ways and in some cases, their sufferings were comparable to those they targeted.

The violation of rights and liberties of the agitators and supporters of the movement by the government was common throughout the period of the movement. Government authorities often employed various harsh repressive measures against ordinary men and women participating in protest agitations. The massive deployment of security forces around protest venues created the impression that the state was preparing for war against enemy countries.

Brutalities perpetrated by security forces in the name of maintaining law and order included lathi-charges, lobbing of teargas shells, firing from automatic guns, as well as arrests and detentions by the police. There were reports of press censorship imposed on local media and draconian laws enacted in the state to contain and control massive protests airing grievances against the government.

For instance, during the week-long mass satyagraha from 12th to 17th November 1979, many peaceful participants of the agitation courted imprisonment and suffered in various ways. Simultaneously, in Nowgong, during a peaceful picketing program led by youth leaders to prevent candidates from filing nomination papers, security forces cracked down severely on picketers on 10th December 1979 when they attempted to prevent Congress (United) candidate Dev Kanta Barua from filing nomination papers. Although picketers successfully prevented Barua from filing in Nowgong, there was a setback in Barpeta. Peaceful picketers standing sleepless in the cold December night were brutally lathi-charged and pushed into roadside drains when they tried to stop Mrs Begum Abida Ahmed, a Congress (I) candidate, from filing her nomination in Barpeta. The government implemented many other repressive measures to suppress the movement. Like the Barpeta incident, at Naharkatia, a teenage schoolboy named Purna Nirmalia became the victim of such atrocities. Dilip Huzuri, a young student, was also killed by army personnel. The people of North Kamrup also endured several cruel acts perpetrated by the government.

Amidst such atrocities, the Duliajan incident reached its peak when CRP men, under the command of police officials and the district administration, opened fire on over seven thousand peaceful picketers squatting in front of the oil installations at Duliajan to halt the flow of crude from Assam on 18th January 1980 in support of their demands. It was reported that thirty rounds of ammunition were fired within a few minutes on the crowd without any prior warning. The Duliajan tragedy resulted in the death of four persons and the injury of hundreds. In Narengi, during the oil blockade incident, thousands of picketers were also arrested in April 1980.

Moreover, there were reports of police and military personnel committing severe atrocities on the pretext of quelling disturbances during the movement. They resorted to wanton and unwarranted lathi charges on peaceful picketers, resulting in many injuries. In another reported incident of police violence in the Dimou area of Nagaon district, three youth leaders—Naren Nath, Bhudhar Deka, and Rajiv Rajkumar—were brutally killed by the police and CRP personnel when they allegedly attempted to stop a convoy of police officials during a Path Bandh (road blockade) agitational program organized by AASU on 31st December 1981. Similarly, in the Path Bandh program at Biswanath Chariali of Tezpur district, agitators Manjit Das, Anukul Kakoti, and Ratna Rajkhowa lost their lives while participating in the protest. Thus, ostensibly, this "rasta roko" program alone claimed seven lives and injured many others. Places like Nowgong and Darrang reportedly experienced the most police atrocities.

Furthermore, people's right to assemble or hold meetings was denied in the name of maintaining law and order during the agitation period. However, such government actions infringed upon the rights and liberties of common people. In most cases, unannounced meetings held at short notice by AASU were forcibly broken up by the police. It was also alleged that women were not exempt from such atrocities, with Indian army personnel and CRP accused of committing violence against Assamese women during the movement. [45]

While there were numerous instances of police excesses and brutalities, the following example, among many others, is cited below to illustrate the repressive measures purportedly adopted by the security forces:

On 27th November 1979, AASU-AAGSP combined called for the closure of all educational institutes and picketing in state and central government offices. Mass picketing was organized in front of all polling offices where candidate nominations could be filed in the first week of December 1979. No candidates were allowed to file nomination papers in the Brahmaputra Valley. On 10th December 1979, the last date for submitting nomination papers, a statewide bandh was declared. The government imposed a curfew in different parts of the state, including the major city of Guwahati. At Barpeta, then IGP K.P.S. Gill led the police force in escorting Begum Abida Ahmed, wife of the fifth President of India, Late Fakhruddin Ali Ahmed, to file nomination papers, and they attacked protestors. A 22-year-old general secretary of Barpeta AASU Unit, Khargeswar Talukdar, was beaten to death and thrown into a ditch next to the highway at Bhabanipur. With this supreme sacrifice, Khargeswar Talukdar earned the unique distinction of being the First Martyr of the Assam Movement. [46]

Even the three-member fact-finding mission, Peoples' Union of Civil Liberties (PUCL), from Delhi, that visited Assam between 9th and 16th February 1980, noted in their report how the army indiscriminately opened fire on peaceful, unarmed Satyagrahis on 27th December 1979. The relevant part of its abridged report, released to the press on 28th February 1980, is quoted below:

"We should place on record here, however, a very genuine incident at Duliajan, in Dibrugarh district, where in front of the refinery, picketing had been in progress since Dec. 27, '79. It seems that on 18th January 1980, the army opened fire on peaceful, unarmed Satyagrahis for a few minutes from 7.50 a.m. to 8 a.m. The official figure of death was 4. Several hundred were reported injured. We gathered that firing was indiscriminate. People were fired at even when they were trying to flee. Some rushed to the nearby petrol pump for shelter. We saw a bullet mark on the pump itself. According to the Gana Sangram Parishad, seven persons are still missing and are feared dead. The tent raised for the picketing Satyagrahis was still lying there when we visited the site on 14th February. **The firing at Duliajan provides one solid example of the peaceful Satyagrahis being victims of the violence launched by the authorities.** [47] (Emphasis by Subir)

According to the Government of Assam Implementation of Assam Accord department: "During this period of six long years of the historic movement, as reported, 855 (later on 860 as submitted by AASU) people sacrificed their lives in the hope of an 'Infiltration-Free Assam' in the 1979-1985 Assam agitation." It has already provided an amount of Rs. 5.00 lakhs to each of the 'next of kin' of martyrs of the Assam Agitation. [48]

Significantly, during the six-year movement, Assam saw five different heads of elected Chief Ministers and three spells of Central (President's) rule, totalling 901 days (2 years 171 days), as represented below:

Sl No.	**Headed by	Period	Duration	##Notable events
1	Golap Bobora, Janata Party	12 March 1978 to 4 September 1979	1 year, 176 days	8 June 1979, AASU sponsored 12-hour state bandh was the beginning of the 6-long years of Assam Movement.

2	Jogendra Nath Hazarika	9 September 1979 to 11 December 1979	93 days	On 27 November 1979, AASU-AAGSP called for the closure of all educational institutes and picketing in state and central government offices. In the first week of December 1979, mass picketing in front of all polling offices prevented all candidates from filing nominations in the Brahmaputra valley for Lok Sabha election of January 1980.
3	*President's Rule	12 December 1979 to 5 December 1980	359 days	18th January 1980 police firing at Oil India H.Q Duliajan killing 4 picketers. It followed by lynching of Dr Rabi Mitra of Oil India who was ranked 2nd in the chain of local OIL hierarchy.
4	Syeda Anwara Taimur Indian National Congress	6 December 1980 to 30 June 1981	206 days	Press censorship imposed on the state's publications. E. S. Parthasarathy, Commissioner of upper Assam division, killed on 6th April 1981 by a bomb planted in his Jorhat office.
5	*President's Rule	30 June 1981 to 13 January 1982	197 days	On 31 December 81, three persons were killed & ten injure in police firing to break a road blockade on NH No.37 in a thirty six hour path band programme. AASU General Secretary Bhrigu Kumar Phukan and its advisor Lalitchandra Rajkhowa held in preventive detention
6	Kesab Chandra Gogoi Indian National Congress	13 January 1982 to 19 March 1982	65 days	Janata curfew declared on 26 January to boycott Republic day Celebration protesting against curtailments of democratic rights of the citizens.
7	*President's Rule	19 March 1982 to 27 February 1983	345 days	Nellie Massacre -18 February 1983
8	Hiteswar Saikia Indian National Congress.	27 February 1983 to 23 December 1985	2 years, 299 days	Bomb blast on 30 March 1983 at Bolatubazar, near Hajo, killing 19 persons on the spot & on 7 November 1983 at Guwahati Railway Station platform killing 18 persons on the spot.

Note: **Source: List of Chief Ministers (CM) of Assam. https://www.mapsofindia.com/assam/chief-ministers.html

#Source- Primarily, inter alia, Research Scholar Falguni Parikh's 1988-thesis on "Dynamics of Assam agitation" presented for award of Ph. D degreeto Gujarat University, Ahmedabad http://hdl.handle.net/10603/49072

* In India, President's Rule refers to the suspension of a state government and the imposition of direct rule of the Centre. The central government takes direct control of the state in question and the Governor becomes its constitutional head. The State Legislative Assembly is either dissolved or prorogued.

During the six-long years of Assam agitation, a new kind of violence emerged in Assam – the bomb blast. The new phenomenon of violence reached its peak in the 1983 election year and then nosedived sharply in the following year, 1984, as could be seen from the year-wise data. Between 1979-84 minimum of 471 cases of bomb blasts were reported to the police. Consequently, at least 101 persons reportedly died at various places in Assam, as per the break-up furnished in a tabular format below:

REPORTED BOMB BLASTS IN ASSAM BETWEEN 1979 and 1984		
Year	Number of	
	Bomb Blasts	Persons Killed
1979	4	0
1980	47	8
1981	81	5
1982	39	27
1983	259	55
1984	41	6
Total	471	101

[49]

Interestingly, as the second of two six-month terms of the President's Rule was about to expire on 12th December, Congress (I) managed to form the government in Assam on 6th December 1980, headed by Syeda Anwara Taimur with the help of defection from other political parties. Anwara Taimur was the first Muslim woman Chief Minister of any state in India. The leaders of the Assam agitation greeted the new government with a call for a general strike, calling it a 'government of defectors'. They refused to recognize the Taimur government as legitimate and launched a 13-day satyagraha on 18th December. The 206 days of the Taimur government saw the crackdown on the local press and large-scale deployment of the CRPF, replacing many Assam Police personnel because of their reported support for the agitation. The period also witnessed an increase in the incidence of violence. For instance, in April 1981, Commissioner of Assam's Plains Division, E. S. Parthasarathy, was killed by a terrorist bomb attack in his office at Jorhat. Parthasarathy was well known for his tough measures against the Assam agitation.

However, the Anwara Taimur government fell on 30th June 1981 when the government failed to get the Assam appropriation bill passed by the assembly. Thus, Assam came under the Central rule for 197 days, for the second time. The factional tussle within the Congress (I), which began with the ouster of the Taimur ministry, was resolved for a while, and the Central rule was revoked with the appointment of Keshab Chandra Gogoi as Chief Minister of Assam on 13th January 1982. Taimur proposed Gogoi for the leadership, and erstwhile rival aspirant Hiteshwar Saikia seconded the nomination.

Keshab Chandra Gogoi was an [1]ethnic Assamese, Ahom by caste, another potential weak link in the Assamese formation. But he was in power for only 65 days. That brief period was characterized by less use of force and the release of the senior ethnic Assamese police official arrested by the Taimur government. However, on 9th March 1982, Gogoi had to resign amid a motion of no-confidence vote against his government. Consequently, the President's rule was promulgated in Assam for the third time. The use of force in administering Assam increased under the Central rule. Given the 'presumed unreliability' of the state police forces, paramilitary forces were brought in from the centre and other states. As a result, Guwahati city and all the major towns in the Brahmaputra valley wore more or less the looks of 'armed camps'. The Republic Day celebration on 26th January 1983, which the movement supporters boycotted, turned into a blatant display of military muscle against the citizens. Amid reports that the government was determined to hold the state Assembly elections in Assam by March 1983, the Central government held the twenty-third round of negotiations with the movement leaders in December 1982. In the last of the series of meetings, the government invited the AASU leaders in Delhi to persuade them to accept 1971 as the cut-off year. When the student leaders did not agree, they were all arrested at Gauhati's Borjhar airport as they returned from Delhi. The elections were announced, and the movement of the largest contingent of paramilitary forces ever sent to any state began. [50]

Note: [1]Ethnic Assamese: "The emergence of the term 'ethnic Assamese' suggests a process that Abner Cohen and other anthropologists have described as a shift from an 'elite group' being culturally invisible to become visible – a result of a loss of hegemony," wrote Professor Sanjib Baura in page 125 of his book "India against itself: ASSAM AND THE POLITICS OF NATIONALITY".

The heightened passion of the agitation was not the opportune moment to hold the state election. However, the President's rule promulgated in Assam on 19th March 1982 would complete one year by the middle of March, and the Indira Gandhi government at the Centre had other plans, as revealed by Arun Shourie in the previous chapter on Nellie. The election was to be held on the basis of the electoral rolls prepared in 1979, which had precipitated the Assam movement. In a sense, the election meant a direct challenge to the supporters of the Assam agitation. Apart from sidestepping all the thorny questions of illegal aliens raised by the agitators, the use of four-year-old electoral rolls was indeed problematic since it did not include the voters who had come of age in the preceding four years. Therefore, the organizers of the Assam movement called for a boycott of the election, dubbing it Assam's 'last struggle for survival'. On the other hand, the so-called 'immigrant' communities, comprising mostly genuine Indian citizens and some legal and suspected illegal immigrants, saw in the election an opportunity to elect a government sympathetic to their problems.

It is vital to note here that after the liberation of Bangladesh, Sheikh Munibur Rehaman, while signing the Indira Mujib Pact on 19th March 1972, stated that he would not take back any of the people of East Pakistan who had crossed over to India before 21st March 1971. India's Prime Minister Indira Gandhi agreed to this. Accordingly, the Government of India insisted on 1971 being the cut-off year for identifying illegal immigrants from Bangladesh. However, it was not acceptable to the leaders of the Assam movement. Their demand was 1951 to be the cut-off year. Thus, the holding of the election in the state legislature in 1983 became the focus of a contest between the Central government on the one hand and the Assam movement leaders on the other. The controversy over the issue divided the people of Assam into two distinct groups – supporters and non-supporters of the election. The fallout of the previous two years of Assam agitation also led to fissures in other links of the Assamese subnational formation, notably between the ethnic Assamese and the plains tribe communities. Besides, apart from Congress (I), some opposition parties also contested the election. In areas with significant numbers of both pro and anti-election ethnic groups, violent showdown surfaced. Its pronounced illustration was the massacre in the Nellie cluster of villages on 18th February 1983, which attracted worldwide media attention and international headlines.

One of the most stringent editorial comments in America's The New Republic, *'There are places – the Indian state of Assam is one – where the slaughter of children is a form of political expression'* is a case in point. Professor Sanjib Barua cited it on page xix in the preface of his book, "India against Itself ASSAM AND THE POLITICS OF NATIONALITY". (Emphasis by Subir)

"The extraordinary election of February 1983 was not going to be an election. It was a tussle between the Assamese people and the Central Government to see if the election could be held. In this, the people were the undoubted victors, but at a terrible cost," wrote Retired (Assam Cadre) IPS Officer E. N. Ramhohan in his book (page 31) "Insurgent Frontiers". He then added,

> "More than 6000 people died in the ethnic clashes and the police firing. The election was a gory farce. The party in power had split the population into two groups, the Assamese on one side and the Bengali Hindus and Immigrant Muslims on the other. The Boros were also divided on the issue. The Saraniya Boros, who were Boros who had taken "Sharan" with the Caste Hindus were with the Assamese, while the Boros, who had remained as tribals were for the elections. The Central Intelligence Agencies had done their nefarious work well. They had been building up this divide assiduously during the run-up to the elections. Political leaders of the ruling party also played a role in this, touring the immigrant Muslim and the Boro areas and instigating both the groups against the Assamese."

As mentioned earlier in this chapter, Retired IPS Officer Ramhohan debunked the myth that the dreaded terrorist organization ULFA *was formed on April 7th, 1979, in Sibasagar.* He narrated the election scenario in his own words as follows:

> "The main fallout of the bloodbath of an election was the decision of the extremist wing of the Assam movement to take up arms. The ULFA has always claimed it was formed in 1979. This was not true. The Intelligence Agencies also confirmed this fiction. It was actually formed in 1983 after the brutal and horrifying election forced upon

> the Assamese people. As Inspector General Operations in Assam from 1990, the commencement of Op Bajrang, till February 1993, I interrogated dozens of ULFA cadres, including several top leaders who all told me the 1979 date was notional. The decision to take up arms was made only after the terrible election of February 1983."

The Retired IPS Officer Ramhohan then continued:

> The entire State Government went on strike from February 2nd, the date set for the commencement of coordinated action across the State. Neither the Central nor the State Intelligence agencies had a clue about this. Mobs of five to six thousand people assembled all along the national highway from Sipajhar to Mangaldoi and attempted to set fire to the two wooden bridges on this road. They also gathered on the road from Mangaldoi to Kalaigaon and Tangla and set fire to all the wooden bridges along the route. A mob of five thousand people even attempted to set fire to a concrete bridge near Mangaldoi. The fury of the mob was such that in some places, armed police from the District simply fled from the scene. The CRPF, led by its officers and the Superintendent of Police Tezpur, opened fire at more than a dozen places before the mobs dispersed. It was as if the people had developed a death wish. The day's toll was 22 killed in police firing. At least, that was the count of dead bodies collected after the mobs were dispersed. It was unknown how many dead bodies were carried away by the mobs. The national highway to Tezpur was open, but the road to Kalaigaon and Tangla was cut off. From the next day, the whole of Assam was under a natural curfew. All vehicles ceased operation, all State Government offices closed, and all shops shut down. A deathly silence descended on the land. It was eerie driving on the roads. The roads were deserted. No human being could be seen, but one had the uncanny feeling of being watched as they drove by. The telephone exchanges were taken over by the Army Signals, and the water supply by the MES. Only the hospitals functioned. Throughout the day, reports came in of bridges going up in flames, and all buildings designated as polling booths being set on fire. Reports of ethnic clashes did not surface immediately because they occurred in the interiors, where all communications had been cut off. I do not believe such a situation has been witnessed by any state in the country before or since. The self-imposed curfew lasted for 19 days. The polling took place on the 7th, 14th, and 21st of February 1983.

Assamese mobs attacked Chawalkhowa Chapori on February 7th. In the clashes, over a hundred immigrant Muslims were killed. North of Malgaldoi was a village called Khoirabari. Here, in a cluster of villages lived a couple of hundred Bengali Hindus, who had been settled here in the lands vacated by Bengali Muslims who had gone to East Pakistan in 1947. For years, the Assamese Hindu villages around them had harboured resentment. After communications to Khoirabari were cut off, the Assamese of the neighbouring villages surrounded them and attacked at night. More than a hundred Bengali Hindus were killed. The rest took shelter in the Khoirabari railway station... [53]

In many places like Chawalkhowa Chapori, Khoirabari, Gohpur, and so forth, Nellie-like clashes occurred during this period, resulting in numerous casualties. After four decades of shameful events, their detailed specifics and statistics are not important. Suffice it to say that in the orgy of savagery, the ethnic divisions along which the violence took place varied from place to place. If in the Nellie massacre, the plains tribe Twias and the ethnic Assamese were on the same side fighting the Muslims of Bengali descent, in another area like Gohpur, which witnessed significant violence, the plains Bodos and ethnic Assamese fought each other. Similarly, in other places, the clashes were between Bodos versus Bengali Hindus and Muslims; Bodo tribes versus Bengali Hindus; Mising tribes versus Bengali Hindus and Muslims; ethnic Assamese and native Muslims versus Muslims of Bengali descent; and so forth. A community may be the victim in one place, yet possibly the same community was the aggressor in another. Clearly, the local perceptions toward a voting bloc – whether a community voted or boycotted the election – determined the pattern of the violence depending, of course, upon the respective communities' available muscle power. According to the government, more than 4000 people died in Assam due to election-related violence in 1983. However, non-government reports suggested the number of deaths was more than 7000. [54]

The 1983 Assembly election brought a new Congress (I) government to power in Assam. It was led by Hiteswar Saikia, who had previously defected from Congress (U) in the aftermath of the Assam movement. He served as a member of the Sinha Cabinet from 1972 to 1978, the Taimur Cabinet from 1980 to 1981, and the Gogoi Cabinet in 1982. Hiteswar Saikia, another ethnic Assamese, was Ahom by caste, following in the footsteps of Kesab Chandra Gogoi. He assumed office on February 27th, 1983, just a fortnight after the infamous Nellie massacre on February 18th, 1983. During his tenure, the

Hiteswar Saikia Government faced a contest between the state and the masterminds of the movement.

The selection of an Ahom Chief Minister for the second consecutive term was significant, as there was a widespread perception that the Assam movement garnered its strongest support from the ethnic Assamese 'upper caste,' and the Ahoms were considered a distinct ethnic Assamese caste. Saikia's immediate priority was to earnestly provide relief and rehabilitation to the large number of victims of election-related violence. Consequently, he formed a broad-based ministry wherein representation from various communities was largely ensured. During this time, the leadership of the movement temporarily called off their protest agitations. However, notably, they refused to acknowledge the legitimacy of the Saikia government and continued to boycott it and its ministers, labelling the government as 'illegal' and denouncing the election as fraudulent.

The Saikia government undertook a restructuring of the entire police force, which was reported to have played a biased role in handling riots in Assam. Through new measures, the government succeeded in mitigating collective violence in Assam. The new government's approach to addressing the agitation combined political manoeuvring and coercion in harmony. It aimed to diminish support for the Assam agitation by favouring groups that constituted the weaker links in the Assamese sub-national structure, already strained by various factors, particularly the numerous incidents of widespread election-related violence. Furthermore, since Anwara Taimur's election as Chief Minister, there had been indications that a section of ethnic Assamese Muslims was reconsidering their participation and support for the Assam agitation. The significant number of Muslim victims in election-related violence, coupled with national and international coverage portraying it as targeting Muslims, distanced ethnic Assamese Muslims from backing the Assam agitation.

By mid-1984, the government became optimistic about reaching a negotiated settlement and extended an invitation to the movement leaders to resume dialogues to break the deadlock. The All Assam Students' Union (AASU) responded positively to the government's outreach and agreed to return to the negotiating table. Several factors contributed to the change of heart on both sides.

a) As foreign countries almost completely encompass the seven states in the northeastern region of India, and centrally located Assam serves as the gateway for the other six states, safeguarding peace and tranquillity in this crucial region, especially in Assam, is always strategically vital for any central government worth its salt. Thus, the

Union Government of India did not want the prevailing stalemate in Assam to continue for long.

b) Although AASU's support base had significantly eroded by that time, the students still retained many followers among certain sections of people in Assam, prompting the government to consider it a powerful force to be reckoned with in the state. As the agitation persisted for a considerable time, an expeditious compromise with the movement leaders became a priority for the Indian government.

c) Given that the movement at that time had lost much of its momentum and the leaders were not in a position to adhere very rigidly to their earlier stance, the Indira Gandhi government in Delhi felt that it was the most opportune moment to resume dialogues with the AASU leaders to reach an understanding, facilitating the return to normalcy in Assam. On the other hand, by winning a two-thirds majority in the 1980 parliamentary election, the Indira Gandhi government was in an advantageous position to negotiate a compromise from a position of strength.

d) In contrast, the AASU leadership, despite their utmost efforts, had already failed to prevent the holding of the 1983 Assembly election in Assam. Congress succeeded in forming a new government in the state, headed by Hiteswar Saikia. This outcome frustrated one section of the movement leadership, leading to introspection on the course the movement should take in the future.

e) The Nellie massacre and other killings during the period generated unfavourable public sentiment, and the growing right-wing influence in the movement upset a large section of the organizers. Internal dissensions eventually arose mainly over these two issues, leading to a breakup of the AASU. Furthermore, these dual issues severely affected the secular credentials of the leadership, resulting in the erosion of their support base and mass response to peaceful protest actions. The emerging circumstances forced the movement leaders to suspend the agitation activities and reflect.

f) Furthermore, most prominent student leaders felt that they could not and should not remain as students for an extended period. By then, some had already spent a decade as post-graduate students. The AASU executive body and various office bearers completed five years in 1984, though they were elected for one year only. Moreover, within the leadership, some questioned the advisability of boycotting and opposing the 1983 election. Some felt that their actions inadvertently helped Congress win the election easily. Several of them believed that the movement's leadership should have participated in the election, as they had a good chance of winning a substantial number of seats, if not the majority.

g) Later on, some leaders also developed apprehensions that the movement would likely meet a natural death soon unless they initiated a rapid paradigm shift in the course of the Assam agitation. [55]

It's noteworthy that a petition was filed at the Supreme Court of India before the 1983 election, seeking a stay on the election, but the apex Court refused to intervene as the election process had already commenced. After the election, another petition was filed at the Supreme Court to declare the 1983 election null and void. The local Assamiya press speculated that the Supreme Court verdict might bring down the Saikia Government. The movement leadership were quite optimistic about a judgment in their favour nullifying the election of the Saikia government. However, the Supreme Court judgment went against their last hope of ousting the Saikia Government from power, severely demoralizing most of the movement leaders.

The emerging situation compelled the leadership to seek a solution more intensely than before. Yet, they were in no position to accept 1971 as the cut-off year, as repeatedly suggested by Congress (I) and other political parties since 1979. Hence, they needed a solution other than a rigid 1971 cut-off year for detecting foreigners in Assam. They now prepared themselves to be flexible in their demand, considering 1951 or 1961 as the cut-off year.

Still, the Government of India and the movement leadership, in the post-1983 election scenario, learned from the earlier experience the futility of talks without some initial preparatory work. Thus, both parties needed to be more cautious in their approach. Several individuals close to the leadership of the agitation and the government acted as intermediaries between the two sides. Even the service of an [1]ICSSR-financed Center was utilized in this connection. It ostensibly organized a seminar in Chandigarh, with significant government spending, for the leaders, where other academics sympathetic to and connected with the movement were invited as guests to participate actively. The intermediaries made full use of the services offered by the seminar. Subsequently, another follow-up seminar was reportedly held at Gauhati University, in which an adviser of the Prime Minister participated. While academics were presenting papers at the seminar, talks were held between the movement leadership and the Prime Minister's adviser. The student leaders continued their informal talks with the Government of India but refused to recognize Assam's Saikia Government. They communicated with the Government of India through the Governor or the Chief Secretary of Assam whenever needed.

[1]Indian Council of Social Science Research

During those days, amidst severe social boycotts, the Saikia government in Assam also gradually made some inroads among a section of the leaders and supporters of the agitation. Consequently, a segment of the Asamiya bourgeois press decided to compromise with the state government to secure various concessions. Their tone of reporting started to change. However, most of the movement leaders still refused to toe the line, and the stalemate with the state government persisted.

On the other side, following disturbing political developments in Punjab, Indian politics underwent a radical transformation. Mrs. Indira Gandhi was assassinated on October 31, 1984, at her Safdarjung Road residence in New Delhi by her bodyguards. Over the next four days, a series of organized pogroms, known as the Anti-Sikh Riots, ensued in retaliatory violence against Sikhs. After Mrs Indira Gandhi's assassination, her son, Rajiv Gandhi, was sworn in as a stop-gap arrangement to the post of India's Prime Minister. In the mid-term poll that followed in December 1984, Mrs Gandhi's Congress party won a landslide victory, securing 404 out of 516 seats where elections could be held. The voting in Assam and Punjab was delayed until 1985 due to the prevailing unfavourable environment. As anticipated, Rajiv Gandhi became the elected Prime Minister of India.

Despite securing a landslide victory, Rajiv Gandhi's inexperience in handling politics in the swiftly changing scenario after Mrs Gandhi's assassination, especially in Punjab and Assam, prompted the Government of India to reconsider its strategy. This led to the signing of the Rajiv-Longowal Accord for Punjab on July 24, 1985. Consequently, the Akali Dal came to power in Punjab through an election that followed the accord. However, the other signatory, Harcharan Singh Longowal, was assassinated, and an ad-hoc arrangement was made in Punjab as per the accord.

The Punjab situation and its resultant crisis exerted added political pressure on the Government of India to seek an immediate settlement of the outstanding issues with Assam student leaders. Consequently, building on at least thirty rounds of talks between the agitation leaders and the central government during Mrs Gandhi's tenure, Rajiv Gandhi, after assuming office as Prime Minister of India, formed a working group of top bureaucrats to resolve the imbroglio stemming from the Assam agitation. After deliberations, the negotiators concluded that the movement leaders might accept 1971 as the cut-off year, with the base year for citizenship set at 1966.

Nonetheless, Assam Chief Minister Hiteswar Saikia believed that no accord was necessary to restore normalcy in the state. However, Prime Minister Rajiv Gandhi felt that some settlement had to be reached to address a demand that still garnered some support. Despite Saikia's efforts to thwart it, Prime Minister Rajiv Gandhi persisted in pursuing an accord. Notably, days before the two parties signed the memorandum of understanding, Hiteswar Saikia set up camp in New Delhi to closely monitor the proceedings. After all, the signing of the accord would mean the downfall of his government. However, negotiating officials from the government side and the team of AASU-AAGSP members maintained absolute secrecy about the negotiations, keeping both the Chief Minister and the Governor of Assam out of the loop.

As negotiations continued, the differences between the agitation leaders and the central government representatives narrowed considerably. The final obstacle to a negotiated settlement with the agitation leaders, however, was the AASU's demand for the immediate dissolution of the incumbent Saikia government, which they deemed illegitimate, having not been chosen by the majority of Assamese people. Finally, the government of India relented on the condition that a caretaker government must be allowed, as it was a constitutional obligation until the Assam assembly poll was held. Thus, the last barrier to a negotiated settlement with the agitation leaders was removed.

On August 13, 1985, the Indian Home Ministry hastily summoned all the executive members of AASU and AAGSP for "a detailed and broad-based discussion on the Assam problem". The first group, consisting of eighteen members, arrived in Delhi around 5 PM on August 14, accompanied by a Central Intelligence Officer, State Chief Secretary P. P. Trivedi, and Hiranya Kumar Bhattacharyya, the IPS Officer of the 1958 batch. Bhattacharyya's vigilance over the electoral rolls of the Mangaldoi Parliamentary constituency as the DIG (Border Police) during the Golap Borbora-led Janata Party regime in the state in 1978-79 had catalyzed the Assam agitation, as discussed earlier in this chapter.

This group waited at the BSF guest house in Tigri for the arrival of another group of six, including Prafulla Kumar Mahanta and Bhrigu Phukan, who had been in the national capital since August 9, negotiating with Government of India representatives. Later in the evening of August 14, another Indian Air Force Flight brought AASU executive member Zoinath (Joynath) Sarma and Bharat Narah, Chief Convenor and Deputy of AASU's voluntary force, Swaccha Sevak Bahini (SSB).

The team of Mananta, Phukan, and the four others returned to the guest house with the final draft of the Accord after spending the day at the Union Home Ministry negotiating a mutual settlement. On August 14, the negotiating team, along with home ministry officials, pressed Prafulla Kumar Mahanta, Bhrigu Phukan, and others throughout the day to reach an agreement since Prime Minister Rajiv Gandhi had decided to announce it in his Independence Day speech at the Red Fort the next morning. Notably, Rajiv Gandhi reportedly appeared to meet the AASU delegation only when Union Home Secretary R. D. Pradhan took the final documents (a Memorandum of Understanding, popularly known as the Assam Accord 1985) for his approval late on the night of August 14-15, 1985.

Upon the return of the 6-member team of Agitation leaders to the BSF guest house, deliberations ensued among all AASU and AAGSP members present. Some members disagreed with a few clauses, particularly the cut-off date of March 24, 1971, which would distinguish foreigners from Indian residents in Assam, an exclusive provision for the state. However, dissenting members were informed that there was no further room for negotiation.

On the morning of August 15, 1985, Prime Minister Rajiv Gandhi, in his inaugural Independence Day address to the nation from the historic Red Fort, announced the formal understanding reached with the movement leaders of Assam. With this declaration, the 6-year-long Assam agitation finally ended on August 15, 1985. [56] [57]

The memorandum of settlement, commonly known as the Assam Accord 1985, signed between representatives of the Government of India and the leaders of the Assam Movement, is reproduced below:

MEMORANDUM OF SETTLEMENT

1. The government has always been deeply concerned about finding a satisfactory solution to the issue of foreigners in Assam. The All Assam Students Union (AASU) and the All Assam Gana Sangram Parishad (AAGSP) have also expressed their eagerness to find such a solution.

2. The AASU, in their Memorandum dated February 2, 1980, presented to the late Prime Minister Smt. Indira Gandhi conveyed their profound apprehensions regarding the ongoing influx of foreign nationals into Assam and the concerns about its adverse effects on the state's political, social, cultural, and economic life.

3. Fully understanding the genuine concerns of the people of Assam, the then Prime Minister initiated a dialogue with the AASU/AAGSP. Subsequently, talks were held at the Prime Minister's and Home Minister's levels during the period 1980-83. Several rounds of informal talks were conducted in 1984, with formal discussions resuming in March 1985.

4. Considering all aspects of the problem, including constitutional and legal provisions, international agreements, national commitments, and humanitarian considerations, it has been decided to proceed as follows:

Foreigners Issue:

5.1. For purpose of detection and deletion of foreigners, 1.1.1966 shall be (Sd/- Biraj Sharma) the base date and year.

5.2. All persons who came to Assam prior to. 1.1.1966, including those (Sd/- P.K. Mahanta) amongst them whose names appeared on the electoral rolls used in 1967 elections, shall be regularised.

5.3. Foreigners who came to Assam after 1.1.1966 (inclusive) and upto (Sd/- B.K. Phukan) 24th March, 1971 shall be detected in accordance with the provisions of the Foreigners Act, 1946 and Foreigners (Tribunals) Order 1964.

5.4. Names of foreigners so detected will be deleted from the electoral rolls in force. Such persons will be required to register themselves before the Registration Officers of the respective districts in accordance with the provisions of the Registration of Foreigners Act, 1939 and the Registration of Foreigners Rules, 1939.

5.5. For this purpose, Government of India will undertake suitable strengthening of the governmental machinery.

5.6. On the expiry of a period of ten year following the date of detection, the names of all such persons which have been deleted from the electoral rolls shall be restored.

5.7. All persons who were expelled, earlier, but have since re-entered illegally into Assam, shall be expelled.

5.8. Foreigners who came to Assam on or after March 25, 1971 shall continue to be detected, deleted and expelled in accordance with law. Immediate and practical steps shall be taken to expel such foreigners.

5.9. The Government will give due consideration to certain difficulties expressed by the AASU/AAGSP regarding the implementation of the illegal Migrants (Determination by Tribunals) Act, 1983.

Safeguards and Economic Development :

6. Constitutional, legislative and administrative safeguards, as may

(Sd/- Biraj Sharma) be appropriate, shall be provided to protect, preserve and promote the cultural, social linguistic identity and heritage of the Assamese people.

7. The Government take this opportunity to renew their (Sd/-P.K. Mahanta) commitment for the speedy all round economic development of (Sd/-B.K. Phukan) Assam, so as to improve the standard of living of the people. Special emphasis will be placed on education and science & technology through establishment of national institutions.

Others Issues :

8.1. The Government will arrange for the issue of citizenship certificates in future only by the authorities of the Central Government.

8.2. Specific complaints that may be made by the AASU/AAGSP about irregular issuance of Indian Citizenship Certificates (ICC) will be looked into.

9.1. The international border shall be made secure against future infiltration by erection of physical barriers like walls. Barbed wire fencing and other obstacles at appropriate places Patrolling by security forces on land and riverine routes all along international border shall be adequately intensified. In order to further strengthen the security arrangements. To prevent effectively future infiltration, an adequate number of check posts shall be set up.

9.2. Besides the arrangements mentioned above an keeping in view security considerations, a road all along the international border shall be constructed so as to facilitate patrolling by security forces. Land between border and the road would be kept free of human habitation, wherever possible. Riverine patrolling along the international border would be intensified. All effective measure would be adopted to prevent infiltrators crossing or attempting to cross the international border.

10. It will be ensured that relevant laws for prevention of encroachment of government lands an lands in tribal belts an blocks are strictly enforced and unauthorised encroachers evicted as laid down under such laws.

11. It will be ensured that the relevant law restricting acquisition of immovable property by foreigners in Assam is strictly enforced.

12. It will be ensured that Birth and Death Registers are duly maintained.

Restoration of Normalcy :

13. The All Assam Students Union (AASU) and All Assam Gana

Sangram Parishad (AAGSP) call off the agitation, assure full co-operation and dedicate themselves towards the development of the country.

(Sd/- Biraj Sharma)   (Sd/- P.K. Mahanta)   (Sd/-B.K. Phukan)

14. The Central and the State Government have agreed to :-

(a) Review with sympathy and withdraw cases of disciplinary action taken against employees in the context of the agitation and to ensure that there is no victimization.

(b) Frame a scheme for ex-gratia payment to next of kin of those who killed in the course of the agitation.

(c) Give sympathetic consideration to proposal for relaxation of upper age limit for employment in public services in Assam, having regard to exceptional situation that prevailed in holding of academic and competitive examinations, etc. in the context of agitation in Assam.

(d) Undertake review of detention cases, if any, as well as cases against persons charged with criminal offences in connection with the agitation, except those charge with commission of heinous offences.

(e) Consider withdrawal of the prohibitory orders/notifications in force, if any.

1.5. The Ministry of Home Affairs will be the nodal Ministry for the implementation of the above.

Signed/-
(P.K. Mahanta)
President
All Assam Students Union

Signed/-
(R.D. Pradhan)
Home Secretary)
Govt. of India

Signed/-
(B.K. Phukan)
General Secretary, All Assam Students Union

Signed/- Signed/-
(Biraj Sharma) Smt. P.P. Trivedi)
Convenor Chief Secretary
All Assam Gana Sangram Parishad Govt. of Assam

In the presence of
Singed/-
(RAJIV GANHI)
PRIME MINISTER OF INDIA

Date : 15th August, 1985
Place : New Delhi.

1. Election Commission will be requested to ensure preparation of fair electoral rolls.
2. Time for submission of claims and objections will be extended by 30 days, subject to this being consistent with the Election Rules.
3. The Election Commission will be requested send Central Observers.

Signed/-
HOME SECRETARY

1. Oil refinery will be established in Assam
2. Central Government will render full assistance to the state Government in their efforts to re-open :-
(i) Ashok Paper Mill.   (ii) Jute Mills
3. I. .I. T. Will be set up in Assam.

AGP.318/15 I.A.A. -3000-1/10/2015 **[58]**

In fine, the above Accord stipulated, among other things, that:

a) All those foreigners who had entered Assam between 1951 and 1961 were to be given full citizenship, including the right to vote.

b) Those who entered Assam after 1971 were to be deported.

c) The entrants between 1961 and 1971 were to be denied voting rights for ten years but would enjoy all other citizenship rights.

d) A parallel package for the economic development of Assam, including a second oil refinery, a paper mill, and an institute of technology (IIT), was also worked out.

e) The central government also promised to provide legislative and administrative safeguards to protect the cultural, social, and linguistic identity and heritage of the "Assamese people," as per clause 6 of the Assam Accord reproduced above.

Strangely enough, the legislative and administrative safeguards the central government promised to the "Assamese people" have become a contentious nomenclature for implementing this vital clause 6 of the Assam Accord. Instead of addressing the age-old grievances of the Assamese people, the interpretation of the term "Assamese people" per se in the Assam Accord has become controversial and debatable. Former Professor of English Literature at Assam's Dibrugarh University, Udayon Misra, in his book "Burden of History: Assam and the Partition – Unresolved Issues", among other things, judiciously broached this topic, hitherto unsettled for nearly four decades after signing the Accord on 15th August 1985. The following couple of paragraphs are quoted from that book for the readers to grasp the controversy surrounding the definition of "Assamese people":

> "Even though the rivalry between the valleys (Brahmaputra Valley and Barak Valley) seems to have subsided and the earlier antagonism between Assamese Hindus and Bengali Hindus has given way to greater understanding, cooperation, and some degree of assimilation, the issue of language continues to occupy central space. Assamese nationalism, primarily language-based and largely dependent on the acceptance of the Assamese language by Bengali Muslim immigrants for the survival of its majority status, still occasionally exhibits anxiety about its continued hegemony. This explains its reaction towards the Bengali language. Though the issue regarding the status of the Assamese language as the official language of the Brahmaputra valley appears to be settled, given the clear majority that Assamese speakers possess over other communities, there seems to be a lurking fear in the Assamese mind that the present situation could change radically if, in some future census, a

substantial section of the immigrant Muslims decide to declare Bengali as their mother tongue. Hence, on the eve of every census enumeration, there is invariably a public debate on this issue, and appeals are often made to the immigrant Muslim community to continue their 'support' for the Assamese language. In the final analysis, it may be said that the status of the Assamese language remains an unresolved issue, despite the fact that pre-Partition politics centred on the idea of a linguistically homogeneous Assamese homeland. With the number of Assamese speakers decreasing with every census, the crisis centred on the linguistic identity of the Assamese is certainly going to deepen, and language politics, which has always superseded religious politics in the state, is bound to take on a new edge.

Another major unresolved issue from the pre-partition days is that of Assamese identity. Just as in the 1940s, in the last two decades or so, there have been acrimonious debates both in the state's public space and in the legislature over the parameters defining Assamese identity. The issue of Assamese identity is becoming more complicated with increasing demographic changes affecting the composition of the state's population, evident in exchanges between members of the Legislative Assembly from the 1990s to the present day. Not only is the question of 'infiltrants' staunchly denied by a section of the members representing immigrant interests, but the very term 'Assamese people' has also become controversial and debatable. It may be recalled that the Assam Accord, which, in one of its clauses, referred to steps calling for the preservation of the identity of the 'Assamese people'. Different plains tribal communities of Assam, starting with the Bodos, raised questions about the definition of the 'Assamese people' and insisted that they did not come under that purview. Other plains tribal communities followed suit, and soon the definition of 'Assamese people' became clouded in controversy. This controversy was reflected in the Legislative Assembly debates, and the government of Assam even had to set up a committee to determine who really constituted the 'Assamese people'. The Asom Sahitya Sabha, in consultation with the Sanmilita Sahitya Manch, made up of several ethnic literary organizations, did not help in resolving the problem because several of the ethnic groups refused to accept it, while some Assamese nationalist organizations felt that by fixing the cut-off date for defining the Assamese, the Sabha had included all immigrants who had gained citizenship up to March 1971. This, many observers felt, distorted the definition of 'indigenous' in the context of the Assam Accord. Moreover, a debate started over the identification of authentic 'indigenous' languages. But, despite the ambiguities and confusions centred on the Sabha's definition, the fact emerged that in any attempt to define an Assamese, the stage had been reached when the immigrant neo-Assamese could not be left out of the ambit – even if this meant alienating the ethnic/plains tribal nationalities. The Sabha was merely accepting the transformation that was taking place with the Assamese nationality. This matter also came to occupy a central place in the negotiations between the All Assam Students' Union and the Centre over the implementation of the Assam Accord. [59]

Anyway, after signing the Assam Accord, as per the directives of the Congress High Command, the incumbent Assam Chief Minister, Hiteswar Saikia, advised the Assam Governor to dissolve the legislature and order a fresh poll. However, he continued leading the caretaker government until the 1985 Assembly election result was declared. Thereafter, Saikia became the leader of the opposition in the Assembly.

Most of the AASU's prominent leaders officially left the Students Union to form a new political party, Asom Gana Parishad (AGP), on October 14th, 1985, with its president Prafulla Kumar Mahanta, who became the Chief President of the Presidium. Two regional parties, AJD and PLP, also merged with the new political party. The new formation of the AGP declared itself a "regional party with a national outlook." However, the strength of AGP fundamentally depended on the workers and the organizations of the AASU. However, after the exit of the senior leaders, the members of the AASU formed a fresh executive body with new office bearers after a gap of more than six years. In the 1985 Assam election that soon followed, it became very difficult to distinguish between the AGP and AASU. In the election to the state Legislature, AGP secured 64 seats in the House of 126. It also received support from 7 independent MLAs, raising its strength to 71 in effect. Thus, the first AGP government in Assam was sworn in, with Prafulla Kumar Mahanta as the Chief Minister. [60]

Significantly, two of AASU's former presidents have already become Assam's Chief Minister. As mentioned above, Prafulla Kumar Mahanta headed the state government from 1985 to 1990; and from 1996 to 2001 again. Similarly, Sarbananda Sonowal was AASU president from 1992 to 1999, and after that, he became a member of the AGP. In 2011, Sonowal joined the Bharatiya Janata Party (BJP). He was selected as the CM candidate of the BJP for the 2016 Assam Assembly Election. After he won on May 19th, 2016, from

Assam's Majuli Constituency, Sarbananda Sonowal formed the first BJP government in the state and became the Chief Minister of Assam. At present, Sonowal is a Member of Parliament in the Rajya Sabha from Assam and a Union Cabinet Minister in the Narendra Modi-led BJP Government in New Delhi.

Dr. Himanta Biswa Sarma succeeded Sarbananda Sonowal as the 15th Chief Minister of Assam and took office on May 10th, 2021. He defeated the three-time sitting MLA Bhrigu Kumar Phukan, the AGP leader, and a former AASU General Secretary, to be elected to the Assam Legislative Assembly from the Jalukbari constituency for the first time in 2001. He has since been representing the people of the same Assembly constituency for five consecutive terms, beginning in 2001, 2006, 2011, 2016, and 2021. On the first three occasions, Sarma was a candidate of the Indian National Congress and then contested as the BJP candidate for the next two terms. [61]

Incidentally, Jalukbari is considered the state's intellectual nerve centre where Guwahati University, once known as the epicentre of the Assam movement, is situated. The Assembly constituency of Jalukbari is a segment of the Gauhati Lok Sabha constituency. Today, it's a part of greater Gauhati (the present name of Guwahati), the most important city not only of Assam but also entire northeast India. Himanta Biswa Sarma's rare feat of repeatedly representing this vital constituency of Assam for more than two decades speaks volumes about his popularity among the people.

On December 10th, 2020, Himanta Biswa Sarma urged the government to reveal the classified documents that contained secret communication between the centre and state government during the Assam movement, which remained a burning issue in Assam and Northeast India. At that time, he was the Minister of Assam Accord Implementation in the Sarbananda Sonowal ministry. In his speech, the (then) Minister of Assam Accord Implementation said that many hidden secrets at the government level were yet to come out in the public domain. Sarma was speaking at the Tathyakosh (data book) launch on Assam agitation in the presence of the (then) Chief Minister Sonowal, reported THE TIMES OF INDIA on December 11th, 2020, under the caption "Secret documents during Assam Agitation must be out: Himanta Biswa Sarma":

> "To date, we know about the Assam Agitation, mostly from the perspective of those who took part in it and the communication between the protesting organizations and the government. But efforts must be made in the subsequent parts of the Tathyakosh volumes that will be compiled at the initiative of the state government to bring to light the then-government strategies to

counter the movement by collecting the relevant documents from the central government through tools such as RTI," said Himanta, showing curiosity to know the counter-strategy of Indira Gandhi, the then PM.

"For an objective and holistic study of the Assam Agitation and its impact on the state, classified information must be declassified," he added.

"We saw the agitation from the agitators' perspective. But what went on inside the Assam secretariat in Dispur at that time, people still don't know. How the government wanted to quell the movement, they planned to find a solution through talks, but the level of sincerity on the part of the government is still in the dark. On what ground 1951 became 1971 (the cut-off date for detection of illegal foreigners from Assam), people should know."

Himanta Biswa Sarma was speaking on December 10, 2020, when the Assam government, along with parties cutting across political lines, observed Martyrs' Day to commemorate the sacrifice of agitators of the AASU-led anti-foreigners' movement. [62]

Coming from a person of the stature of Himanta Biswa Sarma and given his past and present credentials, what the current Chief Minister of Assam said in his speech on the solemn occasion of the Martyrs' Day was momentous, indeed! Now that Sarbananda Sonowal is a minister in the Union Cabinet and Himanta Biswa Sarma is Assam's Chief Minister, more revelations on what went on inside under the guise of the administration at that time of the 6-long years of the Assam agitation are expected in due course of time.

Any material discussion about the Assam agitation wouldn't be complete without a particular mention of Hiranya Kumar Bhattacharyya, the 1958-batch IPS officer. His report on "illegal immigrants" in the state is believed to have created a flutter that eventually started the 6-long years of Assam agitation. The butterfly effect in chaos theory may be an appropriate metaphor for IPS officer Bhattacharyya's act, which is often looked at as having given a fillip to the Assam agitation against 'foreigners'. It culminated in the signing of the Assam Accord – reproduced earlier in this chapter.

Note: The Butterfly Effect is a property of chaotic systems (such as the atmosphere) by which small changes in initial conditions can lead to large-scale and unpredictable variations in the system's future state. For example, a butterfly flaps its wings in Toronto, leading to unpredictable changes in Tokyo weather a few days later. It could be a typical hypothetical instance for the easiest understanding of the phrase 'the butterfly effect.'

During the Assam agitation, Bhattacharyya was arrested and detained twice, in 1981 and 1983, on alleged charges of his support to the agitation under the

National Security Act (NSA). During his first stint in jail, he was dismissed from his post in the police force. Bhattacharyya contested his dismissal and won the case in 1996 after a long court battle. By then, he had crossed the retirement age and couldn't get his job back. The court reinstated his status as a retired IPS officer with all benefits.

Earlier, during the 1971 Bangladesh War of Liberation fought by the people of what was then known as East Pakistan, Bhattacharyya trained many of its Bengali freedom fighters, called the Mukti Bahini guerrillas, to prepare them to fight against the West Pakistani Military forces. "It was a secret affair; there are no official records of it with the Indian government, but those who trained certainly kept a record of it," according to the retired IPS officer. Anyway, in March 2013, when Bhattacharyya became 84 years old, Sheikh Hasina, the Prime Minister of Bangladesh, in recognition of his spirited role in their country's struggle for independence in the early 1970s, awarded him with the Friends of Liberation War.

In an interview Delhi-based journalist Sangeeta Barooah Pisharoty circulated on The Wire website on July 4, 2018, Hiranya Kumar Bhattacharyya reportedly said, among other things, the deportation of those found to be non-citizens is no longer an option, adding, "Even a dignitary no less than the Pope has asked for the sympathetic treatment of the migrants. The whole issue is a human issue, after all." He authored several books, which include Operation Lebensraum – Illegal Migration from Bangladesh (Bloomsbury). It puts the lens on the perennial issue of cross-border immigration in Assam from a "global" perspective. His other book, Betrayal of North East: The Arrested Voice, published in English in 2015, is a testimony of that personal struggle. [63]

On April 5, 2021, Hiranya Kumar Bhattacharyya breathed his last at 86. Describing him, inter alia, as 'The man of steel' and 'a live wire of personality', The Assam Tribune, dated April 14, 2021, remembered the retired IPS officer of Assam for his 'sound knowledge of professional matters, his tactfulness, and his ability to judge criminal behaviour that made him professionally very successful'.

The ensuing paragraphs, reproduced from the book, "Betrayal of North East: The Arrested Voice" by Hiranya Kumar Bhattacharyya, a retired officer of the Indian Police Service, cast a shimmering light upon the intriguing evolutions surrounding the six-year-long happenings of the Assam agitation. Should the revelation echoed hereunder prove genuine, it is indeed a bombshell of exposure on the legendary Assam Movement!

"Having failed in all efforts at bamboozling, Indira Gandhi ultimately visited Gauhati on 12 April 1980, and this time she harped upon a humane approach to the problem and stuck to 1971 as the cut-off date for the purpose of deletion while the movement leadership remained unyielding. Mrs Gandhi did refer to some international obligations, keeping in mind the clauses of the Indira-Mujib Pact, which she had signed without ever taking the country's Parliament or the people into confidence. However, it must be admitted to her credit that in the late evening, of the same day, she did have a little rethinking after having secret discussions with high officials, including the present scribe. Governor LP Singh also participated in the discussion with a positive approach. It was decided to place a fresh proposal before the AASU executive committee, which was meeting the next day. The fresh proposal offered either 31 December 1966 or 1/1/1967, inter alia, as the cut-off date for the purpose of identification. The author, as directed, met the AASU executive committee members the next day along with his staff officer Premkanta Mananta at 10 am but failed to convince the executive committee about the reasonableness of the new proposal and the benefits that would have accrued therefrom. They simply would not budge an inch from 1951 as the cut-off date. If accepted, 1967 as the cut-off date would not have harmed Assam's cause because the PIP scheme was in full operation till 1969 and the success of this scheme hardly needs any elaboration. We failed to understand this adamant attitude at that time; but as the years rolled on and with the unfolding of the subsequent political scenario, it became crystal clear that the then-AASU leaders had a deeper design in lengthening the Assam Movement. It was obvious that with a settlement arrived at, there would be fresh elections in Assam, and if an agreement was made in 1980 or before these student leaders attained the age of 25, they would not be constitutionally qualified to contest in the election. As such, the movement had to be continued until they were eligible to contest. In fact, as it transpired subsequently, the question of solving the foreign infiltration problem was never uppermost in their minds. They had led the entire people of Assam up the garden path, and once they came to power, they dropped the issue like a hot potato on one or the other plea. There were other adverse fallouts also from the rejection of 1967 as the cut-off date in 1980. Firstly, the catastrophic election of 1983 would not have taken place and secondly, the possibility of passing the controversial IMTD Act in 1983 would not have arisen. Above all, being what she was, Indira Gandhi would have honoured and implemented an agreement if it had been arrived at in 1980 on the basis of her latest offer whereas the Assam Accord signed in 1985 is yet to be fully implemented, let alone solve the foreigners' problem. The same set of student leaders made a turn of 180 degrees and accepted 1971 as the cut-off date while signing the Assam Accord on the night of 14 August 1985! For, they had by then attained the age of 25 to make themselves eligible for contesting in elections. What followed next was the historic letting down of an entire people. Still more mysterious, if not intriguing, is the fact that the AAGSP leaders or its executive committee were not taken into confidence while finalizing the draft of the Accord. In fact, some of the AAGSP leaders refused to attend the Accord-signing ceremony and the party thrown by Rajiv Gandhi and instead, left for Guwahati by the first available flight.

What has just been highlighted should suffice to explain why until August 1985, none of the talks held with New Delhi, particularly during Mrs. Gandhi's regime, succeeded. On the other hand, because of such obduracy generated by the absolute self-interests of the handful of student leaders, the people of Assam had to undergo untold sufferings and inhuman atrocities for a long period of six years which witnessed all sorts of repressive measures, including 'community punitive tax', detention without trial, physical torture, and more than 850 deaths resulting from Police firings besides a few thousand killings caused during the communal riots of 1983." [64]

* * * * * * *

Chapter 13.

IMTD Act of 1983

In a rare case in independent India's judicial history, a three-member bench of the highest Court of our country, the Supreme Court (SC), comprising Chief Justice Ramesh Chandra Lahoti, Justice G. P. Mathur, and Justice P. K. Balasubramanyan, pronounced a judgment on 12th July 2005 that struck off from our statute book a law earlier passed by our elected representatives in the parliament twenty years back in 1983, considering various aspects of the situation prevailing in the country during those days. The SC directed that all the tribunals constituted under the IMDT Act would "cease to function" with immediate effect as the Parent Act has been declared unconstitutional. Cases pending before the tribunals would stand transferred to tribunals under the Foreigners Act, the Court said. Thus, the apex court, restoring the status quo ante, brought back the application of the law based on a colonial piece of legislation enacted in 1946 – just one year before the Indians showed the door to the British colonial rulers.

According to the restored law, the onus of proof rested not with the accuser or the police but with the accused if complaints were lodged against them as suspected foreigners. Earlier proceedings were drawn against a certain section of people, which gave rise to a suspicion that the accusers' complaints were driven by the ulterior motive of harassing genuine Indian citizens. Consequently, in 1983, our elected representatives in the parliament considered it imperative to enact a new law to protect these people from such unfair actions. Nevertheless, the Supreme Court of India found the new law of 1983 ultra vires, struck it off, and reinstated the application of the old colonial law that assigned the burden of proof to the person "suspected" of being a foreigner. The judgment virtually endorsed the reversal of a fundamental principle of law that an "accused" is presumed innocent until proven guilty, as envisaged in the Universal Declaration of Human Rights (UDHR) of the United Nations.

Thus, the onus of proving innocence returned to the accused – from the accuser or the police– paving the way for THE GAME CALLED NRC to take place that jolted the whole of Assam like never before. Assam's seasoned Journalist, Mrinal Talukdar, wrote a book with that title and, in its epilogue, rhetorically wrote, inter alia:

"When India will one day realize that almost 9 million people of Assam had moved from one place to another to prove their citizenships, individually spent shocking amounts of money to procure the long lost papers needed to prove their citizenship and in the process ruining thousands of families and killing many, besides spending Rs. 1,500 crores of taxpayer's money to make a list of citizens which no one is (eventually) interested in, they will look up to Assam and its inhabitants as **optimists of the highest order or the greatest idiots in human history.**" [1] (Emphasis by Subir)

The entire residents of Assam had to do this because the [1]onus of proving their citizenship by then returned to the individual inhabitant as per the Supreme Court Judgment dated 12th July 2005 on Sarbananda Sonowal's Writ Petition (Civil) 131 of 2000. [2] The government could dictate the people to do it because the colonial law, THE FOREIGNERS ACT 1946, got a new lease of life consequent upon the Supreme Court upholding Sonowal's Petition. Otherwise, as Mrinal Talukdar satirically termed it, THE GAME CALLED NRC wouldn't have been possible, at least in texts and textures that the people of Assam had been subjected to.

Note: [1]Article 9. Burden of proof, according to THE FOREIGNERS ACT, 1946 reads:

"If in any case not falling under section 8, any question arises with reference to this Act or any order made or direction given thereunder, whether any person is or is not a foreigner or is or is not a foreigner of a particular class or description, the onus of proving that such person is not a foreigner or is not a foreigner of such a particular class or description, as the case may be, shall, notwithstanding anything contained in the Indian Evidence Act, 1872 (1 of 1872), lie upon such person." [3]

In contrast, Article 11.1 of the Universal Declaration of Human Rights (UDHR) of the United Nations states:

"Everyone charged with a #penal offence has the right to be presumed innocent until proved guilty according to law in a public trial at which he has had all the guarantees necessary for his defence." [4] India is a signatory to the United Nations' UDHR.

#Penal offence is a misdeed that can be punished by law.

It's noteworthy that the IMDT Act came into effect only in 1983 when the Anti-Foreigners' Agitation rocked Assam. At that time, the political situation in various states, including Assam, was fluid, and the Indira Gandhi Government in New Delhi faced multiple challenges from various quarters. During those days, before the enactment of the IMDT Act, proceedings were initiated against numerous people in Assam indiscriminately, alleging them to be illegal immigrants, which gave rise to suspicion that these were motivated actions. To protect the people from such unfair actions, the New Delhi Government, in 1983, enacted the IMDT Act.

The forceful deportation of thousands of Muslims to East Pakistan in the 1960s, even though there was no formal agreement with East Pakistan on deportation, has already been discussed earlier in chapter 9 of this book. The border unit of Assam police used to deport hundreds of Muslims without any significant opposition. Former Home Minister and Chief Minister of Assam Hiteswar Saikia had admitted that 1,92,079 persons (the unofficial figure was much higher) were deported under the Prevention of Infiltration of Pakistani (PIP) scheme between 1961-69. The aim of this scheme was to deny entry to any new immigrant from East Pakistan while keeping a watch on existing settlements of migrants and deporting any new migrants. After deporting huge numbers of Muslims to East Pakistan, Chief Minister of Assam Bimala Prasad Chaliha announced on the floor of the Legislative Assembly in 1969 that 'no more infiltrators were to be found in Assam,' and hence, the PIP scheme was to be abandoned." [5]

The PIP scheme drew a lot of international criticism because of the vast powers given to the police officials. In response to the criticism, the Union government created the Foreigner's Tribunals in 1964. These tribunals had the power to take up the case of a person and decide if he was a foreigner or not. The PIP scheme was later renamed as the Prevention of Infiltration of Foreigners (PIF) after the emergence of Bangladesh in March 1971. The new scheme, implemented from time to time, could not deliver the expected results. It was created for the people who were served a 'Quit India' notice by the police officials. Such people could apply to these tribunals and get the chance of a fair hearing. However, this also proved to be ineffective because the whole process was causing excessive delays in identifying and deporting the illegal migrants. [6]

Later, in the midst of political chaos in Assam, the demise of Mangaldai Lok Sabha MP Hiralal Patowary on 12th March 1978 necessitated a revision of the voters' list for the ensuing by-election. A huge controversy erupted over the inclusion of 47,658 doubtful citizens (of which 36,780 objections were sustained) in its electoral rolls. According to Senior Journalist Mrinal Talukdar, two gentlemen met the leaders of the Mangaldai Students' Union and handed over to them the voters' list of 1967 and 1977, persuading them to file objections through Form No. 6, suspecting the families whose names did not figure in the voters' list of 1967 but were included in the list of 1977, as foreigners. Accordingly, Form No. 6, containing objections against 47,658 doubtful people and signed by local student leader Zoinath Sarma of Mangaldai Sub-division Students' Union and one Baruah of Kharupetia, was submitted. The two gentlemen, who met the Mangaldai student leaders, were the DIG of Assam Police (Border), Hiranya Kumar Bhattacharyya and the

Superintendent of Police (Border), Premkanta Mahanta. They were the key founders of the anti-Bangladeshi movement, which eventually became known as Assam Agitation. As the activity picked up quick momentum, a great hue and cry was raised by the Congress leaders from Assam, as well as from outside Assam, and complaints were made to the Chief Election Commissioner, who ultimately called a halt to the operation. But before the exercise was postponed, already 47,658 objections had been filed. Mangaldai Sub-division Students' Union threatened to oppose the election at this juncture.

Till then, the issue of the detection and deportation of foreigners was not on AASU's demand list. They were more concerned about the "outsiders," meaning natives of other regions of India. Against this backdrop, when the Assam Agitation (also known as the Anti-Foreigners' Agitation) against the "outsiders" started a little while later, there was always an anti-Muslim tint on the ground. However, on paper, the Assam Movement was claimed to be a secular movement. The popular concept of an illegal Bangladeshi was of a bearded Muslim with a lungi. The ordinary Assamese was never told that there was an equal number of Hindu illegal migrants residing in Assam. By that time, right-wing political influence had infiltrated into the upper echelons of the Assam agitation leadership. They ensured that the focus remained on Bangladeshi Muslims only, not Bangladeshi Hindus. [7] [8]

Amidst the six-year-long Anti-Foreigners Agitation (1979–1985) that allegedly involved large-scale persecution of minorities, accusing them indiscriminately as illegal immigrants, Assam's law and order situation started deteriorating from bad to worse day by day, reaching its peak in 1983. The Khoirabari massacre, where an estimated 500 so-called "immigrant" Bengali Hindus were killed on 7th February 1983, and the Nellie Massacre of 18th February 1983, which reportedly claimed the lives of 1,600–2,000 supposed "immigrant" Muslims, were only two major instances among a series of scary happenings which had made the Indira Gandhi government in New Delhi push through the IMTD Act on 15th October 1983 in the face of unprecedented situations, as law and order in the state turned wild.

Initially, the seriousness of the prevailing law and order situation in Assam made the Government of India resort to promulgating an Ordinance. In due course, the Indian parliament regularized it as expected by passing a law in December 1983 titled THE ILLEGAL MIGRANTS (DETERMINATION BY TRIBUNALS) ACT, 1983. The main purpose of the enactment was *'to provide for the establishment of Tribunals for the determination,* **in a fair manner***, of the question whether a person is an illegal migrant to enable the Central Government to expel illegal migrants from India and for matters connected therewith or incidental thereto.'*

Among other things, in ACT No. 39 OF 1983, commonly known as the IMDT Act of 1983, it was mentioned that: "….. (2) **It extends to the whole of India.** *(3) It shall be deemed to have come into force in the State of Assam on the 15th day of October 1983 and in any other State on such date as the Central Government may, by notification in the Official Gazette, appoint, and different dates may be appointed for different States, and references in this Act to the commencement of this Act shall be construed in relation to any State as references to the date of commencement of this Act in such State."* [9] (Emphasis by Subir)

As already mentioned, the Indian Parliament reportedly enacted the law to protect minority communities against harassment, alleging them indiscriminately to be foreigners in Assam. Nevertheless, those against it argued that the Act was arbitrary and discriminatory, and made it almost impossible to identify the countless illegal immigrants residing in Assam. Besides, the detractors maintained that the IMTD Act, 1983, was passed in the Parliament at a time when Assam was unrepresented in the Lok Sabha (the lower house of the Indian Parliament) because of the election boycott in Assam. (It can send 14 representatives maximum in the House of 545).

According to Prashant Bhushan, a renowned public interest lawyer in the Supreme Court of India, before 1983, the detection and eviction of foreigners were done under colonial legislation enacted in the interests of the British Colonial rulers, the Foreigners Act of 1940. This Act gave virtually unbridled powers to the authorities, mainly the police, to designate any person as a foreigner and detain and deport him. Anyone disputing his designation as a foreigner had no recourse to a judicial body. Though the Foreigner's Tribunal's order 1964 framed under the Act gave the Government the discretion to refer any dispute to tribunals constituted for this purpose, the Government did not constitute any such tribunals in any part of the country outside Assam. Moreover, in this colonial legislation (the Foreigners Act), if you were alleged to be a foreigner by the authorities, the burden of proving that you were not a foreigner was on you. It was an impossible burden to discharge for most people in the country, especially the poor, functionally illiterate, and uninformed inhabitants who formed the bulk of the population, having predominantly no birth certificates or land holdings. The result was that most people were completely at the mercy of the police, who, in many places, were abusing their powers under the Act to extort money from poor and defenceless people.

Taking note of these problems, in 1983, the Indian Parliament enacted the Illegal Migrants (Determination by Tribunals) Act (IMDT Act), which provided for judicial tribunals to determine disputes about citizenship that might arise under the Foreigners Act. The rules under the Act also provided for an administrative screening committee that would examine the complaints under the Act and reject complaints found to be frivolous. The Act, also for the first time, gave a limited right to any person to lodge a private complaint with the Tribunals under this Act against persons regarding whom they had information of their being foreigners. Such a right did not exist under the Foreigners Act. The right was, however, limited by providing that such a complaint could only be made against persons residing within the same local area and that persons could make a maximum of ten such complaints. [10]

Simply put, the IMTD Act placed the onus of proving the citizenship credentials of a person on the complainant and the police, not on the accused. Besides, it required two individuals living within a radius of 3 km of a suspected illegal migrant to approach an IMDT Tribunal, deposit Rs 25/-, and then file a complaint. (The three km restriction was subsequently modified so that the complainant could be from the same police station limits as the accused, while the deposit sum was reduced to Rs 10/-.) After the enactment of this law, the cases of indiscriminate harassment of minorities in Assam significantly reduced. Likewise, the number of convictions of the alleged 'foreigners' in Assam also came down substantially. Given that this Act was implemented only in Assam and not in other states, some people considered the law to be discriminatory. Eventually, this Act also turned out, as alleged, to be a roadblock in the large-scale identification and deportation from Assam of illegal migrants, ostensibly infiltrating the state illegally, primarily because the IMTD Act 1983 shifted the onus of proof from the accused to the police or the person bringing up the allegation.

It is pertinent to recall here that in the run-up to the signing of the Assam Accord on the 14th of August 1985, hours before the Accord was signed, there was strong resentment among the assembled AASU and AAGSP leaders in Delhi over there being no clear promise from the Central Government on their demand about the scrapping of the IMTD Act. Then, Union Home Secretary R. D. Pradhan told them the Government couldn't discard an Act passed by Parliament just like that, but it would try to create a political consensus for its removal. [11]

Besides, the paragraphs taken from the article "THE AMBIVALENCE OF CITIZENSHIP" by Anupama Roy and Ujjwal Kumar Singh that appeared in a quarterly academic journal, Critical Asian Studies, also provide an interesting perspective on the issue:

> On the 27th of January 1990, the Union Home Secretary and the Chief Secretary of Assam signed a document setting a time frame for the implementation of the Assam Accord. The document explicitly

mentioned that a decision on the repeal of the IMDT Act would be taken by the 28th of February 1991. In a meeting on the 20th of September 1990, between the Union Home Minister, the Chief Minister of Assam, and representatives of AASU, the AASU called again for the repeal of the IMDT Act. The Central Government gave assurance that it would initiate discussion on the issue of repeal with other political parties. The Act remained on the statute books, however, even as the Central Government continued to assure the AASU that the repeal of the Act was under consideration. In a meeting on the 11th of August 1997 with the AASU, the Union Home Minister admitted that the Act's results were indeed extremely poor, and he announced that he had decided to visit the state to take stock of the situation regarding illegal immigration and the inadequacy of the measures taken to prevent it. In the following year, in April and September 1998, the Central Government assured the AASU that it was actively considering the repeal of the Act. This assurance was affirmed in the President of India's address to the Parliament in February 1999. In another meeting held on the 18th of March 1999 between the representatives of the Central Government, the Government of Assam, and the AASU, assurances regarding repeal were given again.

These administrative and political manoeuvres were truncated as the issue of repeal was propelled into the judicial domain in 2000 when a writ petition for the Act's repeal was placed before the Supreme Court by Sarbananda Sonowal. The petition Sonowal submitted stated: "IMDT Act is wholly arbitrary, unreasonable, and discriminates against a class of citizens of India, making it impossible for citizens who are residents in Assam to secure the detection and deportation of foreigners from Indian soil." A reading of Sonowal's petition shows the persistence of a strand within the Assam movement that focused on the resolution of the question of illegal migrants within the framework of the Indian Constitution. Sonowal couches his petition in a vocabulary that may well be termed "constitutional patriotism," identifying with the notion of a political community that is not primarily concerned with cultural and ethnic ascriptions but rests upon constitutional practices and legal principles that define the terms of citizenship. Yet, his constitutional patriotism is qualified insofar as it is hedged in with a concern for securing political boundaries with the more stringent application of immigration laws. Sonowal petitions as a "citizen of India," who happens to "ordinarily reside in Assam," raising issues that he claims "concern all residents of the state of Assam whose rights as citizens of India have been materially and gravely prejudiced by the operation of the IMDT Act, 1983." It is significant that in his petition, Sonowal foregrounds the masked identity of the Indian citizen, relegating the Assamese identity to a mere fact of residence, dissolving in the process the emotive and affective aspects of Assamese identity that the movement manifested in the years 1979 to 1985. Thus the principal grievance of the petitioner that emerges after the ascriptive aspects of citizenship are sieved out was the discriminatory nature of the Act in denying the people of Assam the same terms of membership that other Indians enjoyed. [12]

The Writ Petition (Civil) 131 of 2000 that former AASU President (1992-1999) and AGP member Sarbananda Sonowal (PETITIONER) filed was under Article 32 of the Constitution of India by way of Public Interest Litigation (PIL) where it was contended, *inter alia*,

"The Foreigners Act, 1946, applies to all the foreigners throughout India, but the IMDT Act which was enacted subsequently with the professed aim of making detection and deportation of the illegal migrants residing in Assam easier has completely failed to meet even the standards prescribed in the Foreigners Act. That apart, even those provisions of the IMDT Act which afford some measure of protection to some genuine Indian citizens against illegal migrants are not being properly enforced due to extraneous political considerations in derogation of the rights of Indian citizens living in Assam. The result of the IMDT Act has been that a number of non-Indians, who surreptitiously entered into Assam after March 25, 1971, without possession of valid passport, travel documents or other lawful authority to do so, continue to reside in Assam. Their presence has changed the whole character, cultural and ethnic composition of the area and the IMDT Act creates a situation whereunder it has become virtually impossible to challenge the presence of a foreigner and to secure his detention, deportation or even deletion of his name from the electoral list as they get protection on account of the provisions of the Act. According to the census figures, which have been given in the writ petition, the rate of growth of the population in Assam is far more than the rest of India which shows that a large number of foreigners have migrated to different areas of Assam and have settled there."

The Writ Petition, therefore, prayed for declaring certain provisions of the Illegal Migrants (Determination by Tribunals) Act No.39 of 1983 as ultra vires the Constitution of India, null and void and a consequent declaration that the Foreigners Act, 1946, and the Rules made thereunder shall apply to the State of Assam. The second prayer made was to declare the Illegal Migrants (Determination by Tribunals) Rules, 1984 as ultra vires the Constitution of India and also under Section 28 of the Act mentioned above and, therefore, null and void, and for some more assorted reliefs associated thereto. The Union of India & the State Government of Assam were the RESPONDENTs of the Writ Petition.

Interestingly, the government of Assam under the AGP initially supported Sonowal's move. However, after the 2001 elections, Congress came to power in Assam, and the state government's stance also changed before the Supreme Court. As a matter of fact, in response to Sonowal's Writ Petition, the Central Government filed three counter-affidavits and the Assam Government two in the Supreme Court. In each affidavit, the respective Governments took dissimilar positions harmonious with the standpoints of the different incumbencies:

a) In its first affidavit dated 28th August 2000, Assam's AGP Government focused on the fast-changing demographic profile, particularly the rise of the Muslim population in the state, and claimed that AGP's electoral victory in Assam fought on this plank, demonstrated the people's apprehension on this issue.

b) In contrast, as the Congress Government returned to power in Assam in May 2001, the Assam Government, in its second affidavit dated 8th August 2001, withdrew the State Government's first affidavit to "correct" the earlier position taken by the former AGP Government on 28th August 2000. Reversing the State Government's earlier position, on 8th August 2001, the State Government, in its new affidavit, stated that the law was brought to save Indian citizens from unnecessary harassment and asserted the IMTD Act as constitutional, not arbitrary, or discriminatory. Therefore, the government was against the opinion of striking down or repealing the Act.

c) The BJP-led NDA Government in New Delhi, in its first affidavit dated 18th July 2000, agreed with Sonowal's view that the IMTD Act was discriminatory and inefficient/inadequate. While the Writ Petition focused on the effective legal resolution of the "foreigners' issue," the Central Government emphasized the demographic

change in the state, religious and economic reasons, and implications attaching importance to national security issues.
d) On the other hand, in response to the new affidavit by the Assam Government, the BJP-led Central Government, in its second additional affidavit, reiterated its stand, saying the IMTD Act amounted to preferential protection of the illegal migrants and portrayed the IMTD Act as the single factor responsible for the alarming and growing number of illegal immigrants in Assam.
e) Then again, on 24th November 2004, the Congress-led UPA Government at the Centre, in its third affidavit, totally reversed the Government's stand on the IMTD Act. The third affidavit was in line with the position articulated in the Assam Government's second affidavit that the IMTD Act is protective of genuine Indian citizens by enabling judicial scrutiny. [13]

In 2005, the Supreme Court upheld Sonowal's plea and struck down the IMDT Act, 1983, as unconstitutional. While striking down the Act of 1983, the three-judge Bench comprising Chief Justice RC Lahoti and Justices GP Mathur and PK Balasubramnyan acknowledged the plight of the people of Assam, who were being reduced to a minority within their own state, and unanimously declared the 1983 IMTD Act and rules framed in 1984 as ultra vires of the Constitution. [14] Sonowal had contended that the IMDT Act only encouraged vote bank politics without addressing the problem of illegal migrants. Still, the Congress government in Assam supported the IMDT Act, saying it was fair. The SC directed that all the tribunals constituted under the IMDT Act would "cease to function" with immediate effect as the Parent Act had been declared unconstitutional. Cases pending before the tribunals would stand transferred to tribunals under the Foreigners Act, the Court said – according to The Economic Times dated 13th July 2005. [15]

The Supreme Court also heavily relied upon a report by Assam Governor Lt. Gen. S.K. Sinha (Retired) in deciding the case. Some parts of the Governor's report found place word for word several times in the PIL's Judgement dated 12th July 2005, supporting this assertion. As often happens, selected portions of Assam's 1931 Census report by S.C. Mullan were also quoted in the Governor's report dated 8th November 1998 and the PIL Judgement dated 12th July 2005.

In his 22-page report dated 8th November 1998 to the President of India, the Assam Governor openly stated that there was an unabated influx of illegal migrants from Bangladesh into Assam. The illegal infiltrations threatened to reduce the Assamese people to a minority in their own state. The report further stated, among other things, that the Muslim population in Assam had shown a rise of 77.42 per cent in 1991 from what it was in 1971. Based on population records and not accounting for reasons such as migrations between districts due to floods etc., the report assumed that the rise in the Muslim population must mean a large-scale undocumented migration from Bangladesh. On page 10, paragraph 22 of the report, it was stated that "no misconceived and mistaken notions of secularism should be allowed to come in the way" of addressing the dangerous consequences of large-scale migration.

The Supreme Court, in its judgment, did not only stop at striking down the legislation but also went further in stating that there can be no manner of doubt that the state of Assam is facing "external aggression and internal disturbance" on account of the large scale illegal migration of Bangladeshi nationals. [16]

The 2005 verdict became the bedrock for all future references in the judicial as well as political world concerning the so-called infiltration in Assam. The judgment immediately struck down the IMDT Act and called for all references being sent to Foreigners Tribunals to be decided as per Foreigners (Tribunals) Order, 1964, thus taking away the protection provided to a suspect foreigner. Needless to say, this judgment also formed the basis for deciding many issues concerning Assam and NRC since then. In the 2019 judgment in Abdul Kuddus vs Union of India, when relying upon the 2005 verdict, the Court denied any right of appeal from the decisions of the foreign tribunals. The same threats of the influx of illegal immigrants, relying heavily on the verdict in Sonowal's case, were also found in the 2014 judgment of the Supreme Court in a batch of petitions concerning the constitutional validity of Section 6A of the Citizenship Act, 1955. [17]

"The SC's recent judgment on the IMDT Act betrays such an ignorance of basic legal principles and lack of sensitivity to human rights values, besides using a fantastic interpretation of the Constitution, that it could have extremely far-reaching implications," wrote Supreme Court lawyer Prashant Bhushan. The article appeared in India's current affairs and news magazine, OUTLOOK, updated on 3rd February 2022, which included, among other things, the following lines:

> Being conscious of this limitation, the Judgment written by Justice G.P. Mathur comes up with a brilliant idea. It opines that the Act violates Art 355 of the Constitution, which mandates the Central Government to protect the states against external aggression and internal disturbance! It goes on to say that the onerous provisions of the Act and Rules make it virtually impossible to expel foreigners. Therefore, the Act encourages the infiltration of illegal migrants

from Bangladesh, which amounts to external aggression against India!

Certainly, it's an inspired, original, and breathtakingly audacious interpretation of Article 355 of the Constitution. But then, as a legendary American judge bluntly stated, the notion that judges do not make the law is nothing but a fairy tale. And nowadays, we don't believe in fairy tales.

While considering this interpretation of Article 355 of the Constitution, I wonder whether the Honourable judges were fully aware of the implications of their statements. For instance, India has a treaty with Nepal that permits Nepali citizens to freely enter and stay in India without a visa, and vice versa. Could this treaty be deemed unconstitutional on the grounds that it encourages Nepali migration to India and potentially promotes external aggression by Nepal?

Or consider if Parliament were to amend the Citizenship Act to grant Indian citizenship to individuals from any territory that was part of undivided India upon application. Would such an amendment also be deemed unconstitutional on similar grounds? If so, what about the existing provision that grants automatic citizenship to those born in undivided India? Individuals like Mr. Advani and many others from Pakistan are citizens of India solely by virtue of this existing provision, which would also be deemed unconstitutional based on the logic provided.

Clearly, the remarkable interpretation of Article 355 provided in this judgment could have significant implications for the citizenship and foreign policy of the country, areas that are supposed to be governed by Parliament and the government.

The Court also ruled that the selective applicability of the IMDT Act only to Assam rendered it discriminatory and in violation of Article 14, as other states were not subject to its stricter provisions before designating individuals as foreigners. However, the court overlooked the fact that the IMDT Act applied to the entirety of India, albeit the government had not notified it for areas outside Assam. This was an oversight by the executive, and other pending petitions sought precisely the direction from the court to instruct the government to extend the application of the IMDT Act to other parts of the country. Therefore, the current limited application of the Act to Assam alone was not a flaw in the Act but rather a case of executive inaction, for which the court could issue directives to the government. [18]

In an exclusive interview with journalist and TV commentator Karan Thapar in September 2019, Faizan Mustafa, one of India's top experts on the constitution and Vice-Chancellor of the National Academy of Legal Studies and Research (NALSAR) University of Law, Hyderabad, highlighted significant legal issues associated with the Assam NRC. Mustafa mentioned the following:

> "Starting from the Sonowal judgment, where the court virtually assumed the role of the executive. The issue challenged in Sonowal's judgment—now the chief minister—was the IMDT Act, i.e., the Illegal Migrant Determination Act, 1983. Now, when the constitutionality of a law is challenged, the court's role is to determine whether Parliament had the authority to enact that law or if it violates any fundamental rights. The court did not perform this exercise. Instead, it declared illegal migration as 'external aggression' and held that if the Centre fails to stop it, it is in violation of its duty under Article 355 (duty of Centre to protect states), thus striking it down.
>
> The IMDT Act had shifted the burden of proof onto the state to prove that the accused was a foreigner. I believe the striking down of the IMDT Act was the catalyst for today's crisis, and it was a crisis articulated by the court."

The full transcript of the interview is available on the Indian news website, The Wire, and the video interview can be watched on YouTube. [19] & [20]

Furthermore, there was an earlier discussion in this book regarding the distasteful nature of C. S. Mullan's Assam Census report of 1931, where the British Colonial bureaucrat mischievously employed certain unfounded and unwarranted derogatory expressions against the people and land of India. Unfortunately, in contesting the IMDT Act, certain sections of the same ill-motivated report by the Census Superintendent C. S. Mullan, compiled during the colonial era of India, were also referenced. Given that in the post-colonial period, these expressions from Mullan's 1931 census report have ritualistically found their way into numerous chronicles, accounts, stories, research papers, official reports, and various other forms, discussing the influx of people into Assam, it is unlikely that many would raise eyebrows today against such references.

However, the pressing question at hand is this: Should we condone these words and overlook the fact that such ominous predictions and prophecies—

that the *time was not far off when the Assamese people would be confined to the district of Sibsagar*, laden with derogatory expressions and military terminology like 'conquest,' 'attack,' and 'invasion'—were at the heart of Assam's communal and racial tensions? Are the repeated use of these oppressive texts in numerous important papers and crucial official documents in independent India inadvertently granting these cunning terminologies an undesired legitimacy and perpetuity? Are we not, by echoing Mullan's voice repeatedly, guilty of prolonging the shelf life of these deplorable remarks?

* * * * * * *

Chapter 14.

The Dreaded 'D'
In Assam's Voter list

The agonizing tales are emerging of individuals being branded as Doubtful or 'Dubious' citizens of India after they failed to produce proof of their citizenship, which was never provided to them by anyone in the first place!

If the colour of your skin, the language you speak, the dress, or the beard or the cap you wear is not liked by some 'privileged' people and you are a resident of Assam – you are in great trouble! There are chances of the dreaded alphabet 'D' being put against your name on the voter list, which immediately robs you of your civil rights as an Indian Citizen. It's as simple as that. But, all along, you were under the illusion that the Indian Constitution has guaranteed you these civil rights in India!

Your surname is also an important factor. A typical Bengali surname like Deb, Chatterjee, or Bose carries the maximum risk. A common (with the Assamese) surname like Das, Bhattacharjee carries less risk. If your surname is Barua, a very common surname in the Assamese community, you are perfectly safe even if you hail from the district of Chittagong, presently in Bangladesh. It's a two-decade-long unashamed open exhibition of racism at its worst manifestation in Assam.

You may not even know what is happening behind your back until one inauspicious day, maybe after months or years together, you go to the polling booth. Like any other proud Indian citizen, you arrive there to exercise your invaluable democratic right of casting the all-important vote. But, you receive the rudest shock of your life - you are told that you are a 'D' Voter. It means you earned the dubious distinction of being a "Doubtful" voter! You are placed in the category of voters in Assam whom the government is likely to disenfranchise because of your questionable citizenship credentials. In other words, the authenticity of your Indian citizenship is in doubt or in jeopardy, to be more precise. If you are lucky, you receive a notice, but there is no guarantee. Maybe one dreadful night, there would be Police knocking at your doors. You would be asked to accompany them to the nearest Police Station.

After a little bit of routine questioning thereat, you finally land up in what is 'officially' known as a ¹detention camp. However, in reality, it's out and out a jail where you would be lodged with many other ordinary or hardcore criminals with all the 'facilities,' troubles, and difficulties the Indian prisons are well-known for. You won't know how long you would be there as a 'State Guest,' but you go on counting the number of days you spend behind bars and pray. You have no other choice.

It's neither a description from any mystery novel of a renowned English author nor a narration of any routine occurrences in a notorious banana republic in Africa. But, believe it or not - this is a succinct summary of the harrowing story that has been happening in Assam since the late 1990s. A case in point is an even more frightening real-life story of D-voters, the pertinent part of which is reproduced below:

> "On August 12, 2015, at around 1 a.m., 38-year-old Kismat Ali and six of his family members were asleep in their house in the Sonajuli village of western Assam's Udalguri district when they heard people aggressively banging on their door and calling out, "Kismat! Kismat!" He opened the door to discover that the Border Police of Assam had surrounded his house. The officers forced Kismat to leave with them for the police station without answering his questions about why he was being taken away. On their way, the Police picked up Ashraf Ali, a 40-year-old resident of the same village. At the Udalguri police station, the police officials wrote a Statement and coerced them to sign it. Kismat read the Statement: "Main Bangladeshi hun"— (I am a Bangladeshi.)
>
> "Main Hindustani hun"—(I am an Indian), Kismat recalled telling the Police. "Mujhe Bangladeshi kyun bana rahe ho"—(Why are you forcing me to become a Bangladeshi?) He said the Police threatened Ashraf and Kismat into signing the Statement, following which they were taken over 200 kilometres away to the detention centre in Goalpara district—one of six in the State. The detention centres hold those D-voters, or "doubtful voters"—residents of Assam suspected of residing illegally in the State—who have subsequently been declared foreigners by the State's quasi-judicial Foreigners Tribunals. As of 25th September 2018, a total of 1,037 declared foreigners were being held in detention centres across Assam, according to a report by the human rights organization Amnesty International.
>
> Kismat and Ashraf were declared Indian citizens only after intervention by the Supreme Court and a Central Bureau of

Investigation enquiry. Their cases illustrate how the NRC (National Register of Citizens) alienates suspected foreigners—predominantly Assam's Bengali-origin Muslims, followed by Bengali Hindus—at every stage of the process."

Only a part of the news report titled "Citizens Erased In Assam's NRC, a near-impossible trial followed by inhuman and indefinite detention" by the assistant editor at an Indian English-language monthly magazine The Caravan, Amrita Singh, is repeated above. The full story available on its webpage [1] is too excruciating to believe!

Here is another shocker: "The photo of Ratan Chandra Biswas, chained to the hospital bed of Goalpara Civil Hospital (in Assam) has shaken the Twitterati across the world, once again reasserting that in the name of foreigner's detection, in Assam, the biggest human right violations of modern India have been systematically ignored." The terrible cover photograph of Ratan Chandra Biswas with his two-year-long plight in detention is one among many such heart-rending factual stories of "D" Voters and the so-called "Illegal Foreigners" in Assam, where instances of similar human rights violations are aplenty. An English-language news media portal that caters to English readers and audiences in Assam, Northeast India, and the entire nation, Pratidin Time, showed this unfortunate soul, Ratan, chained to a hospital bed! The terse report of the Pratidin Bureau brought to light one of these ongoing human tragedies underway in Assam. [2]

Yet, on paper, the procedure of branding "D" Voters and identifying "foreigners" in Assam appears to be perfectly legitimate and in order. It is elaborated in Chapter 2.6, Page 22 of the Government of Assam Home and Political Department White Paper on Foreigners Issue (October 12, 2012). [3] But what is happening at the ground level is a different story altogether.

On August 2nd, 2018, an Assamese language newspaper exposed a scandalous revelation about the 'process' of making 'D' Voters' in Assam. An extract of its loose adaptation in English by Subir would read somewhat like this:

"At the Nowgong District Electoral Office in Assam sometime in 2006, one office clerk was struggling to mark "D" against some voters' names in a long electoral roll lying open at his desk. "Look at this long list and just tell me against whose names should I mark 'D'? I know how miserable life would be for those with 'D' marks against their names on the electoral roll. About 80% of the names on this list are Muslims. It is difficult to distinguish between the indigenous Assamese Muslims and the Bengali Muslims in the list merely from the names. But I have been instructed by the officer to mark 'D' at least against ten names!"

The clerk was venting his annoyance and helplessness with these words, the report added. [4]

Reportedly, Assam's border police and some other key Government officials had monthly targets of detecting and detaining foreigners or illegal immigrants from their respective areas of operation. The border police, unique to Assam, is a wing of the state police force set up in 1962 to check the infiltration of people from (East) Pakistan at the border zone.

There are umpteen instances where people were made to suffer even without rhyme or reason in the name of identifying the foreigners in Assam. These were regularly reported in various Newspapers. Yet, the harassment continued unabated. The story of the Indian Air Force (IAF) veteran Shamsul Haque Ahmed who retired in 2014 as a sergeant after serving in the IAF for 35 years, was another case in point. Ahmed was declared 'D-voter' way back in 1997, even when he was in service in the Indian Air Force! For 19 long years, he remained disfranchised and humiliated. On May 27th, 2016, after carefully perusing all his documents, the Foreigners Tribunal declared him an Indian citizen. [5] The story of Kargil war veteran Mohammed Sanuullah [6] and that of 59-year-old retired teacher Madhubala Mondal set free after 3 years of detention due to some 'clerical error' [7] were two more such creepy inclusions, among many others, in the ongoing media reports of licensed harassment focusing on a section of the residents of Assam.

> "The people of Assam, especially the Bengalis, have become so disgusted with the type of 'institutionalized' persecution that they have now started knocking at the doors of Justice to put an end to such harassments". (Loose English adaptation by Subir)

This was reported in a Bengali Newspaper, Jugasankha, on August 27th, 2018. The same newspaper the next day, on August 28th, 2018, reported that an Assam MLA, Kamalakhya De Purakayastha, was contemplating legal action against the NRC authority based on the numerous complaints he received. According to the MLA, there was a deep-rooted "Government conspiracy" to dub a large number of Bengali-speaking genuine Indians as "D" Voters without any notice to them so that their names could be excluded from appearing in Assam's NRC.

Although there are several scary stories, nothing could beat the weird case of the teenager Kishor Nitai Das of 1, Roumari of Baksha District of Assam. The names of all his family members were excluded from the final list of Assam's draft NRC **because**, according to the NRC Seva Kendra, **Nitai was** a 'D' Voter. Interestingly, Nitai was less than 18 years of age at that time, so it's absurd for his name to find a place in the voters' list in the first place - not to speak of him being a 'D' Voter! But that, too, had happened in Assam!

"**How Indians Are Made Into Bangladeshi For Money,**" reported by a leading News Channel of Assam, Pratidin Time, on 7th September 2018, which is reproduced below:

> A foreigner's tribunal meant for detecting foreigners has taken a 360-degree turn and exposed that a **full-scale industry is going on in Assam** to make an ordinary citizen a Bangladeshi to mint money by all sections involved with the affairs.
>
> This sensational revelation came as a judgment from the Foreigner's Tribunal of Morigaon (FT), exposing long-standing suspicions and allegations that innocent Indians were harassed in the name of detecting foreigners.
>
> The judge, through the **formal judgment, exposed** how hundreds of thousands of court notices and summons were not served on those against whom 'foreigners' cases were slapped.
>
> The innocent Indian person has no idea that there is a case lying against him in the FT, as the court-issued summons and notices were either not delivered or hung on the tree of an electric post and, in many cases, signed by ghost receivers.
>
> This forces the court to issue an ex parte order as the other party had no inkling that there was any case hearing under his name. The **racket is so elaborate and rampant** that an FT tribunal has had to issue a judgment, shocking the entire state.
>
> According to the FT tribunal of Morigaon, it is **rampant across the state.** This judgment only confirms the long-standing suspicion that a section of the people is hell-bent on turning innocent Indians into Bangladeshi through the legal maze.
>
> According to the sensational judgment, the whole system is a farce and a money-making industry, with everybody involved in the case only making money.
>
> The angry and distraught judge, in a lengthy order, exposed how the summons were not served to the opposite parties, and judgments were obtained from the Tribunal showing the opposite party absent in the court.

"Foreigner's cases at this juncture have assumed the form of an industry as each and every person involved with Foreigners case have been trying to mint money by any means," said the order. The judgment did not stop there. It also said, "Process server usually hung the notice upon some trees or electric pole despite innumerable cautioning. As a result, the FT orders go ex-parte." The Tribunal made its own investigations and found that the majority of judgments were ex parte as the opposite party did not get wind of the legal development.

In most cases, the opposite party was the alleged foreigners, and they did not get a proper chance to represent their case before the court following court procedures.

The Judgment also said most of the notices/summons were signed without going to the residential address of the party. The process server makes the report at his whims. Notices were hung on the electric poles in the villages, which do not even have electricity.

The Tribunal did try to caution the gaoburah (village headman) and process servers umpteen times, but it was not heeded. "Gaoburah/VDP secretary or president and process server try to get the cases proceeded ex-parte **for some extraneous consideration**, which includes the involvement of a third party."

The Judgment also said dereliction of duty for failing to serve summons in a proper manner compelled this Tribunal to pass orders detrimental to the procedures arrayed in those cases. Various organizations of the Minority have always been saying that **99% of foreigners' cases were false** and only harassed ordinary Indians. This is for the first time a tribunal, through a written and signed judgment, blew off the lid of the whole scam. [8]

Amidst very disturbing reports about the condition of Bengali residents in Assam relating to the process of determining the legality of their citizenship, as well as the legality and conditions of the detention centres where persons deemed to be foreigners are held, a special team on behalf of the National Human Rights Commission visited two detention centres in Assam from January 22nd to 24th, 2018. The members of the team were Harsh Mander, in his capacity as the Special Monitor for Minorities, accompanied and ably assisted by two senior officials, Dr Mahesh Bhardwaj, SSP, NHRC, and Indrajeet Kumar, Assistant Registrar (Law), NHRC. The Special Monitoring Mission also drew upon the assistance of two scholars to aid the team in the research for this Mission, Dr Mohsin Alam Bhat, who teaches at the Jindal

Law School, and Abdul Kalam Azad, an independent researcher formerly with the Tata Institute of Social Sciences, Guwahati.

The team visited two detention centres and met with the detainees. The Mission held meetings with jail and police authorities, district magistrates, and senior officials in the state secretariat. The team also had a series of meetings with civil society groups in Goalpara, Kokrajhar, and Guwahati. During its visit to the two detention camps, the Mission found a situation of grave and extensive human distress and suffering. The detainees were held in the corners of the two jails for several years, in a twilight zone of legality, without work and recreation, with no contact with their families, rare visits from their families, and no prospect of release. In the women's camp, the women wailed continuously as though in mourning.

While listening to the stories of the detainees, the Mission felt that there were many detainees whose cases were either decided ex-parte or didn't get a fair chance to prove their Indian nationality. The Mission observed that as a country, India provides legal aid even to people accused of heinous crimes like rape and murder. But here in Assam, these people are languishing in detention centres without even committing any crime, only because they can't afford legal services.

The Mission recommended, among other things, that the state government ensure that its officials informed the detainees of their rights when they were taken into custody by the border police force. Many of the detainees, it seemed, were not very clear about why they were in detention. Given the widespread concerns about the failures of many persons to receive notices, especially migrant workers, children, single women, older people, persons with mental health issues, and others, the Mission felt that a more humane and legally sound system of ensuring notices was needed.

All the representatives of the students' organizations and civil society groups, as well as the senior citizen, shared their concerns about the process of identifying suspected illegal immigrants. Former Member of the Assam Legislative Assembly and retired professor of Goalpara College, Prof. Joynal Abedin, spoke very explicitly in the meeting about the faulty investigation process and unnecessary harassment of impoverished villagers in the name of identifying illegal immigrants. He alleged that the police didn't investigate the identity of the so-called illegal immigrants properly before sending the cases to the Foreigners Tribunal. Many genuine Indian citizens were tagged as suspected foreigners, which forced those poor people to go through heavy financial turmoil to prove their Indian nationality.

The representative of Jamiat Ulema-e-Hind, Mr. Abdul Hai, gave a written representation before the Mission. In his memorandum, he said that most of the D Voters and the suspected illegal immigrants (Reference Cases) were from the most marginalized section of the society, mostly from the char and chapori areas (river island and river bank areas). Every year tens of thousands of people are affected by floods and river erosion in Assam. In the last 50 years, more than 7 per cent of Assam's land was eroded by the Brahmaputra, which uprooted lakhs of people and forced them to move to upper Assam and other urban areas. Once they went to majority-dominated areas in search of livelihood, they were often suspected as illegal immigrants from Bangladesh because of their identity, culture, and language. The members of local chauvinist groups detained them and handed them over to the police as suspected illegal immigrants. Abdul Hai alleged that police did not duly investigate the claims of those chauvinist groups but registered (foreigners) cases against the inter-district migrant workers. He appealed that the flood and erosion-affected people should get rehabilitation and compensation from the government, not arbitrary cases against them suspecting them to be Bangladeshi.

The Mission expressed their concerns about the issues of children, mental health patients, elderly detainees, payroll/outing, administration of detention centres, and other details to the district and jail authorities. The jailer informed that as per the rule, children above six years who are not declared foreigners shouldn't be detained along with their declared foreign mother. There is a provision for handing over the child to the family members or any other NGOs if they get the order from the competent judicial authority. In the case of mental health patients, the Assam Jail Manual doesn't have any specific guidelines. The Assam Jail Manual hasn't been revised or updated since 1986. The Jail authority informed that they didn't receive any guidelines from the government regarding mental health patients. They also didn't receive the Supreme Court guidelines on mental health patients. Several elderly women detainees complained about colds, illness, food, etc. The jail officials informed that **there were detainees as old as ninety-two years.**

Aman Wadud, a human rights lawyer, alleged that even the Foreigners Tribunal registered cases without properly scrutinizing the credentials of such cases. In one such case, Tufajjal Islam S/O Shohidur Islam, aged about 30 years, a permanent resident of village Baramara under Barpeta Police Station in the Barpeta district of Assam, was sent a notice to appear before the Foreigners Tribunal No. 2, Kamrup (Metro) No.-2 in FT Case No. 1481/2015. In the 'Enquiry Officer's final findings' of the Reference Case sent by the Superintendent of Police(B) Kamrup, it was specifically mentioned that during the enquiry in a premature manner, it appeared that suspected Md. Tafazul Islam was not an illegal immigrant. Moreover, in the Final Interrogation Report On Suspected Foreign National, under the column 'Address in Bangladesh', it was mentioned as 'Not Applicable'. In another column at No. 10, 'Since when he/she is staying continuously in India?' the answer written by the Enquiry officer was 'Since Birth'. But despite this, there was a Reference Case to the Foreigners Tribunal for the opinion of the Tribunal. Tufajjal Islam was finally held as an Indian citizen by the Tribunal. But in the process, he lost his lifetime earnings to defend his citizenship.

Aman Wadud also alleged that reference cases were registered more than once against one person in many instances. He referred to the case of Fajar Ali, son of the late Samad Ali, Vill- Tukrapara, PS- Chaygaon Dist- Kamrup (Assam). He was issued notice by Foreigner's Tribunal No.1 Kamrup(Rural) in GFT(R), Case No.- 866/08 Corresponding to IM(D)T Case No.1620/2003, Police Case No. 435/2006. After receiving the notice, he duly appeared before the Learned Tribunal with all relevant documents. After perusing exhibited documents and cross-examining Fazar Ali, the Tribunal, via Judgement and Order dated 02/07/2010, held him not to be a foreigner. But in 2017, the same Tribunal registered a case against him via F.T. Case No. 408/2017, and he was sent a notice again to prove his citizenship. On both occasions, he was not investigated by any investigative agency. On 25/10/2017, the Foreigner's Tribunal No.1 Kamrup (Rural) held that Fazar Ali is not a foreigner.

Aman Wadud said this sort of gross injustice happened not because of the fault of any individual police officer or members of the Foreigners Tribunal but because of government policy. He alleged that each border police unit is given a monthly target to register a certain number of reference cases. If that unit failed to meet the target, the police constables and officers would face consequences. Senior police officer Louis Aind, DCP Crime, Guwahati, who was earlier in charge of the border police unit, admitted that a monthly target of 6 reference cases from each border police unit was given to the police.

Abdul Baten Khandakar, president of Brahmaputra Valley Civil Society, deposed before the Mission and stated that as per the current modalities of the NRC, the D voters are being excluded from the list. The D voters can apply for the NRC updation process, but their names will be included only after clearance from the Tribunal. Mr Khandakar said there were 1,25,333 D voters in the state, many of whom were still waiting to get their notice from the Foreigners Tribunal. In this process, their civil and political rights were withdrawn for more than two decades. Khandakar drew the attention of the

Mission and suggested that the NRC authority should examine the application and process the same, which will accelerate the disposal of the cases in a time-bound manner. He said that the NRC updating authority had a huge infrastructure of 2500 NRC Sewa Kendra, a three-tier process of scrutiny and supervision, as well as the provision of field verification.

Moreover, the district magistrate was entrusted to supervise the entire process. Compared to the process of the Foreigners Tribunal, the NRC process will be way faster and more accurate in settling the cases of D Voters. It will cut short a huge amount of public money and unnecessary harassment in the process of the Foreigner Tribunal.

Most of the declared foreigners claimed that they were Indian citizens. However, due to a lack of access to proper legal aid, they were declared foreigners through an ex parte decree or couldn't produce the documents before the Tribunal because of their inability to afford good lawyers. The Deputy Commissioner said that every time he visited the detention centre, the detainees complained that they didn't get proper legal service.

Accordingly, the Mission also recommended in its report, inter alia, that the detainees should be provided legal aid through either the District Legal Service Authority or NGOs. Also, the participants felt that in the case of the ex-parte decree, the DFN should get the opportunity to get heard in the Foreigners Tribunal itself.

The full 39-page report is available in the public domain online [9], but sadly, the Indian think-tank in New Delhi was seemingly indifferent or in the dark about the harsh realities prevailing in the state. Only Harsh Mander took some positive steps to rekindle the dying hopes of these condemned persons in Assam. He had drawn the attention of the Supreme Court of India through a Public Interest Litigation seeking Justice for the detainees.

Then, there was a report that Harsh Mander had requested Honorable Chief Justice of India Ranjan Gogoi to recuse himself from the ongoing hearing of his petition seeking the release of over 900 individuals – deemed to be foreigners – who had spent several years in detention under inhumane conditions in Assam. Harsh Mander cited observations made by Hon Chief Justice Gogoi in the course of earlier hearings, which he claimed suggested the Hon Judge had already made up his mind about the subject. However, his request for the Hon CJI's recusal was rejected; instead, the court ruled that Mander's name be struck off the petition and that the matter be argued by the Supreme Court's Legal Services Authority, with assistance from Mander's former lawyer, Prashant Bhushan, whom it appointed Amicus in the case", reported The Wire dated 2nd May 2019. [10] The actual

'Courtroom Exchanges' between petitioner Harsh Mander and the Hon Judges of the Supreme Court Bench are available on Live Law. in, on its website. [11]

On 10th May 2019, the Supreme Court bench of Honorable Chief Justice Ranjan Gogoi and Honorable Justice Sanjiv Khanna ordered that "detainees who have completed more than three years may be released" subject to fulfilling certain conditions, which include, among others, the execution of a bond with two sureties of Rs 1,00,000 each from Indian citizens; providing a specific verifiable address of stay after release; capturing biometric iris scans (if possible), all ten fingerprints, and photos to be stored in a secured database before release from the detention centres. [12]

On 4th July 2019, an English daily newspaper of Assam, 'The Sentinel,' reported, in parts, as follows:

> "Following directives from the apex court, the Assam government prepared the modality of terms and conditions for the release of such FT-declared 'foreigners.' The modality comprises details on how to apply, conditions of release, and other criteria for the declared foreigners to legally leave these detention camps. Before preparing the modality, the State Home and Political Department sought an opinion from the State Law Department on the issue with legal implications. The Law department opined that to carry out the apex court's order, necessary amendments to regulations and orders related to the Foreigners Tribunal were necessary. However, as the subject basically falls under the Central List, only the Central government can bring about the required amendments. Hence, the Home and Political Department forwarded its draft modalities along with the observations of the State Law Department to the Ministry of Home Affairs (MHA). After the Home Ministry carries out the modifications to the Foreigners Tribunal Order and gives its nod, the Assam government will issue the notification for the release of these detainees from the detention camps," [13]

On 26th August 2019, India's one of the major English-language daily newspapers, The Hindu, reported that the Assam Government had conditionally released ten people from the Goalpara centre who had completed more than three years in a detention centre after being declared foreigners. Five were Hindus, and five were Muslims, all of Bengali origin. A Hindu woman, aged 69, was the oldest, and the youngest was a 39-year-old Muslim man. The Foreigners' Tribunal granted them bail. They must report to the concerned police station once a week. [14]

On 17th March 2020, the Lok Sabha was informed that ten inmates of Assam's six detention centres, where declared or convicted 'foreigners' were kept, died in different hospitals during the last year from 1st March 2019 to 29th February 2020. Union Minister of State for Home G. Kishan Reddy said that 3,331 were lodged at the six detention centres in Assam, while another such facility with a capacity to hold 3,000 people was under construction. [15]

[1]Note: Recently, Outlook.com news magazine on 29th January 2023 reported that the Assam government had initiated the process to move declared and suspected foreigners in Goalpara district's newly built detention centre, renamed a transit camp. The largest detention centre in the country, constructed on 22 bighas of land (over 7 acres) 125 km away from Guwahati in Goalpara's West Matia on a budget of Rs 46 crore, became operational two days ago and can house 3000 inmates, including 400 women. Before the new "transit camp", Assam had six detention camps in existing Goalpara, Kokrajhar, Jorhat, Silchar, Dibrugarh, and Tezpur jails.

"The truth about Assam's detention centres: India Today Insight," under this caption, on 10th February 2020, author Kaushik Deka, wrote in the weekly news magazine India Today, among other things, the following:

> In a direct refutation of Prime Minister Narendra Modi's statement (at Delhi's Ramlila Maidan in 2019) that there are no detention centres in India, Nityananda Rai, Union Minister of State for Home, admitted in the Lok Sabha on 4th February to the existence of six such centres in Assam. However, this is not even the first time the Union Home Ministry has acknowledged the existence of detention centres in the country.
>
> So does this mean that there is truth to the allegation often raised during protests against the contentious Citizenship (Amendment) Bill 2019 - that "millions of Muslims left out of Assam's National Register of Citizens (NRC)" are being sent to detention centres? To put it simply, it's not a valid charge. ...... That they do exist is a fact, but the narrative that millions are confined there is untrue.

Kaushik Deka then explained why detention centres exist in Assam. On the question of how many people were kept in these detention centres, he wrote:

> Contrary to popular imagination, the six detention centres house only 834 individuals, of which 559 are Muslims and 275 are Hindus. In April 2019, the Supreme Court ordered the release of declared foreigners who had completed three years in detention provided they fulfilled certain conditions - two sureties, a verified address, and a bond of Rs 1 lakh plus their biometrics. According to government data, 761 individuals were released from detention centres in 2019.

To the question of why the government was then building a big detention centre in Assam's Goalpara to accommodate 3,000 individuals, Deka replied:

"Many human rights activists have questioned the ad hoc provision of state governments setting up detention centres within jail premises as illegal immigrants are not criminals. A visit in 2016 to one of the detention centres--in Kokrajhar--not only offered a glimpse of the pathetic conditions the inmates live in but also raised doubts about the randomness of the functioning of FTs in declaring an individual a foreigner. Ramani Biswas, a 32-year-old woman from Mayong, had been languishing there since 2009 when she, along with her husband, Dilip Biswas, 40, and daughters Kalpana, 15, and Archana, 9, were picked up by the authorities. Her court records show the family ignored notices sent by the FT. What makes the case bizarre is that both Ramani and Dilip's parents are Indian citizens, as are their siblings.

Giving Ramani company at the detention centre were Minara Begum, 32, from Udarband in Silchar; Momirunessa, 45, from Baghbar in Barpeta; Halima Khatun, 40, from Dhing in Nagaon; Gita Biswas, 50, from Shantipur in Baksa; and Basanti Mahanta, 40, from Bongaigaon. These women were the only ones in their family who had been charged with being illegal migrants. Their husbands, parents, and siblings remain Indian citizens.

Legal respite is available to these individuals as FT orders can be challenged in higher courts, but what about being forced to live along with criminals inside a jail? Why can't a foreigner, even if he or she has been living in India illegally, be provided decent living conditions in detention? The Goalpara detention centre, exclusively for illegal foreigners, could actually be a correct executive step towards providing humane living conditions to these inmates. While the Union Ministry of Home Affairs has been instructing the states since 2009 to set up detention centres, one of the circulars sent by the Modi government in 2018 also emphasizes that these centres include modern facilities. So a separate detention centre, such as the one coming up in Goalpara, may be slightly better news for detainees. [16]

Nevertheless, the pressing concerns for a review of the entire process of identifying foreigners in Assam reverberated in the Lok Sabha on 25th June 2019 with the pointed question from the outspoken Trinamool Congress's first-time MP Mahua Moitra:

"In a country where Ministers cannot produce degrees to show that they graduated from college, you expect dispossessed poor people to show papers as proof that they belong to this country?" [17]

"**Detained in Assam and Now Dead,** *Dulal Chandra's Fate Shows the Madness of Official Policy"* - under this caption, Writer, Poet, and Political Science Scholar from New Delhi's Jawaharlal Nehru University, Manash Firaq Bhattacharjee narrated a real-life story of a sixty-five-year-old Dulal Chandra Paul in the backdrop of Assam's pursuit for the illegal foreigners.

Two years ago, the Assam Foreigners' Tribunals declared the sexagenarian an illegal resident. They admitted him to the Guwahati Medical College and Hospital (GMCH) on 28th September 2019 due to his "deteriorating health," where he died on 13th October 2019. **The bizarre story of Dulal Chandra Paul started after he died** in the hospital when neither the state nor the family wanted to own him. "This is the madness that befalls any system that invents a territorial idea of human beings in the name of citizenship," wrote Bhattacharjee in his article that appeared on the news website The Wire on 22nd October 2019. The tragic tale, which progressed from the GMCH since Dulal Paul's death on 13th October 2019, within a couple of months of publishing the final list of Assam's NRC, has been touchingly told by the Political Science Scholar in his article, the pertinent part of which is quoted below:

> "Paul had been lodged in a detention centre (in Tezpur, 175 KM from Guwahati)) for the last two years. There are currently six such centres in Assam that house roughly 1,000 "illegal foreigners." Twenty-four people in Assam's detention camps have died in the last three years. The reason cited for the deaths is "illness".
>
> These are clearly not natural facts about people's deaths. Illness is a natural condition. But to fall ill within the premises of a detention centre is not natural. The term "foreigner" is not a natural but a politico-legal construct. In Assam, "foreigner" has been a politically accusative term since the 1979 Anti-foreigners' Movement. The concept of a "foreigner" in Assam refers to a noncitizen and a politico-legal nonentity. When citizenship claims are at stake, the term "foreigner" entails a political and legal crisis.
>
> The situation of someone who has been labelled a "foreigner" and confined in a detention camp raises ethical concerns. When a human being is deprived of natural rights – life, liberty, and property – the issue extends beyond what they lose to what they become after losing those rights.
>
> Having lost his claims to citizenship, Dulal was stripped of legal and political rights. Dulal was deemed an "illegal foreigner" who was deemed fit to be held in a detention centre until deportation. In her

essay, "The Perplexities in the Rights of Man," [1]Hannah Arendt argues that the loss of citizenship rights deprives a person of human rights. If one is not a citizen, the law does not recognize them as fully human. Being a noncitizen equates to being nonhuman. Dulal was thrust into an extrajudicial space of the detention centre, where, by law, he belonged to another category: the "illegal foreigner."

There is a zoological undertone to a detention centre, where human beings find themselves transformed into another category, falling out of favour with the laws of citizenship. Dulal's nephew, Sadhan Paul, stated that Dulal's siblings and their families made it to the National Register of Citizens (NRC). None of Dulal's three sons were included in the list released on August 31 this year.

It appears that the law has been quite arbitrary in its methods of identifying foreigners and citizens. There is an artificial legal divide within families. The process of identifying "illegal foreigners" (or citizens, for that matter) is evidently flawed. What is even more distressing is how this flawed system manifests itself in the minds and bodies of those detained within closed walls after being labelled foreigners.

Dulal's family introduced a major twist to the story, putting the state in a legal and moral dilemma. They refused to accept Dulal's deceased body, raising a series of questions for the law. Sadhan Paul raised this issue during a telephonic conversation with the Hindustan Times, stating, "How can we accept the body if he is a foreigner? Despite him having legal documents showing he was an Indian, he was declared a foreigner." It was a strategic move – questioning how a family could accept a body that was legally (and by extension, morally) estranged from them.

When officials asked family members to sign documents to claim Dulal's body, they refused. They were aware that by accepting a deceased foreigner, the family was accepting its own (and the deceased's) foreigner status. The family refused to comply with the complex norms of citizenship that the law had imposed on them. By designating Dulal as an "illegal foreigner," the law severed his moral and legal ties with his family. The family requested the law to claim Dulal's body, as it had already assumed complete control over his life, liberty, and nonhuman status.

Manvendra Pratap Singh, the deputy commissioner of Sonitpur district, where Dulal was a resident and where his family currently resides, expressed his dilemma to the Indian Express, stating, "He is not an Indian citizen. I cannot just authorize the cremation. The family has to accept him."

Dulal's deceased body was temporarily deprived of its moral ties with the family and its legal ties with the state. Even in death, like in life, there is a state of statelessness. A cremation is an act of claiming ownership. Neither the state nor the family wanted to claim Dulal. This is the madness that occurs when a system invents a territorial concept of human beings in the name of citizenship.

According to this law, humanity is a documented entity. The definition of a human being is based on legality. Merely possessing documents is insufficient; they must be attested and approved by the law. The law holds the ultimate authority to designate human beings as human. This constitutes a grave violation against the concept of natural rights that human beings inherently possess.

This distortion is facilitated by the delineation of national borders and the concept of citizenship. Those lacking citizenship documents are branded as nonhumans by the state. This is precisely what renders the idea of humanity a territorial, rather than a natural or moral, concept.

Sonitpur Superintendent of Police, Kumar Sanjit Krishna, has said that Paul's family relented after being informed that only the courts could decide Dulal's citizenship status and accepted Dulal's body for cremation. The law saved its skin by transferring its own moral responsibility onto the family. What occurred is a grave divorce between (pending) legality and morality and a division of ownership. The state owns your life (in detention), while the family owns your death.

The nature of Dulal's labour as a resident of Dhekiajuli in Sonitpur district finds no mention in the reports. But this is a crucial aspect. A man's identity as a noncitizen is completely insulated from his years of labour before he was rendered stateless. Isn't his labour part of his identity? Isn't this labour part (and proof) of his belonging? Has labour no bearing on citizenship rights? Once a man loses citizenship status, his years of labour become inessential to his fate?

Dulal's family had earlier claimed that he was "mentally unstable." Imagine the mental condition of people walled inside the socially (and legally) quarantined spaces of detention centres. Doesn't such partitioning of lives affect the mental stability of the sane and insane alike? The medical condition of people who died in detention centres must surely include this fact. [18]

Note: [1]Hannah Arendt (1906–1975) was one of the most influential political philosophers of the twentieth century. Born into a German-Jewish family, she was forced to leave Germany in 1933 and lived in Paris for the next eight years, working for several Jewish refugee organisations. In 1941 she immigrated to the United States and soon became part of a lively intellectual circle in New York. She held several academic positions at various American universities until she died in 1975.

According to a news report dated October 15, 2019, filed by a Senior Assistant Editor of Hindustan Times, Utpal Parashar, based in Guwahati: On Tuesday, October 15, 2019, officials from Tezpur jail, the detention centre where Paul was lodged, came to his house in Dhekiajuli. They brought with them a form where the name of the deceased was written, mentioning him as a foreigner, but the space for the address was left blank. The officials asked Paul's family members to sign the form so the body could be handed over for last rites. Sadhan Paul, the nephew of the deceased person, then asked the officials to include the address so that they knew Dulal Paul was Indian. But as the officials asked them to sign first, they refused. So, the efforts by authorities to hand over the body to the family have failed. Thus, since October 13, 2019, the sixty-five-year-old Dulal Chandra Paul's mortal remains were kept 'rested in peace' at the GMCH morgue. [19]

On November 1, 2019, the [1]CJP Team reported that: The family of Dulal Chandra Paul finally accepted Dulal's dead body for performing the last rites, almost ten days after he breathed his last at the GMCH. Dulal Paul's son Ashok repeatedly asked,

> "They said he is Bangladeshi, so why should we take the body? We have all the documents; how is my father, Bangladeshi?"
>
> The family finally relented only after Assam Chief Minister Sarbananda Sonowal met the family on Saturday, October 19, and personally appealed to them during a meeting with All Assam Bengali Youths Federation members. The family accepted the body on Tuesday, October 22, at about 2 PM, and cremation took place at about 8 PM. But the family's troubles are far from over. Paul's three sons are still out of the NRC, though his widow's name has been included in the list.
>
> In fact, in a cruel twist of fate, even the Gauhati High Court (earlier on January 18, 2019) upheld the Foreigners' Tribunal order declaring Paul a 'foreigner'. [20]

Note: [1]Citizens for Justice and Peace (CJP) is a Human Rights movement dedicated to upholding and defending the freedom and constitutional rights of all Indians.

There was an assurance apparently that submission of a petition to the Supreme Court of India for a review of Paul's case would be facilitated by the local authorities so that, in due course, the names of the three offspring of the deceased find a place in Assam's NRC. However, it is understood that Paul's family has not yet been able to approach the Apex Court even after three years. Their financial condition has deteriorated further, and the family is presently living hand to mouth.

* * * * * *

Chapter 15.

Assam NRC
The story so far ....

How we ended up converting legal citizens into illegal immigrants?

"Since partition, rarely has India seen a man-made calamity as disastrous as this exercise, which resulted in the "othering" of over 1.9 million people. The story is still unfolding and best left for another day". [1]

The NRC is not just an isolated administrative exercise but a process embedded in history and the larger politics of Assamese nationalism, which is principally characterized by hatred towards outsiders, particularly 'the Bangladeshi.' In many ways, Assamese nationalism and its agents are directly responsible for the impoverishment and anxiety experienced by the people of Assam on account of the exercise, according to author duo Angshuman Choudhury and Dr. Suraj Gogoi.

Within a fortnight, the government released the final list of people eligible to be included in the updated version of the 1951-NRC of Assam on 31st August 2019. Angshuman Choudhury, a Senior Researcher at the Institute of Peace and Conflict Studies, New Delhi, and Dr. Suraj Gogoi, an Assistant Professor at RV University, Bangalore, jointly wrote an article on the subject titled "A Narrow Nationalism Again: The Positions Held by Some Intellectuals on the NRC Only Further Legitimize a Rapid Descent into Regional Exclusivism." It appeared in The Hindu newspaper on 12th September 2019. The excerpt quoted above is from that article where, among other things, the author duo also wrote: "With the release of the final draft of the National Register of Citizens (NRC) in Assam, which has pushed over 19 lakh people closer to statelessness, a coterie of Assamese ethno-nationalist intellectuals and their external allies have taken upon themselves the unenviable task of defending the exercise." [2]

Just one week before, on 5th September 2019, renowned literary critic and social scientist from Assam, Hiren Gohain, wrote an article on the same topic in the same newspaper, The Hindu. The caption of the article said: "It is important to contextualize the NRC: Errors aside, the process was rigorous, methodical, and **did not target any particular community.**" [3] (Emphasis by Subir)

And yet, a senior journalist of India's North-eastern region, Mrinal Talukdar, at the outset of his book "The Game Called NRC" wrote inter alia:

> "If for some, the NRC is an absolute necessity in India to weed out the illegal migrants, but for a large section, it is a matter of not only gross human right violation but also 'religious persecution' in disguise" [4]

Between the contrasting views appearing in the public domain amidst huge controversy and protracted debate on updating the 1951 NRC of Assam, which should have facilitated the identification of foreign nationals living in the state illegally, there was confusion, chaos, and chagrin among the commoners, social activists, and the unsuccessful NRC applicants across the board. While the political parties and various social organizations in the state are playing their drums in different bits, by contrast, there is widespread apprehension among civil liberty groups that the process of updating NRC perhaps was not fair. As the final list revealed, it eventually resulted in numerous exclusions of **Muslim minorities and Hindu Bengalis** (unfortunately, this is how the Bengali community is being described by some these days), who are believed to be genuine Indian citizens. Given that the sword of Damocles is hanging over nearly two million people in Assam, it's essential to get to the bottom of the unfolding story so far and make an honest attempt to separate the wheat from the chaff. So, let's begin at the beginning again and try to get a holistic picture of the NRC story of Assam – so far emerged.

The 'National Register of Citizens' is abbreviated as NRC. According to the office of the State Coordinator of National Registration (NRC) Government of Assam:

> "After the conduct of the Census of 1951, a National Register of Citizens (NRC) was prepared in respect of each village showing the houses or holdings in serial order and indicating against each house or holding the number and names of persons staying therein, and in respect of each individual, the father's name/mother's name or husband's name, nationality, sex, age, marital status, educational qualification, means of livelihood or occupation and visible

identification mark. This was done by copying out in registers the particulars recorded during the Census done in 1951." [5]

Notably, only Assam has the unique distinction in the country of having such a register called the NRC, which was the first and the only one of its kind so far, prepared way back in 1951. At that time, the state's population was only 80 lakhs (8 million). As per the latest census report of 2011, Assam's population is now over 3.11 crore (31.10 million). [6]

"Why did Assam prepare the 1951 NRC, which has become a touchstone for citizenship today?" Under this title, the Indian digital news publication Scroll.in published an article on 27th July 2019 written by journalist Ipsita Chakravarty, which, among other things, mentioned that much about the 1951 NRC exercise, its motivations, and uses, was still opaque. The bureaucrats in the census report vaguely mentioned that the NRC would be useful for "administrative purposes" and socio-economic surveys.

Quoting Arupjyoti Saikia, Professor of History at IIT Guwahati, Assam, journalist Ipsita Chakravarty also wrote that the register was born during the chaotic post-Partition moment, which saw vast population exchanges and communal riots. The preparation of Assam's 1951 NRC was partly in response to a Nehruvian India to the immediate post-Partition crisis, especially to extraordinary resistance from Assam to house post-Partition refugees. One of the primary intentions of the NRC was to prepare a village-based inventory of residents, as the Indian states still had federal ambitions to retain their distinct political/cultural characteristics. But very little is known about the political-bureaucratic mechanism put in place at that time to spell out this process because its archival records are yet to be made public. [7]

Even though the historical records are yet to be made public, an informed reader can now easily figure out, or at least make an educated guess, why Assam prepared the 1951 NRC by joining sagaciously certain dots, which emerged out of the earlier discussions, given that some significant developments that ensued just before and after the end of British rule in India involving Assam could now be conceptualized from the deliberations so far made in this book. Most aspects of the 1951 NRC of Assam should, therefore, fall into place by relating to the relevant information, especially those which are encapsulated hereunder:

a) The Cabinet Mission Plan to grant independence without partitioning India collapsed due to Assam's determined opposition to be clubbed in the same group as Bengal, even though both Assam and Bengal were Bengali-majority provinces. It eventually led to the break-up of British India with the formation of Pakistan - a separate homeland for the Muslims.

b) Concurrently, India lost its densely populated Bengali-dominant Sylhet district of Assam in the referendum due to the omissions and commissions of some Congress leaders of the Assam Pradesh Committee.

c) Author Sujit Chaudhuri, in a Seminar Paper titled "A 'god-sent' opportunity?" wrote, among other things: "The transfer of Sylhet to Pakistan was hailed by the Assamese public opinion. The only daily newspaper of Assam, The Assam Tribune, hailed the transfer of Sylhet: 'The Assamese public seem to feel relieved of a burden' (21 July 1947)." [8]

d) Immediately after the Partition, local Congress leaders of Brahmaputra Valley started to float the notion that Assam was only for the Assamese, disregarding the numerous indigenous Bengali-speaking people inhabiting the truncated Assam, as discussed earlier. According to a news report dated 29th August 1947 in The Shillong Times, Assam Chief Minister Gopinath Bordoloi professed the buzzword "Assam for the Assamese". He reiterated it at the Students' Congress held at Golaghat, reported in the same newspaper on 19th October 1947. [9]

e) Assam Governor, Sir Akbar Hydari, echoed this policy[1] of the state government, "Assam for the Assamese", in his address at the Assam Legislative Assembly on 5th November 1947. The following is a quotation from that speech: — "The natives of Assam are now masters of their own house. They have a Government which is both responsible and responsive to them. They can take what steps are necessary for the encouragement and propagation of the Assamese language and culture and of the languages and customs of the tribal peoples, who are their fellow citizens and who also must have a share in the formation of such policies. The Bengalee has no longer the power, even if he had the will, to impose anything on the peoples of these Hills and Valleys which constitute Assam. The basis of such feelings against him as exist is fear—but now there is no cause for fear. I would, therefore. appeal to you to exert all the influence you possess to give **the stranger in our midst** a fair deal, provided, of course, he in his turn deals loyally with us." [10] (Emphasis by Subir)

f) An extract quoted from Assam Government Circular No. 195/47/188 dated 4th May 1948, issued on the question of Land Settlement, also read: "In view of the emergency created by the influx of refugees into the Province from Pakistan territories and in order to preserve peace, tranquillity, and social equilibrium in the towns and villages, Government reiterate their policy that settlement of land should in no circumstances be made with persons who are not indigenous to the Province should include, for the purpose of land settlement during the present emergency, persons who are non-Assamese settlers in Assam though they already have lands and houses of their own and have made Assam their home in all intents and purposes." [11]

g) Author Sujit Chaudhuri, in a Seminar Paper titled "A 'god-sent' opportunity?" also wrote, among other things: "Thus the Bordoloi ministry pursued a policy that **put a ban on the settlement of land not only for the refugees but also for all non-Assamese settlers who might have been living in Assam for generations.** The central government assessed the availability of fallow cultivable land in Assam through a committee headed by Dorab Gandhi, who reported that 18 million acres of cultivable land could be used for the new settlement. This figure is also tallied with the Assam government's own assessment as given in its publication, The Problem of Agricultural Development (Assam Government Press, 1946, Table VI, p. 8) and Industrial Planning and Development of Assam (Government of Assam, 1948). The Census of India, 1951, Vol. 1 also reported that in Assam and adjoining areas **'the percentage of unused land is highest among all the sub-regions of India'** (p. 22). The central government insisted that the vast tracts of wasteland in Assam should be utilized for production, as the available surplus was more than sufficient to accommodate both refugees and indigenous landless people." [12] (Emphasis by Subir)

Note: ¹The Governor's address to the Legislative Assembly is essentially a statement of policy prepared by the Council of Ministers. [13]

On 1st March 1950, the Indian Parliament passed the Immigrants (Expulsion from Assam) Act, 1950, allowing authorized officials of the Centre to eject individuals who had entered the state from territories outside India if their presence, as stipulated by the law, was "detrimental to the interests of the general public of India or of any section thereof or of any Scheduled Tribe in Assam." Significantly, the Indian Parliament thus enacted a law to expel 'immigrants' from Assam in the first year of the Republic of India in 1950, whereas it enacted India's Citizenship Act in the sixth year of the Republic of India, providing for the acquisition and determination of Indian citizenship — five years later — in 1955!

As the problem of refugee influx inherent within the partition proposal itself threatened to neutralize the so-called gains achieved by the removal of the densely populated Bengali-dominated Sylhet district from Assam, Gopinath Bordoloi and his Congress ministry vehemently opposed the central government's attempt to settle these refugees in Assam.

Ironically, all these aforementioned 'refugees in Assam' — as they were called then — were natives of India just the day before, before the country's independence on 15th August 1947. Among them, some were even indigenous men and women of Assam. Due to the cunning political manoeuvres of certain selfish 'leaders,' their Indian citizenships were stripped away. Unfortunately, no one addressed the injustices these unfortunate people endured in the recent past. It is worth recalling that over 43% of the people of Assam's Sylhet district had voted to remain in Assam in the contentious Sylhet referendum on the 6th and 7th of July 1947, which Assam lost to Pakistan.

It is evident from the events recounted thus far that the divisions created by the British administration between the Assamese and Bengali people during their nearly 200 years of colonial rule in India persisted not only until the end of their rapacious rule but also the animosity fostered between the two major communities in Assam remained, if not intensified, even after the chaotic rulers were ousted from our country. Figures like the notorious British civil servant C. S. Mullan, the 1931 Census Superintendent in Assam, who played a key role in instilling divisive sentiments, continue to influence many crucial decisions with long-term consequences through their speeches and writings. We have witnessed this before and will likely see more as the narrative unfolds.

However, on 9th August 1950, Bishnuram Medhi, known as the Iron Man of Assam, had to be sworn in as Assam's Chief Minister due to the unexpected passing of Gopinath Bordoloi on 5th August 1950.

In 1951, the first national Census of independent India commenced. Addressing an army of enumerators in the state on 9th February 1951, Chief Minister Bishnu Ram Medhi said:

> "You have the proud privilege and unique honour of participating in the crucial task of collecting data during the Census operation to enable the Nation to identify its problems and devise a plan for their resolution based on such data. I may also inform you that the first

National Register of Citizens of the Republic of Bharata will also be compiled from the data collected by you during this Census operation."

For the 1951 Census, each respondent had to answer 14 questions on individual slips. Responses to 11 of those questions were transferred to the citizen's register. Three questions were excluded: whether the respondent was a "displaced person," on bilingualism, and whether the respondent was "an indigenous person of Assam." The Census reports do not explain why. [14]

The National Registers prepared during the Census of 1951 were stored in the offices of Deputy Commissioners and Sub Divisional Officers as per instructions issued by the Government of India in 1951. Later, these registers were transferred to the Police in the early 1960s. According to the State Government, "the NRC, when updated, shall become an important legal document for a citizen to reference their Indian Citizenship status. Moreover, as Assam has been facing the problem of illegal migrants from Bangladesh, it is crucial to identify them. Therefore, it is imperative for citizens of India in Assam to ensure the inclusion of their names in the updated NRC. [16]

Interestingly, contrary to popular belief that the Assam Accord mandated updating the 1951-NRC of Assam, in reality, it's an erroneous notion. There was no provision for updating the NRC in the 1985 Accord. It was only stated in paragraph 8.1 of the Assam Accord that "The Government will arrange for the issue of citizenship certificates in future only by the authorities of the Central Government."

The question of detecting Bangladeshis by updating Assam's 1951-NRC was not even considered between 1985 and 1990, even though AASU had demanded the same in their first memorandum to Prime Minister Indira Gandhi on 2nd February 1980. *With emotions running high and typical anti-Bangladeshi Assamese jingoism at its peak in the vernacular media of Assam, no one in the state seemed to be concerned about how the Bangladeshis would or could be filtered out.*' Although almost the entire Brahmaputra valley was on the roads demanding detection, deletion, and deportation of Bangladeshis from the soil of Assam, the NRC was, in fact, not on anyone's mind.

In the numerous meetings that preceded and followed the signing of the Assam Accord of 1985, neither the government nor the AASU or the Assamese intelligentsia were ever serious about raising the matter of NRC, except in the very first memorandum the AASU had submitted to Prime Minister Indira Gandhi on 2nd February 1980, where, among other issues, it was merely stated as follows:

- The National Register of Citizens (NRC) of 1951 should be updated by incorporating any additions to the number of each family since the time of its compilation.
- Comparing the NRC with successive electoral rolls since 1952 will also aid in keeping it up-to-date.

Even in the post-accord years when the AGP government was formed in the state, it never dawned on the AGP leaders or their advisers that, as per the Assam Accord, updating the 1951-NRC could be a starting point to detect illegal infiltrators. Simply put, the NRC was just not on the radar of the AGP. However, the Atal Behari Vajpayee-led government showed keen interest in resolving the core issue, and the arrival of Mr Gopal Krishna Pillai as Joint Secretary (North East) in the MHA in 1998 gave the issue much-needed momentum. Pillai headed a Sub-Committee formed by the Centre to oversee the implementation of the Assam Accord. At the instance of G. K. Pillai, the NRC took centre stage at the 7th Tripartite Talk held on 17th November 1999. He convinced the AASU leaders to prioritize the NRC as a means to detect illegal Bangladeshis. However, with Pillai's exit from the MHA, the impetus was quickly lost. [17]

As a matter of fact, the formal decision to update the NRC was taken on 5th May 2005, twenty years after the signing of the Assam Accord at a tripartite meeting of the Central Government with the representatives of the All Assam Students' Union and the Assam Government. The then Prime Minister, Dr Manmohan Singh, chaired that tripartite meeting. Remarkably, barring the representatives of AASU and its mentors, NO OTHER stakeholders were taken on board while arriving at the two momentous decisions, viz. the Assam Accord (15th August 1985) and NRC Updating (5th May 2005). Both decisions entailed far-reaching ramifications for all the residents of Assam. Yet, all others were kept out while taking these resolutions. The tripartite meeting of 5th May 2005 was also somewhat an 'All-Assam-Affairs'. Apart from the AASU and the Assam Government, former Prime Minister Dr Manmohan Singh, who represented the Central Government and chaired the meeting, was a Rajya Sabha (Upper House of the Indian Parliament) member at that time elected from Assam!

Notwithstanding, the actual process of updating the NRC did not gain momentum right away. In June 2010, five years later, a 'pilot project' for updating the NRC was started in two blocks in the Kamrup and Barpeta districts of Assam. Soon, the All Assam Minority Students Union (AAMSU) objected to these pilot projects mainly for not providing enough documents as options for applicants to prove their permanent residency in the State. The pilot projects had to be abandoned within a month because of serious law-

and-order problems, but not before four youths, Majom Ali, Moidul Islam Molla, Sirajul Haq, and Motlab Ali, suffered martyrdom as a result of indiscriminate lathi-charge and firing by the security forces on 21st July 2010. The incident was reported as the 'Barpeta Incident' in the media. [18]

Again, contrary to popular belief, the Supreme Court was not originally involved in updating the 1951 NRC of Assam. Initially, it was only a political decision taken in May 2005 to update the 1951 NRC that should be the basis on which illegal foreigners in Assam could be sieved. The Apex Court came into the picture much later. According to reports, while hearing a writ petition filed by an NGO Assam Public Works (APW) in July 2009, the Supreme Court had directed the Centre in May 2013 to finalize the modalities for updating the NRC by 16th July 2013. Consequently, when on 5th December 2013, the Registrar General of Citizen Registration issued the notification in this regard, the 1951 NRC of Assam was then literally 'exhumed' for updating in a desecrated, defaced, and numerically depleted condition. Then it came to light that the NRC for as many as six districts of Assam and the complete electoral rolls of 1966 and 1971 were unavailable. [19]

On 17th December 2014, the Supreme Court of India directed the government to resume updating the NRC and simultaneously, the Bench comprising Justice Ranjan Gogoi and Justice Rohinton Fali Nariman took it upon itself to monitor the task, as per the report by Mohsin Alam Bhat, a legal scholar with a focus on constitutional law, minority rights, and law and politics. His research combines ethnographic and socio-legal methods in the study of the law. The report appeared on the news website The Wire dated 7th January 2019. The relevant part of the story under the sub-head, "The paradoxical basis of judicial supervision," is quoted below:

The Supreme Court initiated the NRC update earnestly on December 17, 2014, through an order in the case of Assam Sanmilita Mahasangha v Union of India. The Mahasangha had challenged section 6A of the Citizenship Act, which had been enacted to give effect to the Assam Accord by providing separate rules of citizenship in the state.

Under this provision, in contrast with other states, migrants of Indian origin who settled in Assam before 25th March 1971 could qualify either as Indian citizens or as a route to citizenship. In its petition, the Mahasangha argued that the provision violated the right to life of the citizens in the state by encouraging the "massive influx of illegal migrants" from Bangladesh. It also argued that the distinct regime compromised their right to culture as guaranteed by the Constitution.

A sympathetic bench – consisting of Justice Ranjan Gogoi and Justice R.F. Nariman – recommended that the issue be referred to a larger constitutional bench for final determination. In doing so, the bench raised a serious question on the constitutional validity of section 6A (of the Citizenship Act, 1955). But in the same order, the bench also decided to commence supervising the NRC update, on a court-determined calendar, based precisely on the requirements under section 6A.

The Supreme Court initiated one of the most ambitious judiciary-led bureaucratic exercises in the history of the country on the basis of the rules whose legal validity it is yet to determine! This paradox, which appears to have been completely overlooked in the current discussions of NRC, raises uncomfortable questions for the judicial process.

Should it not have been more prudent for the court to wait for the final legal assessment of section 6A? Has the NRC process made the court's future constitutional bench reference superfluous? Or will finally hearing the reference make the NRC process superfluous? [20] (Emphasis by Subir)

It is worth mentioning here that if a person is born in Assam on or after 25th March 1971 but before 1st July 1987, then he or she is a citizen of India by birth irrespective of the citizenship status of his or her parents, based on Section 3(1)(a) of the Citizenship Act, 1955. However, for inclusion in the National Register of Citizens (NRC), a resident of Assam is mandatorily required to prove his or her ancestor's residency in Assam or elsewhere in the country **before** the cut-off date of 25th March 1971 through documentary evidence. Such compliance is not required to prove one's citizenship according to the provisions under the Constitution of India as well as the Citizenship Act, of 1955. Hence, the cut-off date criteria prescribed for residents in Assam under Rule 4(A)(2) of the Citizenship Rules, 2003, for inclusion in NRC, is a clear violation of both the Constitution of India as well as the Citizenship Act, 1955. Accordingly, the issue of the validity of Section 6A of the Citizenship Act was contested in the case of Assam Sanmilita Mahasangha & Ors. Vs. Union of India in Writ Petition (Civil) No. 562 of 2012 and the matter was referred by the Supreme Court Bench, consisting of Justices Ranjan Gogoi and Rohinton Fali Nariman, to the Chief Justice of India for the constitution of an appropriate Bench to address the questions raised in this regard.

However, pending a decision in this matter regarding the validity of Section 6A of the Citizenship Act, 1955, the Supreme Court Bench directed in their Judgement dated 17th December 2014 to update the NRC in the case of Assam, considering that the same is valid ("As Section 6A of the Citizenship Act must be deemed to be valid until the larger Bench decides these matters, we will proceed, for the purposes of this order, on the footing that Section 6A of the Citizenship Act is valid"). [21]

Incidentally, Section 6A deals with "special provisions as to the citizenship of persons covered by the Assam Accord". It states that all those who came to Assam on or after 1st January 1966 but before 25th March 1971, from the specified territory (which includes all territories of Bangladesh at the time of the commencement of the Citizenship (Amendment) Act, 1985), and have since then been residents of Assam, must register themselves under Section 18 for citizenship. According to a recent news report in the Indian Express dated 11th January 2023, Chief Justice of India D Y Chandrachud is presiding over a five-judge Constitution Bench, which is hearing whether Section 6A of the Citizenship Act, 1955 suffers from any constitutional infirmity. The other bench members are Justices M R Shah, Krishna Murari, Hima Kohli, and P S Narasimha. [22]

By the way, when the first NRC of Assam was prepared in tandem with the Census enumeration in 1951, it was envisaged that the NRC would maintain 'intercensal' continuity. However, that never happened. Had it been regularly updated every ten years, the Government could have avoided putting the entire population of Assam on an unparalleled trial in the manner and with the complexity that the people had to endure in the process. The fault obviously lies with the administration, for which the unfortunate people had to pay dearly.

Furthermore, the Census enumeration of Assam in 1951 was completed hurriedly between 9th February and 28th February 1951, and the enumerators were "unqualified or ill-qualified persons". It was a casual affair prepared without planning, training, or organization. At that time, the NRC was a secret administrative document, not open to inspection. It was also prepared by grossly untrained Census enumerators and completed simultaneously with the Census only in twenty days. With time, even the process of tallying the slips, which formed the basis for the NRC and the NRC itself, was abandoned at the orders of the Registrar General of Census. As is evident from the Census Report, there were many moments of irregularities as the data entered into the NRC were copied into census slips contrary to the established procedure of the slips becoming the basis for the NRC. According to the Census Superintendent, "An important innovation of this Census was the preparation of a National Register of Citizens in which all important census data was transcribed from the census slips with the exception of the Census questions No.6 (displaced persons), No.8 (bilingualism), and No.13 (indigenous persons)".

Moreover, the reliability of 1951 NRC data was doubtful, and the accuracy of its source - the Census Report of 1951 - was also not entirely accurate. The sample verification for the accuracy of the 1951 Census report itself is confirmed on page 12, "The error in the Census count was compounded of cases of clear omissions (making for under-enumeration), fictitious entries (making for over-enumeration), erroneous count of visitors and absentees (which could make for either over-enumeration or under-enumeration), and omission of occupied houses (an error making under-enumeration). Verification of the Census Count of non-household persons was, of course, not possible".

Also, even though the Census of 1951 developed the first and only NRC so far, this document itself became an irregular affair that had never been updated or regularly maintained in the district offices, as initially envisaged. The Assam Government candidly admitted this in reply to a question in the Assam Legislative Assembly in 2015. Earlier in 1970, when the courts in Assam were seized with the citizenship question, the Guwahati High Court held that the 1951 NRC was inadmissible evidence according to the Evidence Act. It is, therefore, clear that both the Census Report and the NRC of 1951 were hardly dependable documents to use as tools for recognizing the 'foreigners' and the 'indigenous' people in Assam. [23] [24]

Despite this, the recent updating process of the NRC in Assam was premised on its 1951-NRC and the electoral rolls till 1971, keeping in view the Assam Accord stipulation that all 'foreigners' who had entered Assam before 25th March 1971 would be recognized as Indians, except the entrants between 1961 and 1971 would be denied voting rights for ten years. The Assam Accord also specified that foreigners who entered Assam on or after 25th March 1971 were illegal immigrants, so their names from the electoral rolls must be deleted.

Thus, the updating process of the NRC rested primarily on 14 prescribed documents on the basis of which a person was asked to show his linkage with his ancestors or his existence within the territory of India before the 25th of March, 1971. Failure to produce such a link would result in non-eligibility to have his name entered in the updated NRC of Assam. Therefore, the official notification stated that:

"There will be two requirements for inclusion of names of any person in updated NRC–

1. **The first requirement** is the collection of ANY ONE of the following documents of List A issued before midnight of 24th March 1971, where the

name of self or ancestor* appears (to prove residence in Assam up to midnight of 24th March 1971): (1) 1951 NRC OR (2) Electoral Roll(s) up to 24th March 1971 (midnight) OR (3) Land & Tenancy Records OR (4) Citizenship Certificate OR (5) Permanent Residential Certificate OR (6) Refugee Registration Certificate OR (7) Passport OR (8) LIC OR (9) Any Govt. issued License/Certificate OR (10) Govt. Service/ Employment Certificate OR (11) Bank/Post Office Accounts OR (12) Birth Certificate OR (13) Board/University Educational Certificate OR (14) Court Records/Processes.

Furthermore, two other documents viz (1) Circle Officer/GP Secretary Certificate in respect of married women migrating after marriage (can be of any year before or after 24th March (midnight) 1971), and (2) Ration Card issued up to the midnight of 24th March 1971 can be adduced as supporting documents. However, these two documents shall be accepted only if accompanied by any one of the documents listed above.

2. **The second requirement** arises if the name in any of the documents of List A is not of the applicant himself/herself but that of an ancestor, namely, father or mother or grandfather or grandmother or great-grandfather or great-grandmother (and so on) of the applicant. In such cases, the applicant shall have to submit documents as in List B below to establish a relationship with such ancestor, i.e., father or mother or grandfather or grandmother or great grandfather or great grandmother etc., whose name appears in List A. Such documents shall have to be a legally acceptable document which clearly proves such a relationship.

(1) Birth Certificate OR (2) Land document OR (3) Board/University Certificate OR (4) Bank/LIC/Post Office records OR (5) Circle Officer/GP Secretary Certificate in the case of married women OR (6) Electoral Roll OR (7) Ration Card OR (8) Any other legally acceptable document.

Points to remember: Providing any one of the documents of List A of ANY PERIOD up to midnight of 24th March 1971 shall be enough to prove eligibility for inclusion in the updated NRC." [25]

Dr Binayak Dutta, Assistant Professor in the Department of History at North-Eastern Hill University, offered an insightful analysis in an article titled "The Illusive Citizen: the Predicament of Determining Citizens between Politics and the Law in Assam," which was published in the Sabrangindia.in news & media website on July 3rd, 2019. The analysis illuminated the precarious situation faced by residents of Assam in proving their Indian citizenship according to officially prescribed parameters.

For instance, an applicant's unequivocal Indian citizenship could be established if their name appeared in either of two crucial documents: the 1951-NRC or the electoral rolls up to 1971. However, it's worth noting that to fulfil this criterion, an individual must have been above seventy years of age by 2015 (when the updating exercise commenced). Considering the average life expectancy in India, recorded as 67.5 according to the 2011 Census, it's evident that a significant portion of the population eligible to have their names listed in the NRC from 1951 or the voters' lists until 1971 would likely have passed away by that time. This implies that more than 90% of the population, predominantly individuals aged 70 or younger, would not be able to readily prove their citizenship using the 1951-NRC or the electoral rolls until 1971.

Furthermore, the 1951-Assam NRC, heralded as the cornerstone document during its recent updating exercise, was prepared under the provisions of the Census Act, of 1948. However, Section 15 of the Census Act specifically states that documents or records prepared under the Act are not admissible as evidence, a position affirmed by the High Court in 1970 (AIR 1970 Assam and Nagaland 206). Even the voters' lists of Assam lack conclusiveness due to significant territorial changes in the province between 1951 and 1971, with records from constituencies falling outside the present state boundaries often being unavailable in other state government offices.

Moreover, the second category of documents could be broadly classified under indicators such as literacy rate, employment records, institutional births, etc., while the third set comprised Land & Tenancy Records. Dr. Binayak Dutta's meticulous examination of each document within these categories, as specified by the government, underscored the extremely limited likelihood of individuals possessing them. [26] Detailed analysis can be found on the aforementioned website link.

Nevertheless, the Assam Government proceeded with the NRC update primarily relying on the 1951-NRC and electoral rolls until 1971, supplemented by the aforementioned documents. The responsibility for this unprecedented undertaking was entrusted to the Home Secretary, Prateek Hajela, an M. Tech graduate in Electronics from Delhi IIT, who was designated as the State Coordinator for the NRC Assam. According to Hajela, the NRC update presented significant challenges. The complexity of the exercise was compounded by the fact that the crucial legacy data, comprising the 1951 NRC and Electoral Rolls of Assam up to March 24th, 1971, were predominantly handwritten or printed in Assamese and Bengali fonts, and were to be maintained by district administrations.

It is noteworthy that in 1951, Assam comprised only eight districts, including the present-day states of Meghalaya, Mizoram, and Nagaland. However, by August 15th, 2015, the number of districts in Assam had increased to 27, and on June 27th, 2016, Majuli, the largest river island globally, was declared a district, thus becoming the 28th district in Assam. [27] To tackle the complexity of updating the 1951-NRC, the government decided to commence anew, opting to develop a digitized system. After approximately a year of conceptualization, another year was devoted to developing the Digitized Legacy Data Development (DLDD) for NRC updating. When tenders were invited for DLDD, major software developers in the country did not respond. However, a local firm, Bohniman Systems, accepted the challenge with guidance from Hajela, as reported by the Kolkata edition of the national newspaper The Hindu on July 29th, 2018. [28]

> "I had two options: to start from scratch and build a digitized system, or to give up," said Prateek Hajela, Assam's Principal Secretary, Home, and NRC State Coordinator, in an interview with The Hindu.
>
> If 2013 was dedicated to conceptualizing the system, the following year focused on digitizing legacy data development (DLDD). Despite major software system developers in the country not responding to the tender for DLDD, a local firm, Bohniman Systems, took up the challenge with guidance from Mr. Hajela, an M.Tech. graduate in Electronics from IIT, Delhi." [29]

Note: [1]Legacy data refers to information stored in outdated or obsolete systems, formats, or technologies. In this context, it includes a combination of the 1951 NRC and electoral rolls of Assam from that year until March 24, 1971.

Note: Digitized Legacy Data Development (DLDD) involves compiling soft copies of legacy data images and their corresponding digitized records.

In 2015, applications were invited from the entire population of Assam for enrollment of names in the NRC. The actual verification process commenced on September 1st, 2015, following the closure of applications on the previous day.

It is surprising that instead of assuming responsibility, the government placed the onus on the PEOPLE to prove their citizenship, framing it as a means to screen illegal infiltrators. The government resorted to an ELIMINATION PROCESS by planning to separate those who could prove their citizenship and potentially declare the rest as "foreigners." Consequently, it mandated the entire population of Assam to "apply" for inclusion of their names in the NRC. The government demanded that the people of Assam establish the genuineness of their citizenship as if all were foreigners. This demand was made in a state where the government itself had never provided any supporting documents to its people regarding their citizenship. When Aadhaar, an individual identity card providing a personal introduction, was issued to Indian citizens nationwide, Assam was excluded from the scheme. This further complicated the task for Assam's inhabitants to establish their identity.

Additionally, Assam presents unique challenges. For generations, many Bengali-origin people have resided in 'Chars' - the fertile sandbars or riverine islands of the Brahmaputra and its tributaries. According to a 1985 Government report, there were 1,256 'Chars' in 11 districts of the Brahmaputra Valley, inhabited by 20 to 25 lakh people. These areas are frequently submerged due to flash floods, forcing their population to relocate swiftly. In such critical situations, it becomes extremely difficult for them to carry even the bare essentials of their livelihoods, let alone decades-old documents to establish their citizenship. Moreover, the mighty Brahmaputra River frequently changes its course, causing floods almost every year, which devastates villages and destroys important papers such as documents supporting Indian citizenship. Therefore, the absurdity of demanding 'legacy data' and 'proof of Indian citizenship' from such people requires no further elaboration.

Yet, the government placed the burden of proving Indian citizenship on individual residents, treating all as foreigners. By applying the Foreigners' Act 1946 Section 9 to all residents of Assam, the government disregarded the minimum legal safeguard of the concept "innocent until proven guilty" under the Universal Declaration of Human Rights, article 11. Due to the government's failure to detect illegal infiltrators through administrative mechanisms and policing, it was presumed from the outset that every resident of Assam was a foreigner. This simplistic approach not only cast suspicion on the entire population of the state, which is detrimental to democracy but also ignored the practical challenges faced by people in proving the genuineness of their citizenship, as discussed earlier.

It is pertinent to recall that earlier, in 2005, the Supreme Court ruled that citizenship verification in Assam – or, for that matter, anywhere in India – must happen under the precept of the Foreigners Act by shifting the burden of proof onto the individual (Sarbananda Sonowal vs Union of India. Writ Petition (Civil) 131 of 2000, judgment dated 12th July 2005). The State, on the other hand, need not prove their suspicion at all. This most lethal blow to due process was a turning point, reversing the International Covenant on Civil and Political Rights 1966, which upholds the right to be presumed innocent until proven guilty. The NRC process extended this logic writ large. The institutional practice of the FTs (Foreigners' Tribunals) showed that they interpreted this (burden of proof on the individual) requirement in ways that sometimes made it practically impossible for individuals to meet. Individuals, most of whom were poor and functionally illiterate, were expected to present error-free and comprehensive documents, often corroborated with oral evidence from relatives and government officials who had to appear before the FTs.

Official orders further exposed the problematic nature of the process, again ratified by India's Supreme Court, which exempted 'persons who are originally inhabitants of the State of Assam' from any 'further proof or inquiry' for automatic inclusion in the NRC (Assam Public Works vs Union of India. Writ Petition (Civil) No. 274 of 2009, order dated 13th August 2019). The category of 'Original Inhabitant (O.I.)' is nowhere defined, but in practice was taken to **exclude** people who spoke Bengali, Nepali, or Hindi, even if they had lived in Assam for generations. [30] Significantly, numerous aboriginal Bengalis like the 'Sylhetis' living in Assam were also not counted as Original Inhabitants (O.I.).

From day one, the attitude of some people involved in the process of updating the NRC was somewhat unfriendly, uncaring, and intimidating towards the non-Asamiya applicants, as if all of them were foreigners or illegal immigrants. Nearly 50 lakh people had initially submitted Gaon Panchayat (G.P.) certificates as a document to prove their citizenship. The Office of the State Coordinator of NRC, Assam, had earlier listed 'G.P. Secretary Certificate in case of married women' as one of the admissible documents in its List B. In March 2017 (i.e., 18 months AFTER the verification process started on 1st September 2015), the Guwahati High Court declared that the G.P. certificate could not be used as a linking document for married women. [31] The judgment is significant considering that the Registrar General of India and the Supreme Court, which kept a close tab on all NRC-related developments, never objected to the use of Panchayat-issued residency certificates. The G.P. certificates were also recommended as a valid link document by a cabinet sub-committee in 2010 and approved by the government soon after. Then, later on in December 2017, the Supreme Court modified this order and granted the use of these certificates, subject to special verification of their content and authenticity. [32] Accordingly, the NRC authorities declared that the G.P. certificate would be verified as per the order of the Supreme Court. Nevertheless, in the actual verification process, officials started asking for alternative documents, thereby creating problems, confusion, and resentment.

Just a couple of months before the final or the second draft NRC was due to be released on 30th July 2018, the NRC authority reportedly sent a notice to all districts on 2nd May 2018, stating that any rulings about the brothers, sisters, and other family members of 'Declared Foreigners' should be put on hold until the tribunals decide their fate. As per news reports, this notice was backed by a year-old Guwahati High Court judgment. There had been speculation that the notification was sent shrewdly at the fag-end of the updating process and just about a fortnight before the Supreme Court took a summer break so that there would be hardly enough time to have any legal relief. It was reported that on 8th May 2018, the Supreme Court had heard some matters relating to NRC, yet the NRC authority did not mention the issuance of this notice on 2nd May 2018, which had vital ramifications for the final draft.

Then, there was a sudden spurt of activity in branding 'D' voters throughout the State just before the publication of the final draft list on 30th July 2018. A huge number of names mysteriously started reaching NRC Sewa Kendras (NSK), alleged to be from the NRC office with Application Receipt Numbers (ARN) and 'D' voter written on them to check whether the concerned person or any of their family members was declared a foreigner. These were written on white paper without any seal or signature. While it was a problem for some of the NSK to respond to such unauthenticated requests, others acted based on the same. [33] Why and how it happened like this is a mystery. The strange coincidence of the issuance of notice by the NRC authority on 2nd May 2018, as mentioned in the previous paragraph, and the sudden spurt of activity in branding 'D' voters throughout the State just before the publication of the final list on 30th July 2018, definitely calls for a proper probe.

When the first draft of the NRC was published on the 31st of December 2017, only 19 million people found their names on the list, with 13.9 million applicants waiting for the second list to know their fate. Interestingly, the names of NRC State Coordinator Prateek Hajela himself and his daughter were missing from the first NRC draft published on 31st December 2017. The two then appeared for a hearing, after which their names were included in the final draft. [34] This speaks volumes about the process, reliability, and efficacy of the system and the software used for the purpose.

The second draft of the NRC, published on 30th July 2018, incorporated the names of only 29 million. However, the fate of the remaining 4 million people was left in limbo as the Central Government avoided commenting on their citizenship status. Of them, 3.6 million people resubmitted their citizenship claims. An additional exclusion list was issued in June 2019 containing 1,02,463 names included earlier in the draft list, bringing the total number left out in the final draft to 4.1 million people.

However, even before the final NRC list was published, the Attorney-General of India reportedly informed the Supreme Court that biometrics were being developed to "catch" declared foreigners (meaning, of course, those who would eventually fail to prove their citizenship) if they escaped to another state. While no level-headed Indian would want any illegal infiltrators to escape, the government's priority at that stage should have been to look for ways and means to prevent genuine Indians from being wrongfully declared as illegal immigrants. No such efforts were reported or visible. Besides, it appeared to be unfair to adopt only the process of elimination to determine whether a person was a foreigner, and that too based solely on the possession of specific papers prescribed by the government. After filtering out the people who could not show or did not possess any of the documents in support of their Indian citizenship, the government could have, on its own, attempted to inquire and ascertain that genuine Indians were not left out from the final NRC list by employing various administrative/investigative machinery. That way, the chances of depriving any Indians of their citizenship rights and the resulting harassment and persecution could be avoided or minimized. Without putting any such efforts, the government was reportedly engaged in developing biometrics to "catch" presumed foreigners. For any civilized democracy, such acts at that time were indeed unexpected and unfortunate!

In the article titled "Assam NRC - A History of Violence and Persecution," author Abdul Kalam Azad wrote at the beginning: "The legacy of anti-immigrant sentiment in the Assamese public sphere for more than a century has created an environment of deadly silence and trauma has taken control over the lives of several million people across the State." In this write-up, author Abdul Kalam Azad painted an alarming picture of Assam under the grip of the updating exercise of the 1951-NRC. While the full story is available in the public domain on the news and opinion website of The Wire, only a small part of it is quoted below for the readers to get a sense of the prevailing prejudice in the entire process. It is an eye-opener!

> "But gradually, the NRC was made another tool for persecuting the Muslim and Bengali Hindus through its range of exclusionary and discriminatory provisions. Though the entire population of Assam had to file the application for inclusion in the NRC, as many as 12 million "indigenous people" were given the benefit of 'original inhabitant' or 'O.I.', a category which may not even hold any constitutional validity and was never part of the initial modalities but **it empowered the lowest level registering authority to include any names even if s/he fails to provide any documentary**

evidence. On the other hand, Muslims, Bengali Hindus, and a few other marginalized groups are subjected to a stringent verification process, including a 'family tree' matching.

Apart from these discriminatory and racial provisions, the NRC authority deployed several exclusionary diktats, mostly beyond the initial modalities, to exclude as many Muslims and Bengali Hindus as possible. Currently, there are more than 1.3 lakh people who are arbitrarily marked as doubtful or D voters, and their cases are pending in the 100 Foreigners Tribunals set up by the Supreme Court across the State. The NRC authority excluded those people from the draft NRC, to which the SC agreed. It also excluded declared foreigners, their descendants, and siblings as well, to which the Guwahati High Court agreed. Even the names of several thousand people who had been declared as 'Indian citizens' by the tribunal were also not included in the final draft." [35]

Similarly, in his article titled, "In the Crosshairs: How Poetry Became a Crime in Assam," Journalist and Author SAMRAT also outlined an unheard-of state of affairs during the days of updating the NRC in the state. The following few lines are quoted from that write-up:

"According to procedures approved earlier by the Supreme Court under (Chief Justice) Gogoi, "indigenous" people were given a shortcut to inclusion in the NRC. They can be included as "original inhabitants" if they can satisfy the registering authority that they are Indian citizens. There is no definition of who is "indigenous" or an "original inhabitant," or how the registering authority, usually a State-government clerk, is to be satisfied with citizenship. Thus, those belonging to an ethnic group considered indigenous are more likely to be declared "original inhabitants," while anyone who happens to be Bengali or Nepali is prone to be considered a foreigner—from Bangladesh or Nepal—until proven otherwise."

The article appeared in the Delhi-Press magazine THE CARAVAN dated 1st August 2019 and reappeared in the 'Sunday Business Standard' (Kolkata Edition), Page 7, on 1st September 2019. [36] [37]

Thus, several "indigenous" or "original" inhabitants in Assam received special treatment during the NRC updating exercise. However, no such privilege was bestowed upon the numerous Bengali-speaking people who were also Assam's aboriginal inhabitants - as documented earlier in this book. This omission was no doubt disastrous to innumerable Bengalis residing in Assam. In hindsight, it appears that the concerned officials entrusted with the task of updating the NRC failed to bring up, wittingly or unwittingly, this vital lapse to the notice of the Supreme Court bench comprising Hon'ble Chief Justice Ranjan Gogoi and Hon'ble Justice Rohinton Fali Nariman that was monitoring and consistently pressing the government machinery to expeditiously update the NRC. It provides an unquestionable attestation of a well-thought-out cover-up of the historical truth.

The relevant parts of the order dated 13th August 2019 in respect of Assam Public Works vs Union of India. Writ Petition (Civil) No. 274 of 2009, which enunciated 'Original Inhabitant' quoted below:

Supreme Court of India

Assam Public Works vs Union Of India on 13 August 2019

ORDER

Item 9. 2. (2) (b) (3)

"The names of persons who are originally inhabitants of the State of Assam and their children, who are Citizens of India, shall be included in the consolidated list if the Citizenship of such persons is ascertained beyond reasonable doubt and to the satisfaction of the registering authority."

Item 10.

"Insofar as clause 3(3) of the Schedule appended to the Rules is concerned, we clarify that the expression "original inhabitants of the state of Assam" would include the "Tea Tribes" and the inclusion of such original inhabitants would be on the basis of proof to the satisfaction of the Registering Authority which establishes the citizenship of such persons beyond a reasonable doubt. Any directions by the Registrar General of India in this regard shall also be followed by the Registering Authority."

We make it clear that subject to orders as may be passed by the Constitution Bench in Writ Petition (C) No.562 of 2012 and Writ Petition (C) No.311 of 2015, the National Register of Citizens (NRC) will be updated.

....

CJI [RANJAN GOGOI] ....J.[ROHINTON FALI NARIMAN]

NEW DELHI
AUGUST 13, 2019 [38]

Note: The full order etc. is available on the website India Kanoon website at the link furnished at source [38]

Significantly, "the category of 'Original Inhabitant (O.I.) is nowhere defined, but in practice was taken to exclude people who spoke Bengali, Nepali or Hindi, even if they lived in Assam for generations," according to legal scholar Dr M. Mohsin Alam Bhat, as cited above. This distinct classification of Bengalis against the "Tea Tribes" implies that all Bengalis were considered outsiders in Assam, whereas, in reality, many Bengalis were the aboriginal inhabitants of Assam, as elaborated earlier in this book.

Thus, barely a fortnight before the publication of the final list of the NRC on 31st August 2019, the Supreme Court bench headed by CJI Ranjan Gogoi, by order dated 13th August 2019, directed that the proof of citizenship for original inhabitants of Assam should be based on the satisfaction of the Registering Authority beyond any reasonable doubt. The original inhabitants included Assam's "Tea Tribes," initially brought by the European Planters from present-day Jharkhand, Odisha, Chhattisgarh, West Bengal, and Andhra Pradesh mostly, but it omitted to mention the numerous indigenous Bengali residents of Assam. A strange resemblance between the Supreme Court order dated 13th August 2019 and the Nowgong (Assam) Deputy Commissioner F.A.S Thomas's order dated 22nd August 1924 thus emerged concerning the "Tea Tribes" vis-à-vis Assam's Bengali population.

For a proper perspective on the distinct classifications, let's quickly look back at history when the British carved out the Bengal Presidency's three districts plus one division and fused them to create a new province in 1874. They called it Assam Province even though 57.34% of its population was indigenous Bengalis. As mentioned by Amalendu Guha in his book PLANTER RAJ TO SWARAJ on page 23, the Bengalis continued to outnumber the Assamese even in the new province well until the partition of Assam in 1947.

Still, on 22nd August 1924, Deputy Commissioner F.A.S Thomas of Nowgong (Assam) had passed a standing order by which persons from all districts of Bengal and the Bengali predominant [1]Surma Valley of Assam were classified as 'immigrants'. Oddly, the order excluded Assam's tea garden labourers and ex-tea garden labourers from the category of 'immigrants'. During those days, the Surma Valley was a part of Assam, and Bengal was its adjacent Province, with no international border separating these two lands. Yet, the term 'immigrant', which stands for a person who comes to live permanently in a foreign country, was tagged to the Bengalis living in Assam then.

Note: ¹Surma Valley, comprising Sylhet district and the plains portion of Cachar district, is the most populated part of Assam and is linguistically and socially a part of Bengal - as per 1931 Census report of Assam p. 21, para 26, Part I, Vol III.

Seven years later, British Census Superintendent C.S. Mullan wrote in the Assam Census Report 1931, among other things, that:

> "…… the **Bengali immigrants** censused for the first time on the char lands of Goalpara in 1911 were merely the advanced guard – or rather the scouts – of a huge army following closely at their heels. By 1921 the first army corps had passed into Assam and had practically conquered the district of Goalpara…...." (Emphasis by Subir)

>> "Probably the most important event in the Province during the last twenty-five years --an event, moreover, which seems likely to alter the whole future of Assam permanently and to destroy more surely than did the Burmese invaders of 1820 the whole structure of Assamese culture and civilization – has been the *invasion* of a **vast horde of land-hungry** Bengali **immigrants**, mostly Muslims, from the districts of Eastern Bengal and in particular from Mymensingh. This invasion began sometime before 1911, and the census report of that year is the first report which makes mention of the **advancing host.**" [39]

The colonial bureaucrat then obnoxiously summed up the report somewhat like this;

> "….. the immigrant army has almost completed the conquest of Nowgong. The Barpeta subdivision of Kamrup has also fallen to their **attack**, and Darrang is being **invaded**. Sibsagar has so far escaped completely, but a few thousand Mamensinghias in North Lakhimpur are an **outpost** which may, during the next decade, prove to be a valuable basis for **major operations.** *Whosesoever, the carcass, have the vultures be gathered together. Where there is a wasteland thither flock the Mamensinghias."* (Emphasis by Subir)

It is not known if the fallacious word 'immigrant' that the Nowgong Deputy Commissioner tagged to the Bengalis living in Assam at that time had induced Mullan, or not, to use the choicest loathsome (military) terminology against a community. Still, one cannot rule out the possibility that one might have led to the other. Such a risk always exists.

Be that as it may, on 20th July 2019, just about one month before the publication of the final list (on 31st August 2019) of people who could provide the requisite proof of their citizenship in Assam to enlist their names in the updated NRC, the Indian national newspaper, The Hindu, brought out an insightful editorial titled "Inclusion over exclusion: on Assam NRC - Fears of a vocal section should not override the rights of NRC claimants to due process," which is quoted below. It is self-explanatory:

> "With the Supreme Court-led process of updating the National Register of Citizens in Assam nearing its deadline of July 31, the complexities involved in the gargantuan exercise have dawned upon the executive. Both the Central and State governments have sought an extension. But it remains to be seen whether the Court, which has insisted on sticking to the timelines, would relent when it hears the matter on July 23. The first draft NRC published on the intervening night of December 31 and January 1, 2018, had the names of 19 million people out of the total 32.9 million who had applied for inclusion as citizens. The second draft NRC, published on July 30, upped it to 28.9 million but left out four million found ineligible. Around 3.6 million of them subsequently filed citizenship claims. An 'additional exclusion list' was issued last month containing 1,02,463 names included earlier in the draft list. In anticipation of millions being ultimately left out, the Assam government is moving to set up 200 Foreigner Tribunals to handle cases of people being excluded from the final NRC, as part of a larger plan to establish 1,000 such tribunals. The State government is also preparing to construct 10 more detention centres; six are now running out of district jails.
>
> A humanitarian crisis awaits Assam whether the final NRC is published on July 31 or after. In the run-up to the final publication, case after case has emerged of persons wrongfully left out of the list. The process has left no group out of its sweep, be it Marwaris or Biharis from elsewhere in the country, people tracing their antecedents to other Northeastern states, people of Nepali origin, and caste Hindu Assamese. The prime targets of this exercise, however, are Hindu Bengalis and Bengali-origin Muslims of Assam — more than 80% of the 4.1 million people named in the two lists belong to these two groups. Yet, the rationale of the Centre and State in seeking a deadline extension, as found in their submissions to the Supreme Court, betrays an exclusionary bias. The joint plea sought time to conduct a 20% sample re-verification process in districts bordering Bangladesh and 10% in the rest of the State to quell a

'growing perception' that lakhs of illegal immigrants may have slipped into the list. This is despite the State NRC Coordinator's reports to the apex court suggesting that up to 27% of names have been reverified during the process of disposal of claims. It hasn't helped that the Central government keeps holding out the prospect of unleashing a nationwide NRC to detect and deport illegal aliens when it has no index to base such an exercise on — the 1951 register was exclusive to Assam. The accent should be on inclusion, not exclusion. The wheels of justice cannot pander to the suspicions of a vocal majority without giving the excluded access to due process." [40]

Anyway, as already mentioned, the first draft of an updated National Register of Citizens (NRC) for Assam was published at midnight on 31st December 2017, listing 1.90 crore names out of the 3.29 crore applicants. Then on 30th July 2018, the complete draft of the NRC, containing names of 2,89,83,677, was published, and 40,07,707 persons were found ineligible for inclusion in the draft NRC. Claims for inclusion in NRC and objections against the inclusion of names were both filed after the publication of the complete draft. The process of disposal of claims and objections was then finalized following due consideration. Before the publication of the final list, the State of Assam and the Union of India raised concerns regarding the genuineness of the persons whose names were included, demanding re-verification of some of the names to check their authenticity. These prayers were examined and found untenable in light of the submission by the State Coordinator that a substantial number of persons have been already re-verified in the course of hearings that took place during the disposal of claims and objections.

Accordingly, on 31st August 2019, the State Coordinator, NRC, Assam, Prateek Hajela (IAS), issued the following press note:

GUWAHATI, 31st AUGUST 2019
OFFICE OF THE STATE COORDINATOR, NRC

Publication of Final NRC on 31st August, 2019

The process of updating the NRC was initiated in the state of Assam as per the order of the Supreme Court of India in 2013. Since then, the Apex Court has closely monitored the entire process. The process of updating the NRC in Assam differs from the rest of the country and is governed by Rule 4A and the corresponding Schedule of the Citizenship (Registration of Citizens and Issue of National Identity Cards) Rules, 2003. These rules have been framed according to the cut-off date of 24th March (Midnight), 1971, as decided in the Assam Accord.

The process of receiving NRC Application Forms began at the end of May 2015 and ended on 31st August 2015. A total of 3,30,27,661 members applied through 68,37,660 applications. The particulars submitted by the applicants were scrutinized to determine their eligibility for inclusion in the NRC. The exercise of updating the NRC is a mammoth one involving around 52,000 State Government officials working for a prolonged period. All decisions on inclusion and exclusion are made by these statutory officers. The entire process of updating the NRC has been meticulously carried out in an objective and transparent manner. Adequate opportunity for being heard has been given to all persons at every stage of the process.

The entire process is conducted in accordance with statutory provisions and due procedure followed at every stage. As per the Orders of the Hon'ble Supreme Court, the Draft NRC (Complete Draft) was published on 30th July 2018, wherein 2,89,83,677 persons were found eligible for inclusion. Thereafter, Claims were received from 36,26,630 persons against exclusions. Verification was also carried out of persons included in the Draft NRC under Clause 4(3) of the Schedule of the Citizenship (Registration of Citizens and Issue of National Identity Cards) Rules, 2003. Objections were received against the inclusion of 1,87,633 persons whose names had appeared in the Complete Draft. Another Additional Draft Exclusions List was published on 26th June 2019, wherein 1,02,462 persons were excluded. Taking into account all the persons already included and after disposal of all Claims and Objections and proceedings under Clause 4(3), it has been found that a total of 3,11,21,004 persons are eligible for inclusion in the Final NRC, leaving out 19,06,657 persons including those who did not submit Claims.

From 10 AM today (31 August 2019) onward, the hard copies of the Supplementary List of Inclusions will be available for public view at NRC Seva Kendras (NSK), offices of the Deputy Commissioner, and offices of the Circle Officer during office hours. The status of both inclusion and exclusion can be viewed online on the NRC website (www.nrcassam.nic.in).

Any person who is not satisfied with the outcome of the claims and objections can file an appeal before the Foreigners Tribunals.

Sd/-

Prateek Hajela, IAS

State Coordinator, NRC, Assam. [41]

In conclusion, the final NRC list revealed that out of 3,30,27,661 applicants, only 3,11,21,004 persons were eligible, while **19,06,657 aspirants were deemed ineligible** for inclusion in Assam's updated National Register of Citizens. Thus, one of the most vital phases of the unprecedented exercise to update the 1951-NRC of Assam came to an end. However, a New Delhi-based rights group termed the exclusion of 19,06,657 people from the NRC as the most significant incident of rendering people 'stateless' in decades, as reported by The Hindu newspaper. [42]

Significantly, three months after the publication of the final NRC list, India's 17th [1]Lok Sabha passed the Citizenship (Amendment) Bill (CAB) on 10th December 2019. The following day, on 11th December, the [2]Rajya Sabha cleared the bill. Upon receiving the Presidential assent on 12th December 2019, the CAB became the Citizenship (Amendment) Act 2019 — commonly known as CAA. With this, the three years of political manoeuvring for the enactment of the CAA by the ruling BJP at the Centre came to an end. The CAB was first introduced in the Lok Sabha on 15th July 2016.

Note: [1]Lok Sabha, the House of the People, is the lower house of India's bicameral Parliament.
[2]Rajya Sabha, the Council of States, is the upper house of the bicameral Parliament of India.

Broadly speaking, as per the CAA, a person belonging to the Hindu, Sikh, Buddhist, Jain, Parsi, or Christian community from Afghanistan, Bangladesh, or Pakistan, who entered India on or before the 31st day of December 2014, shall not be treated as an illegal migrant. One of the qualifications for citizenship by naturalization was that the person must have resided in India or been in central government service for the last 12 months and at least 11 years of the preceding 14 years. However, the CAA created an exception for these groups of Hindu, Sikh, Buddhist, Jain, Parsi, or Christian communities concerning this qualification. According to the amendment, "this clause shall be read as "not less than five years" in place of "not less than eleven years." In other words, for them, the eleven-year requirement has been reduced to five years. Besides, the Act says that on acquiring citizenship: (i) such persons shall be deemed to be citizens of India from the date of their entry into India, and (ii) "...any proceeding pending against a person under this section in respect of illegal migration or citizenship shall stand abated on conferment of citizenship to him." However, in 6B(4) of the Citizenship Act, 1955, as amended now, it is stated that "(4) Nothing in this section shall apply to the tribal area of Assam, Meghalaya, Mizoram, or Tripura as included in the Sixth Schedule to the Constitution and the area covered under "The Inner Line" notified under the Bengal Eastern Frontier Regulation, 1873."

Those who oppose the CAA argue that by privileging certain non-Muslim groups on a religious basis, the CAA threatens to alter the secular foundations of the Constitution for the first time in independent India. Facilitating citizenship to a few communities with the exclusion of the Muslim community, the Act cannot claim to be fair legislation. Instead, the amendment seems to be a kind of belated endorsement of Jinnah's two-nation theory.

Nevertheless, the defenders say that the CAA is not excluding any legitimate Indian citizens. This Act merely includes certain groups of people who were forced to leave their homes in Pakistan, Bangladesh, and Afghanistan under compelling circumstances. There is nothing against Indian Muslims per se in the CAA. Besides, there is no distinction on the religious line in the NRC exercise if we go by the recent example set in Assam. The NRC is a register of all Indian citizens whose creation is mandated by the Citizenship Act 1955 as amended in 2003. As contemplated by the Union Government, a nationwide record of citizens would be handy in detecting illegal foreigners in India. The NRC itself is also not against the interests of any Indian citizens. So, there should not be any reason to be scared of or protest. Nevertheless, the argument is true only if the CAA or the NRC is seen in isolation.

However, to the critics of the CAA in general, the "combo package" of CAA and NRC, as termed by some political leaders, would be a deadly cocktail. That is if the CAA or the NRC is seen together. The detractors say that what is not being told to the people is important. And that has become the bone of contention.

Simply put, with the implementation of the CAA, the undocumented Hindu, Sikh, Buddhist, Jain, Parsi, and Christian entrants from Pakistan, Bangladesh, and Afghanistan who entered India on or before the 31st day of December 2014, shall not be treated as illegal migrants as per the CAA. Accordingly, this group will pass the citizenship test in the prospective all-India NRC. But, for the undocumented Muslim entrants, this escape route won't be available even if they have been in India for nearly fifty years. They would become "illegal immigrants." This is discrimination against Muslims who have been in India since 25th March 1971 (the cut-off date as per the Assam Accord) or any subsequent dates. The people of India are voicing their protests against this inequity incorporated into our Constitution recently. The people are worried because they feel that the secular spirit of our Constitution has thus been tinkered with. They are also upset because of the differential treatment of a few groups of people in Northeast India in the CAA, which is against the concept of "one India, one Nation."

So, as soon as CAB became CAA, there were protests nationwide. It turned violent in many pockets. News of imposition of prohibitory orders under section 144, curfew, and ban on internet services to control the violent protests poured in from several parts of different States. Many State Governments declared their strong reservation against the CAA and NRC.

While religious profiling of displaced persons for granting Indian citizenship, with the exclusion of Muslims, in the CAA was the main ground of protests all over the country, many people in the Northeast were not precisely on the same page. Here, the people protested against regularizing the stay of any more migrants from Afghanistan, Pakistan, and Bangladesh in India through the CAA, irrespective of their religious affinity. In the rest of India, people wanted all persecuted persons, including Muslims, to be accommodated; in contrast, people were generally against accommodating any persecuted migrants in Northeast India. The Economic Times newspaper on December 17, 2019, reported that:

> "Except in Bengali speakers' dominated Barak valley, people in other parts (of the Northeast) fear that CAA will lead to lakhs of Hindus from Bangladesh swamping indigenous communities, burdening resources, and threatening their language, culture, and tradition.
>
> Besides, the CAA has a 2014 cut-off date, but protesters say Assam bore the brunt of immigrants from 1951 to 1971 while other States did not, and it is unfair to impose more on the State. Protesters say they do not trust the Centre and CAA will undo the Assam Accord."

On May 1, 2023, India's daily newspaper Business Standard, quoting a private Indian news agency IANS, reported, inter alia, that Assam Chief Minister Himanta Biswa Sarma said that the implementation of the Citizenship Amendment Act (CAA) could only solve the problems of Hindu Bengalis. The report also added:

> "Notably, though the Citizenship Amendment Act (CAA) was passed in both Houses of Parliament in December 2019, the rules to implement the Act have not been framed till now, which is usually accomplished within six months after the President of India signs on a law. If any ministry or department fails to do so within the prescribed period, they must seek an extension from the Committee on Subordinate Legislation, stating reasons for such an extension. The Union Home Ministry has already taken several extensions to frame the CAA rules."

The Business Standard newspaper, dated May 1, 2023, reported it under the caption, *"CAA is the only solution to Hindu Bengalis' citizenship problem: Assam*

CM". Thus, with the rules to implement the Act yet to be framed, the suspense surrounding the so-called combo package of CAA and NRC is deepening.

Anyway, the updating exercise of Assam's 1951-NRC was undoubtedly monitored strictly over four long years by the special bench of the Supreme Court headed by the Chief Justice of India, who heard relentless objections and suggestions from the stakeholders, including the prominent organizations that led the Assam Agitation. Yet, in the final analysis, about 95% of people out of 3.3 crore (33 million) applicants became eligible for inclusion in the NRC, barring only about 5%, subject, of course, to appeals before the Foreigners' Tribunals, which may bring down the number of excluded persons even less. This abysmally low figure contrasting the earlier persistent claims ultimately busted the myth that Assam was flooded by illegal Bangladeshis numbering 4 million, 10 million, or even more. This vicious campaign about Assam being flooded with illegal immigrants was so oft-repeated that the entire body politic of the country believed that there were numerous so-called foreigners in Assam. The 2005 Supreme Court judgment on the Sarbananda Sonowal Vs. Union of India crystallized that perception further. The judgment was based, among other things, on the Assam Governor's 1998 report to the President of India, which not only stated that there was a serious influx of immigrants in Assam but also that these immigrants mostly belonged to one community, i.e., Bengali Muslims. The precipitation of this narrative into a judicial verdict gave further credibility to claims of large-scale illegal migration in the State. It gave credibility to unassessed apprehensions and formed the basis of subsequent judgments touching upon the fate of millions in Assam. But, with the outcome of the recent NRC updating exercise, the Supreme Court's observations in the 2005 Sarbananda Sonowal vs Union of India case judgment and subsequent judgments that relied upon it should be bound to come under question. [43]

At any rate, as soon as the NRC final list was published on August 31, 2019, Assam's Finance, Health, and PWD Minister Himanta Biswa Sarma, who is presently the Chief Minister of Assam, cried foul over it. He said many illegal immigrants' names were included in the document because of the manipulation of legacy data and numerous names of genuine Indian citizens were excluded as the NRC authorities refused to accept certificates of the refugees who came to Assam before 1971. He demanded re-verification by the Supreme Court of at least 20% of names in the border districts and 10% in the remaining districts for a correct and fair NRC. Earlier in the day, Himanta Biswa Sarma said he had "lost hope" in the National Register of Citizens as the Centre and the state government were discussing new ways to oust foreigners from Assam. He also said: "I don't think this is the final list. There are many more to come." [44]

The Congress leader and former three-time Chief Minister of Assam, Tarun Gogoi, who has been claiming credit for initiating the NRC updating exercise during his tenure, expressed his dissatisfaction, saying, "I am not happy with the way the NRC has been published, with names of genuine Indian citizens left out and foreigners included." Tarun Gogoi blamed the BJP Government in Assam and the Centre for creating hurdles in the path of securing an error-free register. In contrast, Union Home Minister Amit Shah, as BJP President, had accused the Congress of not completing the NRC and had assured that they would bring out a free and fair citizens list. [45] Meanwhile, former Assam Chief Minister Prafulla Kumar Mahanta, who led the six-year-long Assam Movement and was a signatory of the Assam Accord, described 31st August 2019 as a historic day for the indigenous people of Assam, as they could obtain a National Register of Citizens on this date, despite its flaws. However, AASU General Secretary Lurinjyoti Gogoi expressed unhappiness over the outcome of the final NRC list. [46]

The original petitioner in the Supreme Court, Assam Public Works (APW), an NGO, called the final NRC a "flawed document," as its prayer for re-verification of the draft NRC was rejected by the Supreme Court. The NGO president, Abhijit Sarma, wondered **whether the software used in the updating exercise was capable of handling so much data and if it had been examined by any third-party Information Technology expert.** Abhijit Sarma also questioned Hajela's statement regarding the re-verification of 27% of claims and raised doubts **about the efficacy of the computer software** used in preparing the NRC. [47] (Emphasis by Subir)

The Assam Tribune, the most popular and oldest English newspaper in Assam, in its editorial comment dated 1st September 2019, termed the figure of 19,06,657 left out in the final NRC as 'an unrealistically low figure considering the extent of the influx.'

"Whatever may be one's view on the merits of the NRC and its implementation, we must never cease to remain mindful of the fact that it has spawned an enormous humanitarian crisis," said Harsh Mander, a Human Rights Activist. [48]

"The final NRC list should have led to closure, not vexed beginnings," was the editorial comment of The Hindu newspaper on 2nd September 2019 - a couple of days after the publication of the NRC list. A portion of the editorial under the caption: "Citizenship, figured: On Assam NRC final list" is quoted below:

> "The publication of the final National Register of Citizens on Saturday brings no closure to the vexed issue of illegal immigration to Assam yet. Those left out are not foreigners until the tribunals set up to determine their fate pronounce them so. The process could go all the way to the Supreme Court. The Home Ministry has also extended the time to file appeals against exclusion in the Foreigners Tribunal from 60 to 120 days. The point, however, is that the process has yielded an updated register and a figure. It has had its warts and all even as it left over 1.9 million people staring at statelessness — in a continuing saga of glaring omissions, a serving lawmaker, a former legislator, and retired Army man Mohammad Sanaullah, whose case propelled NRC excesses into the spotlight, did not make the cut. But protests across the spectrum expressing concern over the excluded, suggest the judiciary-led process was perhaps largely robust and the errors were more procedural than targeted. The State government and many political parties have promised to offer legal help to those excluded, but such assistance should have been forthcoming from the time the updating exercise was rolled out on the ground in 2015. Instead, it was mostly left to sundry organisations and concerned activists to come to the aid of hundreds of thousands oblivious to documentation novelties such as legacy data.
>
> Beyond that lies the question of what to do with those declared illegal aliens once the quasi-judicial process is done and dusted. The administration is readying detention centres, but only a veritable 'prison state' can house such numbers….." [49]

"A flawed process that pleased none," opined Human Rights Activist Harsh Mander in an article about the final list of Assam NRC on 3rd September 2019 in a Dhaka-based leading English language daily newspaper, New Age. At the outset of the article, the Human Rights Activist wrote:

> "Fear and disquiet have gripped nearly two million residents of Assam, and their loved ones, after their names failed to show up in the final updated list of the National Register of Citizens. But the unremitting tragedy of the Bengali-origin people of Assam is that even those whose names appear on the list have no assurance that they will not be deemed 'illegal immigrants' sometime in the future. They are a people for whom there is still no closure, no prospect of permanent security and dignity of citizenship (as the onus of proof is again back to the accused).
>
> Anxieties about land, culture, and migration have, over decades, created entrenched fissures in the social and political life of Assam.

People on all sides of these bitter divides had hoped that the conclusion of the six-year-long process of updating the 1951 citizen's register in Assam would finally resolve this long-festering dispute. But despite the immeasurable toll of human suffering that the process extracted from millions of very impoverished people, it is evident that it has resolved nothing.

For supporters of the Assam agitation, it is an article of faith that millions of immigrants from Bangladesh have continued to 'illegally penetrate' the porous border which Assam shares with Bangladesh, and that these immigrants will submerge their culture and language and edge them out of their lands and forests. Estimates of the numbers of these 'illegal immigrants' that their leaders have tossed around range from five to 10 million. The final figure of less than two million has sorely disappointed and enraged them. [50]

There were reports about harassment and eviction of the people of Assam following the publication of the NRC. So, the Opposition Leader in the Assam Legislative Assembly, Debabata Saikia, who is also the leader of the Congress Legislature Party, called upon Chief Minister Sarbananda Sonowal to get in touch with the Governments of those States to ensure that such incidents do not take place. [51]

In reality, the bogey of 'illegal foreigners' mushroomed in a few neighbouring states during the days of the Assam Agitation that saw the steady growth of vigilantism under the banner of some extra-constitutional bodies against the so-called 'outsiders'. In the mass media, both print and electronic broadcasting, there were plenty of reports of the unfettered persecution, harassment and expulsion of a certain section of people by some rowdy elements as the updating exercise of Assam's 1951-NRC was nearing completion.

'Is your name in the NRC?' emerged as a slur in some vigilante attacks in Assam while the exercise was underway. In June 2018, a month prior to the publication of the final draft NRC, Bijay Ray, a youth in his early twenties from Gauripur in the border district of Dhubri, had gone to meet a woman in Darrang district, some 300 km away. He was mobbed in broad daylight; his hands were tied and he was thrashed mercilessly.

A widely-shared video of the assault captured Ray being punched, rolled on the ground and kicked. He was abused and asked where he had come from, whether he was Bangladeshi and whether his name was in the NRC, even though only the first draft had been published at that time. He protested, 'I am an Assamese', even as the blows rained on him.

Pankaj Hazarika, the primary accused, as identifiable from the video, was soon nabbed by the police. Later, a journalist who had covered the incident in detail told me that the youth who was attacked belonged to the [1]Koch Rajbongshi community but from his 'appearance' the mob mistaken him for a Bengali Muslim.

A Guwahati-based journalist covering Northeast India for the Indian Express, Abhishek Saha, narrated the above incident in his book, "NO LAND'S PEOPLE: THE STORY OF ASSAM'S NRC CRISIS." [52]

Note: [1]Koch-Rajbongshi people of Assam date back to the Epic period when their kingdom was known as "Pragjyotishpur", according to a long paper prepared in 2007 by the Centre for Koch Rajbongshi Studies & Development (CKRSD). Source: Vappala Balachandran's article dated 13th February 2021 in Outlook India.

Abhishek Saha's account of the torture and trauma endured by Bijay Ray, as described above, was not an isolated incident but rather one of many occurrences in Assam during that period. Furthermore, such brutal incidents were not confined within the state's borders. The effects were felt by 'outsiders' in the neighbouring states as well.

In Assam's bordering states, a similar trend emerged, with reports of increased vigilantism, particularly by various student unions, sometimes in collaboration with political parties or local administrations. This phenomenon was most notable in Meghalaya and Arunachal Pradesh. Reports surfaced of innocent citizens being harassed and humiliated amidst rising ethnic tensions. Dr. Suraj Gogoi, an Assistant Professor at Bangalore's RV University, in his article titled "NRC muddle: a vigilante student union and India's borderlands," explicitly outlined the immediate spillover effects of the publication of the draft NRC in Assam. The article, which appeared in the Hong Kong-based English newspaper ASIA TIMES on August 23, 2018, highlighted the distressing events unfolding in these regions.

The publication of the NRC injected fear, trepidation, and a sense of humiliation into the populace. Border areas of Assam became zones of heightened surveillance, with student unions in neighbouring states intensifying their vigilante activities. Various state governments also heightened border security and deployed additional forces to closely monitor districts bordering Assam.

Following the publication of the draft NRC, the Khasi Students' Union in Meghalaya erected checkpoints in border areas, dubbing them "Khasi Students' Union infiltration gates." This led to widespread disruption as individuals entering Meghalaya were subjected to document checks; those without proper documentation were turned back. The actions of the Khasi Students' Union were deemed unlawful and alarming, particularly considering that no Inner Line Permit is required to enter Meghalaya.

Similarly, the All Arunachal Pradesh Students' Union, through an order dated August 2, 2018, instructed District Students' Unions to launch a joint effort to identify and remove "illegal" immigrants from the state. They set a deadline of 15 days for compliance, after which they would commence "Operation Clean Drive" on August 17. The union emphasized strict enforcement of Inner Line Permit checking and instructed District Students' Unions to enforce the order.

Ahead of Operation Clean Drive, the All Arunachal Pradesh Students' Union engaged with the All Assam Students' Union to address concerns. A meeting between the two student unions, chaired by North East Students' Organization coordinator Pritam Wai Sonam, resulted in assurances from the Assam Union that indigenous Assamese people living in Arunachal Pradesh would not be harassed, while also expressing solidarity.

These instances underscore the significant influence wielded by these student unions, raising questions about the legitimacy of the state's security apparatus as these groups take matters into their own hands. This represents a de facto parallel government that disregards historical precedents, restricts freedom of movement, and dehumanizes individuals.

Arunachal is historically a labor-deficit state. Many wage labourers and sharecroppers, belonging to multiple communities, work in the state, primarily to work and not to own any property. Anyone not belonging to minority Scheduled Tribe communities in Arunachal is not allowed to buy or "capture" any property. There are millions of workers engaged in various state infrastructure projects, primarily roads, bridges, and dams. There are even cases of workers not receiving their due wages or being intimidated by owners and contractors, among others. Many have left the state because of the tyranny of India's permit-license raj (rule).

Writing about Meghalaya, Obadiah Lamshwa Lamare, in a mimeograph, recalls the harassment of workers from Bihar employed in the expansion of Mawlai Nongkwar Presbyterian Church by local youth, despite carrying valid documents proving their Indian citizenship. In that powerful essay, "Democratic Decline," he contextualizes the formation of class in Meghalaya and how a myth of tribal purity is propagated by the Khasi elite, an indigenous ethnic group of Meghalaya. For him, it is also a mechanism to stop the polarization of social class by projecting tribal unity. He reminds us that the Jaintia Hills also have a history of "cultural assimilation, symbiotic, and resembling proto-cosmopolitanism," suggesting co-existence. Lamare also rightly points out that the term "illegal" being attributed to a human body is demeaning and dehumanizing, for illegality is attributed to actions, not persons.

The National Register of Citizens has shown that **we are indeed a racist structure.** This devaluation of human beings is at the core of the National Register of Citizens, and the joint actions carried out by the student unions in various states are but its extension. "Operation Clean Drive" and "infiltration gates" internalize such a philosophy by locating "illegal" bodies and restricting movement. It is extremely shameful that such student bodies and organizations target the working class and push them into cycles of poverty and destitution under various pretexts. [53] (Emphasis by Subir)

Immediately after the final list of Assam's updated NRC was published, at least three FIRs were filed, two against NRC Coordinator Hajela in Dibrugarh and Guwahati, and one against the NRC authorities of Morigaon. Chandan Mazumdar, whose name was not on the final NRC list, filed one complaint at Dibrugarh police station on 4th September 2019, alleging "inefficiency and criminal conspiracy of employees." The FIR held Hajela responsible for the "discrepancies," as he supervised the NRC updating exercise in Assam. An indigenous Muslim Students' Organization, All Assam Goriya-Moriya Yuva Chatra Parishad, filed another FIR at Guwahati's Latasil police station on 5th September 2019, claiming "deliberate" anomalies in the final list. A third complaint was filed by the NGO Assam Public Works (APW) at Guwahati's Geetanagar police station against three declared foreigners, whose names figured in the final NRC, and against the NRC authorities of Morigaon. They were allegedly responsible for including their names. As mentioned earlier, Assam Public Works was the original petitioner in the Supreme Court, which led to updating Assam's 1951-NRC - six years ago. [54]

In a state where there are records of filing some bizarre FIRs, even for penning poetry or writing something critical of the NRC, the filing of FIRs against Hajela is not surprising. It may be recalled that earlier there was an FIR against the former Vice-Chancellor of Assam University, Silchar, allegedly for promoting enmity between different groups and communities for writing an article in a newspaper on 3rd July 2018, on the ongoing updating of the NRC. [55] Then another FIR was filed against ten people for writing poems criticizing the NRC. [56] Such instances attracted intense media attention, creating an atmosphere of fear that made people afraid to voice or write anything on the NRC, 'D' Voters, and many other contemporary issues of public interest concerning the state. There were politically motivated elements operating in Assam whose threshold of tolerance seemed to be extremely low. Consequently, news of many undesirable and unbelievable happenings in Assam never saw the light of day. Then there were some extra-constitutional means and elements ready to prevent people from openly airing their grievances. All these enabled the abusers of human dignity and violators of human rights to get away with their offensive deeds with impunity. **Freedom of speech and honest criticisms, even with reasonable restrictions, thus became the ultimate casualty in the process.**

Likewise, once a Dibrugarh University Professor, Dr. M. L. Bose faced a malicious assault for his seminal work on changes in the social structure of Assam in the British period against the background of the pre-British social system. Dr. Bose, who earned his Master of Arts in History and Doctorate from Jadavpur University, Calcutta, is renowned in the academic circle for a score of insightful papers in different Seminars and Conferences, besides having some acclaimed books published to his credit.

Dr. M. L. Bose was a Reader in History at Dibrugarh University, where he had taught since 1967. In July 1977, when a summary of his pioneering book "SOCIAL HISTORY OF ASSAM" was published in the Journal of Historical Research, Dibrugarh University, serious tension arose in both the University campus and Dibrugarh town. The article's circulation was halted, and distributed copies were recalled. Gradually, the tension spread throughout the state as the news circulated in newspapers. Much of the tension stemmed from rumours spread by individuals who had read the article but lacked the necessary historical knowledge. These rumours offended the sentiments of many who believed the author had attempted to malign the Assamese people and sow discord among different communities. Furthermore, the author was accused of trying to demonstrate the numerical minority of the Assamese people in the State and of holding the Ahoms responsible for numerous ills in the Brahmaputra valley. The rumours gained traction with the withdrawal of the article from circulation and an appeal to the Assam Sahitya Sabha for redress by some University department teachers. In an emergency meeting, the University Teachers' Association condemned the author without examining the context of the article and requested the authorities to retrieve the original from the Indian Council of Historical Research (ICHR), alleging that it contained many distorted facts. They also demanded the author return the money received from the ICHR for the project.

Under pressure from circumstances and at the insistence of some members of the Executive Council, the University authorities had no choice but to suspend the author and the Editor of the Journal from their duties on charges of academic indiscipline. An explanation was sought from the author as to why proceedings should not be initiated against him for writing an article containing "gross distortion of facts" to incite communal discord.

The University's decision to bar the author and the Editor from resuming their duties made headlines in newspapers in Delhi, and editorials supporting the author began to appear in publications such as the Times of India, Economic and Political Weekly, Mainstream Radical Humanist, etc., as well as in local press. There was a clear appreciation for the author's treatment of the subject, and the allegations against him were dismissed as baseless. Subsequently, there was a wave of protests across India against Dibrugarh University's actions by teachers from various universities and by organizations such as the Indian History Congress, Indian Council of Historical Research, Indian Council of Social Science Research, Centre for Studies in Social Sciences, Calcutta, and many others. The Chairman of the University Grants Commission expressed concern over the issue, and the University Chancellor sought information on the matter from the University.

During discussions at Dibrugarh to defuse tension, it became apparent to many that it was not the author who had attempted to create social tension, but rather some individuals had seized the issue to stir disturbances in the State. Thanks to the wisdom of Dibrugarh University students and teachers, the tension was alleviated by distributing Xerox copies of the original report, which effectively dispelled the mischievous rumours and somewhat restored the author's reputation, which certain interested parties had sought to undermine through malicious and false propaganda. The Dibrugarh University Teachers Association subsequently revised its stance on the issue. A new idea and principle of "academic freedom" gained traction, with many asserting that if the article contained any criticism of Assamese society, the author should have the academic freedom to express what he considered correct.

Dr. M. L. Bose recounted this unfortunate incident in the prologue of the same book ("Social History of Assam"), first published and printed by Ashok Kumar Mittal in 1989 and reprinted in 2003, from which Subir traced the episode. [57]

Anyway, returning to the topic of NRC under discussion, Mr Hajela, while releasing the final NRC updated data, recalled that the updating exercise was started in 2013 under the apex court's watch. The process of NRC update in Assam differed from the rest of the country. It was governed by Rule 4A and the corresponding Schedule of the Citizenship (Registration of Citizens and

Issue of National Identity Cards) Rules, 2003. These rules were framed as per the cut-off date of midnight of 24th March 1971, enshrined in the Assam Accord of 1985. The State Home Department officials said though the NRC was called 'final,' the 19,06,657 people excluded would have opportunities to be back on the citizens' list if they appeal against their exclusion and establish their citizenship via courts. Each excluded person will have 120 days to file an appeal at any of the existing 100 Foreigners' Tribunals — 200 more are to be established within a month — which in turn will have to dispose of the cases within six months. The appellant then can approach the High Court and Supreme Court. [58]

According to reports, the majority of the people who could not make it to the final NRC were Bengalis, both Hindus and Muslims, which included numerous genuine Indian citizens. However, the real concern for these nineteen lakh-odd people in the corridors of power seemed to be more or less absent. The concerned authorities in the administration, both at the Centre and the state, appeared to be apathetic about those excluded groups of people, perhaps because these unsuccessful people still had the chance to prove their Indian citizenship through the legal process.

It is true that they were given some opportunities to present their cases before the Foreigners' Tribunals, the Guwahati High Court, and finally, the Supreme Court of India. Yet, these windows might not be of much help to them to establish the authenticity of their Indian citizenship even if they were genuine Indians. In the previous Chapter "The Dreaded 'D' In Assam's Voter List", it is already seen "How Indians Are Made Into Bangladeshi For Money" - under this caption, a 24-hour Assamese news channel, Pratidin Time report dated 6th September 2018 broke an incredible story on the subject and exposed that a full-scale industry is going on in Assam to make an ordinary citizen a Bangladesh and mint money by all sections involved with the affairs. Various organizations of the minority used to say that 99% of foreigners' cases were false and only harassed ordinary Indians. It was for the first time a tribunal, through a written and signed Judgment, blew off the lid of the whole scam.

Accordingly, for the illiterate, ignorant, and impoverished group of individuals, which form the bulk of the left-outs, these options seemed to be insufficient without appropriate legal aid and necessary financial help from the government or elsewhere. Even for those who have the 'papers' prescribed by the government, it would be an extremely difficult proposition to prove their citizenship – not to speak of others who do not possess those 'papers', judging by their experience thus far. Such widespread impressions especially among the minority communities were not without any basis. Rather, they had valid reasons to be pessimistic about their chances to get fair deals through the Foreigners' Tribunals (FTs) in Assam because the ground reports on the functioning of the FTs were terrifying.

Notwithstanding the prevailing mood, the Guwahati High Court had selected an additional panel of 221 members to head foreigners' tribunals (FTs) in Assam barely ten days after releasing the final NRC list. The latest panel of members chosen based on merit included retired judicial officers, civil servants, not below the rank of secretary and additional secretary, with judicial experience, and advocates not below the age of 35 with at least seven years of practice. Aside from handling the cases of applicants left out of the NRC, the tribunals will continue taking up cases of "D" or doubtful voters. [59]

"The foreigner debate in Assam is devoid of reason, with unreliable data, a tie-up with Ahom history that is more fiction than reality leading to an exercise that divides rather than clarifies", wrote Parag Jyoti Saikia and Suraj Gogoi at the outset of their short essay titled, "A register most flawed" on the updating of Assam's NRC that appeared in Fountain Ink, an award-winning long-form monthly on 8th October 2018. In their penetrating composition, the author duo, Parag Jyoti Saikia, a doctoral student in Anthropology at the University of North Carolina, Chapel Hill and Suraj Gogoi, a PhD candidate in Sociology at the National University of Singapore, provided an enthralling perspective on the issue. The following two paragraphs are quoted from the said article:

> "In his book Demographic Trends in Assam 1921-1971, published in 1982, Tushar Kanti Chaudhuri writes, "The NRC was a transcription of certain census information from the 1951 census in Assam. It was a 'secret administrative document, not open for inspection'. Furthermore, it was compiled by 'unqualified or ill-qualified person' and insecurity over the position of Bengali Muslims given the Nehru-Liaquat Pact may well have led to many returning after the register was compiled, in March 1951, leading to under-enumeration." Even then, the number of people identified and deported was not small. On the basis of NRC 1951, under the initiation of B. P. Chaliha, one of the most pro-Assamese Congress chief ministers, 2.4 lakh immigrants were identified, of whom 1.9 lakh were deported in the first three years. What is interesting is that this citizenship register, on the basis of which so many people were deported, was not an admissible document in court as early as 1970.

In a judgment by Justice P. K. Goswami of the Gauhati High Court, the Assam Law Report (ALR) 1970 A&N 206, on pages 208 and 209 states, "...it only shows that the National Register of Citizens is a contemporaneous register prepared by the officers appointed under the provisions of the Census Act in the course of Census operations. If so, Section 15 of the Census Act will make such records of the Census not open to inspection nor admissible in evidence...what is directly prohibited under Section 15 of the Census Act cannot be let in by an indirect method through the agency of a private organization..." How a document that was non-admissible evidence in court becomes the basis for a Supreme Court-monitored process does raise some questions. But the electoral rolls of 1971, the other legacy data, are not beyond question either. Economic and Political Weekly (EPW) correspondent Sujit Choudhury in his article of 1985 "Election Commission and the Assam Accord" writes, "Only in 77 constituencies, out of the total of 126, could the government itself procure full copies of the 1971 electoral rolls; in the remaining 49, these rolls were not available. Moreover, where the rolls were available it was actually impossible to collect a certified copy, particularly for a layman, from a hostile pro-AASU electoral office. For persons who had moved from other states to Assam, it is really difficult to obtain a certified copy from a 15-year-old roll from his erstwhile place of residence." Some of the wall slogans of the Gana Sangram Parishad read: "Indian dogs get out of Assam", "Condemn Indian Army for raping our mothers and sisters in Assam", and "Forget Mother India Love Mother Assam". One can only wonder how such an inadequate set of data became central to determining citizenship. The absence of electoral rolls from 49 constituencies is no joke, yet 1971 remains the cut-off year of legacy data. If this is not a colossal fraud, what is? How does this reflect on the NRC process itself? **It is, by design, a system of exclusion since NRC 1951 or the electoral roll of 1971 by default will keep a large number of people out of its cover.**

The same group of people for whom electoral rolls were problematic have now submitted to the NRC process, which shows the changing goalposts of Assamese cultural nationalism. The anti-rational, anti-fact environment and the xenophobia surrounding the process are no different from the social and political milieu during the Assam movement. Then, too, the media (primarily The Assam Tribune and Dainik Assam), All India Radio Guwahati, and Guwahati University played a huge role in spreading hate and fear, as noted in the PUCL report. Amalendu Guha held that the press in Assam was under the control of the Assamese bourgeoisie since 1978. Similarly, there is an organic link between AASU and the Assamese elite. The PUCL report noted that when the fact-finding team was around, Assam Chief Election Commissioner S. K. Rao was forced to go on leave and "an Assamese-speaking official now presides over this operation adding to the arbitrary and indiscriminate character of decision-making relating to the electoral rolls". Harsh Mandar's resignation from the National Human Rights Commission and revelation serve as an epilogue to such practices of exception in determining citizenship. The report also recorded examples of the chauvinistic slogans that were in vogue. Some of the wall slogans of the Gana Sangram Parishad read: "Indian dogs get out of Assam", "condemn the Indian Army for raping our mothers and sisters in Assam", and "Forget Mother India Love Mother Assam", among others. Is it not ironic that the leaders who were against the Indian army now want the army to be deployed during the publication of the NRC list? As we write, AFSPA is extended to the whole of Assam in anticipation of the troubles that may follow the publication of the draft NRC. Things do indeed come full circle. If one notes the response of Prateek Hajela, coordinator of NRC, to the Avaaz online petition that the Border Police and Foreigners Tribunal (FT), among others, have no link to NRC, the history of the register and appeasement by the Election Commission that led to the Assam accord only shows they are, in fact, connected. The present anomalies were brought to light and the biases in the FT were also observed in the past. One can see how the social and legal processes are closely tied to the NRC process. In essence, the nature of Assamese nationalism and the definition of Assamese have played a significant role in official measures of original inhabitants (OI) and outsiders. Writer Mitra Phukan notes **"We all looked the other way... We were too ready to forgive violence, too ready to find excuses. Terror was all over the place, and we were all victims, though even the most peaceable among us were perpetrators, too, because we kept quiet."** Ordinarily, the idea of who is an Assamese would be an ongoing process, one premised on assimilation. However, with NRC, the narrow cultural definition is now the legal definition, legitimizing the chauvinism that is part of the Assam movement, a process manufactured by the middle class. Anti-Bengali sentiment, as highlighted earlier, was shared socially, politically, and culturally but is now officially legitimate through state mechanisms such as NRC. The anxiety of the people and the suicides, thus, are a result of the cultural exclusion that clouds the skies of Assam. [60] (Emphasis by Subir)

"Claim that updating NRC mandated by Assam Accord false: In this circus, the poor and marginalized are being fed to lions," under this extraordinary title, the author of the article, Debarshi Das, tried to figure out the plausible number of illegal infiltrators in Assam. He wrote:

> "There is a lack of solid research on this. In 2004, the central government said five million illegal Bangladeshis were living in Assam in 2001. It is unclear how this figure was arrived at. A research paper by the noted econometrician Vani Kant Borooah found that between 1971 and 2011 there were hardly any net illegal infiltrations into Assam (according to the Assam Accord, foreigners who migrated since 25 March 1971 are illegal). My own rough estimate, through a different method, arrived at a similar conclusion. The growth rate of the population of Assam has been less than that of India after 1971. This raises doubts about the existence of massive infiltration." [61]

It needs to be realized that Citizenship rights the fundamental to all rights. Without Citizenship rights, all other fundamental rights are lost. So, stripping of citizenship of any genuine Indian in their own country, for all practical purposes, would not be anything less than capital punishment. When the Indian Government could rightly pride itself on NOT being a banana republic and boast of providing sufficient legal aid before hanging even the dreaded Pakistani terrorist Ajmal Kasab, charged with murder and waging war against India; there was no reason why the same Government should not extend similar support to the people against whom no such charge exists. Their only fault was that they could not produce appropriate 'papers' to prove the genuineness of their being Indians.

Yet, the NRC State Coordinator Prateek Hajela had earlier reportedly opined in the Supreme Court on the 1st November 2018 that **"it is better to leave out a genuine citizen than including a non-citizen in the NRC."** [62] However, the Honorable Judges of the Supreme Court took exception to it. Nonetheless, this attitude of Prateek Hajela naturally raised serious doubt about the general approach of the NRC personnel who had been working under his direction on the task of updating the NRC in Assam. (Emphasis by Subir)

Against this backdrop, several crucial questions arise relating to the entire process of updating the NRC in Assam. The most important among them are:

a) There was a report that the Centre had filed an affidavit in the Supreme Court stating that NRC was not required in Tripura as adequate laws existed to identify and deport illegal immigrants. That was in response to a petition calling for implementing the NRC in

Tripura. [63] If that be the case, what was the compelling reason for undertaking an elaborate exercise of updating the NRC in Assam?

b) The reliability of the 1951 NRC data was doubtful as its information source, the Census Report of 1951, itself was not one hundred per cent accurate. The sample verification for the accuracy of the 1951 Census confirmed this on page 12 of its report. Still, the Government decided to update the then-secret document NRC 1951 as a basis for detecting illegal immigrants! Hence, how could the updated NRC be reliable?

c) When the 1951 NRC of Assam for as many as six districts and the complete electoral rolls of 1966 and 1971 were unavailable, how did it become possible then to UPDATE the NRC for all the districts of Assam?

d) Another report in a National English newspaper mentioned: "Major software system developers in the country did not respond to a tender for the DLDD but a local firm, Bohniman Systems, took up the challenge with inputs from Hajela." [64] Consequently, it brought up the questions: (i) What were those "inputs"? (ii) Did it incorporate the concept of "better to leave out a genuine citizen than including a non-citizen in the NRC'1 for developing the DLDD software? This question assumes special significance in the backdrop of (A) Hajela's remarks in the Supreme Court as mentioned earlier and (B) the news report that the names of Hajela and his daughter were initially omitted in the draft NRC.

e) For a man of the stature of NRC Coordinator, it is easy to get errors rectified when his or his daughter's names are omitted. But, given the hurdles that some poor and ignorant people encountered in enrolling their names, one can well imagine their difficulties had THEIR names been excluded in the draft NRC! Was the Government aware of it? If so, what additional precautions did it adopt to take care of this critical issue?

f) According to NRC Coordinator Prateek Hajela, the process of updating the 1951 NRC was a very complicated and unprecedented task that had to be started "from scratch to build a digitized system and improve upon it." It entailed many complex steps, which were never tried before. Nevertheless, India is known for providing extremely complicated software solutions worldwide. Many world-famous IT companies in India are capable of taking up difficult challenges. Yet, there was reportedly a shortage of IT companies to bid for the job. So, the government entrusted the complicated task of this magnitude to a local IT services company that developed the requisite software - **with inputs from Hajela.** It is not known what kind of quality control the software had been subjected to in determining its error margin, checks and balances, and other vital operational areas.

The people of the country naturally would like to be reassured of these critical issues.

Given that the lives and livelihoods of thousands of people depended on the output the software finally generated, it is imperative to review the entire matter before arriving at a satisfactory conclusion rather than relying solely on the computer output to determine the citizenship status of the people. Also, it is essential to delve into (a) the reliability of the locally developed software used and (b) the authenticity of the inputs fed into the system for the identification of foreigners in Assam under Hajela's overall supervision. There must not be any margin of error or anything else. Therefore, a revisit is crucial to the entire gamut of the process, including whether or not the decision taken on 5th May 2005 in the tripartite meeting to update the 1951 NRC of Assam sans other stakeholders in the state was at all justified/necessary.

The Standard Operating Procedure (SOP) was laid down later for both the disposal of claims and objections. It also spelt out the modalities under clause 6 of the Schedule appended to the Citizenship (Registration of Citizens and Issue of National Identity Cards), Rules, 2003, framed under the Citizenship Act, 1955, and was made available on the Government website. [65] However, when the name of a person of the stature of NRC Coordinator Hajela goes missing in the draft NRC, one shudders to imagine the chances, or lack thereof, of ordinary people's names being included in the final NRC. It holds true with the review petitions as well that were subsequently proposed. Given that the same software, same procedure, same people, and everything else would almost be the same and used, which excluded the name of Hajela in the draft NRC, and then 19 million-odd people from the final list NRC; the only pragmatic solution seemed to be to reject the entire list of the NRC because the efficacy of the system and process has been rendered highly doubtful. Yet, it appears that the government would continue to use everything in the same way in dealing with the proposed review appeals too. It's essential to review the position.

"In the initial stage of the NRC updating process, Bengalis (residing in Assam) were both sceptical as well as optimistic. They were sceptical because they were apprehensive that the process would ultimately turn out to be another mechanism, like the branding of 'D' voters, to harass the Bengalis. On the other hand, the finely and scientifically designed software of the NRC instilled a sense of optimism; for the first time, a government mechanism aiming to detect illegal immigrants gave the feeble belief that the process would finally exonerate them from being branded as "Bangladeshis," an abhorred tag that they desperately wanted to get rid of. But as the process began to roll on, the constantly changing guidelines issued by the NRC authorities that were eventually **endorsed by a bench of the Supreme Court headed by a judge who himself is an applicant in the NRC, thereby having his own share of interest, gradually made the optimism get overshadowed by the scepticism.** With the publication of the first draft at midnight of 31st December 2017, the Bengalis were dumbstruck with disbelief as merely 33 per cent could figure in the part document in the minority-dominant districts. With the publication of the complete draft on 30th ¹June 2018 (¹July) where more than 40 lakhs could not make it into the final list, the Bengalis now began to believe that the process was actually aimed at stripping them of their citizenship status and simultaneously establishing the four-decade-long demands of the Assamese chauvinistic forum that at least 40 to 50 lakh Bengalis intruded into Assam after 1971. However, with the publication of the final NRC list on August 31, 2019, Bengalis felt all their agonies, miseries, insults, and wounds were somehow vindicated as less than 20 lakhs failed to make it to the final draft and that too a considerable number of left-outs belong to various *Khilonjiya* (son of the soil) communities." [66] (Emphasis by Subir)

The three paragraphs quoted above are from Mrinal Talukdar's book 'THE GAME CALLED NRC." In an obvious reference to Justice Ranjan Gogoi, who has the rare distinction of being the first judge from Assam to hold the coveted post of the Chief Justice of India, the seasoned Journalist Talukdar seemingly touched upon very ingeniously the delicate issue of the 'conflict of interest' that was often whispered or mentioned sotto voce during those days. "What was correct was not spoken and what was spoken was not correct. This was in respect of both the Union and the state of Assam.", fascinatingly wrote author Ranjan Gogoi in his autobiography, "JUSTICE FOR THE JUDGE: An Autobiography," concerning his 'remarkable experience' in the journey from Court No. 13 to Court No. 1 with Justice Nariman by his side in narrating how this case along with the other connected cases came up before the Bench. [67]

According to the legal journalism platform Supreme Court Observer (SCO), since former Chief Justice of India Ranjan Gogoi was from Assam, he surely was an applicant for registering his name in the NRC. He would, therefore, be personally affected by any judgments in the case. In 2014, Justice Ranjan Gogoi "....... was criticized for not recusing himself from the case." [68] Thus, a 'conflict of interest' apparently prevailed when Justice Gogoi, as one of the two members of the Supreme Court Bench, supervised the NRC updating exercise along with Justice Nariman as the other member of the Bench. The issue of the 'conflict of interest' arises, as we all know, in a situation in which a person is capable of deriving personal benefit from actions or decisions made in her or his official capacity.

According to Mrinal Talukdar, history will always remember Justice Ranjan Gogoi as the man who breathed life into the NRC case pursued it with a dogmatic approach, and made avoidable mistakes by hurrying through and sometimes over-relying on one person – Pratik Hajela, the NRC-State Coordinator. But it was Mr Gogoi who single-handedly drove the entire NRC process and brought it to the point that nobody cared about or dared to go in the previous 40 years. In fact, former Assam Chief Minister Tarun Gogoi had reportedly told journalist Mrinal Talukdar that had it been under Tarun Gogoi's control, the Chief Minister would not have allowed the NRC to be published. Journalist Talukdar asserted that:

> "But the man who made it possible was former Chief Justice of India, Ranjan Gogoi. Even when he was not the Chief Justice, he and the brother judges of his bench took a hawkish stand and started driving the process with passion, removing all the obstacles and giving it the much-needed push – something that neither the state government nor the Centre were willing to give.
>
> In the process, he was often accused of trespassing into the domain of the executive as well as being over-dependent on Prateek Hajela, but his dogmatic pursuit saw the completion of the NRC updation exercise." [69]

It may be recalled that the NRC issue first came up before Justice Ranjan Gogoi on 2nd April 2013 in Court 13, where he was the other member of a two-member bench presided over by Justice H. L. Gokhale. A writ petition No. 274/2009 - Assam Public Works vs. Union of India & Ors – came to be listed before the bench wherein, inter alia, the petitioners sought deletion of the names of all foreigners (post-1971 immigrants) from the voter lists of the state. Then on 8th May 2013, another connected writ petition was also ordered to be heard with W.P. (C) No. 274/2009, wherein the petitioners challenged the provisions of Section 6A of the Citizenship Act and raised the issue of updating the NRC.

Justice Gokhale retired from the Supreme Court on 10th March 2014. Later, once Justice Ranjan Gogoi started presiding over Benches, this case and the other connected cases came up before a Bench consisting of him and Justice R. F. Nariman until Justice Ranjan Gogoi's retirement on 17th November 2019. Notable among the other related cases were:

a) WRIT PETITION (CIVIL) NO. 562 OF 2012 filed by Assam Sanmilita Mahasangha & Ors (Petitioners) vs. Union of India & Ors. (Respondents), and

b) WRIT PETITION (CIVIL) NO. 876 OF 2014 by All Assam Ahom Association & Ors (Petitioners) vs. Union of India & Ors. (Respondents).

Then, the Court sought an undertaking from Hajela to complete the work of updating the NRC within a time-bound program. Subsequent orders of the Supreme Court bench stressed the expeditious completion of the NRC updating task. The bench ensured that Hajela would report directly to it, and no one else could interfere with the work of the Chief Coordinator Hajela. On July 20th, 2014, the Supreme Court ordered Mr. Hajela to prepare a time schedule, marking the beginning of the time-bound focus on the NRC. Later, the Supreme Court took full control of the NRC through a landmark judgment on December 17th, 2014, when it literally took over the implementation of the NRC updating exercise and announced a rather ambitious time schedule. [70] [71] The relevant portion of the judgment on the Writ Petition (C) No. 274/2009 Assam Public Works vs. Union of India & Ors, dated December 17th, 2014, pronounced by Justice Ranjan Gogoi and Justice R.F. Nariman, is quoted below:

> "48. Insofar as Writ Petition (C) No. 274/2009 is concerned, we are of the view that from the date of this judgment, the following time schedule should govern the work of updating the NRC in Assam so that the entire updated NRC is published by the end of January 2016.
>
> The remaining work of updating the NRC will now conform to the following time schedule, which will be strictly adhered to.

Sl No.	Task	Period in Months	Start	End

1	Publication of Records Search/looking up of linkage by public	1	1 February, 2015	February, 2015
2.	Receipt of applications March, 2015 May, 2015	3	March, 2015	May, 2015
3.	Verification	4	June, 2015	September, 2015
4	Draft Publication		1st October, 2015	
5	Receipt of Claims & Objections 1 October, 2015 October, 2015	1	October, 2015	October, 2015
6	Disposal of Claims & Objections	2	November, 2015	December, 2015
7	Finalization of final updated NRC		1st January, 2016	
8	**Total Time Period in Months**	11		

49. All the cases be listed in the last week of March, 2015 to take note of the progress of implementation of the above directions.

...................................J.

(Ranjan Gogoi)

...................................J.

(R.F. Nariman)

New Delhi;

December 17, 2014. **[72]**

By then, the Supreme Court could fully realize the intricacies and complexities of the task. Since then, the two-member bench of the Supreme Court, headed by Justice Gogoi, kept the timeframe under close review and monitoring. It allowed the deadline extension when deemed essential until the final updated NRC list was published on August 31, 2019—only about two and a half months before the 46th Chief Justice of India, Ranjan Gogoi, retired on November 17, 2019.

On November 3, 2019, Chief Justice of India Ranjan Gogoi strongly defended the NRC updating exercise in Assam, calling it "a base document for the future", which is not yet final. Criticizing "armchair commentators" who had raised objections to the drive, CJI Ranjan Gogoi said they were far from ground realities and had presented a highly distorted picture, due to which Assam and its development agenda had taken a hit, reported the Indian Express on November 4, 2019. He was speaking at the inauguration of a book, "Post Colonial Assam (1947-2019)", by veteran journalist Mrinal Talukdar.

According to Gogoi, "The NRC is not a new nor a novel idea. It finds expression as early as in the year 1951 and, in the particular context of Assam, in the year 1985, when the Assam Accord was signed. In fact, the current NRC is an attempt to update the 1951 NRC."

Prior to the exercise, he said, there was "an enormous amount of guesswork" on the number of illegal immigrants in the state, which had fueled "panic, fear, and a vicious cycle of lawlessness and violence". "There was an urgent need to ascertain, to some degree, the number of illegal immigrants, which the current exercise envisages. Nothing more and nothing less. The entire exercise is nothing but a manifestation of one of the most peaceful means by which stakeholders seek to remedy the wrongs and omissions of that turbulence whose effects changed the course of life not only for individuals but also for communities and cultures across the region." Accusing "careless" and "irresponsible reporting by a few media outlets" of "worsening the situation," the CJI praised the citizens of Assam for displaying "magnanimity" and "large-heartedness" in accepting various NRC cutoff dates.

CJI Gogoi said, "It needs to be told and brought on record that people who raised objections... are playing with fire. At the crossroads, we need to keep in mind that our national discourse has witnessed the emergence of armchair commentators who are not only far removed from ground realities but also seek to present a highly distorted picture."

He said the emergence of social media and its tools had fueled the intent of such commentators, "who thrive through their doublespeak." "They launch baseless and motivated tirades against democratic functioning and democratic institutions, seeking to hurt them and bring down their due process. These commentators and their vile intentions do survive well in situations where facts are far removed from the citizenry, and rumour mills flourish. Assam and its development agenda have been a victim of such armchair commentators," he said.

Justice Gogoi added that people must resist the urge to find "wrongs and shortcomings everywhere" and "the constant desire to play to the gallery by demeaning institutions".

Regarding the NRC exercise, he said, "It is an occasion to put things in proper perspective. The NRC is not a document for the moment. Nineteen lakh or 40 lakh does not matter. It is a base document for the future. It is a document to which one can refer to determine future claims. This, in my comprehension, is the intrinsic value of the NRC." [73]

By contrast, in an exclusive interview with journalist and TV commentator Karan Thapar in September 2019, one of India's top experts on the constitution, Faizan Mustafa, vice-chancellor of the NALSAR (National Academy of Legal Studies and Research) University of Law, Hyderabad (India), explained the major legal problems with how the NRC was conducted in Assam. The full interview is on YouTube [74], and its full transcript is on The Wire's news website. [75] Only some selected portions of the interview are discussed below.

In the interview, Professor Faizan Mustafa candidly expressed, among other things, that the NRC is a clear violation of Section 3 of India's Citizenship Act, which grants citizenship by birth. Since the NRC is being conducted under the Registration of Citizens and Issue of National Identity Card Rules, 2003, these rules cannot contravene the Parent Act. Section 3(1)(a) states that anyone born between Republic Day of 1950 and June 30th, 1987, shall be a citizen by birth. The term used here is 'shall,' which in legal terms implies a mandatory requirement. Therefore, while Hajela asserts that individuals' parents 'could' be D-voters or possibly foreign nationals, simply because Hajela thinks there is a possibility that their parents may not be Indian citizens, he cannot deny citizenship or inclusion in the NRC to anybody.

The Professor maintained that the Supreme Court is the guardian of people's rights. Therefore, the Supreme Court has been empowered to strike down a law unanimously passed by Parliament if it violates any fundamental right. 'Administrative convenience' cannot justify the infringement of the most fundamental of all rights. Citizenship embodies a right to rights. If one possesses citizenship rights, they are entitled to several other rights. Starting from the Sonowal judgment, the court has effectively assumed the role of the executive. In the Sonowal case, the constitutionality of the IMDT Act of 1983 was challenged. When the constitutionality of a law is contested, the court's duty is to determine whether Parliament had the authority to enact that law or whether it violates any fundamental right. However, the Court did not undertake this exercise. Instead, it deemed illegal migration as 'external aggression' and held that if the Centre fails to prevent it, it violates its duty under Article 355 (the duty of the Centre to protect States), and therefore the Court struck down the Act. The IMDT Act had placed the burden of proof on the state to demonstrate that the accused is a foreigner. **The striking down of the IMDT Act was the starting point of today's crisis,** and it was a crisis articulated by the court, according to Professor Faizan Mustafa. (Emphasis by Subir)

The Professor continued: Our Parliament has also been diluting the concept of citizenship, and our courts have been supporting it and going several steps beyond Parliament. When the government commits any wrongdoing, we seek recourse in the court for rectification through judicial review. However, in the entire NRC process, the court itself has been making decisions – determining which documents will be accepted, and which will not. Where can people turn then? (Asked the Professor.)

According to Faizan Mustafa, it's a self-inflicted wound in which the court is also complicit because, in a matter as significant as this, the focus should not be on meeting deadlines but rather on ensuring fairness and justice in the most reasonable manner possible. Interestingly, the government was not in a rush. It was requesting the court to extend the deadlines. However, the court did not meet the expectations. The expectation from the court was that it would ensure that people were not denied citizenship if they possessed genuine documents. However, due to the haste and procedural constraints, we have ended up transforming legal citizens into illegal immigrants, which is an injustice. It is both unfair and illegal.

On a similar note, Gautam Bhatia, a Delhi-based constitutional law scholar and prolific writer, asserted that Justice Ranjan Gogoi's tenure would be remembered for the rise of the 'Executive Court,' one that rendered the Supreme Court indistinguishable from the executive. The relevant portions of Bhatia's article, "The Troubling Legacy of Chief Justice Ranjan Gogoi," which appeared in the Indian news and opinion website The Wire dated November 18th, 2019 (republished on March 16th, 2020), are iterated hereunder:

> I will consider some of the important judgments and orders delivered by the ex-Chief Justice during his tenure. My assessment will be simple: ex-Chief Justice Gogoi oversaw a drift from a Rights Court to an Executive Court. That is, under his tenure, the Supreme Court has transitioned from an institution that – for all its patchy

history – was at least formally committed to the protection of individual rights as its primary task, to an institution that speaks the language of the executive and has become indistinguishable from the executive.

The "Executive Court" is evident in the ex-Chief Justice's substantive adjudication [e.g., the NRC case and the Voice Samples case], in his penchant for procedural opacity [e.g., sealed covers], in his contempt for the Evidence Act [e.g., Rafale], in his treatment of fundamental rights as charity rather than entitlements [habeas corpus petitions], and in his judicial rhetoric."

The NRC case

The starting point of any discussion about the ex-chief justice must address the urgent – almost messianic – manner in which he drove the NRC process, even before assuming the role of chief justice. It's important to recall that the National Register of Citizens (NRC) is a state-wide administrative process in Assam aimed at compiling a list of Indian citizens, stemming from the Assam Accord and subsequent amendments to the Citizenship Act. Initially conceived as an administrative process to be carried out by the government and executed by the bureaucracy, in 2014, the ex-chief justice, along with Justice Nariman, effectively assumed control of the entire process under expansive PIL powers. While formally termed as Supreme Court "oversight" over the NRC's preparation, it soon became evident that there was little distinction between "oversight" and "control."

Why was this problematic? Some of the issues have been discussed in detail, and I will now summarize them. The NRC process wasn't merely an ordinary administrative procedure; it pertained to citizenship – the fundamental basis of all other rights, encapsulating the right to have rights. While the NRC itself wouldn't revoke an individual's citizenship, exclusion from the list would significantly prejudice individuals' cases before the Foreigners Tribunals, to which they would subsequently be summoned. Given the gravity of such consequences, one would anticipate the full array of constitutional safeguards to be in place, enforced with heightened rigour. Under our constitutional framework, one of the most crucial safeguards is the separation of powers and judicial review. The executive formulates policies, and if its actions infringe upon individual rights, the courts are tasked with scrutinizing executive actions against the Constitution.

The Supreme Court's assumption of control over the NRC process effectively pierced through this constitutional fabric. It was the Court, in consultation with the state coordinator, that determined the process's conduct, set deadlines, decided on admissible documents, and more. As the Court had assumed the executive's responsibilities, there was no recourse for aggrieved individuals if they felt their rights were violated; after all, whom could they appeal to apart from the Court itself?

This concern is not theoretical; it has concrete implications. For instance, the use of the "family tree" method to ascertain citizenship disproportionately disadvantaged rural women who faced greater challenges in accessing and providing the requisite documents. In a typical scenario – i.e., if this had been purely executive action – it could have been legally challenged under Articles 14 and 15 and struck down by the courts. However, because the NRC's modalities stemmed from consultations between the Supreme Court and the NRC coordinator, these avenues of redress were effectively blocked off. Numerous examples illustrate this, creating a situation akin to the verse from Alice in Wonderland: "I'll be judge, I'll be jury," said cunning old Fury. "I'll try the whole cause, and sentence you to death."

Here, "death" is not figurative; people died due to the NRC. Deaths occurred when the court insisted on unfeasible deadlines for publishing draft NRCs, despite the state – the actual executive – requesting more time, which was denied. Further fatalities followed during the final list's publication, another expedited process despite government requests for an extension being rejected. This culminated in a warning by Genocide Watch around the final list's release – an unprecedented instance where judicial actions in a functioning democracy prompted a genocide warning. In a different world, this would be the moment for a constitutional court to intervene and safeguard rights. However, in a world where the court had become the perpetrator, the norms had long been inverted.

The problems weren't limited to the ex-chief justice's substantive role in the NRC process; they extended to procedural aspects, featuring opaque proceedings where affected parties weren't heard, and decisions were made based on "PowerPoint presentations" by the state coordinator to the court. Furthermore, decisions were based on evidence presented in sealed covers, bringing us to the next issue.

Sealed covers

Right from the beginning, the ex-chief justice's tenure was marked by secrecy, opacity, and the ubiquitous use of "sealed covers". The NRC case, the Rafale dispute, and the Alok Verma litigation were all characterized by sealed covers. Even in the hearing on electoral bonds, sealed covers were employed, and oddly, they surfaced in the litigation surrounding the prime minister's biopic before the election.

I will, again, summarize an argument that I have detailed in previous posts. Sealed covers stand diametrically opposed to open justice, one of the foundational principles of the judicial system. Courts are obligated to provide reasons for their judgments, allowing citizens to assess the soundness of these reasons as part of the democratic framework of accountability over courts. However, when evidence upon which judgments are based is concealed, any form of scrutiny becomes akin to whistling in the dark. Without knowing the rationale behind the court's decisions, individuals cannot form their own opinions about the merits of those decisions. In such a scenario, courts devolve into little more than authoritarian bodies, relying on institutional power rather than reasoned justifications. This contradicts the essence of democracy.

The ex-chief justice's predilection for sealed covers hints at another aspect of the Supreme Court's transition into what can be termed as the Executive Court. Secrecy is intrinsic to the executive branch, as certain executive actions, such as war plans or intricate trade negotiations, must remain undisclosed for their efficacy. However, the crucial disparity lies in the fact that while executive legitimacy for such actions stems from popular elections, judicial legitimacy arises from transparent and public exposition of reasons. [76]

The article also appeared in Gautam Bhatia's "Indian Constitutional Law & Philosophy," titled "A Little Brief Authority: Chief Justice Ranjan Gogoi and the Rise of the Executive Court." [77]

In this ongoing man-made ordeal, many deaths could be attributed to the fear induced by the failure to locate legacy data, while in numerous other cases, overwhelming confusion and misinformation surrounded the updating process of the 1951-NRC of Assam. Reports emerged of individuals taking their own lives upon not finding their names in the draft NRC due to the daunting, confusing, and costly nature of filing claims. Suicides also occurred after exclusion from the final list, and many perished because family members were excluded. Deaths within detention centres were reported, as were fatalities in queues at the NRC Seva Kendras, where individuals sought assistance or clarifications. Additionally, deaths resulted from accidents while travelling hundreds of kilometres for hearings to meet stringent deadlines.

The apprehension of being excluded from the NRC, being labelled as foreigners, and ultimately being sent to detention centres had gripped a significant portion of the population, instilling permanent paranoia among vulnerable communities, particularly the Bengalis (both Hindus and Muslims) and the [1]Neo-Assamese people. This fear-induced intolerable anxiety, leading many to resort to extreme measures. [78]

[1]Neo-Assamese are those immigrant Muslims living in the Brahmaputra valley of Assam who migrated from East Bengal/East Pakistan and declared Assamese as their mother tongue.

Ominously, until December 30th, 2018, the number of objections filed in the NRC Seva Kendras was less than 800. However, on the last day of the deadline, i.e., on December 31st, 2018, around three lakh objections were filed. In the first week of August 2019, notices were issued to thousands of people only 24-48 hours before their hearings, at places 300-400 km away. Overnight, many people sold their cattle and ornaments to hire vehicles to attend the hearings. On midnight of August 5th, a bus carrying 24 passengers (people who received notices) from Kamrup to Golaghat, around 300 km away, was hit by a truck carrying molten tar near Guwahati. Several received burn injuries. In other separate incidents, four people also died in accidents while travelling. [79]

Journalist Sumir Karmakar, covering Northeast India for the Deccan Herald newspaper, reported on January 2nd, 2019, among other things:

> From only 600 in over three months to over 2.6 lakh in 24 hours – objections against possible inclusion of "illegal migrants" in the NRC in Assam took a dramatic leap on Monday. The NRC office here said that the exact number of objections would further go up as one application contains more than one applicant or the entire family. The number of claims by those left out of the draft NRC also went up to 31.2 lakh, and counting was still on. Over 40.07 lakh of the 3.29 crore applicants found their names dropped from the draft NRC released on July 30th.
>
> The claims and objections period for the NRC began on September 25th, but only 600 objections were filed until Sunday. Sources here told DH that Barpeta, a district in western Assam having a sizeable Muslim population, reported the maximum number of objections, which was estimated to be over 65,000. "Most of the objections were

filed by indigenous people, who are worried that illegal migrants from Bangladesh, who entered Assam after March 24, 1971, have made it to the draft NRC by producing fake documents. The objections will be looked into from February 15th, when documents submitted by those filing claims will also be verified," said the source. Sources said that the "mass objection drive" was spearheaded by the All Assam Students Union (AASU), which led the six-year-long Assam Agitation or anti-foreigners movement from 1979 to 1985. [80]

There were cases where people even produced dead bodies to prove a person's citizenship so that, in the end, the offspring of the deceased could escape the risk of being declared foreigners. For instance, the mortal remains of Sonitpur district's Bhelera Village, Balaram Chakravarty, who died on his way to the office of NRC for a final hearing, were reportedly produced to the NRC office.

"Deadman produced at NRC Hearing," under this caption, a leading Assamese News Channel, Pratidin Time, reported on April 3rd, 2019:

> "Sensation prevailed in Misamari of Sonitpur district following an incident where family members living at Bhelera Village allegedly produced a dead person in an NRC Kendra. According to sources, the family was on their way to visit the office of NRC for a final hearing. But on a sad note, the head of the family, Balaram Chakrabartty, had to accept death on his way to the NRC Office. The family members, finding no other solution, had to take the deceased Balaram Chakrabarty to the office, along with the wife, son, and three grandchildren of the Balaram. Balaram Chakrabarty didn't have any illness; his death was a sudden death, as claimed by the family members. Family members asserted that Balaram, on his way to the NRC office, also took part in a family discussion before his death. The family had to reach the NRC office at around 11 am on April 2nd, but the whole incident took place just when the family was 5 km away from reaching the office. The incident took place at Kalakushi Centre in Misamari when Balaram's health condition worsened suddenly. The family tried to contact 108 services, but as they failed to contact them, they themselves took Balaram to Tezpur Medical College (TMC), but the doctors declared him dead. According to family members, Balaram lost his life due to a heart attack. [81]

It is reported that the NRC exercise has so far cost the Government of India dearly. According to rights groups, the exercise also imposed a financial burden on the people in Assam, with expenditures exceeding Rs. 7,800 crore on hearings alone. Given that the entire state was virtually engaged in the process for at least 3 to 4 years, it is speculated that if its human costs could be notionally calculated, the presumptive loss to India would amount to as high as Rupees one lakh crore. Yet, the same people who initially supported it now deem the outcome as 'flawed and incomplete' (AASU); Abhijeet Sarma of the Assam Public Works (APW) is 'unsatisfied'!

A Correspondent for Outlook India and former Analyst at Indian Political Action Committee (IPAC), Syeda Ambia Zahan, in the article titled "Rs 1,220-cr and 10 years later, NRC leaves group favoring exercise dissatisfied, raises doubts over migrant numbers in Assam," which appeared on India's news website Firstpost on 3rd September 2019, summed up the futility of the entire updating operation of Assam's NRC with an eloquent one-liner:

> "The National Register of Citizenship, which took 10 years, employed 52,000 government employees, and cost the Government of India a whopping Rs 1,220 crore, is now being considered as a fruitless exercise by the very same people who sought it" [82].

Reporter Jayanta Kalita in Northeast Diary in Times of India dated 14th January 2023 raised the question: "Is Assam NRC now nobody's child?" The pertinent part of the report is reproduced below:

> More than three years since the NRC was completed, yet the **Registrar General of India (RGI) is yet to notify the list.** Amidst this delay came the CAG report, which is, in fact, a stinging comment on how the NRC Coordinator, Prateek Hajela, handled the entire work.
>
> The audit report flagged issues such as – "exorbitant profit of over Rs 155 crore retained by the System Integrator (Wipro) on operators' wage"; "deviation from the contract" that led to "unauthorized expenditure of over Rs 10 crore in connection with the engagement of third-party monitoring consultations and an excess expenditure of Rs 1.78 crore on project management"; "avoidable expenditure to the tune of Rs 7 crore in **software development through change request";** "haphazard development of **NRC software with a risk** to confidentiality and **integrity of data**", among others.
>
> It is not yet clear what action the government will take against individuals and entities who **made a mess of the NRC exercise.** The state where 860 people sacrificed their lives in the hope of an "infiltration-free Assam" certainly deserves an answer from the ruling dispensation [83] (Emphasis by Subir).

"Assam Govt Registers Case Against Prateek Hajela In NRC Scam," reported Assamese news channel, Pratidin Time, on 12th April 2023. The state government has reportedly filed the case taking suo moto cognizance of the matter following the report submitted by the Comptroller and Auditor General of India (CAG). Assam Chief Minister Himanta Biswa Sarma said, "It would be better if Prateek Hajela took VRS. It would be a victory for the people of Assam if he took VRS," added the Pratidin Time dated 12th April 2023 [84].

Is it the end of the NRC story of Assam, or is there more to it? As far as the constitutional validity of section 6A of the Citizenship Act, 1955 is concerned, a five-judge Constitution Bench of India's Supreme Court comprising Chief Justice of India D. Y. Chandrachur, Justices Surya Kant, M. M. Sundresh, J. B. Pardiwala and Manoj Misra recently deliberated on the issue, leading to a four-day hearing where arguments both in support of and against the provision were presented. After considering the viewpoints of the intervenors and the rejoinders submitted by the petitioners, the proceedings concluded on 12th December 2023. The bench has since reserved its judgement on the matter.

"The story is still unfolding and best left for another day"! [1]

* * * * * * *

Epilogue.
Let There Be Light!

Seven and a half decades ago, when a new country was born, I lost my home! The casualty of the cesarean performed in my motherland was my ancestral domicile. When my dad built a new house for us in Shillong, I could not call it our home. The fact that I was born and brought up in Shillong did not qualify me to be a 'son of the soil' - not only in Shillong, Assam/Meghalaya but the entire North East India. The day this realization sank in me, as I grew up, the quest for my home had started. In my sunset years, I am still looking for a spot where I can have a home of my own. I am still on the lookout to find a place where I can breathe freely and speak in my mother tongue without eyebrows being raised - not for me alone, but for my children too. They must experience for the first time in their life the real taste of staying home. A home we can call our OWN. The search is still on...

I support Asaduddin Owaisi, the President of the All India Majlis-e-Ittehadul Muslimeen, in his demand to arrest all those who call an Indian Muslim a "Pakistani" - whatever might be the provocation. I can feel the pain and agony such an affront could inflict on the psyche of the Indian Muslims. It not only questions the persons' credentials as bona fide Indian citizens but also puts a shadow of doubt over their allegiance to the sacred constitution of our country. I can very well imagine what such an insulting insinuation could do to the people at the receiving end. I know the anguish and the affliction it causes - because I have personally gone through it.

The incident took place in a crowded evening market known as "Batti Bazar" at Laban locality in Shillong, the capital of Meghalaya - one of the 'seven sisters' (State) in the North East region of India. It was a bolt from the blue! A well-educated and dignified 'Kong' [1], who had known me since my infancy, committed a similar transgression against me. In my childhood, I used to visit the market, often holding my father's hands to buy fish from that particular shop. Earlier, her mother used to sell fish, and then the "Kong" took over. The incident occurred sometime in 1979 when the communal tension in Meghalaya was high after the so-called 'foreigners' bogey got imported from Assam. At that time, there were rumours of student leaders from the neighbouring State holding several rounds of meetings with the representatives of the Khasi Students Union (KSU) at Shillong.

For no apparent reason and without any provocation, Kong suddenly flared up and shouted at me, "Jao mein Bangladesh! Aap Bangladeshi log kiew hiana boitha hamlog ka Meghalaya mein?" That was in broken Hindi, commonly used locally. It meant, "Go back to Bangladesh! Why are you Bangladeshis residing amidst us in OUR Meghalaya?"

Earlier, too, there were occasions when I came across such remarks uttered sotto voce behind my back in Assam many times. On those occasions, I dismissed it as flippant off-the-calf comments of some blockheads and did not take any offence. However, coming from Kong, I could not ignore this anymore. It hurt me a lot because we had a kind of special family ties. It existed between our families for many years - perhaps even before I was born.

Once, it happened that my father had severe problems walking when Kong's mother arranged a traditional Khasi massage for him. She personally supervised the treatment visiting our home daily for about a month or so. It had cured my father completely. Since then, there has been a kind of unique bond between our two families. So, when I was called a Bangladeshi by none other than one of their family members, I could not take the insinuation in my stride. I was so heartbroken and shocked that I could not sleep properly that night. With every toss and turn in the bed all night, I told myself: It's time to pack and bid goodbye. I knew that it would be adieu not only to Shillong but also to North East India.

During those days, as I discovered that my Bengali community had become somewhat synonymous with the expression 'Bangladeshis' in the NorthEast, my resolve to bid farewell to this place grew stronger. Now, it hurts ME PERSONALLY when I hear the scream, "KICK OUT THE BANGLADESHIS FROM 'OUR' SOIL; KICK THEM OUT…" and when the yelling voice of the anchor in the TV talk show says, "You (Bangladeshis) can't creep into this country like a rat and then squat here and burn our home, take over our temple land, agricultural land and then murder our people and RAPE OUR WOMEN" and all that, my blood starts boiling at the sweeping insinuations!

The talk show is freely available on YouTube for anyone to watch. [2] I can very well understand now and recognize who those 'Bangladeshis' really are! I know from my years of experience, more than half a century, in Assam that it includes me. Now, I can relate these offensive outbursts to me – rather personally. I feel the 'local' people were being instigated against the Bengalis in Assam as early as the 1920s. At least two members of the Line System Committee had caught similar lies. In their dissenting note of the Report, they mentioned how some FALSE propaganda was unleashed against the poor and the so-called "immigrants" (Apartheid Chapter in this book). Nobody could challenge the authenticity of the note at that time. Also, the Report of PUCL of 1980 (Assam Agitation Chapter in this book) exposed the same type of vicious lies and dangerous propaganda against the so-called "Bangladeshis." Has anyone objected to that Report till today?

Naturally, when sweeping allegations of arson, murder, rape, and more against the so-called "Bangladeshis" are levelled based on some questionable reports, I doubt the veracity of the claim and smell a rat. Now I understand why instead of demanding a thorough investigation and exemplary punishments for those so-called 'Bangladeshi' culprits for the alleged crimes, it is essential for them to scream from the rooftops to make them heard because the truth can never do the talking for them.

It was the 'eureka' moment for us sometime in the late 1990s when I was discussing with one of my Khasi colleagues about the 1979 communal disturbances in Shillong sitting at our office canteen during lunch break. During our discussion, I recalled how, one beautiful morning, our sweeper suddenly appeared at our home and cautioned us against drinking the municipality-supply water. It was quite shocking to learn from the sweeper that some mischievous Khasis had poisoned the drinking water of our locality - reportedly to settle their so-called grudge against the Bengalis. At that, my colleague Syiemlieh almost jumped from his seat and said, "Oh my God! Is it so? Would you believe: We also got agitated with the same rumour on that fateful morning that some mischievous Bengalis had poisoned our drinking water? So, all of us gathered in our community hall. The atmosphere was very tense. By 11 A.M, we came to know that disturbances had already started at some pockets in Shillong!"

Thus, we came to know, by chance, how the horrible communal violence of 1979 was triggered. Those who were living in Shillong during that period may recollect it. In hindsight, I now wonder how silly we, the common men, sometimes turn out to be. It does not require a lot of effort to turn us into a kind of strong-headed bull. Mere rumours like 'poison in water tank', 'beef inside temple' or 'pork in some mosque premises' and so forth are enough to blur our vision and switch off our sanity to start communal riots!

Shillong, where I was born and brought up, was never like this before. It was one of the most beautiful and peaceful towns in the whole of India, where people of different communities, cultures, and faith lived in perfect harmony until the late 1970s. Some of the most beautiful periods of my life were spent in Shillong. I had learned a lot from the Khasis - the most important among those was the real meaning of 'dignity of labour' - that no job is superior or inferior. This is ingrained in Khasi society. A typical example of this, among many lessons which could be learnt from the ethnic societies of North East India, was this highly educated Kong mentioned in earlier paragraphs who did not mind the physical labour involved in selling fish in her retail shop without any helping hand - unlike in many other places in India where such jobs are generally looked down upon. I still have many exceptional Khasi friends in Meghalaya with whom I grew up. I feel bad for the people who can never have those unforgettable days of peace and tranquillity now in the hustle and bustle (and whatnot?) of present-day Shillong.

I know that the customary Khasi Religion teaches its followers: "Ieit la ka jong, burom ia kiwei" (Love one's own, and respect others). Traditionally, a Khasi believed his God was also the God of the Hindu, the Muslim, the Christian and all other people. It is high time now for every Indian, irrespective of their religious affinity, to start following this lovely concept. We need to promote, propagate, and practice this great thought in the entire country. Let us instil this divine notion in us. It will enhance the unity and integrity among the Indians - despite our intrinsic diversity.

I couldn't suppress my giggle while reading an English national newspaper on the morning of June 27, 2018. Naturally, it invited a curious stare from my wife sitting beside me. I was going through an interview given by a well-known journalist from North East India on the recent clashes in Shillong that took place between local Khasis and Punjabi Sikhs on May 31, 2018. The journalist tried to convey that the incident turned into an inter-community conflict because of the fight for economic space. It was asserted that the lack of employment opportunities in Meghalaya was the reason for earlier ethnic clashes. It grew from the perceived notion among the locals that jobs were being taken away by more competitive and competent 'outsiders'. It was a ludicrous explanation, and in all likelihood, the journalist, too, knew this. Alternatively, maybe the journalist was scared of petrol bombs, which are often hurled at the residences of those who speak out frankly against some dubious game plans of a particular group in Shillong.

It is a well-known fact that there would not be any dearth of jobs had Meghalaya only opened its doors to 'outsiders'. I am not sure whether the journalist was wittingly trying to deceive the people outside of Meghalaya decided against telling the truth out of fear, or both. Yet, it seemed to me like an attempt to gloss over reality. Nevertheless, it was quite disturbing since it came from a well-established personality of the fourth estate who specializes in reporting on the North East. But, I understand that one has to be politically correct to survive and serve – especially in North East India. Perhaps that also explains why the unpalatable truths revealed in this book were hardly brought out earlier by established authors and journalists so candidly.

It just so happened that both my daughters had their schooling in Kendriya Vidyalaya (KV), or the Central School as they call it in English. Due to the transferable nature of my job, they had attended different KVs in different States in India. They were quite happy at all the KVs they had attended except one. Their experience at a KV in Guwahati was terrible. They were bullied regularly as Bengali and more so because they could not chat in the Assamese language. Unfortunately, they had to attend that same KV not once but twice on two different occasions because of my two separate postings in Guwahati. While I am fluent in Assamese, my daughters were not - simply because Hindi and English are the preferred languages in all the KVs across India. Also, since I had to shift my family rather frequently from place to place and did not spend much time in any particular station, it was somewhat difficult for my children to pick up Assamese or, for that matter, any other local language.

I was told many years later that my daughters used to return home from that KV in Guwahati, always dejected, often crying but silently, lest it came to my notice, and I took up the issue with the school authorities inviting more trouble to them. Later, they confessed to me that only a handful of students were always at fault while others never involved themselves in such nasty fun. In retrospect, I don't blame those bothersome students who must have been unaware of, at their tender age, the serious distress they had caused to my daughters. Instead, now I pity those KV students for the environment of jealousy, hatred, and hostility in which they had to grow up during their childhood. Now, I shudder to visualize the adulthood activities of those kids who had been bullying my daughters. I am not naming the KV to avoid tarnishing its reputation. However, I wish the school authorities and the guardians, in general, would introspect seriously in the interests of THEIR students/children and act appropriately - as may be deemed fit.

I would have stayed permanently in Shillong, where I inherited a house from my father. I would not have bid farewell to the North East and its exceptional people with whom I had shared many memorable moments of my life. I reluctantly moved away from the 'Seven Sisters' just for the sake of my daughter's future and for posterity. I wanted them to grow up in an environment where their mother tongue does not come in the way of their natural upbringing and career progression. I was yearning for my children to have a level playing field in their life. I longed to provide them with an environment where they need not shy away from telling anyone that they were BengaliSylheti origin. I wanted to be away from the surroundings where one's mother tongue, race, and religious faith matter more than the individual's humility, ability, trait and talent. I wanted my children to be treated as equals, where they wouldn't be 'branded' as Bangladeshi and where their way of life would be more dignified – sans the feeling of ignominy being an 'Indigenous Immigrant.'

Undoubtedly, it was the hardest decision I took in over 70 years of my life. I know that there will be questions. When could thousands of Bengalis still stay in Shillong, Meghalaya, and for that matter, in the entire North East India: what was so extraordinary about me that I decided to take leave? More than anything else, I had to make the decision out of concern for the future well-being of my children and their progeny. Nevertheless, I left Shillong, where I was born and brought up, with a heavy heart. It had pained me a lot to take leave of North East India, where I once thought I belonged to it.

So, to me, it was for the last time over a decade ago:

[1]KHUBLEI, Shillong!

ADIEU, my beloved "Seven Sisters"!

GOD BE WITH YOU, Assam and North East (India)!

Note: [1]Khublei is a Khasi word that conveys many meanings, like: "Thanks", "Hello," "Goodbye," "God bless," and so forth.

* * * * * *

Source / reference

Tribute

[1] Report of the 5-member Commission of Enquiry under the Chairmanship of N. C. Chatterjee, Senior Advocated and Vice-President of Supreme Court Bar Association dated 11th June 1961 https://web.archive.org/web/20131229042659/http://www.unishemay.org/english-pages/lang-content/NCChatterjee.pdf

[2] Bhattacharjee, Tomojit. "Remembering Assam's Barak Valley Martyrs, Who Fought For Their Language" 'Youth Ki Awaaz' dated 19th May 2017. https://www.youthkiawaaz.com/2017/05/barak-valleys-language-martyrs-lest-we-forget/

* * * * * * *

Prologue

Why this book?

[1] A Bengali hailing from the Sylhet District (presently in Bangladesh) of East Bengal is called 'Sylheti'.

[2] In Assamese, 'Bongal' means 'outsider', 'foreigner' (Ref: Hemcosh -14th edition, p 907). In reality, however, 'Bongal' stands for those 'foreigner' who entered Assam from the western side of Assam. So the British were called "Boga (white) Bongal and in the post-independent India, 'Bongal' has become somewhat synonymous to 'Bengalis'.

[3] Amar Ujala India Top 10 Year Book 2019 & New World Encyclopedia. https://www.newworldencyclopedia.org/entry/Bengali_language.

* * * * * * *

Chapter 1

Pre-Colonial Era of Assam

[1] Dutt, Nandana. p. 192-193. "Questions of Identity in Assam: Location, Migration, Hybridity".

[2] Prabhakara, M.S. "In the name of changing names" FRONTLINE dated 16th June 2006. https://frontline.thehindu.com/other/article30209727.ece

[3] Gait, Edward. p. 432. (APPENDIX G) "A History of Assam". Reprint by EBH Publishers, Guwahati, Assam. (2018 Edition)

[4] Sharma, Anushthatri. "Assam". The Critical Script.dated 2nd December 2020. https://thecriticalscript.com/article-details/swargadeo-chaolungsukaphaa-the-architect-of-bor-asom

[5] Barua, Sanjib. p. xvii. "INDIA against itself"

[6] Sudhindra Nath Bhattacharya. p. 19. "The North-East Frontier – The Land, The People and Their Early History". Vol 1, in "Discovery of North-East India: Geography, History, Culture, Religion, Politics, Sociology, Science, Education and Economy", Edited by S. K. Sharma & Usha Sharma. https://www.google.co.in/books/edition/Discovery_of_North_East_India/JUozqyA2e90C?hl=en&gbpv=1

[7] NCERT. p.17 "Assam: Gateway to North East", North East India: People History and Culture .https://ncert.nic.in/pdf/publication/otherpublications/tinei101.pdf.

[8] M. L. BOSE, p.37. "SOCIAL HISTORY OF ASSAM"

[9] Ali, Ibrahim, Md. p.82. Chapter III. "Perso arab relations with Assam and their impact on Assamese language" http://shodhganga.inflibnet.ac.in/handle/10603/66545

[10] SHIN, JAE-EUN. p 25 & 46. "REGION FORMED AND IMAGINED Reconsidering temporal, spatial and social context of Kamarupa" in the book "MODERN PRACTICES IN NORTH EAST INDIA History, Culture, Representation" edited by Lipokmar Dzuvichu and Manjeet Baruah. https://www.academia.edu/35909945/Region_Formed_and_Imagined_Reconsidering_Temporal_Spatial_and_Social_Context_of_K%C4%81mar%C5%ABpa_in_Lipokmar_Dzuvichu_and_Manjeet_Baruah_eds_Modern_Practices_in_North_East_India_History_Culture_Representation_London_and_New_York_Routledge_2018_pp_23_55

[11] M. L. BOSE, p.37. "SOCIAL HISTORY OF ASSAM"

[12] Suresh Kant Sharma, Usha Sharma - 2005, "Discovery of North-East India: Geography, History, Culture, ... - Volume 3", Page 248

[13] Gait, Edward. p 35. "A History of Assam"(EBH Publisher (India) Guwahati 2018 edition)

[14] Word finder. "What is "buranji" https://findwords.info/term/buranji

[15] ASSAMEXAM "Buranjis – Chronicle of Assam History: History of Assam. https://www.assamexam.com/assam-history/assam-history-treaty-buranjis-history-chronicle/

[16] Gait, Sir Edward. p. 78-79. "A History of Assam". Reprint by EBH Publishers, Guwahati, Assam. (2018 Edition)

[17] Baruah, S. L. p 16-19. "LAST DAYS OF AHOM MONARCHY: A History of Assam from 1769 to 1826

[18] Guha, Amalendu. p 6. "THE AHOM POLITICAL SYSTEM: AN ENQUIRY INTO THE STATE FORMATION PROCESS IN MEDIEVAL ASSAM: 1228-1714" *Social Scientist*, Vol. 11, No. 12 (Dec., 1983), https://doi.org/10.2307/3516963

[19] Gate, Edward. p. 147, 149-150. "A History of Assam" Reprint by EBH Publishers, Guwahati, Assam. (2018 Edition)

[20] Goswami, Priyam.p 10-11 "The History of Assam: From Yandabo to Partition, 1826-1947

[21] Nag, Sajal. p 24-26. "Roots of Ethnic Conflict: Nationality Question in North East India".

[22] Ahom–Mughal conflicts, List of Conflicts. From Wikipedia, the free encyclopedia

  https://en.wikipedia.org/wiki/Ahom%E2%80%93Mughal_conflicts

[23] Gait, Sir Edward. p. 142. "A History of Assam". Chapter. The Period of Muhammadan Wars. Reprint by EBH Publishers, Guwahati, Assam. (2018 Edition)

[24] Baruah, S. L. p 1. "LAST DAYS OF AHOM MONARCHY: A History of Assam from 1769 to 1826

[25] Gait, Sir Edward. p. 187-189. "A History of Assam" Reprint by EBH Publishers, Guwahati, Assam. (2018 Edition)

[26] Sharma, Chandan Kumar.p.38-40 "Socio-Economic Structure and Peasant Revolt: The Case of Moamoria Upsurge in the Eighteenth Century Assam." Indian Anthropologist, vol. 26, no. 2, 1996, pp. 33–52, http://www.jstor.org/stable/41919803

[27] Gogoi, Biswadip, "The Matak, Mayamara sect and Moamaria revolt: A brief revisit" The_Matak_Mayamara_sect_and_Moamaria_rev.pdf]

[28] Baruah, S. L. p 32. "LAST DAYS OF AHOM MONARCHY: A History of Assam from 1769 to 1826"

[29] Verma, Rajesh. "BARKANDAZES IN ASSAM." Proceedings of the Indian History Congress, vol. 66, 2005, pp. 717–25, http://www.jstor.org/stable/44145884

[30] Baruah, S. L. p.195 "LAST DAYS OF AHOM MONARCHY: A History of Assam from 1769 to 1826"

[31] Baruah, S. L. p. 207 "Last Days of Assam Monarchy"

[32] Baruah, S. L. p. 231 "Last Days of Assam Monarchy"

[33] Baruah, S. L. p.230- 231 "Last Days of Assam Monarchy"

[34] Baruah, S. L. p. 231 "Last Days of Assam Monarchy"

[35] Baruah, S. L. p. 225 "Last Days of Assam Monarchy"

[36] Goswami, Priyam. p. 15. The History of Assam: FROM YANDABO TO PARTITION, 1826-1947

[37] Gait, Edward. p 37. "A History of Assam" Reprint by EBH Publishers, Guwahati, Assam. (2018 Edition)

[38] Gogoi, Biswadip. p. 2, Foot Note. "Language and Nationalism: Comprehending the Dynamics in Nineteenth-century Assam". https://www.academia.edu/50905736/Language_and_Nationalism_Comprehending_the_Dynamics_in_Nineteenth_century_Assam

[39] Sharma, Chandan Kumar. "Socio-Economic Structure and Peasant Revolt: The Case of Moamoria Upsurge in the Eighteenth Century Assam." Indian Anthropologist, vol. 26, no. 2, 1996, pp. 33–52, http://www.jstor.org/stable/41919803

[40] Baruah, S. L. "LAST DAYS OF AHOM MONARCHY: A History of Assam from 1769 to 1826"

[41] Gate, Edward. p.341 "A History of Assam" Reprint by EBH Publishers, Guwahati, Assam. (2018 Edition)

[42] Baruah, S. L. p 32. "LAST DAYS OF AHOM MONARCHY: A History of Assam from 1769 to 1826"

[43] Baruah, S. L. p 244. "LAST DAYS OF AHOM MONARCHY: A History of Assam from 1769 to 1826"

****

Chapter 2
The Story of OPIUM

[1] Barua, Hemchandra. p. 22. KANIAR KIRTAN https://archive.org/details/in.ernet.dli.2015.451532/page/n19/mode/2up?view=theater

[2] KAWAL DEEP KOUR "On the evils of opium eating: Reflections on Nineteenth Century Assamese Literary Reformist Discourse" EUROPEAN ACADEMIC RESEARCH, VOL. I, ISSUE 2/ MAY 2013. https://euacademic.org/uploadarticle/10.pdf

[3] Kawal Deep Kour – p.145-146. "On the evils of opium eating: Reflections on Nineteenth Century Assamese Literary Reformist". https://euacademic.org/uploadarticle/10.pdf

[4] Pakyntein, E. H. Excise Commissioner, Assam. "Opium prohibition campaign in Assam 1". UNODC. Website: https://www.unodc.org/unodc/en/data-and-analysis/bulletin/bulletin_1958-01-01_3_page005.html

[5] Gita, W V. p 17-18. "History of opium and its impact on society under the British" http://hdl.handle.net/10603/84100

[6] Gait, Sir Edward. p. 381-382. "A History of Assam" (Second Edition)

[7] Guha, Amalendu. "IMPERIALISM OF OPIUM: ITS UGLY FACE IN ASSAM (1773-1921)." Proceedings of the Indian History Congress, vol. 37, 1976, pp. 338–46 ,http://www.jstor.org/stable/44138963

[8] Goswami, Shrutidev. p 622-624. "THE NATURE AND EFFECTS OF OPIUM MONOPOLY IN ASSAM, 1860—1919." Proceedings of the Indian History Congress, vol. 47, 1986, pp. 622–28. JSTOR,http://www.jstor.org/stable/44141612

[9] Guha, Amalendu. p.45-46. "Planter Raj to Swaraj"

[10] Guha, Amalendu. "Planter Raj to Swaraj" Page 71

[11] Chetry, Sanjib Kumar. "Opium: Popularity and Consequences in Colonial Assam, India." International Research Journal of Social Sciences. E-ISSN 2319–3565. Vol. 5(2), 41-45, February (2016) http://isca.in/IJSS/Archive/v5/i2/7.ISCA-IRJSS-2015-319.pdf

[12] Gita, W.V. p 168 chapter IV. "History of opium and its impact on society under the British" http://hdl.handle.net/10603/84100

[13] Goswami, Shrutidev. p. 625-626 "THE NATURE AND EFFECTS OF OPIUM MONOPOLY IN ASSAM, 1860—1919." Proceedings of the Indian History Congress, vol. 47, 1986, pp. 622–28. JSTOR, http://www.jstor.org/stable/44141612

[14] Guha, Amalendu. p. 188-189. "Planter Raj to Swaraj"

****

Chapter 3.

The Emergence of Assam

[1] Bhattacharjee, J. B. p 8-9. "H K Barpujari Endowment Lectures: MAKING OF BRITISH ASSAM"

[2] Dutta, Nandana. "Questions of Identity in Assam". Page192-193.

[3] Guha, Amalendu. p. 1-2. "Planter Raj top Swaraj"

[4] "Ava - ancient kingdom, Myanmar". Britannica https://www.britannica.com/place/Ava

[5] LEXLIFE INDIA THE LEGAL WAY OF LIFE https://lexlife.in/2019/12/16/introduction-bengal-eastern-frontier-regulation-1873/#:~:text=This%20permit%20system%20goes%20back,the%20Bengal%20Eastern%20Frontier%20Regulations.&text=The%20idea%20behind%20this%20regulation,into%20their%20personal%20tribal%20affairs.

[6] Bhaumik, Subir. p 6-7. "Troubled Periphery: Crisis of India's North East" http://14.139.206.50:8080/jspui/bitstream/1/949/1/TROUBLED%20PERIPHERY.pdf

[7] Choudhury, Deba Prosad p 68-69 & p.209-217. "BRITISH POLICY OF THE NORTH-EAST FRONTIER".ProQuest. https://eprints.soas.ac.uk/34099/1/11015915.pdf

[8] J. B. Bhattacharjee p. 24-31. Making of British Assam.

[9] Saikia, Rajen. p. 383-384 "Sectional President's Address: THE POLITICAL GEOGRAPHY OF COLONIAL AND POST-COLONIAL ASSAM : CONSTRUCTION AND CONTESTATIONS." Proceedings of the Indian History Congress, vol. 70, 2009, pp. 380–395. JSTOR, www.jstor.org/stable/44147685

[10] Live History India: "U Tirot Singh & Meghalaya's Fight For Freedom" https://www.livehistoryindia.com/story/history-daily/u-tirot-singh-meghalayas-fight-for-freedom/]

[11] SYIEMLIEH, DAVID R. *"In Pursuit of History, Discussion on Collection and Interpretation of Data"* (NEHU journal publication; Vol XIII) https://nehu.ac.in/public/downloads/Journals/Journal_VolXIII_No2_Jul-Dec2015_A1.pdf

[12] Gait, Edward. p 359. "A History of Assam

[13] Lahiri, Rebati Mohan. p.76. "The Annexation of Assam 1824-1854"

[14] Dutt, K. N. "THE KHASI INSURRECTION, 1829 (Its Real Causes and Character)." Proceedings of the Indian History Congress, vol. 22, 1959, pp. 336–344. JSTOR,

www.jstor.org/stable/44304319

[15] Bhattacharjee, J. B. p. 34-39 "Making of British Assan"

[16] Deryck O. Lodrick. "Nagaland state, India" https://www.britannica.com/place/Nagaland

[17] KETHOLESIE. "British Policy towards Annexation of the Naga Hills". International Journal of Engineering, Management, Humanities and Social Sciences Paradigms (IJEMHS) (Volume 13, Issue 01) Publishing Month: June 2015

https://ijemhs.com/Published%20Paper/Volume%2013/Issue%2001/IJES%2011/IJEMHSJune2015_55_57_Keth.pdf

[18] Saikia, Rajen. p.388. "Sectional President's Address: THE POLITICAL GEOGRAPHY OF COLONIAL AND POST-COLONIAL ASSAM: CONSTRUCTION AND CONTESTATIONS." Proceedings of the Indian History Congress, vol. 70, 2009, pp. 380–95. JSTOR, http://www.jstor.org/stable/44147685

[19] Nath, Monoj Kumar. p.22 "The Muslim Question in Assam and Northeast India"

[20] Chaube, S. K. p. 1. "Hill Politics in Northeast India (Third Edition)

[21] Bhattacharjee, J. B. p. 1024 "THE FIRST PARTITION OF BENGAL (1874)." Proceedings of the Indian History Congress, vol. 66, Indian History Congress, 2005, pp. 1022–29, http://www.jstor.org/stable/44145915

[22] Bhattacharjee, J. B. p. 52-53 "H K Barpujari Endowment Lectures: MAKING OF BRITISH ASSAM"

[23] Pau, Pum Khan. "Reconfigured frontier: British policy towards the Chin-Lushai Hills, 1881-1898." The NEHU Journal, Vol XVI, No. 1, January - June 2018https://nehu.ac.in/public/downloads/Journals/Jan-June-2018/The-Nehu-Journal-Jan-June-2018-7-23.pdf

[24] P. N. Luthra. "North-East Frontier Agency Tribes: Impact of Ahom and British Policy." Economic and Political Weekly, vol. 6, no. 23, 1971, pp. 1143–49. JSTOR,http://www.jstor.org/stable/4382099

[25] MCKAY, ALEX. "The British Invasion of Tibet, 1903–04." Inner Asia, vol. 14, no. 1, Brill, 2012, pp. 5–25,http://www.jstor.org/stable/24572145

[26] Choudhury, Deba Prasad. p 138-139 "BRITISH POLICY ON THE NORTH-EAST FRONTIER OF INDIA, 1865 – 1914"https://eprints.soas.ac.uk/34099/1/11015915.pdf

[27] Choudhury, Deba Prasad. "BRITISH POLICY ON THE NORTH-EAST FRONTIER OF INDIA, 1865 – 1914" https://eprints.soas.ac.uk/34099/1/11015915.pdf

[28] "Kalha, R. S. The McMahon Line: A hundred years on" Manohar Parrikar Institute for Defense Studies and Analysis dated 3rd July 2014.https://idsa.in/idsacomments/TheMcMahonLine_rskalha_030714

[29] Elwin. V p.4 "A Philosophy of NEFA"

[30] Agarwala, Tora, "Explained: At the root of Assam-Arunachal Pradesh border dispute, a committee report from 1951" The Indian Express dated 3rd February 2022. https://indianexpress.com/article/explained/explained-at-the-root-of-assam-arunachal-pradesh-border-dispute-a-committee-report-from-1951-7750914/

[31] Bhaumik, Subir. p 8. "Troubled Periphery: Crisis of India's North-East" http://14.139.206.50:8080/jspui/bitstream/1/949/1/TROUBLED%20PERIPHERY.pdf

[32] Saikia, Rajen. p 383-384 "Sectional President's Address: THE POLITICAL GEOGRAPHY OF COLONIAL AND POST-COLONIAL ASSAM : CONSTRUCTION AND CONTESTATIONS." Proceedings of the Indian History Congress, vol. 70, 2009, pp. 380–395. JSTOR, www.jstor.org/stable/44147685

[33] Bhattacharjee, J. B. p. 113-114 "H K Barpujari Endowment Lectures: MAKING OF BRITISH ASSAM"

****

Chapter 4.
The Colonial Era of Assam.

[1] Goswami, Arup Kumar (Researcher). p. 1-2 CHAPTER I "Waste land settlement in the Brahmaputra valley of Assam 1838 to 1921"http://hdl.handle.net/10603/68403

[2] Manuel, Thomas. p. vii-xii. "Opium Inc. HOW A GLOBAL DRUG TRADE FUNDED THE BRITISH EMPIRE"

[3] "History of Indian Tea". Indian Tea Association. https://www.indiatea.org/history_of_indian_tea]

[4] "Assam: Wildlife, history and native tea" All About Assam Tea - Teabox. https://tea101.teabox.com/the-assam-tea

[5] Duwarah, Julee Researcher p 16-18. "Ethnicity and identity construction a study of the tea community of Assam". http://hdl.handle.net/10603/151279

[6] "BRIEF NOTE ON TEA LAND ADMINISTRATION IN ASSAM" GOVERNMENT OF ASSAM REVENUE & DISASTER MANAGEMENT https://landrevenue.assam.gov.in/information-services/tea-land-administration-in-assam#:~:text=In%201855%2C%20indigenous%20tea%20was,cultivation%20started%20after%20some%20years

[7] Ashfaque Hossain. (University of Dhaka) "Three Bengal Districts and the Making and Unmaking of Assam-Bengal Borders, 1874-1947" https://www.researchgate.net/publication/343675174_Three_Bengali_Districts_and_the_Making_and_Unmaking_of_Assam-Bengal_Borders_1874-1947

[8] Choudhury, Deba Prosad. p 72 "BRITISH POLICY ON THE NORTH-EAST FRONTIER OF INDIA, 1865 – 1914" https://eprints.soas.ac.uk/34099/1/11015915.pdf

[9] Guha, Amalendu. p 278 "Planter Raj to Swaraj".

[10] Guha, Amalendu. p 21, 28-30. Planter Raj to Swaraj

[11] Kar, Bodhi Sattwa. p.37 & 170-172 "Line system and colonial politics in Assam 1920 1947". http://hdl.handle.net/10603/90311

[12] Goswami, Arup Kumar (Researcher). "Waste land settlement in the Brahmaputra valley of Assam 1838 to 1921" http://hdl.handle.net/10603/68403

[13] Goswami, Arup Kumar (Researcher). "Waste land settlement in the Brahmaputra valley of Assam 1838 to 1921" http://hdl.handle.net/10603/68403

[14] Hussain, Eusub. p. 50-52, 63-64, 68, 145 "A history of Muslim politics in Assam" http://hdl.handle.net/10603/160104

[15]] Guha, Amalendu "Planter Raj to Swaraj" p 59.

[16] Molla, Mohammad Kasim Uddin. p.59. "THE NEW PROVINCE OF EASTERN BENGAL AND ASSAM, 1905-1911" https://core.ac.uk/download/pdf/334948095.pdf

[17] Sarkar, Sumit p. 16-18. "The Swadeshi Movement in Bengal, 1903-1908"

[18] Hussain, Eusub. p. 120-121 "A history of Muslim politics in Assam" http://hdl.handle.net/10603/160104

[19] Saikia, Rajen. p 390-391 "Sectional President's Address: THE POLITICAL GEOGRAPHY OF COLONIAL AND POST-COLONIAL ASSAM : CONSTRUCTION AND CONTESTATIONS."Proceedings of the Indian History Congress, vol. 70, Indian History Congress, 2009, pp. 380–95, http://www.jstor.org/stable/44147685

[20] Guha, Amalendu. "Planter Raj to Swaraj. Page 55

[21] Khasru, B. Z. "Politics of language: Why Hindi surpassed Bengali" Countercurrents.org dated 1st January 2022 https://countercurrents.org/2022/01/politics-of-language-why-hindi-surpassed-bengali/

[22] Sharma, Jayeeta. p 142-144 "The making of 'Modern' Assam, 1826-1935"

[23] "What is Dark Age of Assamese language?' https://www.assams.info/answers/what-is-dark-age-of-assamese-language

[24] Barooah Pisharoty, Sangeeta p. 240 – 246. "ASSAM THE ACCORD, THE DISCORD"

[25] Basid, Habib Fazlul. p. 127. "The Assamese Language Issue: An Analysis from Historical Perspective". International Journal of Humanities and Social Sciences. ISSN 2250-3226 Volume 6, Number 2 (2016), pp. 125-133

[26] Sharma, Dr Devabrata. Chapter 3. "Asomia Jatigathan Prakriya Aru Jatiya Janagosthigata Anusthan Samuh" 5th Edition

[27] Das, Nitoo. p. 150-152 "Fabrication of history: construction of the Assamese identity under British colonialism (1826-1920)" http://hdl.handle.net/10603/15168

[28] Sengupta, Madhumita. p. 131-133. "HISTOGRAPHY OF THE FORMATION OF ASSAMESE IDENTITY: A REVIEW". Peace and Democracy in South Asia (PDSA), Volume 2, Numbers 1 & 2, 2006 https://www.repository.cam.ac.uk/bitstream/handle/1810/229189/pdsa_02_01_07.pdf

****

Chapter 5.
Divide et Impera: Genesis of Assamese-Bengali Discord

[1] Pande, B. N. "History in the Service of Imperialism" http://www.cyberistan.org/islamic/pande.htm

[2] The Ancestors of the Saint- The 'Bara Bhuyans', (an (edited) excerpt from 'A History of Assam' by Sir Edward Gait) http://www.atributetosankaradeva.org/barabhuyan.htm

[3] Purkayastha, Bidhan Chandrap. p. 34-35. (Bengali book) "Assame Bangali: Somaj- Itihas-Rajniti."

[4] Maa "Kamakhya Temple" Temples in India information https://templesinindiainfo.com/maa-kamakhya-temple-temple-legend-history-architecture-shebaits/

[5] Chandrachur, Abhinav. p. x-xiii. "REPUBLIC OF RELIGION: The Rise and Fall of Colonial Secularism in India".

[6] Rathee, Dhruv. YouTube video, "India-Pakistan Partition 1947: Why it happened?" https://www.youtube.com/watch?v=r2kKsjZPrVI&t=21s

[7] Amalendu Guha. p 171. "Planter Raj to Swaraj".

[8] AmalenduGuha. p 172. "Planter Raj to Swaraj."

[9] [Guha, Amalendu. 350-351 "EAST BENGAL IMMIGRANTS AND BHASANI IN ASSAM POLITICS : 1928-47." *Proceedings of the Indian History Congress*, vol. 35, 1974, pp. 348–65. *JSTOR*, http://www.jstor.org/stable/44138801

[10] Nath, Monoj Kumar. p.36. "The Muslim Question in Assam and Northeast India".

[11] Nath, Monoj Kumar. p. 41."The Muslim Question in Assam and Northeast India Book".

[12] Bhattacharjee, J. B. "Presidential Address: p. 374. WORLD WAR II AND INDIA: A FIFTY YEARS PERSPECTIVE." Proceedings of the

Indian History Congress, vol. 50, 1989, pp. 365–98. JSTOR, http://www.jstor.org/stable/44146070

[13] Bhattacharjee, J. B. "Presidential Address: p. 377. WORLD WAR II AND INDIA: A FIFTY YEARS PERSPECTIVE." Proceedings of the Indian History Congress, vol. 50, 1989, pp. 365–98. JSTOR, http://www.jstor.org/stable/44146070

[14] MyIndiaMyGlory "Why No Celebration of Azad Hind Govt. this year? Why Netaji Taken Lightly? GD Bakshi" https://www.myindiamyglory.com/2018/04/26/no-celebration-of-azad-hind-govt-this-year-why-netaji-taken-so-lightly/

[15] Mohapatra, Dr. Biswajit. "Subhash Bose and The Battle of Kohima: Mainstreaming the North East into India's Freedom Struggle" in Jamshedpur Research Review, YEAR -VII VOLUME- IV, ISSUE XXXV, July-August 2019, ISSN 2320-2750 https://www.academia.edu/39294429/Subhash_Bose_and_The_Battle_of_Kohima_Mainstreaming_the_North_East_into_Indias_Freedom_Struggle

[16] "Azad Hind Formation Anniversary: Interesting Facts about Azad Hind Fauj and Subhas Chandra Bose" Firstpost dated 21st October 2021 https://www.firstpost.com/india/azad-hind-formation-anniversary-interesting-facts-about-azad-hind-fauj-and-subhas-chandra-bose-10071231.html

[17] Subir. p. 116-123. "Story of Bengal and Bengalis: Ancient to Contemporary Era of Bangladesh & West Bengal"

[18] Arya, Colonel Shailender "The Crown Colony That Never Was" THE UNITED SERVICE INSTITUTION OF INDIA *Journal of the United Service Institution of India*, Vol. CL, No. 619, January-March 2020.https://usiofindia.org/publication/usi-journal/the-crown-colony-that-never-was/

[19] Hussain, Eusub, Research paper "A history of Muslim politics in Assam" p.62. Chapter III http://shodhganga.inflibnet.ac.in/handle/10603/160104

[20] Hussain Eusub, Researcher in Research paper "A history of Muslim politics in Assam" p.69. Chapter III http://shodhganga.inflibnet.ac.in/handle/10603/160104

* * * * * * *

Chapter 6.
Apartheid in India: Assam's Lesser-known Line System

[1] Kar, Bodhi Sattwa, Researcher. p. 88 (Chapter IV) "Line system and colonial politics in Assam 1920 1947" http://shodhganga.inflibnet.ac.in/handle/10603/90311

[2] Kar, Bodhi Sattwa, Researcher. p.1 (Abstract) "Line system and colonial politics in Assam 1920 1947" http://shodhganga.inflibnet.ac.in/handle/10603/90311

[3] Kar, Bodhi Sattwa, Researcher. p. 108 (Chapter IV) "The Immigration Issue, Line System and the Assam Politics". http://shodhganga.inflibnet.ac.in/handle/10603/90311

[4] Dev, Bimal J.& Lahiri, Dilip K. "ASSAM IN THE DAYS OF BHASANI" Page 200.J. Asiatic Soc. Bangladesh (Hum.) xxiv-vi, 1979-81.

[5] Dasgupta, Anindita. p. 152-153. "Remembering Sylhet"

[6] Kar, Bodhi Sattwa, Researcher."The Immigration Issue, Line System and the Assam Politics" Chapter IV. Page 107 to 111. http://shodhganga.inflibnet.ac.in/handle/10603/90311

[7] Dev, Bimal J.& Lahiri, Dilip K. "ASSAM IN THE DAYS OF BHASANI" Page 200.J. Asiatic Soc. Bangladesh (Hum.) xxiv-vi, 1979-81.

[8] Dasgupta, Aninditata. p. 159-160. "Remembering Sylhet"

[9] Kar, Bodhi Sattwa, Researcher. Chapter IV, Page 88. Chapter I. Page 11-12. Chapter IV. Page – 108. "Line system and colonial politics in Assam 1920 1947" http://shodhganga.inflibnet.ac.in/handle/10603/90311

[10] "Line System", BANGLAPEDIA https://en.banglapedia.org/index.php?title=Line_System

[11] Kar, Bodhi Sattwa, Researcher. Page 115-116. Chapter IV. "The Immigration Issue, Line System and the Assam Politics" http://shodhganga.inflibnet.ac.in/handle/10603/90311

[12] "Report of the Line System Committee (1938)" p.20. 1938 Assam Government Publication.

[13] "Report of the Line System Committee (1938)" p.24-30. 1938 Assam Government Publication

[14] "Proceedings of the Joint Sitting of the Two Chambers of the Assam Legislature Official Report" Volume 1, No. 1, 3rd and 4th August 1969 "Assam Agricultural Income-tax bill, 1939. Page 23.

[15] Kar, Bodhi Sattwa, Researcher. p.120-121 Chapter IV. "The Immigration Issue, Line System and the Assam Politics" http://shodhganga.inflibnet.ac.in/handle/10603/90311

[16] Kar, Bodhi Sattwa, p. 176 & 127–129 "Line system and colonial politics in Assam 1920 1947" http://shodhganga.inflibnet.ac.in/handle/10603/90311

[17] Azad, Maulana Abdul Kalam. p.184. "India Wins Freedom: The Complete Version". Orient Blackswan Private Limited (reprint 2022)

[18] Dev, Bimal J. & Lahiri, Dilip K. "ASSAM IN THE DAYS OF BHASANI" p. 217- 223. J. Asiatic Soc. Bangladesh

[19] Kar, Bodhi Sattwa, p. 166-168 & 176 "Line system and colonial politics in Assam 1920 1947" http://shodhganga.inflibnet.ac.in/handle/10603/90311

****

Chapter 7.

The Cabinet Mission Plan

[1] Mansergh, Nicholas and Moon, Penderel (Edit). p. 582-591 "THE TRANSFER OF POWER (1942-7) Volume VII The Cabinet Mission 23rd (item No. 303) March-29th June1946"

[2] Mansergh, Nicholas and Moon, Penderel (Edits). p. 613-615, (item No. 317) "THE TRANSFER OF POWER (1942-7) Volume VII The Cabinet Mission 23rd March-29th June1946"

[3] Mansergh, Nicholas and Moon, Penderel (Edits). p. 646-649, (item No. 346) "THE TRANSFER OF POWER (1942-7) Volume VII The Cabinet Mission 23rd March-29th June1946"

[4] Guha, Amalendu. p 257. "Planter Raj to Swaraj

[5] Noorani, A. G. "Collapse of the Cabinet Mission's Plan." Economic and Political Weekly, vol. 14, no. 47, 1979, pp. 1918–20. JSTOR, http://www.jstor.org/stable/4368164

[6] Constitution of India, a CADIndia Project. "16th May 1946 PreviousNext Cabinet Mission Plan (Cabinet Mission, 1946)" https://www.constitutionofindia.net/historical_constitutions/cabinet_miss ion_plan__cabinet_mission__1946__16th%20May%201946

[7] Guha, Amalendu. p 249-253. "Planter Raj to Swaraj"

[8] Mansergh, Nicholas and Moon, Penderel (Edit). p.669-670. (Item 361) Minutes of discussion on 22nd May 1946 between Mr Abel and Wavell (R/3/1/121: f 60) "THE TRANSFER OF POWER (1942-7) Volume VII The Cabinet Mission 23rd (item No. 303) March-29th June1946"

[9] Mansergh, Nicholas and Moon, Penderel (Edit). p. 76-80 (item No. 35) "THE TRANSFER OF POWER (1942-7) Volume VII. The Cabinet Mission 23rd March-29th June1946"

[10] Guha, Amalendu p 253 "Planter Raj to Swaraj"

[11] Hussain, Eusub. p. 130-131 "A history of Muslim politics in Assam" http://hdl.handle.net/10603/160104

[12] Roy, Monolina Nandy. p 218-219 (chapter VII)."Contradictions and conciliation between nationalism regionalism and localism : the political response of Barak valley to the colonial rule 1874-1947" http://shodhganga.inflibnet.ac.in//handle/10603/93523

[13] Guha, Amalendu. p. 253-254. "Planter Raj to Swaraj"

[14] Mitra, Asok. "The Great Calcutta Killings of 1946: What Went before and After." Economic and Political Weekly, vol. 25, no. 5, 1990, pp. 273–85. JSTOR, http://www.jstor.org/stable/4395903]

[15] Mosley, Leonard. p.41-45 "The Last Days Of The British Raj".

[16] Mosley, Leonard. p.52 "The Last Days Of The British Raj".

[17] Mansergh, Nicholas and Moon, Penderel (Edits). p. 311 Item 204. Telegram, R/3/1/117: f 133 "THE TRANSFER OF POWER (1942-7) Volume VIII The Interim Government 3 July – 1 November 1947"]

[18] Azad, Maulana Abul Kalam. p. 184-187 "India Wins Freedom: The Complete Version"

[19] Mansergh, Nicholas & Moon, Penderel (Edit) p. 239 (Enclosure to Item 141.) "THE TRANSFER OF POWER 1942-47, Volume IX: The fixing of a time limit 4 November 1946 – 22 March 1947"

[20] Mansergh, Nicholas & Moon, Penderel (Edit) p. 295-296 "THE TRANSFER OF POWER 1942-47, Volume IX: The fixing of a time limit 4 November 1946 – 22 March 1947"

[21] Guha, Amalendu. p. 255-256. "Planter Raj to Swaraj"

[22] Azad, Maulana Abul Kalam. p. 190-191 "India Wins Freedom: The Complete Version"

[23] Mosley, Leonard. p.54 "The Last Days Of The British Raj"

[24] Azad, Maulana Abul Kalam. p 205 India Wins Freedom: The Complete Version.

[25] Mansergh, Nicholas & Moon, Penderel (Edit) p. 33-34. Item 27 "THE TRANSFER OF POWER 1942-47, Volume X: The Mountbatten Viceroyalty Formula of a Plan 22 March 30 May 1947"

[26] Mansergh, Nicholas & Moon, Penderel (Edit) p. 522-523. Item 271. "THE TRANSFER OF POWER 1942-47, Volume X The Mountbatten Viceroyalty Formula of a Plan 22 March 30 May 1947"

[27] Mansergh, Nicholas & Moon, Penderel (Edit) p. 344-346. Item 183. "THE TRANSFER OF POWER 1942-47, Volume X. The Mountbatten Viceroyalty Formula of a Plan 22 March - 30 May 1947"

[28] Azad, Maulana Abul Kalam. p. 205-207. India Wins Freedom: The Complete Version".

[29] Dalrymple, William. "The Great Divide The violent legacy of Indian Partition" The New Yorker dated 22nd June 2015

* * * * * * *

Chapter 8.

The Sylhet Referendum

[1] Mansergh, Nicholas and Moon, Penderel (Edits). p.215 "THE TRANSFER OF POWER (1942-7) Volume XII: The Mountbatten Viceroyalty Princes, Partition and Independence 8 July – 15 August 1947"

[2] Dheeraj. "Mountbatten Plan: Introduction, Features and Implementation" https://www.yourarticlelibrary.com/india-2/mountbatten-plan-introduction-features-and-implementation/49351

[3] Mansergh, Nicholas and Moon, Penderel (Edits). p.92 "THE TRANSFER OF POWER (1942-7) Volume XI. The Mountbatten

Viceroyalty Announcement and Reception of the 3 June Plan: 31 May – 7 July 1947"

[4] Mansergh, Nicholas and Moon, Penderel (Edits). p. 107-108 "THE TRANSFER OF POWER (1942-7) Volume XI The Mountbatten Viceroyalty Announcement and Reception of the 3 June Plan: 31 May – 7 July 1947"

[5] Collins, Larry & Lapierre Dominique. p. 262. Part II Reports. "Mountbatten and the Partition of India: March 22 August 15, 1947."

[6] Sengupta, Nitish. p ix Preface. "Bengal: The Unmaking of a nation 1905-1971.

[7] Roychowdhury, Adrija. "A third dominion? How the plans for a United Bengal fell through" The India Express dated 8th April 2021 https://indianexpress.com/article/research/a-third-dominion-how-the-plans-for-a-united-bengal-fell-through-7264511/

[8] Mansergh, Nicholas and Moon, Penderel (Edits). p. 162, ITEM 91, Viceroy's personal report No. 81 paragraph 23 (a) "THE TRANSFER OF POWER (1942-7) Volume XI The Mountbatten Viceroyalty Announcement and Reception of the 3 June Plan: 31 May – 7 July 1947

[9] Jalal, Ayesha. "The sole spokesman: Jinnah, the Muslim League and the demand for Pakistan"

[10] Collins, Larry & Lapierre Dominique. p. 104-105. Part I Interviews. "Mountbatten and the Partition of India: March 22 August 15, 1947."

[11] Mosley, Leonard. p. 246-247. "The Last Days Of The British Raj" https://archive.org/details/dli.ernet.111333/mode/1up?view=theater

[12] Chakraborty, Bidyut. p. 171. "The Partition of Bengal and Assam, 1932-1947: Contour of Freedom"

[13] Lahiri, Dilip: p, 92, 126,107, 108. "Nirbashita Sribhoomi" O Referendum File (Second Part).

[14] ["Conquest of Sylhet" https://www.wikiwand.com/en/History_of_Sylhet

[15] Lahiri, Dilip. p. 1-3. "Nirbasita Sreebhumi O Referendum Fallout (2nd Part)

[16] SYWA4U, "History of Sylhet"

https://sylhetiyouthwelfareassociation.wordpress.com/2013/10/04/history-of-sylhet/

[17] LGED , Bangladesh: "Sylhet" https://oldweb.lged.gov.bd/DistrictLGED.aspx?DistrictID=61

[18] Dasgupta, Anindita. p. 118 "Remembering Sylhet".

[19]] Dev, Bimal J. & Lahiri, Dilip K. "Assam in the days of Bhasani and League politics". Asiatic Soc, Bangladesh (Hum), xxiv-vi, 1979-81

[20] Dasgupta,Anindita. "Remembering Sylhet" Page 118.

[21] HOSSAIN, ASHFAQUE. p 260. "The Making and Unmaking of Assam-Bengal Borders and the Sylhet Referendum." *Modern Asian Studies*, vol. 47, no. 1, 2013, pp. 250–87. *JSTOR*, http://www.jstor.org/stable/23359785

[22] Guha, Amalendu. p. 92 "Planter Raj to Swaraj"

[23] Guha, Amalendu. p 135."Planter Raj to Swaraj".

[24] Dutta, Binayak. "Event, Memory and Lore: Anecdotal History of Partition in Assam", https://nehu.ac.in/public/downloads/Journals/Journal_Jul_Dec14_Art4.pdf

[25] Mahajan, Sucheta (Edit). p.1913. Towards Freedom: Documents on the Movement for Independence in India 1947. Part 2. https://archive.org/details/towardsfreedomdo02maha/mode/2up?view=theater

[26] "WHY WASN'T SINDH PARTITIONED IN 1947?" SOUTH ASIA BLOG Politics and History of the Indian Subcontinent. https://southasiablog.wordpress.com/2014/11/07/why-wasnt-sindh-parititioned-in-1947/

[27] Mahajan, Sucheta (Edit) p. 1040. "Towards Freedom: Documents on the Movement for Independence in India 1947. Part 1"

https://archive.org/details/towardsfreedomdo01maha/mode/1up?view=theater

[28] Choudhury, Mousumi. p. 46. Chpater 2. "Partition in the East resettlement and rehabilitation of refugees in Cachar a case study of Karimganj" http://hdl.handle.net/10603/116402

[29] Guha, Amaledu. p 134 -136. "Planter Raj to Swaraj"

[30] Dasgupta, Anindita. p. 107 to 108. "Remembering Sylhet: Hindu and Muslim Voices from a Nearly Forgotten Story of India's Partition"

[31] Roy, Monolina Nandy; Researcher.Paper "Contradictions and conciliation between nationalism regionalism and localism _ the political response of Barak valley to the colonial rule _1874_1947" Chapter VII Page 219. http://shodhganga.inflibnet.ac.in//handle/10603/93523

[32] Dasgupta, Anindita. p 111-112. "Remembering Sylhet

[33] Chaudhuri, Sujit. "A 'god-sent' opportunity?" https://www.india-seminar.com/2002/510/510%20sujit%20chaudhuri.htm

[34] Guha, Amalendu. p 261. "Planter Raj to Swaraj"

[35] Dasgupta, Anindita. p. 109-110. "Remembering Sylhet"

[36] Dasgupta, Anindita. p. 110. "Remembering Sylhet"

[37] Mahajan, Sucheta (Edit) p. 1907. "Towards Freedom: Documents on the Movement for Independence in India 1947. Part 2" https://archive.org/details/towardsfreedomdo01maha/mode/1up?view=theater

[38] Lahiri, Dilip. p.110. "Nirbasita Sreebhumi O Referendum Fallout (2nd Part)

[39] Lahiri, Dilip. p. 462 & p. 48. "Nirbashita Sribhoomi O Referendum Issue (Second Part)"

[40] Lahiri, Dilip. p. 113-114 "Nirbashita Sribhoomi"

[41] Lahiri, Dilip. p. 100-103, "Nirbashita Sribhoomi"

[42] Lahiri, Dilip. p. 45, 48 "Nirbashita Sribhoomi"

[43] Das, Durga.(Edit) p 25-27. "SARDAR PATEL'S CORRESPONDENCE 1945-50". VOLUME V. (Item 28 & 29)

[44] Sengupta, Nitish. p. 147-148, 156. "Bengal: The Unmaking of a Nation 1905-1971"

[45] Bhattacharjee, J. B. p. 484-485 "The Sylhet Referendum (1947): Myth of a Communal Voting." Proceedings of the Indian History Congress, vol. 51, 1990, pp. 482–87. JSTOR, http://www.jstor.org/stable/44148264

[46] Lahari, Dilip. p. 56, 99. "Nirbashita Sribhumi".

[47] Data: Census of India, 1951, Vol XII Assam, Manipur and Tripura Part I-a Report. p.2. https://archive.org/details/dli.ernet.285650

[48] [Subir. p. 192-195. "Story of Bengal and Bengalis: Ancient to Contemporary Era of Bengladesh & West Bengal".

[49] Balouch, Akhtar. "Jogendra Nath Mandal: Chosen by Jinnah, banished by bureaucracy" Dawn English-language newspaper in Pakistan dated 4th November https://www.dawn.com/news/1217465

[50] Lahiri, Dilip. p. 176 – 177. "Nirbashita Sribhoomi"

[51] Bhattacharjee, J. B. p. 486 "The Sylhet Referendum (1947): Myth of a Communal Voting." Proceedings of the Indian History Congress, vol. 51, 1990, pp. 482–87. JSTOR, http://www.jstor.org/stable/44148264

[52] Mahajan, Sucheta (Edit) p. 1918-1919. "Towards Freedom: Documents on the Movement for Independence in India 1947. Part 2"

https://archive.org/details/towardsfreedomdo01maha/mode/1up?view=theater

[53] Lahiri, Dilip. P 142, 145 & 152. "Nirbashita Sribhoomi"

[54] Lahiri, Dilip. P 145. "Nirbashita Sribhoomi"

[55] Lahiri, Dilip. P 152. "Nirbashita Sribhoomi"]

[56] Lahiri, Dilip. P 106. "Nirbashita Sribhoomi"

[57] Lahiri, Dilip. p. 146-149 "Nirbashita Sribhoomi"

[58] Lahiri, Dilip. p. 178 "Nirbashita Sribhoomi"

[59] Lahiri, Dilip. p. 170-177 "Nirbashita Sribhoomi"

[60] Lahiri, Dilip. p. 178-180 "Nirbashita Sribhoomi"

[61] Lahiri, Dilip. p. 181 "Nirbashita Sribhoomi"

[62] Lahiri, Dilip. p. 182-191 "Nirbashita Sribhoomi"

[63] Collins, Larry & Lapierre, Dominique. p.177 "Mountbatten and The Partition of India: March 22 - August 15, 1947"

[64] Das, Durga (Edit). p 47 & 48. "SARDAR PATEL'S CORRESPONDENCE 1945-50." VOLUME V.

[65] Mosley, Leonard. p 195. "The Last Days of THE BRITISH RAJ" https://archive.org/details/dli.ernet.111333/mode/1up

[66] Mahajan, Sucheta (Edit) p XXX Editor's Introduction. "Towards Freedom: Documents on the Movement for Independence in India 1947.

https://archive.org/details/towardsfreedomdo02maha/mode/1up?view=theater

[67] Auden. W.H. "THE ROAD TO FREEDOM: WH Auden's unsparing poem on the partition of India". Scroll dated 15th August 2014. https://scroll.in/article/674238/wh-audens-unsparing-poem-on-the-partition-of-india#:~:text=Auden's%201966%20poem%20'Partition'%20is,borders%20between%20India%20and%20Pakistan&text=British%20barrister%20Sir%20Cyril%20Radcliffe,time%20on%20July%208%2C%201947.

[68] Page 2. Census of India 1951, Assam Part IA General p 2. Volume XII ASSAM, MANIPUR AND TRIPURA PART I-A REPORT.

* * * * * *

Chapter 9.
Post-Independence Era's Truncated Assam:
Sylhet Gone – Sylhetis Not Gone!

[1] Das, Durga (Edit) p. 235-238. "Sardar Patel's Correspondence 1945-50" Volume IX

[2] Census of India 1951, Assam Part IA General p 2. Volume XII ASSAM, MANIPUR AND TRIPURA PART I-A REPORT

[3] Ministry of Development of North Eastern Region https://mdoner.gov.in/print/infrastructure/inland-waterways-in-ner

[4] Choudhury, Mousumi. 53-56. Chapter 2. "Partition in the East resettlement and rehabilitation of refugees in Cachar a case study of Karimganj" http://hdl.handle.net/10603/116402

[5] Choudhury, Mousumi. 59-60. Chapter 2. "Partition in the East resettlement and rehabilitation of refugees in Cachar a case study of Karimganj" http://hdl.handle.net/10603/116402

[6] Islam, Samsul. p. 85-117 "Muslims Against Partition of India: Revisiting the legacy of patriotic Muslims. 4th Edition

[7] Guha, Amalendu. p. 1701-1703. "Little Nationalism Turned Chauvinist: Assam's Anti-Foreigner Upsurge, 1979-80." Economic and Political Weekly, vol. 15, no. 41/43, 1980, pp. 1699–720. JSTOR, http://www.jstor.org/stable/4369155

[8] Chakravarti, K C. "Bongal Kheda Again" THE ECONOMIC WEEKLY dated 30th July 1960.

https://www.epw.in/system/files/pdf/1960_12/31/assam_disturbances_i bongal_kheda_again.pdf

[9] Chaudhuri, Sujit. "A 'god-sent' opportunity?"

https://www.india-seminar.com/2002/510/510%20sujit%20chaudhuri.htm

[10] Report of the 5-member Commission of Enquiry under the Chairmanship of N. C. Chatterjee, Senior Advocated and Vice-President of Supreme Court Bar Association dated 11th June 1961 https://web.archive.org/web/20131229042659/http://www.unishemay.org/english-pages/lang-content/NCChatterjee.pdf

[11] Chaudhuri, Sujit. "A 'god-sent' opportunity?"

https://www.india-seminar.com/2002/510/510%20sujit%20chaudhuri.htm

[12] Duttachoudhury, Bishu. "Congress Must Fulfill Its Promises Made To The Hindu Refugees: An Open Letter From Bishu Duttachoudhury". Barak Bulletin dated 4th December 2018. https://www.barakbulletin.com/en_US/congress-must-fulfil-its-promises-made-to-the-hindu-refugees-an-open-letter-from-bishu-duttachoudhury/

[13]] Nag, Sajal. "Nehru and the North East"

https://www.academia.edu/38817721/Nehru_and_the_North_East_Sajal_Nag_Nehru_Memorial_Museum_and_Library_2015_NMML_Occasional_Paper

[14] VAGHAIWALLA, R. B. (ICS, Superintendent of Census Operations for Assam, Manipur and Tripura. p.428. "CENSUS OF INDIA, 1951 Volume XII ASSAM, MANIPUR AND TRIPURA PART I-A REPORT"

https://archive.org/details/dli.ernet.285650/page/365/mode/1up?view=theater

[15] VAGHAIWALLA, R. B. (ICS, Superintendent of Census Operations for Assam, Manipur and Tripura. p. 6. "CENSUS OF INDIA, 1951 Volume XII ASSAM, MANIPUR AND TRIPURA PART I-A REPORT" https://archive.org/details/dli.ernet.285650/page/365/mode/1up?view=theater

[16] Osmani, Wazid Reja p. 122-123, Chapter 4. "The historical background of the immigration problems in Assam 1946 to 1983"http://hdl.handle.net/10603/13531

[17] REPORT OF THE STATE REORGANISATION COMMISSION 1955. p. 191 item 707, p. 194, item 719, p. 212 item 783 and 784 https://www.mha.gov.in/sites/default/files/State%20Reorganisation%20Commisison%20Report%20of%201955_270614.pdf

[18] Basid, Habib Fazlul p.131-132. "The Assamese Language Issue: An Analysis from Historical Perspective" International Journal of Business and Social Science. ISSN 2250-3226 Volume 6, Number 2 (2016). https://www.ripublication.com/ijhss16/ijhssv6n2_02.pdf

[19] Saikia, Rajen. p 392 "Sectional President's Address: THE POLITICAL GEOGRAPHY OF COLONIAL AND POST-COLONIAL ASSAM: CONSTRUCTION AND CONTESTATIONS." Proceedings of the Indian History Congress, vol. 70, Indian History Congress, 2009, pp. 380–95, http://www.jstor.org/stable/44147685

[20] Radheye, Sutputra "ONE STATE, ONE LANGUAGE' demands in Assam." COUNTER CURRENT.ORG dated 30th December 2019. https://countercurrents.org/2019/12/one-state-one-language-demands-in-assam/

[21] Deka, S. Kumar. "HALF A CENTURY onto the Assam State Language Bill – The Poison Chalice". TIMES OF ASSAM dated 4th July 2012 https://www.timesofassam.com/headlines/half-a-century-onto-the-assam-state-language-bill-the-poison-chalice/

[22] Bhaumik, Subir.p150-151. Chapter 4 "INDIA'S NORTHEAST: NOBODY'S PEOPLE IN NO-MAN'S-LAND". Internal Displacement in South Asia: The Relevance of the UN's Guiding Principles". Editors: Paula Banerjee, Sabyasachi Basu Ray Chaudhury, Samir Kumar Das. https://www.google.co.in/books/edition/Internal_Displacement_in_South_Asia/VjGdDo75UssC?hl=en&gbpv=1&dq=India%27s+northeast:+nobody%27s+people+in+no-man%27s+land&pg=PA144&printsec=frontcover

[23] Pisharoty, Sangeeta Barooah. "In Language Movements of West Bengal and Assam, a Parallel in Governments' Responses" The Wire dated 8th July 2017 https://thewire.in/politics/language-movements-bengal-assam

[24] Azad, Abdul Kalam. "Assam NRC: A History of Violence and Persecution". THE WIRE dated 15th August 2018 https://thewire.in/rights/assam-nrc-a-history-of-violence-and-persecution

[25] Ahmed, Fakhar Uddin Ali, Researcher. "Arabic studies in educational institutions of Assam since 1947". Page 253-254. Chapter-IV, 'Historical

Background of Assam'
https://shodhganga.inflibnet.ac.in/handle/10603/67546

[26] UPADHYAYA, AMAR (Assistant Professor Dept. of Education, Dibrugarh University) Page 117. "Medium of Instruction in the Schools of Assam: a Dilemma between Self identity and Unification" https://iie.chitkara.edu.in/index.php/iie/article/view/32/14

[27] Ahmed, Farzand "Assam explodes in an orgy of violence between Bodos and non-Bodos, leaves 30 people dead". India Today Issue dated 15th September 1989 https://www.indiatoday.in/magazine/special-report/story/19890915-assam-explodes-in-an-orgy-of-violence-between-bodos-and-non-bodos-leaves-30-people-dead-816490-1989-09-14

[28] Osmani, Wazid Reja, Chapter 5."The historical background of the immigration problems in Assam 1946 to 1983".http://hdl.handle.net/10603/13531

[29] HUSSAIN, Monirul. Researcher. "The Assam Movement: a sociological study" P 172-173: Chapter: 4. http://shodhganga.inflibnet.ac.in/handle/10603/19069

[30] AHMED, Raiul. p 61-62. "Anxiety, Violence and the Postcolonial State: Understanding the "Anti-Bangladeshi" Rage in Assam, India"

http://sam.gov.tr/wp-content/uploads/2014/05/Rafiul_Ahmed.pdf

****

Chapter 10.

Inglorious ill-treatment of students in Assam Valley

A Tiny-Trilogy

[1] Page 5: Report of the Fact Finding Committee Appointed by the People's Union for Civil Liberties (PUCL) on Assam Unrest.- http://www.unipune.ac.in/snc/cssh/HumanRights/02%20STATE%20AND%20ARMY%20-%20POLICE%20REPRESSION/B%20Assam%20and%20the%20north%20east/1.pdf

****

Chapter 11.

NELLIE,

Where Bengalis were Butchered In Broad Daylight!

[1] Hussain, Monirul. p. 244-245. Chapter V, "The Assam movement: a sociological study" http://hdl.handle.net/10603/19069

[2] Mander, Harsh. "The forgotten Nellie massacres. South Asia Citizens Web dated 17th December 2008. http://www.sacw.net/article423.html

[2] Gupta, Shekhar. "Blood, bodies and scars: What I saw after the 1983 Nellie massacre in Assam". The Print dated 18thFebruary 2019. https://theprint.in/opinion/blood-bodies-and-scars-what-i-saw-after-the-1983-nellie-massacre-in-assam/194662/

[3] Gupta, Shekhar. "Blood, bodies and scars: What I saw after the 1983 Nellie massacre in Assam". ThePrint dated 18thFebruary 2019. https://theprint.in/opinion/blood-bodies-and-scars-what-i-saw-after-the-1983-nellie-massacre-in-assam/194662/

[4] Taha Amin Mazumder in NEWS CLICK dated 24th Feb 2019 https://www.newsclick.in/nellie-1983-revisited-victims-say-they-had-been-barricaded-6-months-massacre

[5] Thaosen, Maduli. "Revisiting Assam's Bloody History: The Nellie Massacre 37 Years On" FII - Feminism in India dated 18th February 2020 https://feminisminindia.com/2020/02/18/revisiting-assams-bloody-history-the-nellie-massacre-37-years-on/

[6] Sharma, Diganta "Nellie, 1983: Ahom Andolonor Barbarotomo Gonohotyar 'Hotyo Hondyan." 7th Edition.

[7] Kaushik, Alankar p 155-156. "Violence and Assamese Print Media: A Study of Nellie Violence in 1983"http://hdl.handle.net/10603/253843

[8] Mander, Harsh. "The forgotten Nellie massacres". South Asia Citizens Web dated 17th December 2008 http://www.sacw.net/article423.html

[9] Main Uddin. "Genesis of nellie massacre and assam agitation" Report complied and collected by Main Uddin , Focunder CEO , Indilens News Teamhttps://www.academia.edu/17665743/Genesis_of_nellie_massacre_and_assam_agitation

[10] Times now News dated 5th August 2021. "Enhanced compensation for 1984 anti-Sikh riots victims: Rs 4.5 cr provision made in 2021-22 Budget, says Govt" https://www.timesnownews.com/india/article/centres-rehabilitation-package-for-victims-of-1984-anti-sikh-riots-check-details-here/795236

[11] Bhattacharjee, J. B. p 34-37. "H K Barpujari Endowment Lectures: Making of British Assam.

[12] Alankar, Kaushik Researcher. p 153, Chapter VI. "Violence and Assamese Print Media: A Study of Nellie Violence in 1983". http://hdl.handle.net/10603/253843

[13] Thaosen, Maduli. "Revisiting Assam's Bloody History: The Nellie Massacre 37 Years On." FII (Feminism in India) dated 18th February 2020.https://feminisminindia.com/2020/02/18/revisiting-assams-bloody-history-the-nellie-massacre-37-years-on/?amp

[14] Makiko Kimura. p 70-71, 93 "The Nellie Massacre of 1983: Agency of Rioters."

[15] Makiko Kimura. p 72 "The Nellie Massacre of 1983: Agency of Rioters."

[16] Main Uddin. "Genesis of nellie massacre and assam agitation" Report compiled and collected by Main Uddin , Founder CEO , Indilens News Teamhttps://www.academia.edu/17665743/Genesis_of_nellie_massacre_and_assam_agitation

[17] Alankar, Kaushik Researcher. p 148-149, Chapter VI. "Violence and Assamese Print Media: A Study of Nellie Violence in 1983". http://hdl.handle.net/10603/253843

[18] Azad, Abdul Kamal "In 1983 NAGABANDA MASSACRE AND THE OTHER SIDE OF ASSAMESE INTELLIGENTSIA" in Raiot (a webzine from Meghalaya) dated 18th February 2018.

http://www.raiot.in/1983-nagabanda-massacre-and-the-other-side-of-assamese-intelligentsia/

[19] Main Uddin. "Genesis of nellie massacre and assam agitation" Report complied and collected by Main Uddin , Focunder CEO , Indilens News Team
https://www.academia.edu/17665743/Genesis_of_nellie_massacre_and_assam_agitation

[20] Sharma, Diganta. p 21-22 "Nellie, 1983: Ahom Andolonor Barbarotomo Gonohotyar 'Hotyo Hondyan. (7th Edition)".

[21] Makiko Kimura. p 72-73 "The Nellie Massacre of 1983: Agency of Rioters"

[22] Makiko Kimura. p 137 "The Nellie Massacre of 1983: Agency of Rioters"

[23] Sen, Sumanta. & Dubashi, Jagannath. "Nellie massacre: Assam burns as ethnic violence singes the state" INDIA TODAY dated 23rd July 2013.

https://www.indiatoday.in/magazine/cover-story/story/19830315-nellie-massacre-assam-burns-as-ethnic-violence-singes-the-state-770520-2013-07-23

[24] Main Uddin. "Genesis of nellie massacre and assam agitation" Report complied and collected by Main Uddin , Focunder CEO , Indilens News Team https://www.academia.edu/17665743/Genesis_of_nellie_massacre_and_assam_agitation

[25] "Genesis of Nellie massacre and Assam agitation" by Main Uddin, Focunder CEO, Indilens News Team https://www.academia.edu/17665743/Genesis_of_nellie_massacre_and_assam_agitation

[26] Makiko Kimura. p 93- 99. "The Nellie Massacre of 1983: Agency of Rioters"

[27] Makiko Kimura. p 123 – 124, 154. "The Nellie Massacre of 1983: Agency of Rioters"

[28] Sarma, Diganta. "Nellie 1983: Ashom andolonor borborotomo gonohotyar 'Shotoyo Sondhan'." (Seventh Edition)

[29] Chakravarty, Ipsita. "Why was Assam's Nellie massacre of 1983 not prevented, despite intimations of violence?" Scroll.in dated 18th February 2017 https://scroll.in/article/829682/why-was-assams-nellie-massacre-of-1983-not-prevented-despite-intimations-of-violence

[30] Simon, Thomas W. p.59. "The Laws of Genocide: Prescriptions for a Just World" Chapter 3: GENOCIDE ACT: MASS KILLINGS.

[31] Kimura, Makiko. p 7. "The Nellie Massacre of 1983 Agency of Rioters"

[32] Ahmed, Rafiul. p. 61-62. "Anxiety, Violence and the Postcolonial State: Understanding the "Anti-Bangladeshi" Rage in Assam, India". PERCEPTIONS: Journal of International Affairs. Spring 2014. Volume XIX Number 1.http://sam.gov.tr/pdf/perceptions/Volume-XIX/Spring-2014/perceptions_spring2014.pdf

[33] Bhattacharjee, J. B. p 81. "H J Barpujari Endowment Lecture: Making of British Assam"

[34] Dutta Pathak, Moushumi. p 47. "YOU DO NOT BELONG HERE: Partition Diaspora in the Brahmaputra Valley."

[35] Weiner, Myron. p 284 "The Political Demography of Assam's Anti-Immigrant Movement." Population and Development Review, vol. 9, no. 2, [Population Council, Wiley], 1983,https://doi.org/10.2307/1973053

[36] Weiner, Myron. p 287 "The Political Demography of Assam's Anti-Immigrant Movement." Population and Development Review, vol. 9, no. 2, [Population Council, Wiley], 1983, pp. 279–92,https://doi.org/10.2307/1973053

[37] Weiner, Myron. p. 204-205. SONS OF THE SOIL: Migration and Ethnic Conflict in India"

[38] Goswami, Sandhya. p. 47. "Assam Politics in Post-Congress Era 1985 and Beyond" (SAGE Seiess on Politics in Indian States Volume 4)

[39] Shourie, Arun. "Arun Shourie turns up the most devastating evidence on violence in Assam", India Today issue dated 19th July 2013. https://www.indiatoday.in/magazine/cover-story/story/19830515-arun-shourie-turns-up-the-most-devastating-evidence-on-violence-in-assam-770641-2013-07-19

[40] Choudhury, Angshuman. "Nellie Massacre: 40 Years Later, a Cautionary Tale for Today's India" The Wire dated 23rd February 2023. https://thewire.in/communalism/nellie-massacre-40-years-later-a-cautionary-tale-for-todays-india

* * * * * * *

Chapter 11

The Assam Agitation (1979-1985)

[1] Assam Government, Home & Political Department. p. 11, paragraph 1.7.1. "WHITE PAPER ON FOREIGNERS ISSUE". https://cjp.org.in/wp-content/uploads/2018/10/White-Paper-On-Foreigners-Issue-20-10-2012.pdf

[2] Assam Government. GOVERNMENT OF ASSAM IMPLEMENTATION OF ASSAM ACCORD. First paragraph. "Martyrs of Assam Agitation" https://assamaccord.assam.gov.in/information-services/martyrs-of-assam-agitation

[3] https://assamaccord.assam.gov.in/sites/default/files/swf_utility_folder/departments/assamaccord_medhassu_in_oid_3/portlet/level_1/files/The%20Assam%20Accord%20-%20English.pdf

[4] Gogoi, Tarun. "ASSAM MOVEMENT" https://www.academia.edu/4795710/ASSAM_MOVEMENT

[5] Monirul, Hussain. Chapter I & IV "The Assam Movement: Class, Ideology and Movement". http://shodhganga.inflibnet.ac.in/handle/10603/19069

[6] Rammohan, E. N. p. 11-15. "Insurgent Frontiers: essays from the troubled northeast.

[7] Sharma, Bobbeeta. "How Jawaharlal Nehru's 1962 Speech Was Deliberately Misinterpreted to Mislead Assam" The Wire dated 14th November 2020. https://thewire.in/history/jawaharlal-nehru-birthday-1962-china-speech-assam

[8] Misra, Tilottoma. "Assam: A Colonial Hinterland." Economic and Political Weekly, vol. 15, no. 32, 1980, pp. 1357–64. JSTOR. http://www.jstor.org/stable/4368952

[9] Sharma, Chandan Kumar "The immigration issue in Assam and conflicts around it" https://www.academia.edu/1650961/Immigration_Issue_in_Assam_and_Conflicts_Around_It?email_work_card=view-paper

[10] Dutta, Nandana. p 50. "Questions of Identity in Assam: Location, Migration, Hybridity.

[11] Bhattacharyya, Hiranya Kumar. p.109. "Betrayal of North East: The Arrested Voice"

[12] HUSSAIN, Monirul, Research Scholar. "The Assam movement: a sociological study. Page 177-197. Chapter IV. http://shodhganga.inflibnet.ac.in/handle/10603/19069

[13] Baruah, Sanjib. p. 123. "India against itself"

[14] Dutta, Nandana. p. 112-113. "Questions of Identity in Assam: Location, Migration, Hybridity".

[15] Rammohan, E. N. p.23-24. "Insurgent Frontiers essays from the troubled northeast"

[16] Ashraf, Ajaz. REVISITING ASSAM AGITATION: How two police officers and RSS changed the script of the Assam agitation against outsiders in 1980s" Scroll.in dated 18th January 2018

https://scroll.in/article/865199/how-two-police-officers-and-rss-changed-the-script-of-the-assam-agitation-against-outsiders-in-1980s

[17] Goswami, Sandhya. p.53-54. Assam Politics in Post-Congress Era: 1985 and Beyond."

[18] [Parikh, Falguni. p. 66, chapter III, "Dynamics of Assam agitation". http://hdl.handle.net/10603/49072

[19] Rammohan, E. N. p.23-24. "Insurgent Frontiers essays from the troubled northeast"

[20] Dutta, Nandana. p.71-72. "Question of Identity in Assam: Location, Migration, Hybridity".

[21] HUSSAIN, Monirul.p.194-195. Chapter 4. The Assam movement: a sociological study http://hdl.handle.net/10603/19069

[22] Guha, Seema. India Today dated 30th April 1981 https://www.indiatoday.in/magazine/indiascope/story/19810430-assam-bomb-extremist-bureaucrats-central-bureau-of-investigation-explosion-on-railway-track-militants-772899-2013-11-21

[23] Parikh,Falguni. p.89, 107-208, chapter IV. "Dynamics of Assam agitation." http://hdl.handle.net/10603/49072

[24] Rahman Rukchana, p. 258-263, chapterI VI "Youth activism and democratic politics a study of the Assam movement 1979-85". http://shodhganga.inflibnet.ac.in/handle/10603/169452

[25] HUSSAIN, Monirul. Research Scholar "The Assam movement: A Sociological Study" (Chapter IV) https://shodhganga.inflibnet.ac.in/handle/10603/19069

[26] Kotwal, Dinesh. "The Contours of Assam Insurgency." STRETEGIC ANALYSIS. March 2001 (Vol. XXIV No. 12) https://ciaotest.cc.columbia.edu/olj/sa/sa_mar01kod01.html

[27] Rahman, Rukchana. p. 216, Chapter V. "Youth activism and democratic politics a study of the Assam movement 1979 85" http://hdl.handle.net/10603/169452

[28] [HUSSAIN, Monirul. p.212. chapter IV. "The Assam movement: a sociological study" http://hdl.handle.net/10603/19069

[29] Dutta, Nandana. p. 72-73 "Question of Identity in Assam: Location, Migration, Hybridity".

[30] HUSSAIN, Monirul.p.208 & 195-197. Chapter 4. The Assam movement: a sociological study http://hdl.handle.net/10603/19069

[31] Report of the fact Finding Committee Appointed by the People's Union for Civil Liberties (PUCL) on Assam Unrest

http://www.unipune.ac.in/snc/cssh/HumanRights/02%20STATE%20AND%20ARMY%20-%20POLICE%20REPRESSION/B%20Assam%20and%20the%20north%20east/1.pdf

[32] HUSSAIN, Monirul. Researcher"The Assam movement: a sociological study" Chapter 5; page 238-239. http://shodhganga.inflibnet.ac.in/handle/10603/19069

[33] Kimura, Makiko p. 142-144, 150-152, 155. "Mass Media and Ethnic Formation: Comparative Analysis of Newspaper Reports on the Foreign National Issues in Assam and West Bengal, 1979-1985 https://www.jstage.jst.go.jp/article/jjasas1989/2001/13/2001_13_142/_pdf/-char/ja

[34] Goswami, Sandhya. p. 47. "Assam Politics in Post-Congress Era 1985 and Beyond" SAGE Series on Politics in Indian States. (Volume 4.)

[35] Dutta, Nandana. p. 62-63. "Questions of Identity in Assam: Location, Migration, Hybridity".

[36] HUSSAIN, Monirul.p.246-247. Chapter 5. The Assam movement: a sociological study http://hdl.handle.net/10603/19069

[37] DUTTA, NANDANA, p. 69, 73. "Questions of Identity in Assam: Location, Migration, Hybridity"

[38] Rahman. Rukchana. "Youth activism and democratic politics a study of the Assam movement 1979 – 85" Chapter 5, p. 220. http://shodhganga.inflibnet.ac.in/handle/10603/169452

[39] Udayon Misra. p. 1267. "Immigration and Identity Transformation in Assam." *Economic and Political Weekly*, vol. 34, no. 21, 1999, pp. 1264–71. JSTOR, http://www.jstor.org/stable/4407987

[40] Sharma, Nabanita."Ethnic Boundaries [During And After The Assam Agitation Of 1979-1985" http://www.ijstr.org/final-print/dec2019/Ethnic-Boundaries-During-And-After-The-Assam-Agitation-Of-1979-1985.pdf

[41] Baruah, Sanjib. p.136-137. "India against itself: ASSAM AND THE POLITICS OF NATIONALITY."

[42] HUSSAIN, Monirul. p.216-219, chapter 5 "The Assam movement: a sociological study" http://hdl.handle.net/10603/19069

[43] Baruah, Sanjib. p 136-137. "India Against Itself ASSAM AND THE POLITICS OF NATIONALITY"

[44] Dutta, Nandana. p.47-48. "Questions of Identity in Assam: Location, Migration and Hybridity."

[45] Rahman Rukchana. Chapter V. "Youth activism and democratic politics a study of the Assam movement 1979 85" http://hdl.handle.net/10603/169452

[46] AAI ASSAMI Assam movement https://aaiassami.wordpress.com/2016/10/16/assam-movement/

[47] Report of the fact Finding Committee Appointed by the People's Union for Civil Liberties (PUCL) on Assam Unrest http://www.unipune.ac.in/snc/cssh/HumanRights/02%20STATE%20AND%20ARMY%20-%20POLICE%20REPRESSION/B%20Assam%20and%20the%20north%20east/1.pdf

[48] Government of Assam Implementation of Assam Accord Martyrs of Assam Agitation | Implementation of Assam Accord | Government Of Assam, India.

[49] HUSSAIN, Monirul. p. 248. Chapter 5. "The Assam movement: a sociological study" http://hdl.handle.net/10603/19069

[50] Rammohan, E. N. p. 28. "Insurgent Frontier: essay from the troubled northeast".

[51] Baruah, Sanjib. p. 131. "India against itself: ASSAM AND THE POLITICS OF NATIONALITY

[52] Rammohan, E. N. p. 27. Insurgent Frontiers: essays from the troubled northeast"

[53] Ramhohan, E. N. p 31-33. "Insurgent Frontiers: essays from the troubled northeast".

[54] Baruah, Sanjib. p. 132, 134 "India against itself: ASSAM AND THE POLITICS OF NATIONALITY.

[55] HUSSAIN, Monirul. p. 261-268 "The Assam movement: a sociological study". http://hdl.handle.net/10603/19069

[56] Hussain, Monirul. p. 263 – 268 "The Assam movement: a sociological study" http://hdl.handle.net/10603/19069

[57] Pishroty, Sangeeta Barooah. p. 13-17 & 112. ASSAM THE ACCORD, THE DISCORD.

[58] GOVERNMENT OF ASSAM IMPLEMENTATION OF ASSAM ACCORD: The Assam Accord - English pdf. https://assamaccord.assam.gov.in/sites/default/files/swf_utility_folder/departments/assamaccord_medhassu_in_oid_3/portlet/level_1/files/The%20Assam%20Accord%20-%20English.pdf

[59] Misra, Udayon. p. 150-152. "Burden of History: Assam and the Partition – Unresolved Issues".

[60] HUSSAIN, Monirul. p. 271-274. Chapter V. "The Assam movement: a sociological study" http://hdl.handle.net/10603/19069

[61] Assam Government Portal. "Know The CM - Dr Himanta Biswa Sarma. https://cm.assam.gov.in/know-the-cm

[62] Kangkan Kalita, The Times of India dated 11th December 2020: http://timesofindia.indiatimes.com/articleshow/79678515.cms?utm_source=contentofinterest&utm_medium=text&utm_campaign=cppst

[63] Pisharoty, Sangeeta Barooah. "Assam Has Already Missed the Bus, Deportation of Immigrants No Longer an Option". The Wire dated 4th July 2018 https://thewire.in/rights/assam-illegal-immigrants-interview-hiranya-kumar-bhattacharya

[64] Bhattacharyya, Hiranya Kumar. p. 118-120. "Betrayal of North East: The Arrested Voice".

****

Chapter 13
IMTD Act of 1983.

[1] Talukdar, Mrinal. p 357. "THE GAME CALLED NRC".

[2] Sarbananda Sonowal vs Union Of India & Anr on 12 July 2005 http://www.mcrg.ac.in/RLS_Migration_2019/Readings_MODULE_F/Sarbananda%20Sonowal%20vs%20UoI.PDF

[3] Legislative Department, Government of India. "THE FOREIGNERS ACT, 1946: ACT No. 31 OF 1946 dated 23rd November 1946 https://legislative.gov.in/sites/default/files/A1946-31.pdf

[4] United Nations web portal https://www.un.org/en/about-us/universal-declaration-of-human-

rights#:~:text=Article%2011,guarantees%20necessary%20for%20his%20defence.

[5] Azad, Abdul Kalam. "Assam NRC: A History of Violence and Persecution". The Wire dated 15th August 2018. https://thewire.in/rights/assam-nrc-a-history-of-violence-and-persecution

[6] Rishikesh, S. A. "Critical analysis of the Illegal Migrants (Determination by Tribunals) Act, 1983". iPleaders dated 5th November 2021. https://blog.ipleaders.in/critical-analysis-of-the-illegal-migrants-determination-by-tribunals-act-1983/

[7] Talukdar, Mrinal. p. 50-51 & 58. "THE GAME CALLED NRC".

[8] Bhattacharyya, Hiranya Kumar. p.109. "Betrayal of North East: The Arrested Voice"

[9] Government of India, Legislative Department. The Illegal Migrants (Determination by Tribunals) Act, 1983. CHAPTER I PRELIMINARY 1. Short title, extent and commencement. https://legislative.gov.in/sites/default/files/A1983-39.pdf

[10] Bhushan,Prashant. "An Unconscionable Judgement". Outlook dated 3rd February 2022. https://www.outlookindia.com/website/story/an-unconscionable-judgement/228129

[11] Pisharoty, Sangeeta Barooah. p.4. "ASSAM: THE ACCORD, THE DISCORD".

[12] Roy, Anupama and Singh, Ujjwal Kumar (2009). p. 48. 'THE AMBIVALENCE OF CITIZENSHIP', Critical Asian Studies, 41:1, 37 — 60. http://dx.doi.org/10.1080/14672710802631137

[13] Roy, Anupama and Singh, Ujjwal Kumar (2009) p. 51. 'THE AMBIVALENCE OF CITIZENSHIP', Critical Asian Studies, 41:1, 37 — 60. http://dx.doi.org/10.1080/14672710802631137

[14] India Kanoon https://indiankanoon.org/doc/907725/

[15] The Economic Times dated 13th July 2005 "SC strikes down IMDT Act as Unconstitutional https://economictimes.indiatimes.com/sc-strikes-down-imdt-act-as-unconstitutional/articleshow/1168803.cms

[16] India Kanoon, "Sarbananda Sonowal vs Union Of India & Anr" on 12 July, 2005 https://indiankanoon.org/doc/907725/#:~:text=CASE%20NO.%3A%20Writ%20Petition%20(,2005%20BENCH%3A%20R.C.%20Lahoti%2CG.P

[17] Ayyubi, Fuzail & Mushtaq, Ibad. "NRC busts the myth around massive illegal migration into Assam" The Leaflet: Constitution First dated 2nd September 2019 https://theleaflet.in/nrc-busts-the-myth-around-massive-illegal-migration-into-assam/

[18] Bhushan, Prashant. "An Unconscionable Judgement". OUTLOOK updated 3rd February 2022. https://www.outlookindia.com/website/story/an-unconscionable-judgement/228129

[19] NRC Assam : Karan Thapar interviews Faizan Mustafa for The Wire" dated 10th September 2019. https://thewire.in/law/nrc-citizenship-act-assam

[20] YouTube Link https://www.youtube.com/watch?v=uOfUoG5m670

****

Chapter 14
The Dreaded 'D' In Assam's Voter list

[1] Singh, Amrita. "Citizens Erased In Assam's NRC, a near-impossible trial followed by inhuman and indefinite detention". The Caravan dated 19th December 2018 https://caravanmagazine.in/policy/assam-nrc-near-impossible-trial-inhuman-indefinite-detention

[2] Pratidin Bureau "Chained to hospital bed, Assam ignores worst human right violations" Pratidin Time Updated on 5th November 2018. https://www.pratidintime.com/latest-assam-news-breaking-news-assam/chained-to-hospital-bed-assam-ignores-worst-human-right-violations

[3] Home and Political Department, Government of Assam. "White Paper on Foreigners' Issue" dated 20th October 2012. https://cjp.org.in/wp-content/uploads/2018/10/White-Paper-On-Foreigners-Issue-20-10-2012.pdf

[4] Mukhtiar, Dr. Debendra Nath. "Asomot D voter-or Gopon Rohosyo" ('The strange secret of Assam's 'D' Voters') Assamese newspaper Amar Asom dated 2ndAugust 2018. http://amarasom.glpublications.in//imageview_6710_124447681_4_1_02-08-2018_i_1_sf.html

[5] The Caravan dated 7.11.17 https://caravandaily.com/portal/another-assam-resident-shamsul-haque-declared-illegal-after-serving-35-years-in-indian-air-force/

[6] The Hindu dated 4th June 2019 (Page 11), and dated 10th June 2019 (Page 8) and 3rd June 2019 https://www.thehindu.com/news/national/other-states/witnesses-file-cases-against-assam-cop-who-reported-kargil-veteran-as-foreigner/article27413415.ece

[7] KARMAKAR, RAHUL. "Freedom for Assam woman wrongly sent to jail as foreigner 3 years ago" The Hindu dated 26th June 2019. https://www.thehindu.com/news/national/freedom-for-assam-woman-wrongly-sent-to-jail-as-foreigner-3-years-ago/article61992257.ece

[8] Pratidin Bureau. "How Indians are made into Bangladeshi for money". Pratidin Times updated on 6th September 2018 https://www.pratidintime.com/latest-assam-news-breaking-news-assam/foreigner-tribunal-blow-the-lid-of-own-court

[9] CJP (Citizens for Justice and Peace) website. "Report on NHRC Mission to Assam's Detention Centres from 22 to 24 January 2018" https://cjp.org.in/wp-content/uploads/2018/11/NHRC-Report-Assam-Detention-Centres-26-3-2018-1.pdf.

[10] "Full Text: Why Harsh Mander Wanted CJI Gogoi to Recuse Himself From Assam Case". The Wire dated 2nd May 2019. https://thewire.in/law/full-text-harsh-mander-cji-ranjan-gogoi-recuse-assam-detention-centres

[11] Jain, Mehal. "Learn To Trust Your Judges: CJI To Harsh Mander" [Courtroom Exchanges] LiveLaw.in dated 2nd May 2019. https://www.livelaw.in/top-stories/learn-to-trust-your-judgescji-to-harsh-mander-courtroom-exchange-144720

[12] Nazir, Shayesta. "Detenues Who Have Completed More Than Three Years in Assam Detention Centres Should Be Released: SC. https://www.livelaw.in/top-stories/detenues-who-have-completed-more-than-three-years-in-assam-detention-centers-should-be-released-supreme-court-144987?infinitescroll=1

[13] "Draft Modality: Dispur Moves Delhi For Release of 'Foreigners' ". The Sentinel (Assam) dated 4th July 2019 https://www.sentinelassam.com/news/draft-modality-dispur-moves-delhi-for-release-of-foreigners/?fbclid=IwAR1Lh7_ufnYXQKhHPHpjenDsAsmZSef0P5HexmBegz4kIlWfKVePD6CIiWI

[14] Special Correspondence. "10 declared foreigners released from Assam detention camp". The Hindu dated 26th August 2019. https://www.thehindu.com/news/national/10-declared-foreigners-released-from-assam-detention-camp/article29262234.ece

[15] Times of India dated 17th March 2020. "10 inmates of detention centres in Assam died in last one year; Govt. https://timesofindia.indiatimes.com/india/10-inmates-of-detention-centres-in-assam-died-in-last-one-year-govt/articleshow/74674152.cms

[16] Deka, Kaushik. "The truth about Assam's detention centres | India Today Insight." India Today Updated 10th February 2020. https://www.indiatoday.in/india-today-insight/story/the-truth-about-assam-s-detention-centres-1644836-2020-02-10"

[17] The Hindu dated 26 June 2019 (page 10) under the caption "Maran, Moitra hog prime time", (Also online The Hindu dated 25th June 2019 "Debate on President's address: Dayanidhi Maran, Mahua Moitra hog prime time. https://www.thehindu.com/news/national/debate-on-presidents-address-dayanidhi-maran-mahua-moitra-hog-prime-time/article28138575.ece

[18] Bhattacharjee, Manash Firaq. "Detained in Assam and Now Dead, Dulal Chandra's Fate Shows the Madness of Official Policy" The Wire dated 22nd October 2019. https://thewire.in/rights/dulal-chandra-paul-and-the-madness-of-citizenship

[19] Parashar, Utpal. Hindustan Times dated 15th October 2019 https://www.hindustantimes.com/india-news/won-t-accept-body-until-he-is-declared-indian-says-family-of-foreigner-who-died-in-assam/story-pwgH2L2L68yvDWo22nxExH.html

[20] Team CJP. "Assam Detention Camp death: Dulal Paul's family accepts body". CJP dated 1st November 2019. https://cjp.org.in/assam-detention-camp-death-dulal-pauls-family-accepts-body/

****

Chapter 15

Assam NRC The story so far ....

[1] Ghose, Sanjoy. "What the 'Totality of Facts' Says About Prateek Hajela's Transfer by the Supreme Court". THE WIRE dated 20th October 2019

https://thewire.in/law/heres-what-makes-prateek-hajelas-transfer-order-by-the-supreme-court-rather-interesting

[2] Choudhury, Angshuman & Gogoi, Suraj. "A narrow nationalism again" The Hindu dated 12th September 2019. https://www.thehindu.com/opinion/op-ed/a-narrow-nationalism-again/article29394298.ece

[3] Gohain, Hiren. "It is important to contextualise the NRC". The Hindu dated 5th September 2019. https://www.thehindu.com/opinion/op-ed/it-is-important-to-contextualise-the-nrc/article29334764.ece

[4] Talukdar, Mrinal. p. 11, chapter 1. "The Game Called NRC".

[5] Government of Assam, Office of the State Coordinator of National Registration (NRC), Assam. https://www.nrcassam.nic.in/wha_nrc.html.

[6] Business Standard newspaper dated 9th December 2018. "People not in final list of Assam NRC may be disenfranchised: Officials" https://www.business-standard.com/article/current-affairs/people-not-in-final-list-of-assam-nrc-may-be-disenfranchised-officials-118120900231_1.html

[7] Chakravarty, Ipsita. "Why did Assam prepare the 1951 NRC, which has become a touchstone for citizenship today?" Scroll.in dated 27th July 2019. https://scroll.in/article/931879/why-did-assam-prepare-the-1951-nrc-which-has-become-a-touchstone-for-citizenship-today#:~:text=One%20of%20the%20stated%20aims,eve%20of%20the%20Bangladesh%20War.

[8] Chaudhuri, Sujit. "A 'god-sent' opportunity?" https://www.india-seminar.com/2002/510/510%20sujit%20chaudhuri.htm

[9] The Commission of Enquiry Report dated 11.6.1961. p. 4. Chapter I. WayBack Machine. https://web.archive.org/web/20131229042659/http://www.unishemay.org/english-pages/lang-content/NCChatterjee.pdf

[10] [The Commission of Enquiry Report dated 11.6.1961. p. 4. Chapter I. WayBack Machine. https://web.archive.org/web/20131229042659/http://www.unishemay.org/english-pages/lang-content/NCChatterjee.pdf

[11] The Commission of Enquiry Report dated 11.6.1961. p. 4-5. Chapter I. WayBack Machine. https://web.archive.org/web/20131229042659/http://www.unishemay.org/english-pages/lang-content/NCChatterjee.pdf

[12] Chaudhuri, Sujit. "A 'god-sent' opportunity?" https://www.india-seminar.com/2002/510/510%20sujit%20chaudhuri.htm

[13] Rao, V. Venkata. p. 462-463 "GOVERNMENT AND POLITICS IN NORTH EAST INDIA." *The Indian Journal of Political Science*, vol. 48, no. 4, 1987, pp. 458–86. *JSTOR*, http://www.jstor.org/stable/41855331

[14] Chakravarty, Ipsita. "Why did Assam prepare the 1951 NRC, which has become a touchstone for citizenship today?" Scroll.in dated 27th July 2019 https://scroll.in/article/931879/why-did-assam-prepare-the-1951-nrc-which-has-become-a-touchstone-for-citizenship-today#:~:text=One%20of%20the%20stated%20aims,eve%20of%20the%20Bangladesh%20War

[15] Office of the State Coordinator of National Registration (NRC) Assam. Item 1. What is NRC, 1951. https://nrcassam.nic.in/faq01.html

[16] Office of the State Coordinator of National Registration (NRC) Assam. Item 5. What is NRC, 1951. https://nrcassam.nic.in/faq01.html

[17] Talukdar. Mrinal. p 86-87. "THE GAME CALLED NRC"

[18] Das, Sunil Kumar. "Four die in Barpeta clashes over NRC". The Telegraph dated 22nd July 2010. https://www.telegraphindia.com/india/four-die-in-barpeta-clashes-over-nrc/cid/498813

[19] TNN. "NRC: Six districts don't have complete records. Times of India dated 20th March 2013 https://timesofindia.indiatimes.com/city/guwahati/NRC-Six-districts-dont-have-complete-records/articleshow/19082949.cms

[20] Bhat, Mohsin Alam. "On the NRC, Even the Supreme Court is Helpless" The Wire dated 7th January 2019. https://thewire.in/law/nrc-supreme-court-crisis

[21] Bhattacharjee. D. "NRC for Assam: A flawed design A process with an inherent potential to exclude millions of genuine citizens". CJP dated 7th January 2021. https://cjp.org.in/nrc-for-assam-a-flawed-design/

[22] The Indian Express dated 11th January 2023. "Will first decide on constitutional validity of Citizenship Act's Section 6A: Supreme Court". https://indianexpress.com/article/india/supreme-court-citizenship-act-section-6a-constitutional-validity-8373060/.

[23] Dutta, Binayak. "The Unending Conundrum: The Story of Citizens/Foreigners between Politics and the Law in Assam" PANGSAU dated 31st May 2018. https://pangsau.wordpress.com/2018/05/31/the-

unending-conundrum-the-story-of-citizens-foreigners-between-politics-and-the-law-in-assam/#_ednref4

[24] Vaghaiwalla, R. B. 1951 Assam Census Report: Introduction, page xxxiii-xxxiv and the main report.

[25] Government of Assam, Office of the State Coordinator of National Registration (NRC), Assam. "WHAT ARE THE ADMISSIBLE DOCUMENTS?" https://www.nrcassam.nic.in/admin-documents.html

[26] Dutta, Binayak. "The Illusive Citizen: the Predicament of determining Citizens between politics and the law in Assam". Sabrang dated 3rd July 2019 https://sabrangindia.in/article/illusive-citizen-predicament-determining-citizens-between-politics-and-law-assam

[27] Assam Government. Assam State Portal: District. https://assam.gov.in/about-us/396#:~:text=The%20majority%20of%20the%20newly,also%20declared%20as%20a%20district

[28] The Hindu (Kolkata edition) Page 11, dated 29 July 2018.

[29] NRC update, or a dance of data – CRACKIAS https://www.crackias.com/news_topic.php?news_id=6074&page_no=1&id=468#

[30] Bhat, M. Mohsin Alam. p.192. "Citizenship and the Mass Production of Statelessness in Assam" 2020, India Exclusion Report". India Exclusion Report 2019–2020. https://www.academia.edu/45011722/Citizenship_and_the_Mass_Production_of_Statelessness_in_Assam.

[31] Saikia, Arunabh. "Guwahati High Court ruling on citizenship document will hurt women the hardest" Scroll.in dated 5th March 2017. https://scroll.in/article/830657/guwahati-high-court-ruling-on-citizenship-document-will-hurt-women-the-hardest

[32] Outlook Web Bureau. "National Register Of Citizens: Supreme Court Allows Gram Panchayat Certificates To Be Used As Identity Document For Claiming Citizenship" Outlook dated 5th December 2017. https://www.outlookindia.com/website/story/assam-citizenship-issue-supreme-court-allows-gram-panchayat-certificates-to-be-u/305198

[33] Bengali Newspaper Jugasankha in Page 10 dated 29th August 2018.

[34] PTI. "Meet Prateek Hajela: The man behind NRC in Assam. His own name was missing in 1st draft" India Today dated 3rd February 2022.

https://www.indiatoday.in/india/story/who-is-prateek-hajela-assam-nrc-final-list-1593912-2019-08-31

[35] Azad, Abdul Kalam. "Assam NRC: A History of Violence and Persecution" The Wire dated 15th August 2018. https://thewire.in/rights/assam-nrc-a-history-of-violence-and-persecution

[36] SAMRAT. "How poetry became a crime in Assam". THE CARAVAN dated 1st August 2019. https://caravanmagazine.in/communities/poetry-became-crime-assam

[37] SAMRAT. Page 7, "How poetry became a crime in Assam" Sunday Business Standard (Kolkata Edition), dated 1st September 2019

[38] India Kanoon https://indiankanoon.org/doc/135202420/

[39] Mullan, C. S. p. 49-50, para 50, Census of India, 1931. Volume III, Assam, Part I Report

[40] The Hindu dated 20th July 2019. https://www.thehindu.com/opinion/editorial/inclusion-over-exclusion/article59779747.ece

[41] Government of Assam Office of the State Coordinator of NRC. https://www.nrcassam.nic.in/pdf/English%20-Press%20Brief%2031st%20August%202019.pdf

[42] "Assam NRC final list: Rights group terms it largest incident of making people 'stateless' in decades". The Hindu dated 31st August 2019 https://www.thehindu.com/news/national/other-states/rights-group-terms-it-largest-incident-of-making-people-stateless-in-decades/article61577790.ece

[43] Ayyubi, Fuzail & Mushtaq, Ibad. "NRC busts the myth around massive illegal migration into Assam". The Leaflet: Constitution First dated 9th September 2019. https://theleaflet.in/nrc-busts-the-myth-around-massive-illegal-migration-into-assam/

[44] "Assam BJP minister Himanta Biswa Sarma cries foul over final NRC list, demands reverification" India Today Web Desk UPDATED 3rd February 2022 https://www.indiatoday.in/india/story/assam-final-nrc-list-bjp-himanta-biswa-sarma-cries-foul-demands-reverification-1593829-2019-08-31

[45] The Times of India updated 31st August 2019 "BJP failed to ensure error-free NRC: Former Assam CM Tarun Gogoi https://timesofindia.indiatimes.com/india/bjp-failed-to-ensure-error-free-nrc-former-cm-tarun-gogoi/articleshow/70923781.cms

[46] Kalita, Prabin. "19 lakh left out, final Assam NRC elicits anger and sense of betrayal" The Times of India dated 1st September 2019. https://timesofindia.indiatimes.com/india/19-lakh-left-out-final-assam-nrc-elicits-anger-sense-of-betrayal/articleshow/70930061.cms

[47] PTI. "Original Petitioner APW Unhappy With 'Flawed' NRC" The Wire dated 31st August 2019 https://thewire.in/rights/original-petitioner-apw-unhappy-with-flawed-nrc

[48] The Hindu (Kolkata edition) Page 5 dated 8th September 2019.

[49] "Citizenship, figured: On Assam NRC final list". The Hindu dated 2nd September 2019. https://www.thehindu.com/opinion/editorial/citizenship-figured/article29316557.ece

[50] Mander, Harsh. "A flawed process that pleased none". New Age dated 3rd September 2019 https://www.newagebd.net/article/83368/a-flawed-process-that-pleased-none

[51] The Assam Tribune dated 1st September 2019.

[52] Saha, Abhishek p.190. "NO LAND'S PEOPLE: THE STORY OF ASSAM'S NRC CIRSIS"

[53] Gogoi, Suraj. "NRC muddle: a vigilante student union and India's borderlands". ASIA TIMES dated 23rd August 2018. https://asiatimes.com/2018/08/nrc-muddle-a-vigilante-student-union-and-indias-borderlands/

[54] PTI, "FIRs lodged against NRC coordinator Prateek Hajela". India Today UPDATED: 3rd February 2022. https://www.indiatoday.in/india/story/prateek-hajela-fir-assam-nrc-1595835-2019-09-05

[55] "FIR against former VC of Assam University". Business Standard dated 9th July 2018. https://www.business-standard.com/article/pti-stories/fir-against-former-vc-of-assam-university-118070900960_1.html

[56] Saha, Abhishek "FIR against 10 for poem on Assam's citizenship row" The Indian Express updated 12th July 2019. https://indianexpress.com/article/north-east-india/assam/fir-against-10-for-poem-on-assams-citizenship-row-5825929/

[57] Bose, M. L. p. 7-9. "Social History of Assam". (1989).

[58] Karmakar, Rahul. "Over 19 lakh excluded from Assam's final NRC". The Hindu updated 31st August 2019.

https://www.thehindu.com/news/national/over-19-lakh-excluded-from-assams-final-nrc/article61990870.ece

[59] The Wire Staff. "Days Before NRC Release, Gauhati HC Picks 221 Members to Head Assam Foreigners' Tribunals". The Wire dated 31st August 2019. https://thewire.in/uncategorised/days-before-nrc-release-gauhati-hc-picks-221-members-to-head-assam-foreigners-tribunals

[60] Saikia, Parag Jyoti & Gogoi, Suraj. "A register most flawed". Fountain Ink dated 8th October 2018. https://fountainink.in/essay/a-register-most-flawed

[61] Das, Debarshi. "Claim that updating NRC mandated by Assam Accord false: In this circus, poor and marginalized are being fed to lions," Firstpost dated 2nd August 2018. https://www.firstpost.com/india/claim-that-updating-nrc-mandated-by-assam-accord-false-in-this-circus-poor-and-marginalised-are-being-fed-to-lions-4876881.html

[62] [Mahapatra, Dhananjay. "NRC: SC allows use of 5 contentious documents". The Times of India dated 2nd November 2018. https://timesofindia.indiatimes.com/india/nrc-sc-allows-use-of-5-contentious-documents/articleshow/66468980.cms

[63] Singh, Vijata. "Centre's stand and BJP word differ on countrywide NRC". The Hindu updated 17th May 2019. https://www.thehindu.com/news/national/other-states/centres-stand-and-bjp-word-differ-on-countrywide-nrc/article27165898.ece

[64] The Hindu (Kolkata Edition) page 7, dated 29th July 2018.

[65] Assam Government. SOP for disposal of claims and objections in updation of NRC https://www.nrcassam.nic.in/pdf/SOP-claims-objections-final.pdf

[66] Talukdar, Mrinal. p. 238-239, "THE GAME CALLED NRC"

[67] Gogoi, Ranjan. p 164. "JUSTICE FOR THE JUDGE: An Autobiography"

[68] SCO, Supreme Court Observer https://www.scobserver.in/judges/ranjan-gogoi/

[69] [Talukdar, Mrinal. p 162. "THE GAME CALLED NRC".

[70] Talukdar, Mrinal p. 131-164. "The Game Called NRC.

[71] Gogoi, Ranjan. p. 163-164 "Justice for the Judge"

[72] Supreme Court of India web portal. p. 68-70 https://main.sci.gov.in/jonew/judis/42194.pdf

[73] Express News Service "CJI Ranjan Gogoi says NRC cures a wrong, 'critics are playing with fire' "The Indian Express dated 4th November 2019. https://indianexpress.com/article/india/cji-ranjan-gogoi-says-nrc-cures-a-wrong-critics-are-playing-with-fire-6101568/

[74] NRC Assam: Karan Thapar interviews Faizan Mustafa for The Wire https://www.youtube.com/watch?v=uOfUoG5m670

[75] 'The Wire' https://thewire.in/law/nrc-citizenship-act-assam

[76] Bhatia, Gautam. "The Troubling Legacy of Chief Justice Ranjan Gogoi". The Wire dated 18th November 2019 (republished on 16th March 2020. https://thewire.in/law/chief-justice-ranjan-gogoi-legacy

[77] Bhatia, Gautam. Gautam Bhatia, Indian Constitutional Law & Philosophy https://indconlawphil.wordpress.com/2019/11/17/a-little-brief-authority-chief-justice-ranjan-gogoi-and-the-rise-of-the-executive-court/

[78] Talukdar, Mrinal. p.231 "The Game Called NRC"

[79] Wadud, Aman. "Children out, parents in: The real challenge begins now that final Assam NRC is here". The Print dated 31st August 2019. https://theprint.in/opinion/children-out-parents-in-the-real-challenge-begins-now-that-final-assam-nrc-is-here/284862/

[80] Karmakar, Sumir. "Over 2.6 lakh objections filed against NRC inclusion. Deccan Herald dated 2nd January 2019. https://www.deccanherald.com/national/over-26-lakh-objections-filed-710969.html

[81] Pratidin Bureau. "Dead man produced at NRC Hearing". Pratidin Time dated 3rd April 2019. https://www.pratidintime.com/latest-assam-news-breaking-news-assam/dead-man-produced-at-nrc-hearing

[82] Zahan, Syeda Ambia. "Rs 1,220-cr and 10 years later, NRC leaves group favouring exercise dissatisfied, raises doubts over migrant numbers in Assam". Firstpost dated 3rd September 2019. https://www.firstpost.com/india/rs-1220-cr-and-10-years-later-nrc-leaves-group-favouring-exercise-disastified-final-list-raises-questions-false-claims-on-migrants-7271991.html

[83] Kalita, Jayanta. "Northeast Diary: Is Assam NRC now nobody's child?" The Times of India dated 14th January 2023 https://timesofindia.indiatimes.com/india/northeast-diary-is-assam-nrc-now-nobodys-child/articleshow/96983471.cms

[84] Pratidin Time, dated 12th April 2023. "Assam Govt Registers Case Against Prateek Hajela In NRC Scam" https://www.pratidintime.com/latest-assam-news-breaking-news-assam/assam-govt-case-against-prateek-hajela

* * * * * * *

Epilogue
Let There Be Light!

[1] "Kong" means elder sister. This is generally a formal mode of addressing a Khasi lady.

[2] YouTube: https://www.youtube.com/watch?v=swaSHkHBGuM (special attention 24.17 min)

* * * * * * *

About the Author

Subir

Subir, a science graduate, embarked on his literary journey at the ripe age of 70, making a remarkable debut with a book on Bengal. It inspired him to write this second book on Assam, his birthplace and home, for over half a century.

Starting his career as a bank clerk, Subir climbed the ranks to retire as a senior management officer. His professional journey spanned over 35 years, during which he traversed the length and breadth of Northeast India's seven states. His work required him to interact extensively with diverse communities, each with their unique languages, religions, cultures, and social statuses. Thus he gained chatting skills in several local dialects in addition to his fluency in five widely spoken languages in the region.

Subir's experiences and insight into the region's socio-cultural mosaic have equipped him to weave a comprehensive narrative of Assam in its historical milieu, offering a fresh perspective.

www.ingramcontent.com/pod-product-compliance
Lightning Source LLC
LaVergne TN
LVHW091610070526
838199LV00044B/749